A Novel APPROACH

To Nola
My wonderful
crystal friend

[signature]

For.

Kelly, my own personal hero. Without his tolerance and patience, this book would never have happened. Tricia, Donna, Gail, "Frankie" and Crystal, my personal cheer team.

Acknowledgment.

Starting this endeavor was something I never thought I would be able to accomplish. So much has changed in the past eleven years and I'm finally finding my happy place. Most of this I attribute to my better half, Kelly. He has been my biggest support, fan and peanut gallery. Without him, I would never have been able to accomplish this much.

To Tricia, my own personal Liz. Thanks for the snark that adds some of the laughs.

I also need to thank my amazing circle of friends who have been supporting me and pushing me to get this accomplished. DI Donna, not necessarily the physical push, but a "you can do it" push. Gail, who found fun facts to help improve the book. Frankie, who was my emotional support during those tough chapters. Crystal, who was an inspiration.

I can't forget the Huckleberry Writer's Society. All of the wonderful insight, tips, tricks and information that made this process much easier.

There are many others I would love to thank who read, read and re-read pages to help me make this a story I hope everyone will enjoy.

Glossary of Chinese Names & Words:

NAMES:

Xiao Chen: shee-ow che-ehn

Wei Xian: wey shee-aan

Li Ming: lee-eeh meeh-eeng

Shuai Ming: shoo-aye meeh-eeng

Huang Hu: hoo-ahng hooh

Wu Feng: wooh fah-ung

Tao Xiuying: t-ow xi-uy-ing

Mr. Shun: mister shuhn

Wu Ai: ou eye-ee

Xu Hinge: sh-oo hinj

Lin Bolin: lee-eenh **bow**-luhn

Detective Zhao: detective jah-aww

Dr. Lin Longwei: doctor lee-eenh loh-ong-wey

Ching Wen: ch-uhng weh-ehn

Daiyu: dye yue

Ms. Zhang: ms j-AH-ng

Liu Chaoxiang: l-ee-uu chau-shee-aang

Mama Fu Jing: mama foo jing

Wang Chyou: ouang ch-ay-uw

Vengo Gao: ven-go g-ow

Wang Xiao: shee-ow w-AA-ng

Dilraba Dilmurat: di-luh-**raa**-buh duhl-mr-**att**

Huang Ping: hwan ping

Mr. Luo: mister l-uo

TERMS:

Xièxiè nǐ: syeh-syeh nee - Thank you

Ni Hao: nee haow - Hello, greetings

Jiuniang: juyn-yang - low alcohol fermented sweet rice

Bao buns: bow buns - steamed fluffy treat filled with sweet or savory fillings.

Hanfu: Traditional clothing consists of a robe or jacket worn as an upper garment with a skirt commonly worn as a lower garment.

Cheongsam: also known as a mandarin gown, longer figure-fitting, one piece garment with a standing collar, and asymmetric, left-over-right opening and two side slits and embellished with Chinese frog fasteners on the lapel and collar.

Shūshu: shu shu - Uncle

A Novel

APPROACH

NICOLE POMEROY

章

Chapter 1

Anna Cassidy sat at her desk staring at her computer. She watched as the cursor flashed in her document, taunting her. Searching through the notes strewn about her desk, they weren't giving her any inspiration. Thumbing through pages and sticky notes, there just wasn't anything here that gave her a little push.

Checking the time, she had about an hour until her call. Glancing down at the black keys her fingers rested on, she willed the words to flow through her fingertips onto the screen. Today it just wasn't working for some reason. She decided she needed a little distraction, so Anna took out a photo of Xiao Chen. Today she couldn't talk to him soon enough.

The weekly calls they shared had become one of the highlights of her reclusive life. She was constantly amazed at the relationship that had evolved over the years. Imagine that a famous Chinese actor like Xiao Chen would take time out of his busy schedule to chat with an author from the wilds of Montana, it was still something she had a tough time wrapping her head around. Where had the last four and a half years gone?

Rubbing her forehead to relax the tension she felt building, she contemplated her deadline coming up quickly. There were four scenes in her latest script and twelve chapters in her latest novel that she would need to complete soon. Neither seemed like they wanted any attention at the moment. It might be time to break out her writing playlist, either Electric Light Orchestra (ELO) or a soundtrack from one of her favorite movies. Maybe if that didn't work she should take a little time for some meditation. Something needed to plunge the blockage in her writing pipeline.

Stuck for the moment, Anna slid into a reminiscent mood, thinking back to how she came to be staring at a screen with writer's block.

When they received the news about Anna's husband, Kyle, she had just turned fifty. There were no options, and he didn't have much time left. Anna's daughter Liz, with her then boyfriend Sheldon, moved to Fortine, Montana, to be closer to her mom and stepdad. Helping out when it started to get too painful for Anna to cope by herself. Kyle's family had been crucial support as well. Elaine and her husband Bob were especially there for her when time started to run out.

In six months, Kyle was gone; his illness was just too aggressive. Anna had taken a break from work during those six months, making the most of their time left. Camping, fishing, going on the adventures they had talked about but thought they had years to experience. As the end came closer, and it became more challenging for Kyle to get around, they found the small things to do together that weren't as taxing. Anna would read a book, they would play a game of cards, or sit and watch the sunset together while holding hands.

All too soon he was no longer there. He wasn't there to hold her hand anymore. The emptiness that filled Anna felt like an endless night. Meeting her husband Kyle had been the best thing in her fifty years. The eleven years she spent with him felt like a fairy tale. Life had cheated her. Why didn't she get to have more time with him?

After losing Kyle, Anna lost her interest in life. Hobbies and projects lay discarded and forgotten; the only thing she could do was go through the motions of life. Anna counted herself lucky to work from home; she didn't have to deal directly with people. More often than not Anna's eyes would be swollen from crying herself to sleep the night before. Often she would sit at her computer and sob. She didn't want anyone to see how badly she was doing, so video meetings had been abolished.

Anna kept expecting Kyle to walk up behind her and kiss her neck or shoulders, asking how the day had gone. When he was gone, the sound of his voice, his touch and scent all started fading from her memory no matter how hard she tried to hang on to it.

Besides the obligatory store trip for a few essentials, Anna wouldn't leave the house. Why would she bother? Online shopping gave her the option of not dealing with reality outside her small world. Why leave the home they had built together? Why face people that gave her pitying looks and sympathetic platitudes? She was fed up with the locals; they never had anything to do with them while Kyle was here. Why would they care now? She fought guilt and anger about losing him soon after they had found one another.

Anna's daughter Liz had been a lifesaver for her. She would stop by three times a week bringing Anna's mail and anything she needed that couldn't be delivered.

After six months Liz finally got fed up with Anna's moping. She was putting a halt to her delivery service. "Get your ass out of the house and get it yourself. Your legs aren't broken, and I don't see a cast on your arm. I also know your car works fine; Sheldon looked it over and ensured all the maintenance was done. It would help if you started being a part of the world again. We miss him too, you know."

If it wasn't for Anna's close circle of friends, she might have stayed in her home indefinitely. Frankie, Dana, Gloria and Christie checked on her regularly and tried "jollying" her from her depression.

Drill Instructor Dana was what Anna began calling one of her closest friends. Dana had given her time to mourn, but after the six months, she also became adamant about Anna getting back to life. Dana realized that getting out and getting some exercise would be a massive benefit for Anna's mental state. The gym and spa became two of her usual haunts thanks to D.I. Dana.

Dana wasn't Anna's only support; Frankie, Gloria, and Christie were also there, helping her in their own ways. Gloria made sure Anna ate something other than just ramen and protein drinks. Christie would drag Anna out to fish and see concerts. The outdoors was great therapy. Lastly, Frankie ensured Anna didn't miss her meditations; Anna's extended family with the group also helped with her healing. Frankie's four-legged furry menagerie was remarkable in its own way; though Anna wouldn't have a dog of her own, Frankie's were great surrogates.

During this time, Anna rediscovered foreign television and

movies to distract herself and keep her mind from dwelling on memories of Kyle. They had watched many of the older television shows together and most of the newer offerings didn't appeal to her. Anna had always enjoyed foreign films, though she hadn't watched many Chinese or Korean ones; finding the romantic comedies and epic period dramas from those cultures had a profound effect on her.

After watching many different shows for six months, she found a handful of actors and shows she always seemed to go back to. The series *Eternal Dreams of Love*, which she had watched twenty times or more, was one of her absolute favorites. She could never seem to get enough of it.

Becoming frustrated with reading what the actors said in the subtitles, Anna decided she would begin learning Mandarin. Being a complex language, it took a bit for her to start getting the hang of how the emphasis on different parts of the word affected the meaning. It wasn't long and she began recognizing the actors' words. Soon Anna found herself falling in love with the language, the complexities of it challenging her and keeping her mind occupied.

Finding that a number of her favorite actors had social media accounts, she plucked up the courage to message them to thank them for helping her through a difficult time. Most of the responses were, "Thank you for watching. Please continue to support my work." Perfunctory and sterile, almost as if made by a robot meant to send a cookie-cutter response to any messages.

Xiao Chen was different. He had become her favorite actor so far; sending him a message had taken all her meager courage. Of the actors and actresses she had contacted, he was the only one not to reply at all. Feeling hurt that there wasn't even the robot response, or more than likely a flunky with a keyboard typing a scripted reply, she decided she wouldn't give up. Perhaps he was filming right now and didn't have the time to respond to fan messages.

Each day Anna would write a message, "I hope you are well.", "Thank you for the beautiful movies and shows you have been a part of.", "I enjoy your work so much!". Nothing lengthy, nothing demanding.

After a week of no response, Anna began sending the messages in Mandarin. Perhaps Xiao Chen didn't read English or felt she wouldn't understand if he sent a reply in Chinese. Each note was different but inquired how he was, wishing him well with his projects and making small talk; Anna was hoping he would at least tell her to stop bothering him.

There were times that Anna almost felt like a stalker. She began looking for information about him. What projects was he working on at the moment? Was he filming right now? Could that be why he didn't respond? She tried all social media contact options that she could find for Xiao Chen, and still, after a month there was no answer to any of her messages. It was time to give it one last try before giving up this foolish obsession.

Anna, feeling exceptionally despondent, wrote a long letter to Xiao Chen. She explained what had happened and how she felt until finding several series, *Boys and Romance*, *Destiny of Love*, and her favorite historical drama, *Eternal Dreams of Love*. Watching these shows had started giving her some hope of feeling something again. Three pages later, she finally attached it to a message and hit send, expecting this would be the last time she would send anything to him.

The morning his response came, it caught Anna off guard. A few days after she had penned her heartfelt letter to Xiao Chen, she awoke to a notification of an email from a Chinese email address. Shocked, she stared at her phone in amazement. He had replied, finally. Excited, Anna threw on her robe and slippers and dashed to her office. She wanted to be at her computer if something in the email needed to be translated.

Anna took a deep breath, sat at her computer and began reading. The email was very well written compared to some of the Chinese to English translations she had read over the last few months. Xiao Chen started by apologizing for not replying earlier. He was a famous actor, often getting inundated by letters and messages from fans that were trivial and time-consuming. Not wanting an assistant to deal with some of the personal messages sent to him, Xiao Chen would go through all of them himself in his spare time. After looking back, he said he found all the messages she had sent him over the last month.

The notes touched him as they asked how he was doing; most people sent self-centered messages or made demands on his time.

Xiao Chen explained he was also healing from losing a loved one; his sister had succumbed to cancer just four months earlier. Dealing with her illness and subsequent death had caused a severe slump in his career. He hadn't found a project that spoke to him in some time and he also noticed that mild depression was setting in. The letter Anna had written him shook him out of his funk. Realizing that his work had such a profound effect on someone's life who was suffering pain, he knew he needed to start working again.

Tears rolled down Anna's cheeks as she stared at her screen. Rereading the email several times, she began composing her response in her head, ashamed at herself for a few of the less than charitable names she had called him when sending some of her messages. Replying with concern and support, she hoped they could continue being pen pals if nothing else.

Xiao Chen and Anna began corresponding more frequently as the days went on. What started as simple one or two sentence comments to each other began to morph into a page or two every day.

Writing the emails started to kindle a creative flame that Anna had forgotten years before. Having always enjoyed writing, it was only natural to begin penning the idea that came to her after hearing his story. When she finished writing what had started as a narrative, it had morphed into a novel. Anna sent a copy to Xiao Chen, letting him know he had been the inspiration behind the epic drama.

Shaking herself from her reverie, she stretched and looked out her office window. Catching a glimpse of snowflakes reflected in the light from her porch, she sighed knowing she might have to shovel in the morning.

Catching the clock out of the corner of her eye, Anna realized forty-five minutes had escaped her attention. "Guess I got lost in my thoughts for too long," she mused to herself. There would be just enough time to grab a drink. For some reason, today felt like a Fuzzy Navel kind of day.

章

Chapter 2

Not being a regular drinker, Anna only kept a few bottles of wine and various liquors in her pantry. Walking through the silent house to the kitchen, Anna looked around; maybe it was time to find some new decor. A few new Chinese pieces would look great in the living room after the holidays.

Opening the pantry door, Anna reached in for the bottle of peach schnapps handily within reach. Snagging the bottle with one hand, she left the door standing open. Shuffling her slippered feet across the polished wood floor, she set the bottle on the island in the kitchen.

Anna made her way around the island to the cabinet with the glassware; taking out a tall mug, she sat it on the dark gray granite countertop next to the full bottle of schnapps. Grabbing the fridge handle, she pulled it open, reaching into the nearly empty fridge for the sealed carton of orange juice. Unscrewing the lid as she turned back to the counter, she set the carton down, picked up the glass bottle of liquid peach and poured in two healthy jiggers before adding orange juice to complete the drink. Putting the juice away in the fridge with a soft thump of the door, she mentally added grocery shopping to her to-do list for the week.

Picking up the bottle of schnapps and her full mug, she popped the liquor bottle back into the pantry. Closing the door, Anna took a small sip of her Fuzzy Navel. It tasted like a liquid summer day; just what the doctor ordered on a crisp October evening, bringing a phantom of sunshine. She took another sip and walked into her cluttered office, setting the mug down next to her keyboard. Adult beverage enabled, she waited for her anticipated call with Xiao Chen.

She could have taken the call anywhere in the house, but she may as well work on her script while she chatted with Chen.

Looking at her notes, Anna saw a few questions she planned on asking him while they talked. The scene she was working through was giving her some difficulty. They were friends; Chen always had constructive criticism and didn't pull punches.

Settling in for her call, Anna moved her mug to the right of her trackpad, making it easier to grab. Anna picked up her metal water bottle. There should be plenty; if not, it wasn't a big deal to fill it while talking. Getting comfortable in her office chair, Anna grabbed her earbuds off the desk and quickly popped one in each ear; a significant improvement over holding a phone up to her head for an hour or two. She had tried it one night; the kink in her neck for the next two days hadn't been worth it. Now, headsets or earbuds with mics had become the go-to for calls, especially with Chen. No excuse to get off the phone any earlier than necessary.

As if he knew when she was ready, the phone began to chime with Chen's ringtone. Taking a deep breath and composing herself, Anna tapped the answer button flashing on her screen.

"How are you doing?" Anna asked as the call connected.

Chuckling softly, Chen answered, "I'm doing great. How are things going there?"

"Well, if you could come up with some magic to knock this writer's block loose, I would be ecstatic." Anna laughed.

"Stuck again, are we?"

"Who is this **WE** you mentioned? I'm the one trying to finish at least one of these projects by the deadline. Veronica has been a serious taskmaster when it comes to the new novel. I swear she has hidden cameras stashed around my place and knows if I haven't worked on it in a few days. She will call and guilt me into working on it right then."

Chen laughed saying, "Would it be due to your propensity for procrastination? She realizes your true passion is the screenplays, which frustrates her to no end."

Anna rolled her eyes and sighed out, "You're right, you know. Sure you're not in touch with her secretly? Giving her insider information about how much I've finished on the screenplay or novel isn't fair. I always send you my finished pages daily; you know how much I have accomplished.

Speaking of...how was the last scene I sent over? I'm still on the fence about whether I want to make some changes to it or not. I think it needs a bit more action."

"Action? I didn't think this was that kind of project."

"Okay, maybe not that per se, but it needs some oomph...a bit of a twist perhaps? It either needs death or sex, which do you think?"

After a bit of a pause, there was a tentative reply, " I'd go with the sex; this isn't a good death scene."

"Now to just come up with the perfect passionate interaction," Anna mused out loud.

The call went on for quite some time, just catching up on what had happened over the past week since they had last spoken. Anna took a deep swig of her Fuzzy Navel.

"So what is the beverage of choice tonight? Did you make some of the new tea I sent?" Chen inquired after hearing her pause and swallow.

"It's a Fuzzy Navel kind of night. I thought about making tea but didn't have time before the call. This stupid writer's block needed some lubricant and I haven't received your latest package. I'm excited to try the new blend. I'm sure it is as amazing as the last two you sent. You've got great taste." Anna hoped he could hear her smile through her voice.

"Fuzzy Navel, huh, not familiar with that drink. But, speaking of Chinese tea blends..." Chen began and hesitated. "I have some news for you. How would you like to come and try some blends in person?"

Silence greeted his comment as Anna sat stunned, staring at her computer screen.

"Anna?" Chen asked with a hint of worry in his voice. "Are you still there? Damn crappy service."

"I'm still here," Anna managed to squeak out.

"Good, I thought I may have scared you off with that last question." Chen sighed. "Let me clarify the invitation a bit, or at least let me explain. I hope you won't be mad at me, but hear me out. You are invited to attend the Golden Horse Awards in Taipei City. "

Anna sat stunned in silence as Chen went on, "I know I didn't ask you first, but I took the story you wrote for me and showed it to some of the executives at my studio. They loved it so much that we turned it into a movie. It's been nominated for ten categories at the Golden Horse Awards. It's up for Best Movie, I've been nominated for Best Actor and..." Chen paused, letting the suspense build, "...you have been nominated for Best Writer."

"I'm what?" Anna squeaked.

Chen, unable to control his amusement, chuckled again. "You have been nominated for Best Writer for *The Lost Prince*. That six months that we didn't get to talk as often was because we were filming it. It premiered about six months ago and is a huge hit, so the studio would like to fly you over for the awards and discuss possible future projects. I wouldn't let them do the project without giving you full credit. Anna, this is an amazing opportunity; once in a lifetime."

The tone of Chen's voice became more intense. "I never thought I would get my career back like this. You've changed my life with that story. I must apologize, though; I should have let you know about this sooner. First, it was a surprise that the studio loved it as much as I did; they were excited to bring it to life. Second, we never expected the movie to be nominated for so many awards. *Entertainment* news is going nuts because no one knows who you are, and it's almost unheard of for an unknown to have so many nominations for their first project. Last, but certainly not least, you will have some disposable income to play around with."

"What do you mean by disposable income? My last book left me reasonably comfortable due to the royalties. There was talk about turning *My Twelve Lives* into a movie here in the States; I'm not going to hold my breath on that one. I'd turn purple," Anna joked.

Chen cleared his throat a bit and took a drink. "Well, as far as I'm aware, it's a seven-figure sum."

Anna gasped and slid off her chair, hitting the office floor with a soft thud.

"You said how many figures?" she asked as she picked herself up off the floor, dusting off the seat of her leggings. Pulling her chair back over to the desk and dropping herself in it, the squeak of protest from the chair seemed to mirror

Anna's mind at that moment.

"Last I heard from the studio, it's seven figures, though I don't know exactly which seven."

"Just have to be a smart-ass, don't you?" Anna grumped back at him.

"Sorry, they don't tell me everything," Chen replied apologetically.

"It's okay. Honestly, I'm just trying to wrap my head around this. Nothing like dropping a bombshell at this time of night. You realize I won't get any sleep now, right?" she said, deeply sighing as she looked at the clock. "It's already 1:30 in the morning here; I don't think I will be able to close my eyes. I'm too excited!"

"I'll stay on with you as long as you'd like. I cleared my schedule today knowing you would be wired from the news; I wanted to keep you company, though I wish it could be in person." Anna could almost hear the longing in his voice. Perhaps that was just her imagination.

"You're amazing! You know that, right?" Anna smiled as she imagined his blush at the compliment.

"So you keep saying," came the skeptical reply. "How about we start working on details for your trip? You will be here for two weeks in November. Hopefully, the weather will be nice while you are visiting."

"That doesn't give me much time to prepare; let's get this all figured out." Keeping the excitement from her voice was difficult for Anna. What she was most excited about was finally meeting Chen in person. To sit across a table from him and be bathed in the rich velvet voice she had only ever heard from a TV, computer or phone. During their call, they determined that the first week would be for meetings and the awards; however, the second week had limited engagements and Anna would be open for some sightseeing. So much to do in such a short time to prepare for the trip.

章

Chapter 3

For Anna, the weeks before the trip seemed to compress into just a few days. The preparations for an extended trip kept her busy and distracted. The few calls she managed to make to Xiao Chen were short and rushed compared to their usual conversations. Both were decidedly distracted and busy.

The day before her flight, Anna stood at the edge of her queen-sized bed looking over her list again. She had clothes, shoes, toiletries, gifts and the work that seemed to follow her wherever she went nowadays laid out and ready to go. "I hope these rags will do the trick. I live in northwest Montana; how often do I ever attend a formal event?" Anna looked closely at the borrowed evening gown. "I have a nasty suspicion a shopping trip will be in order, ugh!"

Thud, thud, thud, a muffled noise came from the front, just barely audible over the loud Celtic melody weaving throughout the house. "Siri, volume three." As the music lowered, there were another couple of thuds on the door.

"I'm coming in!" bellowed Liz as she opened the front door. "You better be decent!"

"When am I ever decent? I am, however, fully clothed so you're safe."

"Well, thank you for that, at least." Liz rolled her eyes as she sauntered into Anna's bedroom.

"So, did you just stop by to harass me, or did you come to get last minute instructions for taking care of the monster? Si Ming isn't going to be thrilled with me being gone for two weeks, but he will have to survive. Are the two of you planning to stay at the house or just drop by each day to hang out with His Highness?"

"I figured we'd stay here. Your place is nicer than ours." Liz smirked.

"Well, as long as it's as nice when I get back as it is now, we're good," Anna reminded Liz.

"We're all good!" Liz promised.

"Okay, my flight leaves in the morning; who'll drive me down, or should I just head down to the hotel tonight so you don't have to make the trip? At least the weather is holding and should stay pretty nice for the next two weeks. I'm scheduled to return before Thanksgiving; I should be back in time for the holiday. We can work on the Christmas decorating the weekend after, so make plans. For some reason, I feel like decking the halls this year; I believe it's past time." Anna started to zone out, thinking about decorating plans as she packed clothes and other items in her suitcases.

Liz looked over Anna's wardrobe and wrinkled her nose. "Mom, you need some help with your wardrobe. You aren't seventy. Maybe while you're there, you can find something sexy to wear. You've lost so much weight, and your figure is amazing, but you keep hiding in these baggy old lady rags."

"I know. I figured there would need to be an excursion to the fashion district to find a dress. What I have would cause me no end of embarrassment walking the red carpet. There just isn't a great selection here. I believe I'm in Beijing for a few days before the ceremony, so I should be able to find something there. Want me to let you know when I'm shopping to get your input? You know I don't care much about this kind of thing," Anna said, glancing at the miscellaneous clothing items strewn across the bed.

"Please! I don't want you to feel embarrassed. I hope you find something that will show off those great curves you have now. You worked hard enough to get them; you must flaunt them!" Liz insisted.

"Okay, okay, I get the hint." Anna smiled. "I'll see what I can do. Perhaps the studio has a stylist that can work with me to find something flattering."

"Yeah, that would probably be a good idea. Don't just get an evening gown; get a few other event outfits. I believe you have a signing tour in the new year with your latest book, don't you?"

Grabbing her phone, Anna found her lifeline, the calendar that kept her on track. Scrolling through a couple of pages of dates she found what she needed. "Looks like in March I'll be on the road for a week, possibly two, depending on how the soft launch goes."

"Well, a couple of new outfits for the trip wouldn't hurt." Flipping through Anna's suitcase, Liz shook her head. "Just because you're a widow doesn't mean you have to dress like you're still in mourning. It's been long enough, Mom."

The slow creep of moisture rolled down Anna's cheeks as she sat down on the edge of the bed, sighing, "My head knows this, but my heart is still a few steps behind. I hope I can finally start living again in the new year."

Liz walked over to her mom, wrapped her arms around her, and gave her a long hug. "We miss dad too, but you are still young, and you shouldn't have to live the rest of your life alone. Dad knew that and asked you to find love again. I know it isn't easy, but you must open your heart to the opportunity. Scott Randall has been waiting for you to come out and let him take you on a date."

Shaking her head, Anna thought about it for a few minutes. "Scott is a hunk, for sure. When I first saw him, there was an oddly familiar feeling about him. Having spent time around him though, there is just something that doesn't sit quite right with me. I get odd vibes when I'm around him for too long. It makes me more uncomfortable than I want to be right now."

"I will do what I can to dissuade him then," Liz said, looking determined. "He gets a bit obnoxious asking about you all the time, actually. This was left at the bar, and it has your name on the envelope."

Taking the proffered envelope Liz handed her, Anna gave it a cursory glance and went back to packing. "Thanks, sweetie. I would **REALLY** appreciate any help getting him off my back." Anna gave Liz a quick hug and stood up, walking into her bathroom to wash her face.

Looking in the mirror, Anna still felt like she didn't recognize the person looking back. Having lost one hundred and seventy-five pounds over the last four years, it was hard to imagine she could look like she was in her thirties instead of fifty-five. "Get it together, Anna. You have a huge adventure coming, and you don't need to fall apart at an inopportune moment." Anna rinsed the cloth she had just used to clear the streaks of tears and carefully hung it on the towel bar.

Looking at her reflection one last time, she grabbed the last few items from the counter and turned off the light. Liz sat patiently in her mom's easy chair in the corner, reading the latest pages she had just finished. Anna realized it was almost archaic to do edits on printed pages; she couldn't get past the habit, almost equating it with a superstitious ritual. "This should be an interesting one. Something is missing in this chapter, maybe a make-out scene?" She looked pensively at the page.

Didn't she have this conversation with Chen a few weeks ago about that chapter? "I've thought about that myself. Perhaps while I'm on my trip I'll get inspired," said Anna, winking at Liz.

Liz gave her mom a curious look. "Just what do you have planned for this trip?"

"Well, as far as I know, I have dinner plans with Chen at some point, meetings at the studio for a couple of days, the award ceremony and some sightseeing. I've planned on taking a week and treating it like a vacation. I'd like to see some sights while I'm there. Shopping is definitely on the list."

"Just let me know if we need to stay longer or not. His Majesty will not be overly thrilled about you being gone so long, but we will try our best to keep Si Ming entertained," Liz said, giving her a long face like she was being put out by staying at the house while Anna was gone.

"He'll survive. He's not exactly the most demanding of roommates you know. Speaking of Si Ming, where is that furry tub?" Looking around the room, Anna didn't see a trace of her four-legged furry roommate. The twenty-eight pound Maine Coon who had found his way into her life was one of the most laid-back cats she had ever been around. He was a guard dog, and mood ring, his tendency to gauge her emotions was uncanny. She had been trying to train him not to continue his habit of laying on her at night. His weight was significant, and he was used to when she weighed more and could handle his pudge. Keeping her warm on the cold winter nights was one of his favorite jobs, curling against her throughout the night.

"Not sure where he is now; he knows something is up and has been keeping his distance the last two days. I'll make sure I find him and give him some good loving before leaving." Looking out in the living room to see if he was lounging in his usual chair. Not seeing him curled up on his blanket, Anna figured he may have gone outside for a bit.

"Okay, am I driving down tonight, or am I being driven down in the morning?" Anna asked as she finished packing the last of her clothes and toiletries. Looking over her nightstand, she noticed the letter and grabbed it, tucking it in with the pages for the scene she needed to edit.

"It would probably be better if you stayed at the hotel by the airport tonight. The wildlife has been pretty active in the wee hours, and we would rather not have to come to rescue you in the dark. I'll have Kameron pick up your SUV from the hotel tomorrow and park it at his place while you're gone. He's your son, he can at least do that for you. Then when you return, you'll have your rig handy and won't have to wait on anyone to pick you up." Liz looked at her phone and saw she had about thirty minutes until her bar shift. "I better get going, or I'm going to get an earful for being late. Love you, Mom, have a magical trip." Liz hugged Anna on her way to the front door. "We'll take good care of the place and Si Ming. Oh, and by any chance, do you think you might find a different name for His Highness?"

Giving Liz a dirty look, Anna replied, "You're lucky I didn't name him what I wanted. You'd have a bugger of a time trying to pronounce it. Just suck it up and deal." She hugged Liz again. "I'll keep you in the loop when I know more. I better get on the road soon before it gets too late." Anna turned, taking her phone out of her pocket and looking up the hotel number to make a reservation for the night. "Love you!" she called out to Liz as she left.

"Love you too, Mom!" Liz yelled through the door.

Closing her suitcases, Anna pulled them off the bed and sat the wheels on the floor. Pulling the handles up on the silver case first, then the black case next, she tugged them to the front door. *So, through the house or just take the porch?* Going around the porch route would be much easier, especially for the suitcases. Dragging the full metal boxes on wheels across the boards of her covered porch, she quickly reached the outer garage door. Anna opened the door to the whoosh of warm air carrying slight whiffs of motor oil and gasoline.

Hitting the correct garage door button with her elbow, she yanked the cases to the back of her Subaru Forester. Popping the back hatch, she slung them in the back unceremoniously. Opening the mudroom door, she picked up the last few items she had stashed on the counter. Lined up like soldiers waiting for deployment were her laptop bag, a backpack filled with flight essentials, a gratuitous romance, a buckwheat neck pillow, headphones, snacks and her small purse. Doing one last quick run through her mental checklist, she closed the door.

Time to get on the road. Si Ming hadn't shown his whiskers before she left. That would be another gift she would need to look for while there, something special for her guardian spirit.

—

Wrapped up in her thoughts of the coming trip, Anna didn't notice the dark vehicle parked in the shadows along her road. When he had seen the garage door opening, he had retreated to this distant spot to watch. Where was she going at such a late hour? He sat on the edge of the property most nights, watching until the lights went out. Hoping for a glimpse of her through a window, perhaps even on the porch.

He had watched her daughter leave earlier. Perhaps she dropped off the note he had left for her at Jerry's bar. What would she think of it? Hours had gone into writing the information on that piece of paper. How would she respond? He just wanted her.

—

Driving the curving highway in the dark was one of Anna's least favorite things, but the "road gods" were smiling on her, keeping the large mammals at bay. The route through Whitefish wasn't her preference, but it was the quickest way to get to the airport hotel. Not much further and she could try getting a few moments of shut-eye before she needed to be at the airport. This flight would take a little longer to get through security because she would be traveling internationally.

After a mostly sleepless night, Anna decided she should get

to the airport a little early and just get checked in. The studio had booked her first-class tickets, but she wouldn't get the VIP treatment until she got to Seattle. The flight from Kalispell to Seattle was on a smaller commercial plane without the first-class section, but from Seattle to Beijing, it was nonstop comfort. This flight was the first time she would enjoy the less cramped area of the plane for a change. She usually was squashed into an itty-bitty space in the cheap seats.

Arriving in Seattle, Anna made her way between gates. Navigating through bustling travelers had always been fun for her. It was interesting seeing how differently people traveled today versus thirty-five years ago when she was traveling for the military.

The eight hour layover allowed her time to get to her departure gate casually, so Anna wasn't in any rush. As she window shopped at a store selling different confections, a voice startled her from her inner fight of chocolate or no chocolate. "Anna, is that you?"

It had been almost fifteen years since she had heard that voice. Turning, there he stood. Emotions warred in Anna, elation at seeing her favorite cousin, disappointment at how he had treated her when she had needed him and anger that he hadn't spoken to her during those years. "Hi, Chris," she replied quietly. Her polite nature won out.

"I never expected to see you at an airport in Seattle. Traveling for work?" Chris seemed to be genuinely interested.

"Yeah, heading for Beijing. On your way to visit your folks?" Anna loved Chris's parents. They were among her favorite family members.

"Yeah. Their anniversary is coming up, and I figured it would be good for me to be there," he said and gave Anna a jaunty wink. Checking his phone for the time, he gave Anna a closer look. Just realizing how much she had changed from the last time he had seen her. "You're looking great, by the way."

Giving him a rueful grin she said, "Thanks, I guess being a widow had one positive side effect. I better head for my gate, my flight will leave soon." Anna turned in the opposite direction Chris seemed to be going. Emotions she thought she had finally buried started pushing their way to the surface.

Damn him for showing up today of all days.

"Anna," Chris said as she felt arms wrap around her from behind. "I'm sorry." Quiet words for her ears alone.

"It's a bit late now. I needed you five years ago. You're the one that stopped talking to me, remember? You made your decision, and I'm making mine now." Anna gently pulled away from his arms. Tears silently fell as she walked away from the person that had been her favorite family member.

"Anna?" Chris called after her.

Ignoring the call, Anna stiffened her resolve and kept going. She couldn't let herself deal with this right now. Someday...but not today.

Four hours later, situated in her first-class seat with a drink in hand, Anna messaged Chen. *On my way, should be there in about 12 hours or so.*

I'll be waiting for you at the airport when you get here. Chen replied within moments.

I'll find you as soon as I get off the plane. Unless you've changed dramatically, I should be able to pick you out with no problems, she messaged back while waiting for the plane to take off.

I'm my usual handsome self, he replied with goofy face emojis.

See you soon. Famous last words. Her previous message was sent as the flight attendant told everyone to turn off their devices.

章

Chapter 4

Xiao Chen paced around his apartment, feeling slightly nervous about Anna's visit. They had never had a video chat during the four years they had corresponded. Though he knew that she had reservations about letting him see her, he had hoped she would trust him more by now. Being curious, he had done a little stalking of his own, finding her personal social media page. Not that it helped any as there weren't any current photos. She hadn't posted any photos in over three years. She didn't even have pictures on her publisher's website or books.

Excitement was warring with apprehension. Was there something Anna hadn't disclosed that had kept her from video chatting with him? The photos he had seen showed her brilliant smile and kind eyes; just because there was more of her, she shouldn't have felt so self-conscious with him. He liked her for who she was, her appearance didn't matter. As long as she was happy, he would also be more than satisfied.

Growing up, he had fought with weight issues as well. By college, he had grown out of it and became athletic and fit, which worked to his advantage when he began modeling. Being bullied and teased in school made him a different man; always one to step up, never passing up an opportunity to help others and volunteering for quite a few charity events. He would never say anything to hurt Anna because of her weight.

Anna's flight was due at 8:30 that evening; Chen's schedule for the day should allow him to be there with plenty of time to spare. The flight was scheduled early enough in the evening that he had made reservations at a quiet restaurant that catered to the later night crowd. He didn't imagine that she would have enjoyed the food on the airplane and wanted to treat her to a relaxing meal. The studio hadn't given him all of her itinerary information yet so he couldn't make extended plans.

Chen had dropped a hint to the studio that he would be the best option as a liaison. He knew Anna and spoke English quite well, thanks to their conversations that could last for hours. Anna's Mandarin was also quite passable; she should be able to get around Beijing pretty easily if she had to.

Grabbing his coat off the back of the couch, Chen headed for the front door of his apartment. Unlocking his phone, he checked messages to see if there was anything new for today's shoot. Not seeing anything to make him too worried, he closed the door and headed to the elevator. Oh, how much can change in a few minutes?

Almost the moment he stepped out of the elevator, his phone started having a fit. *Bing, bing, bing,* messages began flooding in. Just as he unlocked his screen to check them the phone rang. Looking at the screen, he recognized the number as that of the assistant producer on his latest project. "Mr. Ching, what's the matter? My phone just started blowing up. I haven't even had a chance to read the messages yet."

A tired and disgruntled voice came through the phone." Li Ming is going to be very late today for filming. Unfortunately, we have to finish these couple of scenes today, we are already behind schedule, and I am getting quite a bit of heat from the studio because they aren't finished. I know you have plans tonight, but I am sorry, they will have to be changed."

Taking the phone away from his ear for a few moments and cursing quietly, Chen put the phone back to his ear. "That conniving little...She knew I had plans; I can almost bet she is doing this intentionally. We should have replaced her in this film a long time ago. She isn't getting the hint that it is over between us and she has no hope of ever being with me again."

Ching Wen sighed, "I know Xiao Chen. I hated making this call, but my hands are tied, and this has to be done."

"I know, Mr. Ching. I'm not holding it against you. Let's film what we can until she gets there. That will keep it from being tomorrow morning before we are finished. I hate keeping the crew there so late. I should be there within the hour. Some arrangements will need to be made for our guest." Chen says as he heads for the front door of the apartment building, nodding at security as he leaves.

One difference between Chen and many other film stars was that he wasn't a pretentious asshole. He didn't have a problem signing an autograph for fans if they were polite in their request and he was on good terms with the security at his building. They were his last line of defense against his ex-fiancé Li Ming. Yes, **that** Li Ming. He still wasn't sure how she ended up being his co-star in this latest movie.

Getting into his Galaxy Blue RS Q8 Audi, Chen took a deep breath, looked up a number on his phone and dialed before pulling into traffic. Putting the call on his car's internal system, he waited patiently for his last hope to answer.

"Yo, dude!" a deep voice boomed over the speaker.

"Interesting way to answer the phone this early, Xian." Chen laughed.

"Well, it is you; how else would I answer?" Wei Xian said with amusement in his voice.

Chen steeled himself to ask his best friend for a huge favor. "Hey, do you have anything going on tonight?"

Xian hesitated for a few moments before answering. "What's up? I thought you had some big plans for tonight."

Chen forced himself not to grit his teeth. "I **DID** have serious plans for tonight, but 'you know who' strikes again!" Trying very hard to keep the anger from his voice, Chen signaled to turn and tried to keep at least half of his attention on the traffic.

Quiet cussing came over the phone as Xian got the gist of what Chen just said. "That bitch! She can't leave well enough alone, can she?"

"Not remotely. I need a significant favor from my closest friend and brother."

Xian cleared his throat, "Anything I can do for you, ask. I would hope you know that." They had been through too much together in their youth for them not to be so close. Chen's sister had been married to Xian for almost fifteen years before she got sick and passed away. He was himself finally getting over her loss.

"Ms. Anna's flight arrives tonight at eight thirty, and I made dinner reservations. I don't think I will be set free until the wee hours of the morning, so is there any chance you could go in my place, pick her up and take her to dinner? I know it's a lot to ask as you don't know her other than what I've told you over the last few years." Chen pulled his attention from the call to maneuver his SUV across traffic and pull up to the studio's gate.

"Chen, not a problem brother. I would happily get Anna from the airport and take her out. I can tell her some stories that will make her think twice about liking a rascal like you. I have a meeting in a few minutes; send me the information and a photo so I know whom I'm looking for," Xian said as he walked into the conference room.

"You're a lifesaver! I owe you one." Chen hung up the phone as he pulled into his parking spot. This situation with Li Ming is going to have to be resolved soon. He didn't want Anna hurt because of her evil behavior, but for some reason, he felt she would cause serious problems in the next two weeks. It would be best if he kept Anna as far from her as possible.

Getting out of his SUV, Chen went across the lot to his dressing room to get ready for filming. Being a period piece this time, it took longer to get into the long wig and makeup that made him look almost twenty years younger. He looked young for being forty six, but needed to look even younger for these scenes. They would be shooting flashbacks that went back decades, so he needed a more youthful appearance.

Once the hair and makeup were in place, Chen inserted the colored contact lenses to make his chocolate eyes look ice blue. He had hoped that Anna could see him in his makeup as she had fallen in love with this script and the part Chen was playing. Usually, a script wasn't allowed to be read outside the pertinent cast and crew, but he had gotten permission for her to read it as she was working on a sequel.

Might as well get a photo, Chen thought as he sat and looked at himself in the mirror. *At least she can see me in my makeup, if not in person.* This was supposed to shoot tomorrow, and she could have been here. The thought made him even more annoyed with the whole situation. Maybe there would be at least one more day of shooting wearing this makeup; his regular makeup and costume weren't nearly this spectacular.

Checking that everything was in place, Chen got up from his chair with assistance from the makeup team. One drawback to the more formal attire was that it was bulkier and difficult to maneuver while wearing. He couldn't help but run his hand over the exquisite silks and brocades used in the costume. It helped that he played an emperor and the elaborate clothing came with the character. Today's scene was a wedding scene for the Emperor, and the costume was even more regal. The reds and golds were striking with his hair and eyes. The outfit Li Ming would be wearing would be equally majestic. What he wouldn't give to see Anna dressed in those delicate and translucent fabrics. Closing his eyes for a few moments to picture the red and gold finery draped on Anna's voluptuous frame.

Making his way cautiously to the set, he found the director Xu Hinge talking with the producer Ching Wen and a couple of the other techs discussing setting up for the upcoming shots.

"Let's get the ball rolling," Chen said confidently and calmly. If he could keep his cool, it would help put the crew at ease, at least for the moment. He knew that once Li Ming arrived on the set, it could be like a tsunami making landfall, so he may as well enjoy the peace while it lasted. This was going to be an exceptionally long day.

章

Chapter 5

The plane touched down only a few minutes later than the flight board had displayed. Xian made sure he had arrived a bit early to have an excellent spot to try and catch Anna's attention as she came through the gate.

Having taken extra care to be dressed to impress, Xian hadn't gone to the extent of formal evening wear. Still, his dark Armani suit, Ferragamo shoes and cashmere coat set him apart from the bought off-the-rack clothing of the people around him. Not that his six-two athletic frame didn't tower over most of them. His square jaw, intense brown eyes, and tousled brunette hair gave him an almost playboy vibe that didn't fit the impeccable threads.

Xian's handsome features drew the attention of many of the ladies, either waiting for passengers or waiting for flights themselves. Over the last three years, he had taken particular pains to stay out of the media as much as possible so people wouldn't ask him about Chandra. A bonus side effect was that people didn't recognize him as the chairman of one of the largest media firms in China.

As the flight began to disembark, Xian watched closely for the woman in the picture. Chen had sent him a photo. The reservations at TRB Hutong were impressive; Chen must have made the reservations as soon as he knew Anna's schedule. This must indeed be an exceptional woman for him to go to such lengths for their first meeting, and Xian felt a bit guilty that he was the one that would be taking her and not his dearest friend and brother. As much as he had teased Chen about telling Anna mischievous stories, Xian would sing Chen's praises as much as possible to help impress the American writer.

Being a constant traveler of late, Xian knew that Anna should have been one of the first off the plane as she had been a first-class passenger. However, after watching most passengers exit the gate, he didn't see anyone who matched the photo except one. This woman was sleek and elegant, in a casual but stylish dress and long overcoat.

The face had some similarities, but that was where the comparison stopped. The rich, deep brunette hair with red and blonde highlights fell in ripples down to the middle of the woman's back; one side tucked neatly behind her right ear.

Her eyes were a rich hazel color that reflected the color of the deep blue coat that nearly reached her ankles. They sparkled with what he could only imagine was a powerful emotion. Her full lips curled into a smile he would never forget, as it seemed to brighten the whole terminal when she looked around.

Why couldn't this vision be Anna? How he would enjoy being able to escort this understated beauty around the city of Beijing. How could he be that lucky? After Chandra's death, he didn't look at women. To Xian, a woman was the same as a man, just individuals to work with, nothing special. This woman had been the first to grab his attention in a very long time. Observing her, he noticed that she didn't act like a stunning beauty; she behaved as though she didn't realize that most of the men were openly staring at her. She was looking for someone, and why couldn't that someone be him?

Turning his head back to the gangway, he almost had to do a double take; walking towards him was Shuai Ming. He hadn't seen Shuai Ming in twenty-five years. While in college, they had been best friends. They had lost touch when her father was transferred to the U.S. for his job. Not able to part with her family, Shuai Ming moved to finish her college education close to them in the States. She was just as pretty now as she had been then; a more mature beauty had settled on her very nicely.

Xian couldn't help but smile when she noticed him, and her face lit up. "Wei Xian?" she called over the din of the other passengers greeting family and friends. "Is it you?"

"Shuai Ming, it has been a long time," Xian said as he walked up and gave her a friendly embrace.

"You're looking rather impressive, Mr. Chairman." She

smiled shyly at him as she stepped back out of his hug.

"Hush, not so loud," Xian shushed her. "I'm trying to be incognito."

"Good luck with that. You stand out like a prize bull in a herd of pigs." Shuai Ming laughed when she saw Xian's expression at her comparison. "Well, that probably wasn't the best way to say it, but you do tend to stand out quite a bit from us common folk." She took his hand in hers to soothe his aching pride.

"I am here doing a favor for Xiao Chen," Xian said as he held her hand in his for a few moments longer. "He has a special guest that was supposed to be on this flight, but I haven't seen her get off the plane." Looking over at the last stragglers coming down the jetway, he became concerned. Chen was going to kill him if he missed Anna. "Have you seen this woman on your flight?" Xian asked as he took out his phone and showed Shuai Ming the photo Chen had sent.

Looking at it closely, she shook her head. "Was she in first-class or packed like sardines in the cheap seats with us poor sods?"

"First-class, I believe. A woman bearing a slight resemblance to Anna disembarked, but the resemblance wasn't enough that I would want to embarrass myself by asking if she was an American author. I believe she speaks Mandarin, but I don't want to risk insulting her by accident." Xian once again looked over the remaining people milling around, waiting for late coming family and friends. The striking woman looked agitated, and her smile was no longer the brilliant shining thing it had been when she had first walked off the plane. She looked like she may be cursing at her phone.

Looking over at her as well, Shuai Ming shook her head. "I pity the person who stood her up. She looks like she could chew nails and spit bullets right now."

Xian shuddered a bit, imagining the tirade someone would experience for leaving her waiting at the airport. Glancing in the woman's direction, Xian noticed her looking in their direction. Picking up her two small bags, she made her way over to them, her dark expression carefully tucked away and a polite smile pasted on her lips.

As she came to stand in front of Xian and Shuai Ming, the woman, speaking in fluent Mandarin, asked politely, "Excuse me, please, would it be possible to borrow your phone, sir? Mine has a dead battery, and my ride doesn't seem to be here. I need to call and arrange for a ride to my hotel."

Looking at her, Xian started digging his phone out of his coat pocket. Unlocking the screen to access the phone, he handed it to her.

"Thank you most kindly." She bowed and took a few steps away from him to gain a modicum of privacy to make her calls.

Distracted by the woman using his cell phone, Xian almost forgot about Shuai Ming's presence. "Shuai Ming, I am sorry. I should find out what happened. Perhaps she ended up on a later flight? Once I get my phone back, I can call Chen and see if he has heard anything from her."

Shuai Ming, seeing how distracted by the woman Xian was, decided it would be better for her to remove herself from the situation and find her cousin, who was supposed to be acting as her taxi. After all, she was there for a funeral and it wasn't time to think about romance. "Look me up if you have a free moment or two before I have to head back to the States," she said, handing him her business card.

Kissing Shuai Ming on the cheek, Xian looked down and remembered the last time a kiss like this had happened. It was also at an airport, but she was leaving him at that point, which was painful for him to remember. "I will, Shuai Ming. I hope to call you soon so we can catch up." Giving her one last hug, his attention turned to the woman borrowing his cell phone. Tonight had turned out to be a bit of an emotional roller coaster. He never expected to see Shuai Ming again, especially at the airport tonight.

章

Chapter 6

As the plane taxied to the jetway, Anna looked at her appearance one last time in her compact. She had touched up her makeup in the first-class lounge and felt pretty good about her appearance. The butterflies refused to settle in her stomach as the plane door opened, and the first-class passengers were asked to disembark.

Putting her coat on and gathering her bags, she carefully made her way along the gangway, avoiding the other passengers as best she could. One benefit of being in first-class was that she didn't get jostled around leaving the plane like she usually would.

Walking into the terminal, Anna smiled in anticipation of finally meeting Chen in person. Scanning over the crowd of people waiting for the passengers from the plane, she didn't see Chen. Perhaps he was running a little late? She knew that he had been filming today and it may have run a little past what he had expected. Putting down her carry-on, she reached into her pocket to pull out her cell phone.

Looking down at the screen, it was black. "What the bloody hell?" Anna cursed under her breath. Pushing buttons, the power refused to turn on. "It didn't charge at all? It must have died somewhere during the flight. Well damn. What do I do now?"

Looking around again, her smile faltered a bit. *I'll give Chen another fifteen minutes*, she thought to herself. She was confused and hurt after planning their first meeting in detail. Hadn't they discussed it into the wee hours of the morning on several of their calls?

Anna scanned the crowd in the terminal and noticed Xian and Shuai Ming. They were some of the last people still talking at this gate; she **HAD** caught him looking at her closely earlier. Was it someone she knew? Nah, that couldn't be possible.

Making her way over to where the two were standing,

Anna, in the most polite voice she could muster and in her best Mandarin said, "Excuse me, please, would it be possible to borrow your phone, Sir? Mine has a dead battery, and my ride doesn't seem to be here. I need to call and arrange for a ride to my hotel."

Startled at her fluent use of Mandarin, the man, without even thinking, unlocked his phone and handed it to Anna to use.

"Thank you most kindly." Anna gave a slight bow and walked a little ways off to make her calls. Dialing Chen's number from memory, she ignored the name that showed up on the phone when the call was connecting. Putting the phone to her ear, she overlooked the "Bro" displayed on the screen. Ringing, eventually, the call went to voicemail. It wouldn't have done any good as the phone was set on vibrate. It had been left lying on Chen's chair on the set. Frowning again, she pulled out the business card Chen had sent her with his assistant's information; dialing the number, she waited patiently. After everything, she just wanted to go to the hotel and sleep.

A polite voice answered the phone. "*Nǐhao*."

"*Nǐhao*," Anna replied. Very glad she had spent so much time learning Mandarin, she used it again to speak with the assistant that answered the phone. Anna requested a car to take her to her hotel, explaining the situation.

"Certainly, Ms. Cassidy." The voice sounded very apologetic. "Someone will be there within ten minutes, ma'am."

"Thank you," Anna replied as she hung up.

While Anna had been on the phone, Xian studied her closely. There was something familiar about the woman; he couldn't put his finger on what exactly. The niggling at the back of his mind was causing him some frustration. He was happy that he had taken a couple of photos of the mystery woman to mull them over later.

After finishing with Xian's phone, Anna went into the call history and deleted the last two calls. Even though she was a bit upset with Chen, she would never leave his number on a stranger's phone; that would be rude. Once again, she wasn't paying close attention and didn't realize that the phone call for Chen said "Bro." After deleting the numbers, Anna returned to Xian and handed him the phone. "Thank you again for your help. A car will be here soon to pick me up."

Xian replied in perfect English, "You're welcome, Ms. I am glad I could be of assistance." Smiling, he bowed his head to her slightly, and she returned the gesture.

A small smile slid across Anna's lips and was gone almost as quickly as it had appeared. The brilliant smile he had seen earlier was gone, and the world looked much darker after its loss.

Anna turned, picking her bags up from the chair she had unceremoniously dumped them on. Glancing around, she found the sign pointing her to the baggage claim. Nodding at Xian one last time, she left to get her bags before the car arrived.

After Anna left, Xian unlocked his phone screen, looking to see if he might recognize the number she had tried calling. Pulling up the call history, there weren't any records of any calls other than the ones he had made and received; the little minx had deleted the call history for those she had contacted. It made him even more impressed with this American. That she valued the privacy of the ones she had called so much she had thought to delete the numbers was very impressive to him. But he was really after the photos he had taken of her. Opening the best of the four, Xian studied the image. Something about her still bothered him. What was it about her that seemed so familiar?

After looking at the photo for a few moments, Xian noticed something he hadn't seen when she was in the terminal; she wore a pair of delicate jade earrings. The earrings were distinctive, but he couldn't put his finger on where he had seen this particular pair. Was it in an ad? Perhaps it was on one of the commercials he had approved for the network? He shook his head over the photo, being out of his character to take a picture of a strange woman. He was glad he had. Turning the screen off, he put the phone in his coat pocket and headed for the front door of the airport and his car.

Opening the door and getting in, he noticed the flowers Chen had picked out for Anna lying on the seat next to him.

Groaning, he realized he was probably a dead man for messing up this favor. Better to get it over with sooner than later. He hit the speed dial for Chen's number. Pulling out from his parking spot, he started driving past the front of the airport, where he saw the woman getting into a luxury sedan; the light glinted off the jade earrings as he passed her. The call finally connected to Chen's voicemail. "Dude, don't be mad, but you better call me the second you get this message."

Sighing, Xian headed his car home, still mulling over what could have happened with Anna. As he drove down the main street of Beijing, a banner caught his attention advertising a charity auction and masquerade gala in a little over a week.

Looking at the banner, it was almost as if a lightning bolt had hit him. His palm smacked his forehead loudly. "I am such a moron! I know exactly where I have seen those earrings! Chen bought them for Anna, so either that goddess was Anna, or she just so happened to have a matching pair of exclusive jade earrings." Looking behind him, it was just too late to return and find her at the airport. Hopefully, they could get everything ironed out in the morning. What a mess, but boy was Chen in for a shock.

章

Chapter 7

Anna arrived at the Four Seasons Hotel with no further issues. Parking in front of the hotel, the driver rushed around to Anna's door, opening it and extending a hand to assist her. Grabbing her purse and laptop bag, she stepped cautiously out of the car, mindful of her dress and heels. She thought, *This would be somewhat awkward at the best of times; how do women do this*? Standing in front of the entrance, she couldn't help but go a bit tourist, staring agog at the main door of what was probably the swankiest hotel she had ever stayed at.

Anna turned to the driver, who had just brought her bags, saying, "I'm not familiar with how this is done. Do I leave you a tip?" She felt slightly self-conscious about asking but didn't want the driver to feel slighted. This was another new experience for her, but her motto was When In Doubt, Ask.

The driver gave her a toothy grin and replied, "No, Ms. But I greatly appreciate you asking. Not many of the people I pick up even think to inquire. I hope you have a wonderful stay with us in Beijing." Handing her an elegant business card he continued, "If you need further services, and not necessarily a limo, even a car to take you anywhere in Beijing, don't hesitate to call. Oh, and it doesn't matter what time of day or night, a number of us are available."

Taking the card, Anna glanced briefly at the metallic letters before tucking the card in her purse where she could easily access it. She had a feeling this was going to come in handy at some point during her stay. "Thank you for being so helpful. I have a feeling this may be a lifesaver at some point." Smiling, she bowed her head slightly to the driver.

Bowing his head in return, his smile ratcheted up even more, turning and waving before getting back into the limo.

Anna turned to the hotel's front doors and entered the lobby. The flower arrangements that greeted her were more exotic than anything she could imagine. The floral scents permeating the air made her think of what a Chinese garden in spring may smell like. Approaching the front desk, one of the desk clerks looked up and smiled warmly at her. "Would you be Ms. Cassidy?" he asked politely.

"Yes, I am Anna Cassidy," she said, impressed. Perhaps the driver had called and informed them she was coming, or even the studio may have given them a heads up that she would be arriving soon.

"Ms. Cassidy, you are all checked in. Here is your room card. Your room is 2315; you are in the Terrace Suite and you will have access to the Executive Lounge and all the hotel amenities. Please don't hesitate to contact the concierge if you need any service. We have twenty-four hour room service and a well-appointed private bar with a wide selection of beverages and snacks. We understand that you will be away from the hotel for one night which won't be an issue. Please enjoy your stay with us."

"Thank you for letting me know. I will head to my room now; it has been a very long couple of days." Anna smiled tiredly. "Can you point me to the elevators, please?"

The clerk gestured off to Anna's left. "Just down that corridor and through the Atrium."

"*Xièxiè nǐ,*" Anna replied to the clerk. It was nice to be able to use her Mandarin a bit. Thank you was an easy one, in any case. Gathering her bags, Anna started to make her way to the elevators.

"Excuse me, Ms. Cassidy, would you like some assistance getting to your room?" the clerk said as he noticed her struggling with her bags.

"That would be wonderful," Anna said, looking relieved; her bulkier suitcase gave her a difficult time. "I have a couple of dresses I need to have pressed by tomorrow afternoon. How would I take care of that?"

"If they are easily accessible in your luggage, you can give them to the porter once you get to your room, or you can call us to pick them up after you have had some time to get unpacked. We can help with that any time of the day or night for you," the clerk said.

"Oh, that will work great. I believe the dresses are right on top of everything. I can send them right down with the porter. That will be a weight off my mind," Anna replied as she handed her suitcases to the porter. He had appeared as if by magic from a semi-concealed doorway.

The elevator ride to the floor of her room took longer than walking to her room. Scanning the key card, the door unlocked and the porter opened the door for Anna. The room was well appointed, the colors very rich and warm, and the decor elegant but not over the top. Anna was happy to see the office nook; this would help with the work she knew she had to focus on during this trip. It wouldn't be easy to concentrate on work with the opportunity to spend time with Chen while she was in Beijing. The work had to be finished, and she couldn't keep putting off those last few chapters and a final couple of scenes on the script; her editor was a slave driver sometimes.

Asking the porter to put her bag in the bedroom, Anna opened her large case and took out the shimmering blue gown and a deep hunter green wrap-around dress she had brought for more casual events. Handing these to the porter she said, "I will need the green dress for sure by noon tomorrow if possible; it just needs to be pressed. The gown I would like to have cleaned and pressed as well." Anna handed him a tip as he walked out of the room; he looked at the money and flushed a little.

"Ma'am, are you sure?" He seemed a bit flustered.

"Yes, young man; what is your name? Would it be possible for me to request you if you're available?" Anna asked. She tried to find staff she could work with exclusively, receiving much better service this way. It had also cut down on paparazzi harassing her in the States. Well tipped people didn't snitch on her nearly as often. It didn't happen often, but it was always a pain in the ass to deal with when it did.

"Ma'am. My name is Lin Bolin." The porter bowed slightly. "If I am available, I will do my best to assist you in whatever you need."

"*Xièxiè nǐ* Lin Bolin," Anna said to the porter as he left carefully carrying the dresses, closing the door gently behind himself. First, she wanted to explore her temporary home for the next two weeks. The suite was more impressive than the house Anna had lived in when she married Kyle. Curious, she went looking for the master bathroom. She was giddy as a schoolgirl; there was a large soaking tub and the shower was huge with a rainfall shower head. *I'm going to be so spoiled*! she thought to herself. "I believe a bath is in order. **AFTER** I get my phone plugged in so I can figure out what in the world happened and let Liz know I'm still alive and kicking," Anna said to herself.

章

Chapter 8

Chen looked at the time after finishing his last scene for the night. "You have to be kidding. It's one in the morning already?" Disgusted with how late it had gotten due to Li Ming's histrionics. He hadn't had a break in hours and he was exhausted. Making his way to his director's chair, he found his phone had been blown up by messages and phone calls. What had happened? Xian tried to contact him about every fifteen minutes for the last four and a half hours. He started to get nervous. Did something happen to Anna?

The calls were all from Xian's number, and a few messages had been thrown in for good measure. Most were along the lines of "Where the hell are you? You need to call me the moment you get this message!" They seemed to get a bit more desperate as the messages went on. Now he was even more concerned; there weren't any messages from Anna. Did she arrive okay?

Cursing softly, Chen hit Xian's number in the list of missed calls. Ringing only once, Xian's harried voice came through the phone. "Where the bloody hell have you been? Didn't you see my calls and messages?"

"Um, twenty-two missed calls is a bit much, don't you think? How's Anna?" Chen tried to lighten the mood a little. He had a foreboding feeling now. Something was wrong; he wasn't quite sure what yet, but there was just an odd itch that he had learned was a good indication that something had gone sideways.

"I don't know how Anna is," came the snappish voice from the phone.

"Why?" Chen's voice trembled as he sank into his chair. "I checked the airline's app; her flight arrived on time, right?"

"The flight was on time; however, there wasn't anyone on the flight that matched the photo of Anna that you had sent me. I would have checked with the hotel if she checked in, but that wasn't one of the details you had provided me," Xian muttered quietly. The strain of the last several hours was telling in his voice. "I have been stressing out trying to figure out what happened."

"Damn. Hold on a minute," Chen said as he took the phone from his ear, putting Xian's call on hold. He dialed Anna's number from memory; the call went directly to voicemail. Trying one more time, again, the call went directly to voicemail. Leaving a short message for Anna to call him as soon as she got the news, he hung up and returned to his call with Xian. "Her phone is off! She said she would contact me as soon as she got in. I need to go and figure out what is going on." His mind raced to decide what he should do first, call the hotel, the studio or go to the hotel itself.

"Go and figure this out, Chen. Let me know when you find something. I am worried now as well. Take care, brother; it'll be okay," Xian said, trying to calm Chen a bit and hung up.

Perhaps his assistant Huang Hu would know something; hopefully, if nothing else, she contacted him. Speed dialing his assistant, his call was answered by a sleepy voice. "Yes, Mr. Xiao?"

"Have you heard from Ms. Anna? Xian couldn't find her at the airport, and I haven't received a call or message from her either. Her flight came in on time, and everything was okay the last I'd heard from her."

"Sir, she did indeed make it in; she said there was no one there to meet her, and her phone had some difficulties. She didn't have an option to contact you. I sent a car to pick her up and take her to the hotel. The driver told me she was polite but seemed very upset." Huang Hu yawned into the phone. "Sorry, Mr. Xiao, I had just fallen asleep when you called."

"It's okay." The relief was evident in Chen's voice. "I'm glad she made it okay and is checked into her hotel. We can iron out the rest tomorrow after some sleep. Oh, by the way, when is Anna's meeting with the studio scheduled?" Due to the excitement, that detail had wholly escaped his memory. Today was Tuesday and the awards were scheduled for Saturday.

"It is 9 A.M. on Thursday. The studio execs wanted to give

her a day to get over the jet lag a bit and settle in. Tomorrow will be soon enough to try contacting her," Huang Hu advised sagely. "I'm sure she is exhausted from the long flight and the ordeal once she got here. Call her in the morning, sir."

"You're right; it would be better if we get some sleep. Tomorrow is going to be a long enough day as it is. We have more shooting because of Li Ming's tantrums today. We couldn't finish what needed to be done, and we are even further behind schedule now."

"I'll be sure to update your schedule, sir. Hopefully, you will be able to finish it soon, or you won't have any free time to spend with Ms. Anna."

"Thanks, Huang Hu; I'll see you on set tomorrow." Chen disconnected the call and rubbed his forehead. What a colossal mess, and he had no problem laying blame at Li Ming's feet. Her childish behavior since they broke up had significantly hindered the shoot, but unfortunately, it was too late to replace her; they just had to muddle through.

He was still annoyed with the studio when they pushed him to go out on dates with her to help promote the newest series. The situation had ended up being a train wreck. The fact that she was his ex-fiancé had made promoting the film very awkward for him as it was. Looking at his phone, 2:05 A.M. glowed dimly back at him. "I better call Xian back."

Grabbing his coat and phone, he made his way through the sound stage and headed for his car. Luckily, he had already changed before checking his phone; he could just leave directly. Getting to his parking spot, he fumbled in his pocket, searching for his key fob.

Settling into the leather seat, he started the car and let it run for a few moments before hitting the speed dial button on the nav screen for Xian. "Hey," he said as the phone connected.

"Hey yourself," Xian replied. "What's the word?"

"She is checked into her hotel. For some reason, her phone had trouble, and she just called the studio to send a car for her." The relief was evident in his voice.

"Good, I can hopefully get a couple hours of sleep," Xian grumped into the phone as he yawned.

"Hey, cut that out. You know it's contagious and I still need to drive home. Besides, you're the chairman; you can take a couple of hours off in the morning if you have to. It wouldn't kill you to take a little break." Chen laughed, feeling almost giddy with relief.

"You would think it was that easy, wouldn't you? Nope, not even remotely. I have a meeting in the morning that I can't miss, so I had better try and get a nap at the very least. You get your ass home and be careful on the way." Xian yawned one last time and ended the call.

Chen looked down at the screen. "That jerk had to get the last yawn in."

Pulling out of his parking spot, he headed toward home. Today was going to be an exciting day, long but undoubtedly exciting.

—

Chen didn't realize it, but his phone conversations had been overheard. The glint of malicious glee that crossed Li Ming's face would have frightened Chen, had he seen it. So far, she had been able to delay Xiao Chen from seeing that witch author. He was hers, no one else could have him, and she would ensure that the author wouldn't have any luck with Chen.

—

While Chen was headed home, Anna woke in her hotel suite. Looking at the clock, it was two thirty in the morning. She was still exhausted, but her phone should have been charged, and she had better call Liz or she would get an earful. Sitting up on the couch, Anna slipped her feet into her slippers and made her way to the office nook of the suite. The room came equipped with a charging station which was a godsend as it appeared that her cord or plug decided to give up the ghost sometime during the trip. She had only sat down on the couch to wait for the phone to get enough charge for her to make a call when she had fallen asleep.

Picking up her phone, she turned it on, waiting impatiently for the phone to complete its boot-up sequence. The lock screen finally showed a load of message notifications and missed calls. *Crap, Liz is going to skin me for not calling earlier. She'll get over it!* Anna was the most concerned about the messages and missed calls from Chen. Unlocking the phone, she opened the messaging app to see fifteen missed messages from Chen and ten from Liz.

"Ugh," Anna groaned. "I'll catch hell over this; I'd better call Liz first. I'm sure Chen is asleep already, and I don't want to wake him." After reading Liz's messages and listening to her voicemails, she pulled up the missed call list and poked her finger at Liz's number.

One, two, three rings. "**HELLO!** Where the **HELL** have you been?" Liz's voice thundered through the phone.

"Calm your tits, daughter. My phone battery died along with either the cord or charging port. I plugged it in when I got to my room but fell asleep waiting for it to charge. I just woke up and got your messages, and I called you immediately," Anna said apologetically.

"Okay, okay, I'll let it slide this time," Liz said, her voice calmer.

Anna filled Liz in for the next half hour on the trip and gave her a virtual tour of her suite.

"I'm seriously jelly, Mom. You should have taken me with you." Liz laughed at Anna's expression of disgust.

"Not likely, girl. This is my first overseas trip in ages, and I want to enjoy it." Winking at Liz, Anna told her good night and ended the call. "I'll look at Chen's in the morning. Hopefully, it'll be easier to deal with after more sleep." After a quick stop at the mini bar and grabbing water, Anna sat down on the edge of the bed. She kicked off her slippers, slid between the sheets and promptly fell asleep.

章

Chapter 9

Anna groaned and rolled over; the clock on the nightstand read 8:04 A.M.; she hadn't gotten enough sleep again, but what she had gotten was better than the previous two nights of travel. Groping around on the stand, she found her phone and blearily unlocked the screen. There were more messages, two from Veronica, a few new ones from Liz and a bunch from Chen. She finally made it through all the messages, flipping through the different apps, voicemail and messenger.

That made more sense now. Chen had sent a message during her flight, no wonder there was confusion last night and she ended up calling the studio for a ride. Someone had been there to pick her up. Something didn't make sense; why didn't they find her? They knew they were supposed to pick her up. Thinking about the situation, Anna groaned and smacked her forehead; he probably had one of her old photos to give them, which probably caused some confusion when she had gotten off the plane.

From the description that Chen had given her, she wondered if the gentleman she borrowed the phone from may have been Wei Xian. There was a good chance that it probably was him. The phone dying yesterday had caused a massive mess for sure. She should have paid more attention and worked less on the flight. At least she had finished most of her script, so she wouldn't have to work on that much during her trip.

Still laying in bed, Anna finished reading messages and listening to the voicemails Chen and Liz had left. Anna was flattered that Chen had been so concerned about her. He had left fifteen messages; the last ten later last night must have been after he found out that she hadn't met up with Xian. They started with a concerned tone ranging to frantic; the most recent, however, was a message that he had found out she had checked into the hotel, so he was relieved, but he wanted her to call as soon as possible.

Anna crawled out of bed, stuffed her feet in her slippers and ambled to the mini-bar. Tea would be great, but a bottle of water would work for the moment until after she spoke with Chen; she just needed something to wet her throat a bit.

Grabbing one of the high-end bottled water in the fridge, she made her way to the plush couch in the room's living area. Sliding the slippers off her feet, she pulled them up on the sofa, tucking them under a light throw she had brought. Anna took her phone out of her robe pocket, took a couple of deep breaths and was about to unlock the screen to call Chen when his ringtone erupted.

"I'm fine," Anna answered as she connected the call.

"I had hoped that was the case," Chen said; the relief she heard in his voice was tangible. "I am sorry things didn't work out last night; I had dinner reservations and everything."

"You have no idea how much I appreciate that. Too bad things went sideways. I was exhausted when I went to the hotel last night and fell asleep waiting for my phone to charge; I finally got your messages this morning."

"It's okay; I ended up filming until after one in the morning because of Li Ming. It ended up being a very long day. She continues to give me serious headaches."

Anna could almost hear the fatigue in Chen's voice. This trouble with Li Ming had been going on for a while. They'd been engaged at one point, but he had broken things off with her because of her selfish attitude and behavior. The studio had pressured Chen to be seen in public with Li Ming because they were co-stars in the latest series. Unfortunately, spending time together had given Li Ming the wrong idea; she had started pursuing him again, much to Chen's chagrin.

"Let's have dinner tonight. I will make sure that I am done in time today. I won't let Li Ming mess with our plans for another day."

"That sounds great. What time should I be ready? I will relax and see if I can get a bit more sleep; the last couple of days have been a tad hectic," Anna replied.

"I'll pick you up in the lobby at 7 tonight. Do you have a

preference for what you would like to eat?" Chen sounded a bit more invigorated.

"You pick your favorite restaurant. I want to experience what you love, and please don't pick a super expensive or fancy one. Let's go where you eat when you need cheering up or want to celebrate," Anna answered. She had never been interested in Chen's money or his fame; she just enjoyed Chen for his conversation and humor. He had made her laugh when Anna needed it most; he had been a shoulder to cry on more than once and she had also been there for him. This was just so exciting that she would finally be meeting him face to face.

"Okay, you should dress comfortably casual for the evening. I have somewhere special I would like to take you then." Now Chen sounded excited. "I look forward to tonight."

"Me too. I'll see you at 7."

"See you then," Chen replied with reluctance.

"Hey now, it isn't that long until tonight. We will finally get to see one another."

"I know; I will tough it out. See you tonight." Chen chuckled as he hung up the phone.

Anna sat her phone down on the table next to the couch, stretched her arms above her head and grabbed the bottle of water; opening it, she took a long swallow. "I believe it is time to get some breakfast," Anna mused to herself. She wandered to the desk to look for the menu for room service. Digging around, it didn't take long to find. Opening the menu, she found a selection that piqued her interest. She picked up the phone, called room service and placed her order.

"Hmm, I doubt I have time for a shower before the food gets here, and that would be awkward to have them come while I'm soaking wet." Picking up the remote for the TV, Anna turned it on and started flipping through the channels. Most of them were in Chinese, and she wasn't in the mindset to try and understand what they were saying. A little background noise was all she was looking for while checking emails and answering messages. Finding a channel that seemed mainly music, Anna left it there with the volume turned low and picked up her phone to finish checking the emails, text messages and voicemails she had received while on the flight with a dead phone battery.

Thoroughly engrossed in her message replies, Anna was startled by a knock on the door. Looking at her phone, she saw twenty minutes had passed and she hadn't even realized it. Pulling her robe tight and retying it, she made her way to the door. Opening it, she was greeted by a trolley with heavenly-smelling food and a beautiful bouquet of tropical flowers. Pushing the trolly with a huge smile was Lin Bolin. "Ms. Cassidy, good morning," he said. "Where would you like this, ma'am?" he asked as he looked around the room for a place to put the cart.

"Good morning Lin Bolin. I'm happy to see you again." Anna smiled as she looked around the room and gestured to the dining area. "Guess that would be the ideal location for it, wouldn't you say?"

"Perfect idea Ms. Cassidy." He pushed the trolly to the table and transferred the dishes to the mahogany surface. "I will take the trolly with me so it doesn't take up space for you. Oh, and these flowers arrived for you this morning. I didn't want to bring them up too early." Putting the vase with the flowers on the table as well.

"They're exquisite." Anna leaned over to smell one of the flowers, looking through the blooms for some kind of clue to let her know who had sent the bouquet. Tucked in the greenery was an elegantly penned card. "To my favorite blossom," it said, but with no name. It had to have been Chen; he would be the only one to know which room she was in.

Feeling warm and tingly, Anna looked over to see Lin Bolin ready to leave the room. "One moment young man. First, please call me Anna; second, please accept this." Anna reached into her robe pocket and pulled out a bill to hand to him.

"Ms. Anna, that is not necessary," he said, blushing when he saw the size of the bill again. "This is too much, ma'am."

"Nonsense, just accept it and smile," she said, winking at him. "I have to tell people that all the time, it seems. Just enjoy it and get yourself something nice."

Nodding to Anna in acceptance, Lin Bolin bowed. He turned quickly and pushed the trolly out of the room before she could see the tear slipping down his cheek. He wasn't used to the generosity and it had touched him.

章

Chapter 10

Chen hung up with Anna and called his assistant Huang Hu. "I have a quick task for you to do right away," he said without taking the time to give a greeting. "I would like you to order one of the most elegant bouquets of tropical flowers and send them to Ms. Cassidy. Sign it 'To my favorite blossom.' I think that will take care of things for now. I am getting ready to head to the studio for the day."

Huang Hu looked at the phone and shook his head. This was a bit out of character for Chen. He typically wasn't quite so animated this early in the morning. For some reason, he was usually dragging so early in the morning for the last few years. He was starting to get an idea why that was the case. Perhaps it was due to him talking to a particular American author most of the night.

"Certainly, Mr. Xiao. I will take care of it immediately," Huang Hu said enthusiastically. "Should your name be on the card with the flowers?"

"No, I don't believe that will be necessary. Ms. Cassidy will know who they're from," Chen said, smiling, thinking of his plans for the evening. "See if they can expedite the flowers. She had a rough day yesterday, and some colorful flowers should make today that much better."

"I believe I know a florist that can handle the order in an expedited manner. I will be going now so I can get on these requests. I will see you at the studio in an hour, sir?" Huang Hu asked, hopeful. It had been a ridiculously long day yesterday.

"Yes, and can you notify the director that I am done at five today? If we aren't, I will walk off the set. I have plans this evening and will not miss them again," Chen said adamantly.

"As you wish, sir." Hanging up, Huang Hu began making

the calls that Chen had requested. It was going to be an interesting two weeks with Ms. Anna around.

Chen finished getting ready to head to the studio; he grabbed his phone and keys from the table next to the door and made his way to where his car was parked. He slid into the seat, buckled his seat belt and popped his phone in its cradle. Pushing the start button, the car purred to life.

He hit the call button on the steering wheel and requested Xian's number.

"Hey, brother dear," Chen said with a mischievous tone to his voice.

"Okay, what did I do now?" Xian asked dubiously. Chen was rarely so flippant when he called unless Xian had done something that Chen found humorous.

"Well, you were in the presence of Anna at the airport. In fact..." Chen paused for dramatic effect as he negotiated the traffic, "...she used your phone."

"Ah, I wondered if that might have been her," Xian replied.

Almost swerving into the wrong lane, Chen recovered his emotions. "**WHAT?**"

"Oops, I didn't mean to mention that while you were driving. Okay, it just so happened that I saw the woman getting into a limo when I was driving past the front of the airport. After seeing her once again, I flashed back to her face and remembered seeing the stunning pair of jade earrings she had in her ears. If my memory serves, they are the same pair you gave Anna for her birthday, and I should remember as I was with you when you won the auction for them. When I realized who it was, it was too late to go back and remedy the situation."

"Talk about an absolute mess," Chen grumbled.

"So, how is she doing? Did she get all checked in, okay?" Xian asked with genuine concern in his voice.

"She's doing just fine. I spoke with her this morning after her phone was charged and she woke up. We have dinner plans tonight as well."

Chen explained what had happened to Anna the night before, and as he finished talking to Xian, he pulled into the studio.

"Okay, I need to get going, so I can hopefully be done by

5:00 P.M. to get ready for our dinner. 7 o'clock can't come fast enough," Chen said, sounding excited.

"So, do you want me to come with you if things don't go well? You know, as an excuse to take her back to the hotel." Xian almost wished he would agree to it.

Chen snorted. "Are you kidding me? You aren't getting anywhere near her now if I can help it."

Xian was shocked and responded with, "What the hell? Why?"

Chen snickered and replied, "Because you are tall, dark and handsome. Women fall all over themselves to be around you, and I like Anna; let's say I'm being cautious. Perhaps after tonight, I will let her get somewhere within a block of you."

"If she likes me better, I guess she has good taste," Xian replied flippantly.

"Keep it up, bud, and you'll be disowned." Chen snorted. Both of them laughed as they hung up.

After hanging up with Chen, Xian was conflicted. Should he send a photo to him and let him know how much difference there was from the picture Chen had to what she looked like now? No! After his comment about disowning him, Chen was on his own. He was, however, considering showing up at the hotel to watch and see what happened. It could go phenomenally or like the sinking of the Titanic, a royal disaster. He wasn't sure how Chen would react to the significant difference.

章

Chapter 11

Chen pulled up to the studio gate and waved at the security guard. The guard smiled and waved him through to the studio parking lot. Lately, it almost felt as though his car knew its way around the lot better than he did; he was constantly there. He saw Li Ming's driver standing off the side of a black Lexus. *Good, at least she is on time today for a change,* Chen thought to himself. If she behaved, they could get something done today.

Parked in his spot, Chen ran his hand through his hair. Picking up his phone, he checked if there had been any new messages while on his way to work. Perhaps a message from Anna? No such luck; he just talked to her not that long ago. He was so anxious for that evening to arrive already.

Huang Hu sent a message informing him that the flowers had been delivered. He also verified that the shooting schedule was pretty light that day; he had notified the director that Chen wouldn't be shooting past five no matter what. However, Huang Hu mentioned that the director wanted to speak with him when he got to work.

Sighing, Chen opened the car door and stepped out to an anxious production assistant waiting for him. *Oh good grief, now what's going on?* Chen cringed at the expression on the PA's face. "How bad is it?"

The PA grimaced and motioned for Chen to follow him. "The director is waiting for you on the sound stage. He'd like to speak to you before you go to your dressing room."

"Certainly. I wanted to speak to him before we started shooting today anyway," Chen said as he grabbed his pack from the passenger seat of his car. "Let's get this over with so there aren't any further delays."

Following the PA, they quickly made their way to the sound stage where they were filming. It didn't take them long to locate Xu Hinge, the director; as he glanced over the scene notes for the first shoot they had scheduled that morning. Looking up at the sound of feet approaching him, he noticed Chen and waved him over.

"Xiao Chen, I heard we have an exact deadline today. I can't say I blame you after what happened yesterday. The American writer is a studio guest, and one of our actresses caused problems for her. I heard Ms. Cassidy had to call for a ride to the hotel."

"So what happened at the airport has become common knowledge? I didn't find out about it until this morning, and she only spoke to Huang Hu as far as I am aware, so where did the rumors get started? Ms. Cassidy is an important guest; she has a couple of scripts that the studio hopes to purchase and produce. This is her first visit to our country; I hope we wouldn't show such dishonorable behavior to a guest. We need to resolve this issue and ensure it doesn't happen again. There's no way we can completely quell the rumors, but I hope we can at least not fuel the fire," Chen said adamantly. He was more than upset; the studio crew seemed to know what had happened at the airport the night before. He was sure to have words with Huang Hu to ensure he hadn't let something slip in passing.

Xu Hinge didn't look happy about it either. "You're right. We must be considerate of Ms. Cassidy. She has come a long way to meet with us, and things have started on a bad footing. We need to try keeping this from Li Ming. For whatever reason, she deeply dislikes Ms. Cassidy, which could make things even more complicated. Let's get these scenes finished quickly. I imagine you plan to meet with Ms. Cassidy tonight, which is why you must finish on time."

"That's what I hope. Our dinner plans ended up being a fiasco, so we will try again tonight," Chen said. "It would be best to keep Ms. Cassidy and Li Ming away from each other if possible. There is a long story behind some of it, and if we ever get a chance to go out for drinks like you had asked back at the beginning of filming, I'll tell you the long, sordid story." Chen laughed and clapped him on the shoulder. "Okay, I'm heading for the dressing room. I believe this may be our last day of the historical garb, so it won't take so long to get ready in the future."

"Li Ming is in makeup, so hopefully, by the time you're dressed and ready for makeup, she will be done and you won't have to deal with her other than while shooting," Xu Hinge told Chen.

"Here's to hoping my luck holds out," Chen said as he turned to leave for the wardrobe department.

It took him less time than usual to get into his costume. When he arrived, the wardrobe department staff had his costume prepared and ready for him. Today it was quieter than usual; the women did little chatting and gossiping. Chen didn't mind; today, he wasn't really in the mood for chitchat; it was better quiet.

When he arrived at makeup, Li Ming was finished and had gone to the set. He didn't need the same makeup time today that she would have required, so it went quicker than usual. The makeup artists were ready and there were extra hands to expedite his preparations.

Finished quicker than he had expected, he made his way to the set. Passing the crew along the way, they were much quieter and more somber than usual, though when he passed by, they smiled and waved. Something was going on and he felt the director made it known that they were pressed for time today.

Chen had always made it a point to be polite and friendly with the crew. They were the ones that helped him look good and kept things running smoothly on the lot. What good was it to be rotten to them? On the other hand, Li Ming was always nasty to the film crew; she treated them like servants below her. Chen had heard some of the names the crew had made up for her; he had even heard the name "Ming the Merciless". Wasn't that from an old American television show?

The day went relatively smoothly with Li Ming behaving and the crew behind him. Chen was shocked at her good behavior, though he was certainly glad. There had been too many days of fighting and strife and the stress had started getting to him. They didn't have much to finish this series, so it was best to push through and get it done as soon as possible.

By 4:00 P.M., Chen was finished. The day had drug on

endlessly, but it didn't help that he had kept checking the time constantly. The crew started laughing and playing along; whenever he would raise his wrist like he would be checking his watch, someone would shout out the time. Soon they had a routine; as soon as the director yelled "Cut!," someone would announce the time.

As soon as he finished his scenes, he made a beeline for the makeup department. The ladies made short work of removing his wig and a few minor prosthetics. One of the drawbacks of shooting pick up scenes was that they spent more time in wardrobe and makeup. Usually, each scene had a different outfit.

As the women buzzed around him, cautiously removing the elaborate hair pieces, Chen contemplated what he would wear that night. He wanted to look impeccable tonight for Anna, but he also knew from their long conversations that she wasn't awed by extravagance. The restaurant he planned to take her to wasn't precisely the formal attire kind of place, but first impressions were important, and he wanted to impress Anna.

Walking through the studio lot, he was lost in his thoughts. Chen had been waiting for this night for the last few years. He could never imagine they would have grown so close after receiving that initial message from her.

After he had received the long letter from Anna, he had gone back and checked, and sure enough, there were the many messages she had sent him. Why hadn't he seen them before? Chen had been touched by the questions and comments she had sent...Was he okay? Had he been eating enough? How was his work? Most of the other letters he would receive from fans were about how he looked and what he could do for them. It was becoming tedious.

Tonight, he would finally get to talk to Anna in person. At first, it had been odd that she wouldn't send photos or have video chats with him. That bothered him for a while; what was wrong with her? Did she have some disfigurement? He had been curious and had done some deep digging on the internet to find several of her older photos. She was beautiful, though she was heavier in weight; her eyes twinkled in the pictures he found. He had even taken the time to have a couple of them printed, framed and hung in his apartment. While Anna was here, he would get new ones to add.

BEEP! Startled, Chen looked up as he heard a golf cart horn blare. Shaking his head, he moved out of the way. Good grief, Chen was too distracted and had better be careful while driving back to his apartment. There were only two hours until he needed to be at the hotel; plenty of time to get back to his place and get ready. How much would she hate him if he messed up a second night in a row?

—

Li Ming watched Chen walking distractedly back to his car and she would imagine he had plans with the bitch. So far, her little tricks hadn't seemed to phase the author. It was time to step up her game. She wasn't giving up on Chen without a fight.

章

Chapter 12

Anna spent most of the morning investigating her room and unpacking her bags. Putting her clothes in drawers and hanging other items in the closet made things feel less transient. Anna wasn't the best traveler; for some odd reason, adjusting to a new place usually took her the better part of a week. The next two weeks would be hectic enough; she hoped to settle in sooner than later.

As the morning wore on, she looked over the hotel's list of services, noticing a spa and salon in the hotel. Calling the day spa first and the salon after, she checked to see if there were openings for that afternoon. As it happened, there were appointments available at both and she couldn't be happier. She was curious to see what a Chinese spa was like. Being a regular at the Finnish spa Relics Retreat near Fortine, she loved going to the sauna and pool. Perhaps she could get some ideas to share with her friend Willow when she returned.

The salon had an opening at 4:30 P.M., giving her plenty of time to get back to her room and dress. Anna scheduled deep conditioning, a style, manicure, pedicure and makeup. The dresses had come back from being cleaned and steamed; the one she planned to wear was lying across the bed waiting for her. On the fence about which shoes to wear, Anna didn't want to wear heels and be taller than Chen. Finding dress shoes that fit her enormous feet had always been challenging, but she had a pair of cute sandals that should work.

Noticing the time, Anna hurried to get ready, finding a blue denim baggy button-up boyfriend shirt and a pair of matching leggings. The simple clothes should be easy to get in and out of while at the spa and the button-up shirt would keep her hair from being mussed when she returned from the salon. Hopefully, being so casual wasn't a severe faux pas; she didn't figure it would matter much at the spa as you usually would wear a robe there.

A little before one o'clock, Anna dug through her purse and found her little wallet, ensuring she had what she needed before leaving her room. She picked up her cell phone and checked for any messages before getting too wrapped up at the spa. She didn't expect anything at the moment, but she hoped she might have a note from Chen. Tonight would be soon enough for her surprise. Her hand on the door handle, she suddenly realized she had forgotten the room key on the table. Talk about a real headache and embarrassing to need help getting into her room if she would have forgotten it. Grabbing the key off the desk, Anna stuffed it in her pocket with her wallet as she walked out the door.

Wandering along the corridor towards the elevators, Anna noticed some artwork she had been too distracted to see the night before. Delicate metal butterflies mimicking flight graced almost an entire side of the mezzanine from the ground level to the roof. She leaned over the railing a little to better look at the intricate insects. Later, when she wasn't so pressed for time, she would get some photos and videos to share with Liz and her other friends. It was rather spectacular.

Entering the elevator, she pressed the number for the floor with the spa. Anna stood pensive, wondering what the evening would hold. It was getting closer to when she would finally see Chen and her nerves were starting to get the best of her. This spa treatment was just what the doctor ordered. She had been so busy getting things ready for the trip that there hadn't been an opportunity to visit Relics Retreat back home. The sauna treatments would have been ideal for relaxing her before the trip. She would have to get in touch with Willow and book an appointment when she got home.

The elevator's chime announced it had arrived, breaking through her reverie. Stepping out of the elevator, the soft perfume of jasmine and lavender permeated the air. The calming scents of the flowers helped to start soothing Anna's hectic mind. Anxious about the dinner tonight, she had begun the self-sabotage she was good at. Something extraordinary was coming her way, and she was trying to overthink it, sinking the ship before getting it to the water.

Walking into the spa, the attendant greeted her. "Good afternoon, ma'am. May I ask your name?"

"Hello, I'm Anna Cassidy, and I have an appointment at 1:30 P.M. for the Emperor's Rejuvenation Ritual, please," Anna said shyly. She had no idea why she was so self-conscious about the visit to the spa. She had been to Relics many times, but they knew her there before she had made her transformation. Here, they were strangers. Would they judge her for her scars and stretch marks? Shaking her head to herself thinking, *I'm starting to do it again.*

Anna smiled and said, "Please take good care of me. *Xièxiè nǐ.*"

The attendant looked momentarily surprised at the use of Mandarin from an American. Smiling, she bowed to Anna and motioned to follow her, leading her back into the spa for her treatment.

Two hours later, after a long relaxing soak, an intense massage at the hands of a talented masseur with one of the most fantastic oil blends she had ever smelled and a foot rub that made her almost melt, she felt amazing. Anna couldn't have been happier with the service, handing the attendant a hefty tip for everyone as she paid for her service. "Thank you so very much for your wonderful care. I will be certain to return before my stay is over," Anna said as she tucked her wallet into her pocket. "Your service has been exceptional, and I couldn't be more relaxed."

"Thank you, Ms. Anna. Please don't hesitate to come again," the attendant said as she beamed at Anna. The staff had fallen in love with Anna and her humble, self-deprecating manner.

"Bye-bye." Anna waved as she left the spa.

Walking out the door, Anna paused to get her bearings. The salon was on the same floor; she just had to walk a little. Making her way down the hall, she contemplated what would be done with her hair. Before leaving Fortine, Anna had visited her favorite hairdresser Jayci and had a color touch-up. Today she just needed a bit of a trim and her highlights toned; her main objective was style and makeup. Anna was not the best with makeup; she knew just enough not to look like a circus clown.

Stepping into the salon, Anna spoke with the receptionist and told her what services she had booked. The hair wouldn't take long, and nails and makeup would be quick. She should have plenty of time to finish getting ready after they were done. Another two hours later, Anna stepped out of the salon looking like a newly minted penny. After hearing the story about how she came to be in the salon, you know how women gossip while getting hair and nails done, they wanted to do something special for her night.

Anna's long hair hung in wavy curls down her back; the sides had been pulled back in an intricate bun with an ornate hair comb. Simple but elegant. She had never looked so put together. Even her makeup was expertly applied. They had consulted her closely on how she preferred it to look. Being someone who rarely wore makeup, they made sure that it looked natural, with just a slight hint of color. Her nails were expertly manicured; they were a neutral color and would match about any outfit she wore. From what she observed, she hoped it would knock Chen's socks off, though they didn't wear much for socks in Beijing.

Looking down at her phone, she noticed she had an hour to get ready for her dinner date. It should be enough time to relax and get dressed to wow Chen.

章

Chapter 13

Anna stood in the elevator, fidgeting with her dress. Why did it take so long to get to the ground floor? She had taken her phone out of her clutch before getting in the elevator; Chen had texted that he was on his way fifteen minutes earlier. How long did it take from his apartment to the hotel? Was she making him wait? Her palms began sweating and the butterflies in her stomach tried to join the ones flying on the wall. Not much longer, and she could breathe easier.

The tone of the elevator reaching the ground floor startled her. She needed to stop spacing out in public places; people would think she had a genuine malfunction. Shaking her head, Anna took a deep breath and stepped out of the elevator. What would he think? Would he be disappointed or surprised? *Stop it, Anna, it will be just fine,* her internal voice tried to reason with her brain. The self-sabotage was trying to do its worst again. Not this time, Anna decided. Standing tall, taking a deep breath, she stepped out of the elevator, excitement conflicting with fear.

Anna didn't notice the handsome gentleman from the airport sitting in a blind corner. His startled gaze followed Anna closely as she walked around the tables and chairs. Was this the same woman? This didn't even look like the person he had seen the night before. Xian felt momentary guilt for not sending a photo to Chen as he watched her nervously make her way towards the lobby, where he knew Chen was waiting for her.

Anna stopped dead. There he was...her imagination hadn't been able to come close to this moment during all of her daydreams. Time stood still as she watched him looking for her. Wavy chestnut hair in a popular style, bangs flopping just above his intense chocolate eyes. His broad nose rested above lips that smiled frequently; she could tell by the laugh lines creasing the corners. A slight furrow between his manicured brows concerned her; she didn't want the smooth masculine forehead marred because of her.

Xian looked to where Chen was standing, fidgeting with his hands in his pockets. He had only been there a few moments, so it wasn't impatience; nerves were trying to rattle his cage. Would this be a success or disaster with an unknown magnitude waiting to happen? He turned just in time to see the expression on Chen's face as he saw Anna for the first time. Xian worried he would need to pick the poor man's jaw off the floor.

Chen's eyes swept the lobby and lounge area again; he should have asked Anna what she planned to wear; it would have made finding her a little easier. That's when he saw a beautiful woman standing a short distance away. Could this be Anna, or was it a fantasy made real?

She was not the extra curvaceous woman he had seen in his gleaned photos; this woman was tall and elegant. Her deep brunette hair was streaked with red and blonde, giving the impression of rich burgundy wine and delicate white chocolate flowing through a river of intense dark chocolate.

Silver chains tipped with jade dangled from her earlobes; they framed her stately neck better than he could have hoped. They were the earrings Chen had sent Anna as a birthday present. Seeing her wearing them, he knew the gift had been the right choice. A simple silver chain hung on her neck, the jade pendant drawing his eye to her ample décolletage.

How could this be the same woman? Flashing back to the photos of Anna he had found, they showed an ample adorable face, kind laughing eyes and full pouty lips; the creature coming toward him was dazzling, elegant and a stranger to his mind. Of all the scenarios that had played through his head, this version of Anna wasn't one of them.

Watching the different expressions flashing across Chen's face caused Anna some concern; this wasn't the expected reaction. Panic gripped her as a weight the size of a ship's anchor started to make its way down her throat, threatening a tsunami in her stomach. Why wasn't this going the way she had envisioned? With some trepidation, Anna took a few steps in Chen's direction. Xian shifted forward on the chair; he was prepared to rush in and hit the track switch so there wouldn't be a major collision.

Chen took a deep breath through his nose, holding it a moment, he willed time to stop for just a moment to sort this out in his mind and heart. This was the same touching woman that had been there through the ugly Li Ming days. The same warm, caring woman who had lost part of her heart and had finally started to open up to him. This glamorous woman gingerly approaching him was still Anna. How could he have set up such ridiculous expectations just on an old photo?

A warm, captivating smile spread across Chen's face as he released his held breath. Xian saw the shift in his disposition and slid back into the chair. This was the Chen he knew, the genuine warmth he expected exuding from his friend.

Anna, seeing the change in his demeanor, relaxed slightly. Still, confusion sketched on her face. The fight or flight response continued warring inside her. *Run, don't put yourself out there; he doesn't want you!* shouted one side in her mind. *Give him the benefit of the doubt. Hadn't he been there during the last four years when you needed someone to talk to?* the opposing voice clamored.

Xian had been so worried about Chen's reaction that he didn't realize he should have been watching Anna's behavior. He noticed Anna hesitate, her expression one of indecision. Quietly slipping to the front edge of the seat again, Xian observed the two locomotives careening headlong on the same track; the crash was imminent if steam wasn't released.

"Damn it, Chen. I didn't want to tip my hand, but..." he growled and sent a quick text message. *YOU'RE LOSING HER! Get your dumb ass over there before she falls apart and runs.*

A message chime erupted from Chen's coat pocket. Startled, he looked down and up again, indecision racing across his face. Should he check it or not?

Xian shook his head with exaggerated motions and punched in another message. If you don't go to her now, she will never trust you again, man. She's terrified you don't like her.

Another chime came from his pocket; quickly, Chen fished for it while keeping his eye on Anna. Glancing down to read the messages, his eyes raised, frantically darting around the area looking for Xian. He had to be there. *Never mind! I'll deal with that jackass later. Spying on me, of all the nerve, I would be fine after I told him,* Chen thought to himself. Xian was right though; if he didn't make a move soon, his friendship with Anna would never be the same.

Five purposeful strides later, Chen wrapped his arms around a trembling Anna. "I am so sorry! I should never have given you any doubt about how much you mean to me," he murmured into her hair. "You're my world, and I was an absolute ass for hesitating."

Anna stood stunned for a few moments; Chen's movements had been swift and caught her off guard. Electrical tingles danced over her skin where Chen touched her. Fingers that had started curling into fists by reflex relaxed of their own accord. His hug had stopped her moments before she had planned to turn and flee. Her soft armor was still delicate and this had added a few extra scuffs to its already fragile, dented shell. *I'm sorry. I'm sorry, I'm sorry...*the litany kept playing through her mind.

Chen stepped back slightly and raised her chin so she would look him in the eyes. Mesmerized by her hazel eyes, the butterscotch and forest green flecked with blues and chocolates were like nothing he had ever seen. Shaking himself, he broke the spell. "Anna, you mean more to me than you realize; I'm sorry for being such an imbecile, making you doubt yourself. I must confess, though, that you caught me a bit off guard. You're stunning!"

Realizing Anna was on the verge of tears, Chen took out his handkerchief and dabbed the moisture from her eyes. "Anna, it's okay. Please don't cry because of my idiotic behavior." Handing Anna the cloth, she dabbed cautiously, not wanting to smear her makeup and make her look like a demented clown.

Chen pulled Anna into his arms again, wanting nothing more than a do-over. Even after all these years, he never realized how many scars she still carried from her first marriage. Kyle had done what he could to help her heal, but he didn't have enough time to heal the more profound wounds. Perhaps, he could be the one to help her finish healing the lacerations to her psyche.

Waterworks under control, Anna handed Chen his handkerchief back. "Sorry Chen, not sure what came over me. At one point, the expression on your face made the crazy in my head start screaming; **HE DOESN'T WANT YOU!** Pretty silly, huh?" A forced laugh and a sheepish smile made Chen's heart skip a few beats. Even as emotional as things had gotten, he felt more protective and possessive of this fragile woman.

"Anna, you never need to be sorry for having feelings and never think I don't want you. Can we start over?" A mischievous smile danced across his lips.

Seeing that smile made Anna think back to several of Chen's dramas. Seeing that grin up close and personal made her feel warm in places she had almost forgotten existed in her body. "What do I get out of it if I give you a second chance?" Her playful response was an attempt to finish diffusing the tense moment.

"Anything your heart desires" His relief was evident even to Xian sitting across the room in his secluded corner.

Xian had finally relaxed after Chen had taken Anna in his arms the second time. This almost ended the train wreck he had predicted, though the wrong locomotive caused the near crash.

Taking Anna's chin between his thumb and forefinger, Chen held her face so she wouldn't look down or away from him. "You are beautiful; I am privileged beyond measure to be able to escort you while you're here for business. Let's go and have that dinner we planned, okay?" His eyes searched hers for approval of his suggestion.

Meeting Chen's eyes, Anna searched for the truth. Was he paying her lip service, or did he genuinely feel something for the broken woman before him? The concern in his deep brown eyes told her yes. She would go out on a limb and believe him. Nodding, a small, timid smile edged its way to her mouth. "Let's go; believe it or not, I'm starved. I forgot to eat lunch."

"We can't have that now, can we? You need to take better care of yourself while you're here." The mischievous grin put Anna completely at ease, finally. "I have something special for you tonight." Tucking Anna's hand in the crook of his arm. "Shall we, my dear?"

"Most certainly," she answered, gripping his arm tightly to steady both her balance and equilibrium.

In all the drama, Xian had forgotten to start recording. He didn't get the scene that unfolded before him for posterity purposes; well, more like blackmail material. Relaxing back against the cushions of the plush chair, he knew he would have hell to pay for revealing himself, but perhaps his texts helped diffuse the bomb, which may earn him a reprieve.

He watched with some relief as Chen and Anna walked through the lobby. The absolute ass-chewing he would get when Chen got his hands on him may be worth a bit less posterior; he hadn't seen Chen this animated or concerned about a woman in quite some time. Perhaps he was finally over the Li Ming debacle; she had soured Chen on any dating for a long time. Maybe an uncertain American storyteller had started demolishing the wall around his heart.

Seeing how his closest friend behaved around this woman, he knew in his head that he should let it go before his feelings became more; however, his heart had other plans. Seeing her again, the chunk of ice that had resided in his chest since the loss of his dear wife began dripping; when had the thaw begun?

章

Chapter 14

Walking out to Chen's Audi, Anna sucked in a breath and let out an almost inaudible "Wow!" The color made her think of the glacial lakes and rivers back in Montana. Chen looked over at her and smiled.

"Like it?"

"Well, it's probably the fanciest ride I've been in besides a limo ride back when my friend Dixie got married," she said as her eyes glanced over the sleek lines of the SUV. "But yes, it's quite impressive. Does she handle as good as she looks?"

"She?" The quizzical look on Chen's face made Anna grin.

"Yes, I always refer to my SUVs as female and trucks as male. Due to an unfortunate conflict with a large four-legged mammal, I owned a pearlescent white minivan with a blue front bumper. I had dubbed her Vanna White with the blue smile."

Chen let out a loud laugh at that revelation. "As in Vanna White on *The Wheel of Fortune*?"

It was Anna's turn to give Chen a shocked look. "You know *The Wheel of Fortune*?"

"I have heard of Vanna White. We don't have the same game show but similar shows modeled after the American *Wheel of Fortune* show."

"That is fascinating. I haven't watched any of the game shows from China, but I have watched your movies and series a FEW times." She hoped he didn't see the sarcastic expression on her face when she said few; the one series he was in she had probably watched about a hundred times...all fifty-six episodes. "I own a digital version of most of them."

"So, would you like my autograph, little girl?"

At Chen's teasing comment, Anna had to cover her mouth to keep from braying like a jackass; she didn't, however, manage to stifle the snort that escaped. Turning away from

Chen for a few moments, she composed herself enough to give him her reply. "Well, certainly, old man. Do I get some candy too?"

The tension surrounding them like a wet, woolen blanket fell away. The deep belly laughs from both cleared the air.

"Okay, Okay. Chen, I need your handkerchief again." Anna reached for the proffered piece of cloth, using it to dab at the tears of joy flowing from the outer corners of her eyes. "Can we go and eat now? If I start to snort while laughing, I'm blaming you."

Chen opened the passenger door for her saying, "Your chariot awaits."

"Why, thank you."

The rest of the trip to the restaurant was like they were having one of their usual phone conversations. Chen filled Anna in on how his day went on the set and Anna regaled Chen about her spa and salon experience. She felt blessed to have found a male friend who would listen to her no matter the topic; he had heard some doozies during their calls.

Pulling into a parking area, Anna excitedly looked around for the restaurant. Not seeing any businesses close by, she gave Chen a quizzical look. "I would imagine parking is a premium in a large city."

"That is certainly the case. Public transportation, walking and cabs are used primarily downtown; however, bikes are primarily used in smaller communities. Some people don't even leave their little community their whole life, though that has changed with the younger generation."

"I looked up some statistics out of curiosity and there are twenty times as many people in Beijing as in the whole state of Montana. The amount of traffic and pedestrians makes my head spin. I'm not sure I'd feel comfortable walking the streets on my own here; I'd get lost." Anna looked out the window wistfully; she had always wanted to explore Beijing. Still, with such a staggering population and how congested everything was, it made her nervous just thinking about it.

"Well, I'd be glad to be your tour guide. We only have a few wrap-up scenes left on this shoot, so hopefully, we can be finished in a day or two; if so, I'm completely at your service next week. We have a brief walk to get there if you're looking for the restaurant. Will that be okay?"

Feeling around the inside door panel, *Where did they put the door handle in this thing?*, Anna searched for a bit. After a few tense moments, she finally located the elusive handle. As she was just about to grab it, the door opened and Chen held his hand out for Anna to take. "If you keep this up, you'll spoil me."

Smiling when Anna took his hand, he said, "A true man should be a gentleman. Let's get to the restaurant; I swear I heard a rumble of protest from somewhere near your stomach."

"Okay, okay! I told you I was starving. I'm looking forward to what you have in store for me." She stood waiting for a cue from Chen about which direction they would be walking.

Stepping to the side so he was closest to the road, Chen offered his arm for her to take. Strolling in silence for a short way, Anna looked around at her surroundings; the bright, colorful businesses along the street and the people rushing to their destinations. It looked like a swarm of psychedelic butterflies, flitting from light to light. Luckily, the restaurant was in a less hectic neighborhood than the main thoroughfare. Food stalls and shops lined the street. The smells made Anna's mouth water and the audible rumble of her stomach made Chen smile.

"We aren't far now. We will feed the rumble."

"I told you I completely spaced out having lunch. At least I ate breakfast a bit late, so it's held me over this long." A smaller growl emanated from her middle.

Hearing her stomach grumble again, Chen grinned, changing their amble to a more lively pace. Anna was glad she was only wearing sandals tonight; the brisk walk would have been more difficult with heels on. She was enjoying just being able to walk with Chen, no matter how quickly they were walking. Perhaps after they ate, they could go for a more relaxed stroll to see some sights.

Turning the corner, a small restaurant was set apart from the rest of the block. Anna would never have guessed the building was home to a restaurant on her own. A nondescript building with red lanterns hanging in the front, the smell that whirled through the evening air was delectable. The meal would be sublime if the food were as good as it smelled. Pulling open the door, the alluring scents blasted over them.

Chen and Anna were greeted by a cherubic, grandmotherly woman bustling over to take Chen's hands in her own. "Xiao Chen, it has been much too long."

"Mama Jing, it certainly has been. Our filming is almost finished so I will visit you more often soon." Bending down, Chen kissed the age-creased cheek. "Mrs. Fu Jing, this is my close friend Ms. Anna Cassidy."

Mrs. Fu's eyes twinkled with excitement. "This is the lady you have told me about over the last few years?"

"Yes, Mama Jing." Winking at the mischief he could tell he was building in this small dynamite package, he cautioned, "You behave now."

Taking Anna's hand, Mrs. Fu pulled Anna to a table that looked like it may be close to the kitchen. "This is the best seat in the house, and you can call me Mama Jing like young Chen does."

Mama Jing's excitement was infectious. Soon Chen and Anna were tucking into delicious homestyle dishes that made Anna's foodie side sigh in ecstasy. The plates were flavorful and varied; being informed that these were all of Chen's favorites, Anna asked Mama Jing about each dish and the ingredients.

A few dishes had made her pause for a few moments; they looked unusual. There was no way she would disappoint Chen and not at least try them; he was putting himself out there. Anna also recognized dishes, though the flavor was much better than she had experienced in the States. Peking duck was a dish she was familiar with; though the Lu Zhu Huo Shao was different, this dish looked much like a stew with mystery meat and a wheaten cake. Chao Ganer was a dish she almost couldn't bring herself to try; she had never been a fan of fried liver, but this dish surprised her. It wasn't something she might eat every day, but it was an interesting treat.

Of course, she couldn't leave out the sweets either. Rolling Donkey was a dish that gave Anna a fit of giggles; it was sticky rice rolled and stuffed with red bean paste. This dish was sweet but not sickeningly so and Mama Jing assured her there was no donkey involved. Wandouhuang was a dessert Anna wasn't sure about. Chen informed her that it was usually a seasonal dish, but Mama Jing knew how much he enjoyed it, so she would make it even during the off-season.

By the time they finished with the seemingly unlimited dishes, Chen and Anna were groaning; they were so full. Mama Jing kept pressing them to try more. Laughing, Anna finally had to put her foot down and tell the woman, who reminded her of her grandmother, that she was too full to enjoy another bite.

She looked disappointed for a few moments, but it didn't last long; she must have had some idea dawn on her. "Ms. Anna, please make sure you return before you leave China. I will be making a special meal for you."

How Mama Jing treated Anna proved what Chen had known from very early in their friendship, she was one in a million. Mama Jing wouldn't even speak to Li Ming when he had brought her to meet the feisty surrogate grandmother, which should have set off alarms. He'd always trusted her opinion of people from that point on.

"Yes, Mama Jing, I will be sure to bring her again before she goes home. I will call and let you know when we have time next week. We will play tourist and do some sightseeing too," Chen assured her.

"Good, don't you forget your Mama Jing. Make it a night you can stay for a while. It will be memorable."

章

Chapter 15

Having finished with their meal, Anna and Chen gave Mama Jing a big hug, Chen placing a kiss on her plump cheek. They assured her again that they would be back to see her before Anna left town.

They were assailed by the sights and sounds as they stepped out of the cozy restaurant. "Would there be a quiet place we can go and walk?" Anna asked hopefully. "I must stretch my legs and walk off the eight million calories Mama Jing forced on us."

"You got off easy. Normally Mama Jing sends several boxes of extra food with me." Chen shook his head, remembering the last time he had eaten there. He had gone home with five full containers of leftovers; he had even given Huang Hu some.

Anna chuckled at that. "I have a lovely Filipino woman like Mama Jing back home. She always gives me about four meals worth when I order from her," she said, thinking of her dear friend Ely.

Taking Anna's hand and pulling it to the crook of his arm again, he walked on the traffic side of the sidewalk. Few men were gentlemen of this caliber in this day and age. "Where are we off to now?" Anna looked at Chen for a clue.

"I'm going to take you to a quiet park not far from my apartment so that we can walk off some of those...how many calories did you say the meal was?" A soft chuckle let her know he was teasing her again.

"You are just so funny tonight. I believe it was somewhere around eight million." Her answer made Chen laugh outright. "Okay, maybe not really that many, but it felt pretty darned close."

Starting to feel playful, Anna turned around and started walking backward to look at her companion. "It was amazing food is all I can say. She reminded me of my dad's mother;

short, plump and full of love. I wish we had more restaurants near me with fabulous food like that. Do you think she would teach me a couple of the dishes?"

Chen pulled Anna towards him since she walked right for a post and several pedestrians. "Anna, if you're going to walk that way, you need eyes in the back of your head. As for Mama Jing teaching you dishes, she just might." Stopping, he took Anna's hand and tugged her in front of him, looking into her eyes as he waited for the passerby to move along. Standing so close to her, he could smell the product they used in her hair; it also allowed him to see how the earrings swayed from her lobes.

"Ahem." Anna cleared her throat. "I believe this could be construed as PDA," she remarked, arching her brow at Chen.

"Not really, but we should get to the car if we plan to have our walk. We have our meeting with the studio tomorrow, and it needs to go well, so you should get to bed early tonight and get some sleep. I'm sure they will love you." Spinning Anna so she was beside him again, Chen tucked her hand back in the crook of his arm and led her back to the car. Unlocking the door with a click of a key fob, he opened her door and helped her in.

"Are you trying to spoil me?" Anna asked when Chen had gotten in on his side; he reached across her, pulled her seatbelt across and latched it.

"If possible, you will be spoiled rotten while you're here. You are much overdue." Chen winked at her as he put the car in gear and pulled out into traffic, pointing them towards the park he had in mind.

Anna loved being in the passenger seat for a change. She didn't get to watch the surroundings often as she was usually behind the steering wheel. Watching out the window, all the bright signs and interesting architecture fascinated her. Leaving the main thoroughfare and turning onto a side street, the traffic dropped dramatically; the single lane was lined on both sides with white fencing.

"Now, these are interesting," Anna commented on the barriers. "I've never seen anything like them."

"Those barriers keep accidents between vehicles, motorbikes

and bicycles down; they use them in the residential areas more than the main business district."

Pressing her face closer to the window, she looked up at the apartment buildings lining the street. "Wow, how many floors are there? I guess I'm a total bumpkin. I grew up on a farm in a pretty rural area and even when I did move to the city, it was just Bismarck which is tiny compared to Beijing. There are probably more people in a couple of blocks here than in the whole city of Bismarck. Heck, Beijing dwarfs even our large cities."

Chen looked wistful. "I grew up in a smaller community on the outskirts of Beijing, so it was quieter than living in the main part of the city. My aunt and uncle raised my sister and me as my parents were too busy with their corporation. I spent most of my school years at a private school in the dorms. I'm sure your life was way more fun than mine." A distant look crossed Chen's face. Anna could only wonder if he was reliving some painful memory.

"Now, I would not understand what that would be like. I didn't even have the usual college experience." Anna mused, "I started college when Liz was two and I had to quit after one year. During the summer break, I worked for a delivery company; I injured my hand due to stupidity and dropped a truck cab on my right wrist. After that, I couldn't go back to school; our curriculum called for most of the design work to be hand done. For most of my career, I got there on my own. I can't remember all my jobs over the years, everything from making burgers to building windows. Thanks to you, I believe I finally found my calling, writing stories for you to share with people. Perhaps I need to think about writing a new movie script; want to collaborate with me?"

Hearing what Anna said, Chen glanced over at her with surprise. "I'm no writer Anna. I just act them out."

"But that is why I think we could write something amazing. Isn't there a story you would like to tell your fans?" Anna asked.

"Well, there is actually. I never thought I'd do anything about it, though." Chen looked thoughtful.

"So why don't we? Do something about it, that is."

Reaching out her hand to touch his arm, those phantom sparks shot through her fingers again.

Arriving at the location Chen had in mind for their evening stroll, he pulled into a parking spot, shifted the SUV into park and shut off the motor before looking directly at the woman sitting next to him. He had felt those sparks at her touch. Chen had never felt anything like it when touching women before, and there had been a few in his profession. Looking closer at Anna, he could see the hope and excitement in her eyes. He wanted to see that look every day for the rest of his life.

"When do we start?" Chen said softly.

Excited, Anna launched herself across the seat at Chen, throwing her arms around his neck as much as she could in the confines of the front seat. Hugging him tightly for a few moments before remembering herself and pulling back, she blushed hotly. "Oh Chen, I am so sorry for that. It was inappropriate."

Still gaining his composure after the attack hug, Chen smiled and reached over to take her hand. "If I were that excited, I probably would forget myself too. It's not like I minded the hug either."

"Okay, let's go for that walk so I can walk off those calories and some of this excitement," Anna said as she unbuckled her seatbelt and opened the door.

Chen walked around the SUV and grabbed Anna's hand; pulling her to his side, he offered his arm for her to hang on to again. He may have seemed to be acting the gentleman by doing this, but he had an ulterior motive. Walking this way allowed Chen to touch Anna, to feel her warmth as she walked next to him. Sneaking a glance at the smiling beauty next to him, his right hand reached over to cover her hand on his arm; he never wanted this night to end.

———

Headlights of a dark luxury car followed them as they walked; Chen and Anna were so wrapped up in one another that they never noticed it. The hostility radiating from that vehicle would have made any sensitive person cringe. Tears of anger and frustration blurred the driver's vision; why had he never shown her this kind of attention? Even when they were engaged, he had never shown her the kind of courtesy he was giving that foreigner. Li Ming would make him return to her; if she had her way, that American would leave and never return.

章

Chapter 16

Returning to the hotel, Chen parked and jumped out. He dashed around the SUV to get Anna's door before the valet could open it. Holding his hand out for her, he kept her hand in his and led her to the hotel's entrance.

Slowing her step, Anna halted their forward momentum. "Chen, I have a question for you. I don't want to be too forward, but would you come with me to my room? I need your opinion on something."

Stopping to consider Anna's question, Chen turned back to her with a sober look on his face. "Madam, what do you take me for? An easy man?" At the look of shock and dismay on Anna's face, Chen quickly grabbed her hand as she made to rush past him. "Anna, please stop. I was just teasing you. Of course, I will be happy to go with you to your room, and I can also come in. Unless you plan on taking advantage of me." Chen attempted joking again.

This time Anna played along saying, "Are you sure I won't?" Winking, she turned and pulled him toward the hotel.

Arriving at her room, Anna scanned her card and opened the door. Walking in, Chen looked around, assessing the decor. This was a room worthy of Anna; he would have moved her to one of the larger suites if it had failed his approval. The polished dark wood of the furniture gave the room a warmth that went well with the rich browns and creams of the fabrics. The giant plush throw pillows on the couch looked inviting. Seeing the office area, he approved. She should be able to work well there.

Tossing her purse and key on the dark cherry sideboard next to the large curved screen tv, she asked, "So, what do you think of my temporary digs?" Walking to the minibar fridge Anna pulled out a juice bottle. "Can I get you anything? Coffee, tea, me?" She was mentally banging her head on a wall at that last comment. Why in the world had she said that? He probably wouldn't get the movie reference.

Chuckling, Chen walked over to inspect the options available; taking a beer and cracking it open, he took several long swallows. "I believe a beer will do the trick."

Anna could feel the moisture develop on her upper lip from watching his throat as he swallowed; she imagined running her tongue along his throat. Shaking herself, she always had a thing for men's Adam's apples. Turning back to her desk, Anna picked up the pages of the chapter waiting for Chen's feedback. Wending her way around the furniture, Anna sat the pages down on the coffee table, giving Chen easy access to them while she changed.

"I have two favors to ask," she said, turning to address Chen but avoiding looking him in the eye, she was still a little off-kilter after those borderline naughty thoughts. "First, would you mind reading that scene and let me know what you think? I made some changes before leaving Montana and wanted your feedback. The second may be a bit of a stretch." Anna paused, she was working through how to phrase the request.

Chen piped in before she could continue, "You can ask me any favor, don't worry about it."

"Okay, you asked for it. How much do you know about fashion?" Anna asked as she fidgeted with her dress, avoiding his gaze.

"Well, I know a bit, though Xian is more knowledgeable than I am on women's fashion. Why are you so nervous about fashion?" The curiosity was beginning to eat at him.

"For the award ceremony, it's normal for women to wear evening gowns, right?"

Hearing that question, a realization dawned on Chen; Anna had never been exposed to the awards. Of course, she wouldn't know what is expected other than what she may have seen in movies or on TV.

"Typically, yes. Some actresses have designers fight over who will wear their latest creations. Do you have anything to wear? I should have thought about that sooner; I'm so sorry, Anna." Chen was immediately apologetic.

"Well, yes and no. I borrowed a dress from a friend, but I

don't know. It's not me, but I'm not sure what is. I've never worn an evening gown." Sighing, she just gave up being embarrassed; what was the point? "Can you look at my dress and tell me if I need something different?"

Chen secretly smiled; he was flattered that she would ask him for his advice. "Bring it out and let's have a look."

Ducking into the bedroom, Anna came out with the blue gown on a hanger and held it up for Chen's inspection.

"Sorry Anna, I think you will need to put it on for me to judge; it's too hard to tell on the hanger. I'll look over these pages while you slip into it. Let's kill two birds with one stone." Chen picked up the pages she had asked him to look over, sat on the couch and looked at the first page. Trying to hide his pleasure at getting to see Anna in what he figured would be a pretty skintight gown.

Rolling her eyes, she took the dress back to the bedroom. Trying it on in Montana, it had been just a little bit snug; it may be snugger after that fabulous meal made by Mama Jing. Sliding the zipper down, she stepped into the gown. Granted, it may not fit right without the proper supporting garments, but that was fine; it was just to give him an idea of the fit and style. Being a strapless gown, Anna was self-conscious about wearing it. Stretch marks and scars from surgery would be out there for the world to see. Would they be noticed?

Zipping the dress about halfway up, Anna just couldn't manage to close it the rest of the way. "Hey Chen, can I get some assistance? I'm not part octopus. These dresses are **NOT** meant to be put on without a team of help, I swear." Holding the top of the dress over her breasts with one arm, she grabbed the hem of the skirt with her other hand to have Chen help with that stubborn zipper.

Shuffling cautiously into the living room, Chen's eyes couldn't leave Anna as she made her way toward him. She had finally let down her guard and became the Anna he had talked to for so long. Stepping up to Chen, she turned her back to him, so he could help finish zipping the glittering gown.

Setting the pages aside, he found the delicate zipper pull and gently tugged it upwards, smoothly, then with more difficulty as it reached the top. "Don't take this the wrong way but suck it in, Anna; it's getting difficult to finish zipping up." At those words, Chen could feel Anna's grumble as she exhaled and made herself as small as possible. That was just enough to allow him to finish zipping it.

Finally able to take a breath, it just wasn't a deep one; she was undoubtedly bustier than the dress's owner. This dress wasn't going to work; she felt as though something was going to tear if she took a deep enough breath. Walking to the floor-length mirror in the bedroom, Anna checked her reflection from different angles. Shimmering in the soft light, the color was one of her favorites, but it didn't quite work with her hair and skin tone. Tugging the dress up, she adjusted the girls to settle in the cups better; they still didn't fit quite right.

Snickering from the doorway made Anna turn and glower at the handsome peeping tom. "And what is so damn funny?" Her hip cocked to one side, arms folded across her ample cleavage.

"Sorry, I shouldn't snicker; it reminded me of my sister Chandra getting ready for some gala. I don't believe that dress will work; as much as I love seeing you in that skintight gown, it leaves so little to the imagination. I doubt that is the look you want; it may give the wrong impression. You are an unknown and showing up dressed like this could be spun the wrong way. We're going to need to shop before Saturday. Do you happen to know what time your flight leaves Saturday morning for Taipei?" Chen pulled his phone out, looking up his flight information.

"Can I get out of this rib crusher first? It's a challenge to breathe in this thing." Anna turned her back to Chen. "Would you mind reversing the process you just went through?"

If she had known the thoughts flitting through Chen's mind at that moment, she might not have been so nonchalant about having him unzip her. It took restraint on his part not to reach out and caress her creamy shoulders and back. He could picture running his fingers from the nape of her neck down her spine, his hands slipping around her waist, pulling her back against him.

Shaking his head, he quickly tugged the zipper down. "Anything else you need? I'm going to go finish those pages."

He turned and walked out of the room without her answer. He needed to put some space between them. Seeing her in that dress was almost more than his willpower could handle.

Grabbing the pages from the coffee table again, he settled back on the couch to finish going through the scene. Completing the first two pages, Chen found an envelope tucked between the pages. Not seeing any writing on the envelope, he checked it, figuring perhaps she had mistakenly grabbed an empty envelope from her desk.

Inside, he found a sheet of neatly folded paper. Fighting his curiosity, it won; he pulled the sheet from the envelope, giving it a cursory glance. What he found on that page doused his ardor in moments. Reading through the printed page, he started to feel dread. Who had written this letter? Had Anna read it? He highly doubted it; she would have mentioned it if she had, wouldn't she?

"Hey Anna, do you happen to know where this envelope came from? It's tucked in with your scene pages."

Anna poked her head around the bedroom door and scrutinized the envelope Chen was waving at her. "Oh, someone left it at the bar for me. Liz dropped it off right before I left. Is it anything interesting?" Pulling her head back into the room to finish dressing.

Looking around, Chen found a sheet of blank paper on the desk. Folding it, he tucked it into the envelope. The sheet with the distressing words disappeared into an internal pocket of his jacket. She didn't need to see this right now, not that anything could be done about it at the moment.

"It's just a notice for an event happening while you're here. I'll take care of it for you."

"Thanks, Chen. One less item to deal with now."

Shaken, Chen needed to talk to Xian. First, he would ask him to take Anna shopping for her evening gown. Xian had taken Chandra shopping for dresses on more than one occasion; he had impeccable taste, which may come from dealing with all those designers and models for the company.

Anna picked that moment to walk out of the bedroom wearing a baggy denim boyfriend shirt and a pair of black leggings with lace panel inserts at the hips and below the knees.

She had also taken the time to brush out her hair and throw it in a messy bun. Anna might have been in trouble if it hadn't been for that letter cooling the heat he felt; she looked cute in that baggy shirt.

Chen zoned out for a few moments, contemplating what Anna might look like wearing nothing but his dress shirt and a tie. Shivering, he shook his head. He couldn't stay much longer. He thought back to the letter, and once again, it put a wet blanket on his desire.

"You were wondering about my flight Saturday?" she asked as she walked to the desk to check her laptop calendar. Using her laptop was easier than trying to find it on her phone at the moment. Checking, she saw she flew out at five in the morning. "Looks like my flight leaves at 5 A.M., First-class. I should be there by 10 A.M."

Chen sighed in relief; she was flying with him. The studio must have booked all their tickets together. Oh man, did they book Li Ming on the same flight? That wasn't a good idea.

"Let me give Xian a call. I would like him to take you shopping Friday. We're so close to finishing this shoot I'm hoping Friday will be the last day. Besides, he is more of a fashion guru than I am; I can only tell you what I like."

"Well, as long as it is okay with him. Would this be the Xian I was supposed to meet last night?" Anna looked curious.

"The same." Chen took out his phone, dialing the man in question.

"This better be good." Xian yawned as he answered the phone.

"Grumpy much?" Chen teased.

"Well, as it was mostly your fault, cut me some slack," came the grumbled reply from the other end of the phone.

"Yeah, I owe you a big one and I am adding more to the tab. I have another favor to ask." Chen watched Anna thumb through some of the printed pages on her desk. Quietly, turning his back to keep Anna from hearing everything he was saying to Xian, he said, "I'll call you back after I leave; I have a couple of situations that I need your assistance with involving Anna." Speaking louder again he continued, "So, would you be willing to escort a certain fashion-challenged writer on a shopping trip?"

Hearing what Chen said, Xian's lassitude evaporated. Chen was rarely that serious; something was happening besides a clothing emergency. "Certainly, I would love to give her my fashion expertise. When do we need to do this?"

"We have a meeting tomorrow morning. Depending on how long it goes, I was going to ask her to watch the filming tomorrow. How about we meet for dinner tomorrow night, I can formally introduce you and we can make plans. Hey, were you going to the awards? I thought I remembered you saying something about attending." The relief was evident in his voice. He trusted Anna's safety with Xian.

The letter must have been from Montana, but he couldn't forget there was also Li Ming to deal with here. They needed to be cautious now—no telling what that crazy woman would do.

"Come to the house tomorrow night; we can relax at my place. That bat crazy woman you were engaged to can't just show up here. As stressed as you're sounding right now, it's probably the best option."

Xian knew Chen too well. He had found a resolution to one of Chen's most nagging concerns at the moment, keeping Li Ming away from Anna as much as possible. That letter reminded Chen that there was crazy in China they needed to contend with.

"What time tomorrow night?" Chen asked.

"Will 7 o'clock work okay for you?" Xian inquired.

"Hey Anna, do you have any plans for tomorrow night? Xian invited us over for dinner."

"You're my event coordinator while I'm in China, so do I have plans tomorrow night?" Anna smiled at Chen's expression of mild irritation. Taking pity on Chen, she said, "No, I don't have any plans other than what we've made so far."

"Okay, Xian, tomorrow night it is. I'll talk to you later." Chen stressed the last sentence.

"Don't make it too long; I need a few hours of sleep once in a while," came back the snide response from Xian.

"Certainly. Have a good night. Bye," Chen said as he disconnected the call. He needed to call Xian back soon. Resources he had, though some explanation may be in order if he utilized them.

"Anna, I better call it a night. We haven't been getting much sleep the last few days and we have a long day tomorrow again. Are you ready for the meeting?" Chen tried to steer the conversation in a safer direction.

Anna gave Chen an appraising glance. Something was up. Chen's demeanor had shifted and he was suddenly rushing to leave. What didn't she hear on Xian's end of the conversation? "That sounds like a good idea. I'm pretty wiped out. Why don't we meet for breakfast and finalize our plan? My meal this morning was impressive. We can either eat here in the room or down in the restaurant."

"Let's plan on eating in your room. Reduces the risk of eavesdroppers." Standing up, he adjusted his jacket; reaching inside, he touched the folded paper in his pocket.

Anna got up from the desk and walked over to Chen; taking his hand, she led him to the door. "I had one of the best nights in a very long time. If the rest of this trip goes as well, I may not want to leave," Anna confessed and gave Chen a shy smile.

"I wouldn't complain if you stayed." Chen's tender gaze made Anna's knees go wobbly.

That statement caused a hitch in Anna's breath. "Good night, Chen." Anna needed Chen to leave; if he didn't go in moments, he wouldn't be leaving for the night. That wasn't how she wanted the night to end. Well, she did...but they weren't even dating. She had rushed into bed in too many other relationships when she was young and reckless; being older, and hopefully wiser, she didn't want to repeat the same mistakes.

"You better get going. I don't trust myself right now," Anna said as Chen made to hug her, putting her hand on his chest.

After that admission, Chen closed his eyes and tried to think of anything but staying with Anna that night. It was this difficult already and she had only been there one day. Could he make it the entire two weeks?

"Okay, I'll be here at 7:30 A.M. for breakfast. Our meeting has been changed to 10 o'clock, so that should give us plenty of time." Leaning in, he kissed Anna's cheek as he opened the door. Stepping through, he closed it quickly and leaned against it attempting to regain his composure. Anna's admission rattled his self-control; he could feel his heart beating in a wild staccato in his chest.

Pushing himself away from the door, the sound of paper rustling in his pocket brought reality crashing around him. Damn, that letter! He made it down to his car in record time. He had better go see Xian; this shouldn't be discussed over the phone.

As Chen was heading to Xian's, Anna poured herself a tub of hot water; she needed to soak the sexual tension away. It had been such a long time and her body reminded her of that every time Chen got close to her. After the long hot bath, the bed called her. As excited as she was, exhaustion won and she was out within moments.

章

Chapter 17

Chen had broken a few speed limits and was lucky he wasn't stopped. It didn't take long to reach Xian's condo; the contents of that note kept haunting him during the drive. What was with this individual? They were undoubtedly disturbed. Pulling up to the gate, Chen entered his private code and sat impatiently waiting for the heavy black iron gate to finish opening.

Chen saw Xian waiting at the front door as he pulled up to the house.

"So, what's the big emergency?" Xian asked from where he casually lounged against the doorjamb.

Chen pulled the folded offensive paper from his pocket, handing it to Xian. "Read this, and don't think you're off the hook for that stunt you pulled earlier."

Reading the letter as they walked into the house, Xian cringed when Chen mentioned the incident at the hotel. Stopping, he looked at Chen and waved the paper asking, "Where did this come from?"

Chen ground his teeth as he replied, "She received this in Montana right before she left; someone had dropped it at her daughter's workplace. The real concern is that very few people know this information about her. She's an extremely private person."

"There isn't much we can do from here. This happened in another country, and we have no idea who wrote it. Do you think Anna's daughter may have an idea who left it?" Xian asked, running his hand through his tousled hair. He hadn't officially met Anna, but with what Chen had told him throughout the years and meeting her at the airport, he had a vested interest in keeping her safe.

Walking into Xian's home office, Chen dropped into his usual plush armchair. He had sat in the chair many nights playing Go when Chandra had been alive; Xian must have been working in the office when Chen called. A rocks glass of what he assumed was bourbon sat next to the keyboard; crystalline condensation droplets slowly slid down the glass. Ice cubes clinked as they settled when Xian accidentally bumped the desk slightly as he sat down.

"Not sure if I can get a hold of her without her mother knowing. I don't have her contact information," Chen said, wracking his brain for an idea on how to contact Liz. Where did Anna say she worked? Some bar in the same town Anna lived in. There couldn't be too many of them, could there? Pulling his phone out, Chen googled bars in Fortine, Montana. Two came up, but the one didn't sound right. It had to be Jerry's; the name sounded familiar.

Opening the clock app on his phone, he checked the time; there would be a distant chance that he would be able to catch Liz this early in the day. Chen would need to wait until the following morning; it would afford him the best opportunity to see her at work.

"I'll have to try her in the morning; it's the wrong time right now to try calling her work. If I call on my way to have breakfast with Anna, someone at the bar should get me in touch with Liz. Xian, if I find a name, do you have any contacts in the States that can look into this?" Chen looked up to see why Xian was so quiet. "Xian!"

"Huh? Oh yeah, I believe I have some people over there that can investigate," Xian said, completely distracted by something on his phone.

This wasn't like Xian, being so distracted when discussing something serious. Quietly, Chen crept up behind Xian, looking over his shoulder. Xian was pricing out video surveillance systems. "You don't have enough security around your place?" Chen asked teasingly.

Startled, Xian quickly closed his phone screen. "I'm looking into it for a friend."

Chen had known Xian since he was five years old; Xian wasn't forthcoming about whom he was pricing those cameras for. Chen had an odd suspicion that Anna would have some seriously beefed-up security if Xian had anything to say about it by the time she returned home. Why? Xian had met Anna for about five minutes the evening before and he hadn't even known it was her. Curious.

"Well, I would imagine they'd appreciate having Big Brother installed in their home. Do you think that system would fit Anna's house?" A bright crimson color crept over Xian's face. *Bingo!* He had been looking at it for Anna. Chen couldn't get mad; he had asked for help.

Xian got his emotions under control and calmed himself down. Chen had almost caught on. That letter frightened Xian. This person was disturbed; his obsession was aimed at Anna and he had to help Chen protect her.

He'd never been one to buy into the "love at first sight" nonsense, but this almost had him convinced. Even when Chandra was alive he hadn't been this concerned with her safety. Coming from an affluent family, danger from competitors and rivals was always a risk; having grown up with these risks, Chen and Chandra had known how to deal with them from a young age. Anna didn't have the benefit of their training and experience.

Not able to do much more about it that night, Chen needed to try contacting Liz very early in the morning. Her workplace business hours were primarily during Beijing's overnight hours. Getting all this coordinated would be challenging, but he would get it done considering whom it was for.

Xian was on his computer now. Chen guessed he was finding an even more sophisticated system; he wouldn't put it past Xian to get one that he could monitor from anywhere as long as it kept Anna safe.

Standing up and stretching, Chen walked to the wet bar Xian had tucked in the corner of the office. Backlighting behind the bottles lent their soft glow in the dimly lit room. Accent lights on the shelving added to the relaxing atmosphere. A glass of scotch and he would be ready to go home and sleep. Anna was depending on him tomorrow. It was a monumental meeting for her.

Pouring three fingers of Xian's best scotch, Chen returned to Xian's desk to spy on him more. Sipping the amber liquor, the notes of smoke, oak and peat blended on his pallet as he rolled the room temperature spirits throughout his mouth. It was one of his favorites. His nerves finally calmed to a dull roar; he looked over Xian's shoulder at the latest security system he was investigating. "Have you found something that will work?"

"I believe so. It will take a bit of doing, but it can be set up unobtrusively; no one should know the system is even installed as long as no one observes it being connected. Liz will need to let the installers in when I get it scheduled. I wonder what obscene amount of money can expedite this in the next couple of days, especially so close to their Thanksgiving holiday?" Xian continued perusing the specifications of this latest system. "How much trouble will we be in?"

Brows creased, he considered the question. Chen thought about it for a few moments. "Well, she will either appreciate it or won't speak to us again. You take your pick. If she saw this letter, she would be happy for the help. Do we dare show it to her? I've never read anything like it."

"Let's get this done then. Anna's safety is more important than her talking to me. I will take the fall for it if she gets furious." Xian was going to protect her. It may be time to tell Chen the truth about Chandra as well. She had forbidden him from telling her brother, but he may have to know.

章

Chapter 18

Chen didn't stay much longer, the morning would come fast enough and he was running on energy fumes already. Getting to his apartment, he was glad he had picked up after himself before leaving. Mrs. Hu would appreciate him making that much of an effort. His housekeeper was a miracle worker and she only had a few rules: #1. Don't leave the kitchen in a huge mess if you happen to cook, #2. Do **NOT** leave dirty clothes in the common areas of the apartment, #3. He would receive her resignation if she found a naked woman in the apartment.

After getting a royal ass-chewing over him breaking rule number one, he had been exceptionally cautious about further rule-breaking. She could be intimidating, and she kept his apartment immaculate; he couldn't afford to offend her. He's not sure why she even included rule three. He hadn't been with a woman since Li Ming. Having finally found the woman he truly wanted to be with, he would take his time and not mess it up.

The morning came quicker than he had hoped. Sunday would be his first opportunity to get some much-needed sleep.

Looking at the clock, he would have time to call and try to locate Liz before meeting Anna for breakfast. Bringing up the Google search he had done the night before, he initiated the call; hopefully, someone would answer. Sitting down on the couch he waited for the call to connect.

"Hello Jerry's, Liz speaking, how can I help you?" Liz's cheery voice answered the phone.

"Hello Liz, I know this will sound odd; please don't hang up until I can explain the situation. I know your mother." Chen started.

"Xiao Chen, is that you?" Liz asked, curious why he would be calling her. "Why would you be calling Jerry's on a

Wednesday afternoon?"

"Yes, it's me. It's a long story, but we don't have much time now. I need your help."

The seriousness of Chen's voice put Liz on high alert. "What can I do to help? Does it have something to do with mom?"

Chen quickly explained the situation and why they wanted to put the security system in. Liz was appalled at what had been in the letter. "Did you tell mom about this? Does she know how bad that letter was? Is she being protected while she is in Beijing? How about that nasty Li Ming and her bullshit? Has she done anything other than making both of your lives miserable?" The rapid-fire questions shot at Chen.

"No, I didn't want to let her know until she was home. Her trip shouldn't be ruined by someone that far away." Chen walked around his apartment, picking up his wallet and keys, preparing to head for Anna's hotel. "I need to go meet your mother for breakfast. We have our meeting at the studio this morning, then I will ask her to stay with me on set for the rest of the day. We have plans with my brother-in-law for dinner tonight, so someone will be with her at all times unless she is in her hotel room. Give me your number and I will add it to my phone to chat with you or call. We will need to get the security install team in; I'll let you know what time and date. As for Li Ming, I am doing what I can to keep them from running into each other."

Liz rattled off her cell number for Chen and let him know both Sheldon and herself would be behind him one hundred percent on installing the security cameras. She had always been nervous about her mom living alone in the woods.

"Thank you, Liz. I will also need your help for a few other things; this is the most pressing at the moment." Chen stood up, grabbing his wallet from the couch table, he headed for the door. "I'll be in touch in a day or two. I have some holiday plans that will require your assistance."

"Whatever I can do to help. You make my mother the happiest she has been since Kyle passed. Just let me know how I can assist." Liz was thrilled that Chen was making this much effort for her mom. Anna had been the leading family supporter for a long time and it would be great for someone to take care of her for a change.

——

If Liz had known she was being eavesdropped on, she might have been more cautious about what she had said. Scott took his phone out and began looking for flights to Beijing. This Xiao Chen was going to be a problem. What was Anna doing in China? There hadn't been anything posted on her numerous social media accounts. But that explained why she hadn't been home and why her daughter was staying at her place.

Sitting at the end of the bar, he had listened carefully; Liz was loud enough that he could hear some of both sides of the conversation. Why in the world would she leave their picturesque community to travel halfway around the globe?

He had to go and get her back; perhaps this Li Ming could be of some help. It seemed as though she didn't want to see Anna and this Xiao Chen dude together any more than he did. From the way Liz spoke, she was making trouble for them. That was a good thing, right?

Seeing Liz finish the call, he thought he would feel her out for information. "Hey Liz, when's your mom going to be in? I haven't seen her in a while. I had hoped to take her to dinner."

Did she just wince? "Sorry Scott, mom won't be in for a while. I told her you were waiting to see her. I'm sure when she's not so busy she will get back to you."

Watching her closely, he could tell she was behaving differently towards him. Liz had been all for him going out with her mom before this point. Narrowing his eyes, he wondered if she read the letter he had left for Anna. That could be a problem, but he would deal with that later. He needed to get Anna back.

Flipping through screens on his phone, he found a flight, and he should be in Beijing late on Friday. Hopefully, he could locate the Li Ming she mentioned; it was time to throw a wrench in someone's plans.

章

Chapter 19

Chen arrived at the hotel with ten minutes to spare, plenty of time to get to Anna's room for their breakfast meeting. Now to keep his composure while they were eating.

This meeting could easily change both of their lives. Each of the scripts could easily be made into long-running dramas, which would require considerable work on Anna's part. Perhaps they might find an assistant to work with her so it wasn't so daunting.

Arriving at Anna's room, Chen stood there for a few moments; his palm pressed to the door. *Get yourself together, man.* Wrapping his fingers into a fist, he knocked on the door. He cringed as the sound echoed through the empty hallway loudly.

After a few moments, the door cracked open. Anna poked her head around the door and smiled shyly at Chen. "You know I am still having a hard time getting used to seeing you up close. After hearing your voice for many years, I almost regret implementing the video chat ban. Come on in," Anna said, opening the door for him to enter the room.

Chen saw Anna's back as she walked to her desk; she wore a long silk robe. "Um, you're not dressed yet?"

"Well, as I can be a klutz when I'm eating, I decided that the best option is to eat first and then finish dressing. The face and hair are all handled. I am very fast when I need to be." Anna rooted around on the desk, looking for the menu; her notes and papers had taken over the space. Finding the printed folio with the room service menu, Anna handed it to Chen. "Let's get breakfast ordered; we can discuss the meeting while waiting. I already know what I want."

Chen glanced over the menu, choosing a light breakfast option.

"Okay, now that is out of the way. Can you tell me what I should expect at this meeting?"

Chen was about to answer when his phone started vibrating on the table. Anna could tell Chen was reluctant to answer the call; picking up the phone, he replied curtly, "Hello, this had better be good."

Anna looked at Chen with shock; she had never heard him be that brusk before.

The look on Chen's face screamed volumes to Anna; something wasn't right. The color had drained from his face to be replaced with a deep crimson. "They **WHAT**?"

A sneaky suspicion began to develop in Anna's mind. As a writer, she couldn't believe she didn't see this coming; bad guy 101, mess with the heroine at every turn. This had Li Ming written all over it. Anna laid her hand on Chen's arm, willing her calm to flow to him. "Chen, what's wrong?" she asked as he hung up the phone.

Taking a few moments to regain what little composure he had left, Chen closed his eyes and took a few deep breaths before explaining. "Our studio meeting has been moved to 8:30 this morning. You had better dress; I'll call room service to cancel our meal. We must leave in a few minutes to get there in time."

Cursing under her breath, Anna, who could have made a sailor blush at one point in her life, rushed into the bedroom to dress. She was so glad she had taken the time that morning to lay out her clothes and do her hair before Chen's arrival. One positive aspect from her upbringing, she could be ready and out the door in ten minutes or less; she had managed it in about four once. Being in the military and the volunteer fire department had given her excellent training too.

Dressed, Anna looked herself over in the mirror and nodded; she marched into the living area, putting her shoes on as she walked.

When Anna walked out of the bedroom, Chen was texting Xian about the meeting change. He almost had asked where Anna was before looking closer. Wearing a stylish black pantsuit with a blush-colored camisole under the jacket and a pair of low heels, she looked professional and almost severe.

She would knock those executives for a loop.

Picking up her clutch and folio from the desk she asked, "Chen, would you be a dear and grab my phone from the table for me?" Checking to make sure she had the pages she had printed explicitly for the meeting.

"Ready?" Chen asked.

"As I'll ever be," Anna replied, taking a few deep breaths to calm the herd of horses stampeding through her stomach at the moment. It was probably better that she didn't eat before the meeting; otherwise, it may not have ended well.

Staying at a hotel close to the studio had been a distinct advantage. It hadn't taken long for them to reach the administrative offices of the studio.

Opening Anna's door and helping her out of the car, Chen was impressed with how poised and relaxed she appeared. He, however, knew better; below that placid surface there was a tsunami blowing. On the drive from the hotel they had gone over critical points of the scripts that Chen felt would interest the executives and possible angles they may throw at her.

Taking Chen's proffered arm, Anna composed herself, stood tall and walked with confidence she, in truth, didn't feel. This trip had been continually throwing her off her game. One curveball after another continued to be thrown at her; it was a good thing she could hit one out of the park on occasion.

Walking into the offices, Chen and Anna were greeted by the secretaries who offered to take their coats and directed them to the conference room where the meeting would be held. Walking into the room, they were greeted by a long glass table with breakfast snacks and bottled water. Chen pulled out a chair and offered it to Anna; taking the chair next to her, they sat and waited for the executives to arrive.

"Nervous?" Chen asked, taking Anna's hand in his.

"How did you guess?" Anna said, mentally doing relaxation techniques.

"Well, it may be the perspiration on your upper lip or your intense look of concentration. Honestly, take a deep breath; these guys don't bite," Chen assured her.

"I know; this is my first experience with something like this. I'll be fine." Anna looked at him and smiled. She was so fortunate to have him with her as her support system; doing this alone would have been overwhelming. She pressed the back of her hand against her lip to blot off the sheen of moisture.

The door to the conference room opened, admitting three men all dressed in business suits. An older gentleman that had dark hair with silver around the edges, and creases of age on his face, sat in the middle of the table across from Anna and Chen while the two younger men took a chair on each side.

"Mr. Xiao, it is a pleasure to see you again," the older gentleman said.

"Mr. Shun, it is a pleasure to see you," Chen replied. "Mr. Shun, I would like to introduce Ms. Cassidy."

Mr. Shun stood and offered his hand to Anna. "Ms. Cassidy, it is indeed a pleasure."

Anna stood, taking his hand and shaking it briefly. "Mr. Shun, I am very honored to meet you," she replied in perfect Mandarin.

Mr. Shun sat down, smiled and laughed heartily, switching to Mandarin himself. "I look forward to working with you, Ms. Cassidy. Your story for *The Lost Prince* was exceptional and we look forward to seeing more of your work."

"Mr. Shun, I sent the two new scripts to your office to review. I hope you liked those storylines as well. I had also considered doing a follow-up story to *The Lost Prince* in the coming year." Anna settled back in her chair.

Chen sat back in his chair, watching Anna and Mr. Shun discuss the scripts she had sent and the premise for her follow-up. He wasn't sure why she had felt so nervous; she seemed right in her element.

After a lengthy discussion and negotiation, the studio bought both scripts Anna had pitched and the rights for the follow-up script to *The Lost Prince*. Anna almost fell out of her chair when they told her what she would receive for *The Lost Prince* story. Anna had tried to object, feeling it was too much, but Mr. Shun had insisted on the amount.

Anna gave Chen a side glance, trying to convey, *We are going to have a long talk.* Chen nonchalantly gave an almost imperceptible shrug as if to say, *It isn't my fault.*

One of the critical points in the negotiations was that the

studio wanted Anna to be in China while filming for any possible rewrites that might need to be made. They didn't have to press her hard to agree to this stipulation. She had fallen in love with China; it wouldn't be an imposition for her to live there for a year. Chen hadn't looked brokenhearted about finding this out either.

Finished with the meeting, Anna stood and gave Mr. Shun a bow. "Thank you, Mr. Shun, for your time. I look forward to working with the studio for a long time. Please take good care of me," she said, pulling from her Chinese lessons on how to address him adequately.

Returning the bow, Mr. Shun looked quite impressed. "Ms. Cassidy, it has genuinely been a pleasure to make your acquaintance. I believe we will have a very beneficial partnership in the future. You are here in China for a while longer?"

Chen answered Mr. Shun, "Yes, the awards are on Saturday and she will be here for the following week. Next Tuesday, we have a meeting to finalize what we have done here. I hoped to take Anna with me on set today while finishing some scenes."

Mr. Shun smiled. "I will call and make the necessary arrangements for her to join you. It may give her even more ideas for future scripts."

Chen nodded and added, "That and it may give her more insight when she writes to see how we film."

"True, true. Mr. Xiao, you have an excellent idea. We'll make it happen." Mr. Shun made to leave the room, one assistant furiously texting on his phone while the other spoke quietly into his phone. Hanging up, the assistant said to Chen, "Everything is arranged, Mr. Xiao. There will be a visitor badge for her at the gate."

Chen bowed to Mr. Shun. "Thank you, sir."

"Don't mention it, Mr. Xiao. Both of you have made the studio a tidy sum with *The Lost Prince*; we owe you both for your diligent work. Now I must leave you; I have another meeting soon," he said as he left the conference room followed by his assistants.

Anna looked at Chen and mouthed the final figure they had agreed on. "2.75 million?"

"Did I hear that right?" She gasped as a minor panic attack hit her. She had never contemplated that kind of money ever in her life. "Plus royalties from the future shows as well. Chen, I need some air. Are we finished here?"

Noticing Anna's distress, Chen took her hand and pulled her to the door. They picked up their coats from the assistant on their way out of the building. Chen put his arm around Anna's waist, giving her moral support more than physical support. Finding a bench near the cars, Chen guided her to sit down.

"Are you okay?" he asked, concern in his voice.

"I'll be fine. I just need to wrap my head around it. I've made a nice amount with my books, but nothing of this magnitude."

"I believe *The Lost Prince* has grossed them a significant amount, so that is just a pittance of what it costs to film one of these dramas. Besides, that is for the three stories, so that isn't so bad." Chen did his best to downplay this to help calm her.

After a few minutes, Anna finally calmed down. "So, when were you going to mention the set visit?" she asked, waggling her eyebrows at Chen.

Rubbing a hand across his neck, trying to look innocent he said, "Didn't I mention it earlier? It must have slipped my mind, you know, with the meeting time change and all."

At the mention of the time change for the meeting, Anna looked at Chen thoughtfully. "Do they tend to make last minute changes to meetings like that? We would have been late if you hadn't come for breakfast."

"You know, it's not normal now that you mention it." Chen looked at the sky in thought. Soft, fluffy gray clouds chased past. "Give me a few moments; I will be right back." Getting up, he walked back to the office.

After a short time, Chen returned to where Anna waited, a murderous look on his face. At that moment, it may have been humorous to lip-read Mandarin; she could probably learn a few good swear words by the look on his face. There was a sinking feeling in her stomach as she waited for Chen to reach the bench. "Are you okay?" she asked.

"No, not even remotely okay." Chen fumed as he sat next

to Anna. "So Mr. Shun received a phone call early this morning from Ms. Li. After the call, the meeting was moved from 10:00 A.M. to 8:30 A.M. I don't think this will be the last time she makes trouble for us while you're here."

Putting her hand on his knee, Anna reassured him saying, "I'm a big girl; I should be okay."

"I'm sure you will." *I hope,* he thought. Chen placed his hand on top of hers. "Did you want to change before we go to the set? We'll probably be there until about 6 o'clock; then we'll head to Xian's. Perhaps you would like to get changed for hanging out and bring clothes to change into for dinner tonight. I bet I can talk to the ladies in hair and makeup to doll you up or down if you prefer." He tried to look serious about that last comment.

Anna's laughter made his mood improve. "Let's stop at the hotel; I'll change and grab a dress for tonight. Hair and makeup help. I'd take that all day long. Did you honestly think I managed that amazing look last night by myself?"

Peals of laughter on both sides lightened their mood; however, it completely crushed the observer lurking behind a nearby bush.

—

Early that morning, Li Ming picked up her phone, scrolling through her long list of phone numbers looking for the one that would do the most damage at the moment. As the call connected, she cleared her throat. "Good morning Uncle Shun. It's Li Ming," she said, playing on the fact that Mr. Shun was a friend of her father's.

"Good morning, Li Ming. What can I do for you today?" Mr. Shun's deep voice came through the phone.

"Uncle Shun, I wondered if you could come to the set today? There was an issue with the script that I couldn't get cleared up with the director and producer. Would it be possible to meet at 10:00 A.M.?"

"I have a meeting scheduled then. Could we do it earlier or later?" Mr. Shun inquired.

"I'm sorry, Uncle Shun, but it is about scenes we plan to film today." Li Ming wheedled and whined. She was pulling out the tricks she used when she was a child.

"Okay, I will change my schedule and meet you on the set at 10 o'clock." Mr. Shun chortled.

Li Ming's glee at messing up Anna's day was exquisite. Every opportunity she could find, she would do her best to make that author bitch miserable.

Watching Chen and Anna walking to his car laughing, she couldn't figure out how her plan had gone so wrong.

章

Chapter 20

After a quick stop at the hotel, Chen and Anna arrived at the set with about thirty minutes to spare. Huang Hu met them at the parking lot with Anna's visitor's pass and Chen's shooting schedule for the day. Anna grabbed her dress from the car's back seat and slung it over her shoulder.

Chen looked at her and shook his head. "Give me that please." Taking the light garment bag from Anna and handing it to Huang Hu. "Are you sure you wouldn't rather leave it in the car until later?"

"I thought I would save time by keeping it in your dressing room?" Anna made puppy dog eyes at Chen and stuck out a pouty lip. "Please?"

Chen couldn't help but laugh at her childish antics. "Okay, we can certainly put it in my dressing room but it's more of a trailer than a room." Grabbing Anna's hand and tucking it in the crook of his arm, they set off towards his dressing trailer.

After dropping the dress off at his trailer, Chen took Anna on a brief tour of the wardrobe, hair and makeup departments. Last he showed her where they were shooting for the day. "You can watch us from here." He led her to his chair. There she would be away from the chaos behind the cameras. "I hate to leave you alone, but I need to get into wardrobe and makeup; luckily, one of the pick up scenes we have to film today is one with my best wardrobe. I'll see what I can do, perhaps we can get you all dressed in a matching costume and we can take some photos."

"That would be amazing. I've always wanted to try on a Hanfu." It took Anna a bit of research to find that most of the period garb for the shows was called Hanfu; there were just different versions of the traditional clothing depending on the person's status.

"Let me see what kind of strings I can pull. As long as the shooting goes well, we should have some time this afternoon." Looking around and not seeing anyone nearby, Chen leaned down and kissed Anna's cheek. "I didn't get to do that earlier. Congratulations on your meeting this morning; I'm so proud of you. Don't hesitate to text Huang Hu if you need anything at all. If anyone gives you a bad time, let him know as well. When we have a few moments, I'll introduce you to Ching Wen, the assistant producer. I often work with him on projects; he'll more than likely be working on your projects when they start."

"I look forward to it. Go, get all dolled up. I can't wait to see you in your formal attire; the photo, I'm sure, didn't do it justice." Anna motioned to kick him in the butt to get him going. She hadn't felt so young in years. She wasn't sure why she felt like behaving as though she was sixteen with Chen. It was fun being around someone who didn't mind teasing one another and being playful.

Relaxing in the chair, she started going through messages and missed calls. She would need to call Veronica at some point in the day. She had sent over her latest manuscript to be edited; she was just waiting to make the final corrections. Hopefully, Veronica had some excellent news and there would be minimal changes.

Scrolling through her social media, killing time, Anna noticed a number of the film crew observing her. She could hear the murmurs and whispers as people walked by, bustling around the set preparing to film. She noticed some swords being carried by what must have been the props master. Chen had mentioned earlier that there would be an action scene this afternoon; he would be filming a sword fight. The morning shots were mostly courtyard scenes and a few in the palace. Anna was still blown away by the complexity of the set for his latest project.

After checking messages, Anna noticed Liz had tried calling her while in the meeting at the studio. Checking the time difference, she may still be at work, but she would certainly still be up. Tapping the call button, Anna looked around, watching the beehive activity of the crew. It completely floored her to watch how the film crew interacted; it looked like a choreographed dance.

"Well, about time you remember you have a daughter," Liz said as the call connected.

Anna rolled her eyes, letting Liz know how unimpressed she was with her comment. Anna waved at Liz's grumpy face. "You'd never believe where I am right now. Wanna try guessing?"

The grump left Liz's demeanor. "Well, from what little I can see, you're outdoors somewhere in China. Oh, and how did the meeting go?"

"The meeting was fabulous. I sold the two scripts I hoped to; they also commissioned me to write a follow-up story to *The Lost Prince*. So do you give up?" Anna moved her phone a little to give Liz a peek at one of the buildings behind her.

"Are you on a movie set?" Liz's face was almost pressed on the phone like she could crawl through the screen and be with Anna. "And congrats on the sale. Are you going to tell me how expensive your work is now?"

"Sorry, I can't tell you. We will be finalizing the contracts next week. Have to keep it hush-hush until then. Only Chen knows how much at the moment, other than the studio execs. As for where I am, yes, I am on the set of Chen's latest project. I'm getting some insight for future projects. It's more that I'm waiting for Chen; we have dinner with his best friend tonight."

"Oh, you're having dinner with Xian?" Liz asked without thinking. Realizing what she just said, she caught herself before she cringed. At that moment, she couldn't remember if Anna had mentioned Xian's name or not in her previous calls. *Damn, me and my mouth,* Liz thought.

Anna scrutinized Liz's expression for a moment. How did Liz know about Xian? She couldn't remember if she had mentioned his name or not before. Raising an eyebrow she asked, "When did I mention Xian?"

Mentally Liz was still kicking herself. Damn, that woman was observant. "After your date with Chen, you had told me about the mess up at the airport." Whew, would she believe it? Chen had filled her in on the mess up at the airport more than her mom had. Liz was getting to like Chen. He was very concerned with her mom's safety and happiness; that alone made him okay in her book.

Anna squinted at Liz as if trying to read her mind from thousands of miles away. "Well, as I've been almost a walking zombie for a few days, it's more than possible that I told you and it slipped my mind."

"Mom, you need to get some sleep. Don't you have a big weekend coming up? You should see if you can find a toning mask and use it Friday. Or at the very least, get some cucumber slices and put them on your eyes to reduce the dark circles. I can see it from here. Good grief, woman, have you been sleeping at all?" Liz looked more closely at her mother.

"I'm fine. I'll get sleep tonight. I don't need to be up early tomorrow, that I'm aware of. Xian is taking me shopping. Do you still want me to call when I get to the dresses? You may need to hang out with Xian while I'm changing if he will entertain the idea of holding you up while I'm modeling gowns."

"Never hurts to ask. If Xian's game, just let me know roughly when. I'll stay up if I need to; I should be available. I better go; it's almost closing time. Better get things finished." Liz waved at Anna. "See you later, Mom."

"Night, sweetie, love you." Anna waved and blew a kiss.

Ending the call, Anna noticed there was more activity and noise. Stretching in the seat and looking around, Anna turned in the direction of the wardrobe trailer and almost fell out of her chair. Chen was making his way toward her.

So this is what a Chinese god would look like embodied in human form. Chen's garment was breathtaking in detail. The deep blue fabric had ornate gold stitching on the long flowing sleeves of the overcoat; the stitch work on the piece was immaculate from what Anna could see. All she could do was keep her seat and not jump on Chen. What grabbed her attention was the long hair and ornate crown. She couldn't remember the name of that particular part of the outfit; it had been a while since she had researched it for a script.

As Chen approached, Anna stood, wanting to give him the use of the chair; the multiple layers in this costume had to be heavy and difficult to move around in. Stuffing her hands in her jacket pockets to keep her hands off Chen; perhaps once he was finished filming she could touch him.

"Hi, handsome," Anna called to Chen as he got close.

Smiling, Chen cautiously turned in a circle, giving Anna a look at the whole costume. "I would say this has been one of my absolute favorite roles; this Hanfu has been one of the most ornate I've worn."

"Can I just say yum?" Anna could have used a tissue at that moment. She swore there was actual drool dribbling down the side of her mouth. "Okay, don't be offended by this, but there is only one character I like better in a Hanfu. That would be from a series you were in some time ago."

Chen shook his head and cringed saying, "You don't have to tell me; let me guess, he has white hair?"

Caught, Anna blushed hotly. Clearing her throat and looking anywhere but at Chen, she asked, "How did you guess?"

He shook his head. "You're not the first woman who's had a thing for that character. I didn't exactly have a large role in that series. If I remember correctly, you told me it was one of your favorites."

Anna could tell he was feeling down, perhaps thinking she didn't find him handsome. Leaning over so she could whisper in his ear, "You are fortunate that I know I can't touch you. I just said I liked his character in the Hanfu." Leaving it at that, she stepped back from Chen; the temptation was great to touch the rich fabrics and the man inside them. She hadn't felt this kind of attraction since she first met Kyle. Anna stuffed her hands deeper in her pockets, fighting the overwhelming urge. She was such a tactile person.

Chen, startled, looked at Anna. A crimson was coloring his ears and cheeks. He felt a strong urge to fold his hands over his lap at that moment. "Anna, that wasn't fair. You could have waited until I was finished filming to drop that little bombshell on me."

Ashamed of herself, Anna blushed and looked down at her feet. "Sorry Chen, my filter went out the window when I saw you walking towards me. The explanation will have to wait until **MUCH** later. Trust me on this one."

Chen and Anna continued chatting about the scene he

would be filming shortly. Wrapped up in one another, they didn't notice the whispers they caused and the looks they were getting. Not realizing they were being observed by the one person doing her best to ruin Anna's trip. The red creeping across Li Ming's cheeks had nothing to do with a feeling of embarrassment; it was pure anger and hatred. Chen had never looked at her that way; what did this American have she didn't? Anna didn't know Chen as Li Ming did.

—

Li Ming knew her plan to mess with the upstart author that morning had backfired. Noticing the garment bag that Huang Hu was carrying...perhaps this might be an opportunity to play with that bitch from the States.

章

Chapter 21

The day went quickly, almost too fast for Anna's taste. She had a fabulous time on the set. Many of the crew she had contact with were wary at first, but after seeing her interact with Xiao Chen and how well she treated anyone she came in contact with, they warmed up to her quickly. Soon, a few of the crew gathered by Anna's chair. Anna wasn't the best with names, so she apologized if she didn't remember everyone.

Whispers about the American author spread like wildfire; all praised Anna's cheery disposition, politeness and thoughtfulness. The craft food staff nearly tripped over themselves catering to Anna's every whim. Not that she had any, but she loved being able to chat in Mandarin.

After the morning shots, Chen changed three more times in the afternoon for the pick up scenes. Anna quietly observed while scenes were shot but had lively discussions between shots with the director, Xu Hinge. After Chen had introduced Anna, Xu Hinge invited her to sit with him while they filmed. He had been the director of *The Lost Prince* and had loved the story. There weren't many projects he had worked on recently that he had enjoyed as much. When Anna hinted there might be a follow-up to the series, Xu Hinge was ecstatic.

Anna felt humbled when he asked for her information to keep in touch with her. Xu Hinge also informed Anna that if she got stuck on any scenes in the future, she could get his input.

Chen stood back and watched Anna interact with the different people on the crew. She treated everyone equally, whether the director or a grip. He hadn't seen everyone this relaxed and having fun since the week that Li Ming had been away. He had a suspicion that once people found out about the upcoming projects, there would be a clamor to be included;

especially if Anna was going to be on set during the filming, which was his hope. Perhaps by then...only time would tell if that dream would become a reality.

After the final scene was shot it was only two in the afternoon. It was a blessing that Li Ming only had two scenes that needed to be reshot. He thought there would be more she would need to redo for how much drama she had continually put the crew through. Chen only had one scene with Li Ming on the schedule and there was little direct interaction.

It finished quickly without all of the Li Ming drama and the crew being in such a great mood. Xu Hinge attributed the great day to Anna being there. She was great for putting the cast and crew at ease.

Chen had asked Xu Hinge about dressing Anna in one of the Royal Court Hanfus; he would also put his Hanfu back on so they could take some promo photos with Anna. Because of the contribution to the day's filming, he gladly approved as long as they had one that would fit Anna. He had one of the PAs run to wardrobe and makeup to give them a heads up about what was happening.

Once word circulated that they planned to make Anna's wish to wear one of the royal costumes happen, the key costumer in charge of Chen's wardrobe was more than happy to find a female version of Chen's blue and gold Hanfu in Anna's size. After looking for a while, they found they didn't have a blue and gold version; however, blue and silver was available. A rush was placed on the garment to get it to the wardrobe trailer.

While waiting for the clothes, Chen and Anna were parked in the hair and makeup chairs. Chen already had his wig on; they just needed minor modifications for the more elaborate crown. Chen didn't tell Anna that the particular Hanfu they would be wearing were the wedding costumes for the project they were just finishing. Having thought about this all afternoon, he had an ulterior motive for her wearing a matching outfit.

After finishing his hair, Chen sat and watched as the women flitted around Anna like butterflies. The wig and makeup took less time than usual; all the available staff was there helping to make Anna look as stunning as possible. An elaborate wig and a hairpiece that would have been accurate, and would have cost more than her house, adorned her head. When her hair and makeup were finished, the Hanfu arrived and the costume department whisked Anna away to complete the transformation.

Decked out in the blue and gold court costume, Chen waited patiently for Anna to be finished. Two assistants came out and asked, "Are you ready, Mr. Xiao?" The girls giggled as they helped Anna step out of the trailer.

Chen staggered, finding a post to steady himself. Anna was dazzling. During filming he had imagined Anna playing opposite him in all of the intimate scenes; there was no way he would have been able to get through filming with Li Ming otherwise. Seeing Anna in the full costume proved his imagination was slipping; she was resplendent in the ornamented skirt and jackets. Anna in this costume made Li Ming look like a dirty sock. Why couldn't Anna have been his co-star?

The long black hair coiffed in elaborate braids, and the ornate hair piece accentuated the silver embroidery on the blue fabric. Layers of white, peach-soft materials were beneath the embellished jacket. Walking with help, they had to use men's slippers due to Anna's non-dainty feet, but they were covered with the length of the Hanfu. Cautiously moving in the heavy garments, Anna walked up to Chen.

"Do I look okay?" He could feel the giddiness radiating from her as she asked.

"Anna, I don't even have words. Will you marry me?" Chen asked, only half joking. "You're dressed for a wedding. Be my empress?"

"If I thought for a moment you were serious, I may be tempted to say yes. If I ever get married again, I would love to wear this. I have never felt so beautiful as I do right now." Anna demurely looked down at her folded hands in front of her.

Chen wondered how much the studio would charge him for these costumes once the filming was complete. They usually sold the more elaborate costumes because they would be too difficult to reuse. He wished he could genuinely propose; how perfect it would have been at that moment, but it was too soon. They needed more time together before she was ready, he could tell. Taking Anna's hand in his, he said, "Come with me; we found the perfect location for photos."

Chen led her to a lotus pond with flowering trees. Anna looked around, astonished. "How can these be flowering in fall?"

Chen smiled as he plucked a flower from one of the branches, handing it to Anna. She was amazed at the detail in the petals that were fabric. "Wow, the blossoms are all fabric? Doesn't that take forever to create?"

"Not all of them are this detailed. The ones that may show up in close-up shots are this elaborate. They pale in comparison to your beauty, though." Caressing her cheek, careful not to disturb Anna's makeup, her skin looked like porcelain. "You can't even imagine what I felt seeing you dressed this way."

"I have an excellent idea. I had a very similar reaction when I saw you earlier. There was a reason I kept my distance from you." Anna blushed prettily. "You just didn't see the full reaction because I got most of it out of my system before you reached me. Let's just call it a tie."

Chen pulled Anna into his arms; how could he have read her mind? She had wanted to do this all day. Cautiously she laid her head on his shoulder.

How could she crave his touch so much after only two days? Then again, it shouldn't surprise her; she was the queen of unconventional relationships. Knowing they couldn't stay like this all night, Anna stepped back and looked around. Not realizing they had an audience, she blushed hotly, especially at the round of applause.

Chen laughed and held his hands up. "Come on now, Ms. Anna isn't used to having such an attentive audience for her acting. Where would you like us?"

Taking Anna's hand, he led her to the spot the photographer indicated. They had gone all-out getting the studio's still photographer to take the shots. Chen would have been just as happy to have them on his phone. However, he made sure several photos were taken on both of their phones for easy access later.

Chen caught a photo of Anna deep in thought while gazing into the lotus pond, watching the koi lazily glide through the water. That photo would be the wallpaper on his phone from now on.

After almost an hour of photos, they both reluctantly went back to wardrobe and makeup to have the magic removed.

A large number of the crew had stayed to watch the photo shoot. As Anna and Chen had made their way across the set, many had said their goodbyes to Anna.

"You made a few friends here, I'd say," Chen said as a key grip came up to Anna and bowed.

"They have all made my day fascinating. I may be doing the wrong job. Perhaps I should go to school for the filming aspect instead of writing the stories?" Anna joked with Chen; as if she could ever give up storytelling.

As they sat in hair and makeup, Anna looked over at Chen. "Chen, is Huang Hu still here?"

"Yes, he won't leave until we do," Chen said, his curiosity piqued as to why Anna would need Huang Hu.

"Could you have him get my garment bag from your dressing room? I figured I would change into my dress after getting out of the Hanfu. It doesn't make sense for me to change twice. May as well just do it while I'm almost naked anyway," Anna said casually.

Anna hadn't noticed that Chen had just taken a drink of water right before she made her naked comment. It was good there wasn't anyone in front of him; the makeup table was sprayed with water as he choked and gasped.

The women removing their hair broke out in laughter at Chen's reaction to Anna's comment.

Blinking innocently, Anna asked Chen, "Are you going to be okay?"

He covered his mouth as he coughed to clear the last bit of errant water from his airway. Holding up a hand, he replied hoarsely, "I think I'll be fine." Picking his phone up and wiping droplets of water from the screen, unlocking it, he found Huang Hu's chat thread and asked him to bring the garment bag from the trailer to the wardrobe and have them steam the dress for her to make sure it looked as good as possible for their dinner with Xian.

"Okay, madame, your gown shall be awaiting you." Chen bowed comically in the chair.

"Thank you, Your Majesty." Anna returned the bow. The trailer filled with the laughter of everyone in the room. The women whispered among themselves. "Why couldn't Ms. Anna have been the lead for this series? She fits much better with Mr. Xiao."

It had taken a while, but Anna finally talked most of the crew into calling her Ms. Anna.

In Chinese culture, it was considered disrespectful to call people by their first name unless they were close friends or had permission. It took Anna a bit to get used to the fact that the first name pronounced was the surname and the second name was the given name, backward from how it was done in the States. She wasn't used to hearing Ms. Cassidy all the time, so she had finally made it widely known to the cast and crew that if they couldn't just call her Anna, then at the very least, they should call her Ms. Anna. This had been adopted by all of the crew that had fallen in love with her.

Finished with hair and makeup removal, Anna made her way to the wardrobe trailer with Chen's assistance. She loved the elegant finery, but it was time to put on something less restrictive and lightweight. To fit the inner jacket properly due to her ample breasts, they had loosely bound her chest; she was ready to be able to breathe normally again.

Walking into the trailer, Anna was greeted by a sight that disappointed her. Her steel blue hanky hem dress was covered in black spots. Looking at the dress hanging on the stand to the side of the room, Anna almost overlooked one of the young girls sitting in a chair sobbing.

Rushing to the young woman, Anna cautiously kneeled beside her to determine why she sobbed so desperately. "Ms. Anna, I didn't ruin your dress, I promise! It was that way when I took it from your garment bag. Not only that, someone took the clothes you changed from," she gasped out between sobs.

Anna hushed the inconsolable girl. "Please, sweetie, don't sob over a forty-dollar dress. I have had that old thing for years, and this is finally a good excuse to replace it. I have a handsome man taking me on a shopping trip tomorrow; I am sure I will find something suitable to replace it, probably way better than I had. As for my other clothes, they were nothing special either. I have plenty in the hotel room. I came with way more than I needed. My daughter thought I would stay for a month with how much I packed," Anna said as she wiped the tears from the girl's cheeks.

Chen had waited for Anna's magic to calm the young assistant's nerves so he wouldn't lose his temper and frighten her even more. "Excuse me, Anna, I need to step out for a moment. Please just wait for me."

Still dressed in the full regalia, Chen stepped outside the trailer and cursed a string of expletives that would have significantly impressed Anna. Unlocking his phone, he dialed Huang Hu. "Where are you?" he said between gritted teeth when Huang Hu answered.

"I am waiting in your trailer for you, sir." His confusion was evident in his voice. He couldn't figure out why Chen was so angry after the beautiful photoshoot. They looked so regal together in their costumes. "Is anything wrong?"

"Was my trailer locked all day?" Chen asked, trying to get to the bottom of the dress incident.

"Yes, as far as I am aware. When I came to retrieve the dress, the door was locked. Mr. Xiao, is there something wrong?" Huang Hu was very concerned now. He could almost feel the anger through the phone.

"Anna's dress was completely ruined and someone stole her street clothes from the wardrobe department. It must have been while we were doing the photoshoot. We had quite the audience." Wracking his brain for some kind of option. "Hu, get over here. I may need a favor," Chen said as he hung up on the young man. Finding the number for Ching Wen, he initiated the call. "Wen, how many favors do you owe me?"

"Chen? I know I would have to use both hands and most of my toes to count them. Do I need to take my shoes off?" Sensing something was wrong, he had tried levity to lighten the mood.

"Wen, I need a favor that may wipe out five of your

favors," Chen explained the situation.

"Are you sure it was her?" Ching Wen sighed; when would this headache be over with Li Ming? Xu Hinge had texted him a photo of Chen and Anna; he had been floored by how they looked together. Now, if only Anna were an actress as well as a writer.

"Well, as she messed with Anna's meeting with Mr. Shun this morning, I'm fairly positive. With a fair amount of certainty, I'd say that she hates Anna with something close to animosity." Chen sighed. They still had to get through the awards on Saturday; dealing with Li Ming would be more stressful. "The problem I have right now is that Anna doesn't have anything to wear without running back to her hotel or going out to a shop and buying something. We have dinner plans with Wei Xian tonight, so we will be pressed for time now."

"I have an idea; how do you think she would look in a cheongsam?" Ching Wen mused, thinking about the other series that had just wrapped filming. A decent number of the 1920's inspired dresses were coming back in the more affluent circles. The sheath-style gown would look elegant on Ms. Cassidy's curvaceous figure.

"Wen, you aren't pulling my leg, are you?" The excitement in Chen's voice almost made Ching Wen laugh.

"Would I do that to you right now? Chen, we have worked with each other too long for me to do that to you. Get Anna's size from the wardrobe department and I will send over the best selection of that size for her to pick from. The dress will be hers, so don't worry about returning it to the studio; it's the least we could do for her since her clothes were damaged and stolen." He would speak to Mr. Shun about buying out Li Ming's contract. She continued to embarrass herself and the studio she represented. Again, he wished Anna lived in China; even though she was American she looked stunning in the period costume. "I do have one stipulation. You must send me a photo of Ms. Anna in the dress."

Chen's eyebrows shot up in amazement. That rascal. Chen wondered if Xu Hinge had sent photos to Wen. "Certainly, Wen! You're a lifesaver."

One crisis averted. It was good that Anna would be going on a shopping spree with Xian tomorrow. Chen would pay for all of her purchases; she deserved a day of pampering after the headaches Anna continued to suffer on his behalf.

章

Chapter 22

After trying her top three choices, Anna found a light blue cheongsam with a silver phoenix; it could have been the modern version of the Hanfu she had just worn. One of the hairdressers had heard the commotion and came to investigate. Ms. Yan had worked on Anna's hair earlier and was shocked to find out what had happened. As soon as Anna was dressed, she was whisked away to have her transformation completed. Chen was banned from seeing her until Ms. Yan was finished.

Impatient, Chen paced outside the trailer; the day had been going so well. Anna looked so happy while they were taking the photos. As a special gift, he had plans to have a number of the images framed.

Fifteen minutes later, Ms. Yan brought Anna out. Her long hair was pulled up in an intricate updo with an ornate hairpin; long silver chains with jeweled beads hung to her shoulders. Self-conscious, Anna stood with her hands folded gracefully before her.

Again, Chen's heart contracted and started beating funny. Anna looked striking in Chinese clothing. He had seldom seen anyone look so good in that style of dress. Maybe it wasn't such a good idea to have dinner with Xian tonight; Anna was so alluring that he may have difficulty resisting her charms.

Chen motioned Anna to spin around for him, interested to see the rest of the phoenix pattern. Silver Phoenix and lotus blossoms trailed down the front of the dress and along the lower hem in the back. His eyes followed the pattern as Anna slowly turned in a circle, his eyes rising to meet hers as she faced him again.

"You are so lovely." Stepping forward, he took Anna's hand and kissed it.

"I think your opinion is jaded," she commented softly. "We

better head to Xian's. This whole clothing debacle has us running a little behind schedule." Turning, she hugged Ms. Yan and kissed her cheek. "Thank you so much for making me look beautiful today. I've never felt so special." Quickly turning to dab at errant tears trying to form. She couldn't let Ms. Yan's hard work be wasted on frivolous emotions.

"Ms. Anna, you are most welcome. You brought joy and laughter to our day; it was special for all of us. I hope we will meet again," Ms. Yan replied in Mandarin. While she had worked on Anna's hair, they had a lively conversation getting to know one another. Anna had felt like she was in the chair speaking with her dear friend Jayci in her salon, warm and comfortable.

"Ms. Anna!" an urgent voice called as she made to leave with Chen. Turning, she saw the young girl from the wardrobe department running to catch her. Anna noticed some cloth draped across her arm. "Ms. Anna, you don't have a coat; please take this to keep the chill off." Draping a silk wrap that complimented Anna's dress over her shoulders.

"I can't wear this; it's too fine for me." Anna objected to the gift.

"Ms. Anna, it was our fault your street clothes disappeared. We wanted to ensure you didn't get cold in the cool air, especially since the dress is short-sleeved. Please accept the gift," she said as she bowed to Anna.

Unable to resist her midwestern upbringing, Anna walked over to the young lady and hugged her. "Thank you. I will cherish this. It is so beautiful. I hope I will see you again sometime."

Taking Chen's arm, they walked to his car. Chen whispered to Anna, "Can you ever forgive me? I should have thought to offer you my coat. It's a cool evening."

"To be honest, I forgot about it, so don't think anything of it. Besides, I received a wonderful gift. It was so sweet and thoughtful of the costumers."

Chen opened Anna's door and helped her get in; she wasn't used to wearing a formfitting dress. She was glad the weather was warmer in Beijing than in Fortine. Back home, this dress wouldn't have been her first choice for an evening in the fall.

"How far to Xian's place?" Anna asked once they were on their way.

"We should arrive in about twenty minutes if traffic isn't too heavy. We're going to Xian's condo, not his estate, or the trip would take us roughly an hour," Chen replied, watching the traffic as he changed lanes. "Anna, I can't apologize enough for the loss of your clothes. I, unfortunately, have a suspicion about who the culprit was. The studio will be sure to replace what was lost."

"Chen, you don't have to worry about it. What I wore wasn't my best; I had dressed for comfort. A pair of joggers, a baggy sweater and a light jacket aren't that much. I told the young girl it wasn't a big deal; Liz gave me a lot of grief over how much I packed." Anna laughed because she might start to cry if she didn't. Today had felt like she was back in school being bullied. That was a memory she would rather stay buried deep.

Chen glanced at Anna; something in her voice didn't sound right. He had gotten to know Anna's voice very well; the hours of phone calls had given him insight into this complex woman. Today had affected her more than she would admit. Perhaps it wasn't a good idea to have dinner with Xian. No, dinner would help take the day's events off her mind, it would be a good distraction for her.

A companionable silence fell over the car. Anna enjoyed watching the lights of the streets and businesses as they drove. She didn't mind being chauffeured around; she was usually the one driving.

Quicker than she had expected, they pulled up to a luxury condo. "Xian lives here?" Anna was suitably impressed. "So, is your apartment as impressive?" Anna teased.

"It's even better than Xian's," Chen boasted. "No, it's not really. I have a nice place but not as large and modern as his." He laughed. "Hopefully, I can show you my place Sunday after we return from the awards."

"I would love that." Anna was curious about Chen's apartment.

Stopping at the security gate, Chen rolled his window down, reached out and punched in a six-digit code on the keypad.

"You even know his security code to get in?" Anna asked.

"Of course, who do you think brings him home when he drinks too much while we're out? I usually check on his place when he's away on business. He has staff that could, but he'd rather I do it; he trusts me more." Chen drove to Xian's assigned parking spaces, taking the empty one next to a luxury sports car Anna didn't recognize.

Anna put her hand on the door, but Chen reached across and stopped her before she could open it. "Chen, I can open a door for myself. I appreciate you being a gentleman, but it isn't necessary all the time. I'm not used to this kind of attention," Anna protested.

"Please, just let me do this for you." Chen took her hand in his. "Let me explain. My aunt and uncle raised me; they were pretty strict about polite manners. My grandfather treated my grandmother as a gentleman would every day they were together. I watched them grow old and saw how much they loved one another. My grandmother could open doors for herself, but she knew how much pleasure it gave my grandfather to do these little things for her. As I grew older, I began understanding why my grandfather made these small efforts. Don't get me wrong, not every woman I'm acquainted with is afforded the same courtesy. Only two other women have enjoyed this treatment in my past. So please, while you are here, let me do this for you. Let me treat you as a lady on the silver screen. Opening doors and offering you my arm are small trifles, straightforward ways to show my sincere friendship and admiration."

Anna saw a wisp of sadness in him for a moment; if she hadn't been concentrating on his words so closely she might have missed it.

"Thank you, Chen; when you get used to doing everything for yourself for so long it feels strange to have someone make an effort." Anna wanted nothing more than to caress his cheek at that moment, wiping away the wayward tear she barely glimpsed. It was too soon for such intimate gestures, but she wanted to be his comfort. "Well, sir, will you open my door, or will we enjoy the evening sitting in your car? I believe we will just make it if we get our butts in gear, as we would say in

America." She smiled, inclining her head to the door.

A smile and a glint of amusement were all she saw as he stepped out of the car and opened her door. Chen stood there with a mock haughty look. "Madame, shall we sally forth?"

Laughter escaped Anna's lips at the comical expression on Chen's face. "Lead on McDuff."

Chen raised an eyebrow at the reference.

"Okay, Okay, it's a cheesy reference. Thank you for salvaging the day for me. This trip has not been what I expected so far. Let's hope the rest goes smoother." Anna took Chen's arm. Standing there, he gazed at her for some moments.

"Come on; now you're just stalling. Does Xian have some horrible disfigurement or is he an absolute lech? You almost seem to be delaying our entrance on purpose."

"Xian is an amazing guy. He's been getting over my sister's death, so he has his moments. For the most part, the man can be charming and polite when he isn't trying to take over a company or mess up a favor for his best friend," Chen joked.

"I look forward to meeting this paragon of virtue." Anna snickered.

Joking back and forth, they walked up to the door of Xian's condo; Chen knocked briskly.

"Coming!" a deep male voice yelled from somewhere inside.

As the door opened, Anna inhaled sharply and restrained herself from giving a low whistle of appreciation. Xian was handsome in his sweater and khaki pants. He was taller than Chen by about four inches, and his dark tousled hair was made for someone like Anna to run her fingers through it. Looking at him a little closer she exclaimed, "It **WAS** you!"

Xian cringed and let out a self-deprecating laugh. "As I was leaving the airport, I saw you were getting in the car and it dawned on me a few moments later that you were the one I was sent to fetch." He emphasized the word fetch.

Chen made to kick his best friend in the shin for his comment. "So are we invited in, or do we stand in the doorway and dine?"

"Where are my manners? Come in, come in. Make yourself at home. Ms. Cassidy, I do apologize for the mixup at the airport. I'm pleased to meet you again." Xian took Anna's hand, pressing his lips to it.

Anna, momentarily at a loss for words, blushed hotly. "The feeling is mutual, Mr. Wei," she responded once she got her voice back.

Chen cleared his throat. "Well, we made it in the door; NOW, we'll be doing great if we can just make it inside." Giving Xian a look that said, *Hands off, buddy! She's mine!*

"Sorry, please come in." Xian chose to ignore Chen's glare. Anna wondered if the interior had been featured in a home interior magazine. This was the first time she had been in a home with fresh-cut flower arrangements placed throughout the rooms.

"May I take your wrap?" Xian asked.

In the cheongsam, Anna dazzled Xian as she pulled the wrap from her shoulders; he hadn't seen one that looked so good on the wearer.

"You look stunning in that dress," Xian complimented Anna as she handed him the wrap.

"Thank you. Your home is impressive, Mr. Wei. Thank you for inviting me for dinner." Anna gazed around the room.

"Ms. Cassidy, please call me Xian. You are a dear friend of Chen's, so a good friend of mine. It makes me feel like you're either a colleague at work or addressing my father when you call me Mr. Wei," Xian said.

"In that case, please call me Anna. I don't hear Ms. Cassidy very often and it makes me feel old," Anna replied.

"Okay, now that's settled. Let's eat. I don't know about you two, but I'm famished," Xian said, tucking Anna's hand around his arm and leading her to the dining table.

Chen followed, glaring sullenly at Xian's back. Xian was his best friend and brother-in-law, but he was also a man who recognized how special Anna was, just as Chen did. He needed to keep a close eye on him.

"I heard you are going to be my shopping guide tomorrow?" Anna asked Xian.

"Yes, Chen knows I have better taste than he does," Xian said, teasing Chen.

"Haha, pick on the actor." Chen rolled his eyes.

Seating Anna at the table, Xian took the seat next to her, while Chen chose the chair opposite. Let Xian sit next to her. This way, he could gaze at Anna all night.

A young woman began bringing dishes out and putting them on the table family style. Chen gave Xian a questioning look. This was out of the ordinary for meals. Usually, they would be served restaurant style, everything already artfully arranged on the plate by the chef.

"Anna, in your honor, I asked that they serve the dinner family style. I gather that is more in holding with what you're used to," Xian said, offering the first dish to Anna.

Anna took a small amount of a dish she didn't recognize and handed it to Chen. "Well, as I typically eat alone, I don't eat that way very often. Thank you though, you didn't need to do anything special for me."

"It's a nice change of pace. Something different for us jaded bachelors." Xian winked at Chen.

Chen gave him a slight grumble under his breath. Thinking to himself, Just take a deep breath, man. Anna doesn't know Xian as she knows you; you're fine.

Dinner continued and Xian asked questions of Anna, wanting to learn more about her. Anna obliged and kept her answers cursory, not going into extensive detail. Chen sat across the table and fumed. Xian was trying to horn in on his girl. Well, okay, not officially his girl...Yet!

After finishing dinner, Anna stood and started gathering the dishes.

"What were you doing?" Xian jumped up, taking Anna's hand to stop her from stacking the dirty plates and silverware and leading her to a cozy nook with several chairs and a comfortable-looking couch.

"Sorry, a force of habit," Anna mumbled.

"Xian, why don't you open one of those bottles squirreled away for special occasions," Chen hinted.

"Chen, that is a fabulous idea." Xian excused himself, returning with a crystal decanter filled with a honey amber liquid and three rocks glasses. "I believe this 20-year-old, single cask scotch should do the trick." He poured the golden spirit into each glass.

"Please, only a small amount for me; I'm a teetotaler." Anna laughed. "If I drink, most alcohol makes me turn very bright red and I get uncomfortably hot. Having a snort now and again with close friends is a pleasure." Picking up the glass, she inspected the libation with delight. It had been quite some time since she had enjoyed anything this old.

She had a bottle of 60-year-old Crown Royal tucked away at home; she'd been saving it for a visit from her favorite cousin...and now she would need to find someone else to share the special bottle with. It had been some time since she thought of that bottle.

When Anna broke from her musings, Xian and Chen had their glasses in hand.

"What shall we drink too?" Anna asked.

"To Anna! Cheers!" Synchronous voices blended with the sound of crystal glasses clinking.

Taking a sip of the scotch, the warmth of the liquor spread throughout Anna, starting from the stomach up. This was certainly not the quality Anna was used to; notes of honey, chocolate, vanilla and hints of fruits filled her pallet. "There aren't enough O's to describe how smooth this scotch is."

Chen and Xian laughed at Anna's praise.

Over the better part of the bottle, stories were told and tears spilled, both happy and sad. Xian told Anna stories of Chen when they were going to school together. Anna told them stories of growing up on a farm.

Anna noticed the alcohol was beginning to go to her head. "Xian, would you happen to have bottled water in this fancy place?" A slight slur snuck out.

Chen gave Anna a surprised look. "Anna, are you getting drunk?"

"Um, maybe. I told you I was a teetotaler. I haven't been drunk since I was twenty-two." Anna definitely slurred this time. "Water is certainly required now."

Xian returned with two bottles of water. "Anna, you better drink these and no more scotch for you."

Chen smiled and watched as Anna finished an entire bottle of the proffered water. "Thirsty?"

"Yes! Very much so. I miss my well water at home." Anna

cracked open the second bottle and took a deep swallow.

"Not sure I've ever had water that wasn't over-treated by chemicals, other than bottled water."

Xian watched Anna and Chen as they bantered back and forth. They had something special for sure.

"Xian, what are the plans for tomorrow?" Anna asked, squinting slightly.

"Ah, the shopping trip. What time would you like to head out in the morning? We have to find the perfect dress for Saturday. I have some ideas about where to go," Xian said thoughtfully.

Anna contemplated the answer for a few moments. "Is nine too early or too late? I don't know exactly what you have planned."

"Most of the fashion boutiques I plan on taking you to are near one another, making things easier. I believe they open at ten in the morning for most of them. Shall I pick you up and take you to breakfast? Can't have low blood sugar while we are shopping." Tipping back the last of his scotch, Xian sat his glass down.

"I, however, received notice that several more scenes need to be reshot. I'm stuck working with Li Ming tomorrow. Anna, think you'll be up to a late dinner with me after your shopping trip?" Chen asked.

"Chen, I would go anywhere with you." Anna smiled, weaving a bit on the couch.

"And on that note, I believe it's time for me to take this young lady back to her hotel." Chen stepped up to Anna. He offered Anna his hand to pull her to her feet. She swayed and fell into Chen as she stood, his quick reflexes catching her before she hit the floor. "Anna, are you all right?" he asked with concern evident in his voice.

Raising her hand to her forehead she said, "I did drink too much tonight. Time for me to turn into a pumpkin." Giggling to herself, they probably wouldn't get the reference.

Laughing now, Chen was tempted to pick her up and carry her out of the apartment.

Xian handed Chen Anna's wrap, helping him walk her to the door. "You have this?" he asked.

"Got it, you meet her at the front of the hotel in the morning," Chen said as he supported Anna.

"Good night, Chen," Xian said as he watched Chen walking Anna cautiously out to his car.

"Night, Xian." Chen waved over his head as he negotiated the stairs with a weaving Anna.

The ride back to the hotel was quiet. Anna's head swam with the blurring lights as they drove. Closing her eyes to avoid feeling the nausea that the colors and lights threatened. "Chen, please don't let me drink like that again. Now I remember why I don't get drunk."

Reaching over, Chen took Anna's hand to lend her comfort. "Anna, I am so sorry for letting you drink so much. Are you feeling okay?"

"I'll live if my head doesn't fall off my body and explode." Anna groaned softly.

Pulling up to the hotel, Chen knew he needed to help Anna to her room; he contemplated how wrong it would be to put her on a luggage cart to haul her to her room.

"Come on, Anna, let's get you up to your room," Chen said as he helped her out of the car.

After a few stumbles, groans and curses, Chen used Anna's key card to open her room door. "Anna, we're here."

"Mmmrrphh," came the reply.

"Anna?" Chen looked down to see a nearly unconscious woman under his arm.

Now, what should he do? He didn't want to leave her in the dress; it would be uncomfortable for her to sleep that way. Chen was sure he could do this.

Laying Anna on the bed, Chen opened the closet finding her robe; at least he could put her in that.

Undoing the buttons, he discovered Anna had a camisole under the dress. At least she had undergarments; he wouldn't see her naked, but he wished he could. Getting the robe placed on the bed, Chen moved her in place after removing the dress, pulling the robe on, tying it and pulling the sheet and duvet over Anna. Going to the minibar, Chen grabbed a bottle of artisan water and sat it on the nightstand next to Anna. Chen brushed Anna's hair from her forehead before gently kissing it.

"Good night, my angel," he whispered as he looked at Anna sleeping peacefully. He looked at her, debating if he should stay to prevent an accident if she got sick. No, he didn't know how she would react. Perhaps they could enjoy a night together before she went home, but tonight was not it.

章

Chapter 23

Muted bamboo flute music floated from somewhere Anna couldn't find. Groaning, she rolled over and swatted the covers, looking for the music. The sound disappeared for a few moments and began again. Squinting, Anna looked around and saw her purse at the foot end of the bed and her...dress. Her dress?

Startled, Anna looked down. How did her dress end up at the foot of the bed? Her phone continued ringing in her purse. Scrambling to grab it, she dug her phone out to see Chen calling.

"Hello?" Anna croaked.

"You don't sound so hot." Chen's sympathetic voice came through the phone.

"Well, I feel like I was scraped off the bottom of a shoe." Anna groaned.

"Sorry, I didn't realize you had so much to drink last night."

"It's okay. I rarely drink. Oh, and I remember why now. I'd laugh, but my head couldn't handle it. Um, Chen, can you tell me something?" Anna wasn't sure how to phrase the question.

"Sure." Chen inwardly cringed. He had a feeling he knew what she was going to ask.

Drumming up her courage she asked him, "How did my dress end up at the foot of the bed, not on me?"

Pretty much exactly what he had expected her to ask. "You were in no shape to do it yourself. I knew you couldn't sleep in that dress; getting comfortable would have been difficult. Not only that, you don't know how to remove that kind of dress alone. I'm sorry, I should have told you about it right away."

"It's okay. Thank you for taking care of me. I'm so embarrassed. The last time something like this happened, I didn't have anyone there for me." Anna just wanted to hug

Chen at that moment.

Chen cleared his throat a little. "I almost spent the night, but I didn't want to be too forward. However, I called to ensure you were up and ready for your day with Xian. We planned for the two of you to meet in front at 9 o'clock. I wasn't sure if you had set the alarm or not, so I wanted to make sure you were awake. Let me know when you finish shopping so I can meet you at the hotel for dinner tonight."

Anna yawned and stretched. "If I had woken to find you in the room, you would have been fine."

"Thanks, but it wouldn't be proper as we aren't a couple," he said with a tinge of longing in his voice.

"One of those things we should discuss at some point." Sighing, Anna looked at the time. "I better go. Xian will be here in thirty minutes."

"Okay, let me know what you pick out. I can't wait to see what you find. Bye, Anna," Chen said as he hung up the phone.

Anna laid back on the bed for a few moments, taking deep breaths. Looking at the nightstand, she saw a bottle of water. Chen was sweet and thoughtful and why couldn't he have stayed the night? Drinking half the bottle, Anna felt a touch better.

Dragging herself out of bed, Anna threw her hair up in a bun and jumped in the shower. Fifteen minutes later, Anna was freshly showered, dried off and dressed. Slipping into a simple sheath dress, Anna wanted to be wearing something easy to get in and out of when trying dresses. The silk wrap she received the day before matched her dress well enough to wear while shopping.

Anna walked through the hotel's front door at nine on the dot. Parked in front was a graphite gray Bentley. Xian stood by the passenger back door.

"Your carriage awaits." Xian bowed.

Anna gave Xian a quizzical look. "My carriage? I didn't peg you as the knightly type." Her eyes swept appreciatively over the sleek lines of the luxury sedan.

"I've had a passion for all things medieval since I was a kid. You should see my house; I have a room filled with armor, swords and everything of the era. My dreams were always filled with dragons, knights and damsels in distress." Xian waxed nostalgic for a few moments. "So, therefore, your carriage awaits Milady." He held his hand out for Anna to take.

"Certainly, Milord." Anna delicately placed her hand in Xian's. When their skin touched, Anna waited for the spark she felt when she touched Chen. It wasn't there. Xian's hand was warm and assuring, but it felt like a friend's or comrade's hand. But even more, he felt like family.

Xian helped Anna into the car. "Are you ready for an adventure?"

"Five years ago, I would have said a resolute no. Today, I am quite ready for an adventure." Anna threw Xian a slightly less brilliant smile than the one he had seen for a fleeting moment at the airport.

"Wu Feng, let's follow the plan we discussed on the way to the hotel," Xian said as he settled into his seat behind Wu Feng. "I hope you don't mind; we can eat on the way," he mentioned as an afterthought to Anna.

"I'm at your whim today," Anna commented, curious how they would be dining en route. She hoped he didn't plan a trip through a drive-through.

Smiling with an impish grin he said, "I don't think breakfast will disappoint. Excuse me, but I have a few loose ends to tie up before I am free for the day. I have a few emails and a call or two. Please forgive me for not entertaining you while we travel."

"Don't stop what you need to do on my account. I am perfectly content to watch the scenery go by. I don't get the chance to be a passenger often, so I will enjoy it." She smiled graciously.

Watching the city fly by in the daylight was quite different from the view at night. Towering buildings crammed into limited space made her think of the forests of home that she missed. It was difficult for Anna to imagine living on the fiftieth floor of an apartment building. Marveling at how congested it was, made her feel homesick for the mountains and even the open plains where she grew up.

After an hour of driving, the car pulled up to heavily fortified gates with a guardhouse situated to the left of the iron structure.

A muscular man in a well-appointed guard's uniform looked at the car; apparently recognizing either the vehicle or Wu Feng, he opened the gate and waved them through.

Now Anna was confused. This certainly didn't look anything like a shopping district. If Anna's memory served her well, the buildings they were driving past resembled plane hangars, though they were much fancier than any she had seen.

"Xian? This doesn't look like the Beijing fashion district," Anna said as she craned her neck to see where they were heading.

"Well, how spectacular do you want to look?" Xian asked nonchalantly.

"Have you met Li Ming?" Anna asked, watching Xian's face while he answered.

Cringing almost imperceptibly, Xian answered truthfully, "Yes, I have, unfortunately."

He didn't want to remember the unpleasant encounters with Li Ming. In society, it was always frowned upon when a man attempted to force himself on a woman, but they rarely addressed when a woman tried to force herself on a man. Li Ming had thrown herself at Xian one evening when Chen brought her. Being Chen's fiancé didn't stop her pursuit of Xian. Whenever she could fabricate a reason to be alone with Xian, she aggressively pursued him.

It was one of many reasons Chen had called off the engagement. One night he had walked in on Li Ming cornering Xian, one of her hands poised to caress the front of his suit pants. Her other was pressed to his chest. He counted himself lucky he was so much taller than Li Ming; it made it impossible for her to force kisses on him.

"She was Chen's fiancé at one point. We have met each other on a few occasions." His voice tightened with the memory.

"My goal is to make everyone see me and ignore her. Is that a good enough goal?" Anna gave Xian a sympathetic pat on his arm without thinking. Realizing what she had done, she yanked her hand back and folded her hands in her lap. She had to learn to restrain herself while in China. They weren't as familiar as she was used to.

Grabbing Anna's hand, shocking them both, Xian took it between his own. "Don't ever be afraid to touch me casually. We have only met briefly, but Chen's told me so much about you over the years that I feel we're dear friends."

Anna's breath caught in her throat for a few moments. "Xian, I am honored to have your permission. I grew up in a very touchy-feely family. My cousin had a tough time as he has one of those hundred-dollar word aversions to being touched. Hugging and casual touch are normal for me; I will strive to keep my 'groping' to a minimum." She laughed softly.

Laughing with her, Xian released her hand. "Chandra taught me that touch was necessary for sanity. I hope you can feel comfortable enough with me that just touching as you would a close friend isn't too far of a stretch."

"I don't think that will be an issue at all." Anna patted his arm in affirmation of her comment. "Now, would you mind filling me in on where we are going?" she said, feeling more comfortable with Xian.

"We are going dress shopping. I have a few appointments set up for us in Shanghai. Hope you don't mind the trip." The impish grin had returned.

"Are you kidding? I never thought I'd have an opportunity to make it to Shanghai on this trip. So, being the deductive writer I am, I assume we are abusing your position as chairman and using the company jet?" Anna could barely contain her excitement at the prospect of flying on a corporate jet.

"No, we aren't using the company jet...we are using my private one." Xian's expression was that of a kid bragging to his classmates about the newest toy his parents bought him.

"Aah, if you ever chose to visit Montana, you wouldn't need plane tickets." Anna was suitably impressed.

Xian got a thoughtful look on his face for a few moments. "I guess so. When I fly to the States, I typically just fly first-class on one of the commercial airlines."

"Mmm, must be rough," Anna murmured under her breath.

Xian raised a manicured eyebrow; humor sparkled in his eyes. "Plane envy?"

"Flight envy in general. When I fly, usually, I'm in coach or economy. Flying first-class was an unexpected perk on this trip, but now I'm spoiled. How can I go back to the sardine seats?"

At Anna's description of the coach seats, he couldn't help but laugh.

Wu Feng saved him by announcing they had arrived at the hangar. A bright white Gulfstream jet sat on the tarmac waiting for the passengers to arrive.

Assisting Anna from the car, he took her hand and tucked it at his elbow as though channeling Chen. "Shall we?" he said while escorting her to the stairs.

Stepping into the plane, Anna was thoroughly impressed. The tan leather seats looked like they would completely engulf her when she sat down. Walnut tables sat between two chairs; a lounge area was further back in the plane. A beautiful young woman in a sharp uniform greeted Anna and motioned her to find a seat. Taking the forward seat, Anna sat her purse down on the table and buckled herself in.

Wu Feng entered the plane; a costly messenger bag slung over his shoulder and took his spot across the aisle from her. Xian followed and took his seat across the table from Anna. "Once we get in the air, we'll have brunch, if that's okay with you."

"Oh, I think I could force myself to eat." Anna winked at him.

Smiling, Xian gestured to the attendant to take off as soon as the pilot was ready.

Within moments the door was closed and sealed. Anna's ears felt a slight pressure, similar to when she would drive to the higher elevations—working her jaw back and forth for a few moments to relieve the pressure.

Xian sat and watched her with curiosity as she moved her lower jaw around. "Interesting technique," he mused.

"Old trick from home," Anna replied. "We have some amazing places to visit if you don't mind some elevation. If you ever visit, I'd be concerned that you may get elevation sickness. My daughter had it for a week after she first arrived."

"That would be understandable as I live primarily at sea level or below. I wonder if there would be a way to avoid something like that." He lapsed into silent thoughtfulness.

The slow, gradual movement pulled Anna's attention to the window, watching the dark asphalt slip past as the plane taxied to the assigned runway. Taxiing along the black surface, the plane suddenly surged forward, pressing Anna back into her seat. This was certainly different than a commercial flight. Easing into the air, the aircraft climbed at a steep elevation, gaining cruising altitude quickly.

The pilot's voice came across the intercom informing them it would take about two and a half hours for the flight. The weather may be a little rough closer to Shanghai, so there may be turbulence, but he hoped they had a comfortable flight.

Shortly after the announcement, the young woman appeared with two covered plates on a tray. Cautiously setting the plates on the table, she pulled the covers off to reveal delicate crepes and a small omelet that seemed to be made of air. Champagne flutes filled with what Anna would guess was a Mimosa followed the plates.

Anna's mouth began to water at the smell of the gourmet food.

"Please dig in." Xian gestured to begin eating.

Taking a bite of the crepe, Anna was sure she had died and gone to food heaven. The light buttery texture of the paper-thin pancake was like nothing she had ever tasted. Groaning with satisfaction, Anna slowly, savoring every bite, cleaned the plate.

"My compliments to the chef. I don't think I've ever eaten anything that org...er heavenly. You realize you are spoiling me terribly." Anna sighed in delight as the attendant cleared the dishes from the table.

"I'll be sure to pass your compliments along. Though for some reason, I get the feeling you had a different word in mind other than heavenly." Xian leaned forward, looking intently at Anna.

Xian's expression caused a fit of giggles from Anna. After a few moments of getting a grip on herself, she could only smirk and shake her head and cover her face, trying hard not to giggle again.

In Xian's opinion, the rest of the flight went way too fast.

Anna had chatted openly about her background and how she had become friends with Chen. Xian was impressed that Anna had optioned rights for a sequel to *The Lost Prince*. When Chen had shown him the manuscript, he fell in love with the plot, just like all the lucky others to read the story. Anna deserved to win the award for that tale.

The intercom announcement interrupted Anna from filling Xian in on her first marriage. Xian was glad for the distraction. After hearing parts of her past, he had become furious, wishing he could have been there to deal with the problematic situation.

"Ready to shop?" Xian inquired.

"Ready as I'll ever be," Anna sighed.

章

Chapter 24

Anna had texted Liz during the flight, checking to see if she still wanted to help with the dress decision. *OF COURSE!* came the return text.

Getting into Shanghai a little after noon, Xian and Anna had forty-five minutes to arrive at their first fitting. Liz would need to stay up to be available for the two appointments. Xian had graciously agreed to hold the phone so Liz could join the shopping trip. He had been there with Chen when he had called Liz at one point. He may have an opportunity to get some insight into Anna from her daughter.

Arriving at the dress salon, it was evident to Anna that Xian was well known there. The staff escorted them to a private lounge area with a small walkway at the front of the room. Was this a private fashion show for her benefit?

Anna watched Xian for cues about what would happen. He was speaking Mandarin too quickly for her to catch all of it. Anna was almost sure she heard the number twenty and dresses and a few other numbers. The staff escorted Anna to a chair that looked to be designed for fashion rather than comfort.

Anna gave him an inquiring gaze.

"Patience, you will find out soon." Xian settled in a matching chair.

Flutes of champagne appeared on the table between the chairs. Xian picked one up and took a sip, almost like his hand was on autopilot. Anna would love to have a glass but knew she would pay for it. The Mimosa on the plane hadn't been too bad; the orange juice helped cut the carbonation.

Anna leaned toward Xian, motioning him to lean closer so she could speak to him in hushed tones. "Xian, I can't drink champagne. I'll explain later. The glass on the flight was an exception to my usual rule. Could I get a bottle of water?"

Startled at this request, Xian motioned a clerk over and

spoke to her in a whisper. She nodded and hurried away to return with a glass bottle of water.

"Thank you," Anna said to the clerk as she resumed her position at the side of the room.

Soft music filled the room as young women dressed in elegant gowns appeared before Anna and Xian on the walkway. Deep blues, blacks, creams and grays; the dresses were colors that Anna would have picked for herself. Each was more elegant than the last.

Watching the models, there were three or four options Anna could see herself trying. The first was a cream-colored flowing gown, rhinestones glistened on the bodice and long sleeves. The second was a long black sheath gown with a single black lace sleeve. The last was a dove gray gown with a layered gauzy skirt with lace appliqués on the bodice. She liked the latter as it had half sleeves. These three were the only ones she picked out of their selections.

After making her choices, they led Anna to a private changing room, got her measurements and brought her the corresponding dress in each style she requested. Trying the cream gown first, she looked at herself in the mirrors in the room; that was a definite no. The sleeves didn't fit her well, nor did the bodice; she was too endowed for the gown, and they were too pressed for time to alter it. She wasn't even going to show Xian.

Trying on the gray lace and gauze gown next, this one she liked; this dress fit her much better. It flattered her new curves. Anna messaged Xian to let him know she was coming out and that he should put that call in to Liz. Little did she know Liz and Xian had been chatting while she was in the dressing room.

If a relationship between Chen and Anna didn't work, Liz was all for Xian being a possibility. She was impressed with his concern for her mother's safety and well-being. Liz had told him that the security firm had contacted her and the system was scheduled to be installed the following Monday. She wasn't sure if Xian or Chen should be the one to hear that Scott hadn't been around the last two days, which was unusual for him. Perhaps it was nothing; she would wait and see if he showed up in the next few days before mentioning it. The last she had seen him was right after she had spoken to Chen for the first time. There wasn't a correlation, was there?

Anna walked out of the dressing room and strode confidently to stand in front of Xian. She let Xian and Liz look at the gown before trying on the final dress.

Finally, she tried on the black silk gown with the lace sleeve. Astonished, the dress fit as though tailored for her. Elegant and simple, she loved how the dress fit but wasn't sure this was elegant enough for the red carpet at the awards. She was more self-conscious in this dress as it was formfitting, showing her curves too clearly for her taste.

She was less confident walking into the salon wearing this gown; a slit to the knee in the skirt allowed her to walk somewhat normal as she strode into the salon, one hand holding the skirt off the floor as she didn't have the heels on that would make the dress the perfect length. Being in her bare feet helped her feel more confident.

Xian inhaled sharply when he saw Anna enter the salon. "What?" Liz's concern emanated from the screen. "Is mom okay?"

"She's better than okay!" Xian turned the camera to face Anna as she glided into the room. This dress was perfect for her, Liz's gasp confirmed his assessment that this was undoubtedly a dress in the running. "That can't be my mother," Liz said. "She has never looked so stately."

"That is most certainly your mother. Chen had better treat her like the goddess she is." Xian took a few photos of Anna in the gown.

"Anna, you look stunning in that gown. What happened to the cream gown? You didn't come out in that one." Xian was curious; he had liked the flow and glitz of that gown.

"The fit wasn't right and we don't have time for alterations. The gray and this black one fit me like a glove. I will take the gray dress for other occasions. I like this one, but I'm not in love with it. You said we have an appointment at another salon after this? Why don't we see what they have before I make a final decision." Anna turned and returned to the dressing room.

Xian told the attendant, "Please have the gray gown

brought for Ms. Cassidy; I would like the black one she last wore wrapped in a gift box." Xian then waved his hand in dismissal.

Anna returned to the salon in her casual dress and wrap. "So, what did Liz think?" Xian had ended the call with Liz and told her he would contact her when they reached the next salon.

"She liked both of the dresses. Her preference was the black gown; it was mine as well. You looked very regal in that gown," he replied.

"I like the black gown, but it didn't 'speak' to me. Let's pay for that gray gown and go to the next appointment," Anna commented as she pulled her wallet from her clutch.

Xian took her small wallet and tucked it back into her purse. "The gowns are on Chen and me. Just call them a welcome gift for visiting us." Inwardly he groaned at the lame reason for paying for her purchases today.

"Thank you, Xian. It isn't necessary, in any case. I have a bit of disposable income, especially after the meeting with the studio." Anna smiled, trying to pull her wallet out again. This time, Xian snatched it from her hands and tucked it into his inside breast pocket in his suit jacket.

"I said we were taking care of all of your purchases today. Anna, you would probably be disgusted at how much money I have. I need to spend it somewhere and what better way than to spoil a sweet friend?" Xian wanted to say much more but knew he had best keep his growing feelings to himself. Finding out more about Anna, his feelings for her were becoming more than a friendly admiration.

Still suffering from a slight hangover, Anna pouted prettily, arms folded over her middle.

"You can try all you want, but I'm immune to it. Chandra tried the same tactic on me several times as well. Trust me. I'm more stubborn than you are." Xian winked at her and escorted her from the salon so she didn't notice two bags being loaded in the car.

"How long do we have until the next appointment?" Anna asked, curious to see if they were on schedule or running late.

"We are right on time," Xian said as he texted Wu Feng to

notify the next boutique that they would be there shortly.

The short ride to the next salon didn't allow Anna to see much of the city; the following location was only a few blocks from the previous salon. This salon was for a famous clothing line Anna had heard of but had never seen.

Excited to see what this salon offered, Anna opened the door and stepped out almost as Wu Feng parked the car. Xian was caught off guard as Anna didn't wait for the door to be opened. Quickly, he opened his door and walked around the vehicle to stop Anna before she stormed the store.

"A bit impatient?" Xian joked.

Anna smiled up at Xian. "Not for the reason you think. I am not a fan of shopping. I would much rather just get this over with."

Giving Anna an appraising look, this woman continued to surprise him. He couldn't remember a woman who didn't take advantage of his offer to pay for a shopping spree.

"Well, let's see if we can find something that tickles your fancy. I imagine we will need to find you footwear after choosing the gown."

"Sure, as long as you know somewhere that sells shoes for drag queens," Anna said offhandedly.

Xian turned and gave her a questioning look. "Drag queens?"

Her hand rubbed her forehead for a few moments. "I have enormous feet. I wear an eleven and a half to size twelve men's shoe. Women's sizes are difficult to come by. They make larger sizes for men who dress as women, though they can be ridiculously high heels."

"Ah well, that makes some sense. I will find you the perfect shoes," Xian replied, winking at Anna.

Escorting Anna into the shop, the proprietor met them at the door. "Mr. Xian, we have been awaiting your arrival. I have the specifications you sent and the dresses are ready to view. Please follow me." The woman led them to a private salon with mirrors on the walls.

She showed Anna and Xian to plush chairs and called the models to display the dresses, ensuring they were settled.

Once again, the gowns' colors were deep blues, deep greens,

grays and blacks. Xian had excellent taste.

Watching the ladies walk through and give a spin, Anna watched each closely. A nude sheath dress with a black lace overlay grabbed Anna's attention. That was a serious contender. Watching the rest of the dresses, she liked a deep blue flowing gown.

Letting the attendant know her selections, Anna was escorted to a changing room to try the two gowns. She put the blue one on. It wasn't her favorite of the two, but she liked it.

Walking out to the salon, Anna spun for Xian and Liz. Anna could hear Liz say, "Nope, not a big fan of that one."

Xian nodded in agreement. "Sorry Anna, that one just doesn't suit you."

"I wondered. After putting it on, I just wasn't feeling it either," Anna called over her shoulder as she went to the dressing room again.

Slipping into the nude silk and lace gown, Anna could tell this was the one. It fit her as if it had been sewn for her alone. Turning and looking at it from every angle, Anna decided this was it.

Anna walked into the salon, gliding gracefully across the room. Xian sat at attention; he noticed that Anna's demeanor had changed dramatically in this dress. Her confident energy filled the room.

"Anna, that gown is amazing on you!" Xian said breathlessly.

"Hey! Don't forget me!" Anna could hear Liz's muffled voice yelling from the phone.

Startled out of his daze, Xian lifted the phone so Liz could see how stunning Anna looked. "That's the one, Mom! You have never looked so amazing."

Anna beamed as she turned one way and then another, admiring how the dress moved.

Xian spoke softly to Liz before he hung up the phone. He stood up and strode over to Anna, standing behind her. "You look beautiful, Anna." Standing in front of the mirrors, they made a striking couple. Though it wasn't formal, Xian's suit went amazingly well with the dress.

"So, now for shoes. Oh, and let me get a photo for Chen or

I'll never hear the end of it," Xian said. Activating his camera app, Anna posed so he could take several photos.

Xian texted them to Chen immediately. He figured Chen would tell Anna his opinion when he saw the photo.

Xian had been on his phone while Anna was getting changed. She was correct that finding designer shoes in a size that would fit her would be a daunting challenge, but he would rise to the occasion.

He made a few more calls and found a shop with designer shoes in larger sizes. They would need to get to the shop quickly as it would close soon.

Anna finished changing back into her casual dress; the feeling was different from the gown she had just removed. That dress was unique. She picked up her clutch and heard Chen's text tone. Checking the message, Chen texted that Anna was the most beautiful woman he had ever seen. Silent tears brimmed in her eyes; dabbing quickly, she stopped the imminent flood.

Anna was touched beyond words, not having felt that way in some time. His words made her day incredible. How could she be so lucky to have a fantastic friend?

Chen had finished one of the day's last scenes on his call sheet. Today should be it, finally. He was ready to be done with Li Ming and her machinations. Chen checked his phone; he hadn't heard from Anna since earlier in the day. He hoped her trip with Xian had been going well. A text message from Xian had come through a few minutes before; he finally had good timing.

Opening the message, Chen saw an image that made his heart melt. Anna was beyond stunning in that gown. He could see them walking the red carpet with one another. He needed to find a suit matching her dress to a tee.

He stared at the photo for a few more moments before sending a message to Xian. *Thank you.*

His message to Anna was well thought through. *You're the most beautiful woman I've ever seen.* Now he couldn't wait to see her wearing that stunning gown. Dinner tonight should be memorable. Tomorrow was a momentous day for Anna and he wanted to celebrate beforehand because he knew she would win. Time to make some plans.

—

Wrapped up in his phone, staring at the photo of Anna, Chen didn't see Li Ming walk up behind him. She glanced over his shoulder and saw Anna in the gown; her blood began to boil. How could that upstart American look so good in a Chinese-designed dress? She knew how to get that same gown, proving that she would look even more spectacular. Walking away quietly, Chen didn't realize she had even been there.

章

Chapter 25

The afternoon flew by for Anna. Xian had found an exclusive shop that had designer shoes in her size. Taking advantage of the rare opportunity, Anna picked several pairs she had only dreamt of. Three pairs of heels and two pairs of flats joined the dresses. Xian also made a point to remind her she needed a stole or wrap as there may be a chill in the air the following evening.

Asking Anna if she trusted him, Xian arranged to stop by another shop as they headed back to the airport. A boutique representative was waiting at the curb as the car pulled up, Wu Feng accepted the bag and they continued to the airport.

Chen had texted Xian that he had reservations at eight that evening and needed Anna by then. Xian had finally mentioned to Chen that they were in Shanghai, which annoyed Chen that he hadn't told him his plans earlier. Anna was a grown woman, and they were only friends at this point; Chen had no right to dictate what she did.

The plane trip back to Beijing was much like the earlier flight. Xian and Anna exchanged stories of their past. Anna told him about her life before she had married the first time, telling him about her two children and their partners; she also gave him the abbreviated list of jobs held before she became an author. Anna never expected to be an author, and being a screenwriter was even more of a surprise for her.

Xian was fascinated by the experiences Anna had growing up. He had always led a charmed life in comparison. Xian had gone to private schools from the beginning, his parents had pushed him and continued to do so. He couldn't even imagine what life had been like for her. Xian couldn't fathom living paycheck to paycheck, struggling to make ends meet and ensuring your children had food before you fed yourself. He sat quietly, listening to Anna open up about her past. Xian wasn't used to people confiding in him, but that was most likely because he didn't have any close friends beyond Chen.

Xian looked at Anna in an entirely different light by the end of the flight. The success she had garnered had been due to her work. She had fought tooth and nail to get where she was today. What impressed him most was Anna's humility. When Chen first told Xian about Anna, he had done the overprotective friend thing and had looked into Anna. The investigation found that she had written several screenplays and several popular books. Even with all of her success, Anna was genuine and unconceited. Chen better not screw up this relationship, or Xian would be there to step in and sweep this angel off her feet.

Anna stood beside the car, amazed at the stack of packages unloaded into Xian's car from the plane. "Did I buy all of that?"

Xian laughed saying, "Well, you did have a bit of help. A few in there aren't yours. I picked up some gifts while shopping. Being a chairman doesn't afford me much time for leisurely shopping trips; I have to take advantage of the situation when it presents itself." Cocking his head to the side in contemplation he said, "Actually, I should thank you. I had forgotten how much I missed being with a beautiful woman."

Turning, Anna looked up at Xian. "You must have women falling at your feet and certainly more extraordinary than me. I'm a simple girl who grew up quite rurally compared to Shanghai and Beijing. I don't believe I'm beautiful at all, either. You are a lovely man Xian; I am sure there is some goddess worthy of you."

Anna climbed into the car's back seat and sat quietly as Xian sat in the seat next to her. Anna pulled her phone out of her clutch and sent a text to Chen, letting him know they were back in Beijing and she would be at the hotel in roughly an hour; he could pick her up from there.

The silence in the car on the trip back was almost palpable. Xian continually berated himself during the ride. Why couldn't he keep his mouth shut? He had possibly ruined any chance of being with Anna by being too candid. After the story of Anna's romance with Kyle, he had hoped there could be that kind of spark with her.

Wu Feng looked in the rearview mirror and cringed. Mr. Wei and Ms. Cassidy stared silently out the windows. The day had been going so well; Ms. Cassidy had laughed frequently and he hadn't seen Mr. Wei smile this much since his wife had died. He had even laughed several times. Hopefully, they could figure this out and it wouldn't ruin their friendship. Wu Feng didn't want to see Mr. Wei lose the ground he had gained today.

Pulling up to the hotel, Anna smiled to see Chen standing at the entrance, dressed in a charcoal silk suit with a burgundy shirt and black tie. Xian noticed Anna's change of demeanor as they parked. Then he noticed the reason and his spirits fell. Chen had finally brought a smile back to Anna's face. All Xian wanted was to see Anna smile this way; if it was with Chen, so be it. Chen deserved to find that one particular person, finally.

Chen had nearly as bad of luck with relationships as Anna had. He had never found his female version of Anna's Kyle, so he could have that happiness no matter how brief it may have been.

Chen walked up to Anna's door and opened it as the car stopped. Offering his hand to assist her, he raised the hand to his lips and kissed it before folding her in his arms.

"I missed you today. The set wasn't the same without you. Everyone was asking about how you were doing," Chen said as he stepped back from the embrace.

"Missed you too. I did have a good time; Xian has impeccable taste." Anna grinned as Xian walked around the back of the car to stand next to them.

Looking over at the stack of bags and boxes held in Wu Feng's arms, Chen raised his eyebrow. "You did do some shopping, didn't you?" he gently teased Anna. He knew how much she disliked shopping. He had repeatedly heard her complain about it.

Blushing in frustration, Anna softly punched Chen in the shoulder. "You know I dislike buying new clothes, though that last dress was worth the trip." She winked at him.

Chen looked at his wrist; they would be pressed for time. "We need to get your bags to your room. Let me talk to the manager and have them delivered to your room. If we don't get going, we will be late for our reservations."

Wu Feng followed Chen through the doors to the lobby, leaving Xian and Anna standing in awkward silence. "Thank you for today," Anna said, looking at him for the first time since leaving the airport. "You have no idea how much I appreciate it." Hoping to erase some of the hurt she noticed creeping into his eyes, she stood on her tiptoes and kissed Xian's cheek. Resting her hand on his chest for a few moments, she looked into his eyes. "You are a true friend. If only..." Anna stepped back and turned to wait for Chen.

Xian started to reach for Anna. He wanted nothing more than to pull her back to him, kiss her and confess that he had fallen hard and fast. Thinking better of it, he dropped his hand. He couldn't do that to either Chen or Anna. Frustrated, Xian leaned back against the car, sliding his hands in his pants pockets while waiting for Chen to return. He should have just left, but it would be rude to leave Anna alone while Chen was inside talking to the manager. Besides, Wu Feng was still inside with Chen, so he could use that as an excuse to spend a few more moments with Anna.

Staring at the ground, Xian ignored the whoosh of the automatic door when Chen and Wu Feng returned. Chen stopped, giving Xian an appraising look. Since high school, he hadn't seen that expression on his friend's face. What had happened between Xian and Anna during the trip? Looking closely at Anna, her smile didn't reach her eyes; it felt like she was doing her best to force it. Chen had a feeling he didn't want to know. Best leave it be for now.

Striding past Anna, he grabbed her hand. "We will be late for our reservation if we don't leave right now," Chen said, explaining his behavior to Anna.

"Xian, thank you, man, for helping Anna today." Chen held out his hand to shake Xian's.

Xian stared at Chen sullenly before mentally shaking himself and taking the proffered hand. They would be at the awards together tomorrow; he had to keep the peace for the moment. "You are welcome. Anna was a pleasure to be with. I better go as well; I've had a few calls and texts about some issues at the office that need to be addressed today. Are you flying commercial tomorrow with the rest of the studio execs, or are you going to fly with me?"

Chen contemplated the offer. "Would it be alright for Anna and me to fly with you? It will keep us away from Li Ming."

Xian was afraid Chen would suggest that. Both of them on the same plane with her for four hours would be a challenge to his composure. But it would also be an opportunity for him to spend time with Anna, as painful as that may be. "Sure. Have Huang Hu contact Wu Feng and coordinate the schedule for tomorrow. The ceremony starts at 7 P.M., but I imagine there will be pre-award photos and interviews to deal with."

Chen was thoughtful for a moment. "We could go early and get checked into the hotel. Anna will need to have her hair and makeup done to get ready. She is one of the first Americans to be nominated. There aren't many foreigners writing Chinese movies or television. *The Lost Prince* movie was unique. Anna is bound to be at the center of attention."

Chen looked at his wrist again. "We do need to leave right now." He started guiding Anna to his car.

"Good evening Xian; thank you again for today," Anna said as she got into Chen's car. Settled into her seat, she waved at Xian.

Xian raised his hand in response to Anna. *Tomorrow was going to suck!* he thought.

Dinner was a nice reprieve from the long hectic day for Anna and Chen. They decided to keep it a short evening as the next day would be quite long. After finishing dinner, Chen took Anna back to the hotel to get some sleep. The morning was going to come early.

Huang Hu sent Chen a text message telling him they would need to be at the airport by seven in the morning to arrive in Taipei early enough to prepare for the ceremony. He informed the studio that they would fly privately and meet them at the hotel by one o'clock. Chen replied to Huang Hu that he and Anna would be there a little early.

Arriving at the hotel, Anna was ready to call it a night. The emotional roller coaster of the day had finally caught up to her. Liz had texted her a few times while she was having dinner with Chen. Anna would try calling her when she got up in the morning for the flight. Liz should be awake by then.

The evening had been a little tense. Anna was still out of sorts from Xian's behavior earlier; and Chen could sense something had happened, but he didn't want to push for an explanation. He had dealt with Li Ming most of the day, so his mood wasn't the best either. Once the awards were over, they could spend some quiet time together.

Getting out of the car to open Anna's door, he wished he could just stay with her and cheer her up. She wasn't frowning, but he could tell something had bothered her. "I'll be here at 5:30 A.M. to pick you up. The flight to Taipei is about three and a half hours, so you could catch a nap on the plane if you like. Would you like me to call before I leave my apartment?" Chen asked as Anna tugged her skirt into place.

Distracted, Anna started walking to the hotel doors. "Anna," Chen called, trying to get her attention.

"Huh?" Anna was startled and looked back at Chen. "Sorry, what did you say?"

"Anna, are you okay? You've been off all night. Did something happen I should know about?" Chen was concerned now.

"I'm just tired, Chen." Anna walked back to where Chen was standing by the car door. Laying her head on his shoulder for a few moments, she raised her head and kissed his cheek. "Thank you for dinner tonight. It was delicious. Good night, Chen." She turned and walked through the hotel doors.

Stunned, Chen stood there a few minutes before realizing Anna had left. What just happened? They needed to have a chat tomorrow, perhaps on the plane.

———

If Anna hadn't been so distracted, she might have recognized the middle-aged man with salt and pepper hair standing by a pillar having a cigarette. He had found her hotel, but she was leaving for Taipei in the morning. Now she was traveling there? He had just arrived and she was leaving for another city?

He was on the fence about following her to Taipei or just waiting in Beijing. Turning to get his rental car, he noticed a woman watching the car that Anna had gotten out of. She looked as mad as he felt; perhaps it followed the adage, the enemy of my enemy is my friend.

"Excuse me, ma'am, do you know that gentleman?" he called to the woman.

The woman replied in stilted English, "Yes, I do. Who wants to know?" Her haughty attitude made him smile. He might have just found an ally here in Beijing.

"Can I buy you a cup of coffee, or perhaps something stronger?" he asked as he walked closer to her.

"How do you know Xiao Chen?" she asked him, curious now.

"I don't. I know Anna. She's my fiancé," the man said confidently.

Li Ming gasped. Was Chen interested in an engaged woman? This might allow her to get rid of that interloper once and for all. "Hello, my name is Li Ming. Let's have that drink. I prefer stronger."

"Scott Randall, I believe we may be able to help one another. How much do you know about that Chen character? I don't want Anna around him."

"That is two of us," Li Ming responded in broken English.

章

Chapter 26

In Anna's opinion, morning came ridiculously early. After returning to her room the night before, she unpacked the bags and boxes from her purchases. Figuring she'd get a jump on things, she packed her smaller suitcase with her overnight essentials; she would wear comfortable casual clothes for the flight. She wasn't used to dressing up this much. Anna planned to shower and finish preparing once they arrived at the hotel in Taipei.

Packing last minute items in her bag, Chen's text chime dinged on her phone. *On my way, be there in 10 minutes.*

Good timing as she was just finishing packing her toiletries. Anna checked her reflection quickly, her baggy, cable-knit burgundy sweater paired nicely with the black leggings with lace insets up the sides of the leg and a pair of slip-on black shoes. Anna was lucky she had thrown the woven wrap in her bag; she would need to invest in a new casual jacket since hers had disappeared from the wardrobe department at the studio.

Anna had thrown her long hair in a messy bun, with no makeup or jewelry, trying to be low-key. She still looked great, even this casual. Nodding, she grabbed her bag and headed for the lobby.

Anna walked out the front doors moments before Chen arrived. As soon as the car stopped, Chen was out of the vehicle, taking Anna's bag and putting it in the rear compartment.

Huang Hu was behind the driver's wheel today; he would accompany them to the awards. He would be invaluable in keeping in touch with the studio people before the ceremony.

Anna didn't wait for Chen to open her door; getting in the back seat of the large SUV, she waited quietly while Chen closed the hatch and settled into his seat.

"How are you?" he asked Anna.

"A bit tired and nervous about tonight. This is a first for me," Anna said past a yawn.

"You should be able to rest on the plane," Chen replied, concerned at why Anna was so quiet and subdued. It wasn't like her. Watching her from the corner of his eye, she browsed her phone, sending a text message.

Anna put her phone down for a few moments. She stared out the window watching the city pass. Early morning was certainly quieter than the evening, though it was still busier than she was used to.

Raise Your Glass by Pink suddenly blared from Anna's phone, breaking the awkward silence in the SUV. Answering the video chat she greeted her daughter, "Hi Liz, how is Montana today?" Anna forced herself to smile, not wanting Liz to worry about her.

"It was a beautiful fall day. We still had temps in the fifties so unseasonably warm, would have been great fishing weather." Liz turned her phone to show Anna the cotton candy sunset. Montana had some of the most spectacular sunsets; the deep blue fluffy clouds looked like an artist's brush had just swiped magenta across the bottoms. Yellows, oranges and purples made it picturesque.

"That sunset looks spectacular as always. Miss it right now." Anna sighed a little.

Chen leaned in slightly to catch a glimpse of what Anna was sighing over. He had never seen such a spectacular sunset. It was another incentive to make the long trip to the wilds of the mountains.

"Oh Liz, this is Xiao Chen, my good friend I've spoken of ad nauseam." Anna pulled Chen closer, so he was on the screen.

Liz waved hello to Chen. "Hello! Are you taking good care of my mother?"

"Liz, how rude can you be?" Anna shook her head.

Laughing, Chen said, "I'm taking great care of her, I hope. I have also had a little help from my best friend, Xian." Chen winked knowingly at Liz.

"Good, I didn't want to have to come over there and have words with you." Liz smiled to show the threat wasn't genuine.

For the remainder of the trip, Anna and Chen talked with Liz, filling her in on the awards. Anna had found that there would be a live feed of the red carpet on YouTube; as soon as she could get the link information, she would send it. Liz was excited at the prospect of seeing her mother walk a red carpet.

Huang Hu cleared his throat. "Sir, we are almost at the airport."

"Thank you, Hu," Chen said, checking his phone for messages. One from the studio verified the hotel they were booked at and when Chen and Anna had to be available for hair and makeup. Chen replied that they would be there a little early if possible. They had to be there at one o'clock; it should allow for a light lunch when they arrived.

"Liz, we need to go; we're at the airport waiting for Xian. I'll be in touch with the link. Love you, Tribbles." Anna snickered at the face Liz made hearing her nickname.

Chen leaned over for a quick moment to say his goodbye before Anna ended the call.

"Your daughter is pretty cool," Chen said.

"I got pretty lucky with both my kids. You haven't had a chance to chat with Kameron; he's usually super busy and on the go, so I don't get to talk to him often. Heck, he used to text me for everything, now he has a fiancé and she is his world. I imagine you will have an opportunity to chat with him at some point if you like." Anna smiled. Talking to Liz had lightened her mood and she felt much better overall. She knew she was having some homesickness contributing to her foul mood. Well, that and Xian.

Arriving at Xian's hangar, Huang Hu found a parking spot close to the jet. Wu Feng was exiting the plane as Chen stepped out of the SUV.

"Mr. Xiao, Mr. Wei is onboard awaiting Ms. Cassidy and yourself. I will assist Huang Hu with your luggage; please feel free to board the plane and get comfortable," Wu Feng said as he pulled a garment bag from the back of the SUV.

Chen opened Anna's door, smiled at her and mouthed, "Thank you."

Anna cocked her head at an angle in confusion. "For?" she inquired quietly.

"For indulging me," was his simple statement.

The lightbulb flickered for a few moments before roaring to life. *Ah, I got it.* "You're welcome. I don't mind being spoiled a little. Thank you, d..." Anna stopped before finishing.

Chen stopped and looked at Anna. "What were you going to say?"

"I have a habit that I've been watching closely. I'm not sure how it would go here in China," Anna said quietly.

"Okay, now that you have my curiosity piqued, spill it." Chen nudged her.

She let out a soft laugh. "Okay, okay, so I use the endearment 'dear' quite often. I do it with close friends when I'm at home. I didn't know how it would go over here, so I watched closely. I didn't want to be too familiar," Anna explained.

Looking thoughtful, Chen answered, "You can call me dear anytime you like. I won't mind at all. It may be better if you don't do it while around anyone other than Xian or Hu. Now, let's get on this plane and go get your award."

Beaming at Chen, his words blew away the last dark cloud that had followed her since the previous afternoon. "Let's go, dear." Anna laughed, grabbed his hand and pulled him towards the stairs.

Chen laughed with her; this was more like his Anna.

Neither noticed Xian observing them from the door of the airplane. Today was going to be a rough one for him. He would have to watch Chen and Anna together. He couldn't help how he felt and it certainly wasn't something he had expected to happen. Xian was usually more reasonable about his feelings. He thought about the gifts he had stowed as a surprise for Anna.

"Hey guys, let's get the lead out," Xian called to Chen and Anna.

Chen and Anna looked up at Xian and let out peals of laughter.

Xian wasn't sure if he should feel hurt or join in. The infectious laughter decided for him; his deep voice added to the raucous sound. Stopping for a few moments, Xian said, "Hey, what are we laughing about?"

The question only spurred them into more thunderous peals of laughter.

Anna held her hands up in capitulation. "Please, we need to stop this already. My sides and face hurt from laughing."

Chen and Xian looked at Anna and the tears rolling down her cheeks. Trying hard to stop, Anna snorted, spurring them into another round of chortles.

"Enough, I can't breathe." Anna flopped into the same seat she had used the previous day.

Chen took the seat previously used by Xian, snuffling as he attempted to contain the levity. "I'm okay now, I think," he said, then taking a deep breath to calm himself.

Xian's amusement died quickly when Chen sat across from Anna. He should have made Chen take a commercial flight. Grumbling under his breath, he sat across the aisle from Anna.

Anna didn't know how long she could keep her eyes open; the laughter had given her a short burst of energy that fizzled quickly. "Sorry guys, but I feel like I'll nod off," Anna said drowsily, stifling another yawn.

Xian thought for a moment. She could undoubtedly stretch out on one of the couches at the back of the plane; it would be better than trying to sleep in the chair.

The attendant had just closed the door and was heading to her seat at the back of the plane. Xian caught her attention as she passed, motioning her to lean over so he could ask quietly, "Do we have any blankets and pillows on the plane?"

The attendant nodded in affirmative. "Good, please pull a pillow and blanket out for Ms. Cassidy once we are underway. Thank you." Xian motioned for her to take her seat.

"Certainly, Mr. Wei," she replied as she made her way to the back of the plane.

A short time later, the plane cruised at altitude and the attendant let Xian know she had the couch ready for Anna.

"Anna, why don't you stretch out on one of the couches in the back," Xian suggested. Noticing her massive yawns, he wondered if they hurt. They were so forceful.

"Oh, thank you, Xian. I can barely keep my eyes open," Anna mumbled as she unbuckled her seat belt and made her way to the back of the plane.

Anna found a soft fluffy blanket and a plush pillow on the couch. Stretching out, she didn't realize Chen had followed her. Taking the throw from her, he shook it out and covered her, tucking the edges around her and placing a soft kiss on her forehead.

"You are too sweet," Anna said through another yawn.

"What was that?" Chen smiled at Anna's cute yawn.

"You heard me." She poked his chest in accusation.

"Okay, okay, I heard you." Laughter threatened to bubble to the surface once again.

"Out!" Anna pushed him. "Go entertain Xian."

"I got the hint; you don't want me." This time a snicker did escape.

"Chen, you have about three seconds to get back to the front of the plane, or I won't talk to you for the rest of the trip." Her mock fury almost set Chen off again.

"I'm going," he called over his shoulder as he returned to his seat.

Sitting down, he couldn't help but smile to himself. Anna was getting more comfortable with him and sounded more like the Anna he had talked to the last four years.

Xian looked at Chen, questions dancing on the tip of his tongue. He was still curious about what had evoked the hilarity earlier. They had time to kill so Xian would find out.

"So, what was so funny earlier?" Xian was prepared to grill Chen for the answer.

"To be quite honest, I'm not even sure myself. Something set Anna off, and she suddenly became playful and giddy." Chen shrugged in confusion.

Not getting anywhere with Chen, Xian decided to finish some work he had neglected, so he was lost in his laptop for most of the trip. He would ask Anna about it later if he remembered. Curiosity was eating him and there was nothing he could do about it. Nothing short of an emergency would make him wake Anna.

Deep in thought, Chen spent the time going through emails and messages. Since Anna arrived, he had neglected his correspondence. The four-hour trip didn't feel like it was nearly enough to finish it all. He would at least put a dent in the fan emails and correspondence from the studio about his next project. The new project wouldn't start until after the new year. He needed a break before starting the grueling process over again.

"We are about 15 minutes out, Mr. Wei," the pilot notified the passengers. Chen leaned into the aisle, checking if Anna was awake yet. She was still out; he thought he had occasionally heard a snore from the back. He had snickered quietly each time, seeing Xian doing almost the same thing; he must have listened to the cute snores too.

Walking to the back of the plane, Chen gently touched Anna's shoulder, shaking her lightly to rouse her. Snuffling and yawning, Anna's eyes slowly opened. Seeing Chen, her smile was beatific. "Hi, handsome."

Chen's eyebrows shot up in surprise at Anna's comment. "Hi, beautiful," he replied.

Anna tried to close her eyes, sleep pulling at her.

Chen tenderly pulled the blanket off the sleepy woman. Pouting, Anna tried to grab the blanket and curl up in it. Rolling his eyes, he tugged the blanket with more force this time. "Anna, you must get up. We will be in Taipei in a few minutes; you need to get back to your seat."

Groggily, Anna sat up, rubbing the sleep from her eyes. "You're no fun," she grumped, sticking her tongue out at him.

Chen wondered why Anna had become so playful; he would figure it out later. "Come on, sleepy. Let's get you back to your seat," he said as he pulled Anna up then gently pushed her towards the front of the plane.

"You are such a party pooper, Chen," Anna muttered as she stomped back to her seat.

"Someone has to be the adult," Chen teased.

"Keep it up; you're gonna be in trouble." Anna yawned and slid into her seat, pulling the strap across her lap.

Xian looked up from his laptop. "Anna, how did you sleep?"

"Great, not nearly long enough, but it was much needed or I'd be worried about dozing off during the awards," Anna answered, a residual yawn sneaking out.

"Are you hungry?" Xian inquired.

"Famished, though I don't want to eat anything too heavy. My nerves are already singing. They're strung a tad tight at the moment," Anna said as she looked out the window, watching the ground change from residential areas into taller, more elaborate buildings.

"Wu Feng, can you find us somewhere to grab a bite on the way to the hotel?" Xian asked his assistant.

"On it, sir." Wu Feng whipped his phone out, searching for options.

Landing, Anna watched as they taxied up to a hangar on the airfield. How would she go back to using commercial flights? She noticed two limo vans parked by the hanger waiting for their arrival.

Half an hour later, the bags moved into the vans, Xian, Chen and Anna piled into one while Huang Hu and Wu Feng loaded the luggage and themselves in the second.

Wu Feng had sent a breakfast location to Xian. The restaurant was only a few minutes out of their way to the hotel. They could all use some food to keep them going; it would be a stressful enough day not to have food in their stomachs.

Anna looked over the menu and ordered a light meal so her stomach didn't get upset from being nervous. They had congee on the menu, which made her happy. Hopefully, it was close to her recipe. Chen and Xian ordered large meals; it was almost as if they were trying to compete to see who could eat more.

The ride from the airport to the restaurant had been tense. For whatever reason, Xian and Chen had significant tension between them. Now they were taking it to a new level with the meal.

When the food arrived, Xian and Chen tucked in; they competed to see who could eat it faster. Anna wasn't sure if they were even tasting the food as they shoveled it in. She was amazed at the number of dishes they were polishing off. Anna cringed, thinking of what kind of upset stomach they would end up with.

Anna tried the congee, which was a little blander than she was used to, but it hit the spot. It did the trick settling her stomach.

Having finished her meal, Anna pulled Huang Hu to the

side as they waited for the oversized kids to finish their meal. "I'm riding with you and Wu Feng to the hotel. I just thought I would warn you. Those two need to talk."

Huang Hu looked at Anna with admiration. She dealt with the situation better than he could have. The tension between Mr. Xiao and Mr. Wei made everyone uncomfortable; something had to give. "Ms. Anna, you are welcome to ride with us. Will you warn the gentlemen you will be going with us?"

"I've been debating if I should or not. I was just on my way in to discuss it with them. This childish behavior needs to stop before we get to the hotel." Steeling herself, Anna walked back into the building to confront Xian and Chen.

When Anna returned to the table she found Xian and Chen had finished and stared daggers at one another.

Standing by the table with her arms folded across her middle, she looked from one to the other. "If I didn't know you two were best friends, I'd swear you were bitter enemies. So, you will be riding with one another to the hotel. I will be riding with Huang Hu and Wu Feng. You two **FIX** this by the time we get to the hotel!" Anna stomped her foot. "I need you guys for support later, and if you're going to behave like this I'll just go back to Beijing." Turning on her heel, her bun slipped and her hair flew out behind her.

Chen and Xian looked at one another, realizing how immature they'd behaved. Xian cringed and gave Chen a sheepish grin. "I'm sorry. I started this. Can we let it go, at least for now? We will need to talk later, though." The smile slipped from his face.

"Yes, we will need to discuss this later." Chen nodded as he put his hand out to shake Xian's. "Truce?"

"Truce." Xian shook Chen's hand.

"So, do we let Anna ride with our assistants?" Xian glanced towards the restaurant's entrance.

Chen considered the options and decided it was better for them if Anna had a break from them. "I think she's better off going with them. She can cool down for a bit. I haven't seen Anna that irritated before, even when Li Ming stole her clothes."

"Li Ming did what?" Xian was on the alert. That troublemaker just didn't know when to quit.

"Damn, man, I forgot we didn't fill you in on all the drama from the studio on Thursday night. I'm surprised Anna didn't tell you yesterday on the trip." Chen's brow furrowed, thinking back on the prank she pulled on Anna. He had to deal with Li Ming today and it would take most of his self-control not to send her back to Beijing. "I'll fill you in on the way to the hotel."

章

Chapter 27

On the drive from the restaurant to the hotel, Chen filled Xian in on the events at the studio. Xian's mood darkened with each mention of what Chen suspected Li Ming of doing. As they pulled up to the W Taipei hotel, Chen and Xian discussed options to keep Anna as far as possible from her.

Arriving at the hotel, they were greeted by a queue of vehicles waiting to off-load their cargo. Other studios must have also used the W Taipei as their staging ground for the awards. Actors and studio executives piled out of various luxury vehicles and light flashes strobed as actors entered the hotel.

Lovely, the Paparazzi were in full force. Chen was concerned about Anna and the vultures circling the hotel entrance. Thinking about the situation for a few moments, it was a blessing she rode with Huang Hu and Wu Feng; she could slip in as a tourist. Chen texted furiously as their vans were next in the queue. *Hu, hold back while Xian and I distract the paparazzi. We'll keep them busy while you get Anna in the hotel.*

Yes, sir. I had considered that option myself. That was one reason Chen worked with Huang Hu for years. Huang Hu's concern for Anna earned him a raise once they were back in Beijing; he deserved that much, at least.

Xian sighed as they arrived at the hotel; the media was out in force. Within moments of leaving the van, Chen was surrounded, reporters and paparazzi all trying to get their piece of the proverbial pie. Xian was glad he had kept a low profile throughout the years, or it wouldn't just be Chen getting all of the attention. Xian took a surreptitious glance back at Anna's van and saw it was, for the most part, being ignored by reporters and paparazzi.

Chen kept the horde of press busy as Wu Feng and Huang Hu assisted Anna with luggage. Anna had also devised a plan. She hauled her bags into the hotel; what celebrity would realistically schlep their bags at a luxury hotel? None of the pack of jackals surrounding Chen paid any attention. Why go after a guppy when there was a great white handily available?

One of the studio PAs was waiting for Chen and Anna inside the lobby since Huang Hu had notified the studio that they were arriving. Anna made it into the building with little to no attention. "Ms. Cassidy?" The voice startled her; she had been soaking in her surroundings for future use in a book or script. Anna was fascinated by the hotel's interior, it was ultra-modern with simple lines and warm lighting.

Looking around for the body the voice belonged to, Anna noticed a young man in a suit bowing to her. "Yes? I'm Ms. Cassidy."

"Ms. Cassidy, please follow me. The studio has reserved a few meeting rooms for hair and makeup; wardrobe assistance is also available. You can do your main preparation in your room and come to the rooms to finish preparing. Do you have a gown with you? If not, the studio has several available options," he politely filled Anna in.

"I have my own. I'll dress in my room but would be glad for the hair and makeup help."

Bowing again, he gestured for Anna to head for a hallway leading into the depths of the massive hotel. "One moment, please, can we wait for Chen to join us?" Anna looked back at the front doors, still catching light bursts from the cameras.

"If you wish, Ms. Cassidy." He straightened and turned to watch the front doors.

An eternity passed before Chen managed to break free from the crowd and enter the hotel. Xian had managed to skirt the throng of press and followed a few steps behind Chen. Xian clapped his hand on Chen's shoulder and spoke in a low tone that didn't quite reach Anna.

Anna cocked her head and raised an eyebrow. *Did those two finally kiss and make up? Hmm, a kiss? Oh, good lord Anna, that last novel had gotten a little graphic.* She had read part of the steamy novel on the flight to Beijing and the interaction between Chen and Xian reminded her of a particularly bawdy chapter. A jolt broke her out of the twisted erotic daydream that tried playing itself out in her mind. Anna shivered with a pent-up frustration she had rarely experienced.

After Kyle passed, Anna wasn't sure how to cope with the urges that haunted her. Kyle and Anna had enjoyed an exceedingly intimate relationship. Suddenly, not having that touch had added significantly to the depression that nearly sunk Anna. Her meditation leaders, Debra and Jeff, had done wonders in helping her cope with losing both mate and touch. Her meditations had calmed the physical side of her needs, but her mind was not so easily persuaded.

Chen walked up to Anna, noticing her decidedly crimson complexion. What on earth would have Anna blushing so intensely in the lobby of a hotel? "Anna?" Concern tinged his voice.

"Huh?" Anna startled guiltily, the crimson darkening even further when she saw Chen.

Xian had finished speaking to Wu Feng and had wandered over to see what the fuss was about. Noticing Anna's ruddy complexion, his curiosity was clamoring for attention. If Anna blushed any hotter, she might burst into flames. "Anna, are you okay?" His curiosity was warring with his concern.

"I'm fine," Anna replied, using her clutch to fan herself. "It's just warmer in here than I'm used to. Perhaps it's a bit of a hot flash." Grabbing her rolling bag, she followed the PA, trying to avoid looking directly at either of the men.

Chen and Xian looked at one another and shrugged. Anna had been acting odd since the previous afternoon and neither could quite put their finger on the exact cause. Being a bit short-sighted, how could they realize they were to blame for Anna's behavior?

Following the production assistant through the hotel, they came to the block of meeting rooms the studio had reserved. A few of the other studio actors already had makeup and hair finished. Realizing a sizable number of talents would require photos, the scheduling had been staggered between studios. Chen and Anna needed to be ready by five thirty for the still photos before leaving for the event.

Chen pulled the PA aside for a few questions. "Did Li Ming arrive? If so, where is she?"

The PA looked around the room before answering. "She must be in her room. I saw her about ten minutes ago talking to one of the wardrobe assistants."

A wave of relief washed over Chen. There was a reprieve at the moment. Now to get Anna to her room and avoid Li Ming.

Huang Hu walked into the room carrying a few keycards. "Mr. Xiao, I have taken care of the rooms as you requested." Chen had been on the ball, and the moment he knew they would be coming to this hotel for the awards, he had booked a couple of the well-appointed suites before they were all spoken for. Anna's room should be the most impressive, a suite with a corner balcony.

So far on her trip, the moments he had been able to treat Anna to something special had been overshadowed by the evil that was Li Ming. Hoping the room would help make up for some of it, Chen accepted the keycards from Huang Hu. Xian, Anna and Chen were in three consecutive rooms next to one another. Chen wasn't sure what Xian had done to pull off that neat trick.

"Anna, let's get you up to your room. Huang Hu, please take Anna's dress to the wardrobe staff and get it steamed. I want it to look perfect for Anna," Chen requested. He trusted his assistant to take good care of the dress.

Bowing to Chen, he replied, "Certainly, sir." Finding the garment bag with Anna's dress, he left for the temporary wardrobe department.

Having stayed in the W Taipei, Chen knew his way around roughly. Their rooms were on the twenty-fifth floor; finding the closest elevators, the ride was quiet. Chen, Xian, Anna, Wu Feng and their luggage made Anna feel confined. She wasn't claustrophobic, but she was feeling somewhat cramped. Arriving on their floor, Anna made sure to be the first out of the tiny box.

Arriving at her room, Chen handed Anna her keycard and pocketed the extra as a backup if something happened. He hoped it wouldn't be necessary to use the spare, but it would be inconvenient if something happened and they would have to wait on staff to open the door. It would also be convenient if Anna forgot something, to have one of the assistants retrieve it for her.

Anna walked into her suite and marveled at the modern interior. She was more at home with log furniture and hardwood floors, but how could she expand her horizons without trying something new? She took her bag from Wu Feng and wheeled it into her bedroom to get situated. Chen and Xian followed her in, looking around the room, covertly inspecting the room for any sign of tampering.

Not seeing any glaring issue, Xian told Anna he would be next door if she needed anything. He had to get himself ready as a studio guest.

Chen walked into the bedroom to speak with Anna before going to his room. "Hey, sorry about earlier. Xian and I get a touch competitive at odd times and you ended up in the middle of it." The half-truth was better than explaining to Anna that they were fighting over her. He stood looking down at his shoes, waiting for Anna's response.

Anna walked up to Chen and put her arms around his neck. "You are one of my best friends. It will take more than a bit of childish behavior to get me **REALLY** pissed at you," she said while hugging him. As she stepped back from the hug, she gave him a swift kiss on the cheek, shocking Chen. "Now, get out. Unless you plan on scrubbing my back." A mischievous grin spread over her lips.

Eyebrows raised in surprise, Chen spluttered, "Uh, I better not; we'd be late. Let me know when you're ready for your hair and makeup. Huang Hu will bring your dress when it's been steamed. I'm going to go and get ready myself. Have a good shower." He turned and left before Anna could see the blush creeping up his face.

Anna laughed as she finished unpacking and headed for the shower.

.

章

Chapter 28

About twenty minutes later, there was a loud knock on the door. Anna pulled her robe shut and walked through her suite to answer it.

Huang Hu stood in the hall with her garment bag on a rolling rack. Handing the bag to Anna, he gave her a slight bow. "Ms. Cassidy. I need to check on Mr. Xiao, but don't hesitate to call if you require anything."

"Thank you, Huang Hu," Anna said as she took the garment bag. Checking her watch, it was almost 4:30 P.M., and she would need to have her hair and makeup completed before their photos in an hour. "Can you check with Chen and see how soon he'll be ready? I know it won't take him long to have the finishing touches applied, but it may take a bit longer for me. I'll slip into my dress so we can head down when he's ready."

"Certainly, Ms. Cassidy." Huang Hu bowed again.

"Huang Hu," Anna put a hand on his arm to stop him from leaving. "Can you please just call me Anna? Or even Ms. Anna, at the very least, please."

"Ms. Anna, I can if you like. You may call me Hu if it makes you more comfortable when we are not in public." Huang Hu gave Anna a timid smile.

"I would like that very much, Hu." Anna smiled back. Huang Hu was a great help to Chen and she liked the young man immensely. "Text me and let me know how soon Chen will be ready." She closed the door and took her dress to the bedroom, carefully laying it on the bed.

Unzipping the bag, Anna pulled the nude and lace creation out and lifted it to inspect the delicate fabric for any creases or wrinkles. Not a crinkle or wrinkle anywhere.

Anna finished her final preparations before she slipped the gown on. She would need some help with the zipper if she remembered correctly. When she tried it on at the boutique she could get it pulled up most of the way, but a few inches at the top were awkward.

The moment Anna had been waiting for since she picked out the exquisite dress had come. Unzipping it, she stepped into the sheer fabric, sliding it up her body and slipping her arms through the sleeve holes...something wasn't right. Anna stepped over to the mirror in the bathroom and stared in horror at her dress. It wasn't her dress! It looked like it, but it was a knock-off at the very least.

Looking closely at the lace, it was not the delicate lacework she appreciated when she had tried it on. Terror started to grip Anna; why now? How could her gown have been sabotaged? Frantic, Anna searched for her phone. Had she laid it on the bed? No, it wasn't there. She found it on the coffee table in the suite's living area.

Rushing to the coffee table, she grabbed her phone; frantically, she texted Hu. *Emergency!*

Pacing in the substandard garment, Anna's anxiety was growing by the moment. Where was her dress?

Thunderous pounding on her door startled her from the panic attack that threatened to overwhelm her. Rushing to the door, she flung it open to a frantic half-dressed Chen and a concerned Huang Hu.

"Anna, are you okay?" Chen pushed into the room. Grabbing Anna's arms he looked her over for any sign of blood. He had feared she had cut herself or had fallen.

When Huang Hu's phone had dinged, and he had turned to rush from the room, Chen had questioned him. Seeing the message from Anna, his heart dropped to his stomach. Running from his room to Anna's, he hadn't even finished buttoning his shirt.

Tears that had been just behind the surface welled and spilled down Anna's cheeks. "Chen, my dress...this isn't my dress." Her voice was shaking with emotion.

"What do you mean? It looks like the dress you showed me." Chen looked at the gown on Anna closer. "Wait, that isn't the dress you showed me." The details weren't correct. There should have been delicate black floral appliqués to almost the top of the shoulders on a textured nude fabric. The floral appliqués were of poor quality and the jewels on the original weren't there either. It was a shoddy knock-off of Anna's designer gown.

Chen pulled Anna into his arms, doing what he could to comfort her. Damn! He had tried so hard to keep any further mishaps from following Anna, only to have this ruin her big evening. "Huang Hu!" Chen said through gritted teeth. "What happened to Anna's gown?"

Bowing low, Huang Hu stood trembling with anger. How did this happen? The gown had been in his sight for all but a few moments. He would find out what happened. How could anyone have it so in for this sweet woman who had done nothing but treat him with kindness and respect? "Mr. Xiao, I will get to the bottom of this." Turning, he left the room to find the answers.

Anna stood trembling in shock. She couldn't go to the awards dressed in this shabby gown. Chen helped Anna to the couch; he could tell her legs wouldn't hold her much longer as he could feel the fine trembling in her body.

Chen pulled his phone out and texted Xian, *We have a huge problem! Anna's room now!*

Within moments there was a loud pounding on the door. Chen opened it to a breathless, agitated Xian. "What happened?"

Chen led Xian into the room, where Anna was sitting in a daze on the couch. Xian rushed to Anna's side and took her hand. "Anna, what's the matter?" He looked at her closely to see if she was injured. She was dressed in the gown she had picked for the awards. Wait, it wasn't the dress; it was a shabby imitation of the gown she'd chosen. "Where is your dress?"

Xian looked at Chen, questions in his eyes. Chen could only shake his head in silence, his fists clenched. He was suspicious of what had happened but wouldn't act on it until he had proof. Huang Hu would get to the bottom of it. Unfortunately, they were under a time crunch and had to be down at makeup and hair within the next fifteen minutes.

"Anna, the studio has gowns available in the wardrobe area. Let's go see what they have available in your size," Chen said gently.

Anna had shut down for a few moments, her emotions taking her on an uncomfortable trip. She wouldn't allow them to win. Anna lifted her head, straightened her back and strode towards the door. They wouldn't win this time or ever again. Not entirely sure who "they" were, at least the voices in her head wouldn't win again.

Chen and Xian looked at one another and followed Anna. "Chen, I need to go to my room and finish dressing. I will be down to the prep rooms shortly." Xian looked thoughtful as he left Chen, heading back to his room.

While he had waited for Xian, Chen had finished dressing the best he could. When Huang Hu was back, Chen would have him grab the suit jacket he had forgotten when he rushed to Anna's room. All he could do was follow Anna, she didn't even have her shoes on and her dress was half zipped. "Anna, wait a moment." Chen tried to catch up to her.

"I can't stop right now or I won't be able to do this, Chen." Anna marched forward, her back ramrod straight.

"Anna, your dress isn't zipped, and you have no shoes." Chen tried again.

"It's not **MY** dress!" Anna growled through gritted teeth.

Chen finally caught Anna at the elevator. "Anna, the dress is half-zipped and you are barefoot."

She turned and looked at Chen saying, "I doubt I could even finish zipping the dress; it won't fit my chest. As for shoes... hard to say if the dress I end up with would match my shoes. Chen, this is a disaster."

"We will figure this out, Anna. I promise!"

The elevator doors opened to a panting Huang Hu. "Sir, you aren't going to like this."

"Is it what I had thought?" Chen's temper was boiling right under the surface.

"I'm afraid so, but it's worse than expected." Huang Hu looked down, keeping his anger from being noticed by Anna or Chen.

The elevator ride down was quiet, the fury in the car palpable between the three of them. Once the doors opened, Huang Hu led the way to the makeup room, opening the door after reassuring the attendant they were part of the studio.

Sitting in the makeup chair was Li Ming, wearing Anna's gown.

Anna stopped in her tracks. Chen nearly ran her down, she had stopped so quickly. Looking at the makeup area, he knew why.

Fury vibrated through Anna, she shook with rage. Stepping forward, she intended to rip the dress from that cow's body. This was the last straw.

Chen grabbed Anna's arm, sensing her intent. "Anna, don't. We will get this dealt with."

"Chen, it's my dress. How can she be wearing my dress?" Anna wanted to cry but wouldn't give that witch the satisfaction.

"Let me handle this," Chen growled. He had enough. It was time to put an end to this farce.

Chen walked past Anna and headed directly for Li Ming. The makeup artist that was working on Li Ming's face saw the thunderous expression on Chen's face; she put down her brush and told Li Ming she needed to get a different color shadow.

Li Ming was on the verge of chastising the woman, but Chen's reflection in the mirror stopped her verbal diatribe.

"Chen, are you ready to escort me on the red carpet?" Her sickly sweet tone made Chen's skin crawl.

"Only if you return Anna's dress to her, and even then, it's debatable," Chen snapped at her.

Anna could see the veins on Chen's forehead throb. He needed to calm down. The dress wasn't worth him getting this worked up.

"Chen, let's just go," Anna called to him. She could only contain her ire a few moments more. Li Ming would be bald if she stayed much longer; Anna would gladly rip every strand out of her head.

As Anna pulled the door open to leave, Xian fell into her. Boxes flew into the air spilling black fabric on the floor. Scrambling, Xian cautiously lifted and examined the material for debris or creases.

"Xian, are you okay?" Anna kneeled beside him, curious about what was so imperative. Inspecting the item in his hands closer, it looked familiar somehow.

"This wasn't how I had hoped to give this to you," Xian lamented. He stood with the black lump of fibers in his hands. Delicately he shook it until it began to resemble a gown.

Anna gasped, recognizing the shape that materialized.

"Xian?" Eyes wide in disbelief, Anna sank to the floor.

"It was meant as a gift for when you won your award. I guess it's a preemptive good luck token now," Xian said with a sigh. "This is the dress you should have chosen in the first place."

Chen had watched the tableau unfold before him. Xian had come to Anna's rescue. Would he ever be the one? He could only stand and watch his best friend salvage the situation.

Xian handed the gown to one of the assistants giving them instructions to steam and return it immediately. Xian also warned the girl that she would never work in the film industry again if anything happened to the dress. He watched as she rushed from the room.

Turning his attention to Anna, he bent over and picked up the smaller velvet case by her knee. Anna had been so distraught that she had missed the package.

Opening the case away from Anna's sight, Xian fiddled with something. When he was satisfied with the arrangement, he snapped it shut. Seeing Anna's curiosity, he just smiled.

"You need to wait to see this one." Xian carefully tucked the case into his pocket.

Shaking her head, the case became an afterthought. Li Ming was whom she needed to deal with.

Anna turned to Chen. Her eyes pleaded with him to help her resolve this. The situation would get ugly quickly if she dealt with it alone.

Chen turned back to Li Ming. "This is the last straw. Li Ming, you overstepped this time. It's no longer a simple prank. You've stolen Anna's property on two occasions now. I will be speaking to the studio about this." His fists clenched, Chen fought with the urge to strike a woman. His grandfather had taught him better than that.

Everyone jumped as the door to the room slammed open. Several studio executives rushed into the room, making a beeline for Chen and Li Ming.

"What's going on?" Mr. Shun thundered.

Chen bowed to the studio president. "Mr. Shun, we've had an issue with Ms. Cassidy's dress." He inclined his head towards Li Ming. "Li Ming took it without Anna's permission."

Mr. Shun turned his glare toward Li Ming. "Is this true?"

Li Ming suddenly realized she **HAD** taken it too far and faced severe consequences.

"Uncle Shun, it was in the wardrobe room, which I was told had gowns available for us to wear for the night," Li Ming simpered at Mr. Shun.

"Mr. Xiao, is there any truth to what she's saying?" Mr. Shun asked. He could feel the headache building behind his eyes.

Chen took a deep breath to keep his composure. He answered Mr. Shun, "It was for a few moments while steaming it for Ms. Cassidy. Li Ming must have known it wasn't one of the stock dresses. This is a dress from a designer we don't use. At the set Thursday, we had an issue where Ms. Cassidy's dress was damaged and her street clothes stolen. I'm appalled at how Ms. Cassidy has been treated since she arrived. Besides that, the dress doesn't fit Li Ming properly at all. You can tell the dress was never meant for her."

Mr. Shun turned to Li Ming. "Explain yourself."

Li Ming stood and sidled up to Mr. Shun. "Uncle Shun, I saw it hanging in the wardrobe room and thought it would be striking on the red carpet. I'll be walking with Mr. Xiao; I needed a dress to help me stand out."

Chen hissed; he had forgotten he was supposed to escort Li Ming that night. Chen had tried getting the studio to change who accompanied Li Ming, but because of the project they were finishing, the studio was adamant about him walking with her. Anna was going to be livid. He hadn't told her yet.

Anna stared at Chen, disbelief pasted on her face.

Mr. Shun turned to speak with Anna. "Ms. Cassidy, what can we do to make this better?"

Anna just stood staring at Chen, hurt replacing the disbelief. She couldn't deal with being in the same room with Li Ming or

Chen at the moment. She turned and walked out the door.

Xian was only a few steps behind. Once in the hallway, he caught her arm and stopped her.

"Anna, stop, please." The pleading in his voice stopped Anna's flight.

"Xian, how could he do this to me; tonight of all nights?" Anna couldn't decide if crying or screaming would make her feel better.

"Anna, give him the benefit of the doubt. I imagine the studio is giving him his marching orders. Chen would never willingly escort that snake anywhere." Xian tried his best to calm Anna.

"I can't do this right now. Can you find my gown so I can get changed? Let's get this night over with. I may cut my trip short and fly home after Tuesday's meeting." Anna's voice was thick with emotion. Tears were held back by sheer force of will.

Xian wanted nothing more than to reassure her. He knew she needed comfort.

"Give me a few minutes; I'll figure out where it is." He rushed off in the direction of the wardrobe room, leaving Anna alone with her thoughts.

Anna walked over to the wall and leaned against it. Feeling a chill on her back reminded her that the gown was only half-zipped. What else could go wrong? She was mortified.

Wrapped in her misery, Anna didn't hear the door open.

"Anna?" Chen's tentative voice called to her.

"You're the second to last person I want to speak to right now," Anna said quietly.

"Anna, I explained this earlier. Because of the project we just finished, the studio wants us together to promote it. I don't want to be anywhere near her." Chen took a step toward Anna. His heart hurt. Anna's face told him he was better off keeping his distance. "I tried to persuade Mr. Shun to change his mind, but he wouldn't budge. I only have to walk with her on the red carpet; we can be together after that."

"Chen, I don't think we can." Anna's face was flush, her eyes starting to get puffy.

"What do you mean?" Chen started to panic.

"After tonight, I think I should return on the commercial

flight. I'll be changing my reservations to return home on Wednesday." Anna sniffed. She was getting stuffed up—an annoying side effect of getting so emotional.

Anna straightened, stepping away from the wall. "I need to go find Xian and get changed. I don't think it would be a good idea showing up in this rag."

Chen stretched his hand out to Anna's back as she walked down the hallway. It was all he could do to keep his feet. How did this go so wrong? Tonight was supposed to be Anna's big night.

A hand touched his shoulder. "Sir?" Huang Hu asked hesitantly.

"What do you want, Huang Hu?" Chen asked, his voice cracking with emotion.

"What would you like me to do about the plans you had for tonight?" Huang Hu hoped Chen wouldn't give up. Anna was what he needed; they needed to get past this.

Chen cringed. In the middle of this disaster, he had forgotten his arrangements with the hotel to surprise Anna.

"Just keep the plans as they are. I'm not giving up so easily." Determination kicked the despair to the curb.

"Yes, sir!" Huang Hu sighed with relief.

—

In the wardrobe room, one of the assistants looked around to see if anyone was paying close attention. Switching the garment bags on two dresses, she took the one Li Ming had requested and delivered it to her room. Nervous about what might happen, it had taken some convincing to get her to help with Li Ming's scheme. Would the large sum of money Li Ming offered be enough to offset the chance she may need to find new work? It would probably be best if she just quit and found a new studio to work for before they found who had made the switch.

章

Chapter 29

Anna stumbled blindly down the hallway, barely able to see through the tears. Deep down, she knew Chen was doing what he needed to, but it didn't mean it hurt any less.

The wardrobe room was only a few doors away from makeup. Anna gathered herself and walked into the room. Xian was there talking to one of the assistants. People were scurrying about preparing last-minute wardrobe pieces for the actors and executives.

"Xian," Anna called, her voice thick with emotion.

Xian turned, the concern on his face nearly started the waterworks again. She already needed to have some intense makeup work done before walking the red carpet.

"Good, you're here. A magnificent black gown is ready for you." Xian took the gown from the assistant and handed it to Anna.

"Go put your gown on. Seeing Li Ming in the nude and black gown made me realize how garish it would make you look. This is more elegant and stately; it matches the woman I have come to know and respect." Xian's heartfelt statement made Anna's heart beat faster.

Stiffening her resolve, she stepped into a changing area, removing the hideous knock-off gown. Throwing it over the partial wall she said, "Please ensure this is returned to Li Ming." She couldn't help but overhear the snickers and claps from the costumers working in the room. A small smile crept past the hurt, curling one corner of her mouth.

Slipping into the black gown, the sheer material clung to her curves. Anna was glad she had lingerie on that worked with the dress. Sliding her left arm in the lace sleeve gave her comfort; it would cover the scar on her left elbow.

Pulling the zipper as far up as she could on her own, she

called for help to finish. Putting her back to the curtain of the cubicle, gentle hands tugged the zipper the rest of the way.

"Thank you." Anna turned and started when she saw Xian standing there. "Oh, I didn't know it was you. You're a lifesaver."

"There is part of the outfit missing yet." Reaching into his jacket pocket, he drew out the velvet case. Handing the case to Anna, he watched expectantly as she opened it.

Anna had never seen so many carats in one spot; a matching necklace, earrings and bracelet gleamed at her. She had never seen a blue diamond, let alone four. The focal stones of each piece were a sizable pear-shaped blue diamond.

"Xian, this is too much!" Anna gasped.

"I think it isn't nearly enough with all you've gone through," he said. "Your gown is the perfect backdrop for these stones." Taking the necklace from the case, he motioned Anna to turn around. Reaching around her neck so he could put her necklace on, his hand brushed against her bare skin and Anna felt sparks tingling over her body.

Now Anna was confused. There had been a slight tickle when she had touched Xian before, but this was a full zap. But Chen was the one in her heart...or was he? Was it possible to have a connection to them both at the same time? After all she had been through the last few days, she didn't know anymore.

With her necklace clasped and settled over the lace at her neck, Xian took the bracelet and fastened it to her bare wrist. They decided it was best to wait with the earrings until Anna finished her hair.

Letting out a low whistle he said, "Anna, you are stunning. I can barely put it into words." Xian's eyes took in each detail of Anna's attire. One thing was missing yet, her shoes. Taking his phone from his pocket he quickly texted Wu Feng to bring the shoes.

Moments later, a slightly breathless Wu Feng arrived with a black shoebox tied with a white ribbon. He handed the box to Anna, who gave Xian a half-hearted glare. Opening it, Anna was dazzled by the pair of black corset heels with tiny rhinestones glittering on them.

"Are you sure they will fit?" Anna's eyes were huge. She

had always wanted a pair of this style of designer shoes but never had luck because of her foot size.

Smiling at Anna's evident pleasure, he assured her, "Yes, they are the same size as the pair we had found for the other gown." Xian took the box from Anna's hands and knelt to help her into the eye-catching footwear. Xian smiled at Anna's glittery toenails. "Interesting toenails."

Anna giggled. "When you have big feet, you need to distract from the size with some bling," she informed him and began wiggling her toes so Xian would notice her toe ring.

"What in the world is that?" Xian inspected it with fascination.

"It's called a toe ring. Jewelry for the feet." Anna had some of them for the summertime when she lived in open-toed shoes.

"Fascinating." Xian looked the ring over for a little longer.

"My toes or the ring?" Anna teased.

Xian looked up and winked. "Both."

They both chuckled at that comment. Anna offered Xian her hand to help him to his feet.

"What's that for?" he questioned as he looked at her hand with curiosity.

"You knelt to put my new skis on; the least I can do is give you a hand up. One thing you will need to realize about me, I'm not a delicate flower. I've picked a man about your size up and carried him about 500 feet." Anna struck a bodybuilder pose.

Catching Xian off guard, he coughed and choked a moment before letting out a huge guffaw. "You surprise me at every step," he finally managed to say once the laughter subsided. Xian took Anna's hand and allowed her to assist him to his feet.

"Let's get you to makeup and hair so you can knock some socks off." Xian offered Anna his arm. "Wu Feng, please make sure all of Anna's belongings are carefully watched. Her possessions will be safe from now on."

Xian led Anna from the wardrobe room to hair and makeup. Motioning Anna to wait for him, he looked in the room to verify that it was cleared of anyone but the personnel assigned there. The room was empty other than the makeup and hair artists. Xian motioned Anna to enter quickly and stood guard by the door; they would surprise everyone. Anna was going to make a statement.

The hair magician finished styling her hair in an elaborate updo; her makeup was simple but accented her natural beauty. The earrings were the final piece of her outfit. Slipping them on to each ear, the diamonds dangled close to her shoulders. Looking into the mirror, she almost didn't recognize herself. They had worked magic.

Anna asked one of the assistants to get Xian. Standing in the middle of the room with her head bowed, she waited for his reaction. A loud gasp let her know their efforts had paid off. Anna looked up to see Xian standing awestruck; he might just start drooling if his jaw dropped further.

"Xian?" Anna looked for affirmation. "Does it look okay?"

Three giant strides and Xian reached her. Gently placing his hands on her cheeks, he gazed into her eyes. "Anna, you may be one of the most beautiful women I've had the pleasure to know. Chen is a fool for making you doubt that for even one moment." With no warning, his lips were pressed to hers.

Sparks, lots of them. Anna expected to hear fireworks exploding. The shocks she had felt at his touch earlier were nothing compared to how the kiss affected her. Anna's hands reached up to pull him tighter into the kiss; her fingers entwined in the hair at the nape of his neck.

Breathless, Anna pulled back from Xian, embarrassed that she had let it go that far now that her brain was back online. Her heart was the traitor. Chen was still the one her heart wanted most, wasn't he?

Xian lifted a hand toward Anna, not wanting the kiss to end. When Chandra had died he'd felt like a shell of himself; this was the first time he felt like a complete man since then.

"Xian, we can't do this." Anna placed her hand on his chest. "I have feelings for Chen. This is wrong."

Shame combated with desire. Xian wanted to take Anna in his arms and protect her from the nastiness that Li Ming continued to dish out. But how could he do that to his best friend and brother? Stepping back, Xian turned and walked a short distance away.

"I'm sorry, Anna. There is no excuse for my behavior," Xian's voice quaked with emotion.

"Xian, it's okay. It has been an emotional week for both of us. Let's get this night over with, so our lives can get back to normal." Anna walked to a mirror, checking her hair, makeup and dress. This should give them something to talk about.

Chen couldn't get the look on Anna's face out of his mind. The disappointment and pain he had seen made his heart hurt. *Damn, how could everything go so wrong?*

When Anna had left the room, Chen had turned to follow her immediately, but a voice clearing stopped him.

"Chen, what has been going on?" Mr. Shun pulled him to the side, wanting clarification. They couldn't afford to lose the deal with Ms. Cassidy, especially if they won many awards tonight.

Chen gave Mr. Shun a down and dirty explanation of what had happened since their meeting Thursday morning. Shaking his head, Mr. Shun had an aggravated grimace on his face. "That explains the phone call Thursday."

Chen looked at the studio president, questioning the comment. "What do you mean, Mr. Shun?"

"Li Ming called me on Thursday morning saying she needed to meet with me, and it had to be the time we had set our meeting for initially. That's why the meeting was bumped several hours earlier. It makes sense now; she was causing trouble for Ms. Cassidy. Chen, when we meet on Tuesday to finalize the deal we will discuss the Li Ming issue further. Do you think Anna will still go through with it?

Chen contemplated the situation for a moment before answering the older gentleman.

"Anna is a woman of her word. She won't back out of the deal as long as we handle the situation with Li Ming. She was excited about working with the studio on the new projects and had discussed options for her living here during the process."

"Good, good!" The relief was evident on Mr. Shun's face. "Now, let's get through tonight. We will try keeping Anna and Li Ming as far apart as possible."

Chen nodded in agreement. He wasn't sure how Anna would react if she were allowed near Li Ming. Whatever it might be, it certainly didn't bode well for the self-entitled actress.

章

Chapter 30

A nna, finished with her hair and makeup, was trying to avoid watching the time too closely. She didn't have butterflies in her stomach, bats perhaps, but certainly nothing as dainty as butterflies.

Xian had Wu Feng run to Anna's room to fetch the black silk wrap they had purchased the day before. It matched her dress perfectly.

Precisely at 5:25 P.M. Anna and Xian entered the staging room used for the photos taken before leaving for the ceremony. Chen and Li Ming stood in front of the muslin backdrop they had set up. Anna could tell Chen was forcing a smile; it looked unnatural on him. Li Ming beamed as though she had won the best actress award — until she saw Anna.

Anna stood quietly by the door, hurt she wasn't the one standing next to Chen right now.

A hush gradually crept over the room. Everyone associated with the studio knew what had happened earlier between Li Ming and Anna. Rumors had spread faster than a plague. However, the hush wasn't entirely due to rumors. As people noticed Anna, the silence spread. Anna's presence could be felt throughout the room.

Whispers could be heard cropping up in corners. "Who is that?"

Chen noticed the change in the atmosphere of the room. Whispers circulated the room about a beautiful woman standing by the door, barely loud enough for him to hear. She wasn't someone he was familiar with, or was she? The bright lights made it difficult to make out who it was. A few moments later he felt Li Ming tense. She had also seen the woman by the door and heard the whispers. Was it Anna? From Li Ming's reaction, it could only be her.

"Enough already, people. We need to finish these photos;

you must leave for the awards in fifteen minutes," the photographer chided everyone. "Mr. Xiao and Ms. Li, just a few more and we will be finished." The room had fallen so quiet you could hear the whir and click of the camera as the photos were taken.

Anna waited patiently for her turn; she had decided turning her emotions off for the moment would be best. How embarrassing would it be to start sobbing in front of the cameras? She had to hold it together for a few hours; she would come unglued when she returned to her hotel room later.

——

Li Ming's smile faltered as she stepped behind the lights. That annoying American was there and she looked even more spectacular in her new gown. She was pissed that she had seemed to help Anna. But Chen was still hers for the night; that's all she cared about.

——

Chen walked to Anna, hoping to speak with her before leaving for the ceremony.

"Chen," Li Ming called. "We need to head out to the lobby; our car is waiting for us." She wasn't going to allow Chen to speak to Anna.

Indecision was written all over Chen's face. He needed to fix the situation with Anna, but the ceremony came first tonight. Afterward, he would catch up with her and get everything ironed out.

"Can we talk after the awards?" Chen asked Anna as they walked past her.

"Not sure at the moment," Anna replied, brutally honest.

"Okay, I understand." Chen left the room feeling dejected.

As they stepped into the hallway, Xian was leaning against the wall, his arms casually crossed over his chest while waiting for Anna. Seeing Chen and Li Ming, Xian nonchalantly dropped his arms and stepped away from the wall, alert for any possible drama. Chen acknowledged Xian with a nod of his head and kept walking.

Xian sighed with relief once they were out of sight. Anna must have an iron fist on her emotions at the moment not to have come completely unglued at the sight of those two. After the awards, he would need to keep a close eye on her to make sure she didn't do anything she would regret later.

Anna had her "I'm okay" smile pasted on her face. She had perfected it after Kyle had passed. Photos went quickly, the photographer complementing Anna on her grace and style. The photographer's assistant called Xian into the room; she wanted to have a few pictures with him as a memento. She had hoped to take photos with Chen, but that wasn't in the cards. The photos they had taken at the studio while in costume would have to suffice.

"Ms. Cassidy, your car is ready to take you to the awards," the PA said after he entered the room.

"Thank you," Anna said, picking up her wrap and following the young man.

Xian followed Anna, not wanting to invade her space. Her tension was palpable; he could almost feel the apprehension radiating from her. It would be a miracle if they would get through tonight without "Mount Anna" erupting. As they reached the lobby, an idea dawned on him. He could text Liz. She may have an idea of how to defuse the impending explosion.

Pulling his phone out, he quickly sent a text message to Liz. Any ideas on how to defuse your mom's temper? I'm concerned there may be a Mount Anna eruption. Hopefully, she would have some kind of idea for him.

Anna walked through the throng of reporters and paparazzi in front of the hotel, not batting an eye. They glanced at her with curiosity but didn't give her a second look. Little did she know that would change after the awards. Xian followed, not garnering much attention either. He had done an excellent job keeping out of the limelight. That would also change after tonight. Walking an award ceremony red carpet with someone of Anna's notoriety would rob him of some of his privacy, but it would be worth it.

Getting in the backseat with Anna, he took her hand in his, feeling a slight tremor run through her. He looked at her closely. "Anna, are you okay?"

"I'm doing my best to keep it together. I've done about ten breathing exercises I learned from meditation. It seems to be helping a little, but I'm still beyond nervous," Anna said with a tremor also evident in her voice.

"You're going to rock this. I deal with celebrities regularly, and you are cool as a cucumber compared to some." Xian chuckled as a memory surfaced. "We had one actor literally shit himself; he was so scared."

A soft snort came from Anna's side of the car, followed by raucous laughter.

Xian looked at Anna, checking to see if she was okay. "It wasn't **THAT** funny," he mumbled.

Gasping for air, Anna coughed and hiccuped. "I think it's because of my nerves," she managed to say between hiccups. A look of panic on her face. "I have the hiccups and am supposed to walk the red carpet in a few minutes."

Xian took both of Anna's hands in his. Pulling her to look at him he assured, "Anna, you've got this. Just stop and take a deep breath."

Anna nodded, taking a deep breath and exhaling noisily through her nose. Hiccup. Damn it!

Remembering an old trick that worked for her ninety percent of the time, Anna's face lit up. Taking a deep breath, she carefully swallowed three times while holding it. Slowly she let the air out, keeping it steady. Once the air was expelled, she cautiously took a few shallow breaths to experiment. Ten more breaths confirmed the hiccups had left the car.

Sighing with relief, Anna leaned back in the seat. She just needed to focus on keeping her breathing steady and calm. She gave Xian a side glance. "Let's not say anything funny till after the awards, please?"

Holding his hands up, Xian capitulated and made a serious face.

Anna snorted and looked out the window avoiding his antics, or she would start braying like a mule.

Traffic was moving at a turtle's pace because of the awards. Their car, however, made it to the lane that had been designated for celebrities. Anna's car was queued in front of Chen's car and a limo bus with the studio's other artists and minor executives. She was glad Mr. Shun's car was in front of hers; she wasn't sure what to do.

Quicker than she had expected, she was assisted from the car's back seat to the dazzling flashes from dozens of cameras clicking steadily. Dazed, she waited for Xian to offer his arm before attempting to move forward.

"Remember to smile," Xian whispered, patting her hand.

Breathing deeply through her nose, she cranked up the wattage of her smile to ten and strode forward with confidence that was a facade. Stepping up to where Mr. Shun waited for her, she fell in step with him, walking at a stately pace down the walkway.

At that moment, a flash of cattle walking through a chute flashed through Anna's mind. Her eyes widened and she clamped her lips shut to keep the hysterical giggles from escaping. She didn't want to see the photos they may have gotten of her expression at that moment. She kept up with Mr. Shun until they reached the interrogators–no, she meant the interviewers–of whatever show was covering the awards.

Anna was glad she knew Mandarin; otherwise, she would have made a fool of herself. When the questions were directed at her, she responded clearly and concisely. As Anna fielded each question like a pro, Mr. Shun beamed like a proud father.

They asked her impression of the country and people, if she had plans to write more scripts and a few other innocuous questions. Anna answered that she had fallen in love with the country and the people, with a few exceptions, giving the host a wink and causing an enthusiastic response from the crowd. The applause was thunderous when she revealed that she would be writing more scripts for the studio, to which Mr. Shun nodded enthusiastically and announced, much to Anna's shock, that they would be working on a sequel to *The Lost Prince*.

Anna thought she would be blinded as the cameras flashed at the announcement. It caught the interviewers off guard as you could see them regroup and redirect, tossing questions at Mr. Shun. Chen was blindsided when Mr. Shun announced that he would be the lead in the sequel and the next project of Anna's that they hoped to start early the following year.

Li Ming's fake smile faltered when there was no mention of her. Each host questioned Chen about the film he had just finished and if he was looking forward to his next project.

Chen gave Anna a questioning glance. Was he looking forward to his next project?

Anna gave an imperceptible nod. No matter what happened between them, the scripts had been written with Chen as the lead. At the very least, they would work together as friends once she cooled off.

Chen's smile became more genuine after seeing the nod. His hope was renewed that she could forgive him for not protecting her better from Li Ming.

—

Li Ming was furious as they were escorted to their seating. They had all but ignored her. She was the lead actress to Chen's lead actor, yet they didn't interview her. That damned author kept ruining her life. Chen hadn't said more than five words to her since the incident in the wardrobe room. Anna wasn't going to win; she would see to that. She was looking around for her new favorite American. Li Ming saw him seated a few rows back and to the left of where they were seated. Hopefully, their plan would work.

Scott watched as Anna was escorted to her seat by another man. Now, who was this guy? Wasn't it bad enough she was messing around with one man, now she was on the arm of another and looking happy about it? The plan he had cooked up with Li Ming should work. He didn't want to see Anna hurt, but she deserved it after leaving him the way she had. And for not saying goodbye. It was time for her to return to Fortine.

—

章

Chapter 31

The awards went quicker than Anna had expected. What she had seen on TV was pretty much what happened. Categories were called, the nominees for each and the winners. *The Lost Prince* had been nominated for most of the categories, so the studio attendees had high expectations.

Moments into the ceremony, their first category was called. Anna held her breath. It wasn't her category, but it was still for her story. And the winner is...not *The Lost Prince*. Anna groaned in disappointment.

As each category *The Lost Prince* was nominated for was announced, Anna held her breath, groaning if it lost and applauding loudly if it won. Before she realized it, they announced her category. Xian squeezed the hand he had been holding through each category announcement.

"And the winner for Best Original Screenplay goes to... Anna Cassidy for *The Lost Prince*." Silence greeted the announcement. Anna stood, her heart in her throat. Xian squeezed her hand in reassurance and support. Closing her eyes for a moment, she gathered her courage.

One set of hands clapped; a moment later, another joined and another. In moments thunderous applause surrounded Anna. She smiled at Xian and slid past Mr. Shun. As she slid past Li Ming, a foot hooked Anna's ankle. Chen saw Anna stumble and quickly caught and steadied her, much to Li Ming's ire. Anna mouthed "Thank you" to him as he gave her a thumbs up.

Making her way to the stage, her nerves tried to get the better of her. She nearly tripped as she took the steps to the stage. Standing in the bright lights, she couldn't see much of the audience, but she knew roughly where her group was seated.

In clear Mandarin, Anna began her acceptance speech; they

had told her she could say a few words. "I would like to thank Beijing Golden Film Studios for this opportunity. Without them, my dream would never have been achieved. But most of all, I must give my deepest appreciation to my inspiration and the one whom the story was for, Xiao Chen. Thank you." Anna bowed in his direction and allowed the young woman to escort her from the stage bathed in deafening applause.

Only a few categories were left; the movie had been nominated for each. One was Chen's for Best Leading Actor, Xu Hinge for Best Director and the studio for Best Feature Film. Anna would join everyone on stage if it won the Feature Film category.

"And the winner for Best Leading Actor is...Xiao Chen for *The Lost Prince*." Again there was deafening applause as Chen took the stage to accept his award.

"Thank you, Beijing Golden Film Studio, for allowing me to star in this movie. It has been the closest to my heart. I need to thank the one responsible for *The Lost Prince*; thank you, Ms. Cassidy." Chen bowed and allowed his escort to lead him from the stage.

When Chen was shown the photo area, Anna had just finished her photos with the award. Seeing him, Anna smiled and gave him a thumbs up. Chen smiled back and returned the gesture. Anna waited while they bumped Chen to the head of the line as they needed to be available when they announced the Feature Film category.

Anna hugged Chen, her excitement momentarily erasing her disappointment with him.

"We did it. We both won." Anna glowed with her excitement.

"We wouldn't even be here if it wasn't for your story Anna. It was special and that's why it has done so well tonight." Chen hugged her tighter; he didn't want to let her go now that she was in his arms.

Tingles chased over Anna's limbs. Why was she feeling them for both Chen and Xian? Her body was a traitor, especially when she was upset with Chen. Giving up trying to figure it out, Anna leaned into Chen; she had missed his scent.

"Excuse me, are you Ms. Cassidy and Mr. Xiao?" a young

woman in a sparkling pink gown inquired.

"Yes, we are," Chen replied.

"You're wanted by the stage. The announcement for the winner of Best Feature Film is coming up," she said as she led the way.

Anna held onto Chen's hand as they walked through the crowded backstage. Standing in the wings out of view, Chen and Anna waited, holding their breath as they announced the nominees for Best Feature Film. "And the winner of Best Feature Film is...*The Lost Prince.*" Anna and Chen hugged one another, jumping up and down. Stopping and regaining their composure, Chen offered his arm for Anna to hold as they made their way to the stage. The whole group from the studio made their way on stage. Li Ming pushed her way to the front. Even though she had a minor role in the movie, she desperately wanted some attention.

Chen and Anna were escorted to the front to stand with Mr. Shun and the director, Xu Hinge, who had also won his category. Mr. Shun accepted the award and handed the gold horse statue to Anna. Bowing to her, he clapped with the rest of the studio.

The whole group was ushered to the backstage area for photos. Soon they were finished and were being escorted to the after-party. Xian had his backstage pass and followed a few celebrities who didn't have the best luck that night. If he didn't find her soon, he would just text Anna. Oh hell, that wouldn't work; he had Anna's clutch with him, which meant he had Anna's phone and money.

Xian saw one of the young women that escorted celebrities off stage. Perhaps if he asked her, she could help him locate Anna and Chen.

"Excuse me, do you know where the group from the Beijing Golden Film Studio might be?" he politely inquired.

"Certainly, would you happen to be Mr. Wei?" she asked him.

"Yes, is someone looking for me?" Xian hoped it was Anna.

"Mr. Xiao asked me to keep an eye out for you. He's so dreamy," she sighed, showing a bit of inner fangirl.

"Yeah, Chen is a regular Don Juan." Xian rolled his eyes.

The young woman looked at him with skepticism. She led Xian through the din of the backstage until they reached a spacious conference room set up with a bar, comfortable lounging areas, tall tables with stools and a live band getting ready to start playing. Looking around the room, there wasn't a significant number of people milling around yet. Give it another fifteen minutes and the place would be packed.

The young woman gestured to a corner of the room where a group congregated around a table. It wasn't a challenge to pick Anna out. She stood as tall or taller than most of the group. Hopefully, she didn't notice. Her heels put her a couple of inches taller than Chen even. She was laughing and chatting animatedly with the director of *The Lost Prince*.

Xian was almost loath to interrupt her; the day had been so stressful that it was great to see her back to some normalcy. Walking up to her, he slid an arm around her waist, letting her know he was there.

Startled, Anna turned to see who was taking liberties, ready to make their day unpleasant. Finding Xian, she smiled and gave him a quick hug.

"I won, Xian!" Anna gushed.

"I know, Anna. Congratulations!" Xian kissed Anna's cheek.

"Thanks. It's a relief the whole thing is over," Anna said with a sigh. "Now, I have to rub elbows with celebrities for a bit, and I can go back to the room and get some sleep." A colossal yawn punctuated her comment.

"What, you didn't get enough sleep on the plane?" Xian teased.

"Ha Ha, you're funny. Hey, we aren't leaving super early in the morning, are we? Can I sleep in a little?" Anna made a pleading face with puppy dog eyes.

Xian laughed and said, "No, we can leave whenever her Highness is ready to depart." Bowing low to Anna.

Anna chuckled and slapped Xian's shoulder. "Aren't you just the chivalrous one?"

Mr. Shun chose that moment to walk up to Anna. "Can I borrow you for a bit, Ms. Cassidy? There are quite a few people that are interested in meeting you."

"Certainly, Mr. Shun, lead the way." Rolling her eyes behind Mr. Shun's back.

Xian covered his snicker with his hand and went to find the bar; he needed a stiff drink. As Xian made his way through the crowd, he saw Li Ming behaving more peculiarly than usual. Following the snake through the throng, he noticed her speaking to a strange man. Where had he seen that man before? Xian couldn't put his thumb on it; he stood and watched them for a while. Those two were acting cagey.

About fifteen minutes later, they parted company and Li Ming made her way towards where Chen was talking with a man and woman Xian had seen in the news recently. Xian lost the man in the crowd. Where was Anna? Xian had a bad feeling about this.

Xian realized he was closer to Chen and made a beeline for him; he needed to be warned and intercept Li Ming.

Catching Chen's attention, Xian motioned him over so they could talk privately.

"Chen, Li Ming is up to something. I saw her meeting with a suspicious man. I'm getting a bad feeling," Xian spoke in a hushed voice to avoid being overheard.

Chen, alarmed, looked around the room for Anna. He didn't see her. "Where did Anna go?"

"Last I saw her, she was with Mr. Shun," Xian said as he scanned the room for Anna.

"We need to find her." Chen grasped Xian's arm. "I've messed up enough today. I can't let something else happen to her."

"We'll find her, Chen." Xian was trying not to panic himself.

"You go right; I'll go left. Text if you find Anna." Chen headed into the crowd, not waiting for Xian's response.

Xian headed in the opposite direction, texting Wu Feng to watch for a foreign male and warn Huang Hu. Xian figured Chen would be too distracted to ask his assistant for help. For once, his height had an advantage; he was taller than most people in the room tonight. His eyes skimmed over the room, looking for Anna's telltale hair.

Finally, he saw her speaking with a group of older men off

to the side of the room. Texting Chen, *I found her!*, he started working his way toward the group.

"Did you hear that Cassidy woman slept with the studio executives to get her movie made?" That wisp of conversation caught Xian's attention. Looking around for the origin of the offensive comment, he noticed a group of women glaring in Anna's direction.

"Shit!" Xian grumbled. If Anna heard that, the eruption he had been trying to avoid might just happen. He had a sneaky suspicion that Li Ming was behind the vicious rumors.

Making his way through the crowd towards Anna, he heard more snippets of rumors circulating. *Damn it! he thought.* Xian texted Chen to keep an ear out for any possible grumbles on his side of the room. "Can you believe she is trying to date one of our men? How presumptuous of her." It was getting worse and worse as he moved through the groups. They needed to get Anna out of the room before she heard these vicious lies.

"Where is that viper?" Xian heard a loud voice from Anna's direction. Crap, he hadn't made it in time. The best he could hope was that they could corral Anna before she attacked Li Ming.

Xian's phone chimed that he had a new text message from Chen. *Was that Anna?*

Yeah, I'm afraid so. She must have heard the rumors circulating in the room. After Li Ming's stunt earlier, she will be toast. Xian replied in a long message.

"Excuse me. Pardon me," Xian repeated, moving through the crowd as quickly as possible. Anna was pissed; he could tell even from where he was. A deep male voice was attempting to calm her down. Xian wasn't sure how many people close to Anna were fluent in English. They were certainly getting an earful if they were.

"I want that cow's head on a platter. No more Ms. Nice Guy." Chen reached Anna to hear her latest demand. After the ugly comments he had heard passing through the room, he couldn't blame her. Li Ming had dug her own grave this time. Mr. Shun stood close to Anna, attempting to soothe her ruffled feathers. It wasn't going well.

"Ms. Cassidy, we will get this straightened out. There is no need to get violent," Mr. Shun assured Anna. "Li Ming acted in her last project with this studio or any other in Beijing if I have any say in the matter. It isn't worth your effort to punish her yourself."

"But Mr. Shun, the satisfaction of seeing her squirm would soothe my soul after what she's done to me since I've arrived. She will reimburse me for the clothes she either stole or damaged. Whether or not I give her a black eye is another matter entirely." Anna seethed, looking around the room for the snake in a designer dress.

Chen walked up to Mr. Shun and Anna, much to Mr. Shun's noticeable relief. "Mr. Xiao, I will leave you to convince Ms. Cassidy not to beat Ms. Li into a 'bloody puddle of goo' I believe, is how Ms. Cassidy put it." Blanching at the thought, he left to find the target of Anna's fury.

"Anna?" Chen reached out to comfort her.

"Chen, you were just starting to get back in my good graces. Stopping me from taking out some of my frustration on Li Ming will put you back in the dog house." Anna took advantage of her height, looking for the gown she had lost to Li Ming. Spotting it in a group of affluent looking women, Anna barreled at her with a full head of steam.

Desperately texting Xian, Chen asked him to head her off if possible.

Xian saw Anna heading in his direction. Swinging around he saw Li Ming was a short distance from him, whispering to a group of gossip-mongering executives' wives. If he could get to her before Anna did, there was hope.

"Li Ming, come with me." Xian stepped up behind her. Taking her arm firmly in hand despite her protests, he maneuvered her to a door close to where they stood. Xian could hear Anna's curses following him as he conducted Li Ming through the door.

"What are you doing, Xian?" Li Ming protested finally.

"That's Mr. Wei to you," Xian growled. "Your previous relationship with my brother-in-law doesn't entitle you to use my name informally." He pushed her to a secluded section of the hallway then heard the door open and close behind them; Anna wouldn't be far behind.

"Where is that bitch?" Anna's angry voice came from behind them. Li Ming turned to run in fright.

"You have every reason to be afraid." Xian held Li Ming in place. "Just face the music, Li Ming. You brought this on yourself."

Anna reached them and, not missing a beat, slapped Li Ming so hard her head whipped to the side and a red handprint marred her cheek. "That was for the ink on my dress," Anna growled. Like a snake striking, Anna slapped her other cheek as hard, if not harder. "That is for my street clothes you stole." And without further warning, Anna rabbit punched Li Ming in the eye. "And **THAT** is for my gown you stole. You will be reimbursing me for the stolen and damaged clothing. Good luck ever working again in the film industry." Anna glared at her, waiting for a response.

"You think you've won?" Li Ming laughed manically. "Bitch, you haven't seen anything yet. Chen is **MINE!** Keep your filthy foreign hands off of him."

Chen recoiled at the insanity he could hear in Li Ming's voice. Turning away from them, he called Huang Hu to have an ambulance summoned to take Li Ming to a hospital for observation. He knew she had always been a bit erratic, but now it was evident she had severe instability. Chen tried to convey to Xian with a look to keep a hold of Li Ming until the authorities arrived.

Li Ming made her move at that moment, straining against Xian's grip, her fingers shaped in claws. She intended to mar Anna's face so Chen would never want to look at her again. Anna stood out of her reach sneering at Li Ming's threat.

Anna stepped forward, taking Li Ming's hair in her hand and holding her still for emphasis. "Listen bitch, Chen is an adult and can choose whomever he likes. He isn't your private property," Anna growled at Li Ming. "Leave us alone. I won't warn you again." Li Ming, struggling, yanked her head to the side, leaving a hunk of hair dangling in Anna's hand. Li Ming's luxurious ponytail was fake. Anna snorted in delight. She had counted her first coup. Resisting the urge to dance around in a circle, swinging the hair over her head, Anna leaned close to Li Ming.

"We're done, Li Ming. I never want to see you anywhere near Chen or me, or this will look like a love tap." Anna indicated the darkening bruise on Li Ming's eye. "She's all yours," Anna said to Xian and Chen as she turned on her heel and walked away.

Xian and Chen watched Anna's back as she stormed down the hallway. For both men, the need to deal with Li Ming warred with the urge to follow Anna. Xian quietly cursed under his breath. He still had Anna's clutch in his jacket pocket; she didn't have her phone. He hoped she wouldn't do anything stupid until they dealt with the squirming woman. Li Ming kept trying to reach out to Chen, begging him to protect her from the "psycho American". She had been attacked viciously without provocation; that damned author needed to be imprisoned. Her ranting became more and more hysterical.

They could only wait for the ambulance to arrive. Perhaps they would have a sedative that would help calm the erratic woman.

章

Chapter 32

Anna was done. It was time for her to head back to the hotel room to cool down. She couldn't wait to take a long bath and relax. Stopping by the cloak check room, she realized Xian had her clutch with the ticket for her wrap, her phone and money. Being from Montana, she wasn't concerned about the walk. Pasting her best false smile on her lips, she requested directions to the hotel from one of the young male attendants at the entrance.

Shakily, the young man explained how to get to her hotel. Anna had to genuinely smile at how flustered the young man got from speaking to her. "Are you sure you wouldn't rather have a car, Ms. Cassidy?" he stuttered as he asked.

Shaking her head, Anna thanked the young man and began walking toward the hotel, explaining she needed fresh air and a walk. She hadn't gotten far when the tinkle of the bracelet reminded her she had a ridiculous amount of diamonds draped on her. Stopping for a moment, she carefully removed the necklace and bracelet, tucking them in the only place available...her bra. Not trusting the earrings to stay put, and she didn't relish the idea of being jabbed in tender areas, Anna decided to keep them safely grasped in her hand.

Anna strode purposefully towards the hotel, using her right hand to help manage her dress. Damn, the designer shoes were not meant for hiking, even over a short distance.

Sirens and flashing lights sped past Anna heading toward the venue; the ambulance was most likely on the way for Li Ming. She wondered how long until the unstable woman completely snapped. Taking a deep breath, Anna slowly resumed her determined but painful walk.

While Anna made her uncomfortable way toward the hotel, Xian and Chen wrangled Li Ming. When the ponytail had been snatched from her head, something had snapped in her mind.

Cursing and ranting, Li Ming made ever-worsening threats toward Anna. Chen blanched at a few of her more colorful suggestions. She had gone completely off the deep end.

Shortly after Anna's departure, uniformed attendants arrived to deal with the unstable woman. Xian and Chen gave them details of Li Ming's breakdown while the woman spit and cursed Anna's name. The two men were shocked at a few of Li Ming's vile comments.

As gently as possible, each attendant took an arm and led Li Ming to the waiting ambulance. Xian and Chen watched them load her into the vehicle; they didn't want to take any chances of her escaping. Now to find Anna. Had she returned to the party?

Chen cursed when Xian informed him he had Anna's claim check for her wrap, her clutch with her phone, money and room key. They needed to find her.

"We need to split up again and find Anna," Chen said as they turned back into the venue.

"Excuse me, are you looking for Ms. Cassidy?" a timid voice asked from beside the door.

Turning, Xian and Chen saw the young attendant looking concerned. "Ms. Cassidy asked for directions to the W Taipei hotel. She left about ten minutes ago on foot."

Chen and Xian looked at one another. Without a word, Chen turned and ran in the direction Anna had gone.

Xian watched as his best friend ran after the woman he was coming to love. He would let Chen have this one. Xian had scored a win with the dress and jewelry today.

Someone needed to fill Mr. Shun in on Li Ming's latest escapades and how they had dealt with them. Xian made his way back into the party amid whispers and surreptitious looks from the partygoers. It was a good thing Anna had headed back to the hotel; if she had stayed, who knows the rumors that would have started flying.

Finding Mr. Shun, Xian asked him for a few moments of his time; he wanted to fill him in on what had happened. Once Xian had given him a recount of the altercation in the hallway, he described the meltdown they had experienced. Before he finished, he also informed Mr. Shun that Chen and Anna would be returning with him on his private jet.

Mr. Shun nodded and let Xian know he would arrange for Li Ming to be transferred to Beijing. Monday morning the studio board of directors would be meeting to discuss the final details of Ms. Cassidy's contract with the studio; at that time, he would address the Li Ming situation. As far as he was concerned, she was finished with the studio. Being the board president had some advantages. Even though he had been friends with Li Ming's parents, even before she was born, he couldn't overlook her behavior this time.

Xian thanked Mr. Shun. Making his excuses, he let him know it had been a long day and he would be heading back to the hotel. Now he remembered why he avoided spectacles like this; the rumors spread through the room like wildfire. Mr. Shun was doing his best to deal with the fallout from Li Ming's smear campaign. Little did they know there was another rat in the room fanning the flames.

—

Scott had been concerned when he saw Li Ming being escorted from the room by the taller interloper. Anna was his; how dare they make such fools over her. Li Ming had planned to smear Anna's name; in their minds, this would force her to return to the States a wreck. Scott had agreed, believing he would swoop in, comforting her when she returned. At least, that's how the plan had begun. Anna's guard dogs had been too quick to step in and minimize the damage. Now he wasn't sure where Li Ming had been taken. He would find her. They would have to come up with some other option.

—

章

Chapter 33

While Xian did damage control and retrieved Anna's wrap, Chen raced after Anna. A woman dressed in an evening gown on foot could be a target for any unsavory types lurking about. Glad for his weekly workouts, by the time he finally caught up with Anna she wasn't far from the hotel.

"Anna, wait up," Chen called to her as soon as Anna was within earshot.

Stopping and turning back, Anna was surprised to see a sweaty, breathless Chen running in her direction.

"Chen, what in the world are you doing?" Anna's voice carried to him.

Coming to a halt next to Anna, Chen noticed she was covered in goosebumps. Taking his suit jacket off, he slung it around her shoulders to keep the chill from her bare skin. Thankful for access to pockets, Anna slipped the earrings she had been tightly gripping in her hand into Chen's jacket.

"Are you okay?" Chen asked, inspecting Anna.

"I'm fine, Chen." Anna turned to continue her trek back to the hotel. If she quit now, her feet wouldn't make it the rest of the way.

Falling in step next to Anna, Chen walked silently beside her. After a few moments, he noticed her slight limp.

"Anna, what's wrong? Why are you limping?" Chen attempted to stop her.

"Chen, if I stop moving, my feet will win and I won't make it the rest of the way to the hotel." Anna winced.

Without a word Chen stopped, sweeping Anna into his arms. They were still a few hundred yards from the hotel, and as shocked as she was having her feet leave the ground, she was thankful to him for coming to her rescue. Her pride wouldn't allow her to ask for help after everything that day.

"Anna, are we okay?" he asked, not sure he wanted to know the answer.

The silence was his answer.

"I get it; I messed up pretty badly today. The studio shouldn't have dictated whom I would escort," Chen continued. "Especially when it was Li Ming, with everything she had done to snub and hurt you at every turn. I'm so sorry I didn't protect you better."

Anna wrapped her arms around Chen's neck. "I shouldn't have held it against you. I knew the studio wanted to promote the new show, but it hurt after what she had done. I like you too much to stay mad long. I just wish you had been able to walk me down the red carpet. Our photos together would have looked amazing," Anna lamented.

Silent for a few moments, a thought came to him. "We can always take our own photos," Chen offered. "I think I have a selfie stick in my room somewhere."

Anna laughed at the thought of them taking photos with a selfie stick. "That sounds fabulous." Anna snuggled closer, it was a novel experience being carried this way.

Anna was nervous as they approached the hotel. She wanted to ask Chen something, but she wasn't sure how he would react to her proposal. Anna, lost in her thoughts, noticed a change in Chen's body language. She wondered what had suddenly caused him to become so tense.

Chen cringed as he noticed a few photographers lurking about the hotel entrance.

"Anna, I'm going to distract the vultures. Can you make it into the hotel on your own?" he asked with concern tinging his voice.

"I should be able to make it. Your chivalrous act gave my poor tootsies a break." Anna smiled as Chen cautiously set her back on her feet.

"Okay, I'll head in first. Arriving on foot should stir the pot with them," Chen said, kissing Anna's cheek. "Meet me in the lobby."

"All right," Anna said. She pulled his jacket closer around herself. *Damn! Chen's jacket, those leeches would have a field day with that one.* "Chen, one moment," Anna called and handed his coat back. "Those sharks will smell blood in the water if you arrive with no jacket and I walk in with it over my shoulders."

"Anna, you're a miracle in heels." Chen slipped his jacket back on and headed for the main door.

As Chen predicted, the few paparazzi lurking in the shadows came out of the woodwork to get their final shots of Chen.

"Mr. Xiao, where is your car?" one of the paparazzi questioned.

"It was a beautiful night; I thought I would take a walk and get some fresh air after the awards. Winning Best Lead Actor was a huge honor for me." Chen charmed the reporters taking photos and tossing questions at him.

Chen imperceptibly motioned Anna to make a run for it. Nonchalantly, she made her way to the doors and entered the lobby; the shutterbugs focused on Chen and didn't even pay her any mind. Once in the lobby, one of the chairs in the lounge area called her name. Sinking into the chair, Anna waited for Chen to break away from the surrounding group.

She didn't have long to wait. Chen came whistling into the lobby, hands in his pockets. Heading for the elevators, he winked as he passed Anna, figuring she would follow him.

Anna chuckled to herself. Cheeky monkey. Standing as gracefully as her sore feet would allow, she gingerly walked to the elevators. It wouldn't be much longer and the lovely but uncomfortable shoes would be removed. Stinging in her heel reminded her of a line from a movie, "the more expensive the shoe, the shorter the distance you can walk in them." How true.

Chen was holding the elevator when she arrived, allowing the doors to close once she had stepped in.

"Are you all right?" Chen asked, noticing her fidgeting.

"I'll be fine in about five minutes," Anna said, intently watching the floors' numbers.

Stepping out of the elevator, Anna winced again. You must break in shoes before walking half a mile in them. Better yet, never walk that far in heels again, **EVER**. She nodded to her internal monologue.

Chen noticed Anna's wince. Picking her up again, he made his way to the door of her room. Pulling the spare keycard from his pocket, he opened the door to dim candlelight and soft music. Huang Hu had done his job well. Rose petals were strewn across the king-sized bed, a dozen roses in a crystal vase graced the nightstand next to the bed and lit candles covered many surfaces of the room, giving it a soft glow.

Anna inhaled sharply, seeing the room. It was an incredibly romantic gesture. Chen carried her to the bed, setting her down tenderly. Lifting each foot, he unfastened the offending footwear. Anna couldn't help but give a deep sigh of relief.

"I don't know if removing my shoes has ever felt so good." Anna grinned down at Chen. She reached for him, he took her hand and allowed her to pull him up to sit next to her on the bed.

Looking around, Anna noted the work it took to set the room up. A heavenly fragrance scented the air as the bamboo flute music filled the room with a soft melody. Chen may not have done the work himself, but she could tell much of it was his idea. It made asking the question she'd been fretting over that much easier.

Turning, Anna looked at Chen squarely. "I want you to stay with me tonight." It had been a long time since Anna had been intimate with anyone and her nerves tingled with anticipation.

"Are you sure, Anna?" Chen could barely disguise his excitement. He had wanted this for a long time. Over the last four plus years, Anna's friendship had morphed into something more in his heart. Chen had fallen in love with Anna some time ago, before ever laying eyes on her; he had never dared admit it to her.

Taking his face in her hands she said, "I am very sure, Chen." Anna gave him a definitive answer by kissing him.

Delirious joy suffused Chen. He pulled Anna to her feet, wrapping his arms around her waist; he lifted her off the floor and swung her around.

"I've wanted to do that from the first moment I saw you." He pressed his lips to Anna's, taking her breath away.

"Well, what took you so long?" Anna grumped. A giddiness filled her, escaping in giggles that ruined her sullen look. She wrapped her arms around his neck, fingers ruffling his hair. Perhaps she should warn Chen that she had a bit of a hair fetish, loving to run her fingers through a man's hair.

Pulling her into his embrace, Chen kissed Anna until they were breathless. Pressing against Chen's chest reminded Anna she had precious cargo stashed.

"Chen, hold that thought; let me slip into something less designer and more comfortable. Yup, I know, how cliché." Anna slipped from Chen's arms to dig in her suitcase; she pulled out a couple of silky garments. "Can you unzip me?" She turned her back to him.

Anna's zipper slid down easily; Chen resisted an urge to run his hands over the exposed smooth skin. Soon he would be able to touch all of it. *Patience.* Leaning forward, he placed a kiss between her shoulder blades. His hand slid down Anna's bare right arm.

As Chen's kiss stoked that primordial fire in her body, Anna shivered with desire. Composing herself for the moment, she stepped away from him.

"Give me a moment, dear," Anna said as she walked toward the nightstand. Sliding her arm from the sleeve of the dress, it dropped to the floor in a silken puddle. Stepping from the silky circle, Anna bent over to retrieve the gown, draping it over a chair in the corner of the room.

Making to reach behind her back to unfasten her strapless bustier, Anna felt Chen's warm hands undoing each hook. The bracelet and necklace fell into her hand as the cups shifted away from her chest.

Standing beside the bed, her left arm held the bra in place as she slipped her jewelry into the nightstand drawer. Anna turned to face Chen wearing only a pair of black silk and lace panties, her black strapless bustier and her scars. She looked into his wide eyes, looking for his reaction to the stretch marks, loose skin and scars that covered her body.

In answer to Anna's questioning look, Chen removed his jacket and laid it across the chair Anna had left her dress on. Deliberately, he slowly unbuttoned the blue dress shirt, aware Anna watched him closely. Anna gasped as his chest and back were exposed. Dropping the bustier, no longer self-conscious, she rushed to Chen, wrapping him in her arms. His stretch marks and scars rivaled hers.

Tears filled her eyes as she felt the raised welts on his back. "What happened? You never mentioned this."

Chen sighed, "It's not something I talk about easily. I told you that I was heavy when I was younger, right? Well, I was exceptionally heavy. I still have stretch marks from the weight loss. They've improved over the years, but they are a constant reminder. As for my back, that's a bit more painful. While I was attending private school, we had a headmaster that was sadistic. The more I gained, the more he would attempt to correct my behavior. Just so you aren't shocked, the ones on my back aren't the only scars."

Tears quietly streaming down Anna's cheeks, she walked behind Chen, tracing the fleshy ridges with her fingertips. How could anyone do this to a child? Anna's tender touch sent threads of desire surging through Chen. He wouldn't be able to control his body's response to Anna much longer. Turning swiftly, Chen caught Anna's hands and pulled her into a crushing embrace. His mouth captured hers in a passionate kiss.

Anna wanted more; she fought the urge to climb Chen like an oak tree. Her hands fumbled with the button and zipper on Chen's dress pants, a frustrated groan escaping between deep kisses. Chen quickly remedied the situation. He let them fall to the floor and stepped out of them, wrinkles-be-damned.

Pressed flesh to flesh, Chen in his boxer briefs and Anna in her silk and lace panties, she took the initiative and pushed Chen onto the bed. Straddling him, she bent to kiss him. Her tongue teased the corners of his luscious lips. Kissing, nibbling, her tongue danced over more of his skin, exploring the texture and taste.

Chen groaned under her exploration. "Anna, I don't know how long I can hold out if you keep up what you're doing. It's been a while."

"I know; it has been for me as well." Anna stopped flicking her tongue over his hard nipple.

Chen growled, no longer resisting, he flipped Anna on her back. He situated himself between her legs, hands exploring her petal-soft skin. In an almost gymnastic move, Chen stripped himself of his boxer briefs.

Anna's look of hunger at the sight of the whole package drove Chen into a frenzy. He lifted her legs and slid the damp lace and silk panties along her legs and over her feet. He flung them somewhere in the room.

"Anna, this may not be as slow and gentle as I'd like our first time, but your touch has made that impossible." Chen grasped Anna's hips, sliding himself into her warmth. Stroking deep and swift, he held on as long as possible, waiting for her to meet him at the climax.

"Chen, now!" Anna gasped as the explosion of sensation began surging throughout her body. Feeling Chen's explosive release sent Anna spiraling as another wave of passion crested over her.

Chen collapsed on Anna, his body spent. Kissing her gently, he moved to roll away. Feeling Chen's intent to move, Anna wrapped her arms and legs around him, pinning him where he was.

"Just where do you think you're going?" Anna joked.

Leaning on his elbows, Chen looked down at Anna saying, "Nowhere, it seems," while wiggling his eyebrows at her, setting off a round of giggles.

"So, do I get to have my bath now?" She pulled Chen down to her, kissing him thoroughly.

Sometime later, a thumping on the door roused Anna from her stupor. Wrapped in Chen's arms, they had been soaking in the warm water for some time. She had filled the tub shortly after they had made love for the second time.

"Chen, do you think that might be Xian? He still has my clutch with my phone and money in it." Anna stood up and water cascaded down her bare body.

"Well, if it is, don't invite him in." Chen slapped Anna's bare ass as she stepped out of the tub, wrapping herself in an oversized towel.

She stuck her tongue out at Chen as she stepped into the living area to answer the door.

"Who is it?" Anna called through the door.

"It's Xian; I wanted to check on you. Can I come in?" his

smooth baritone voice responded through the door.

"Only for a moment; it's not a good time right now." Anna opened the door.

"Here's your clutch and wrap..." Xian started before he saw her attire. "Um, I see why you said it wasn't a good time." His throat went dry as he watched the beads of water trickle down her arm, dripping on the floor.

"I needed to soak after everything that happened today," Anna said, taking her clutch and wrap from Xian's hand.

"Are you okay? Chen found you?" Xian wasn't sure which answer would make him happier.

"Chen found me and ensured I returned to the hotel in one piece. I got creative about my jewelry, though, so I wasn't a target. I'll fill you in on the flight back tomorrow," Anna said, going to the door, hand on the handle. "Xian, I am doing good. I just need some time to unwind and get my head on straight. I said some things today I wasn't proud of."

Xian got the hint, heading to the door he kissed her cheek as she opened it. "See you in the morning."

"Good night, Xian," Anna answered as she closed the door behind him.

Letting out an explosive sigh, Anna dashed back to the tub. Her skin had chilled from the cool air on her damp skin. Chen was just in the process of warming the water for her. Dropping her towel, she stepped into the tub, slipped between his legs and leaned back against him.

Having a giant tub at their disposal had been fun and offered much-needed relaxation.

"I better check my phone. I bet you he will text me in the next few minutes," Chen murmured into Anna's neck.

"I know better than to take that bet. I'm sure he'll want to grill you about what happened once you caught up to me. So, what do we tell him about tonight?" Anna asked, knowing Xian's feelings.

"That's not an easy one," Chen mused. "I know he has feelings for you." Breathing in her intoxicating scent, he wrapped his arms and legs around her. "Right now, you're mine."

They sat looking out the large glass windows at the city's

lights. Anna had almost felt like an exhibitionist walking naked through the room. It gave her a wicked thrill knowing someone might be watching her. Floor-to-ceiling windows surrounded the bed and bathroom area. During the day, it wasn't such a rush, but someone might see it at night with the candlelight as a backdrop. They would certainly get an eyeful tonight.

章

Chapter 34

Morning found Anna tired and sore. Even with the blinds closed it was still bright enough to make sleep difficult. Rolling over to a warm body sprawled on the bed next to her, it had been a long time since that had happened. It was kind of comical; neither of them was used to sleeping with someone so they had spread out on opposite sides of the bed. Once Anna had thrown in the white flag of surrender, they enjoyed cuddling before falling asleep. It had been such a long time. It was almost guaranteed she might walk a bit funny today.

Sitting up, Anna stretched. She hadn't had that kind of workout in at least fifteen years. A hot shower was exactly what the doctor called for. She got out of bed, cautious not to disturb Chen. Padding barefoot to the bathroom, she turned on the water, waiting for the temperature to be just short of cooking your skin off. Soap check, shampoo check, conditioner check and the water was the perfect temperature.

Anna didn't hear the bare feet entering the shower behind her as she stood under the warm cascading water. Eyes closed, she stretched her hand out for the shampoo bottle, confused when it wasn't where she'd left it. Fingers began running through her hair, massaging her scalp. Suds slid down her body as the fingers worked the shampoo into her long hair.

"Darling, that feels amazing," Anna murmured as the fingers continued working the shampoo through her long tresses.

Watery kisses were sprinkled across her shoulders as the gentle hands began rinsing the shampoo from her hair. Water ran clear of soap as arms slid around her waist, a firm chest pressed against her back and a reminder that someone was happy to see her.

"Morning, dear," Anna said softly.

"Morning, *Baobèi*," Chen said playfully, using a Chinese term of endearment.

"Baby, huh?" A chuckle escaped Anna's lips. "If I'm not mistaken, that means you like me a little bit."

"Oh, I think more than just a little. I'm saving the more serious endearments until we've been together longer," Chen murmured into Anna's neck.

Turning in Chen's arms, she wrapped her arms around his neck, pulling him in for a long, lingering kiss. One kiss led to another. Soon, the shower was forgotten as the pent-up, sexual frustration of four years crashed over them.

After they finished with their passionate play, Chen and Anna needed to actually shower and finish packing Anna's belongings before Xian called looking for them.

"Okay, so now you need to help me wash up." She teased, "At least we don't need to worry about being sweaty."

"You are so funny," Chen quipped back. "So, does this mean we're seeing one another now?" She couldn't help but hear the hope in his voice.

Leaning back against his hard chest, Anna closed her eyes for a few moments as his arms snaked around her waist. "I think we might want to wait until I come back to China. I'm not sure either of us needs a long-distance relationship right now."

The pattering of water filled the awkward silence as they stood, the warm drops falling on their heads like warm summer rain. After what felt like eons, Anna turned in Chen's arms, studying his face and searching for a clue about how he was feeling. His eyes were closed with streams of water cascading down his cheeks. Anna wasn't sure if it was only water or if there were tears there.

Anna's hand reached up to cup his cheek. Her answer was the right one, she was sure of it, but she never wanted to hurt him.

"Are you okay?" she tentatively asked him.

"I'll survive," came the quiet answer. "Did you regret last night?" She could tell the question pained him to ask it.

"Never think that I regret anything we do. I'm just not sure I'm ready for an over 5,500 mile relationship. I'm just starting to feel ready to jump back into the relationship pool; that kind of distance would be like jumping in an ocean," Anna responded earnestly. She didn't want Chen to feel the same rejection she had known most of her life.

"I like you too much to strain our friendship," Anna said as she gave him a gentle kiss before grabbing one of the washcloths and soap. "Are you going to finish washing my back?" She playfully dangled the washcloth in front of him. "I know I had asked you to a while ago...the offer still stands," she said, winking at him through the water streaming down her face.

Grabbing the cloth he said, "Thought you'd never ask." Chen smiled, playfully squirting soap at her. She didn't say no, just not right now. He wasn't finished trying. He had a little over a week to convince her.

"What time did Xian say we would be leaving this morning?" Anna inquired casually while towel drying her hair.

Kneeling on the floor looking for one of his errant socks, Chen shrugged. "I didn't have much opportunity to ask him about it last night. I was kind of busy."

Anna saw Chen's sock on the floor, picked it up and threw it at his head. "Looking for this?"

He grabbed the sock out of the air and pulled it on his foot.

"Hey, is my phone on that side of the bed?" Chen asked, looking around where he was.

Looking, Anna didn't see it. "Sorry, dear, I don't see it over here. Let me try calling it." Grabbing her phone, she called Chen's.

A faint jingle sounded somewhere in the bedding. Anna and Chen looked at one another, laughed and dug for the phone.

"You looking for this?" Anna held up the elusive electronic device.

"Thanks. See, you came to my rescue now." Chen took the phone from her hand and kissed her cheek. "You know I'm unsure if I can handle being unable to touch you whenever I want."

"I'm sorry, Chen, you just need to wait a bit longer. There are some conflicting emotions I have to sort out and that whole 5,500 mile distance thing." Anna's expression was pained for a few moments.

"Well, I've waited this long. A little while longer won't kill me," he mumbled, less than happy. Before their evening activities, being close to Anna had been a tease. He knew what he'd been missing now; this would be sheer torture.

Checking his phone, Chen noticed a few messages from Xian. He knew he would have some explaining to do, though he had noticed an expression on Xian's face the night before that he hadn't seen in years. Xian was developing feelings for Anna. How much more complicated would the situation get?

Hey, what's up? Chen replied to the messages.

Chen watched Anna as she flitted about the room finding pieces of clothing they had thrown. She dressed in a pair of leggings depicting cute little men with hats and a hoodie. Anna was going for comfort, not fashion today. Chen wasn't sure if he should warn her about the press or let her figure it out for herself. After her win yesterday, she was going to be newsworthy now. At least in Beijing, it may not be quite as bad.

"Anna, I need to warn you about something." He thought for a moment about how to explain her new reality. "You just won a major award. On top of that, the studio announced you would be writing a sequel to one of the biggest box office movies of the year. You may not want to dress so casually unless you think you can become completely inconspicuous."

"What do you mean? I'm just some unknown author from the States."

"Not anymore. How much would you care to bet you're headline news this morning?" Chen smiled and shook his head, it had been similar to when he won his first award. However, Anna's situation was more complex. Her movie had garnered seven wins out of the ten nominations; for an unknown, that was big!

"Nah, even with the win, they will focus on the studio and you. I'm just the writer; you were the Best Leading Actor. I'm guessing our site seeing is going to be compromised a bit. We won't be able to go out in public easily," Anna said and pouted.

Chen checked his emails and messages. His phone had

blown up overnight. His agent Tao Xiuying had called several times, leaving messages that Chen had numerous scripts sent to him and endorsement opportunities. Wow, it hadn't been this big a deal when he won his first Best Actor award. What was so different about this one?

Sending brief replies to the most urgent messages and emails, Chen wanted to spend the last few moments of peace with Anna before the chaos began. Sending a text to Huang Hu, Chen asked him to pack anything in his room and be ready when Xian wanted to head out. He hadn't unpacked much since he had only gotten dressed in his room.

Moments later, Anna's phone began ringing. Checking the time, Xian had been true to his word and had let Anna sleep in. It was almost 11:00 A.M. and checkout time.

"Morning," Anna answered in a chipper tone.

"Morning. After last night I wasn't sure how you would be doing this morning," Xian said. There was thumping and rustling in the background.

"I'm doing better than I expected. I figured out some stress relief last night that helped calm the...how did you put it? 'Mount Anna'?" Anna barely stopped herself from laughing, seeing the expression on Chen's face. Chen mouthed "Mount Anna?" to her while pulling her case off the bed.

A loud groan came through the phone that even Chen could hear.

"You weren't supposed to hear about that," Xian grumbled. He was going to have words with Liz for snitching on him.

"Sorry, Liz left me a message this morning and she was laughing so hard I wasn't sure if she would be able to finish what she was trying to say." Anna started snickering now. "Thanks for trying to help diffuse the situation last night. Li Ming had just pushed too many buttons and needed to be put in her place. But let's not ruin what has begun as a beautiful morning by discussing that person."

"You're right, Anna. I'd rather not discuss her either. Anyway, we can leave anytime you're ready. Did you want to do any sightseeing before we fly back?" Xian asked, half distracted by something on his end.

"I'm not familiar with the city, so I'm not sure what

sightseeing there is. Chen brought something up though. With our wins from last night, the media may be looking for an opportunity to pester us. It might be a good idea if we find some low-key food and head back to Beijing. At least there, I can blend in easier. You won't be immune to any of this either. Walking me down the red carpet brought you more into the spotlight," Anna said as she gathered the last minute small items around the room.

"Sure, rain on my parade. That completely slipped my mind. We may need to be cautious when we head back to your hotel. If the paparazzi determine where you're staying, they may camp out." Xian sounded concerned now. "We still don't know where that foreigner Li Ming worked with last night went."

"What foreigner?" Anna's attention was entirely on Xian now.

"Didn't Chen tell you about him?" Xian asked.

Anna gave Chen a dirty look. "No, he didn't say anything about it. You can tell me, or I can interrogate Chen about it."

A snort of amusement from the other end of the phone made Anna smile. "We saw a guy talking with Li Ming last night. He may be an American, he spoke English fluently and I didn't notice any unusual accent."

"Can you tell me what he looked like? Did you happen to get a photo by chance?" Anna wondered who that viper Li Ming might be working with now.

"He's slightly taller than you with salt-and-pepper shorter hair. He also had a beard and mustache and was built pretty sturdy from what I could tell." Xian thought about it for a few more moments. Not sure what else to say, he shook his head even though Anna couldn't see it.

Wracking her brain, Anna tried to furnish someone with those features. Nothing was coming to her. "I just don't know offhand. I'll have to think about it for a bit. So when are we leaving?"

"Well, as checkout time is now, are you ready to go?" Xian was making noise while finishing his last minute packing.

Anna mouthed at Chen, "You ready to go?"

Chen looked down at his formal wear from the night before,

motioning to Anna that he better go and change first. He sent Huang Hu a message and told him not to go too far with his luggage.

"Give me fifteen minutes, and I'll be ready," Anna replied to Xian.

"Okay. Text me when you're ready," Xian said before ending the call.

Chen was almost to the door by the time Anna finished the call.

"Just one moment, you." Anna put a hand on Chen's shoulder as he was about to open the door, pulling him back into the room for a deep kiss.

"Once we leave this room, we must keep our hands and lips to ourselves. I want one more soul searing kiss before we leave." Anna cupped Chen's cheeks in her hands. Her lips captured his one last memorable time. The following week would be a challenge. She wanted to be with Chen, but it would be hard not to touch him for months. It just wouldn't work right now.

Chen wrapped himself around Anna and didn't want to let go. Perhaps there could be some kind of option so they could be together? He could see Anna's point about the distance, but that didn't make it easier.

Pulling away, he opened the door and walked through. He would have stayed in the room for the rest of the day, given half a chance. It was best they stopped things where they were right now—Chen pulled his keycard from his jacket pocket and opened his door. Too wrapped up in his thoughts, he didn't see Xian in the hallway just leaving his room.

Unfortunately, Xian did see Chen wearing the same clothes as the night before, leaving Anna's room. He had a suspicion that was the case. He had knocked on Chen's door late last night, hoping to share a bottle of good scotch with his closest friend. When there wasn't an answer, he knew. Why should he be so upset about it?

Anna had come to China for Chen. She would never have met Xian if it hadn't been for Chen. Even though there was little hope for him to be with Anna, he would care for and protect her as long as possible. It would be difficult being around her knowing she was with his friend; she haunted his dreams and thoughts. She had taken over his world in a few days.

Once they returned to Beijing, he would have some of his security detail assigned to Anna. There was still an unknown man somewhere; who knows what his intent was?

章

Chapter 35

Anna had slept through the uncomfortable flight to Taipei; she wasn't so fortunate on the return flight. Chen sat staring at his phone, moping and lost in his thoughts and Xian was working on his laptop across the aisle from her. With the quiet, she decided to catch up on a bit of her work, checking messages and emails.

The night before, she had sent text messages to Liz and Kameron, letting them know about her win. They were the only two she had communicated with as Xian had her phone most of the night. While they had breakfast earlier, Anna had sent messages to both of them, letting them know she would send a video invite once they were on the flight back and she had service.

Trying to get the guys out of their moody funk, she introduced Kameron to them. Xian politely waved and said hello before returning to work. Chen offered to join their conversation. Not wanting to disturb Xian they went to the back of the plane, sitting on the couch next to one another.

Anna and Chen described the details of the ceremony. They took turns elaborating on some of the outrageous outfits they had seen. Liz and Kameron gave them both their congratulations. Kameron yawned, he would need to be up for work soon.

"It was nice meeting you, Chen. Good night, Mom; see you when you get back. Love you," Kameron said before ending his connection to the call.

"Hey Mom, now that Kameron has hung up, I thought I would mention something possibly disturbing. Someone overheard Scott making flight arrangements for Beijing." Liz cringed when she saw Anna's expression.

A lightbulb had flashed on in Anna's mind. "Well hell! Xian! I know who that guy is now," she yelled to the front of the plane.

Liz gave Anna a dirty look. "I need these eardrums, you know."

Anna gave Liz an apologetic smile. "Sorry, sweetie. I didn't mean to deafen you."

Xian came hurrying back. "What do you mean you know who he is?"

Chen looked between Xian and Anna, the realization dawning on him exactly whom Liz was referring to. Damn it! That sick bastard was in Beijing? The one that had written that letter? He had even followed them to Taipei. Somehow, he had found Li Ming and they had combined forces. Anna was in real danger now. It wasn't just Li Ming's petty pranks. Scott was a sick individual and he was obsessed with Anna.

Looking at Xian, he motioned with his head for them to go upfront to the seats so they could talk.

"Liz, it was great talking to you. Hope we can chat again soon." Chen gave her a surreptitious wink before getting up and heading for the front of the plane with Xian.

Anna gave the guys an odd look as they went forward, deep in conversation.

"What was that all about?" Anna mused at Liz.

Liz had carefully schooled her expression as soon as her mom had yelled. Well, shit. Scott had found her already, her and her big mouth. He must have been eavesdropping when her mom had called the bar that one night. Now he was in Beijing and causing trouble there.

When Chen had told her about the letter, they had discussed possible culprits. After investigating on her end, she found out that Scott had been the one to drop off the envelope for her mother. Chen had given her a glossed over version of the letter but didn't tell her all the details. When he explained it, the look on his face had made her angry at first, then terrified. She needed to talk to Chen later.

"No idea," Liz lied. "I better get going as well, Mom. Lots to do at the moment. You don't have to rub in the whole private jet thing."

"Hey, cut your mom some slack. I deserve some fun once in a while," Anna said. "It hasn't been a total picnic here either.

That Li Ming has made my life challenging so far. But last night made up for some of it." Anna started to feel her face getting flushed.

"Mom, you got some!" Liz crowed.

"Shush!" Anna hushed her. "It's all kinds of complicated. Fill you in later. Love you."

"Love you too! I want all the juicy details." Liz smirked at her mother's discomfort.

"Yeah, yeah, goodbye." Anna ended the call. Staring at her phone's wallpaper of her and Chen in their period garb, she thought about what it meant that Scott was in Beijing. No wonder she had felt the creepy crawlies at the awards. Scott had been there and had ganged up with Li Ming to continue making her life difficult.

Chen and Xian were deep in discussion in the front cabin, trying to keep it quiet enough that Anna wouldn't overhear them.

"That guy you saw was the sick bastard that wrote that letter." Chen's anxiety had kicked in. That creep had even been at the awards last night.

"Chen, we need to keep cool heads and not tip Anna off that we know something about that horrid man." Xian wanted to call him unpleasant names, but what good would it do? He would probably feel better, but he didn't need the negative karma.

"Did you ever find a security company to install everything at Anna's?" Chen asked.

"Yeah, I will let Liz know tomorrow. They will be there on Wednesday to install it." Xian checked his email to verify the time.

"Our Wednesday or theirs?" Chen wanted to verify. Hopefully, they could convince Anna to stay instead of leaving early.

"Theirs, did Anna tell you if she planned on staying? Or is she still planning on returning early?" Xian had heard Anna telling Chen she had thought about returning after the Tuesday meetings.

"I hope she will stay, but I don't have a solid answer to that." Chen wanted to start moping again.

"Well, we need to convince her to at least stay until the weekend. Did you two have any plans?" Xian asked, not wanting the answer.

"Nothing solid. I know Anna wants to go back and get some sleep and relax. She's been on the go almost nonstop since she arrived, and it hasn't exactly been a walk in the park." Chen looked at Xian with suspicion. "Why do you ask?"

"We need to make sure she stays long enough that they can finish the installation. The company told me it could take a few days. We need to propose some good reasons for her to stay until her scheduled flight. When is she supposed to head back?" Xian wondered if he would have more time with her.

Chen craned his neck to see if Anna was still on her call. It appeared she may be finishing; they better wrap this up quickly.

"Anna is almost finished. We can develop a plan after we drop her at her hotel. Let her get some rest tonight," Chen said as he kept an eye on her.

"I'm sure there are enough sights she wanted to see. Hopefully, we can keep her well and truly busy for a week. Do you know of any interesting events we can get her involved in next weekend? I saw a banner for a charity auction next weekend. We could spend money for a good cause," Xian mused.

"I know Anna had planned on sightseeing for sure. Let's plan to take her to some of the big ones. I don't have anything on my plate for this week. The last day of filming for the series was Friday and I plan to take Anna to the wrap party. She has become well loved by most of the crew for only spending a day on the set." Chen smiled, remembering the crew members asking how she was doing.

"Sounds like we should have plenty to keep her on the go." Just in time, Xian looked over his shoulder to catch Anna making her way forward. She stopped to chat with Huang Hu and Wu Feng, thanking them for their help at the hotel earlier.

Heading out of the hotel, there had been a gauntlet of the press to navigate. Right in his element, Chen charmed the media and paparazzi with his smile. While he had been schmoozing, Anna, wearing a baseball cap with her leggings and sweater, walked right past, completely ignoring the chaos and getting in the limo van before anyone noticed her. Xian, however, hadn't been quite so lucky. He had tried the same tactic as Anna but had been stopped on the edges by a perceptive reporter. Xian had politely declined the interview and made his way to the van.

The tricky part had been getting Chen in the van without them realizing that Xian and Anna were also in the same van. Huang Hu and Wu Feng had devised a plan; Xian and Anna would leave the hotel with Wu Feng and Chen would take the van with Huang Hu. They would then meet up at a restaurant on the way to the airport.

The plan had worked well. Xian and Anna were quiet on the way to the restaurant; Anna avoided questions about the night before and Xian avoided finding out for sure that Chen had spent the night not only in her room, but with her.

Wu Feng had watched the two of them, wondering what had transpired to cause the friction between them. There was undoubtedly more tension in the van. With Xian's save the night before, he had thought Anna would be warmer towards his employer. He would need to talk with Huang Hu and see if he knew what happened.

The rest of the trip to the airport was also quiet. They had stopped for a quick brunch on the way and this time the guys behaved. Both were somber and introspective, though. They would need a bit to work through what had transpired over the weekend.

She thanked them again for helping keep her out of the main focus of the media. Veronica would be ecstatic to hear Anna had won. She would find a way to spin it to help with book sales for her new novel. It didn't hurt to have an award, even in a foreign country.

Slipping back in her seat opposite Chen, she gave both guys a curious look. They had been in a deep discussion for a while and now they looked as though they were ignoring one another. Her instincts were telling her something was up. They both had given her concerned looks when they heard about Scott.

"Okay, you two, what do you have cooking?" Anna gave them both inquiring glances.

Xian and Chen both seemed to squirm in their seats. Now she was even more suspicious. They were looking more guilty all the time.

"Well, darn it. It was supposed to be a surprise. You caught me; I planned to invite you to our wrap party on Friday. The crew would be ecstatic to see you. There is also a charity auction and masquerade gala on Saturday night that we had hoped to take you to. That would give you Sunday to rest before flying out on Monday," Chen blurted out.

A momentary expression of amazement flashed across Xian's face, only to be replaced with satisfaction. Hopefully, Chen's declaration would assuage Anna's curiosity. That woman could be tenacious.

Glowering at both of the guys, Anna turned back to her phone as she heard several notification sounds. She hadn't looked at her social media page in a while, but today she constantly noticed people following her author page. It was hard to imagine that due to the award, she was suddenly famous. The last time Anna looked at her followers, there were only 13,350. Now, there were close to 48,000. She was having a difficult time processing the change. *Veronica must have posted an article or video...if not, Veronica, perhaps Liz must have.*

"Hey Chen, is your social media page getting a sudden surge of popularity?" Anna asked with genuine curiosity. Was it just her account, or did Chen also notice an increase?

Chen began flipping through screens on his phone. "Looks like I had a few new followers. Why?" Stretching across the table to check the screen on Anna's phone.

A low whistle escaped Chen's lips. "Certainly nowhere near as many new followers as you. I may need to steal Veronica to help my career." A sly look crossed his face. "Or I just need to keep acting in a certain rock star writer's projects."

Rolling her eyes at the blatant flattery, Anna checked for the new posts that may have incurred the influx of new followers. Sure enough, there was an article and a short video of her accepting the award. The language was, of course, Mandarin, but it had English subtitles. Xian had been so dead-on; the black dress had made Anna stand out. Li Ming looked dowdy beside her.

Checking the post, there were thousands of comments already. Trolls were posting anti-Chinese sentiments. Why would an American author be writing for a Chinese studio? There were more comments, some worse, but the praise made up for the nastiness.

There was considerable clamoring for her to publish *The Lost Prince* as a novel, or perhaps the movie could be remade by an American studio. At the very least, there was interest in having the film available on the larger streaming platforms.

This was great for the studio. Anna was glad she had retained some of her merchandise rights so that she could see some residual income from the movie. It was still a lot for her to take in. Her life had changed overnight, it seemed. Her notoriety in the States wouldn't have increased much, but she would have to be cautious while still in China; being an American writer and winning the award set a new precedent.

Putting her phone down on the table, she watched the clouds. Small peaks of towns and rural areas shown through the heavy cloud cover. A few of the comments weighed heavily on her mind. She would need to contact Veronica about new moderators for her social media. There would always be good with the bad, it came with the territory. For some reason, today, they bothered her more than in the past.

Xian looked over at Anna's stoic countenance. What had her so morose suddenly, especially after her triumph the night before? He would have thought she would be riding more of a euphoric high from her win. Even with the drama Li Ming caused, he thought Anna should be more upbeat.

"Anna, we were discussing sightseeing options for the next week. Do you have any special requests?" Xian figured he would distract her from whatever was raining on her parade at the moment.

Anna continued staring into the distance having not heard Xian's question. Everything that had happened since she arrived in China was finally catching up to her. Anna's mind was thousands of miles away.

"Anna?" Chen waved a hand in front of Anna's eyes. "Are you in there somewhere?"

"Huh? Oh yeah, I'm here, I guess."

"Xian asked if you had any sightseeing musts before you head home. You seem a bit distracted, though." Chen reached out his hand to gently take Anna's. Her fingers had a slight chill to them. Pulling her hand between his, he rubbed vigorously to get warmth flowing.

Anna's distracted gaze shifted to watch Chen attempting to get the circulation moving in her fingers. His hair had flopped over his eyes so that she couldn't make out his expression very well. Focusing on his hands, Anna hadn't paid much attention to them before now. Manicured nails tipped long, graceful soft fingers. Self-conscious, she pulled her hand away from Chen. Her hands were rough and calloused from working around her place.

"I didn't have anything specific in mind for tourist locations. Whatever you guys think are the must-see locations are fine with me. However, I would like to visit a temple or two," Anna said quietly as she stared at her hands.

Chen exchanged a concerned look with Xian.

Anna needs some rest, Chen thought and mentally cursed whatever had dampened her inner light.

"We will be landing in Beijing in about fifteen minutes." The pilot's voice crackled across the intercom system.

Startled by the voice, Anna looked around.

"Excuse me," she stood up and rushed to the plane's restroom. She made it to the small cubicle before the tears escaped. Hot salty drops rolled down her cheeks as she silently cried. Emotions held in check began to overwhelm her. How was she going to cope with the next week? Being close to Chen and Xian was difficult enough; would Li Ming and Scott wreak more havoc in her life during her remaining time in Beijing? Most likely, yes.

Giving herself about five minutes of a personal pity party, Anna dug down for some intestinal fortitude and got a grip on her emotions. She couldn't do much about the red puffy eyes, taking a moment to wash her face. Where was a pair of sunglasses when you needed them?

Making her way back to her seat, she met four pairs of eyes —varying degrees of curiosity and concern in each set. Buckling into the chair, she kept her gaze averted. She had let her hair down before leaving the bathroom to help conceal her blotchy face.

章

Chapter 36

Once the plane landed, it didn't take long to get the bags loaded into the waiting vehicles. Chen and Xian had agreed that Chen should take Anna back to her hotel, though Chen had contemplated just letting Huang Hu take her. He had some thinking to do.

What could Chen do to help Anna change her mind about their relationship? Four years of waiting had been hard enough when he didn't know what was at stake. Now that he had spent time with Anna, he wasn't sure he wanted to waste any more time.

Without a word, Anna hugged Xian and kissed his cheek. Not waiting for Chen to open her door, she climbed into the back seat of the SUV and waited so they could head back to the hotel.

"Take care of her," Xian quietly murmured to Chen as he gave him a brusque, brotherly hug. "We'll talk later and figure out plans after you get her settled."

Nodding, Chen climbed into the SUV sitting next to the taciturn woman.

What had felt like a short trip on the way to the airport drew out endlessly as they traveled to the hotel. Anna spent the trip deliberating the choice to stay or return home before she was scheduled to go. Leaving so early would be admitting defeat and letting Li Ming win. However, how much more could she take?

Chen used his phone as a pretense to cast sidelong glances toward Anna. He was becoming more concerned because she had shut down. The few monosyllabic words she uttered since the plane landed were primarily polite responses to questions. He was at a loss; what should he do to cheer her up?

"Mr. Xiao!" Huang Hu disrupted Chen's thoughts.

"What's the matter?" Chen looked up from his phone.

In front of the hotel, a media circus had set up camp. Reporters and paparazzi milled around the front doors of the hotel, watching every patron that entered or exited the building like scavengers. Chen hadn't seen this kind of mob in some time. Did the studio plan a press conference for Anna without consulting them first?

No, that couldn't be it. Something else was going on.

"Huang Hu, call the studio and see if they had anything to do with this." Chen was just glad the windows of the SUV were dark enough that they could pass by the hotel without being recognized.

Continuing past the hotel, Huang kept driving as he attempted to reach his contact at the studio. After a short conversation, he was even more confused.

"Mr. Xiao, the studio has nothing to do with the crowd at the hotel. A very limited number of people knew she was staying here." Huang Hu was flustered and Anna could tell.

"Huang Hu, head for my apartment." Chen was already looking for the hotel's phone number.

"Yes, sir." He maneuvered the car between the steel bodies traveling in unison. Slipping between two compact cars, he didn't notice a dark sedan following several car lengths behind.

"Hello, may I please speak to your manager?" Chen queried as the phone connected with the front desk at the hotel.

Anna's tension increased as she listened to half of the conversation.

"What do you mean you can't provide any security for Ms. Cassidy? Is there another entrance we can use to at least retrieve her belongings?" Chen was getting more irritated as each moment passed.

Anna could have sworn she heard his teeth grind as his jaw clenched.

"When can we get access to her room?" Chen paused to hear the response. "We will be there in a few minutes. Please have someone there to greet us when we arrive." If the phone had been one of the old Bakelite rotary phones, he would have slammed the handset in the cradle.

"Huang Hu, head back towards the hotel, but don't go to the front. There is an alley around the side of the building that is used for deliveries. We will go in that way and get Anna's possessions. She can't stay there any longer. They've found odd people wandering on her floor and the floors above and below her room."

"Want to make a wager on who leaked my hotel to the media?" Anna's anger began building, replacing the apathy.

"We won't even have to go there; I'm sure I know too. If it wasn't Li Ming, it could very well have been Scott. Did he know which hotel you were staying at?" Chen turned, observing Anna. Her long fingers clenched in fists, he could see the crescent-shaped indents on her palm from her nails.

"Not sure, but I would imagine if Li Ming knew then she told Scott. So now where am I going to stay?"

"You can stay with me," Chen replied as soon as she posed the question.

"And you think that's a good idea?"

"Well, at least for the night it should be fine. You're planning on living over here for more than a year in a few months. We can do some apartment hunting and perhaps find something while you are here. That should save you from having to stay in a hotel while getting arrangements made." Chen looked quite pleased with himself. He felt they had a pretty solid plan.

Chen unlocked his phone and tapped on the screen. Within a few moments, there were several text message notices. Looking at the screen, he nodded to himself and tapped a reply.

Huang Hu was pulling into the alley, approaching the hotel from a back road, out of view of the mob. The dark sedan parked along the street as their SUV parked by a large roll-up garage door.

As soon as they had parked, a smaller door popped open and Lin Bolin poked his head out. Looking around for any observers, he waved the three into the freight area of the hotel.

"Ms. Cassidy, are you okay?" Lin Bolin asked, genuine concern in his voice.

"Lin Bolin, I'm all right. Unfortunately, I can't continue staying at the hotel. Now that the media has been tipped off, I wouldn't get any peace and quiet for the rest of my trip. Thank you so much for being so helpful during my stay."

"Ms. Cassidy, please don't mention it. It has been my pleasure to assist you. Let's take you up the service elevator. It isn't accessible to the public so we should be able to sneak you into your room," Lin Bolin said as he pulled out a key card to unlock the elevator.

Anna was glad for the extra space in the elevator. Built to haul large mattresses and furniture, it wasn't the polished glass and brass of the guest elevators, but it was more comfortable for her. She had dealt with freight during one of her many jobs growing up.

Arriving on the twenty-fifth floor, Lin Bolin checked the hallway before allowing Anna to step from the elevator. The coast was clear as he led the group down the carpeted hall. Four sets of feet made little noise as they cautiously made their way along the dim hallway.

Noticing they were getting close to her room, Anna pulled her key card from her purse. Arriving at her door, she waved her plastic key in front of the sensor. Hearing a click, she swung the door wide ushering everyone in as quickly as possible.

Gasping, Anna's room was in total disarray. Cushions were thrown on the floor and clothing was strewn around the room. Clothes that had been meticulously hung in the closet were unceremoniously dumped on the floor in the bedroom. Papers from the desk were scattered all over the office area.

Rushing to the desk, Anna looked for her computer but it wasn't on the desk. Searching she found it on the floor only to discover the screen was cracked; who knows what other damage had been done. Luckily she had the whole computer backed up on the cloud as well as on her portable drive.

Having taken extra precautions due to having scripts and her manuscript on her computer, the documents were all password protected with 128-bit encryption. Even if they did get the files, it would take them a lifetime of lifetimes to hack them. It seemed like overkill to have such heavy encryption but nowadays, you couldn't be too careful.

Anna checked the room's safe to verify that her thumb drives with the extra files for her book and other scripts were still intact. At least the safe was unmolested from what she could tell. She carefully tucked the drives into her messenger bag after pulling them from the lockbox.

Looking around the room, she wasn't even sure where to begin. Clothes? Papers? Sinking into the office chair, Anna put her head in her hands. Breaking down at that moment wasn't an option. Time was of the essence. Gathering her fragmented thoughts she looked up to see the men still in shock.

Lin Bolin's face had a purple tinge.

"Ms. Cassidy, please excuse me. I will return momentarily," he said as he abruptly rushed from the room.

Chen squared his shoulders and looked around, assessing what he and Huang Hu could handle. Picking up a piece of clothing from the floor, he tried to gather them from the room's surfaces.

"Chen, stop a moment. We need to report this, don't move anything else. Can you please contact the authorities?" Anna's pragmatic side pushed its way to the surface.

"I believe the manager is the first person we need to contact." Chen looked for the room phone to call the front desk.

He picked up the handset but just as he started dialing a loud pounding came from the door.

Anna stood from the office chair, heading for the door. Chen intercepted her, grabbing her and pushing her behind him.

"Huang Hu, get the door," Chen barked the order. He would apologize to Huang Hu later for his tone. He didn't want Anna anywhere near that door until he was sure who was on the other side. Both Huang Hu and himself were martial art experts and could easily protect Anna if necessary unless a firearm was involved.

"Ms. Cassidy!" a familiar voice called through the door.

"Huang Hu, let him in. It's Lin Bolin." Anna pushed past Chen.

The door was opened to a nervous, middle-aged shorter man with glasses and graying hair. He looked fit, though at the moment he was a bit winded.

"Ms. Cassidy, this is Mr. Luo, our hotel manager," Lin Bolin said, introducing him to Anna.

"Mr. Luo, thank you for coming so quickly. I believe you spoke with my associate Mr. Xiao earlier?" Anna pointedly introduced Chen.

Mr. Luo bowed deeply. "Ms. Cassidy, I am so sorry. We have no idea how someone accessed your room. The security is beginning to review the video footage from the hallway while you were gone. It was only yesterday and today, correct?"

"Yes, Mr. Luo. I left early Saturday morning," Anna said, trying to remember the exact time Chen picked her up that morning.

Chen chimed in, "I believe it was about 5:30 A.M."

Mr. Luo pulled his phone from his pocket and made a quick call. Speaking in Mandarin too fast for Anna to make out much of it, she looked to Chen for a clue.

"He's giving his security staff a dressing down," Chen whispered close to Anna's ear.

"I'd say it's deserved," Anna glowered at the manager.

Finished with his call, Mr. Luo turned to address Anna again.

"Ms. Cassidy, forgive me, but we must involve the authorities. This has never happened that I'm aware of at our hotel. I can't express how embarrassed I am." Mr. Luo bowed deeply again.

"So what am I supposed to do while waiting to deal with this? I would imagine I can't clean anything up or move anything, correct? This day just keeps getting better." Anna turned away and grumbled under her breath.

"Mr. Luo, can we at least take a few clothes so Ms. Cassidy can change into something clean? If there is something that hasn't been soiled." Chen walked to the bedroom, checking the closet and drawers, finding there were no clothes left in either. Everything had been pulled out and strewn around.

"Anna, we will stop and pick up a few things for you when we leave. It will all need to be cleaned. Mr. Luo, you **CAN** handle that, correct?" Chen put extra emphasis on the question.

"Certainly, Mr. Xiao! Our staff will pick up and clean all of her garments. We can also pack them so all of her belongings can just be picked up from the front desk versus making Ms.

Cassidy return to the hotel." Mr. Luo looked around the room, assessing what staff would be required.

"Mr. Luo, I would prefer Lin Bolin handle my belongings. I will only deal with you two. Lin Bolin, would you be willing to handle this for me?" Anna asked him, her eyes pleading for help with the situation.

Bowing deeply, he replied, "Certainly, Ms. Cassidy. I will be happy to assist you with anything you require."

"Thank you, Lin Bolin. I will trust you to take good care of my belongings. I seem to have difficulty with them being damaged, disappearing or stolen. Heck, I may end up with a new wardrobe yet. This trip just keeps throwing curveballs at me."

"Excuse me, ma'am?" Lin Bolin looked confused.

"It's a colloquialism from the States." Anna gave him a small smile. Her first in many hours.

"Huang Hu, can I speak with you?" Anna motioned for the young man to join her in the bedroom for privacy. "Can you check into Lin Bolin? I believe I'd like to hire him as an assistant while I'm in China. I can't keep depending on you and Wu Feng for help. Lin Bolin has really impressed me."

"Yes, Ms. Cassidy. How quickly do you need to know?"

"Sooner is best. I realize it may be a stretch, but I would like to offer Lin Bolin a job before we leave if possible."

"If that's the case, may I have your permission to contact Mr. Wei? He has resources that could facilitate that request much faster."

"Actually, I better call Xian and discuss it with him first then. I think he will handle it better coming from me. He's going to be super protective as it is when he hears about this. May as well let him know sooner than later," said Anna, sighing as she pulled her phone out.

Xian picked up her call after only one ring.

"Anna? I didn't expect to hear from you so soon" Xian sounded wary. "What happened this time?"

"How much time do you have? First and foremost, I have a favor to ask."

"Certainly, Anna. Anything I can do for you, just ask."

"There is a young man employed with the hotel and I would

like to offer him a job, but I would like to know a bit more about him before I make the offer."

"How quick do you need this?" Xian was curious now.

"Soonest. Within an hour if possible. It doesn't need to be super in-depth, just curious if there is anything glaring that I should be wary of."

"That is certainly possible."

"Thank you. You have no idea how much I appreciate it. I'll text you the young man's name. Just give me a moment." Anna flipped through the screens on her phone and sent the message.

"Give me one moment, don't hang up," Xian said. Anna could tell Xian had muffled the phone and was most likely giving Wu Feng instructions regarding Lin Bolin.

After only a few moments Xian said, "Okay, I'm back. Now, what's going on?" She could almost hear the tension in his voice.

"I'm not sure where to start. First, the hotel has become media central, there's a zoo down in front of the hotel and we had to sneak in through the freight entrance. To top that off, my room was ransacked."

"**WHAT?**" Anna was sure that if Xian could have come through the phone, he would have been there in the blink of an eye. "I'm on my way."

"Wait, Xian! The manager is here and we are just waiting on the authorities. Once I make my statement, we will head for Chen's apartment. I'll let you know when we're ready to leave here and you can meet us there. I will be checking out of the hotel and need to figure out where I'll be staying the rest of my trip."

"You'll have one of my apartments," Xian said with a tone that brooked no disagreement.

"Xian, I couldn't put you out like that." Anna liked Xian's apartment, it was modern but homey at the same time.

"I have several apartments. One is in a secure building, so it will be difficult for the press or paparazzi to bother you. My staff will also be at your disposal. I have a housekeeper who is an amazing cook on staff there. It isn't far from the studio or Chen's place either. It's your best option unless you stay in Chen's one bedroom apartment. Someone would be on the couch." Rather, Xian hoped one of them would take the couch.

"We can talk it over at Chen's. I believe it may be my best option at this point." Anna felt less nervous, knowing she would have a good alternative.

"I will have Mrs. Wang prepare for your arrival tomorrow." Xian was already making plans. He would have his housekeeper clean and freshen the apartment for Anna's arrival. Mentally, a list started in his head; he would have Wu Feng do some shopping before she moved in.

"It'll take a couple of hours for us to get to Chen's. I need to stop and shop for a few clothes when we're done here. Every piece in the room has been strewn all over. And I would imagine it will be evidence or, at the minimum, it needs to be cleaned, which the hotel said they would take care of."

"I can help with that, at least. I know your size and I can stop and pick up a couple of outfits. Is there anything specific you will need?"

"I think I'm good as long as I have access to your washer and dryer once I get to the apartment. I can do a small load of the items from the trip. Though a robe would be a nice option if possible." Anna thought about it for a moment to see if there was anything she would need in the next day or two. "Oh yeah, I need to shop for a jacket. Mine was stolen from the studio, and I've been using a wrap that's not practical."

"Okay, don't worry about it. I'll take care of the clothes for you. Just take care of yourself. I'll make sure you have anything you need here. What about your laptop and other electronics?"

"Oh yeah, the laptop…" Anna cringed. She had forgotten the state of her laptop. "I need to shop for a new one. Mine was damaged and I haven't tried turning it on to see how bad it is yet."

A loud knocking let Anna know someone had arrived.

"Someone's at the door; I imagine it's the police now."

"Let me know when you're done. I'll see you at Chen's. Are you sure you're okay?" The concern in his voice came through the phone and felt like a warm blanket wrapping around Anna.

"I'm not okay, but it's kind of par for the course after the rest of this weekend. I'll call when we get to the SUV. Bye, Xian," Anna said as she ended the call.

The police took Anna's statement about being in Taipei for the awards. One of the officers had recognized both Anna and Chen. He had watched the ceremony and had seen them on the red carpet as well as accepting their awards. When his superior wasn't looking, he asked them to sign an autograph for him. Anna looked to Chen for guidance; she didn't have experience with fans requesting autographs.

"Certainly, Officer Ma." Chen winked as he signed the officer's notebook. "Our secret. Right, Anna?"

Taking the notebook, Anna added her autograph to another page. Handing the notebook back she said, "That's my first autograph as a screenwriter." Anna smiled for a few moments before being reminded why they were there.

"Ms. Cassidy." Detective Zhào came over to talk with her. "Unfortunately, we will need to take your belongings as evidence while trying to figure out the situation. How long will you be in Beijing?"

"I have a flight next Monday to return to the States. Then I will be returning in January for an extended stay. How long will you have to keep my belongings?" Anna had a sinking feeling she would be without most of her wardrobe for the better part of her trip, if not all of it.

"I'm not sure, ma'am. Much of this depends on if we can find security evidence." Detective Zhào looked uncomfortable. He couldn't imagine how difficult this would be for the poor woman.

—

Anna had left that morning, her room would be empty at least today. He needed to find out if she had brought the letter with her. Li Ming had given him a large wad of bills to access the room. He bribed one of the hotel maids for her keycard and entered her room.

Scott looked around to get his bearings. He searched around the office area and then wandered into the bedroom. She had left most of her clothes in the closet and drawers. Digging through her drawers, he found a pair of her underwear, stuffing it in his coat pocket. Searching through the drawers he started getting frustrated and angry upon seeing the lingerie. Did she bring it to wear for that Asian asshole?

Pulling it from the drawer, he threw it on the floor and stomped on it. She had traveled halfway across the globe to see this foreign jerk but couldn't be bothered to have a date with him. He saw red; pulling everything out of the drawers and throwing it around. Why couldn't she see him? He was right there in Fortine. But she hadn't seen him all those years ago either.

Looking in the closet, there were fancy gowns and some of the normal clothing he had seen her wear before. Never had he seen her wear anything this fancy. Why did she need it now? Fortine was quiet and she wouldn't need anything so elegant. Pulling them from the closet he threw them to the floor, grinding his heel on it.

The more he thought about her being with what's his name...Chen? Yeah, the one Li Ming wanted so badly, he became angrier. Picking up the clothes he had thrown on the bed, he took them to the main living area and tossed them around on most of the surfaces. Where was the letter? Damn, he had been drunk when he wrote it and left it for her. If she disappeared, that letter could be used as evidence against him. He had to find it.

The office area was the last place he needed to look. Flinging papers as he looked at them, it wasn't there. Had she left it in Fortine? No, there was the envelope it had been in but inside was a blank piece of paper. What? Where was the letter? Shit, this was going to be a problem. In a fit of pique, he threw her laptop to the floor and stomped on it. Damn it! He just wanted to be with her. Why was it so difficult?

Ding. A message displayed on his screen. We need to leave for the airport. Did you find what you were looking for? Li Ming inquired.

Replying to her text, *No, the envelope is here but not the letter. She either has it on her or one of those men has it.* Shit, he had to go. When he caught her, he would make her give it to him or tell him where she had it stashed. The award ceremony would afford him an opportunity to see her in formal wear, he knew she would look beautiful. Now to make her his.

章

Chapter 37

After an hour, Anna, Chen and Huang Hu were allowed to leave. Xian had sent a message to Anna about Lin Bolin. He checked out. The young man attended college and worked at the hotel to help with his tuition and living expenses. He was in the top ten in his class and had glowing recommendations from teachers and previous employers. His family owned a small business in his hometown and were well-liked in their community.

This was the best news of the day. As Lin Bolin escorted them back to the freight area, Anna pulled him aside.

"I have a serious question for you. I'll be moving to Beijing next year for work. Would you be interested in being my assistant? It would allow you to work with a movie studio and actors. It may require you to be able to travel to the States on occasion as well. You don't have to give me an ans..."

Anna didn't even have a chance to finish her last comment before he interrupted her.

"I would get to work with you? And travel?" Lin Bolin blurted out.

"Yes, do you have a passport?"

"Not at the moment; I can certainly get one. When would I start?"

"So, I'd take that as a yes?" Anna laughed softly.

"Absolutely, yes!" Lin Bolin grabbed Anna's hand and pumped it with enthusiasm.

"Give me your information, and I'll be in touch Tuesday when I know when I'll need to be back in Beijing."

Lin Bolin took no time giving Anna his phone number.

"Thank you again, Ms. Cassidy."

"No, thank you, Lin Bolin." Anna patted his shoulder and followed Chen and Huang Hu out to the SUV.

Once Anna was settled in her seat, she called Xian. "We are

just leaving now. I will need to get a laptop tomorrow. Mine is in evidence."

"I can have Wu Feng pick one up for you if you'd like."

"No. I'd rather pick that up myself." Anna was thankful for the offer. "Tomorrow will be early enough; I'll need it for Tuesday's studio meeting."

"I'll take you shopping tomorrow," Xian offered.

"That sounds like a good idea, we can make plans at Chen's apartment."

Anna looked over at the serious Chen. He hadn't said much the whole time at the hotel. She would wait until they were at his apartment before poking the bear.

Chen was fuming internally. So much had gone wrong. Anna's privacy had been violated again, worse than before. He had a hard time believing it was Li Ming this time. She had been in Taipei for the awards, though Scott had been as well. He could have taken a later flight. If they could figure out which flight he had been on, that would give them more to go on. Perhaps he should let Detective Zhào know about the letter, though they still weren't one hundred percent sure he had left it. They needed more proof.

Quiet was the best tactic for him; he knew if he said too much at the moment it would push Anna away. He was close to losing his cool, which wouldn't do any good. He was hurt and furious that Anna had turned to Xian for help without asking him. She had even gotten Huang Hu involved, but she hadn't asked him for his assistance. Time and a stiff drink would help.

The trip to his apartment went quickly. There was security at his building to an extent. You needed a code to access the parking garage, but that only kept people from driving in, it didn't keep someone from walking in. Elevator access was also restricted by code, but that hadn't completely stopped intruders. When Xian got there, they would need to formulate a plan for Anna's safety. Xian had offered the use of a bodyguard, but Chen had disagreed at the time. He felt the constant supervision would stifle Anna. After this? He was all for it. The more, the merrier if he had any say.

Pulling into the garage, Huang looked around discreetly

after parking. No one seemed to be in the area, he motioned that Chen and Anna could get out.

"Mr. Xiao, Ms. Anna, please feel free to head to the apartment. I will bring the luggage up," Huang Hu said as he led them to the elevator.

Chen punched his six-digit code into the keypad next to the elevator, his foot tapping as he impatiently waited for the car to arrive.

Anna stood just behind and to the left of Chen staring at her feet, the events of the last few days clamoring in her mind. As each mishap, misunderstanding and prank swirled through her mind, her heart began to race faster. Breathing was becoming an issue as it felt like a bag of cement had landed on her chest.

Anna grabbed Chen's hand, gripping it as though her life depended on it. She felt like it was a lifeline to keeping her sanity. In a brief moment of clarity, she realized her hands had become cold and clammy. She attempted to pull her hand away from Chen's, not wanting to share her cold sweat.

Chen felt Anna grab his hand tightly, her desperation transmitted through her touch. He turned to Anna, questions on the tip of his tongue until he saw her. Face pale, sweat glistened on her forehead and he noticed that her breathing had become rapid and shallow. If she didn't calm herself soon, she would hyperventilate.

"Anna, what's going on?" He kept her hand gripped in his. No matter how hard she tugged, he wouldn't let it go. He suspected that if he did, his chances to be with her would slip away with her hand.

Anna couldn't respond. In the grips of a panic attack worse than she had experienced in almost twenty years, she couldn't articulate the words to let him know what was happening.

As the elevator arrived, the doors whooshed open quietly, and a loud *ding* sounded. Anna couldn't breathe. The thought of stepping into that tiny metal box terrified her at that moment. Caught in the throes of a panic attack, her mind didn't allow her reason.

Chen turned to step into the elevator, trying to pull Anna with him. Her feet wouldn't move. She was rooted to the concrete of the garage floor. Deep panting breaths made her feel light-headed. Eyes closed, Anna sank to her knees.

"Anna!" Chen yelled as he watched her crumble to the floor.

Huang Hu had just pulled the luggage from Chen's SUV when he heard his employer's cry.

"Mr. Xiao?" He looked in the direction of the elevators. Laying on the polished concrete was Anna.

"Ms. Anna!" Dropping the suitcase he had in his hand, he rushed to Chen's side.

Chen looked at Hu with fear in his eyes. He didn't understand what had happened. Anna had started acting strange when they approached the elevator, but that didn't explain why she had collapsed. Still grasping her hand, he pulled Anna onto his lap.

"Hu, help me get Anna to the apartment. We can call Dr. Lin and have him come here. Taking her to the hospital won't help unless it's an emergency. All we need is the media having a field day over it." Chen tried to gather Anna in his arms to carry her to the elevator.

"Mr. Xiao, you're shaking and it isn't going to help Ms. Anna. Let me carry her and you get the elevator and doors." Huang Hu gently lifted Anna from Chen's lap, shifting her so he could comfortably carry her.

"You need to let go of her hand, sir." Gently he pulled Anna's hand from Chen's. That seemed to rouse Chen from his daze. Hu was worried that Chen was showing signs of shock and he didn't need to have two people to care for. Anna was his priority at the moment.

"Mr. Xiao! Get yourself together. We need to help Ms. Anna!" Hu hoped to goad Chen into action.

"Huh? Oh yes, sorry, Hu. Let me get the elevator." Chen visibly steeled himself, got off the floor, rushed to the elevator keypad and entered his code.

Moments later the door noisily slid open; Hu shifted Anna one last time, ensuring he had a good grip, before stepping into the small space. Chen pushed the door close button before punching the button for the twenty-ninth floor.

Xian, where was he? Chen needed him to be there. Pulling his phone from his pocket, he sent a text message to him.

Emergency! Anna! My apartment, now! Hitting the send button, he hoped Xian would act first and ask questions later. He realized Xian had feelings for Anna, but her health was the priority right now. They could work out their issues after she was okay.

What? On my way, be there in 10. The reply came a moment after Chen sent it.

Walking through the boutique, Xian picked out several outfits he knew would look good on Anna. He realized she would most likely be upset and annoyed that he had purchased lingerie for her. That was a minor issue to deal with after the fact. Easier to get forgiveness than to obtain permission.

Xian's phone chimed with the tone he had explicitly set for Chen. Looking at the screen, he blanched, a hundred questions warring with one another. The message was terse and unlike Chen. There was something seriously wrong. Fear began to make him shiver. So much had already happened to Anna, she didn't need more now.

"Wu Feng, we have to go now," Xian called to his assistant standing at the counter, paying for the clothing they had picked for Anna. "There is an emergency with Anna."

Wu Feng had come to appreciate the spunky author. He didn't want to see anything happen to the woman helping his boss heal.

"Mr. Wei, I will have the car waiting for you at the door if you can finish this," Wu Feng said as he handed Xian the credit card and rushed toward the parking garage.

"Hang in there, Anna," Xian whispered as he stepped up to the boutique counter.

The clerk wondered if he had a girlfriend. There was some woman he cared for by the look of his purchases. Why couldn't she find a man like this?

章

Chapter 38

Wu Feng was lucky he didn't get a ticket during their mad rush to Chen's apartment. Xian hadn't heard anything further from Chen and he was beside himself with worry about Anna. As they pulled into the parking garage, Xian noticed Chen and Anna's luggage on the floor next to Chen's SUV. Now he was terrified. Huang Hu wasn't the type to leave his employer's belongings.

"Feng, grab those bags, please," Xian barked as he headed for the elevator. Punching in Chen's code, he stood impatiently waiting for the doors to open. Xian looked back at Wu Feng to see if he had grabbed the suitcases.

"Coming, sir." Wu Feng wheeled the cases towards Xian.

They waited a few moments before the doors whooshed open to reveal a pale Huang Hu.

"Thank you, Feng; I was just coming to retrieve the luggage." Huang Hu's voice was tense.

"What's going on with Anna?" Xian fired the question at Huang Hu.

"Mr. Xiao and I got her into the apartment and have her resting. We aren't sure what happened exactly; she collapsed while they were waiting for the elevator."

Xian and Wu Feng stepped into the elevator; Huang Hu punched the button to close the door and hit floor twenty-nine. If the car had been any larger, Xian would have been pacing. His patience was paper-thin at the moment. Damn, he knew that Anna wanted to be with Chen, but why did she have to suffer so much? Surely, he could protect her better...or could he?

As soon as the elevator stopped on the twenty-ninth floor, Xian was out the door and it took what self-control he still had not to run the distance to Chen's apartment.

Huang Hu punched in Chen's code and opened the door.

Xian pushed past him into the apartment.

"Chen!" Xian called loudly, heading towards the bedroom. She must be there, as she wasn't on the couch.

Chen popped his head out of the bedroom and put his finger to his lips in a hush gesture.

"Keep it down, you ass. Anna's resting at the moment." Chen glowered at Xian.

"What happened?" Xian tried to push his way into the bedroom to check on Anna.

Chen blocked his way.

"Let's talk out here first; then we can go in and you can check on her," Chen said quietly as he took Xian's arm and pulled him towards the living room.

With a sullen growl, Xian followed. What right did Chen have to keep him from Anna's side? Chen sank slowly onto the couch, the stress of the weekend starting to catch up with him as well. He needed a vacation.

Xian paced in front of the large windows of the living room.

"Anna and I were waiting at the elevator when she began hyperventilating. She suffers from panic attacks. Over the years I've helped talk her down from a few over the phone, but this one came on so suddenly that I didn't have time to do much before she collapsed. So much has happened since Anna arrived...it's just caught up with her. Now she has to deal with her hotel room and finding new lodgings for the rest of her stay."

"That's been addressed already. Didn't Anna tell you?" Xian stopped to scrutinize Chen. "We spoke about it while on the phone at the hotel."

Chen shook his head.

"No, she didn't say anything to me about it. I didn't give her a chance. The trip from the hotel was pretty quiet." Mentally, Chen berated himself. No wonder she panicked. After everything that happened at the hotel, he gave her the cold shoulder.

"I told Anna she could use one of my properties and I can stay at the house or another apartment while she's here. With the security of the apartment complex, and the security detail assigned to her for the duration of her trip, I can only hope she can have some relaxation."

Chen sat forward on the couch, shoulders slumped and his head bent in resignation. Xian had won this time. As long as Anna was safe, it didn't matter. An opulent apartment with a staff to care for her would be ideal for Anna. Chen didn't have dedicated staff because he liked having privacy.

"You're right. Anna would certainly be better off at your place."

"I think the penthouse has the best security of my properties. We can set Anna up there with a full staff and bodyguards, even if it's just for another week." Xian pulled his phone out of his pocket and sent Wu Feng a message to arrange it.

Xian sat down next to Chen and patted his knee. They were both anxious about Anna.

"Chen, she'll be okay. We know her home isn't the only place we have to worry about now."

Looking at his friend, Chen tried to be mad with him. Xian couldn't help that he was handsome and a billionaire. Chen wasn't one hundred percent sure if Anna knew about the extent of his wealth or not. Not that Chen was broke by any means; he just didn't have quite the unlimited resources Xian did. His family, on the other hand, was nearly as wealthy. He had distanced himself from them when he was in high school and had started acting. He built his own wealth.

"Can I go see Anna now?" concern laced Xian's voice as he asked.

"Sure, she's in my room." Chen sat back on the couch and closed his eyes.

Xian looked down at his friend as he started for the bedroom. He hadn't noticed before how tired Chen looked at the moment. He almost thought he saw a few gray hairs trying to push their way through the thick brunette hair. He overheard Wu Feng and Huang Hu talking and Hu had mentioned how he had carried Anna to the apartment because Chen had been shaking too hard to hold her.

Chen needed a break. He had been a changed man for the last two years, more gregarious and cheerful. Now Xian understood why. Anna just had that effect.

Leaving the exhausted man on the couch, Xian went to the bedroom. Anna was stretched out on the king-sized bed, a white duvet covering her. He noticed a fine sheen of sweat on Anna's forehead as he approached the bed. Stepping into Chen's bathroom, he pulled a clean cloth from the cabinet and ran it under cool water.

Gingerly, Xian sat on the edge of the bed. Anna suddenly thrashed under the blanket. She had thrown the cover across the bed with her flailing. Grabbing her hand, he pulled it to his lap and began doing a pressure point massage. Within a few moments, Anna calmed. He pressed his thumb into another pressure point, rubbing a few moments before moving to another. The technique he had learned when Chandra was in the worst of her pain came in handy once again.

A deep sigh escaped from Anna when he finished. He laid her hand on the bed, wiping her brow with the cloth. Xian gently dabbed her forehead; the escaping drops of perspiration rolled down her cheeks to her neck. Getting up, he stepped into the bathroom again to rinse the cloth. The transparent walls of Chen's master bath made it convenient to keep an eye on Anna.

Sitting next to Anna again, he mopped the moisture from Anna's cheeks and neck. Finished, he refolded the cloth and laid it gently across her forehead. Not able to resist, he cupped Anna's cheek in his large hand, brushing his thumb across Anna's soft lips. The lips he had kissed, the lips that haunted his dreams. He wanted to taste those lips one more time.

Xian didn't realize it, but he had an observer. Chen leaned against the door jam watching Xian's tender care of Anna. Xian was a pro at it. He had nursed his wife the last year of her life as she fought leukemia. Cancer had ravaged her body. As Chandra had lost strength during her treatment, Xian had been her primary caregiver: bathing her, dressing her, doing her hair and all other necessary tasks.

Chen couldn't give up on Anna, but if there ever were a man he would trust to care for her, it would be Xian. But it was up to Anna. She would need to decide which man she wanted to be with. With all of the drama she had gone through, he wasn't sure if she would desire either of them.

Tiptoeing, Chen turned from the touching scene and went to the kitchen. The sky had become a deep indigo blue as the sun exited for the night. Looking out at the city's lights, he had hoped Anna's first trip to his apartment would have been under different circumstances. He had planned an intimate dinner for the next night. The plans dissolved like tissue in water.

A chime brought Chen back from his internal musing. The doctor had made good time. On numerous occasions, a physician who would make house calls had been a lifesaver. Being a celebrity, it seemed as though the paparazzi were constantly watching for some medical scandal.

Dr. Lin had been working with Chen for many years now. When Chandra had first been diagnosed and when Chen had caught pneumonia five years ago. Trying to keep any rumors from hitting the tabloids, he had found a doctor that agreed to house calls if necessary.

"Dr. Lin, sorry to call you out on a Sunday. Someone dear to me collapsed. Can you please have a look?" Chen's voice trembled for a moment. He brushed the few errant tears from his cheeks.

Dr. Lin had known Chen for a while now, and he was curious who had caused the overload of emotion in the ordinarily stoic actor. Even as Chen's sister neared the end of her life, he hadn't shown this much emotion to anyone except his brother-in-law Xian. They had called Dr. Lin on a few instances where Chandra needed extra pain management. The middle-aged physician had become close with the family during that time.

"Chen, you never need to be sorry for calling me. Where is the patient?"

"She's in my bedroom. Please follow me."

She, that's what Chen had said. That word gave Dr. Lin the illumination he needed. Chen had finally found someone and was terrified. Putting a hand on Chen's shoulder, Dr. Lin nodded and motioned for him to lead the way.

章

Chapter 39

Dr. Lin was shocked when he entered the bedroom and found Wei Xian sitting with the woman Chen had apparent feelings for. Looking closely at Xian before announcing his presence, he saw that Chen wasn't the only one with deep feelings for this woman.

"Mr. Wei, it has been a while," Dr. Lin stated to announce his presence, trying not to startle Xian.

"Dr. Lin, I'm glad Chen could have you come and look at Anna. Has he filled you in on what's happened?"

"He gave the cliff notes version. To be quite frank, I'm amazed this poor woman didn't collapse before this."

Chen had filled Dr. Lin in on the highlights of the stressors Anna had experienced over the last five days when he called. She hadn't even been in Beijing for a week yet and had gone through enough drama for a lifetime.

"She's a strong woman, but even the strongest can only withstand so much before the body calls a time out." Xian caressed Anna's hand before moving to make room for the doctor.

Settling beside Anna, Dr. Lin noticed she was flushed and breathing rapidly. Running the few tests he could without a lab to confirm his suspicions, he concluded a few things. First and foremost, the stress of the last few days had been enough to overload an elephant and this woman had weathered it. Second, she was mildly dehydrated. He would be sure to give her an IV before he left, which would help. He would remind the two men pacing in the other room to ensure she drank more fluids too. Third, he would bet his retirement money that this poor woman was conflicted by two well-meaning but emotionally needy men.

When Dr. Lin had requested that both of the glowering children remove themselves from the room so he could examine

Anna, he thought they would have tantrums on the spot. He didn't envy the woman recuperating in that bed. She was going to have a difficult decision to make at some point. Those two men were close, and having something like this come between them would be difficult for them and the person they were lavishing their attention on.

It took a little to get the IV started, but once it ran for a few minutes the doctor noticed Anna's color improving and her breathing began to calm. He may run two IVs to be on the safe side. Now to go figure out how to deal with her two paramours.

Dr. Lin stood in the hallway watching Chen and Xian; both of them agonizing in their own way. Chen sat slumped on the couch, his elbows propped on his knees. His forehead was resting in trembling hands. Xian paced the room like a caged tiger, flexing his hands into fists and releasing. He had to reassure them that Anna would be okay after some fluids and rest.

"Okay, you two! Xian, if you don't stop, you'll wear a hole in Chen's floor. Chen, sit up or your back will be screaming at you after all the work we've done on it."

The doctor's voice snapped Xian out of his trance and he stopped dead in his tracks, turning to face the doctor. Chen's head popped up and he jumped to his feet.

"How is she?" The question was nearly simultaneous for them both.

"Resting, which she needs to do for a day or two. Her blood pressure was a bit elevated and she was dehydrated. I can understand both of these issues. With all the stress over the last few days, I could understand the blood pressure elevation. And being from out of the country, it's easy to get dehydrated. Chen, I believe your assessment of a panic attack is quite likely. If possible, try to keep her stress level as low as possible. That means stress from you two, as well." He gave Chen and Xian meaningful stares.

Realizing the cheerful older man had caught them in their dilemma, each looked sheepish. Chen rubbed a hand on the back of his neck. He realized that Anna must have been feeling the strain from their attentions, but not to this extent. Chen leaned against the counter with his outstretched arms, looking over at Xian. Different expressions chased across his face as he wrestled with his own emotions.

Relief was foremost in both of their minds at the moment, however. When Anna collapsed, Chen had flashbacks to when Chandra first became ill. Those had been some of the most challenging days for all of them. Hearing that Anna should be fine with some rest and fluids was a huge weight off their shoulders.

Xian was trembling with the release of the horrid thoughts that had plagued him since he first saw Anna lying in Chen's bed. Now he just wanted her to smile, snort or yell at them. Something.

"Dr. Lin, would you be averse to a drink? I think Xian and I both need one," Chen inquired softly.

"Only if it's not the good stuff. Let me check Ms. Cassidy's IV." Dr. Lin looked in the bedroom and saw the IV about half empty.

In the living area, Chen had an old bottle of amber liquor sitting on his coffee table with three glasses.

"The good stuff?" Dr. Lin could almost taste the aged booze from where he sat.

"The best I have, Dr. Lin." Chen poured a healthy jigger into all three glasses.

Xian sat down next to Chen and picked up one of the glasses. Swirling the honey amber liquid in the glass, he deeply sniffed and whistled with appreciation.

"Chen, is this **THE** bottle?" Xian looked at Chen with amazement.

"Yeah. It's the Karuizawa 35-year-old' Emerald Geisha' bourbon. This is my absolute best." Chen held his glass up for a toast. "To Anna, a whirlwind in a skirt."

Quirking an eyebrow, Dr. Lin tapped his glass with Chen and Xian. "Cheers."

Xian shook his head and chuckled softly at Chen's description of Anna. It did fit her.

"So, where is my glass?"

Three heads whipped towards the bedroom. Standing unsteadily in the doorway, holding the IV bag, was Anna.

"I was thirsty, but this is going a little overboard Chen." Anna smiled crookedly.

Chen beat Xian to Anna.

"Are you okay? How do you feel?" His concern warmed Anna through.

"Well, I've felt better, to be honest. Mostly I feel tired and a bit sore. What happened?"

"You scared us is what happened. You collapsed in the parking garage." Chen took her hand and helped her to the couch. Taking the IV bag from her, he lifted it above her head and held it while she sat across from Dr. Lin.

Looking at the doctor with curiosity Anna asked, "I guess I have you to thank for the on demand fluids?"

"That is an interesting take on it." Dr. Lin chuckled. "Yes, my name is Dr. Lin. I've been close to Chen and Xian for several years now. How are you feeling, my dear?" he asked as he moved next to Anna, checking her pulse and respiration.

"Better, thank you. I haven't had a bad panic attack in a few years." Anna looked down at her hands, rubbing them together self-consciously.

"I would imagine it was a doozy. If you're okay with it, I'd like to give you another bag of fluids when this finishes. Bolstering your fluids should help you feel better even quicker."

"Certainly, Dr. Lin. I've been bad about fluids," Anna mused.

"You must keep on top of that if you don't want another episode like this. Dehydration isn't good for you at the best of times, and being under significant stress and lacking fluids is a recipe for ending up in the hospital. As I'm sitting here versus you being in an ER, I guess Chen didn't want that to be the case."

Chen cleared his throat. "Anna just won an award at the Golden Horse Awards. She's gained some notoriety since Saturday night. The media would have a field day with Anna ending up at the hospital."

Xian nodded in agreement. "We are trying to keep Anna out of the limelight as long as possible."

Dr. Lin took a sip of his bourbon. Watching how Chen and Xian were attentive to her every word and move, he decided she would either be the best thing in the world for them or the absolute worst. Only time would tell which of his assessments would hold.

章

Chapter 40

Topped off with saline solution, Dr. Lin gave Anna one last quick check and reminded the group that Anna needed to have quiet and rest for a day at least. Huang Hu and Wu Feng had returned from their errands in time for the speech from the affable doctor. All of them swore they would do their utmost to keep as much stress as possible from Anna's life for the duration of her visit.

Chen showed the doctor to the door, shaking his hand and bowing.

"You don't need to do that, Chen. I'm just glad it wasn't anything more serious. You found a good one, don't let her go." Dr. Lin had come to appreciate Anna while spending some time visiting with her as the IV replenished her much-needed fluids.

"That will all depend on her. Anna needs to do what will make her the happiest. I'd be ecstatic if she decided that was me, but I will be happy for her if it happens to be Xian."

Shaking his head, the doctor could tell that last sentence cost him to put it out there in the universe.

"Just be yourself, don't try too hard. She will see the gem you are." Clapping Chen on the back, Dr. Lin turned and left the apartment.

Anna was back in bed, propped up with several pillows.

"So, what does it take to get something to eat?"

Xian could hear a loud growling noise from the vicinity of Anna's middle.

Laughing in relief, Chen sat on the foot end of the bed.

"What can I get you, your Majesty?" Chen bowed.

Raising an eyebrow at the honorific, Anna pondered the question.

"Any chance I could get some porridge?"

"Have a preference?" Xian asked as he pulled his phone out, searching for a restaurant nearby that had porridge this late in the day.

"Can you hold on for about two hours?" Chen asked, putting his hand on her foot.

"I believe so. Why?"

"Because that's how long it takes to make a good porridge."

"Chen, don't go through all that trouble for me. Is there somewhere you can just pick some up to-go?"

"It's no trouble. I can bring you something to nibble on to hold you over." Chen stood, heading for the kitchen.

Xian sat next to Anna, taking a deep breath before the mini tirade he planned to unleash.

"Why didn't you tell us you were so overwhelmed? You scared about five years off my life. I don't need to be five years older than Chen, he already teases me that I'm older, even though it's only by a few months. I can't even imagine how Chen feels right now. You have come into our lives and turned them upside down for the better, and we want you there for a long time to come."

Anna hadn't been ready for the heartfelt confession. How could she have made such an impact in such a short time? A blush crept up Anna's neck, coloring her cheeks a faint rose.

"I'm sorry, Xian, everything hit all at once." She took Xian's hand and looked him in the eye. "I never expected the emotional minefield I've had to try navigating. It might have been worse if it hadn't been for two amazing men coming to my rescue repeatedly. I don't know that I can ever thank you two enough for all you're doing for me. I feel like a burden. Are you sure I shouldn't just head home Wednesday? I'd be out of your hair."

"Don't you dare!" Chen's gruff voice answered her from the door. "That's what Li Ming wants. Don't give in."

Chen entered the room carrying a tray with cut fruit and a glass of water.

"You know she is doing everything possible to get you to leave Beijing. We've devised a plan; hopefully, it will keep the chaos in check." He sat the tray down on the nightstand.

"I don't want to be a bother. Xian is letting me stay at his apartment. That will be an inconvenience. Plus, I'm sure shopping for me was also a pain."

"Anna, I will set you up in my penthouse, which isn't used often. It's kept for company VIPs and any family who want privacy without staying in a hotel. So it isn't an inconvenience at all. As for shopping, I enjoyed shopping for you." Xian squeezed her hand.

Bamboo breakfast tray deposited on her lap, Anna looked over the fresh fruit Chen had provided and it looked delicious. A loud gurgle erupted from her stomach at the smell of the sweet flesh. Melon, apple, pear and grapes were laid out on a plate. The cute shapes he had taken extra time and effort to prepare made her smile.

"Thank you, Chen. This looks amazing."

"Your porridge will take a while, but this should take the edge off." He smiled at her evident delight with the extra effort he had put into her snack.

"Would you two like a bite?" Anna offered a bite to Xian and Chen.

"Thanks, but I snacked a little while cutting it up. You know, the chef has to taste test." He winked cheekily at her.

Xian looked wistfully at the fruit chunks as his stomach let its displeasure be known. He hadn't eaten since that morning either. He was eyeing the piece of apple that Anna waved in his face hungrily.

"Sorry, Chen," Xian said before his mouth engulfed the apple chunk.

Giving Xian a disgusted look, Chen walked back into the kitchen and returned with a small plate of fruit chunks. He handed it to Xian.

"Don't eat all of Anna's fruit."

"Thank you, Chen." Xian quickly tucked several pieces into his mouth.

Anna finished her fruit, chatting easily with Chen and Xian between bites. She was relieved that the guys had come to some understanding and calmed their petty behavior.

Finished with the appetizer, Chen took Anna's tray back to the kitchen and checked on her porridge. While Chen was puttering around the kitchen, Xian retrieved the bags from his shopping trip earlier. He figured Anna would like to get comfortable after washing and drying the new clothes.

"Anna, I picked out a few outfits and some comfy clothes to hold you over for a few days until we know more about the situation with your belongings. Check them out."

Pulling the largest bag onto her lap, Anna started pulling garments out. Shirts, skirts and leggings. She began to feel like she was pulling from the magical bottomless bag. Finally reaching the bottom of that one, she picked a smaller decorative bag next.

Curious about what would fit in such a small bag, she looked inside and couldn't figure it out. Taking a closer look, she pulled out the first item. Once it unfolded, it revealed a cream-colored silk camisole. Peach soft, Anna couldn't help but rub her cheek on the buttery fabric. Reaching in again, she pulled out a stretch lace bralette. This time Anna blushed. Xian had picked out lingerie for her. Kyle hadn't bought her any underwear during their marriage. This was a new experience for her.

"I think I'll save the rest of that bag for later," Anna mumbled.

Xian grinned. He never expected her to get shy about simple lingerie.

"Here, try this one. I think you'll find some pieces that you can use now," Xian said while handing her a large fabric bag.

Peeking into the bag, almost nervous about what she might find, she saw something soft and fuzzy. Anna pulled it out, revealing a voluminous robe. Beneath the robe, there was a pair of silk pajamas.

"Ooooh," she squealed, pulling the silky nightwear from the bag. It was a short-sleeve button-up top with matching shorts. "These will be a nice treat when I'm not alone. I usually don't worry about pajamas." Anna watched Xian closely as she made that last statement. Sure enough, the middle-aged man turned slightly red, not quite blushing.

"That was revenge for not warning me about the lingerie," Anna teased. "Serves you right."

Chen had walked back into the room just as she dropped that bombshell on his poor friend. He knew better, having spent the night with her. Anna, in her usual PJs of nothing, was preferable. However, if she stayed in the penthouse with on-site staff, she would be more comfortable wearing something.

"Those look very comfortable, Anna," Chen said, announcing his presence before something more embarrassing could transpire.

"I look forward to the robe. It feels so fluffy," she announced, then buried her face in the fuzzy robe.

Taking the garments from Anna, Chen carried them to his compact washer and dryer combo. He was careful to read the instructions, not wanting to damage the new clothes. He threw the robe and pajamas in first. At least shortly after the porridge was ready, she could take a long hot bath and have clean clothes to wear. He had planned to offer her one of his pajama sets to wear. Xian ruined his fun.

Picturing Anna wearing his blue and white striped pajama set made his pulse quicken. His pulse wasn't the only part of his body that reacted to her image in his clothes. Anna had slipped Chen's shirt on in the hotel to run to the ice maker; she had looked so sexy that he couldn't wait to see it again.

Calm down, Chen; you're only making this harder on yourself. He shook his head and went to check the porridge.

"Hey Anna, would you rather take a bath now or after you eat?" Chen called to the bedroom.

"I'll wait until after. If I took a bath, I'd fall asleep before finishing my porridge. I'm looking forward to trying your cooking, Chen."

Smiling, Chen stirred the porridge, which had about thirty minutes left. At least she would be staying at his place that night. He wondered if Anna would allow him to at least sleep in the bed with her as long as he promised to behave himself. He just wanted to hold her while she slept. Getting Xian to leave for the night was the tricky part. Anna would be at his place tomorrow, that was soon enough. He couldn't believe they had been intimate just that morning. It felt like weeks ago.

The rest of the night went quickly. Anna had crawled out of bed to eat at the table when the food was ready. Xian and Chen had protested loudly about her getting up but Anna squashed their protests quickly.

"Chen, I am a klutz when eating. Do you want to have to

change your bedding tonight?" Giving them both piercing glares. "I am **FINE!** It was a panic attack. I feel much better now."

Begrudgingly they let her get up, stipulating that Xian would carry her to the table and back. Rolling her eyes, she agreed so she could finally eat.

Anna enjoyed the porridge that Chen made. It was a savory grain porridge different from what she made. He would have to teach her the recipe for it. Finished, Anna wasn't overly upset about Xian carrying her back to the bed; she didn't realize how exhausted she was.

Settling back into the bed, Anna motioned Chen to come closer while Xian cleaned up the dishes from the meal.

"Chen, I know my clothes aren't done yet. Would you happen to have a set of pajamas I can wear for the night? I don't think I'm going to get that bath in. My batteries have depleted pretty fast."

Chen couldn't believe his luck. His dream was coming true.

"Certainly, Anna." Chen turned to head for his walk-in closet.

"Chen, wait. I'll change after Xian leaves. I don't want to hurt his feelings by not wearing his gift tonight. I will have plenty of opportunities. However, I have one more request." She hesitated for a few moments. "Would you sleep with me tonight? As long as you can behave yourself, that is."

"Will you allow me to hold you while you sleep, at least? I'll be a gentleman. You need your rest."

"Deal, I don't want to be alone after that attack earlier."

"Okay. Now we just need to get Xian to go home. I swear he wants to sleep on the couch."

Anna groaned. She liked Xian quite a bit but wanted some alone time with Chen.

"I'll convince him to go home," Anna said as she ran several excuses to convince Xian that it was time for him to go home.

"Xian, are you finished?" she called out.

"Just finishing, Anna, one moment."

Xian walked into the room, wiping his hands on a towel.

"What can I get you, Anna?"

Anna's heart warmed at the sight of him being domestic.

She shook her head and bolstered her resolve.

"Xian, I'm ready to go to bed. I think it's time for you to head home so I can rest."

"I had thought about staying on the couch if you needed anything," he said, looking hopeful that she would agree.

"Chen will be on the couch; I'm sure he will be here to help me if I need anything."

Crestfallen, Xian knew when he was beaten. There wasn't any good reason for him to camp out on the couch. She would be moving into his penthouse tomorrow. That was enough for him at the moment.

"Okay, Anna, I'll finish in the kitchen and head home." Kneeling on the edge of the bed, he bent over and gave her a soft kiss on her forehead.

"Good night, Xian. I'll call when I get up tomorrow. We can shop for my laptop then."

Xian had almost forgotten that she needed to pick up a new computer. He would be able to spend a good part of the day with her then.

"Sounds good. Good night, Anna."

章

Chapter 41

Anna awoke in an unfamiliar room. The faint scent of cotton-scented laundry soap and men's cologne lingered on the pillow. She took a deep breath, remembering where she was. An unfamiliar pressure across her waist reminded her that she had asked Chen to sleep with her. His firm body pressed against her back.

Lying there, she soaked in Chen's warmth. Soft breaths puffed against her neck as he slumbered. Anna, feeling safe and cared for, snuggled against his chest, but nature had other ideas and she desperately needed to move.

Shifting slowly, so she didn't disturb her bedmate, Anna tried to wiggle away from the possessive arm wrapped around her middle. As she tried to move, the arm holding her tightened. Not only did the arm pull her closer, but a leg also swept forward to capture hers. It was apparent Chen had no intention of letting her go. For much of the night she'd been held this way and she wasn't going to complain.

Giving up, Anna finally had to rouse Chen. Her bladder wasn't going to handle much more delay.

"Chen." Anna rubbed his arm to wake him gently.

"Mmmph," a muffled grumble emitted from the snoozing body.

"Chen! I need to get up **NOW**!" Anna struggled, prying Chen's arm from her abdomen.

"I'm not stopping you," came a husky voice filled with amusement.

"The hell you're not. I have to pee! Unless you want to be changing some bedding, you better let me move now." Anna shot from the bed, dashing to the bathroom.

Being a gentleman, Chen rolled over to face away from the transparent walls, giving Anna a bit of privacy.

"Is there some reason for the clear walls in your master

bath?" Anna called from her perch on the bidet.

"Came with the apartment. You're the first woman to spend the night here, so I haven't had to deal with it before now. Does it bother you? I may need to find a new apartment."

"Why would you look for a new apartment?"

"Well, if I have a girlfriend who needs privacy in the bathroom, I should find something with opaque walls. Not that watching you in the shower wouldn't be entertaining."

Anna smiled to herself. He was serious about them being together. That was a decision she still couldn't make. She cared about him so much, but some factors made it complicated. Finished with her call of nature, Anna washed up and leaned against the opening to the bathroom.

"Well, as you don't have a girlfriend I'm aware of, you should be just fine."

Chen rolled to his back and grabbed his chest as though he had been shot with an arrow.

"Overdramatic much?" Anna laughed at his exaggerated death throes.

"Hey, I'm an actor; what do you expect?"

Anna crawled back on the bed, sat on her knees and looked down at the lounging man. It wouldn't be hard for her to look at his handsome face every morning.

"You look good in my pajamas." Chen smirked. "I hope I'll see you wear them again sometime."

Flopping down on her stomach next to Chen, she rested her chin on his chest.

"You are a persistent one, aren't you?"

Chen grabbed Anna's shoulders and rolled her over on her back so he was on his stomach, looking down at her instead. His eyes were intense as he gazed down at her.

"Anna, I won't give up unless you tell me it is over for good. Even then, I might still try. We have something special and I don't want to throw that away over something so insignificant as distance. Can't you at least give me a chance?"

"No fair making this so difficult. I need some time, Chen. Before I arrived, I would have said yes in a moment, but with everything that's happened...I'm just not sure. Will I have the same issues if I move here during the filming? Will I be harassed constantly?" Anna pushed Chen over on his side and sat up. Pulling her knees to her chest, she wrapped her arms around them and rested her chin there.

Chen sighed, Li Ming had done damage as she planned. Anna's confidence was shaken. Would she still come back to work on the movies? It almost sounded like she might decide not to return to China. As much as he loathed the idea, he would need Xian's help to change her mind. He had finally found that person who made him feel complete. Letting go now without a fight wasn't an option.

"Anna, I can't guarantee there won't be issues. You'll need to decide by tomorrow if you plan to return or not. I'm biased and don't even want you to leave. I'm hoping the rest of the week will help convince you."

"I know, there is a lot I need to consider by the meeting. I'll give you a hint, don't push me. Being a Taurus, I can be a tad stubborn. The more you push me, there is a good chance I'll say no just to be a pain. Just keep that in mind."

Chen groaned internally; he had forgotten that about Anna. Over the years, he had experienced it several times. So he would have to modify his plan of attack.

"We better get moving. You have a big day. Shopping and settling into the penthouse." Chen stretched and rolled off the far side of the bed, making his way to the bathroom.

Anna realized Chen's destination and gave him a mischievous grin.

"Shall I turn my head, or should I just keep watching? I could leave the room."

"I'm not shy. You've seen it all already. It just depends on how comfortable you are." He returned her grin. Seeing Anna blush and turn her head, he knew he had taken the right tact with her. Chen quickly finished in the bathroom.

"Need a shower?" he called to Anna as she hid her face.

"I probably should. I stress sweat, and I swear I smell funky." She lifted an arm and sniffed the offending armpit.

Chen shook his head. Anna was becoming more and more comfortable with him. He can't ever remember seeing a woman sniff her armpit.

"Would you like your back scrubbed?"

"I don't know if I dare. Chen, I don't want you to get the wrong idea. We need to stop this until I make up my mind."

"Anna, it's okay. Shower all on your own. Can I watch?" Chen laughed as he dodged the pillow Anna threw.

"Very funny. Get out." Anna laughed as Chen left the room pouting. "Any chance there may be tea when I'm done?" she called before he could close the door.

"Your wish is my command," came the reply.

Checking her phone for messages, Anna noticed Xian had sent a text asking when she would be ready to go shopping. Checking the time, it was already 9:30 in the morning; she had slept in a little later than she had hoped—time to get motivated.

Anna opened the door and poked her head out.

"Chen, think an hour should be enough time before Xian picks me up?"

"That should be fine. Get in the shower then." Chen's mood darkened knowing Anna was leaving with Xian. She was a grown woman. It was her choice.

"Okay, I'm getting in!" Anna shouted through the door.

Thirty minutes later, washed, dried and wearing one of the outfits Xian had bought for her, Anna found Chen in the kitchen finishing breakfast preparations.

Heavenly aromas filled the air, savory with a touch of sweetness. Anna couldn't quite put her finger on which food each smell associated with. Numerous dishes were laid on the table and covers were on several to keep the contents warm.

Chen didn't hear Anna so much as he sensed her when she entered the kitchen. To him, it felt like a warm summer day walked into the room; the room brightened and warmed with her presence. *Oh man, he had it bad.* He found Anna wearing a baggy, cream-colored cable-knit sweater over a pair of black leggings. She looked casual and comfortable, just her style. Damn Xian for choosing such appropriate clothes for her.

"Something smells divine. My stomach has informed me that I'm ravenous. Is there anything I can help with?" Anna looked at the kitchen area, checking for other dishes that might need to be placed on the table.

"I think I have it all. Sit down and dig in. I made a more

traditional Chinese breakfast. See how you like it."

Lifting lids from the dishes Anna found steamed buns, noodles, congee from the previous evening and rolled omelets. Delicious aromas wafted from each dish causing Anna's mouth to water. Picking up the chopsticks next to her plate she chose a bun to try first, curious if it was the savory or sweet variety. Taking a bite of the soft dough, the filling was decidedly delicious. Pork and vegetables with a mild seasoning filled the fluffy dough.

"Mm, did you make all of this?" Anna managed to mumble between bites. After that first bite manners had gone out the window. She hadn't realized how hungry she was.

"Well, I bought and steamed the buns, but the rest I made. I hope you enjoy it."

Taking samples of each dish, she was delighted. Flavors she was unfamiliar with tantalized her taste buds. Sighing with delight, she savored each bite. Heck, staying with Chen was a definite advantage if he could cook like this.

Chen laughed watching Anna's reactions to each dish. These were simple staple dishes but she treated them like gourmet creations. He only had rudimentary cooking skills, but he was glad Anna enjoyed the meal. Perhaps she would like to learn how to make the dishes.

"Anna, would you like to learn how to make these? I'm sure you could pick them up easily."

"Honestly, I'll just keep you to cook for me," Anna joked with him. "I'd love to learn the recipes."

"I like the first option best, actually." Chen grinned at the thought of being Anna's house boy, cooking and cleaning for her. It might be an exciting change from acting. "Need a cook when you head home?"

Anna gave Chen an appraising glance. Just how serious was he about that comment? Too tempted by the idea, Anna stuffed a large piece of the omelet in her mouth to delay her response.

Chiming music distracted Chen. *Saved by the bell*. His inquiring gaze had been getting quite intense. Now he had someone at the door to deal with and Anna was off scot-free.

"Don't think this gets you completely off the hook. It's just a reprieve." He laughed at her surly expression when she realized he would still want an answer.

Since when had he started reading her mind? They became increasingly in tune with one another as they spent time together. To have someone that was in sync with her was a little disconcerting.

"Go answer the door and stop picking on me." Anna stuck her tongue out at Chen's back.

"Stick that tongue out any further and see what happens." Chen didn't even turn around.

Anna sat and stared dumbfounded at him, causing Chen to laugh.

"Be nice to me, and I may reveal my secrets," he said.

Chen was still chuckling as he opened the door and ushered Xian into the living area.

"Seems I missed the fun." Xian looked from Chen's grinning face to Anna's irritated scowl.

"I just realized Chen must have eyes in the back of his head," Anna groused.

Xian raised an eyebrow in curiosity. Chen just stood, arms folded across his chest, smirking.

"I'm not giving up all my secrets."

Rolling her eyes, Anna headed to the bedroom for the bag Chen had given her for the clothing Xian had bought her. Pulling it off the bed, she checked to ensure she had everything. She looked for the pair of pajamas she had worn the night before, thinking she would sneak them into her bag to take with her. They smelled of Chen and were so comfy. He must have already put them in the laundry. Perhaps she would try to get a pair later.

Wheeling the bag into the living area, Chen and Xian were whispering. Now, what were those two up to? She wasn't sure if she trusted leaving them alone anymore. They had a way of coming up with plans that involved her...and they didn't go well.

"Xian, you ready? We have quite a bit to do today." Anna walked up to Chen, throwing her arms around his neck and kissing his cheek. "Thank you for everything. You have no idea how much it meant to me."

"I believe I do know. It meant a lot to me as well. Let me

know when you get to the penthouse. I'll drop by to check on you," Chen said as he wrapped his arms around Anna and lifted her feet off the floor in a huge hug.

Seeing Chen and Anna, Xian sighed and took Anna's bag.

"Anna, we better get going. We have a bunch to do before we head to the apartment." Xian wheeled the bag to the front door, giving them a few moments of privacy.

Anna stepped away after one last hug and followed Xian out the door.

Once Anna and Xian had left Chen went to the bedroom to ensure he still had the pair of pajamas Anna had worn. Opening a drawer in his closet he discovered them right where he left them. While Anna was eating, Chen had excused himself for a few minutes to use the bathroom. He noticed the pajamas neatly folded on the bed. Grabbing them, he'd squirreled them away. They had Anna's scent so he wouldn't let them be washed, at least for now.

When he had finished tucking the pajamas in the drawer earlier, Chen found the pair he had worn, folded them neatly and opened Anna's case to tuck them in with her clothes. It would be a surprise for her, whether a good one or not remained to be seen.

章

Chapter 42

The first stop on shopapalooza was a new laptop to get her through until hers was released from evidence. So much had happened in the last two days that Anna was still reeling. It was hard to imagine that she had been on the red carpet of an award ceremony, slept with one of her favorite actors, had all her possessions put into evidence and had a massive panic attack in two days. From now on, Anna would just roll with whatever came her way.

Chen had invited her to his movie wrap party on Friday. In what world would a girl from rural Montana be included in a wrap party for a television series? A dress for the occasion would be in order. Her beautiful cheongsam and dove gray gown were in evidence lockup. Hopefully, they weren't damaged in the rampage through the hotel room.

Luckily, there were Apple stores in Beijing. This was an excellent excuse to upgrade her laptop. The relic she had been limping along with for some time had caused her delays; the speed had been getting slower and slower. It wasn't that she couldn't afford a new computer, but the laptop she had was the one she had first started her writing on. She hung on to it more for sentimental reasons than anything else. Upgrading to the new processor alone would improve performance and the speed should be a considerable upgrade.

Carefully looking over the models in stock, Anna found a beefed up MacBook Air. This was a big difference from the clunky MacBook Pro she had been lugging around for years. Xian was impressed with Anna's knowledge of Apple products. He gave her his opinion when she requested it, usually that she needed more peripherals. The external trackpad, a larger monitor, a laser printer with wifi capability, a new laptop bag, extra cords and external drives were all added to the pile on the counter.

"Are you sure I need all of this, Xian? I'm only here for another week before I head home." Anna looked dubious at the pile of boxes she had accumulated.

"Yes. I'm sure. There is an office at the penthouse and I want you to have everything you need to work if necessary. As for only being here for a week, weren't you supposed to return in a few months for a longer stay? You will need all of this equipment for a long-term office; you may as well buy it now. The penthouse is now yours as long as you need it. It's not like I don't have twenty more properties around Beijing and other cities. It's nice to have someone using it for a change. It's been empty for quite a while now."

"Xian, I can't just accept a penthouse apartment. That's too much." Anna looked distressed at the thought of accepting such an extravagant gift.

"Wait until you see it before you turn it down." Xian winked at her; she had no idea what she was in for. Chen had shown him photos of Anna's home in Montana and this wasn't as rustic, but she would be safe and comfortable. Security at that apartment complex was some of the best in the city.

"Okay, my curiosity has been piqued for sure. How will we get this pile of electronics moved to the apartment?" Anna looked at the large boxes for the thirty-two inch monitor, the colossal laser printer Xian had insisted she needed and the pile of smaller boxes and packages with other peripherals.

"It's been taken care of. All of the boxes should be waiting at the apartment when we are finished with our shopping. We still need to get more for your wardrobe and the essentials: shampoo, conditioner, feminine supplies, makeup and other hair care items. Did I miss anything?"

Anna laughed at Xian's list of items to use as examples.

"Well, clothes and some beauty supplies will be good; but as for feminine supplies, I haven't needed those in almost thirteen years. The plumbing is all gone, I had to have it removed. Xian, we don't have to buy everything in one trip. I love this part of the shopping experience, but the rest...not so much. You are looking at one woman who is not even remotely interested in fashion and makeup. Though it was fun when we went dress shopping, I can't deny it completely."

"Well, you do need clothes for tomorrow. Your meeting with the studio is important enough that you should dress for it. I believe a stylish business suit will impress them, though I'm not sure you could impress them any more than you did at the awards. You were the talk of the ceremony." Mentally, he slapped himself, wishing he could take that last sentence back.

"Thanks for the reminder Xian." Anna's buoyant mood sank. Anna could still hear the snide comments that circulated with the rumors Li Ming had started. *No! She wasn't going to let that over-manicured leech ruin her day*. Anna looked stunning on the red carpet. Photos of her and Xian had been popping up on numerous media sources. So far, they had been lucky not to be recognized by anyone.

"I'm sorry, Anna, I meant to say that you were one of the most stunning women at the awards. Few could hold a candle to your beauty."

Blushing at the compliment, Anna took Xian's arm and asked a difficult question.

"Where to next?"

The next few hours were a blur for Anna. Xian whisked her through boutique after boutique. They found individual pieces that would work well so she would have a multitude of options. What had excited Anna the most was the black, pinstripe three-piece suit. She had fun looking for a tie to match the suit with Xian's help. Trying the suit on had made her feel powerful yet sexy. Chen was in for a surprise with this one.

Finding the casual clothing and sundries, it was time to focus on the formal attire she would need for the rest of the trip. A cocktail gown for the wrap party would be just the ticket. Xian had decided she needed a formal evening gown as well.

Xian had looked into the charity masquerade gala that Saturday. He had planned to attend with Chen but thought Anna might enjoy the opportunity to spend his money for a good cause.

"Anna, why don't we find a formal evening gown," Xian hinted.

"Wouldn't that be overkill for a wrap party? I'm already going to look fancier than I usually do. I've told you how comfortable I am in evening wear." Anna rolled her eyes in sarcasm.

"I actually thought you could wear it for a charity auction and masquerade gala on Saturday. After Chandra died, I usually attended with Chen, but you would be a delightful substitute. You could spend my money for a good cause." Xian wondered if Anna had any idea how much he was worth. That might make her run away in fear. This was one woman who didn't care about his fortune; in fact, it might work against him.

"What's the cause?" Anna asked curiously. She supported and helped with several charities back home.

"Orphaned children. We are raising money to rebuild one of the schools for children waiting for adoption. Chen and I have held this charity near and dear to our hearts. Chandra and I could never have children so we spread our love to children without parents. We were in the process of adopting when Chandra got her diagnosis. I never had my opportunity to be a father."

Anna saw the pain in Xian's face. She could only imagine. For years, children had been a sore spot with her, complicated feelings that were best left buried. Anna wrapped her arms around Xian in the middle of the sidewalk.

"I'm so sorry, Xian. I can't imagine how you feel. I would love to help support such a worthy cause. I'll even go through the torture of shopping for another evening gown. The dove gray one I bought would have been perfect. Let's not fly back to Shanghai to find one. There have to be boutiques here that would carry what I need. Oh crap! My shoes were confiscated too. **DAMN!**" Anna pulled away and stomped her foot in aggravation.

Xian grabbed Anna's hand, trying to calm her.

"Anna, it's going to be okay. I have already found a store that carries shoes in your size. They have assured me that they have quite a selection. Why don't we go find your next dream dress and some shoes to match?"

This was the closest to heaven Xian had been for many years, escorting Anna while they shopped and talked. It felt so familiar, almost like it had been with Chandra. He felt comfortable walking with Anna chattering in his ear about stores they saw and odd people crossing their paths. Chen was right, they had to convince Anna to return to China. Xian wasn't sure if he could lose Anna from his life now that he had found her. But Chen was in love with Anna too. This wasn't going to end well for one of them.

Reaching the boutique he had in mind, Anna immediately was drawn to a blue lace cheongsam gown. It wasn't the traditional style, but it looked amazing. It would be the perfect dress for Chen's party; she would need to get a photo so Chen could find something to match. She looked forward to upcoming events for the first time in a few days.

Now that she had found the dress for Chen's party, she needed one for the masquerade gala. Browsing through the gowns displayed throughout the store, Anna found one that caught her attention. A wine ombre strapless gown hung on a mannequin towards the back of the boutique.

"Excuse me, do you have this dress in my size?" she inquired. Anna worked with the clerk to figure out her size for that designer.

After checking the stockroom, the attendant returned with the wine-colored ball gown. Anna went into the dressing area to try it on. *Please let it fit* was the mantra running through her head as she slipped into the gorgeous garment. With help from the clerk, Anna could fit into the dress. It would need a few minor alterations but Anna was assured it could be accomplished by Friday.

Another clerk had brought the blue cheongsam for her to try as well. Anna thought about showing Xian the wine ombre dress before changing, but she wanted to surprise him. He had been otherwise occupied when she inquired about it, so hopefully he didn't know this was her pick for the masquerade gala.

Trying on the blue lace marvel was a little more challenging. Anna had the clerk teach her how the dress needed to be adjusted once she had it on. It was almost perfect; Anna's ample chest made it a little snug, nothing the proper undergarments couldn't remedy. Needing the photo for Chen, Anna had the clerk summon Xian to the dressing salon to see what he thought.

"You look stunning, Anna." Xian was jealous of Chen enjoying Anna's company in this beautiful dress. "Is that for the gala?" he couldn't stop himself from asking even though he was sure he knew the answer.

"Sorry Xian, I already have the gown for the masquerade gala," Anna said in an offhanded tone, not realizing her words had bowled Xian over.

"What do you mean you have the gown for the gala?" Xian sputtered.

"That was the first dress I chose. It needs a few alterations, but they assured me it would be delivered to the apartment by Friday." Anna grinned, pleased with herself.

"Where did you put Anna? You can't be the same timid woman I had to almost carry into the salons in Shanghai."

"I had a good teacher. He was kind, patient and considerate of a shy backwoods woman's feelings. Thank you." Anna kissed Xian's cheek.

"You're so very welcome. I'm happy to see you so confident."

"It's great! I haven't had this kind of confidence in a very long time. I believe you and Chen have something to do with it."

"Glad we could help. Now that we have the dresses, let's go find you some shoes," Xian said, still beaming from the compliment Anna paid him.

章

Chapter 43

Yawning, Anna watched out the window as buildings flowed past the SUV. Passing by apartment buildings taller than most buildings in Montana, she marveled at how much of the city had built upward. Looking over her shoulder, she could only be awed at the number of bags and boxes stashed in the back of the vehicle. She couldn't believe how much she had purchased in one trip. It was all Xian's fault.

Whenever she thought she had enough, Xian would come with another sweater, skirt, tunic or some other piece of clothing and then would make her fall in love with it. That man was evil when it came to shopping. Anna could only hope that there would be enough room to store her new wardrobe. She definitely wouldn't need to bring anything with her when she returned. She would undoubtedly be the best dressed she had ever been.

Wu Feng pulled up to a grand portcullis entrance at what Anna had confused for a luxury resort. Anna was floored at what she saw; it was more elegant than the hotel she had stayed at. Stopping in front of the main doors, Wu Feng came and opened Anna's door.

"Welcome home." He bowed.

"Well, at least it is for a week. Xian, are you trying to spoil me?" Anna asked as she looked around.

"Nothing's too good for you. I just hope you enjoy your time here," Xian said as he opened the door to the building.

Walking into the lobby, they were greeted by a pleasant receptionist. Xian stopped and notified them that Anna had arrived and would be in residence for the next week. The young woman behind the desk beamed at Anna and welcomed her. She told them that three different women would be staffing the desk and she would inform the others that Anna would be coming and going and receiving guests. After thanking the sweet woman, Anna looked around the lounge area while Xian finalized the arrangements.

Taking Anna's hand, he led her to the elevator and handed her a keycard. "You'll need this to access your floor. Chen and I have cards for the apartment, but that is all. Call security immediately if there is a knock on the door and it's not one of us, or you're not expecting a guest. This building has CCTV in the elevators and hallways to keep people from wandering through the facility. You will have access to the pool, exercise room, sauna, spa, restaurant, bar and the kitchen available to prepare residents' meals. I figured you could use that service to save you from some of the cooking. It could come in handy for breakfasts."

Anna was suitably impressed. When the elevator arrived at the correct floor Xian swiped the keycard and the door whooshed open to an ornate foyer. Anna noticed a CCTV camera in her entry which reassured her; she liked knowing it wouldn't be easy to get in without her invitation. Opening the double door to the apartment, Anna was underwhelmed until she stepped further into the apartment.

"Xian, where do you keep the slippers?" Anna looked for a place to remove her shoes.

"Don't worry about it right now. Let me give you the tour first and get you settled. You can leave them next to the entrance chair for now. The apartment has five bedrooms, but one is set up as an extra office and the other is a surprise. Where would you like to start? Bedroom or kitchen area?" Xian motioned left to the bedroom and right to the kitchen.

"Why don't we start to the right and work our way from there." Her imagination was working overtime. So far, all she had seen was the hallway.

Pulling her down the hall to the right, he led her to the kitchen and informal living room. A small sitting area with a brown leather couch covered in lavender and silver throw pillows nestled against the wall beneath a large wall hanging. Two dusty purple sitting chairs sat across a simple coffee table from the couch. Looking around, there were several doors and hallways leading to other rooms. It looked almost like the hub of a space station. The kitchen looked like it could fit in a science fiction movie, modern and shiny.

Right off the sitting area, Anna found a room filled with a desk, office chair and a plush couch. The boxes that held Anna's office supplies and laptop were on the desk; they had been delivered before expected. She was suitably impressed. This would be a perfect workspace, close to the kitchen with great light. She mentally laid out the desk, deciding how she wanted to set up the electronics.

Down the hall from the office were two guest bedrooms, though she didn't expect to need those. They were both decorated with purple accents that matched the sitting room. She was glad to know there was a bathroom handy across the hall from one of the guest rooms, so she wouldn't have to go to the opposite end of the apartment while working. Convenience was key.

"Xian, this place is huge." Anna peeked into each of the guest rooms.

"You haven't seen anything yet." Xian grinned as he grabbed her hand again and led her to the dining room.

Walking through a short hall, they entered the formal dining room. An immense polished wooden table sat in the center of the room with a large glass turntable. She could only imagine the dishes that could be served at the huge table. It was overkill for just herself. She would most likely eat at the coffee bar by the kitchen. Anna wasn't sure if she knew enough people in Beijing to fill the table if she wanted to entertain.

"So, you could certainly throw one heck of a party," Anna mused.

"We've had a few informal gatherings here. The spare rooms are handy for those who tend to overindulge and shouldn't drive."

Turning, she noticed there were stairs leading up from the dining room.

"Where do the stairs lead?"

"That's a surprise. Let's see the rest first," Xian said, leading her past a wall and into the formal living room.

What caught Anna's attention before anything else was the view. The cityscape at night would be spectacular and she had a fantastic panorama. Walking to the window, she looked out over the city.

"Guess I must close the drapes if I decide to walk around the apartment naked," Anna mused to herself.

Xian snickered. Anna was like no other woman he knew. She had little to no filter at times. "I don't believe that will be an issue if you **REALLY** want to walk through the apartment nude. You're above most of the closest apartment levels."

Having seen enough of the cityscape, she looked around the living room. The purples were carried through this room as well. Throw pillows scattered on couches and chairs matched those in the smaller sitting area. Anna estimated that at least fifteen people could hang out comfortably. A flat panel television was inset into the wall between the living room and dining room; it was a little larger than the one she had at home above her fireplace.

"Xian, there is so much space here. I'm not sure what I'll do with it all." Anna continued to marvel at the room.

"Just wait until you see the bedroom." Xian winked at her.

Anna found a door outside the main bedroom while walking down another short hallway. Looking inside, she discovered it was a masculine study. Dark wood paneling and shelving made it feel warm, but it was too dark for Anna's taste. She would undoubtedly use the brighter room for her office. Anna noticed a large selection of books on the shelves; she would assuredly browse through and see if there was something to help when she couldn't sleep.

"Last, but certainly not least." Xian showed her the master bedroom.

"Wow!" Anna exclaimed as she looked around the room. A king-sized bed was the focal point of the room. The purples carried into the bedroom as well. Blonde wood shelves covered the far wall and numerous knick-knacks resided there. In front of large windows at the foot of the bed was a couch and TV. The view was as spectacular from the bedroom as the living room. Soft lighting in the bedroom didn't detract from the lighted city outside the windows.

Finishing her investigation, a glass curio cabinet perched atop a dresser along the wall between the two doors to the room caught her attention. Anna would have to be cautious around all that glass. She could see herself bumping into that and breaking something. Either in the cabinet or herself.

"Xian, as pretty as that curio is, can it be stored while I'm here? I'm a notorious klutz and I can see myself falling into that during the night. I don't think we want an ER visit at odd hours."

Xian quirked an eyebrow. At least she was proactive. He would contact the maintenance department and have them put it in storage for now. He had never been a big fan of the piece.

"That can certainly be arranged. It will probably be tomorrow. I'll try to schedule it during your meeting. What time is it again?"

"Um, I'll have to text Chen. I'm not sure." Anna pulled out her phone and sent Chen a text message asking about the time. At the last moment, she remembered to let Chen know she was at the apartment. She was surprised that he wasn't there already. It would have been like Chen to be there waiting to surprise her.

"Check out the closet and bathroom. I hope they will work for you." Xian was interested to see how her new togs would fill the closet. Thinking about all they purchased that day, he mentally did a forehead slap; of all the clothing they had purchased they had once again forgotten to pick up a couple of coats. He could see Anna wearing a long cashmere coat to go with her business attire.

Anna entered the vast walk-through closet; it rivaled the one she had at home. She started mentally cataloging all the different clothing pieces she had purchased today; this closet would easily organize the various pieces to her wardrobe puzzle. Xian was a whiz regarding women's clothing, picking pieces that could be mixed and matched to make endless outfits.

She was most excited to wear the formal business attire for tomorrow's meeting. Xian had urged her to pick out several ties that matched the three-piece outfit. He had even commented that a business suit never looked so good.

Entering the bathroom, Anna let out a low whistle. The marble throughout the room had a calming effect. Finding a sizable tub, Anna was excited about a long soak. It was a bummer that the tub wasn't quite as large as the one in the W Taipei hotel. It would be a tighter squeeze to fit two people. An errant daydream put Anna and Xian soaking in the tub, snuggly fitting in the warm water. Shaking herself, she quickly left the bathroom before her libido caught up.

"Xian, this place is amazing. So, what is the surprise you have hinted at on several occasions? I believe the stairs from the dining room had something to do with it."

"You're an impatient one, aren't you?" Xian chuckled.

"Sweetheart, you haven't seen the half of it," Anna snarked back.

The sweetheart comment elicited a raised eyebrow. Anna seemed to become more casual and comfortable around him as time passed. Bantering back and forth with Anna had been a joy. What would he do when she returned to the States? He would miss the rapport they had developed.

"Okay impatient one, let's go see the surprise."

He took Anna's hand and led her to the stairs leading upwards to another floor.

"Can I trust you to keep your eyes closed, or should I find something to cover them?" Xian stopped at the foot of the stairs, searching Anna's face for the answer to his question.

"I think I can keep them closed. I'll behave, I promise."

"Close your eyes. I'll lead you up and don't open them until I tell you it's okay." Xian wrapped his arm around Anna's shoulders, gently guiding her to the steps. Helping her, he ensured her footing was secure before going forward. Finally, after some moments of cautious climbing, they reached their destination.

"Ready?" Xian's excited voice teased Anna.

"Yes, you don't even want to know where my imagination has gone." Anna cringed a bit at some of the ideas that had slid through her mind while climbing the stairs. The wildest was a room straight out of *Fifty Shades of Grey*. Shaking her head slightly Anna took a long deep breath, holding it a moment before letting it out slowly.

"Go ahead and open your eyes."

Opening her eyes, Anna gasped at the "surprise." This was

Anna's favorite room in the apartment. At the top of the stairs, Anna looked around the airy room; comfortable furniture surrounded a low table covered in delicate looking dishes of aromatic foods. Six doors opened out onto an oasis in the city.

Patio furniture was situated around an oriental looking brazier for cool nights. Candles and fairy lights lit every surface of the room and patio so that flickering light painted the room. Fresh cut flowers added their aroma to the ambiance. Vases of exquisite orchids, lilies and other hothouse flowers dotted the area.

"Xian, this is amazing. I love it! Did you do all of this just for me?" Anna was still trying to take it all in.

"I hope you like it. After the long day, I figured a quiet, casual dinner would be welcome...especially after yesterday."

"Thank you, it's wonderful. Is this just for us or will we include Chen in this? I let him know I was moved into the apartment."

"Well, I had hoped it would just be us, but Chen is always welcome."

"Let's eat. If Chen gets here in time, he will get to share; otherwise...too bad." Anna laughed and sat down to enjoy the meal Xian had prepared for her.

章

Chapter 44

Xian and Anna made short work of the meal. Anna started to wonder if Chen was even going to reply to her; it had been almost two hours since she had sent him the message. Deciding she had waited long enough, she sent another.

Hey, where are you? A little worried here.

Anna chatted with Xian, discussed their day and made plans for Saturday's upcoming gala. Checking her phone, she still had nothing from Chen. What was going on? He hadn't gone this long without answering her texts unless he had an extra busy filming day. Anxiety began cropping up and she wasn't sure which technique to use to calm herself.

Anna got up from her chair and walked out to the patio, breathing in the fresh air as she began pacing the confined area. Seven steps and turn, over and over. Xian watched from the couch, curious about what had Anna so anxious. He checked his phone since he hadn't heard anything from Chen either, not even after sending the picture of the dress Anna was going to wear for the wrap party. Xian was starting to get concerned.

Time to call in reinforcements. Xian sent a text to Wu Feng.

Can you check with Huang Hu where Chen is? Anna and I are both getting concerned.

Indeed, sir, I will notify you when I hear anything. Oh, all of Anna's clothes have been delivered and placed in the master bedroom. Will there be anything else?

Not at the moment. I'll let Anna know. It might give her a distraction to go through the clothes.

Xian watched Anna a little longer. He couldn't tell what she was saying to herself, but he felt some of it was cursing Chen. It wasn't like his friend not to reply to his messages, let alone Anna's. He could understand her concern after everything that had happened recently.

His phone chimed as Xian walked toward the patio to talk to Anna.

Mr. Wei, it's not good. Please meet me downstairs.

Torn between having Anna come with him and letting her continue to work off some of her nervous energy, he opted to let Anna continue her path. Quickly going down to the living room, Wu Feng was there with Huang Hu.

"Huang Hu, what's going on? Where's Chen? Anna's beside herself."

"Mr. Wei, Mr. Xiao is in the hospital," Huang Hu said, his voice unsteady.

"**WHAT**? Tell me everything." Xian looked up towards the room where Anna continued to pace the confined space.

"Mr. Xiao was on his way here earlier. He wanted to have a surprise set up for Ms. Anna when you arrived. However, he didn't make it. There was a hit-and-run on his way. His car was hit on the passenger door side. Mr. Xiao isn't seriously injured, but he must stay in the hospital tonight."

Xian sank into a chair. How could anything happen to Chen? He couldn't lose him as well. Chen was the closest thing he had to family–as his own had nothing to do with Xian after he stood by Chandra when she became ill. According to his family, she couldn't produce an heir so what good was she? He should just divorce her and find a wife who could provide the heir to the Wei Group. Xian shook his head to help focus on the present.

"I know this might sound crass but have you called the studio to make arrangements? I doubt Chen will be up to attending the meeting with Anna tomorrow. I know it's a big meeting for her. Perhaps I could attend with her. Do you happen to know the time of the meeting?" Xian had already begun making plans in his head. He could reschedule his appointments for the next day. His office had been forewarned that he would be in and out during Anna's visit.

"Their meeting is at noon tomorrow. It was meant to be a business lunch. I can contact Mr. Shun and see if it will be okay for you to attend in place of Mr. Xiao," Huang Hu said.

"Feng, can you please notify the office that no matter what

happens I won't be in tomorrow until the afternoon, if at all. Do I have an overnight bag in the car?" Xian had decided that Anna couldn't be left alone that night. They would head for the hospital in a few moments so she could see Chen. This wasn't how the day was supposed to end. Hadn't Anna been through enough already?

"I will run to your apartment and get what you need. Will you be staying in the master bedroom or a guest room?" Wu Feng couldn't quite keep the hope from his voice.

"The guest room with the bathroom. I'm going to go get Anna so we can see Chen. Huang Hu, can you drive us?"

"Certainly, sir. Mr. Xiao may be awake now. I took his phone, though. He isn't supposed to use any electronics tonight as he has a concussion."

"Well, that explains why he didn't reply to Anna. She's upstairs wearing a path on the patio floor." Xian took the steps two at a time, his long legs making it easy for him to take them quickly.

"Anna, can you come here for a moment?" Xian was loath to explain what had happened. She wasn't going to take it well.

Anna stomped her way towards Xian. She knew she was acting like a spoiled toddler, but damn that man! He had her stomach tied up in knots with anxiety. Chen was going to get an earful for not replying to her before now. Didn't he realize how worried she was?

Xian was wary of Anna's thunderous expression. This wasn't going to end well if he wasn't careful.

"Come downstairs please; your clothes were delivered. Wu Feng put them in your bedroom," Xian said, stalling for time. Before he broke the news, getting Anna down the stairs was a good idea, right? He imagined her barreling down the stairs at breakneck speed and hurting herself. Wasn't she the self-proclaimed klutz?

"That's great," she answered in a distracted voice. "Any word from Chen?"

Xian had already started down the stairs so he avoided that question for a few more minutes. He was already nervous about the fallout from not telling her immediately. Her safety was his main concern at the moment, and now Chen's as well, it seemed. It was suspicious that after everything that had happened recently, Chen just happened to have an accident on his way to the apartment building.

Reaching the bottom of the stairs, Anna nearly ran Xian over. She had been trying to get him to answer her question. With both of her feet firmly on the main level, Xian finally felt he could tell her the news. Huang Hu picked that moment to return from the bathroom and Anna spotted him. All color drained from Anna's face. Huang Hu was there but Chen wasn't...something was very wrong.

"Anna, you better sit down." Xian tried to tug her to one of the plush chairs in the living room.

"No, I want to know **NOW!**" Her anger found a new target. Xian wasn't telling her something important. She had been suspicious when he wouldn't answer her on the patio or all the way down the stairs.

Bracing for what came next, Xian explained to Anna what had happened with Huang Hu's help.

Crumpling to the floor, Anna felt like she couldn't breathe.

"No...No, no, no, no..." the litany spilled from Anna's lips. "He's okay, right?"

"Yes, Ms. Anna. He is recovering from a mild concussion and a few minor cuts and bruises. Nothing that will keep him down for long," Huang Hu reassured Anna. He knew they had better get to the hospital before Chen woke up, or he would be looking for a new job for taking his boss's phone with him.

"Mr. Wei suggested I drive you to the hospital to see him. Do you need anything before we go?"

Helping Anna from the floor, Xian looked at her, his concern evident even to Huang Hu.

"Anna, why don't you get your purse and wrap from the bedroom and we'll head for the hospital now. I'm sure Chen will be waiting to see you." It hurt his heart to say that, but he couldn't begrudge Chen Anna's comfort.

"I'll be ready in a few moments," she said. Anna dashed the tears from her cheek. Rushing to the bathroom in her bedroom to wash her face and brush her hair. She couldn't let Chen see her in such a state. It would only cause him more stress.

Finished cleaning up, Anna met Xian at the door.

"Huang Hu has gone down to get the car for us."

"That's good," Anna replied in a distracted voice.

Standing in the foyer waiting on the elevator, Xian pulled Anna into a hug. Startled, Anna stood still for a moment before wrapping her arms around his waist. Fighting the sobs that threatened to escape her iron control, she had just cleaned herself up and didn't want to look a mess.

Pulling away when the door to the elevator opened, she stepped in and waited for Xian. He pushed the *L* button for the lobby.

Long minutes passed as Anna watched the declining numbers. They were going down; why did it feel slower than when they had gone up? Grabbing onto Xian's arm, she held on tight.

Reaching the lobby, they quickly made their way to the front doors. Huang Hu must have been quick as he was parked under the apartment portico waiting for them. He moved to get out and open the back doors. Xian waved him to stay and opened the door for Anna. They slid into the back seat, Anna holding Xian's hand for comfort.

"We're ready, Huang Hu." Xian touched the man's shoulder in reassurance and said, "Let's go see Chen."

章

Chapter 45

Chen awoke in an unfamiliar room. A machine to his left was making quiet beeping noises. Looking around, nothing was familiar. Dull throbbing behind his temple confused him. He wasn't prone to headaches; this made no sense.

The last thing Chen remembered was making some calls to arrange a surprise for Anna at her new residence. Now he was lying in a hospital bed? How did he end up here? Where was Huang Hu? How was Anna? She hadn't messaged at all. Xian had sent the photo of a spectacular blue dress that Anna planned to wear on Friday.

Getting his bearings back, Chen looked for his phone. Not seeing it anywhere he was concerned something had happened to it. How would Anna reach him if his phone wasn't with him?

Laying there trying to replay the afternoon in his mind only caused the pain to increase gradually. Better just let it go for now. Someone should be in to check on him soon.

Moments later, his wish came true. The door opened to a frantic Anna and somber Xian. Seeing Chen awake, Anna rushed to his side.

"How are you feeling?" Anna took the hand that didn't have the IV.

"Well, if you find the truck parked on my head, beat the driver mercilessly," Chen attempted to joke. He didn't dare laugh, it would only worsen the intense throbbing.

"Ha, not funny, Chen. Do you have any idea how worried I was about you? I hadn't heard from you all day. You're just trying to add gray hairs, right?"

"No, Anna, the last thing I want is you worried about me. I'm supposed to worry about you, remember?"

"I believe I'll be doing enough of that for the both of you."

Xian finally made his presence known. "Brother, you had me just as concerned. Especially when you didn't respond to the dress photo I sent."

Chen closed his eyes and dredged up the image of Anna in the blue cheongsam. He had wanted to tell Anna in person that the dress was perfect. For a short time, the dread of having to attend the party had overshadowed the day until the photo came. Groaning, he remembered they had a meeting with the studio the next day.

"Chen, I can tell by your expression you're worrying about tomorrow, aren't you?" Xian pulled up two chairs.

"Yeah, I'm concerned for several reasons." Chen bit his lip. He needed to discuss this with Xian but not with Anna in the room.

"Anna, could you please find the nurse? I need to use the bathroom." Chen squeezed her hand.

"Sure, I'll find Huang Hu and get your phone back too." Anna squeezed his hand back before leaving the room.

"Xian, you need to go to that meeting tomorrow. We have to get the arrangements made so Anna will return. This couldn't have happened at a worse time."

"I'm beginning to wonder if it was an accident at all. Huang Hu is contacting the studio to determine if I can step in for you at the meeting tomorrow. I've worked with Mr. Shun and several of the other executives before, so they know me well. You'll need to give me the pertinent details so I sound like I know what I'm talking about."

"When Huang Hu gets here I'll have him forward the pertinent documents. Damn, what happened to me anyway? Last I remember I was heading for the florist, then everything went black."

"From what I understand, as you drove through an intersection you were struck by a hit-and-run in the passenger door. I'll check with the police to see if they have CCTV footage of the vehicle. I hate to say this...but I don't think it was a simple accident. With everything that has happened recently, it's too suspicious." Xian stood and walked to the window with agitation.

"You're not the only one wondering the same thing. Isn't Li

Ming still under observation? I wonder if she's even been transferred back to Beijing already? What about that Scott character? Any word on where he might be?"

"No, that's the frustrating part. I've had my security details keeping an eye out for him. The apartment staff has been briefed that if anyone requests to see Anna, they must show ID. They know Huang Hu, Wu Feng and you, so you shouldn't have to worry about it. It would be a huge help if we had a photo of this Scott person," Xian replied and began pacing while he thought.

"Would Liz possibly have some information? Possibly a photo?" Chen brightened at the thought.

In a flash, Xian had his phone in hand, fingers flying over the screen sending Liz a message. He had looked at some of the social media for the bar, checking where Anna's daughter worked. There had been many photos from different events. Perhaps Scott was in one of them? If he remembered correctly, he was supposed to be a regular.

Before they could continue the conversation, the door opened again admitting Anna, Huang Hu and a scowling nurse.

"Why are you all in this room disturbing Mr. Xiao?" the disgruntled nurse questioned the visitors.

"Nurse, please don't chase my fiancé and brother-in-law out. I need to make some arrangements since I'm here until tomorrow." Chen poured on the charm, hoping the nurse would cut them slack. He looked at Xian and cringed. Shock and hurt raced across his face, rivaling the surprise on Anna's. He tried to make a face conveying his purpose for the lie.

Harrumphing, the nurse told them they had fifteen minutes. After that, they had to leave. She assisted Chen to the bathroom and checked his IV and vital signs before leaving the bewildered Anna and Xian alone with him.

"What the hell, Chen?" Xian exploded as soon as the nurse left the room.

"Fiancé? Hell, we aren't even dating," Anna spluttered.

Chen held his hands up in capitulation, he knew he was outgunned.

"I didn't want you to be kicked out immediately, but I know they only allow family past visiting hours so I had to come up with something on the fly. I'm pretty good at improvising, huh?" He smirked for a moment until he saw the expressions on the faces of the two most significant people in his life.

"I'm sorry. I wasn't thinking straight. With Anna, it's more about wishful thinking." Chen's buoyant mood dampened.

Anna walked over to the bed and handed Chen his phone. She wasn't sure how to feel at that moment. When she first heard him say it, it gave her an immense burst of joy...until she saw Xian's face. Despair or anger, Anna wasn't sure which was winning the battle in Xian. This was getting so complicated, she didn't want to be what came between the two of them.

"Here, there are probably some important messages you may need to check before taking it away for the night. Doctor's orders, no phone tonight. You need to rest." Anna sat in the chair farthest from the bed. She was still trying to process her emotions after Chen's comment.

Watching Anna distance herself caused Chen more pain than his head. Why did he keep screwing this up? This time it wasn't just Anna, Xian was also caught in the backlash of his rash idea. Sighing, he knew he would need to fix this somehow; he just needed to be out of the hospital first.

"So, when will I be able to get out of this place?" Chen looked at Huang Hu.

"Sorry, sir, it will be tomorrow at least and longer if you don't behave." His assistant glowered at him. "That's why Ms. Anna will be keeping your phone tonight."

Chen looked to Anna for confirmation. He hadn't talked with the doctor so he had no idea if what Huang said was accurate or not. Anna shrugged when she saw Chen giving her a questioning look.

"Sorry, Chen, I haven't had an opportunity to talk to the physician yet. The nurse now believes I'm your fiancé, so I could go find someone and get some details," Anna said and stood to head for the door.

"Anna, I'm sorry," Chen whispered to her back as she walked out.

Xian watched Chen and Anna. He could tell Anna was upset and Chen was kicking himself for his rash decision. Fate just seemed to have it in for the three of them. One thing after another made it difficult for Anna. Now they were going after Chen **AND** Anna; he would have to step up the search. Xian's gut told him that Scott creep had a role in this.

"Xian, I messed up," Chen confessed.

"And then some. You knew Anna was having issues with her feelings for you and had to push it. Don't get me wrong, I understand why you did it, but it was a bonehead idea."

"Did you have a better one? I needed to see Anna for more than the two minutes that harridan would have allowed. She's the air I breathe. I don't know what I'll do if she isn't in my life," Chen said fervently.

Seeing Chen in a different light, Xian's heart squeezed painfully. How could he interfere with his brother's happiness? Xian had time with Chandra; why couldn't he walk away and let Chen have this? Because as much as he loved Chen, he wasn't sure he was good enough for Anna. Did Chen really know Anna? Xian wondered when he made such rookie mistakes with her.

"Chen, I will play devil's advocate here; how well do you know Anna? After talking with her for so long, how could you not know how much that comment would hurt her? I haven't even known her for a week and I know that much about her already."

"Xian, I do know Anna and she knows me. It's a bit more complicated than you know." Finally realizing he needed to come clean with his brother, Chen disclosed what had happened in Taipei between him and Anna.

"When I caught up with Anna after the awards she asked me to spend the night with her. When I asked her if we were a couple the next morning, she told me she couldn't get involved because of the distance. We had discussed possibly dating when she returned for filming, but if I keep screwing it up, I don't know if she will even agree."

"Thanks for telling me; that does explain a few things." Xian's guess had been correct. Chen had spent the night with Anna. It also explained some of the tension between them on the return trip. There might be hope for Xian yet.

Moments later, Anna returned with the doctor on duty. He

looked over Chen's chart, noting the mild concussion.

"Mr. Xiao, I'm Dr. Li. How are you feeling?"

Chen eyed the doctor with mild suspicion. Who else was out to get him?

"Other than a mild headache, I'm not doing too bad. When will I be able to leave the hospital?"

Referencing the medical chart he carried in his arms, the doctor hemmed and hawed.

"Tomorrow evening at the earliest. We would like to have you under observation for at least twenty-four hours after an accident, especially when a concussion is involved."

Xian eyed the doctor with suspicion as well. Something felt off.

"What was your name again, doctor?" Xian moved closer to the bed, getting a good look at the man in the white lab coat. "Dr. Li, was it?" He wanted to get a look at the man's hospital ID.

Fidgeting, the man pulled his phone from his pocket.

"Sorry, I must take this call," he mumbled as he hurriedly left the room.

"Anna, where did you find the doctor?" Xian watched the door close behind the man.

"He was at the nurses' station inquiring about Chen. I figured it must have been his physician," Anna answered in a concerned tone.

Chen and Xian looked at one another and Chen began trying to remove the IV.

"What's going on?" Anna asked as Xian moved to help Chen.

"Something's fishy. I've played better doctors in my TV dramas." Chen managed to get the needle removed. Xian helped Chen sit on the edge of the bed. "I'm not staying in this hospital another minute if I can help it."

"Let's take you to Anna's apartment and call Dr. Lin. I trust the security there better than at your place Chen. You can have the other guest room. I'm staying in one already."

Anna and Chen both gave Xian calculating looks. This was the first Anna heard about this. It was Xian's apartment. How could she say no? Chen wondered if Xian was already trying to make moves on Anna himself.

The surly nurse came back into the room prepared to evict Xian and Anna; she was none too pleased to find Chen unplugged from the IV and looking for his clothes.

"Just what do you think you're doing, Mr. Xiao? You should be in bed resting."

"Sorry, ma'am, please get my discharge papers ready. I won't be staying any longer."

"One moment, Mr. Xiao, let me get your doctor."

"Nurse, I don't want to talk to Dr. Li again," Chen replied emphatically.

"Who is Dr. Li?" The confusion on the nurse's face confirmed their suspicions.

"A Dr. Li came in and told me that I wouldn't be allowed to leave the hospital until tomorrow evening. I also wouldn't be allowed my phone during my stay. I have a private physician that will finish my care. My assistant will give you the information to send my records to him."

"Mr. Xiao, I must protest. Who is your physician?"

"Dr. Lin Longwei is my physician."

"**THE** Dr. Lin?" The nurse blanched. "I will have your discharge paperwork ready in a few moments."

"Thank you," Chen said as he grabbed the clothes Huang Hu handed him.

"I'll be outside," Anna said as Chen started dressing.

"Let's get you out of here. That was not a real doctor; I would bet you anything." Xian helped Chen put his shirt on.

———

Dr. Li stepped into a room down the hall, a well-dressed woman was lying in bed and a middle-aged man sat in a chair next to the bed.

"I informed Mr. Xiao that he would have to stay until at least Tuesday night and he isn't allowed phone access due to his concussion. During the night, I will administer the drug to his IV. Where are we transferring him once he is unconscious?"

"I will get that information to you shortly. My associate will make sure you have the address and your payment."

"Yes, ma'am." Dr. Li bowed and left the room.

"He will be a loose end. Are you okay taking care of him as

well? You did a great job with the accident. We are getting closer to our goal."

"I'm sorry about your car. I'm quite impressed with the number of shady people you know," Scott commented.

"They've come in handy over the years. I didn't get where I am today just with my good looks and acting. After what they did to me at the awards, I will get my revenge." Li Ming looked at the door, she would need Dr. Li to sign her discharge pages before she had Scott dispose of him.

章

Chapter 46

Dr. Lin met the group in the lobby of the apartment building. Xian cleared him with the receptionists and added him to the guest list for the apartment.

"Can you please have the head of security report to the apartment? We may have a situation," Xian spoke quietly to the woman behind the desk. He kept his voice low so Anna and Chen couldn't hear him.

"Certainly, Mr. Wei. Will the morning be okay or do you need him tonight?" she asked, obviously concerned.

"Morning will be fine. It is rather late now and we need to get some rest."

Xian joined Dr. Lin, Anna and Chen at the elevator. Huang Hu and Wu Feng bowed slightly to them.

"We'll take the next car up. Mr. Wei, I have my key card. Is there anything more you need tonight?"

"No, Wu Feng. I believe we are good for the night," Xian said as he stepped into the car.

Silence, no one spoke on the ride up. Dr. Lin hummed in appreciation upon entering the apartment, it was an impressive residence. Suitable for a man of Wei Xian's status. The fact he had all but given Anna the apartment spoke volumes.

"Where is Mr. Xiao going to be staying?" Dr. Lin asked. "He needs to lay down soon; he's had a rough day."

"Take a right and go down the hall. It's the first bedroom off the sitting area. Huang Hu should have brought what he needed for a few days," Xian said. He was glad he had decided to stay so Anna wasn't alone with Chen.

"Mr. Xiao, let's get you checked out. Your records show it is just a mild concussion and some bruising. I want to see how extensive the bruising is so I know if we need to keep a close eye on it." Dr. Lin motioned for Chen to proceed him to his room.

"I'll come and check on you in a few moments, Chen," Anna said. "Let me put my stuff in my room and give Dr. Lin a chance to check you over."

Chen looked over his shoulder at Anna as he walked down the hall. Another plan to woo Anna had failed, this time pretty spectacularly. Now he was staying at Xian's apartment with Anna and Xian; this was not how he envisioned the week. At least he was here and Xian wasn't alone with Anna.

Xian walked into the living room and settled on one of the couches. He figured it was best to wait for Dr. Lin to give him an idea of how Chen was doing. That fake doctor at the hospital had him concerned. It was time to do some serious investigating. First, a hit-and-run accident sent Chen to the hospital, though it wasn't severe. Second, a questionable doctor checked on Chen, telling him he would have to stay in the hospital until after their meeting and no phone access to boot. It was all too fishy.

Huang Hu and Wu Feng came into the living room, waiting to hear what Dr. Lin had to say.

"Wu Feng, we need to start an investigation of our own if the police aren't of any help. Tomorrow we need to check on Anna's case and see if they plan to investigate Chen's accident. See if the hospital has footage of that doctor that came to Chen's room. Something isn't right—one last item on that to-do list. Find out where Li Ming is. I suspect she may have had a hand in all of this."

"Certainly, sir." Wu Feng bowed to Xian.

"Sir, I would also like to help. I have a few resources that may be of some help," Huang Hu chimed in. "It was my employer that was injured."

"Thank you. It means a lot that you care enough to help Chen, Huang Hu."

"Mr. Xiao has been good to me; I want to repay his kindness somehow. Helping find the responsible parties is the best I can do right now." Huang Hu bowed as well.

Dr. Lin walked into the living room at that moment.

"Chen is fine. What the hospital sent was probably accurate. He seems to have a mild concussion and does have some bruising but nothing we should have to worry about too much. Chen's been up long enough; he must rest for at least a day. I heard he was supposed to have a meeting at the studio tomorrow. He shouldn't go. Rest is what he needs right now," Dr. Lin said.

"It's okay, Dr. Lin. I had planned to go in place of Chen. Huang Hu has sent me the documents for the meeting; I may be able to negotiate an even better deal for Anna. Chen has focused on modeling and acting, so he hasn't kept up on his business training. I believe I can negotiate a better price for her scripts, and with the movie winning seven of the ten awards it was nominated for, it's now worth more than what they've offered."

"Anna's lucky to have you on her side," Dr. Lin observed.

"Actually, I'm lucky to have her in my life. Anna is an exceptional woman," Xian mused, thinking about the scripts she was pitching to the studio. Xian had briefly looked them over, and they had the potential to be as good, if not better than *The Lost Prince*. Anna deserved more and he would fight to get it for her. Chen was right, Anna needed to come back while they were filming. He would be happy if she didn't leave at all; he would gladly gift her the apartment if it meant she wouldn't go.

"Dr. Lin," Anna called from the hallway.

"In the living room Anna," Dr. Lin answered.

"Dr., how is Chen doing?" Anna inquired. She wanted to know before she went to say good night to Chen. She figured if there were any rules he needed to follow, she might have more leverage to get him to stick to them.

"He will be just fine. He should rest for at least twenty-four hours. Try to keep the excitement to a minimum, so tomorrow's meeting is off-limits to him.

"I figured as much," Anna said in a resolute tone. She would make sure that Chen behaved and rested. "I'm going to go and tuck him into bed for the night."

Anna left the living room, stopping by the kitchen where she grabbed a glass of water to put by Chen's bed for the night. She pulled a bottle of water from the fridge and sat it on the counter so she could grab it on her way back to her room. Walking across the sitting room, she heard Chen talking to someone.

"No, I'm fine. I will be staying with Xian for a few days until I'm back on my feet. Dr. Lin doesn't want me to stay alone...you don't have to come and see me. I'm fine, honest." Chen continued to try convincing whomever it was that he didn't need to have a visit from them.

"I will call you tomorrow and let you know how I'm doing. Have a good night." Chen disconnected the call.

Anna peeked her head in the room saying, "Up for a short visit?"

"For you, always." Chen smiled, then winced.

"I brought you some water. I hope it helps a bit. Did Dr. Lin give you anything for the headache?"

"No, he said that medication wasn't a good idea with a concussion. Rest and fluids are what the doctor called for." Chen laughed at his joke and winced again.

After handing Chen the glass of water, Anna sat down on the edge of the bed.

"I didn't think my trip would take so many unexpected twists and turns. Seeing you like this almost makes me regret coming to China. I feel like it's all my fault."

"Are you kidding? I wouldn't have had it any other way. I waited four years to get to see you in person, finally. You surprised me in so many ways, all good. Tomorrow I can't go with you. Will it be okay if Xian takes my place?" Chen looked hurt to concede to stay at the apartment, but with his injury it was best that he not push himself.

"I'm sure Xian will do fine with Mr. Shun. Guess you won't get to see the new suit I purchased for the meeting." Anna gave a mock sigh of regret.

"New suit? You had better stop by my room to let me see before you leave or I'll be seriously put out." Chen mock scowled in return, though Anna wasn't so sure his scowl was as playful as her sigh.

"Your wish is my command." Bowing to Chen, Anna winked.

"Okay, you scamp, I'm tired. Get out and get some sleep yourself." Chen yawned to confirm his statement.

"I'm going. Sleeping in a strange bed will be difficult again.

This is the fourth in as many days. I can't wait to get home to my bed."

"Perhaps someday I will sleep in your bed like you got to sleep in mine," Chen said and gave Anna a cheeky grin.

Walking to the door, Anna looked over her shoulder. "You just never know. Good night, dear."

"Good night, Anna," Chen called after her.

Heading along the hall to her bedroom, Anna heard Xian and Dr. Lin speaking in the living room.

"I don't think it was an accident. Chen's injuries were enough to put him in the hospital for a night. That odd man who claimed to be Chen's doctor also raised warning flags. There was something very suspicious about his behavior. That and telling Chen he couldn't have contact with anyone for 24 hours was also very odd. It isn't adding up," Xian said as he paced the area by the couches. The floors in the apartments have been getting extra wear and tear the last few days.

Dr. Lin sat on the couch looking pensive.

"I'll check with friends at the hospital and see if I can find anything on my end. At least he is here and safe now. I am also prescribing a good night's sleep for both you and Anna. It's almost midnight."

"Yeah, we have an important meeting tomorrow. A lot is riding on it. I'm going to tell Anna good night. Would you like me to see you out?"

"Thanks, Xian, but I know my way. I'll stop in tomorrow and check on Chen. We need to keep any excitement limited as much as possible," Dr. Lin said as he shook Xian's hand. "Get to bed. Dr.'s orders."

"Yes, sir." Xian smiled as he pulled the doctor in for an unexpected hug. "Thank you for caring for the two people who mean the most to me."

"You never have to thank me for caring for Chen; I owe him that much...and more." Dr. Lin headed for the foyer. Anna ducked down the hall before he could see that she had been eavesdropping.

Xian cared for her. She had suspected, but what he said to Dr. Lin confirmed it. Now what to do? For starters, get through the meeting tomorrow, the party Friday and the gala on Saturday. Once she was home, she would have time to sort through the conflicting emotions that plagued her.

"There you are, Xian. I was just going to bed. I wanted to say good night and thank you," Anna said upon entering the living room.

"For what?" Xian looked perplexed.

"For everything you've done for me. For one, letting me take over your penthouse apartment. And taking me on two major shopping trips in one week is a miracle," Anna laughed.

"I would do that and so much more, Anna." Xian stepped closer to her, giving her a comforting hug and a kiss on her forehead. "Go get some sleep. Tomorrow's a big day. Did you need to get your laptop set up for the meeting?"

"I won't have time. Do you have one I can use for about half an hour to transfer some files?"

"Sure, I'll have Wu Feng put it in your office; you can use it in the morning. The password is Chandra," he cringed slightly when he said it.

"Xian, are you sure?" Anna touched his cheek, seeing a glimmer of pain.

"Yes. Now, go to bed. I'll be at the other end of the apartment if you need anything."

Anna turned and walked back to her room, closing the doors. She put her suitcase on the couch to get a pair of pajamas. Perhaps the ones Xian had bought her?

Opening the bag, Anna rifled through the clothes she found neatly folded. Tucked under several of the outfits was a pair of men's pajamas. After pulling them out, Anna held them up and recognized them after a moment. They were the ones Chen had worn the night before.

Holding them up to her face she inhaled deeply; Chen's scent filled her nostrils. Sitting on the edge of the bed, the tears began falling and wouldn't stop. Carefully putting the pajamas back in the suitcase, she dug around and found the set Xian had purchased for her. Tears still streaming, she went into the bathroom to change and wash her face.

Inhaling deeply through her nose and exhaling with a sigh, she used a meditation technique she had learned with her friends Jeff and Debra to help calm her down. Finally, after using the breathing technique several times, the tears abated. She needed sleep; that would help, right?

Changed and face washed, Anna crawled into bed. She had grabbed her tablet from her messenger bag before slipping between the sheets. Opening one of the streaming services, she found one of the series Chen had acted in and started watching. It had always worked at home to calm her; perhaps it would work here.

Her eyes slid shut sooner than she guessed and much needed sleep took her.

———

Back at the hospital, there was an uproar. The body of a middle-aged man was found in the room Xiao Chen had been in. His head tilted at an unnatural angle. The nurse who had begrudgingly signed Chen out was trembling in the doctor's lounge. She recognized the body; the man who claimed to be Dr. Li. If something like that happened to him, was she also in danger? Perhaps they didn't realize she had been the one to release Mr. Xiao from the hospital. She had been paid handsomely to keep it quiet until late the next day. Was it worth it?

———

A vase shattered as it hit the wall. Li Ming had been thwarted again.

"What do you mean he's gone?" The shriek must have been heard several rooms away.

"When I accompanied Dr. Li to administer the sedative, the room was empty. No one has any idea where he went," the gruff voice that replied was none too happy either.

"All of my plans are completely down the tubes again! That woman will not leave China alive if she keeps interfering in my plans."

"Hey, she leaves with me, remember? Anna's mine!" The maniacal look in his eyes even frightened Li Ming. He was more unstable than even she was. This partnership would either get her what she wanted or end her. Either way, unless she could have Chen, life wouldn't be worth living anyway.

"There is always the party on Friday," she mused. Not sure if she would even be allowed to attend. The studio hadn't extended an invitation to the wrap party. Her agent had informed her that she was on probation pending a board meeting. It was all that Americans' fault. If she thought her life was difficult so far, she hadn't seen anything yet...

—-

章

Chapter 47

Morning came with the smell of bacon. *Bacon? Did she actually smell bacon?*
Pulling on the fluffy robe Xian had picked for her, Anna stuffed her feet in fuzzy slippers and ambled down the hall to the kitchen. The sight that greeted her made her regret not grabbing her phone. Xian was wearing an apron and finishing cooking the bacon that had woken her.

"So, a chef as well as a business mogul?" Anna sat at the counter to watch Xian work.

"Not so much, but I can at least prepare breakfast for a pretty woman." Xian saluted her with his tongs.

"Would you like some help?" Anna grimaced when she saw how well cooked the bacon was. Crispy wasn't even close to describing the pork flesh. But to give him some credit, it wasn't wholly burnt either.

Laughing, Anna got up and walked into the kitchen. "Is there another apron around here somewhere?" she asked as she started going through drawers, looking for another apron to use.

"I believe I have one here you can use." Xian walked to the far counter and shook out another piece of fabric. The red plaid fabric had black words printed on the front, Kiss the Cook.

"So, did you pick that out just for me? Guess it will give you a good excuse to kiss me?" Anna teased Xian.

Xian looked flustered for a few moments until he saw what the apron said.

"Wu Feng picked it up. You had me confused. Kissing does sound good, though."

"How about we get food finished and not worry about lip-locking."

Anna checked to see what foodstuffs were in the fridge. It

looked like there was a carton of eggs, a few vegetables and some cold rice. There was enough to make rolled omelets or fried rice and fancy scrambled eggs; there were options. She pulled the carton of eggs and veggies from the futuristic refrigerator. Heck, it was one of those you could watch TV on while you cooked.

Xian looked on with curiosity; he wondered what Anna had in mind. It was his turn to sit on the stool at the counter while Anna flitted around the kitchen. Some of the tools took her a bit to locate, but she found everything they needed to finish the meal.

Anna finally settled on rolled omelets. She could make a more western-style breakfast another morning; she had too much to do this morning to get fancy. Anna would go shopping for what was needed or create a shopping list for Huang Hu or Wu Feng to pick up for her. She was looking forward to having her own assistant, she was even tempted to contact Lin Bolin to see if he would be available to return with her.

Anna also found a couple of apples, peeled and cut them up, adding them to the plate with the extra crispy bacon and the rolled omelets. She set a plate in front of Xian and waited nervously while he took a bite.

"This is fabulous, Anna. Not the bacon, but the omelet. It's as good as I've had here in one of the better restaurants."

"Xian, flattery will get you almost everywhere." Anna winked as she dug through the cabinets, looking for a tray. "Hey Xian, is there a breakfast tray here somewhere? I figured our invalid is entitled to at least one meal in bed."

"Yeah, one should be in the bottom cabinet next to the fridge." Xian started to get up and get it for her.

"Just sit your butt back in that chair. I've got it." Anna bent down and rummaged in the cabinet. There it was, tucked in the back.

Tray loaded with juice and his plate of food, Anna carefully balanced the breakfast as she carried it to Chen's room. Using her foot, she tapped on the door to see whether or not Chen was awake. After a few moments, a groggy "Come in" let Anna know he was at least conscious.

"Breakfast is ready, sleeping beauty."

"Hmph, do I have to wake up?" Chen grumbled as he pulled the duvet over his head.

"Do you want the breakfast I just made for you?" Anna's patience was struggling a little. She had work she should be doing but had taken time to make him food. How about that for gratitude?

"You made it? I thought Xian cooked and his cooking scares me at times." Chen peaked out from under the covers.

"You're safe for the moment. I made this, well, all of it but the bacon. Xian was a little enthusiastic while he was making it."

"Xian means well, but his cooking skills leave a bit to be desired. Chandra did the cooking if they ate at home. I know he can cut up fruit and make instant ramen."

"Isn't that something like bachelor chow? Instant ramen is huge for college kids and young single people or broke couples in the States." Anna snickered. "I've eaten a few packages in my day."

Sitting up, Chen arranged the pillows to support him while eating.

"Okay, sir, you are not an invalid, so I will leave you with your food. I have a load of work to finish before the meeting. Just shout if you need anything. Are you good?" Anna checked the tray to ensure there were chopsticks, a napkin and a small fruit fork for his apple.

"I should be good, Anna; go eat so you can get ready for that meeting. I know Xian will be a big help," Chen grumbled as he took his first bite of omelet. "This is delicious. You made this?"

Anna rolled her eyes. "Why do you two make it sound like I'm a horrible cook? I cook for myself quite a bit. There are few good Asian restaurants near my home and I eat more Eastern cuisine than Western. It agrees with my digestive issues much better."

"Good to know. I'm good. Go eat." Chen threatened to throw an apple slice at her.

Laughing, Anna went back to the counter and sat next to Xian. Glancing at his plate, she was shocked to see it was nearly clean.

"Were you starved?"

"Well, not starved, but quite hungry. That omelet was just the ticket. I'm looking forward to that Western-style breakfast you mentioned."

"I'm on the fence if I want to make French toast or pancakes. I'm leaning towards French toast. I doubt that is something you eat much of here."

"Come to think of it; I don't think I've ever had French toast." Xian looked thoughtful.

Anna stuffed a piece of the omelet in her mouth, watching Xian wracking his brain for any memory of eating French toast. She had missed this kind of interaction. It had been five years since she had made breakfast for a handsome man, let alone two of them.

"Well, as I have a ton of work, you're on dish duty," Anna said as she pulled off her apron and hung it in the pantry.

"That I believe I can handle." Xian smiled as he gathered the plates.

Anna gave him a peck on the cheek. "Thanks, Xian, you're a sweetheart." She headed for the office across the sitting room.

Walking into the room, Anna felt overwhelmed by the number of boxes and packages strewn over the desk and floor. Good grief, did they buy all this yesterday? Her week had turned into one giant blur. So much had happened in such a short amount of time. When Anna got home, it would all catch up to her if it didn't happen before.

Anna moved a few boxes to find a MacBook Pro sitting on the desk.

"Hey Xian, is this MacBook Pro yours?"

"Yeah, that's mine. Remember the password?"

"Yeah, I got it. Thanks for the help." Anna opened the laptop and hit the power button. She would let it boot up while she ran to her room for her messenger bag with her backup drives and thumb drives.

Anna was ridiculously cautious about her files after writing a thriller that dealt with espionage. The scripts she planned on handing over today weren't on her laptop, they were on an encrypted thumb drive.

The goal was to check the script files and ensure she had all of her edits completed. If these two projects were significant, she might switch to script writing and just write novels as a hobby.

Returning to the office, Anna found the laptop on the login screen. Typing in the password Xian had told her, it opened on a scenic background.

"Hey Xian, are you in love with the wallpaper on your laptop?" Anna called.

"No, it's pretty generic. Why?"

"Just wait and see." Anna smiled as she pulled her phone out, looking through some of her more scenic photos from home. One of those would make a fitting wallpaper. Then it would remind him of her.

After she was finished playing with Xian's wallpaper, Anna plugged in the thumb drive with the scripts. Typing in her password, the files opened and looked good. Scrolling through the pages, she found the key spots she needed to change. Making her quick edits she saved the files again without password protection this time. She would throw in the thumb drive with what the studio was paying for the scripts.

Anna was wrapped up in what she was doing and didn't notice Xian leaning against the doorjamb watching her. Wu Feng was out picking up Xian's suit for the meeting, he planned to match Anna's style. If he had his way, she would be making considerably more for the scripts she was selling than Chen had told him they planned to pay.

Leave it to an actor to try and negotiate something this important. Anna should receive, at the minimum, a million more. If this studio didn't pay what he had in mind, several studios would jump at the chance. Especially with Xian's company backing them. He planned to finance these projects, so Anna would need to be involved.

After watching Anna for some time, Xian finally cleared his throat to alert her to his presence.

"Anna, it's about time and you must get ready for the meeting. I have a hairstylist that should be here in about thirty minutes. Jump in the shower if you're ready and she will do your hair for the meeting. I believe your minimal makeup look will be beneficial for this meeting. Oh, which color tie did you plan to wear?"

Anna mentally ran through the ten ties she had purchased. The robin's egg blue shirt with navy accents and the navy tie with white accents would go well with her suit.

"I'm wearing a light blue shirt with a navy and white tie. Don't you think the outfit will make me look striking with the red in my hair?"

"Any of the color combinations we picked would make you look striking. I think your hair will mostly be up in an elaborate French twist with some loose strands."

"Xian, will you be my personal stylist? I could never come up with such an impressive look. Guess it comes from being the head honcho at a large media firm."

"Speaking of being head honcho, would you be willing to come with me to the office later? I have some work I need to get done this afternoon and Chen needs his rest. You've seen Chen in action; now it's my turn. Do you have work you need to finish? Bring my laptop with you and you can use it for whatever you need. You can get your computer started tonight." Xian secretly liked this plan. Perhaps he would impress her.

"Really? I can come and see your office?"

Anna was quite excited about the prospect of seeing the empire that Xian was king of. She had dug to see if she could learn a bit more about her mysterious benefactor. Xian was quite reclusive. There was little information about him other than he had a family that wasn't close. Having come from a large family, she had difficulty fathoming what it would be like to have such a small family.

"Absolutely, would you like your own office or think you can work in mine? There may be interruptions."

"Don't go to any special trouble. Just stick me in a corner with my earbuds and you'd be amazed at what I can tune out. When Kyle and I lived in our tiny house I worked from home and he was there most of the day; I became good at tuning out distractions."

"Well, I hope I'm not that kind of distraction," Xian teased.

"No, you're fine. I'm excited to hang out at your office for a bit. I feel bad for keeping you away from your work so much."

"I've needed the break. I can't remember the last time I took time off. Besides, it's only been two days. I've already warned them I would be in and out this week. We don't have anything pressing."

"Okay, I'm still feeling guilty about taking over your apartment. How will I go back to my shack in the woods?" Anna sighed dramatically.

"Shack in the woods? Is it that same shack Chen showed me photos of? Heck, I'd be tempted to trade you. You can have this apartment and I'll take your house."

"Not sure you would want the roommate you would inherit with it. He can be a tad cranky at times."

Xian stopped and gave Anna a searching glance. Roommate? He hadn't heard about any roommate. Could it be another rival? It's bad enough Chen was competing with him for Anna's attention.

"Roommate? I didn't know you had one." His voice cracked a bit. Damn, he couldn't let on that he was jealous.

"Yeah, twenty-two pounds of crabby fur." Anna laughed as she pulled out her phone and found a photo of Si Ming. Showing Xian, she missed the look of relief that crossed his face.

"That is quite the handsome roommate. I'm not sure if he would approve of me," Xian said sagely. Growing up, he never had a pet; his parents didn't believe someone of his status should have pets.

"Hard to say. Si Ming has a mind of his own. He's a Maine coon, and they are a unique breed. I had Bengals years ago and they weren't your run-of-the-mill alley cats either. They're a mix between an Asian leopard cat and a domestic. Beautiful cats with some interesting quirks. Si Ming has been a lifesaver, however. He kept me together after Kyle passed." Anna's face clouded over for a few moments, the memories pulling at scabs on still healing wounds.

"Well, I hope I get to meet your honored roommate sometime. Hopefully, he will approve." Xian looked at his watch. "Anna, you have about thirty minutes to finish your shower."

"How little you know me. I can be in and out of a shower and dressed in fifteen minutes. Granted, the hair is still wet, but I'm fast. Unless I've planned to take a leisurely shower, I get in and get out. The reason for that is a long story, perhaps when I've had a few ask me. It's funny for sure."

Anna closed the laptop and stuffed it into her messenger bag.

"Xian, can I ask a favor? It's not a small one." She stepped closer to Xian.

"You don't even have to ask. Just let me know what you need." Anna's heart clenched when she saw how genuinely he felt those sentiments.

Holding up the silver thumb drive she asked, "Can you keep this with you? These are the scripts and the treatment for the follow-up movie to *The Lost Prince*. I can't afford to have them disappear or get damaged. I seem to have someone gunning for me and if they get that key, it's a year's worth of work totally down the toilet."

Holding his hand out, Anna placed the thumb drive on his palm and he curled his fingers around it.

"Please guard this with your life. Oh, good grief, did I just say that? How overly dramatic can I be? Don't guard it with your life; just take good care of it, please."

Xian smiled as he tucked the drive into his pants pocket. He would genuinely guard that thumb drive with his life if necessary, but he wouldn't tell her that.

章

Chapter 48

Anna emerged from her room; the dark pinstripe suit was very contemporary. She felt powerful. The stylist had created a sleek French twist with her hair. Xian had suggested having some loose tendrils, but Anna had nixed the idea.

Xian had even picked a pair of chic heels that matched the suit better than anything she could have chosen. The man had impeccable taste, that's for sure. Anna couldn't get over how much her style had changed since meeting the gregarious man. As much as he avoided being in the public eye, he was exceptionally outgoing.

It wasn't hard to break past her anti-social barriers and view the world differently with his help. Her feelings for Xian became more complicated as her time with him continued. Her heart was torn in two directions. She still loved Chen, but was it romantic love or a love for a close dear friend? No time for this puzzle right now; they had a meeting to attend.

Anna knocked on Chen's door. She wanted to get any last details he could give her to help with the meeting.

"Come in," came the drowsy voice.

"Did I wake you?" Anna asked with concern. He was supposed to be resting.

Chen sat up quickly when he saw Anna. Dressed in business attire, she looked like an entirely different woman again. Anna had so many sides and he wanted to spend the rest of his life discovering them. One of the drawbacks of developing their friendship online was that he hadn't seen her complexity.

"No, I will probably go back to sleep once you leave. Xian was here a bit ago going over the details for the meeting. You'll own the studio before long if he has his way." A small smile quirked Chen's mouth. Xian had been persistent in asking questions Chen hadn't even considered when they had begun the negotiations. He almost felt bad for Mr. Shun; he had no idea what would be hitting him.

Anna tamped down the urge to go and hug Chen, he looked so dejected at the moment. She knew he'd been invested in this deal because he would star in the movies. Now that he was injured, he would be relegated to the sidelines for the duration.

"I want you to rest while I'm gone. You have to be better by Friday so I can attend that wrap party with you. The dress I picked will knock their socks off."

"Heck, you almost knocked my socks off. You're going to knock them dead on Friday. I may need to hire bodyguards to keep the other actors at bay. Oh, and I will have a surprise for you Friday as well. Just remember you liked me first, okay?" Chen hinted.

"What are you up to now? You realize the surprises I've had the last week have all but driven me to drink, right?"

Groaning, Chen fell back on the bed, grabbing his chest. The overdramatic death throes were so cheesy that Anna couldn't help but laugh.

Anna rolled her eyes. "Didn't you try this one on me already?"

"You wound me so deeply, Anna. But to be fair, you do have a point. My track record has been pretty abysmal. I'm hoping Friday makes up for all of it."

Grabbing one of the pillows from the bed, Anna chucked it at Chen's head. "If this one goes sideways, you're not allowed to give me a surprise ever again, got it?" Anna's mock anger made Chen chuckle. Good, she was loosening up. When she had walked into the room earlier it had felt like someone in her family had died, she was so tense and uptight.

"Sorry, no promises. I'm going to get it right one of these days." Chen plastered a cheesy grin on his face.

Anna checked her watch and saw that she needed to meet Xian in the lobby.

"I need to go, Chen, any last suggestions?"

"Just be yourself. You've won over so many people here already. Mr. Shun is already one of your biggest fans and I think you'll do great. Come here before you go." Chen crooked his finger at her.

Anna walked around the bed to where Chen was propped up with a pile of pillows. Chen grabbed her hand and pulled her down in his lap when she was close enough. Looking at her deeply in the eyes, he wanted to keep her like this and make time stand still forever.

He kissed her on the forehead, careful not to muss her hair or suit. Chen held her there a few moments more before letting her get to her feet.

"Knock 'em dead," he said as she walked from the room in a daze.

Damn you, Chen, Anna thought to herself. Why did he have to pull that stunt right before her big meeting? Now his upcoming surprise was all she could think about.

When Anna reached the lobby, Xian noticed something off.

"Anna, are you alright? Did something happen?"

"I'm fine. I just had a nagging issue on my mind and got distracted. Let's go sell some scripts." Anna regrouped and pushed Chen from her mind for the time being. She needed to concentrate on this meeting.

Back in the apartment, Chen was on the phone.

"Are you sure you can make it Friday? I know you've been anxious to meet her, and I figured it would be a great opportunity. Otherwise, you might have to wait. She's on her way to negotiate with the studio on the two scripts I told you about and the sequel to *The Lost Prince*." Chen sat and listened to the voice on the other end of the phone for a few moments.

"You want to be involved with these new scripts? I know she would be ecstatic. I believe you can ask her on Friday. One of the key negotiations was that she would have a say in who is part of the projects. Li Ming is banned from any of her projects, so you don't have to worry about her. Besides, she seems to have developed an obsession with me now so you're off the hook."

The conversation lasted for a while longer; Chen was glad he could make the arrangements that would give Anna the best surprise. Hopefully, he wouldn't regret it.

章

Chapter 49

Wu Feng pulled into a parking spot at the studio headquarters and jumped out to open Anna's door. Xian stepped out from his side and walked around to take Anna's bag.

"Xian, you shouldn't be carrying my bag." Anna glanced around to make sure no one was paying attention. "You're a company president, not my porter."

"I'd rather keep this in my possession. Important documents are in this bag. I'd have Wu Feng carry it, but he is dealing with the car, so I will hang on to it until he returns. At this point, I only trust Huang Hu or Wu Feng to handle your possessions. Too much has happened this last week." Xian offered his elbow for Anna to take.

"Well, since you put it that way." She took the proffered elbow. Anna still couldn't believe her luck. She had been escorted by two of the most handsome men she had ever met. Her confidence was at an all-time high.

Walking through the glass doors of the office building, they were met by Mr. Shun's assistant. "This way, Mr. Wei and Ms. Cassidy. Mr. Shun is waiting for you in the conference room."

Following the young man, he led Xian and Anna in a different direction from how she had gone with Chen last week. She didn't have to wonder long about why they weren't taken to the same small conference room as before. Ten men were sitting around the table waiting for them. Anna could see all the middle-aged to older men chatting around the glass table.

Xian noticed Anna stumble slightly. He glanced at the conference room and realized that she must be daunted by the group of men around the table. Taking a few moments to assess the situation, Xian was relieved to know all the men. He had dealt with all of them throughout the years and there was only one he wasn't thrilled to see. That one could make trouble for Anna and he wouldn't allow it.

Arriving at the door to the room, the assistant bowed slightly to Xian and Anna. "Please go ahead."

Entering the room, Xian was in his element. He dealt with meetings like this weekly. This was a pleasure because these were all, with the one exception, men he admired when he dealt with them. Walking into the room, he smiled at the men with genuine pleasure.

Anna wasn't as calm about the situation. She forced a smile as a fine tremor shook her body. Only Xian would have noticed it; she did her best to control it so the gentlemen before her wouldn't see.

"Good afternoon, gentlemen," Xian started. "It's a pleasure to see all of you."

"Mr. Wei, it is indeed a pleasure to see you." Mr. Shun stood and motioned for Xian and Anna to take the two chairs at the head of the table. "It's unfortunate that Mr. Xiao couldn't be with us. I know he is very invested in this deal as well."

"Mr. Xiao has entrusted me to represent Ms. Cassidy and himself in the negotiations; I hope that is acceptable to all of you?" Xian assisted Anna to her seat.

"Mr. Wei, I'm sure we have all worked with you and your company. I believe I speak for all of us when I say we are honored to have you working on this deal with us. There were rumors that you plan to invest heavily in these projects if all goes well." Mr. Shun raised an eyebrow at Xian, wondering if it wasn't because of the striking woman sitting by his side.

Anna Cassidy took him by surprise once again. When he had last seen her at the awards, Anna had lost her temper, not that he could have blamed her after the behavior of Li Ming. The awards had been a fiasco for her and he had heard there had been more mischief when she returned to Beijing. Chen may not have known it, but Mr. Shun had a few individuals keeping an eye out for Anna. She would be a significant investment and he wanted to protect it.

Today, Anna had a slightly shell-shocked look about her, not that he could blame her. Talk about throwing her in the lion's den. All these gruff men may be daunting to her—time to put her at ease. Knowing Anna, she would have these men wrapped around her finger in no time.

"Ms. Cassidy, it is a great honor and pleasure to have you with us today. We look forward to working with you for some time if you're willing and Mr. Wei gets his way." Mr. Shun winked cheekily at Anna, helping to put her at ease.

"Mr. Shun, it is indeed a pleasure to see you again. I must apologize for the scene I caused at the award after-party. I believe you know the circumstances, but it doesn't excuse it." Anna stood and bowed to Mr. Shun.

Shocked, Mr. Shun sat down and reassessed the American. She had just hit a home run with that move. The other men had discussed that exact situation before Anna and Xian arrived. They had all agreed, with one exception, that Anna was goaded into the action she took and they couldn't blame her. There had been one dissenting voice Mr. Shun would prefer wasn't involved; but as he was on the board for a few more months, he didn't have much choice.

"Shall we begin?" Mr. Shun motioned to the assistant stationed at the door to bring the food in.

Over the next two hours Xian not only negotiated two million more on the royalties for the movie, but he also got an extra million for the three scripts–two that were written already and the third that Anna would have finished within nine months. Another crucial point that he negotiated was that Anna would have complete creative control over the scripts. She would have the final say on any changes or rewrites.

Anna appreciated Chen for getting this all started, but without Xian she wouldn't have been nearly as well compensated or have much say in her works. With the creative control he stipulated, she would have to be there for the filming. Xian had secretly discussed this with Mr. Shun earlier about including that part. Granted, it was self-indulgence on his and Chen's side; they wanted her to be there for the filming.

Anna leaned over and whispered to Xian, "Why am I getting so many concessions suddenly? Not that I'm complaining, just curious."

Xian smiled saying, "Perhaps because *The Lost Prince* was nominated for three more awards, one in the United States. I believe you're familiar with the Oscars. It's been nominated for Best Foreign Film."

"It's **WHAT**?" Anna squawked a little louder than she expected.

Mr. Shun and most of the executives smiled and chuckled. They had learned about the nominations that morning. He was impressed that Xian had the intel as well.

She was processing the information Xian had just imparted, leaving her in a daze for a few minutes. Well, one good thing had happened out of all the crap. Anna never expected to have the movie become such a big deal. It was humorous that she had to write a story that was made into a film in a foreign country to be nominated for an Oscar. She wondered if they would want her to attend those awards as well.

"So what you're saying is because the movie has been nominated for so many awards, it's worth more?"

"Pretty much, I would have been able to get you a good part of what we did accomplish without them, but it helped cement the creative control. Unfortunately, you will need to be here and on location when the studio begins shooting the new properties. They even discussed having you write a few television series and new movies."

"Hmm, I have a few ideas for a series, but that is something I've never tackled before. There's always a first time for everything. Now that I know, I can start putting some ideas together." Rummaging in her messenger bag, Anna pulled out one of her journal books, jotting a few notes that came to mind right then.

Mr. Shun looked on with interest. It looked like whatever Xian had said to her gave her some inspiration. He was invested in this writer now. With the amount of capital Wei Xian had insinuated he planned to invest in her future projects, how could they go wrong? It didn't exactly hurt that her first project for them had won seven awards. He had writers that didn't accomplish that after years of writing.

"Ms. Cassidy, are we ready to agree on the terms?" Grinning widely at the prospect of having Anna writing almost exclusively for the studio.

"I need to clarify one point. There shouldn't be an issue

with me continuing to write my novels, correct? You know how contracts work and I have one with my publisher that I need to fulfill. As for movie scripts, your studio is the only one I will be writing for until I have fulfilled my obligation. Then we can renegotiate." Anna paid close attention to the men around the table and gauged their willingness to agree to her stipulations.

Conferring with the others at the table, Mr. Shun nodded in acceptance.

"Then we have a deal." Standing, Anna offered her hand to her new partner. Mr. Shun gladly stood and took her hand, impressed with how Anna shook his hand, not too firm, but with good pressure.

"I look forward to a lucrative partnership." He bowed slightly to Anna, showing his gratitude and respect.

Returning the gesture, Anna made a slight bow to each executive. They would begin working on the timetable for the first project to begin. There would be preparations that would need to be made. While working with the studio, she would need to find a residence here in Beijing as a base of operations. A sneaky suspicion itched at her mind that Xian probably had an option in the works.

Making it clear that she had arrangements that would need to be made before she could begin, the executives were more than happy to put off filming until January of the following year. That would give Anna a month to get her affairs in order back in the States. They also need to start the paperwork allowing Anna to stay for extended periods in China. Xian had experience with the forms and processes as he had several employees from various countries who regularly worked for his company.

"If we have finished here, Ms. Cassidy and I have a pressing engagement we must attend to." Rising to his feet, he offered Mr. Shun his hand. "It's been a pleasure doing business with you, Mr. Shun. I'm sure we will have good fortune with this deal."

"Ms. Cassidy, when it comes time to renegotiate, please leave Mr. Wei at his office. He's too sharp for us poor old men." Anna barely contained the giggle that wanted to escape due to Mr. Shun's attempt at looking pitiful.

Giving Xian a sideways glance she replied, "Mr. Shun, I'm not sure I will leave home without him when I have any bargaining to do. His skills are invaluable. I plan on staying on his good side as long as possible."

A quiet snort came from her right. Anna had a feeling she was going to pay for that comment later.

"Ms. Cassidy, I will be your negotiator as long as you will have me." Xian winked surreptitiously at Anna. "Shall we go? We need to do much as you don't have long before you need to return to the States."

"Gentlemen, until we meet again." Bending slightly in another bow, Anna turned and left the room.

———

As soon as Xian and Anna had left the room, the one executive fighting against this deal began texting furiously. The response he received made him cringe. Someone's head would roll and if he wasn't cautious, it would be his. There wasn't much more he could do on his end; it was up to her to find an alternative.

章

Chapter 50

Floating on cloud nine, Anna was still reeling from the meeting results. "I can't believe they agreed to all of my concessions."

"And why wouldn't they? What we offered and what we requested weren't unreasonable. Besides, an opportunity to win more awards was a no-brainer for them. I'm glad we added the clause in that they would give you a housing allowance while you are in Beijing, though you won't need it. Why don't you just keep the penthouse? It's mine, and it's rarely used."

Stopping in her tracks, Anna gave Xian a dubious stare. "You have got to be kidding me. Your penthouse? Wouldn't that put you out?"

Rolling his eyes, she still had no clue of his net worth. If she realized he wasn't a millionaire but a billionaire, would she be so cavalier? "Trust me, Anna, it's not putting me out in the slightest. If you like it, please accept it as a gift."

"Xian, I can't accept that as a gift; it's too much."

"I insist. I'll feel relieved if you stay there with everything you've been through. The security will keep you safe." Xian took Anna's hand and continued, "You mean a lot to me and I would be devastated if something happened to you. Please, Anna, give me peace of mind and accept."

Anna's reasons to decline the apartment were smashed to bits by Xian's heartfelt plea. She let out a long sigh and said, "One condition, you're welcome to use it anytime. Oh, make that two conditions...I can do a little redecorating?"

"Certainly, make it your own. I realize it isn't your beautiful cabin in the woods, but it can be your oasis in the city." Using her hand as leverage, he pulled her close, wrapping his arms protectively around her. "If you gave me a chance, I would give you the world," he whispered into her hair, softly enough he hoped she wouldn't hear.

Melting into the hug, Anna caught part of what Xian whispered. Conflicted, perhaps she should decline his offer after all. Would this give him the wrong idea? No, she was going to accept graciously. She had turned down business propositions for most of her life because she felt she wasn't worthy. Now, she began to feel respected. She had worked hard to have this opportunity and she would grab it with both hands.

"Then, I accept." Grunting as Xian squeezed her after her answer. "Careful. I still need to breathe."

Releasing her, Xian took her hand and tucked it in the crook of his arm. He couldn't be happier. She had agreed to return and she would be safe in the apartment. As for Chen, they better give him the good news; he was probably stewing in the penthouse waiting for details.

"Who's going to break the news to Chen?"

"Let's wait until we get to your office and have some privacy. There are too many ears around here, and **YOU** may be fine with discussing my plans here in the open. I, however, am not. Especially after all that's happened in the last week."

"By all means, let's away to my castle, fair damsel," Xian said. Pulling Anna with him, Xian headed for the car and Wu Feng.

"So, can I contact Lin Bolin then? I would like to get him on board to help coordinate things over here while I'm getting everything arranged in the States. Speaking of which...would you and Chen be willing to be with me when I call Liz? She may blow a gasket because I'll live in Beijing for at least two years." Remembering how Liz had felt when Anna had gone on a short vacation by herself a few years before, she was dreading that call.

"Certainly. Hopefully, we can help her realize this is a huge opportunity for you." Reminding himself mentally to contact Liz and warn her not to give their conversations away. He had been in touch with Liz daily, filling her in on her mother's activities, especially since Anna had been so distracted lately.

"Oh, I have one huge question, though. What about Si Ming?" Turning to Xian with concern.

"Who is Si Ming?" A fit of jealousy tinging his voice

without his realizing it.

Quirking her eyebrow at his tone, Anna snickered while saying. "He's my four-legged furry roommate, remember? I'm sure I mentioned his name this morning. Will it be difficult to bring him with me while I live here? He's already neutered, so that shouldn't be an issue and he is up to date on his shots. I wonder how he will do moving into the city...though, he's a pretty independent feline."

A wave of relief washed over Xian when she reminded him of her furry companion. He felt stupid for his childish reaction to her requesting help to bring her support with her. "We can always see how he does. If he isn't happy with living in the penthouse, perhaps he could come and live at my estate. You would at least be able to visit him."

Xian's heart swelled when he saw the look of relief that flickered across Anna's face. If he had realized that was one of the only stumbling blocks to her agreeing to move to Beijing, he would have suggested the option sooner.

"Okay, now I'm excited. Do you think Chen will be well enough to celebrate tonight? Or should we wait until tomorrow to celebrate?" Excitement and anxiety warred with each other in Anna's psyche. Anything to try and distract her mind from the million-mile-a-minute ideas flooding her.

"Why don't we wait and see what Dr. Lin says when he checks on Chen this evening? Why don't we invite Dr. Lin to dine with us? He's done us a great service and has been a close friend to Chen and me for many years now."

"Certainly, can you make the arrangements? I am still making a shopping list for ingredients. I had planned to make a special dinner for us. I would like to invite Wu Feng and Huang Hu, as well as Dr. Lin and his wife and Lin Bolin. Would that be all right?" Mentally going over the menu she had in mind, deciding if they would like it or not.

Astonished by Anna's consideration for the assistants that made his and Chen's lives easier, he couldn't see any reason not to invite anyone she wanted. "Certainly, I don't see any reason you couldn't invite them. I'm sure Wu Feng would be happy to take you to a market so you can purchase any of the supplies you might need. Oh no! Another shopping trip." Xian made an expression of mock horror.

"Ha, nice try. I don't mind grocery shopping." Anna slapped Xian's shoulder. "You just feel like you need to tease me, don't you?"

"I love seeing you smile, so get used to it if it takes a little teasing." Winking at Anna, Xian noticed Wu Feng waiting for them outside the car. "Are we ready to head to the office?" Xian asked Wu Feng.

Opening the back door for Xian and Anna, he replied, "Certainly, sir. I hope the meeting went as planned."

"Even better. We'll fill you in on the drive. Oh, and Wu Feng, would you be willing to give Anna a lift to a market to do some shopping later? She has some plans and needs supplies."

Giving Anna a slight bow he said, "Certainly, Ms. Anna. Just give me an idea of what you will be looking for and I'll take you to a market that carries it."

Anna put her hand on Wu Feng's arm. "Please don't feel you need to bow to me; though I thank you for your consideration. I do have a request. Would you join us for a meal tomorrow night? I would like to make something special to celebrate."

Astonished at Anna's offer, Wu Feng took a moment before he replied. "Certainly, Ms. Anna. I would be honored. We will find the best ingredients available. Would tomorrow morning be okay for shopping? I can take you after I deliver Mr. Wei to the office. He is required for a few meetings tomorrow that he can't duck out on, or I suspect he would accompany you tomorrow."

"Tomorrow morning will work great. I'm sure the supplies I require won't be too difficult to find." Anna slid into the back seat of the luxury car and scooted across the backseat to make room for Xian. Would she ever get used to driving herself after this royal treatment?

——-

A dark SUV followed Xian's car as it traveled to his office. The message she had received wasn't what she wanted to hear. Now that bitch would be returning. Wei Xian was becoming a thorn in her side. He kept interfering and protecting the

American. Checking to see how her compatriot handled the situation, she noticed his white knuckles from his clenched fists. She would continue using this fool. His obsession blinded him to the fact that their antics were becoming more serious.

章

Chapter 51

Driving to Xian's office went quickly as they filled Wu Feng in on the meeting. Hearing that Anna would be living in Beijing for at least two years made him excited for Xian. It was a chance for Mr. Wei to woo her properly. Would there be a fight between Chen and his boss? Wu Feng needed to converse with Huang Hu about how to handle this.

Arriving at the headquarters of the Wei Group and leaning back to try and see the top of the building, Anna almost felt like she would tip over. "How many floors are there? I'm not sure I've been in one quite so tall before."

"It's only 65 floors. We had considered more, but for safety reasons we decided not to go any taller. There are television studios for several programs on different floors, as well as a recording studio and publishing company. I guess I never really explained how large my company was." Pride in what he had built was evident to Anna. "Once you return I'll ensure you get the full tour, though it may take a full day to see it all."

"So what you're saying is that if it's related to media, it's housed somewhere in this building?" Awe crept into Anna's voice.

"Something like that. We have a few other buildings that house the large printing presses for the magazines we publish and the books we print. The one media we don't have of our own is a movie studio; that's why I negotiated a contract with the studio to work with them."

"If you were trying to impress me, you've outdone yourself. Let's get to your office. We have some calls to make." She grabbed her bag from the back seat and waited for Xian to finish talking with Wu Feng.

Seeing Xian was finished talking with his assistant, Anna slung the strap of her bag over her shoulder. She made a mental list of the calls she would need to tackle immediately. After discussing it with Xian, Lin Bolin was one of the first calls she had to make.

Before anything else, they would need to call Chen. He deserved to hear the good news as his groundwork made it all possible. Hopefully, he'd gotten some rest. It should have been quiet in the penthouse and Huang Hu was going to deliver lunch to him.

Following Xian closely, Anna watched the people rushing about passing through a security checkpoint. "Xian, is there going to be an issue? I don't have my ID with me."

As an answer, Xian took Anna's hand and walked through the checkpoint. People slowed down and watched them walk through the lobby; she noticed whispers beginning to circulate. "Xian, we're causing a commotion," Anna said while trying to pull her hand away.

"So? What's your point? Let them talk. Besides, there are photos of us all over in the media from the awards. Our publications have some great photos I'll need to show you." He turned and smiled at her; it was easy to tell she wasn't used to being in the spotlight.

Pulling her closer, he tucked her hand in the crook of his arm. If the employees were going to talk, they might as well give them something to talk about.

Stepping up to the elevators, the crowd parted, allowing Xian and Anna to have the car. Murmurs of "Good afternoon Mr. Wei" chorused through the group. Anna had noticed the head bows and greetings as they passed through the main lobby area. Xian would incline his head in acknowledgment of certain employees.

While waiting for the elevator, Anna did her best not to fidget under all the scrutiny. She whispered in Xian's ear, "Are you sure you want the rumors this is going to start?" Anna was feeling the pressure from the growing crowd around them.

Winking at Anna, Xian grasped her hand tighter to keep her from bolting. He had experienced her desire to flee before at the hotel. It would cause an even bigger spectacle if she ran now. "We're almost there. Just hang in there a few minutes more. My floor is much quieter," Xian whispered back to

Anna.

The elevator picked that moment to announce the car's arrival, and the crowd of people flowed around Xian and Anna as they exited. Pulling Anna with him, Xian punched a button and watched as the group smiled, giggled and whispered while watching the power couple standing in the elevator. Speculation circulated and Anna caught snippets of gossip. "Who's the woman with Mr. Wei?" "Wow, where did Mr. Wei find such a knockout?" "Is she his new girlfriend?" Anna could feel her face begin to flush.

Thankfully the doors closed, giving her a reprieve. She pulled her hand from the crook of Xian's arm and slapped it, though it was a bit harder than she had planned. "Were you trying to embarrass me?"

Xian studied his shoes as the car rose through the floors. "No, that wasn't my intention. If they saw you as someone of interest to me, your chances of being harassed by the flocks of single men employed by the company would drop dramatically."

Arriving at their floor, Xian stepped out of the elevator and was greeted by a woman wearing a casual suit. "Mr. Wei, you have a meeting in an hour and several calls that should be returned today."

"Get the notes for the meeting and give me thirty minutes with no interruptions. I have an important call. Ms. Zhāng, please get Ms. Cassidy some bottled water and make sure we aren't disturbed," Xian spoke to his secretary as he walked toward his office.

"Certainly, Mr. Wei, I will return with your notes and the water in a moment." Ms. Zhāng hustled away down a hall.

Following Xian, Anna looked around the modern interior; the warm grays and tans made it feel comfortable. Opening a door, they entered a room bigger than several of Anna's previous homes. The gray and tan carried through the space. She liked how there were three distinct areas though it was one room.

Anna eyed a small meeting area with a table and chairs; it was set apart from Xian's desk, so it would afford them a bit of privacy to do their work. Comfortable couches were in the same area as Xian's desk. If she sat down on one she wouldn't be getting up anytime soon; they looked too inviting.

"So, this is what the office of a media mogul looks like," Anna murmured as she spun slowly to take it all in. The bookshelves beside the couches had awards the company had won and books that had been printed on their presses. Curiosity drew her to look over the nooks along the wall across from Xian's desk.

"Not too shabby, huh? I like it." Xian took Anna's bag from her and set it on the table. "Let's get this call with Chen over with. Did you want to discuss Lin Bolin before or after?"

Sauntering over to a chair in front of Xian's desk, Anna daintily lowered herself to the seat. "Why don't we discuss Lin Bolin first? Then we can call Chen. After that, I have some emails and calls I will need to make and I believe you have a meeting shortly?"

"Had to remind me, didn't you," Xian grumbled as he settled into the chair opposite Anna's. Leaning forward, he rested his elbows on his knees and gave Anna his undivided attention. "What would you like to know?"

After discussing the situation, Xian came up with a plan. He would hire Lin Bolin as an executive assistant to the studio liaison.

"Wait, if he's the executive assistant to the studio liaison, how does that help me?"

"Because Ms. Anna Cassidy, you are officially my liaison with the studio. Hiring you for a position like that allows me to process your work papers more easily. If you only go through the studio, you would be a contractor and it's more complicated. What do you think? Oh, and the position comes with an executive assistant, a luxury apartment, a car and a salary." Xian sat back, pleased with himself.

Anna sat staring at him with a deer in the headlights look. "Xian, I don't know the first thing about being a liaison."

"There's not much to know. You'll be working on the films, correct? So you'll know what's going on. You would need to give me a report once a week. If I have any input, you will relay it to the staff at the studio. Not too difficult."

Rubbing the back of her neck, Anna tilted her head giving

Xian a calculated look. "Why do I feel you have an ulterior motive for this job appointment?"

"I have no idea what you're talking about. After we call Chen, call Lin Bolin and ask him to come to my office tomorrow. I will have him start here and train him by the time you return. If you would like assistance now, you could borrow Wu Feng. I know he wouldn't mind one bit." Xian stood and walked around the desk to his leather office chair.

"We **WILL** be discussing this later," Anna warned Xian as she found Chen in her recent calls and touched the green button. Putting it on speaker, as she figured it would be easier for them to answer questions.

"About damned time! What took you so long?" came the irritable voice over the speaker.

Anna and Xian shared a look and both silently laughed. "Sorry, we just got to Xian's office a few minutes ago. We didn't want to call from the car. So, do you want to hear how it went or be a total grouch?"

"Sorry, with everything happening lately, I was worried. How did the meeting go? I'm betting Xian worked his magic and you are leaving with way more money than you expected." Chen's tone was apologetic.

"Well, you aren't wrong. Xian did wonders. Too much to go into over the phone. Needless to say, I'll be back in Beijing in the new year for a while."

Anna would have laughed joyfully if she had seen Chen dancing around the room. She would be back! "That's fantastic, Anna! We must go apartment hunting this week."

Cringing, Anna looked at Xian for an idea of how to break the news that she would be staying in the penthouse when she returned.

"That's been all sorted already. Anna's new job comes with accommodations," Xian cut in.

Anna looked at Xian, murder in her eyes. "What do you think you're doing?" she mouthed at Xian. That wasn't the type of help she'd been looking for.

He smirked and shrugged his shoulders. Getting one up on Chen felt good for a change. Knowing he would be in deep water with Anna anyway, he figured he might as well jump in with both feet. Get it all over and done with, like ripping the band-aid off. "She will be staying in the penthouse. It comes with her new position with the Wei Group." Raising his eyebrow, he dared Anna to dispute his claim.

The silence continued from the other end of the phone and Anna was concerned. "Chen?"

After a pause, a quiet voice broke the silence, "That's great, Anna. Everything worked out in your favor. We can talk about it when you get home. I'm tired, I should get some rest before you return." The call ended without a goodbye.

"Xian, if you had any clue how pissed I am right now...you didn't have to break it to him like that. We could have done it in person, at least. Please don't make me regret my decision to agree with this plan." Anna was worried about Chen. It couldn't have been easy to hear that she would be working for his best friend **AND** living in his penthouse.

After everything Chen had tried to do for her that had gone wrong, this was rubbing salt in his wounds. Hopefully she could explain the reasoning when they returned to the apartment. She hoped making a special meal tomorrow night would help soothe the hurt ego too.

Picking up the notebook she had grabbed to make notes, she gave Xian one last hurt gaze before walking to the table and chairs to call Lin Bolin and work on answering her emails and messages that had been piling up.

Xian cringed when he saw Anna's hurt eyes. He had gone too far and he knew it, but he wasn't used to losing. Whatever he wanted, he found a way to get it one way or another. Why was he acting this way? Was it just because Chen was interested in Anna and he was competing with him like they had since school, or did he truly have feelings for Anna? Leaning back in his chair, he sat with his fingers steepled, contemplating his feelings.

If he had seen Chen at that moment, he might have felt worse. Chen lay in the guest bed in the pair of pajamas Anna had worn at his apartment. He could still smell her scent on them, one of the only comforts he had at that moment. Growing up, Chen and Xian had always been competitive, but this went above and beyond. Xian knew how much he cared for Anna. Why would he intentionally pursue her as well? *Because Anna's an incredible woman, that's why.*

Right now, he still wanted to cry. Xian had finalized the deal he had started, getting Anna more money and better control of her scripts. He had also found a way to talk Anna into living in his penthouse apartment. All Chen had done was introduce Anna to a man that could make her dreams come true. All he did was cause her trouble because of his ex-finance. Friday night had to go smoothly. His relationship with Anna depended on it.

章

Chapter 52

Not long after Xian and Anna had finished the call with Chen, Ms. Zhāng knocked and came into the office with the notes for his upcoming meeting. Taking the folders, he murmured to her before excusing her. Perusing the documents, Xian made notes on a pad that he tucked into the folder.

Glancing at his wristwatch, Xian decided it was time for him to head to the meeting. It was with one of his distributors and it shouldn't take long. There had been a snafu, and once in a while, the big boss needed to clean up the mess. Leaning forward, Xian tried to glimpse Anna. There was a small gap in the room divider; perhaps if he leaned just right he could see her. He could barely glimpse her laptop on the table as he stretched forward. Listening, he thought he heard low murmurs. She must be on the phone.

Xian stood, grabbed his folders and walked past the table. He almost felt Anna's glare directed at his back as he opened the door. *Oh, I messed up!* He was at a loss...when he messed up with Chandra, he knew what to do. Anna was a different creature entirely. He wouldn't be able to buy her forgiveness with money. Chen would have been the best option to figure out the resolution for this situation, but he had hurt his friend as well.

Anna watched Xian as he left the room. How could he treat his best friend with such contempt? Sure, kick the guy when he is recovering from an injury. They could have broken the news to Chen in a better way. Hopefully, Xian had realized he had been too rash. She had to find a way to make it up to Chen. Just because her heart was a traitor and had started softening towards Xian didn't mean she didn't care about Chen. The last thing she would ever want is to see Chen get hurt.

Looking through her contacts she found her number for Lin

Bolin. Hopefully, he could talk so she could fill him in on the latest developments.

"Hello, Ms. Cassidy; how can I be of assistance? Do you have a return date yet?" Lin Bolin asked excitedly.

"Lin Bolin, please slow down a bit. First off, are you sure you would like to be my assistant? If you would rather stay at the hotel, I will understand."

"Oh no, Ms. Cassidy. I would like the job," Lin Bolin replied enthusiastically.

"Well, report to Mr. Wei at the Wei Group main office tomorrow afternoon if you want the job. Will that be a problem? You will begin training immediately, so you'll be ready when I return in January. Your official title will be executive assistant to the studio liaison." Anna couldn't help but grin at the title. It was indeed a mouthful and sounded important.

Silence. Did the call drop? A shaky voice replied, "Ms. Cassidy, who is the studio liaison?"

Sighing, Anna filled him in on her new position and his job. Lin Bolin had agreed to show up at Xian's office at 1:00 P.M. sharp the following afternoon. Anna was glad she would get to see the young man in person before she had to leave to return to the States.

At the last moment, Anna remembered what she had planned. "Lin Bolin, do you have plans for tomorrow evening?"

"Not that I know of," was his hesitant response.

"I would like to invite you to an informal get-together at my new apartment. It's a celebration of my new position and finalizing the deal with the studio. Since you will be working with me, I would like it if you could come to celebrate with me," Anna said, unsure if it was too much too soon.

"I'd be honored, Ms. Cassidy." Lin Bolin sounded excited again.

"I'll give your information to the receptionist. Check in when you arrive and come up to the apartment; I'll expect you at 7:15 P.M."

"Okay, Ms. Cassidy, I will see you tomorrow. Thank you so much for this opportunity. I'll do my best." She could almost hear him bowing over the phone.

"As long as you do your best, I can't ask any more than that. My one request is that if you ever have anyone approach you about turning against me or spying, please let me know no matter how much they might offer. You would be in for a huge bonus. Loyalty is important to me."

"Ma'am, even though I will be working for Mr. Wei's company, I will be loyal to you first and foremost." His earnestness touched Anna, especially after Xian's behavior.

"Lin Bolin, thank you. I look forward to tomorrow evening. See you then. Goodbye," Anna said as she ended the call. She was glad the young man would be her assistant; he had shown a hint of his potential and Anna wanted to cultivate it. There wasn't any reason he couldn't be on par with Huang Hu or Wu Feng.

Sitting down with her laptop open, Anna started tackling the backlog of correspondence she had neglected for the last week. Veronica was at the top of the list. Reading through the emails from her, Anna realized that she had better do some writing. Her latest manuscript was nearly finished and the publisher was pushing to get the draft for proofing. That meant she would be working on her laptop that night so she could finish the chapters. Letting Veronica know there should be completed chapters by the end of the week, Anna felt good getting that dealt with.

Next on her list was social media. Since the awards her social media had continued to have mind-boggling attention. Anna wasn't sure how to take it all. After living such a quiet life, she had been pushed into the spotlight and it was a tad overwhelming. She realized most of these people had probably never read her other works. They were just following the latest trend. Anna knew she had a true circle of fans; the new ones were like empty calories.

Finished with her work emails, Anna decided to send some personal messages to friends back home. With the chaos that had surrounded her lately, she had been distracted. Her four closest friends were probably wondering what had happened to her.

She grabbed her phone from the table and sat on the couch.

They looked a little more comfortable than the office chairs around the table. Looking at the time, Anna decided she would send text messages; it was almost 5:00 A.M. back in Montana. Her friends might be awake but she would wait until later that night to call them. They were almost at opposite hours of day and night.

She took a few minutes to send each a message, letting them know she was still alive and kicking. Anna asked them what the best time for a call was; she missed her support system. Liz had left Anna a few messages so she had better answer those as well.

Messages addressed and emails sent, Anna opened one of her phone games for a distraction from a hectic few days. Matching bright-colored symbols was a mindless escape for her, giving her fifteen minutes of distraction. Flipping symbols back and forth on her phone screen, she began to nod off. Her eyes just couldn't seem to stay open.

When Xian returned to the office, he got worried when he saw Anna's laptop open but no sign of her. The relief was staggering when he found her snoring softly on the couch. Quietly, he approached the slumbering woman. Sitting next to her, he gently brushed loose hair from her face. Snuffling, Anna had changed her position and was sitting at an odd angle. Tucking himself close to Anna's side, he tenderly shifted her head to his shoulder. Xian sat there for thirty minutes browsing social media and taking a break from his hectic schedule. The warm body next to him relaxed him more than any soporific could.

As loath as he was to move, he realized it was close to 5 o'clock and he needed to fix things with Anna and Chen. He had been agonizing over it all afternoon, which was somewhat new to him. Before he would have just been blunt and left it. Seeing Anna so hurt by what he had said, he regretted it. Time to rouse her and see if she would forgive him.

"Anna," a gentle male voice called her back from a dream that made her blush.

Startled, Anna awoke to Xian sitting next to her on the couch with her head resting on his shoulder. Looking around she saw the light outside the windows had darkened. "What time is it?" Anna looked at her watch; two hours had passed. Slowly, she sat up; the couch wasn't as comfortable as it looked.

"It's almost 5 o'clock. Sorry, my meeting went long. After that, I was pulled to several different departments to deal with a few proverbial fires...Anna, can you forgive my earlier behavior?" Xian looked pained. Anna could see he had been agonizing over what had happened. "I was so distracted today, a couple of my department heads even mentioned something to me. Knowing I hurt you ate at me all afternoon. I shouldn't have blurted your business out as I did."

Having some quiet earlier, Anna had the time to reflect and calm down. Wrapping her arms around the arm she had been leaning on, she put her head back on his shoulder. "I'm not sure what kind of magic you used on me, but I can't seem to stay angry with you very long. It's been a long time since I've had a man to care for me, and to add to the confusion, I have two amazing men who have been pursuing me."

Xian looked down, trying to formulate his reply. The last thing he wanted was to cause Anna to pull away. It was so comfortable sitting with her like this.

"So you have some other guys chasing you? Where are they? I'll take care of them." Xian hoped levity might diffuse the heavy mood.

Smirking, Anna figured she would mess with Xian as payback. "Yeah, they are exceptionally handsome and sexy. I'm even considering asking them to return to Montana with me for a vacation. I'll need a diversion after my trip here."

As Anna spoke, she felt Xian tense up. Her words were making an impact. "I'm supposed to have dinner with them tonight. Would you mind if I borrow Wu Feng to drive me?" Anna sat up and looked at Xian with a straight face. Keeping the sober look was challenging. She wanted so badly to laugh at his stoic glare. Shifting her gaze down, she noticed he was even clenching his jaw.

Xian had it wrong; the mention of Anna having dinner with two sexy men nearly made his head explode. Mustering any shred of control he had, he answered Anna, "Wu Feng is at your disposal as long as he isn't involved in some errand for me. If he is busy, I imagine Huang Hu would be available."

"But I don't want to pull the guys away from their jobs. I could always take a cab or the bus even," Anna said in a matter-of-fact tone.

Xian exploded off the couch and pulled Anna up to her feet. Wrapping his arms around her he hugged her so tight she had difficulty drawing a deep breath. "You will **NOT** take a bus **OR** cab while staying here. Please don't ever go anywhere without one of us to protect you. As for the two men you're meeting for supper, who are they? Where did you meet them?"

It was becoming more challenging to keep her straight face. Anna almost felt guilty about her trick, but he had it coming. His high-handed behavior earlier deserved some payback. "Xian, I need to breathe. The guys were just two men who came to my rescue once or twice. I figured I'd treat them to dinner to thank them for what they've done for me."

Loosening his hug just a little, Xian still wasn't satisfied with Anna's answer. "Where are you meeting them for dinner? How late will you be out? Do you need me to accompany you?" He held Anna at arm's length to watch her face as she answered him.

She just had to hold out a little longer. "I'm not sure where I'll meet them; I need to check with them first. As to how late I'll be out? Hard to say…it depends on how much fun we are having. I was thinking of perhaps trying karaoke. We have it in the States, but it looks much more fun over here. I don't know if you can accompany me or not. Do you think Chen would like to go with us?" Anna was getting close to cracking, but kept her innocent face. Wasn't Xian going to get the hint soon?

"Why would we disturb Chen to go out with you and two strangers for dinner?" Xian looked frustrated.

"Well, what if it wasn't Chen, you and two strangers? What if it was just you and Chen? Would you let me take you two to dinner to thank you for everything you've done for me?" Anna asked him, keeping her face as neutral as possible.

Letting go of Anna, Xian had turned to begin pacing. He wanted to rant at Anna about how dangerous it was to meet strange men for dinner and karaoke when the light bulb finally came on. The dumbfounded look on his face was worth Anna keeping her cool. "We're the two men?"

"Xian, as intelligent as you are, sometimes you can be so dumb. Who else would I be asking out to dinner? The number of people I know well enough, and trust to have a meal with me, I can count on one hand. You and Chen are too important to me. So, I'm going to call and invite Chen. Hopefully he got some rest today and will be up for a meal. Do you have a suggestion for a restaurant?" Anna pulled her phone from her pocket and found Chen's number.

Standing and watching Anna call Chen, Xian shook his head and rubbed his neck with his tacky hand. He had been so upset that his palms had started to sweat. Why did Anna shake him up so bad?

"Chen, I'm so sorry about earlier. Can I make it up to you? Would you be up for having dinner with Xian and me? He would like to apologize for the tactless way he let you know what was happening. There are reasons we set it up this way. I had hoped to be sitting down with you when I explained it, not speaking over the phone so bluntly."

"Anna, I didn't blame you or Xian. I'm used to him being a bonehead. What did you have in mind for dinner?" Chen sounded better now than he had earlier.

"I had asked Xian for suggestions, but he hasn't been forthcoming with anything yet. Do you have any ideas?" Anna was relieved Chen had agreed to go.

"Hey Xian, how about our usual makeup place?" Chen asked Xian.

"Sounds good to me. Want to meet us there?" Xian went behind his desk to shut down his computer for the night.

"Um, excuse me!" Anna interrupted. "I would like to go and change into something less business attire. Especially if we are going to karaoke."

"Okay, okay. I'll have Wu Feng drive us back so you can change. One perk to the penthouse's location is that it's pretty central to my office and the studio." Grabbing keys off his desk, he went to the table holding Anna's bag and the laptop. He stuffed everything in her messenger bag and slung the strap over his shoulder. "Shall we?"

"Chen, we'll be back to the apartment shortly. We'll go

together from there. Bye." Hanging up her phone, she followed Xian as he left the office. "Are you mad at me?"

Stopping so Anna could catch up to him, he took her hand in his, leading her to the elevators. "A little, but I deserved what I got. You did pretty well. You had me going good."

"Well, it took everything I had not to break down and start laughing. I swore you were going to pop a blood vessel. Are your teeth okay? If you ground them any harder, I was worried one would break from the pressure." The laughter Anna had to hold in earlier escaped. "So, was that an example of your jealousy?" Anna asked, enjoying the feeling of her hand in Xian's. Was he indeed that jealous at the thought of her with another man?

Pushing the down arrow on the elevator, Xian turned and looked at Anna while waiting for the car to arrive. "I don't know that I've ever been that jealous. I was ready to find those two men and do bodily harm. That is so out of character for me. It's bad enough I have to compete with Chen, but to have two other 'handsome and sexy' men to deal with? I'm not sure I wouldn't end up in jail."

Anna reached out with her free hand and placed it on Xian's shoulder. "I would never intentionally string you or Chen along. You have done so much for me; I will be forever grateful. We will have to sit down and discuss where things are going, but not tonight. Let's go celebrate our success and let me thank you two for being my knights in shining armor."

Pulling Anna's hand to his mouth, he kissed her knuckles. "Certainly, Milady."

章

Chapter 53

Arriving at the apartment, Anna dashed down the hall to her room. Nature had been screaming at her for the last ten minutes. She had thought of stopping on the way up, but she could hold it that long.

Digging through the outfits she had picked out with Xian, Anna found a blouse and skirt that looked dressy enough while still having a casual feel. She was excited to try a pair of her new strappy sandals with the outfit. Well, damn it! They had forgotten one item in their shopping, a coat. Pulling her suitcase out, she opened it to find the silk wrap; it went with almost everything she had bought.

The smoke gray pencil skirt paired well with the turquoise silk shell and gray cardigan. Anna felt more at ease in the outfit, though she had loved wearing the suit. That would be one of her favorites for meetings.

Time to see if the guys were ready to go. Making her way to the sitting area by the kitchen, Chen was already there waiting on Anna and Xian. Lounging on the couch, Chen wore a pair of dark gray pleated dress pants, a lavender dress shirt and a gray sweater. He looked relaxed as he sat browsing on his phone.

"Any sign of Xian?" Anna asked as she walked into the room.

"Are you kidding me? That prima donna? Good luck if he's ready in the next thirty minutes. I swear he takes longer than most women, no offense. You get ready faster than 95 percent of the women I've known. Even my sister Chandra was ready faster than Xian most of the time. Anna, you look lovely; even after that smoking hot business attire from earlier."

"You don't look too bad yourself. How are you feeling?" Sitting down next to Chen, she took his hand in hers. "Can you forgive me for earlier?" Anna searched Chen's face for any sign that he was still upset with her.

Engulfing Anna's hand in both of his he said, "I was hurt that I didn't get to help you make the decisions, but I understand. It was a shock to hear that you would work for Xian and the studio."

"It worked the best this way. Being an employee of Xian's company I will have fewer hassles with moving here; and hopefully, Si Ming will be able to join me." The relief Anna felt when Chen told her he wasn't mad at her was nearly euphoric. Chen had been her rock for the last four and a half years; she knew she **COULD** live without him, but it would hurt if he wasn't part of her life somehow.

"I had almost forgotten about Si Ming; how do you think he will manage here?" Chen knew Anna's sidekick might not enjoy living in a penthouse apartment in the city; used to roaming the woods of Montana, it may be too much of an adjustment.

Sighing, Anna shrugged. "If he doesn't adjust to the apartment, Xian offered to let him live at his estate where he would have the run of the place and I could visit him there. I'm even considering leaving him with Liz, as much as it would suck leaving him behind."

"Well, from what you've told me over the years, he sounds resilient. We will hope for the best."

"The best what?" a new voice interjected into the conversation.

Xian walked into the room, pulling on a dust blue long jacket over black dress slacks and a white collarless shirt. How could Anna be so lucky to go to dinner with two exceptionally handsome men? She may need to purchase a baseball bat to keep the women at bay while out with them.

"We were just discussing the possibilities of Si Ming adjusting to living in an apartment after having the run of the forest back home." Looking up at Xian, she saw he must have showered; his hair seemed slightly damp. "Did you take a shower?"

Suddenly looking uncomfortable, Xian avoided Anna's gaze. "Yeah. I needed to calm down a bit after your prank earlier."

Curiosity piqued, Chen sat forward and looked between

Xian and Anna. "So what happened?"

"Just getting a little revenge for Xian being an ass earlier," Anna stated as she folded her arms and gave Xian a look that simply said, *Apologize! Now!*

"Chen, listen man, I'm sorry. What I did was petty and childish. I swear we bring that out in one another. Can you forgive me?"

Giving his best friend an appraising stare, Chen noticed Xian looked more haggard than usual. Had he been sleeping at all the last few days? How could he stay angry with Xian when he deeply cared for Anna?

"I forgive you, but you owe me one." Chen felt better after clearing the air with Anna and Xian.

"So, now that we're one big happy family again, where in the world are we going for dinner? I don't have to dress nicer than this, do I?" She looked down at her outfit.

"You might be overdressed." Chen laughed, and shortly after, Xian began laughing as well.

"Okay, so do you plan on letting me in on the joke?" Anna huffed.

"You'll find out. Let's eat so we can hopefully get a decent night's sleep for a change," Xian said and headed for the foyer.

Holding Anna's hand, Chen helped her up from the couch. "You'll enjoy it, I promise." His smile was infectious and she couldn't help smiling back at him.

"Not even a hint?" Anna wheedled.

Rolling his eyes, Chen headed for the door, dragging Anna with him.

Xian and Chen weren't cooperating with Anna. They absolutely wouldn't give her any hint about where they were going.

"Really? Come on, guys. Some idea, please?" Anna begged. "Why did you laugh when you mentioned the restaurant?"

"We're almost there; you just need to wait," Chen told her again.

"Humph," Anna grumped. Surprises weren't her favorite, though they could be fun at times.

Wu Feng pulled the car to the end of a long entrance walkway. Sitting in the front seat, Xian got out and opened

Anna's door. He would be the one to escort her in and Chen would get to escort her out. They had played a silly game to determine the outcome; at times like this, it wasn't hard to see that these two had been close most of their life. Having grown up with one another, it made sense.

Taking Xian's arm, Anna was led down a long corridor to an ornate gate. Fascinated by the colors and lights, Anna felt like she was being transported back in time. Women and men dressed in costumes from a bygone era greeted the visitors. Walking through the gate guarded by stone lions, they were transported back three hundred years.

Xian requested one of the garden pagodas if one was available. It was kind of chilly to be out in the garden area, but these pagodas had glass around them. Guests could see the gardens and stay warm. He wanted them to have privacy and the pagodas were set apart from the main building.

An attendant dressed in period garb led them through the winding paths. Gardens and ponds lined the walkways between the different buildings and tables with guests dotted throughout the grounds as well. Their passing caused a stir with the patrons. Anna could hear murmurs as they passed. "Who is that woman?” “Isn't that Xiao Chen?” “She's nothing spectacular; why is she with those gorgeous men? Westerners think they are so impressive.” “I wonder which one she's sleeping with."

Xian and Chen steeled themselves, ignoring the comments. Anna wasn't so lucky; the whispers brought her back to the award ceremony and the horrid rumors Li Ming had spread through the crowd. Why couldn't she be happy and enjoy the evening out with the guys?

Leaning towards Xian, Anna whispered to him, "Let's go find somewhere else to eat." She turned to retreat the way they had come.

Putting a hand on her shoulder to stop her flight, Chen popped earbuds in Anna's ears. He then stepped up and took Anna's other arm; sandwiched between Xian and Chen, Anna had no choice but to continue. Soft music flowed from the small electronics in her ears, she couldn't hear the comments but she could see the glances and whispers. It was apparent they figured that with her being a Westerner, she wouldn't know Mandarin as well as she did.

Unfortunately, Chen taking Anna's other arm didn't stop the comments from the patrons; it only succeeded in causing more grumbles and whispers. The women made jealous remarks about how a Westerner couldn't be good enough for the men she was with. The men seemed to think it wasn't fair that these two had found such an attractive Westerner to dine with. Xian and Chen kept their expressions as neutral as possible. Hopefully, Anna wasn't hearing the comments now.

They arrived at the glass-enclosed pavilion, surrounded by placid water and floating plants; it was quiet, and the whispers and murmurs were gone. Their attendant patiently waited for Xian to help Anna with her chair and take their seats before offering the menus. Chen rattled off their order without looking at the proffered menus; simply stating they would like the Royal Supper.

With an incline of the head the attendant hurried off to fill their order. Xian and Chen looked at Anna with concern. "Anna, are you okay? Why did you want to leave?" Xian asked her. He had been disturbed when she had tried to pull away.

"Was it the comments from the patrons?" Chen voiced his suspicion. He had heard some of the mutters and whispers as they had passed. Chen ignored it and kept going about his life, but he was used to being in the spotlight. It wasn't the same for Anna; she was new to the gossip and whispers that occurred when she passed by. Being as strikingly beautiful as she was, it made the situation more complex because she was noticed more easily.

Ashamed at how easily she had wanted to run away, Anna nodded to Chen as she pulled the pods from her ears. "Do you ever get used to the whispers? I'm used to comments about how big I was, not how I don't deserve to be with the men whose company I'm with."

"You deserve to be with us just as much as any other woman might, in fact, more so. Don't ever feel like you aren't worthy of either of us." Xian grasped Anna's hand in reassurance. Chen nodded his agreement with Xian's statement.

"Thanks, guys. After the last week, what meager self-confidence I had built has been stomped on repeatedly. Sorry, I guess I'm feeling sorry for myself. I'll throw myself a pity party later and be fine." Her self-deprecating smile worried Chen.

They would need to make a detour on the way back to the apartment; Chen needed some supplies. Anna wouldn't need to have a pity party on her own; he would be there to support her. If he had anything to say about it, they would climb into her bed, watch a silly show and eat ice cream.

Trying to distract Anna, Xian thought of a way to divert her attention. "Anna, do you have your shopping list ready?" He was curious about what Anna had in store for them.

"I believe I'm close. I need to check the pantry at the penthouse to see if there are any supplies there. I want to be cautious about what I purchase. I'll be gone for almost two months before I return, so I don't want to get anything that might go to waste."

"But what are you making?" Chen tried again to get her to divulge the menu.

"It's a surprise! I may kick you two out while I'm cooking so you can't peek." Snickering at the looks of disgust that crossed the men's faces, she said, "You two need to learn patience."

Rolling his eyes at her last comment, Xian noticed the attendant returning with their first dishes. The following two hours were spent enjoying the "royal" fare that the restaurant specialized in. This restaurant's particular meals would have been served to the royalty of a previous era. Anna was especially partial to the Palace Pastry and the Six Spells, dainty bite-sized treats. Yinpin Tofu and the Organic Fungus were unusual, though they were tasty. One of her favorites was the Aromatherapy Venison. Now, if she could find a recipe for that one, she would make it at home with some of the whitetail deer she harvested.

Seeing both Xian and Chen enjoy it, Anna decided that if they ever came to visit she would make them bacon-wrapped back straps. Most of the meat she harvested ended up in sausage; that would be a great breakfast, biscuits and gravy. Those two wouldn't know what hit them. The difference between Eastern and Western cooking was quite noticeable.

After finishing the meal, they sat and chatted for a while, discussing the meeting and how Xian had talked the board into allowing Anna to have creative control. Chen was the most excited about that; it meant that Anna would be able to work with some of her favorite actors and actresses on the projects if they were available. She would be blown away from his surprise on Friday if all went according to plan.

Anna's mood had improved dramatically. Xian and Chen had done wonders in raising her spirits. "Pity party has officially been canceled. You two are better than a pint of ice cream."

Rising to leave, each hugged Anna to cement her good mood. Chen carefully put the earbuds back in Anna's ears. At least she wouldn't have to hear the whispers on the way out. It was darker now and she wouldn't notice the looks and glances either.

—

Sitting in a small room across the garden from the pavilion, Xian, Chen and Anna were unaware of their audience.

Li Ming and Scott sat watching the interaction between the three and seethed. Both had become increasingly determined to undermine the relationship between the group. The actor, hired to pretend to be a doctor, had signed papers to discharge Li Ming before Scott made sure he had an unfortunate accident falling down several flights of stairs at the hospital. It had been a genius idea on Li Ming's part to leave the body in a hospital bed. It had taken hours for them to discover the body. She hadn't been pleased to find Chen had slipped through her grasp yet again. Now the bitch author was living in a secure apartment and it would be nearly impossible to get to her there.

Scott had been following Li Ming's orders. He wasn't familiar with Beijing and the customs, so he was okay with doing her dirty work...for now. As long as Anna was going back to Montana, where he could finally realize his plans, he would continue working towards the actress's goals. Li Ming had heard that Anna would be working with the studio starting in January, which meant she would leave Montana for a couple of years and he had to stop her plans.

章

Chapter 54

Wednesday morning dawned under a heavily overcast sky. The threat of rain weighed on Anna's mind. The meal she had in mind for that evening would go well with the gloomy weather. Now, she just hoped the guys would like it. She was going to be seriously outnumbered by the men that night. Perhaps one of them might know a woman to invite?

She would bring it up to Chen and Xian at breakfast, if Xian hadn't left for the office already. It was hard to determine his schedule because she had messed it up so badly. Wu Feng had mentioned going to the office at ridiculously early hours of the morning. At least with her around, he's taken a little break.

Going through her shopping list in her head, Anna figured soup and the main course would be good on such a gloomy day. Now, if she could get the ingredients her dishes called for, then the meal would be fabulous. She never thought that she would be cooking while here so didn't think to bring some of her spices along.

Dragging herself out of bed, Anna pulled on the fuzzy robe Xian had picked out for her and stuffed her feet in her slippers. Before she returned, she was going to make sure she had a pair of Merrell slippers; their flip-flop versions were ok but she missed her sherpa-lined slip-on moccasins.

Shuffling down the hall, the apartment was very quiet. Looking at her watch, it was 8:20 in the morning, Xian must have left for the office already and Chen must still be in bed sleeping. It was still a bit early for her to be thinking about breakfast, she might as well start working on her laptop so she could return Xian's.

The guys' end of the apartment was all quiet. Chen's door was closed, so she was most likely correct in her assumption that he was still resting. Concussions didn't heal overnight and he had gone out with her the night before which was probably pushing it. They did have a good time though...other than the whispers of the other patrons. Anna wasn't sure if she would ever get used to being scrutinized like that.

When they returned to the penthouse, they had all gone their separate ways. Chen and Xian had been talking quietly with one another and Anna was just done for the day. It was time to curl up with her iPad and continue watching the next episode of the current series she was bingeing. She had woken up several hours later to her iPad on the nightstand and her blankets pulled over her. One of the guys must have checked on her at some point.

Stopping by the kitchen, Anna snagged a bottle of water from the fridge and ambled to her office. Now that she would move in for a while, she would start making the space hers. First, the laptop needed to be set up. That was easy enough; she would just need to unbox it, get all the password information entered and let it do its job pulling the Time Machine information from her backup.

Taking a long swig from the bottle, Anna wasn't paying close attention to the room around her. She sat the bottle on the desk and looked for the laptop box. Pulling the package from the pile, she opened it and removed all of the protective plastics from the sleek aluminum electronic. Uncoiling the cords, she wanted to ensure the plug was compatible with the outlets. Plugging everything in, she pushed the power button and heard the Apple start-up sound. Setting up a new computer was a joy for Anna. For most of her computer career, she had typically bought used or refurbished systems. On the occasions she had splurged for a brand new machine, it was a big deal.

Once Anna had become a serious writer and had the extra funds available, she splurged and purchased one of the bigger Apple computers and had a pretty sweet setup in her office back home. This was an upgrade for her, it had the latest and greatest processor and the current operating system. The laptop currently collecting dust at the police station was soon to be retired anyhow, sometimes it was a good thing to be forced to update the old hardware.

Clicking through all of the setup screens, Anna plugged in

her backup drive and started the import process. It would take an hour or better so it was time to get dressed and find some breakfast.

Feeling more herself, dressed in a pair of comfortable jogger pants and an acid-washed hoodie, Anna started digging around in the kitchen. Realizing there weren't many foodstuffs in the apartment, she fought the urge to go shopping to supply the place. If she could pick up a few items, she should be good; whatever was leftover, perhaps either Wu Feng or Huang Hu could use.

Speaking of the assistants, Anna had asked Xian and Chen to invite them, but she hadn't heard a definite answer if they were coming. Lin Bolin had confirmed that he would be attending, he wanted to visit with Anna more before she had to return to Montana.

Pulling her phone from the kangaroo pocket on her hoodie, she first sent a message to Huang Hu asking if he would be coming for dinner. Anna next sent a text to Wu Feng, she wanted to find out if he was ready to go shopping. Depending on what they found, she may need to start cooking soon. Her soup was best if it was allowed to cook most of the day.

Waiting for the responses, Anna popped into her office to check the migration process. It was showing it still had thirty minutes to go. Where was the reply text from Wu Feng?

Looking around the room, Anna was surprised to see a bouquet of flowers on a table next to the plush couch. It was possibly the most enormous bouquet she had seen in a long time. Did Xian's house staff supply these? Tucked in the blossoms was a card, "A flower cannot blossom without sunshine, and a man cannot live without love." Anna wondered who had googled that particular quote. It was charming. No signature, though. Was it Xian or Chen?

Anna took a picture and texted it to Liz with the message, *So, which of those two stinkers put these in my office?*

Within moments, Liz replied, My guess would be Chen. Didn't he send you those amazing flowers when you first arrived **AND** all the beautiful flowers at the hotel in Taipei?

Flopping down on the couch, Anna wasn't up for another mystery. Couldn't those two just sign their name already? Not that she didn't appreciate the beautiful blooms in her office, she was just getting sick of the guessing games.

Knowing Liz was available, Anna gave her a FaceTime call. "Evening, daughter dear."

"Hey Mom, wasn't expecting a call from you. Give me a moment." Liz put the screen on pause for a minute but quickly returned. "Okay, what's up? I thought you had a big dinner to cook for tonight."

"Yeah, I'm waiting on Wu Feng to text me back. He's my ride to the market today. I'm cooking knoephla soup and curry roasted chicken. I had toyed with making my signature roast beef but over here beef is a precious commodity. I did however have some lip-smacking venison last night. Actually, the reason I called was to let you know how the meeting went yesterday."

"I figured it went pretty well since you didn't call me crying," Liz said and stuck her tongue out at her mother.

"Funny kid, you may not laugh quite so hard after you hear this one." Anna decided to rip the band-aid off and announced, "I'll be moving to Beijing for at least two years."

Liz sat and stared at her mom for what felt like hours. "Two years? I figured like six months or so, how did it end up being two years?"

"Xian worked his magic and wrangled creative control for the scripts. With that being said, I will need to be here while they are filming with the exception of my book tour and appearances that were already scheduled. So, would you like to see my new digs for the next couple of years?"

"You already have an apartment and you just found out about this yesterday?" Liz said skeptically.

"So, not only did the meeting with the studio go well, but I also became the newest employee of Wei Media. Xian hired me to be the liaison from his company to the studio. The position comes with a comfy salary, an assistant, a car and..." Anna trailed off as she walked into the area between the dining room and living room; she flipped the screen so Liz could see the two rooms as Anna panned the phone around, "...this penthouse apartment," Anna finished.

"What the bloody hell?" Liz squeaked. "Joanie, Berta, Heather come look at this!" Liz yelled to her co-workers to see

Anna's new residence.

Anna spent the next fifteen minutes giving the ladies a brief tour of the apartment, saving Anna's favorite part for last. The terrace overlooking the city would be Anna's favorite no matter what. Looking over the city, she could enjoy the sites without much sound.

The ladies were excited to hear how Anna had scored such a fantastic apartment, so there was a short recap of how everything had gone with the studio. Excitement and congratulations went all around. "Okay, ladies, I better get going. I have some serious shopping to attend to." Waving to the girls as they headed back into the bar.

"Before you go, how are you doing Mom? What happened on Sunday? Your message was pretty brief."

Anna spent another ten minutes filling Liz in on the last few days. Pausing here and there for Liz to make the appropriate ooh, aah and oh my gods. "So, I have a wrap party with Chen on Friday night and a benefit masquerade gala with Xian on Saturday night. I believe Chen and I will go to dinner with Mama Jing on Sunday night before I leave. Tomorrow is my only real down day the whole time I've been here. Maybe I'll just stay in bed."

"Don't you dare! Enjoy it while you can. Once you get home, you'll have plenty to do. What do you plan to do with the house?"

"Well, what do you think of staying there while I'm gone? I'm sure you wouldn't mind moving out of your tiny place. Perhaps by the time I'm ready to move back, there may be other options for you two. **BUT** you would have the guest room. I will be back on and off and you can't live in my room."

The excitement on Liz's face said it all. "Not only yeah, but **HELL** yeah. You know we wouldn't turn down an offer like that. When are you supposed to be back in Beijing?"

"Mid January. I will have a little less than two months before I need to be back here. I'm not sure what I'm going to do about Si Ming. I believe I'm going to try bringing him over here and if he doesn't handle it well he will come back to live with you two. I hate doing it to my buddy, but I can't pass up this opportunity." Anna sighed. Her life was changing so quickly.

"Just enjoy the ride Mom. I better go, my break's over. Love you. See you next week."

"Love you too. Don't break Sheldon's heart too much." Laughing, Anna ended the call. The kids would love living in Anna's place for a while as long as they took good care of it. It wasn't good to let a house sit empty for that long.

Flipping back to her main screen, Anna noticed she had a text message from Wu Feng. *Ready whenever you are Ms. Anna.*

Come and get me. Let me know when you're downstairs, Anna replied. She better check on Chen before she left. She didn't dare go without letting him know, not with how protective those two were.

After the loud call with the ladies during their tour, Anna would have been amazed if Chen was still asleep. Still, knocking gently on his door she wasn't sure if she would get an answer or not. She was still surprised to hear a soft, "Come in."

Opening the door just enough to poke her head in, Anna saw Chen covered up to his chin with the white duvet. "Chen, are you okay? How are you feeling today?"

Chen was glad Anna had knocked first. He didn't want her to see him wearing the same pajamas again, the ones she had worn...and she was worried about the guy stalking her from Montana. He had enough time to pull the blanket up to his chin before answering. He had enjoyed listening to her conversation with Liz and the other women. Peals of laughter throughout the apartment had been a nice change of pace.

"I'm doing alright. Going out last night wore me out. I'm going to spend the day in bed resting. What plans did you have?"

"Wu Feng is on his way to take me grocery shopping. I need to pick up supplies for the dinner tonight. Did Huang Hu let you know if he could make it or not? I tried sending him a message with no luck." Anna checked her phone for any possible messages she might have missed. Still nothing from Huang Hu.

"He planned on coming from the last I heard. I'm excited to find out what you plan to make. I know you said something about dishes that you've made for years?" Chen was quite curious about what Anna had planned, but she still wasn't giving him any hints.

"Yes. I'm **STILL** not going to tell you." Winking, Anna pulled the door shut. Walking a few steps, she remembered she wanted to ask Chen about the flowers. Turning the doorknob, Anna heard a slight commotion from the bedroom. Throwing the door open, Anna expected Chen to be on the floor. Instead, he was still in bed with the covers pulled up to his chin.

"Are you sure you're okay? I heard a loud noise." Anna looked around the room for any evidence of an earthquake or some other disaster that might have explained the noise.

"I'm fine. I knocked a book on the floor. I'll pick it up when I go to the bathroom." Chen tried to cover up his mistake. After Anna had closed the door, he had planned to get up and use the bathroom. He hadn't expected Anna to throw the bedroom door open so he had dove back into bed and covered up.

"Okay, as long as you're fine. The reason I came back, do you know anything about flowers?"

"Flowers? No idea. Did you need to order some?" Curiosity tinged his voice.

"Nope, just curious if the staff supplies fresh flowers to the apartment," Anna said, flustered that she didn't get an answer. Xian must have left them. She would find out later. "Get some rest. Sorry I disturbed you."

"Anna, you never disturb me that way. In other ways, it's another story." Chen waggled his eyebrows at Anna.

"You're incorrigible," she laughingly responded as she closed the door. Good to see he was feeling better.

"*Do or do not, there is no try,*" blared from her phone. Checking the message, Wu Feng was just pulling up to the front door. Anna texted that she was on her way as she slipped on her casual shoes. She wondered if she would have time to shop for a jacket as well. She was dressed warm enough for the moment, but that could change. At some point, she would need to get some kind of coat for the weekend as well. It would need to go with both of her dresses. Perhaps the wrap would be better for those nights.

章

Chapter 55

Wu Feng was waiting next to the car. "Morning, Wu Feng. How are you doing?" Anna greeted the young man.

"Doing pretty good, Ms. Anna, looking forward to dinner tonight. Mr. Wei said you were making something special." Wu Feng opened the back door of the sedan.

"Can you do me a favor today Wu Feng? Can I just sit in the front seat? I'm not used to sitting in the back all the time. It feels odd, especially when we just go to the grocery store. Oh, and could we possibly find a clothing store nearby? I really need to find a jacket, especially for when I return home. We could have snow when I get back."

Closing the back door, Wu Feng opened the front passenger door. "I'll make you a deal. You can ride in front, but I open your door and we don't say a word of this to Mr. Wei or Mr. Xiao."

Sticking her hand out to shake his, she said, "Deal." Anna smiled as Wu Feng shook her hand.

"Let's get this done. I have some cooking to do."

"What kind of groceries are you looking for?"

"I'll need whole chickens, flour, eggs, carrots, potatoes, celery, chicken stock, milk, butter and seasonings; plus a few other odds and ends. Will that be difficult to find?"

"No, those are pretty easy ingredients, honestly. We won't have to go far to find great quality. As for the coat, I believe I know a place. Is it for casual use or a special occasion?" Wu Feng pulled out into traffic, watching the oncoming vehicles.

"Both. I'd like something that could be used for business in a pinch." When Anna was finally home, she planned on shopping for her dream coat. She had been looking for a knee-length Shearling coat for ages. Perhaps she would just have to have one made for her. It would be overkill for Beijing, though.

"Ms. Anna, I believe I know just the place. Why don't we go there first and get groceries right before we return."

"Hey, did you have breakfast yet?" she inquired as her middle section began making embarrassing noises.

"I had a cup of coffee. Mr. Wei headed for the office pretty early this morning." Chewing on his bottom lip, Anna knew there was something he wasn't saying.

"Spill it, Wu Feng. What's up?"

"If Mr. Wei hears about this, I'll be in trouble. He asked me to bring a bouquet of flowers early this morning. I had to pull some strings to get them that early. Did something happen yesterday?"

Ah, so Anna had her answer. Xian was trying to make up for his screw up. "Did you put the card in the flowers or did Xian?"

"I just provided a blank card. I'm not sure what Mr. Wei wrote on it."

Xian wasn't going to make this easy on her. The quote and flowers hit all the romantic notes with Anna. That man knew what he was doing.

Anna shook herself and thought about food. *Keep your mind on food, Anna.* She didn't need to contemplate relationships at this moment. Turning, she stared out the window as buildings blurred past.

Wu Feng pulled into a parking area near an upscale boutique. "Ms. Anna, there should be coats here that will fit what you're looking for. Do you need my assistance?"

"I believe I've got it. Thanks for getting me here." Stepping out of the car, Anna walked into the shop.

Twenty minutes later, Anna left the boutique with two coats. It had taken some serious convincing for her to purchase the two items. Two phone calls later and the clerks finally believed that she had the financial means to purchase clothing in the shop. Looking at the tags, Anna could understand their hesitation. The black cashmere duster she had picked out for evening wear was $3,500.

Usually, Anna would have gasped and told Wu Feng to find her a department store. Being around Xian and Chen was wearing off on her. She knew she would never be able to wear clothing from any of the big box stores anymore. The quality of the clothing Xian had purchased for her was exceptional, so much so, that putting on her old clothes had felt like wearing sandpaper compared to the new finery.

Wu Feng opened the sedan's trunk and put her packages in carefully. "Wu Feng, we may want to put those in the back seat. I'm not sure I'd like my new coats riding in the same space as the chicken I plan on buying."

Rubbing the back of his neck, Wu Feng looked at the two boxes and realized Anna had a good point. High-end clothing may pick up odors from the food, best to keep them in the back seat. Pulling the boxes out of the trunk, Anna opened the back door for him and he carefully put them in. "Thanks, Ms. Anna. I should have done that."

She clapped Wu Feng on the shoulder, startling him. "You better get used to me. I open doors for people and help where I can, especially when it involves me. So, you can either get used to my odd Western behavior, or I find another driver." Cocking her head to the left, Anna watched him process what she had just told him.

"Okay, just don't do it in front of Mr. Wei or Mr. Xiao, or you're gonna get me in trouble. Is Lin Bolin going to be your driver as well as your assistant?" Opening the car door for Anna and getting in himself. Wu Feng decided that whoever was associated with Anna would need a heads-up about her quirks.

Anna pondered Wu Feng's question for a few minutes. "Actually, I'm not sure. I can check with Xian this afternoon. I'd like to be there for Lin Bolin's interview with Xian, but I need to babysit the meal."

"Speaking of food. Why don't we go find that brunch you were talking about? I swear I just heard some creature making noise around your middle."

Rolling her eyes at Wu Feng, Anna smirked and agreed with the idea of food.

章

Chapter 56

Arriving at a building that looked like a high-end department store a few minutes later, Wu Feng parked the car and opened Anna's door. "After you, Ms. Anna."

"Where are we?"

"This is one of the best markets in Beijing. It has a great little bistro right in the store, we can grab something to eat and then go shop for what you need. I'm going with you this time. If anything happens to you while you're in my care, it'll be my job, if not my life. I think Mr. Wei and Mr. Xiao would skin me alive." Shivering, Wu Feng pictured both of the men chasing him with sharp knives. Well, that might be a bit drastic, but they would certainly fire him.

Taking Wu Feng's arm, Anna said, "Let's go."

Shaking off the shock of Anna grabbing him, he smiled and walked into the store. It wasn't often he had a beautiful woman on his arm. If Mr. Wei and Mr. Xiao hadn't been so enamored with Anna, he would have been interested himself. She was a breath of fresh air, treating him better than any other woman Mr. Wei had dated. Not that there had been many.

Stopping for a quick bite, Wu Feng and Anna chatted about the rest of her week. Not having anything planned for the next day, Anna was at a loss. Perhaps she would finally be able to do a bit of sightseeing. Knowing she would return in two months, it wasn't a high priority anymore. It would be easier for her to go when the weather was warmer. But she had hoped to see something historical before she left.

Wu Feng ran back to get a shopping trolley from the store entrance. When Anna asked about a shopping cart, Feng informed her that they called them trolleys. Walking toward the store's produce section, Anna began looking for the vegetables she needed for her recipes.

Picking through beautiful carrots, she heard soft whispers behind her. Trying to just ignore it, she moved on to find some celery. She would have to wait for Wu Feng to choose the potatoes, the varieties were different here, and she needed to find one that would hold up well in her dishes.

Again, she heard whispers as she moved through the aisles marveling at the variety of fruits and vegetables. Some of which she wasn't familiar with. Where was Wu Feng? He was supposed to be helping her. Not wanting to carry a bunch of vegetables around she put them back until he showed up with the trolly. What was holding him up?

Glancing around, women were pointing in her direction then to the front of the store and whispering. Turning in the direction they were looking, she saw a large crowd had assembled. Anna swore she saw camera flashes in the group. Was that Wu Feng standing in front of them? Looking around, there was a growing number of people pointing to her and looking at their phones.

Pulling her own phone from her pocket, she saw a message from Wu Feng she had missed. Ms. Anna, head for the restroom. Stay there until I message you. Someone tipped off the media.

Frantically looking for the restrooms, she saw a young woman wearing a smock with a name tag reading Daiyu. Anna hoped she was an employee that could direct her to a possible safe area.

"Excuse me. Could you point me in the direction of the restrooms?" Anna asked in Mandarin. The employee she had thought was an older woman turned out to be a young girl, possibly just out of high school. Startled by the Western woman speaking Mandarin, the girl pointed to the front of the store close to where the mob was growing.

"Damn," Anna muttered under her breath in English. That wasn't going to help. "Daiyu? Is that your name?" Anna spoke softly, switching back to Mandarin.

Nodding, the girl seemed to be getting her bearings. Clamoring from the media at the front of the store distracted her. "How can I be of assistance, ma'am?" she asked when she looked back at Anna.

"Do you see that group of people by the front door? I have a bad feeling they are here because of me. Is there somewhere I could go so they won't disrupt your store? Perhaps you could find your manager for me?" Anna led her towards an aisle with a less direct line of sight from the front door while she spoke.

"Certainly, ma'am." Looking around, the girl pulled Anna towards a nook holding cooking wines. "Please wait here. I will return soon." She darted away, heading further into the store.

Peaking around the shelves, Anna saw Wu Feng losing ground. He had experience wrangling the paparazzi and media, but these were like rabid dogs on the scent of fresh meat. Prospects of getting the first photos of the now-famous screenwriter Anna Cassidy were too much of a draw. He didn't dare even try sending a message to anyone for help, or they might slip past him.

Pulling her phone out, Anna wasn't sure to whom she should send a message. Chen was supposed to be resting and Xian was at work. Huang Hu would know what to do. Touching his contact number, the phone rang twice before the pleasant male voice came through the phone. "Hello, Ms. Anna. How can I help you?"

"Huang Hu, help! Wu Feng and I came to a market to pick up ingredients for dinner tonight and someone tipped off the vultures that I'm here. Wu Feng is holding them off by the front door, but I'm not sure how long he can keep them at bay. One of the clerks from the store is getting her manager and I'm hiding in a wine aisle, trying to stay out of their direct sight." Not sure if she should be angry or scared, Anna moved further into the nook, trying to stay hidden.

"Ms. Anna, do you know which market you're at?" Huang Hu's voice was strained now. How ridiculous was it that she couldn't even go out to get groceries without being harassed?

"To be honest, Hu, I'm not even sure. We had just finished eating at a little bistro in the store. Wu Feng said the market wasn't far from the apartment." Anna craned her neck, looking for some store sign to give her an idea.

Anna could hear the relief in Huang Hu's voice when he said, "Ms. Anna, I believe I know the store you're at. Hold on. I'll get the calvary."

"Hu!" Anna called before he could hang up. "Don't you dare disturb Chen! He is still recovering from the accident."

"He's not the calvary I was thinking of. Please trust me, Ms. Anna." With that, the call ended.

Trying to devise options to disguise herself, Anna pulled up the hood of the sweatshirt over her hair, the red and blonde of her highlights stood out. Perhaps covering it would help. Wrapping her arms around herself, she leaned against the end of a shelf. She waited, avoiding the glances of patrons shopping for their own items. Remembering she had a mask in her pocket, Anna pulled the mask over her face, further helping her disguise. Not much she could do about her five-foot ten-inch height; she stood a few inches taller than most women in the store.

Contemplating an exit strategy, Anna was working on a plan when a harried middle-aged man in a white dress shirt, blue tie and dark slacks rushed up to her. "Are you Ms. Cassidy?"

Nodding, Anna pulled her mask down. "Yes, how did you know my name?"

Looking around, he motioned for her to follow him. "Please come this way, ma'am."

Following the furtive man, he led her further into the store to a hallway leading to what must have been the employee lounge. Standing and looking out a window was Xian. Hearing footsteps, he turned to see Anna. The look of worry on his face was replaced with relief. Doing his best not to ruin his chairman persona, Xian calmly walked to Anna and looked her over. "I can't let you out of my sight for five minutes, can I?" His scolding tone hid the fear that tried to creep into his voice.

"Yeah, like I'm a fan of being harassed by the media," Anna growled at Xian. "I just wanted to pick up a few groceries for dinner tonight. How could I know there would be a paparazzi flood."

"Send your grocery list to Wu Feng. Your shopping spree has been cut short," Xian said and shoved his hands in his pockets. He desperately wanted to wrap Anna in his arms and protect her. That was the last thing she needed right now. It was bad enough that they knew of her, but if they found out she was involved with him in any way other than business, she would never get any peace.

"Xian, I would have had him pick the stuff up for me anyhow, but there are seasonings I need that I'm not sure they have here. Is there some way I can at least get to that aisle? The rest is easy enough, meat and vegetables mostly."

Xian looked at the manager standing by the door. "Would it be possible to clear the spice aisle for fifteen minutes?" Xian looked to Anna to see if that would be enough.

Nodding, Anna wrapped her arms around herself again. So much drama for a few groceries. She decided she wouldn't do any more shopping while in Beijing, at least not on this trip.

Nodding, the manager bowed to Xian and rushed from the room so he could make arrangements for that aisle to be blocked off. Now that they were alone, Xian grabbed Anna and wrapped her in his arms. "What am I going to do with you?" he murmured into her hair.

"What can you do but love me?" Anna joked. Tension was radiating from Xian. He was scared and that worried Anna. "What's wrong, Xian?"

"How did they know you were here? I haven't had a chance to talk to Wu Feng yet. Did anything out of the ordinary happen?"

"No, we stopped at a boutique a few blocks away so I could pick up a couple of coats, then we came here and had a bite to eat before we started shopping. Wu Feng had gone to get a trolley and didn't come back. I was picking out produce when I noticed the mob growing by the doors. At least a young clerk helped me hide. She ran to get her manager to help. While I was waiting, I called Huang Hu and I'm guessing you're the cavalry he mentioned."

"Riding to your rescue again." Xian hugged her closer. "Yeah, Huang Hu called me when he hung up with you. Knowing the neighborhood, we figured this must have been the market you were at. I verified it with my news department as well; there had been an anonymous tip that the award-winning screenwriter Anna Cassidy had been seen at this store. Since you haven't really had your photo taken, other than in Taipei, the vultures are clamoring for a chance to get the first photos of you." Xian had raked his staff over the coals about it. There was a standing order for all of his publications not to harass Anna.

Leaning her forehead on Xian's chest, Anna tried to let some of the tension melt away. "I just wanted to make a special meal and this happens. Do we have a plan to get me out of here?"

"Working on it. Let's get your spices first and then go from there," he said, tucking a bang that had escaped her ponytail behind her ear. Xian didn't want to let her go.

Hearing steps coming in their direction, Xian reluctantly stepped away from Anna. The manager appeared at the door, bowed and waved for them to follow.

Leading them into the store she saw there was an aisle blocked by employees. Anna ducked through the line and looked over the extensive selection of spices. Some day she hoped she could come back and spend more time in the fragrant aisle. Finding the main herbs and spices that would work, she handed them to the manager and followed Xian back to the employee area.

"I'll message Wu Feng the rest of the ingredients. It's pretty simple, but it's frustrating that I can't even get groceries without drama." Anna began pacing around the room.

Xian checked his phone and saw that Huang Hu had messaged him that they had an exit plan. They would sneak Anna through the freight area of the store. From what they could tell, the media wasn't covering that entrance. Huang Hu had picked up one of the limo vans that the Wei group used for transporting celebrities to different events. With the dark windows, they should be able to get Anna out and back to the penthouse.

"We have a plan. Now, to get you to the freight area without being noticed by too many customers."

"I have that covered." Anna pulled her hood up and put her mask on. "Does this help?"

Giving Anna the once over, Xian took his jacket off and had Anna put it on over her hoodie. Now she looked like many of the women in Beijing trying to keep low-key. It covered her hair and most of her face, making her stand out less. If she would keep her hands in her pockets and look like she was browsing on her way to the hallway across the store, they might be able to pull this off.

Xian let Anna know he would go and help Wu Feng tame the circus that had blocked the store's front doors. Huang Hu was waiting for her by the store's loading dock and watching closely for suspicious vehicles.

Checking down the hallway, Xian saw the young clerk that had helped Anna earlier. She stood at the end of the hall watching for any suspicious patrons lurking around. He motioned her closer. "Are we ready to help Ms. Cassidy?"

Bowing slightly, she replied, "Yes, Mr. Wei. As the media is blocking the doors, we can get customers out but not back in, so the store is pretty empty. If we hurry, we should be able to get her through without much fuss." She motioned to Anna.

Anna started to follow but turned back, pulled her mask down and gave Xian a peck on the cheek. "My knight in shining armor again." Turning, she followed the young woman down the hallway.

Touching his cheek where Anna had kissed him, Xian battled the urge to follow her. Unfortunately, he had the media to wrangle.

章

Chapter 57

Huang Hu waited with the van door open for Anna as she came rushing out of the freight door, almost diving into the back of the van. She leaned back in her seat and sighed, glad to be in a safe space for the moment. Huang Hu climbed into the driver's seat, then he turned and checked on her.

"Ms. Anna, are you all right?" He knew that Chen would read him the riot act when he found out what happened, but he had orders from both Anna and Xian not to disturb him today. The doctor had said no excitement, but that wasn't an option with Anna around.

"Thanks to you, Wu Feng and Xian, I'm fine now. Someone has been tailing us though; there has to have been for them to know what grocery store we were at. We didn't have a problem at the boutique, but it wouldn't have caused even close to the scene it did here. I'm just glad they didn't tip them off earlier. I had hoped to do some sightseeing tomorrow, but I doubt that is an option now."

Huang Hu turned back to watch out the windshield for suspicious vehicles. He was waiting for the go-ahead from Mr. Wei, though it might be a good idea to make a run for the apartment with all of the paparazzi and media busy in the store. Wu Feng and Xian ran interference, trying to get the group to disburse. Now that Anna was safely out, they would allow the media hounds to roam the store looking for her.

Huang Hu's phone started ringing; looking at the screen, he groaned. Chen was calling. He wasn't sure if Mr. Xiao knew what was happening, but Huang Hu would bet his next month's wages he did.

"Hello, Mr. Xiao," Huang Hu answered. Glancing back at Anna, he held a finger to his lips. Perhaps if Chen didn't hear Anna's voice, there was a chance to salvage the situation.

"Huang Hu, when were you going to tell me?" Anna could

hear Chen's angry voice from her seat in the back of the van. Cringing, she didn't envy Huang Hu at that moment.

"I'm not sure what you mean, sir."

"Is Anna okay? Why do I see rumors all over the internet saying that Anna Cassidy is holed up in a shopping market? I tried calling and messaging her with no luck. **WHAT IS GOING ON?**"

Hearing that Chen had tried contacting her, Anna checked her phone to find her ringer was turned off. She had forgotten she had flipped it on silent mode while hiding in the wine section. Her phone ringing would have tipped off people where she was. Five missed calls and three times that many text messages were on her phone. Anna lifted her phone and showed Huang Hu the evidence of Chen's concern.

"Mr. Xiao, Ms. Cassidy is just fine. With Mr. Wei's assistance, Wu Feng was able to fend off the media and paparazzi. She should be returning to the apartment in less than half an hour," he replied with a look at Anna to see if that sounded reasonable. Nodding, she motioned to her phone. "Why don't you try calling her again? I believe they have the situation under control now and she should be able to talk to you."

"We will talk about this later. I should have been notified immediately that there was an issue," Chen groused as he disconnected the call. Huang Hu leaned forward and rested his forehead on the steering wheel. He was in deep shit.

Moments later, Anna's phone started to vibrate. Looking at her screen showed it was Chen. "Hi Chen, how are you feeling?"

"Well, the doctor told me to have a mellow day, no serious excitement. I'm not sure what I'm supposed to do when I see the name of the woman I care for plastered all over the internet. Are you okay? Please tell me you're safe." Anna felt terrible; the concern in his voice made her heart skip a few beats. Could she make it until Monday without giving into her feelings again?

"Chen, I'm fine. Wu Feng was my hero. He kept the mob at bay until the store manager could sneak me out the back door, so to speak." She continued to do her best to reassure Chen that she was fine.

"Get your butt back here right now. You aren't allowed out without either Xian or me escorting you. No offense to Wu Feng or Huang Hu, but they weren't equipped to deal with this kind of situation. Did you get what you needed?"

So much for her sightseeing. "No, but Wu Feng has my list. We need to return to the apartment so I can start cooking. It's going to be cutting it close as it is. I had just started my shopping when the horde descended on the store. They suspect that Li Ming had something to do with it, though how can that be? I thought she was under observation in the hospital."

A pregnant pause on Chen's part had Anna concerned. "Chen? Are you there?"

"Yeah, I will do some investigating until you get home. Just hurry back so I can see that you're in one piece," Chen said and the tension in his voice as he spoke worried Anna. He was supposed to be resting and not getting stressed.

"I'm on my way. See you soon, dear." Anna hoped calling him "dear" would help calm Chen a little.

"Just hurry," were the last words before the call ended.

"Hu, we need to go now. I need to get back to the penthouse before Chen does something rash. I'll call Xian and let him know to meet us there." She hit Xian's name in her recent calls.

A few moments passed before Xian's voice answered, "Anna, are you safe?"

Smiling, Anna wanted to reassure him. "I'm fine. Huang Hu has me ensconced in one of the limo vans. Chen found out what happened; I need to get back to the penthouse before he does something stupid. So much for keeping his stress at ground level. We are heading back now."

"Good, I'll be there shortly. I'm doing an impromptu press conference before I leave. Some of the more aggressive press is adamant that you are still hiding somewhere in the store."

"Well, I'll remove myself from the premises, and hopefully, that will help the situation. See you back home." It felt right to hear herself use the word home after Chen had also said it.

"See you at home," he echoed, hanging up the call. Xian stared at his phone; Anna had used the word home. He hadn't used that word in a long time. Saying it to Anna made him feel warm. It would be Anna's home for a while; why wouldn't she refer to it that way?

Fifteen minutes later, Huang Hu pulled up to the front door of the apartment complex. "Ms. Anna, I will let you out here and return the van to Wei Media. Will you be all right to get up to the penthouse on your own?"

Checking around to see if she saw anyone, Anna nodded. "I should be fine. It looks like the coast is clear."

Opening the van's back door, she looked in both directions before she quickly walked to the sliding glass door of the building. The whooshing of the automatic door startled her for a moment; her nerves were strung tighter than a violin. Stepping into the lobby, she found she had good reason for being so jumpy. Sitting in a chair near the reception desk was Scott.

Anna was amazed at her self-restraint at that moment. She usually wasn't one to use a large number of expletives. Still, having been in the military, and worked in the freight business, Anna could curse a blue streak with the best of them. Could she make it past without him noticing her?

"Ms. Cassidy, you have a guest waiting for you," the young woman at the desk said, trying to be helpful.

Pulling her phone from her pocket, Anna made the motions as though she was replying to a text message. Instead, she typed a statement, *Call security* **NOW!** showing it to the woman.

Panic crossed the woman's face for a moment before her training kicked in and her composure slid into place once again. Pretending that she was returning to work, she sent a message to the security team on duty, letting them know there was a possible emergency. Once that was completed, she also sent a message to Mr. Wei. His guest was visibly trembling at the sight of the man.

Throughout the interaction with the receptionist, Anna kept an eye on Scott. How had he found her? They had thought no one knew where she was.

———

Having heard the receptionist greeting Anna, Scott lazily turned to ensure it was the woman he wanted so badly. It has been almost a year since he first saw Anna at Jerry's. Not knowing much about the quirky author, he started probing the regulars and asking innocuous questions. As he learned more about her, his obsession grew.

After a few months he realized she was it; the one he had lost while he had been in the military. They had been stationed together during school and hung out together. She had suddenly disappeared just when he had planned to ask her out and had been devastated. But now, he had found her again. It had to be fate. He would be the man to fill her life with happiness. Couldn't she see that?

——

Trying to determine the best way to stall, Anna smiled reluctantly as she greeted the man who gave her the heebie-jeebies. Being this close to Scott made her skin crawl.

When he had first started hanging out at the bar, Anna hadn't spoken to him much since he made her uncomfortable. As time passed, the unease she felt if they happened to be at the bar together continued to grow. Anna had even started calling Liz to ensure he wasn't there before stopping by.

"Hi Scott, you're quite a ways from Fortine. What brings you to Beijing?" Anna's voice had a tremor and she hoped he wouldn't notice it. She couldn't tip her hand before the security arrived.

Grinning as though Anna called him by an endearment rather than just his name, Scott stood and walked around the chair. "I came all this way to see you. Congratulations on your award win. I'm guessing your quiet existence in Fortine ends when people discover where you live." The thinly veiled threat was dangling out there.

Squinting at his blatant disregard for her privacy she said, "Why would anyone find out where I live? I doubt they've even heard about this back in the States, let alone in Fortine, Montana. No reason for them to find out about it now."

Anna wasn't sure if she had ever seen a look of sheer evil like the one that flashed across Scott's face for a brief instant. She might never have seen it if she hadn't concentrated so closely on him. Fine hairs on Anna's neck stood on end and goosebumps covered her arms. Being sensitive to emotions, she could almost feel a wave of malevolence emanating from him. How long until security reached her? Why did she let Huang Hu leave without walking her in?

Smirking at Anna, Scott moved a few steps closer. "Anna, why would you treat your fiancé this way? I haven't seen you in a couple of weeks and you're treating me like I'm a stranger."

Using the last of her sheer willpower, Anna stood her ground. Thinking to herself repeatedly, *I can't tip him off; someone will be here soon.*

"Well, as you aren't her fiancé, I could see why she would be uncomfortable with you calling her that." Anna had never been so relieved to hear a voice in her life. She was going to read him the riot act when she finally had him alone, but she knew that he would either help or make things ten times worse at the moment.

Taking several giant strides, she wrapped her arms around Chen's neck and kissed him as though her life depended on it. At that moment, it had.

Scott's pleasant mask slipped as he watched Anna kissing that damned actor. Quickly catching himself, he pulled his cheerful facade back to the forefront. Kicking himself, he should have just ambushed her outside; letting her make it into the building had been the mistake. She was on their turf now.

Caught off guard, Chen wouldn't let the opportunity pass him by. His arms circled Anna, returning the desperate kiss, pulling her into his protective embrace. Finally, breaking away from the kiss he whispered in Anna's ear, "Is that whom I think it is?"

Nodding imperceptibly, Anna didn't want to move from the safety of his arms. Chen was there; he came to her rescue. "Forgive me," Anna whispered to him before facing Scott once again. "**THIS** is my fiancé, Chen. I'm not sure where you got the impression we were engaged. I can count on one hand how many times I've had a conversation longer than ten minutes with you."

This time the anger couldn't be hidden on his face. "You're

MINE!" Scott growled. "Why do you hide behind that Chink?"

Before either knew what happened, the sound of Anna's hand slapping Scott's face reverberated throughout the lobby. She had no idea how she had moved so quickly, crossing the distance to defend Chen. "Obviously, you don't know me well at all. I don't tolerate racial slurs, so I think you should leave. You're not welcome at this apartment complex and it would be best if you return to Montana."

Anna stepped back from Scott to put her out of arm's reach. There was a crazed look inching over his face.

"You need to come home with me. Anna, you don't belong here with them. I'm the one who can take care of you." The deranged man's voice became more strained as he moved to grab Anna's wrist.

Before he could reach Anna, a wall moved between them. "Excuse me, ma'am, is this person bothering you?" She looked up at the hulking man in a security uniform. Muscles in his chest and biceps strained against the black fabric. The square, clean-cut jaw beneath the broad nose and intense brown eyes made Anna swallow hard. Heck, she was a woman, and this man was a prime specimen.

Bringing herself back to the situation, she said, "Yes, that man isn't welcome here. If he doesn't leave, please detain him for the police." Anna spoke up to the six-foot-four-inch powerfully built guard.

Bowing his head in acknowledgment, the guard turned to Scott. "Excuse me, sir, you're not welcome on the premises. I will have to contact the authorities if you don't leave."

Glaring at Anna, Scott raised his hands in quiescence. "I'm going, but Anna, you will be my wife." He turned and walked towards the door. "This isn't over," he said as he looked over his shoulder one last time before stomping through the doors.

"Thank you..." Anna stared up at the guard.

"Liu Chaoxiang, ma'am. Sorry, it took me a few minutes to arrive. Will you be okay now?"

"Thanks to you, Liu Chaoxiang, I'll be fine. You came at the perfect time. Can you get a copy of his image from the security footage and tell everyone he's not allowed? If I'd known he would be so brazen, I would have brought it up earlier." Anna held out her hand to shake the guards.

Her hand was engulfed in a grizzly bear paw-sized hand. "You're welcome, Ms. If you need further assistance, please don't hesitate to contact the receptionist."

Nodding her head, she grabbed Chen's hand and pulled him toward the elevator. She wasn't sure what would happen, but she planned on giving Chen at least one more light the volcano kiss before they reached the apartment.

章

Chapter 58

When the elevator doors closed, Anna leaned against the wall. Her plan of kissing Chen was totally blown out the window because her body revolted. Trying to calm herself, she closed her eyes and took deep breaths. *In through the nose, out through the mouth.*

Chen pushed the floor button, entered the code that allowed them to go directly to the penthouse's foyer and stared at the numbers, his mind in shock over the events in the lobby. Anna had apologized, then called him her fiancé and kissed him as he had never been kissed before. How was he to take that? On the flip side, he knew what Scott looked like now, which was good.

With a soft ding the door of the elevator opened. Finally, Anna calmed her breathing, grabbed a stunned Chen and pulled him to the apartment door. With the limited access to the floor she felt safer. Entering the door code, she tugged Chen inside, slamming it behind her. She could finally breathe easier. She had been uncomfortable around Scott up to this point; now she was terrified.

"Chen, snap out of it," Anna said and shook him, hoping to get a response. After Anna had kissed him in the lobby he had shut down. He hadn't said a word after his gallant entrance.

"Huh? Where? Anna?" Chen looked around, unsure how he had gotten from the lobby to the apartment.

Seeing Chen returning to himself, Anna headed to the sitting area by the kitchen and slumped on the couch. "I need a drink. A really stiff one. Possibly a lot of them."

"You don't drink. That wouldn't help the situation," his voice of reason tried to dissuade her from getting bombed off her ass at one in the afternoon.

She gave Chen a dirty look while saying, "You're a party pooper!" Grumbling, Anna slouched back and folded her arms over her middle. Her nerves were still rattled from the morning. "Thanks for coming to the rescue. I'm not sure what I would have done if you hadn't shown up to distract him when you did. The poor girl at the desk looked pretty freaked out."

Sitting next to Anna on the couch, Chen decided to broach the subject of what Anna had told Scott. "Soooo..." Chen started, drawing the word out, "...what was that all about? Especially the part involving me?"

Rubbing the bridge of her nose, Anna was dreading this conversation. "There was a reason I said sorry first. I couldn't think of a way out of the situation other than calling you my fiancé, hoping he would get the hint. No, we aren't engaged. I still can't even say I'll be your girlfriend."

"I see." The sound of dejection in Chen's voice made Anna's heart ache. She still couldn't say she would date Chen. Not when she had confusing feelings about Xian too, especially after today's rescue.

Leaning back on a pillow, Anna closed her eyes, trying to cope with the day's drama; and she still needed to cook as soon as Wu Feng showed up with her groceries.

"Anna, wake up." Someone shook her shoulder.

"Who? Huh?" Groggily, Anna looked around to see who had shaken her. Wu Feng stood in front of Anna with an odd look.

"Feng, when did you get here?" she asked. Looking at her watch, it had been almost thirty minutes since they returned to the apartment. Looking to her right, the couch was empty. Chen had left her sleeping on the couch. She wasn't surprised after she had thrown his world upside down. Again.

"I just arrived with your groceries. Mr. Wei had to return to the office and finish a few things. I got an odd message from Mr. Xiao saying he was returning to his apartment. Why do I get a bad feeling something else happened?"

Anna just sat and looked at Wu Feng blankly. She knew she had hurt Chen badly this time. Anna rested her head on her knees for a few minutes before she gathered herself together and got up. She needed to get cooking. That would take her mind off the mammoth-sized mess her life had become.

"You could say that. I need to talk to Xian before I fill you in. I feel he may already know what happened, but I need to explain things." Digging in her pocket, she pulled out her earbuds and popped them in. At least she could work on dinner while she talked.

"Call Xian," Anna instructed her phone. She wasn't sure it rang before she heard Xian's stressed voice.

"Anna, what in the world happened? I received a call from the security team at the apartment building."

"It's a long story...I'm trying to get food started. I'm not sure if Chen will be here tonight. That's the complicated part of the story." Anna explained to Xian what happened in detail. "To try and help diffuse the situation, I kissed Chen and called him my fiancé after apologizing first. He didn't take it very well. I told him after that I still can't commit to dating him... and I think this time it really hurt him." Anna had put a pot of water on to start cooking one of the chickens for soup.

Due to the lack of time, she had requested Wu Feng pick up a pre-cooked chicken to add to the stock. It wouldn't be the best she had ever made, but it would suffice.

"You're not going anywhere without one of us for the rest of your trip. We need to contact the detective handling your case at the hotel. I have a strong suspicion that Scott was involved. Now we have a picture of him we can turn over to the police."

"Well, there goes my sightseeing this trip," Anna sighed out as she finished cutting up the vegetables for her soup and the main dish.

"Sorry, Anna, perhaps we can do a little tomorrow."

"I'm not holding my breath, dear. Let's get through until Monday. Then I'll be out of your hair for almost two months. Perhaps everything will calm down by the time I return."

On the other end of the line, hesitation made Anna wonder what Xian was thinking right then. She was just a burden to the guys right now; and to top it off, feelings were being hurt and that wasn't her intention. As much as she felt closer to being ready for a relationship again, she wouldn't if it broke those she cared about.

Trying to distract herself from the feelings aspect of the day, Anna figured she should find out if Lin Bolin showed up for the interview and started his new training. "Hey Xian, did Lin Bolin arrive to meet with you?"

"He did. I'm quite impressed with him. Due to the market incident, I was late returning to the office; he had arrived on time and patiently awaited my return. His first concern was if you were all right. The story was plastered all over the internet and he had seen it. I believe you invited him for dinner tonight. He is excited to attend." Hearing his approval of her choice in an assistant made Anna grin.

"Well, if you want to eat tonight, I better get on with my cooking. I noticed I had already missed a step I would normally have done. I still need to figure out what to do about Chen. He went back to his place, so I'm not sure if he will be here tonight or not. Thanks for letting me vent, Xian. Oh, I have one more thing to discuss with you. Do you have any female friends you might invite? I'm feeling seriously outnumbered as it would be me with six men. I've invited Dr. Lin and his wife, but I'm unsure if she will attend." Anna was hoping to have some female conversation.

Usually, Anna was more comfortable with male company; she had been since she was young and a tomboy herself. Since she had become close with Dana, Gloria, Christie and Frankie, she missed having women around on a rare occasion.

"I might know of someone. I'll see if she is available. I'll hang up first; see you when I get home." Xian wondered if Anna would notice that he had referred to the penthouse as home. It slid off the tongue naturally after such a long time. He hoped she could feel like it truly was her home.

Vegetables in various states of preparation were laid out on the counter. Anna looked them over and added what she needed to the stockpot on the stove. It was good that she had noticed the lack of cookware and had Wu Feng purchase it.

Reaching a point where she needed to wait, Anna checked on her computer installation from that morning. Checking the screen on the laptop, the data had successfully migrated over. Now she just had to finish the updates to the software on the computer. Having just done a restore from a Time Machine backup, it didn't require much tweaking on her part.

Sitting there, Anna stared at the screen as the final updates finished. She should work on her book. That was pressing, but her heart wasn't in it right now. Chen leaving without letting her know bothered her. To be fair, she hadn't tried calling him either. Was it worth dragging up more emotions? Yes. She had to see if they were okay.

Initiating the call, Anna almost thought he wasn't going to answer. Just before it should go to voicemail, a resigned voice came through the speaker. "Hi."

"Where are you? I've been worried about you." Salty pools of tears began welling in Anna's eyes. She was terrified that Chen wouldn't be back.

"Sorry, I had some stuff to take care of. I should have woken you before I left, but I know you're exhausted with everything. You didn't sleep well last night."

"No, I didn't, but how did you know?" Had Chen been the one to cover her up?

Avoiding the question, Chen changed the subject. "What time is dinner tonight?"

A wave of relief rolled over Anna; he planned on being there. "I was figuring 7:30 P.M. I'm hoping it will be finished in time. I took a shortcut I've used before; it won't be my best meal, but I hope you will like it."

"If you've made it, I'm sure it will be great. Anna, I'll be there, but I need to go and finish what I'm working on. Please don't go out unless Xian or I are with you. We got lucky earlier." Anna hadn't heard Chen so earnest before.

"No, I won't go anywhere. If I need something simple, I believe there is a market in the apartment complex." Curiosity over what Chen could be up to almost made Anna ask. It wasn't any of her business what Chen was doing. Hadn't she just affirmed that they weren't dating?

"Don't leave the apartment alone. Someone got into your locked hotel room; I'm not completely sold on the fact that they can't get into the apartment building. Do this for me, please, Anna." Trying to control the emotion in his voice, Chen couldn't let her know he was on the verge of tears after what he'd recently found out. "I need to go. Anna, promise me."

"I promise," Anna said before the call ended. What was Chen up to? Why did it feel like they had both been on the verge of crying? She was going to find out later, one way or another, what was happening.

Looking at the blank phone, Chen knew he should have told Anna that Li Ming was at large. He had stopped at the hospital to see how she was doing and if they had a diagnosis, only to find that a Dr. Li had discharged her. He would bet his newest award it had been the same Dr. Li that had tried to force Chen into seclusion. It would be difficult to verify as the doctor had disappeared suspiciously.

When Anna had called, he was sitting in the office of Detective Zhào. Chen wanted to check on how the case was going with the break-in at the hotel. Before he had left the apartment building, he had stopped at the security office and retrieved a photo of the intruder. Chen had wanted to notify the officers about what had happened at the apartment and give them a picture of Scott, hoping they could then find him in the video at the hotel.

Scott had been in the security footage the morning of the hotel break-in. While looking through the footage, they had seen Scott and Li Ming in front of the hotel shortly after Chen had left the night before the break-in as well. He had been lurking around the hotel since Friday morning of the previous week. Now that they knew who was to blame, they would just have to catch him.

Chen's emotions had been close to overwhelmed when he realized how close Anna had been to being kidnapped or worse. Of course, with Anna's fantastic luck, she had picked that moment to call. Choking back his anger and fear, he answered his phone.

Realizing she was in grave danger not just from Li Ming but also from this Scott character made him finally admit to himself how much he loved Anna. Whomever Anna chose, it was okay with him; he just wanted her alive and happy.

Chen had also discussed with Detective Zhào what had happened to him after the accident and the suspicious doctor at the hospital. Hearing what had happened, the detective informed Chen that a man had been found dead in one of the hospital rooms the morning after he had been discharged. He would almost bet it had been Chen's room where the man had been found. He was going to have security look into that as well. Having seen the man, Chen offered to go and see if it was indeed the fake physician.

Now that the police had proof of who the intruder had been, they could watch for him. At this point, they only had him on breaking and entering charges. He hadn't done anything illegal at the apartment complex so they couldn't go after him for that. Because of the threat to Anna's life, they agreed to station an officer to watch the apartment building. If he tried getting to her there once, he might return for another attempt.

Knowing they had planned a couple of very public events to attend on Friday and Saturday with Anna, Chen also told the detective they had plans to get extra security. When Chen had called Xian about Li Ming's disappearance from the hospital, they had agreed that more security was necessary. Xian would get several security specialists who would be with Anna when he and Chen couldn't be.

Anna's safety was their main priority. They just hoped she would understand the extra precautions.

章

Chapter 59

Checking her watch, it was almost 7 o'clock and no one was there yet. There were no calls or text messages about anyone being late or not coming. Were they all going to show up a few minutes before the meal? Anna tasted the soup, it had a slightly different flavor than she was used to, but it was still fabulous. She made her usual massive batch, hoping they were all hungry.

Checking the chickens in the oven, she found they had about twenty minutes left and would be done in plenty of time to let them rest before carving. Looking through the cupboards, Anna had located enough serving dishes for most of the meal. Remembering a trick she had seen on some cooking show, she put all the plates through the dishwasher to warm them right before she put them on the table.

Wanting this to be a special evening, Anna had set the large table in the dining room. This would be her first time entertaining in Beijing and she wanted everything to go smoothly. Not knowing how many would attend, she set the table for ten people, as many chairs as available. If one of the settings wasn't used, it wasn't the end of the world.

Waiting for the chicken to finish, Anna took the time to duck into her bedroom and change into a soft, ankle-length flowing skirt and a long-sleeve gauzy blouse. Slipping on her brand new pair of lace-up sandals, she checked her outfit. She looked sophisticated, not a word she ever thought she would use to describe herself. Her hair was done in a simple braid as she wasn't in the mood to do anything fancier.

A loud noise started blaring from the kitchen. The timer had gone off, letting Anna know the chickens were finished and ready to take out so they could rest. She knew the meal would be a hit when she could smell the honey and curry from her bedroom, the scent permeated the whole apartment.

Pulling the crispy-skinned fowl from the oven, she ladled on the final basting of the curry and honey mixture. Using a knife and spatula, she transferred the plump birds to the large cutting board, the smell tempting her not to share with anyone.

She had been lucky, the kitchen had most of the dishes and utensils she had needed for the meal, but there were a few items she would either need to shop for or ship from home. Some of the creature comforts she was used to having while preparing food would help make the transition easier.

Anna started carving the chickens, slicing the breasts and cutting the legs, thighs and wings. Using the platter she had found, she kept one of the chickens whole while positioning the cut pieces around the whole bird. Carefully, she selected vegetables to display with the birds, taking extra time with the presentation.

Picking up a sliver of the chicken, she tested it for moisture and flavor. It was spot on. Juices dripped down her wrist from the piece she had tasted, it was so moist.

Sliding the platter into the warm oven, she covered it to keep it from drying out before she served it. Dipping a spoon into the soup, she tested the dumplings and potatoes wanting to make sure they were cooked through. Anna was curious what they would all think of her offering. This meal would be different from the usual local fare.

Looking at her phone, it was now 7:10 P.M. and still nothing. Anna had begun to suspect something was going on. At least one of the guys should have contacted her or shown up by now. She decided to give them five more minutes before she started making phone calls.

Those five minutes passed and still no one had arrived. *That's it!* Anna decided she needed to make some calls. **SOMEONE** should have been here by now.

As she picked up her phone, she heard voices and the door of the apartment opening. Laughter filled the apartment as several people arrived. Did they all show up at once? Not sure if she should be happy, sad or hurt, Anna continued with her meal prep. She decided on being pissed off at that moment. Xian and Chen knew how important this was for her and they showed up a few moments before the meal. How rude.

"Something smells divine," a female voice said, carrying into the kitchen.

Anna smiled; good, Dr. Lin had brought his wife with him. At least she wouldn't be the only woman there that evening. Picking up the platter Anna had set down, she took a deep breath of the fragrant meat. Curry was one of her favorites and the smell lingered in the kitchen. The yellow hue of the vegetables came from the turmeric in the curry powder. Anna had dyed her counter and clothing with the bright yellow of the curry on more than one occasion. Perhaps one day, when she finally decided to get back into her crafting, she could use it as a dye for wool.

Taking the platter to the dining table, she sat it down next to the other dishes that had already made it to the table. Steam from the Chicken Knoephla soup curled into the air, carrying the earthy scent of the celery she had used. Anna had been careful when she added her vegetables to the broth; if she added the carrots too early, the soup could have a sweeter flavor. Liking a little bit of heat, she usually added a small amount of cayenne powder for a little extra kick.

Returning to the kitchen, Anna smelled something off. She didn't believe there was any pan or pot on the stove. How could anything be making such a pungent odor? Checking the stove and oven, she noticed a few drops of food had fallen on the hot element causing the acrid stench of burnt food to permeate the air. Anna doubted the windows opened; how would she get that smell out before the party?

Digging through the kitchen cabinets, Anna located a candle. Perhaps with it burning it might pull the slight funk from the air. Finding a match in one of the drawers, Anna lit it, watching the flames flicker and dance on the end of the wooden stick. Touching the flame to the fresh wick, it caught immediately, flames licking over the cotton and wax.

Notes of vanilla soon wafted throughout the kitchen and blended with the scent of the curry. At least that disaster was averted. The laughter and chatting flowed from the living room area of the penthouse. Wow, they couldn't even check to see how she was doing and offer her help? After everything that had occurred earlier today? Disappointment and hurt overshadowed her previous anger.

Dishes arranged on the turntable in the middle of the dining table, Anna removed her apron and sent Xian and Chen a text message. *Foods on the table. Enjoy.* Peeking into the living room, she saw a young woman talking with Chen and Xian.

Quietly, Anna took the back hallway to her room, avoiding the living and dining room areas. She didn't want to see any of them at the moment. They ignored her to entertain another woman. Anna would bet that wasn't Dr. Lin's wife. Closing and locking both doors, Anna sat down on the bed, tears of frustration threatening to fall. Could just one thing go right?

Grabbing her wrap from the bed, Anna decided she needed to get out of there. Damn the promise she made Chen; if she didn't get some air, she might say something she would regret later. She was livid. Opening the door to the back hallway, Anna carefully checked to see if anyone was in that part of the apartment. Seeing no one, she slipped to the front door, opening it as quietly as possible and pulling it shut behind her until she heard the faint click of the latch.

Pressing the button for the elevator, she waited impatiently for the car to arrive. She needed to get away before they discovered she was gone. Anna didn't want to talk to any of them at the moment. Despite her efforts to put together a special meal, they ignored her all afternoon and arrived minutes beforehand. The door of the left elevator opened and Anna stepped in. Pushing the lobby button, the doors slid shut just as the right elevator doors opened for Dr. Lin, his wife and Lin Bolin.

Dr. Lin knocked on the door as his wife and the young man who had introduced himself as Ms. Cassidy's new assistant chatted. He had informed them his name was Lin Bolin and he would work with Anna as her assistant when she returned to Beijing in January.

"Coming," a voice called. Opening the door, Huang Hu saw the doctor, his wife and Lin Bolin; swinging the door wide, he grinned widely. "Dr. Lin, Mrs. Lin, it's so nice of you to come. Please come in." Seeing the young man from the hotel, he deduced this must be Ms. Anna's new assistant. "Lin Bolin?"

Nodding and bowing his head slightly, Lin Bolin recognized Mr. Xiao's assistant. "Yes. Ms. Cassidy invited me tonight."

"Certainly. Come in. Dinner is ready. We are just waiting on Anna." Huang Hu ushered the couple and young man into the living room where Xian, Chen, Wu Feng and a young woman sat chatting.

"Something smells amazing," the doctor commented when he entered the room.

Chen looked up and saw Dr. Lin. "Dr. Lin, Mrs. Lin, so nice of you to come. Anna will be so pleased to see you."

"Where is Ms. Cassidy? Being this is her party, I had expected her to greet us." Dr. Lin looked around.

Chen and Xian exchanged embarrassed glances. "We aren't sure, actually. We haven't seen her since we got here a few minutes ago."

He gave both of the men a long stare. "You haven't seen her? Didn't you greet her when you arrived? I saw the food set out on the table. Didn't she do that?"

Xian looked down at his phone. *Foods on the table. Enjoy.* He looked at Chen, who had also just seen the message. *Anna?* Xian sent a reply. Not receiving a response, Xian excused himself and hurried to the kitchen. Extra dishes were on the counter, but there was no sign of Anna.

Rushing back to the living room, Xian caught Chen's attention motioning with his head to follow him. Chen got up and excused himself from chatting with the young woman, leaving her to talk with Huang Hu and Wu Feng.

"What's up?" Chen asked.

"Anna's not in the kitchen and isn't replying to my message."

An uneasiness settled over both men. Looking down the hall, they saw that her room door was closed; thinking perhaps she was just freshening up for their guests, they both sent messages. *Everyone's here. Shall we eat?* Chen messaged.

The food smells great, Xian sent.

Minutes passed with no response. "I'll go check; you go entertain our guests," Chen told Xian.

Knocking on Anna's door, there was no answer. Sending another text, Chen heard the alert chime she had set for his messages. "Anna?" Chen called through the door. No answer. He tried the doorknob and the door swung open. Looking in the room, Anna's phone was on the bed, but there was no sign of Anna.

Not finding her, he sent a text to Xian. *Anna isn't here.*

Turning, he rushed down the hall to Anna's office. Empty, her laptop's screensaver showed the photo of Chen and Anna in period garb.

Xian found Chen there. "When did you last speak to Anna?"

"Around 2:30 this afternoon, I believe." Chen checked his phone. "What about you?"

"Probably 2 o'clock." Checking his phone as well to verify it. Cringing, neither had spoken to her all afternoon.

"So you're saying no one has spoken to her all afternoon and we showed up fifteen minutes before the meal started with another woman? Oh, we messed up bad," Chen said.

Fear gripped both men. Where had she gone? After her day, how could they have left her alone with her thoughts?

"You go tell the guests to start eating. Just say Anna ran to the market for something. We don't need to worry them. I'll check with the receptionist and find out if they've seen her. With Scott and Li Ming out there, we have to find her," Xian told Chen as he was pulling up the number for the front desk.

Chen walked back into the living room. "Everyone, please sit down and start eating. Anna had to run to the market; Xian and I are going to check on her. Please, enjoy while the food is warm."

Dr. Lin gave Chen a calculating stare. He knew Chen too well and could see the frantic fear around his genial grin. "Come everyone, let's not waste Anna's hard work." Pulling his phone from his pocket, he sent a message to Chen. *What's going on? What did you two do to Anna?*

Chen looked at his phone when it chimed and winced. We screwed up and left her home alone today after the media tried to mob her and her stalker tried to grab her in the apartment's lobby.

Dr. Lin saw the message and glared at Chen. *You idiot, go find her.*

Nodding, Chen left the room to find Xian waiting for him by the door. "The receptionist saw her about ten minutes ago. She left the building."

Both cursed under their breaths. Chen brightened and said, "There's supposed to be a policeman watching the apartment complex. We can only hope they saw her when she left. Contact the security office and ask if Liu Chaoxiang is working. He helped rescue her from Scott earlier. Perhaps he can be of some assistance."

Waiting for the elevator was agonizing. Each minute Xian and Chen waited was a minute more that Anna could be in danger. Xian was on the phone with the security office and Liu Chaoxiang was indeed on duty. He remembered Anna, and when he found out about the situation, he checked the security cameras around the property. He didn't see Anna. "I will be off work in fifteen minutes; I'll be happy to help look for her."

Chen and Xian quickly walked to the front doors; if only they knew which direction she had headed. Chen noticed a vehicle parked across the street to the entrance with a surly-looking man sitting behind the wheel. Rushing to the car, Chen recognized officer Ma. "Officer Ma, thank goodness. Did you see Ms. Cassidy?"

Recognizing Chen, Officer Ma's expression changed. "Mr. Xiao, are you referring to the lovely woman from the hotel? Is she the one I'm supposed to be protecting? Well damn! Detective Zhào didn't tell me it was Ms. Cassidy. He just told me to watch for a caucasian male with salt and pepper hair."

"That's Anna's stalker. He followed her from Montana in the United States. He was here earlier in the lobby, causing trouble. Scott's the reason you're here on a stakeout. Did you happen to see Ms. Cassidy leave?" The anxiety was beginning to break through Chen's calm expression.

"No, I wasn't watching for people leaving; I was only watching for the man. Give me a moment." Officer Ma used his radio to contact the department requesting that they check the CCTV for a caucasian woman with dark brown hair with red and blonde highlights. Being dark, it might be difficult for the cameras to catch the colors, but there wouldn't be many lone women walking in the neighborhood at this time. It wasn't late yet, but there weren't many pedestrians out at this time of the evening during the fall.

Xian and Chen paced while Officer Ma waited for a reply. How far could she have gone in just fifteen minutes? Five minutes later, an answer came over the radio; a lone female walked five blocks to the South. A burly man was following her and gaining ground. Officer Ma thanked the officer on the other end. "I'm not supposed to do this, but get in. You won't get there in time on foot," directing Chen and Xian to get in the car.

Revving the motor, Officer Ma pulled a U-turn in front of the apartment complex and raced in the direction they had indicated Anna had gone. Turning on his siren and lights, he flew through the intersections, quickly reaching where the officer had stated a lone female had been walking.

Lost in her thoughts, Anna didn't notice she was being followed. She was focused on processing her emotions at that moment. The searing anger had burned down to a smolder. Now the hurt was winning out over the rage.

Though Chen and Xian kept telling Anna how much they cared for her, they had left her with her ugly thoughts all afternoon. It didn't pay to be so mad. She knew that they had other things to address, but couldn't they have checked on her once? But hadn't she caused them loads of trouble since she arrived? They would have been much better off if she had left and returned to the States long ago. Now, her special dinner was ruined. Perhaps she should go back.

She should stop feeling sorry for herself and thank the two men who kept showing up and rescuing her. Fumbling in her pocket for her phone to let them know she would be back shortly, she noticed it wasn't there. *Oh crap.* Chen and Xian had made her promise not to leave the apartment without one of them and now she was several blocks from the apartment without a phone.

Now that Anna was focused on her surroundings as she walked, she heard heavy footsteps behind her. She picked up her pace and started walking faster, keeping ahead of the ominous footfalls. The sound of footsteps was getting closer. Not wanting to tip her hand to whoever was following her,

Anna began to pick up her pace more.

When the footsteps were almost upon her, she wanted to run, but her legs wouldn't move any faster. Prepared for nearly anything, Anna turned to face her shadow...no one was there and a car with flashing lights was speeding in her direction. Just now, she finally noticed the siren warning other vehicles to move from the speeding car's way.

Grateful for whatever had distracted her follower, Anna turned and retraced her steps towards the apartment building. The car slowed and came to a halt twenty feet from her. The headlights blinded her so she couldn't see the two men that clamored out of the car and raced toward her.

Suddenly Anna's feet left the ground and she was hugged hard enough that she was amazed he didn't crack a rib. "What in the hell?" she managed to croak out.

"DON'T YOU EVER DO THAT AGAIN!" That was what she heard in stereo. Xian put Anna down so Chen could pick her up and swing her, hugging her almost as hard as Xian.

Each of them took one of Anna's hands, not wanting to let go. They explained what had happened with Officer Ma and the guard Liu Chaoxiang. Her guests, especially Dr. Lin, were waiting for her.

"Please, come home Anna," Xian claimed Anna from Chen, hugging her tenderly this time.

Wrapped in Xian's arms, Anna could smell his particular musky scent. Home, what did that mean to her anymore? What was a home that wasn't shared with anyone? Tears that Anna had fought all afternoon found a crack in the dam and began pouring forth. Sobbing on Xian's shoulder, Anna felt a warm body behind her. Suddenly she was sandwiched between two men, which made her heart beat faster, her breathing quicken and her palms sweat.

This is what Anna felt home meant. Warmth and security. Strong arms that held you together when the world wanted to unravel. Chen's clean, crisp scent mingled with Xian's musky scent and Anna wanted to roll around in that fragrance like a dog in a pile of something disgusting. Through her sobs, she could feel these two rocks keeping her grounded. They formed an island that Anna could cling to and weather the flood of emotions overwhelming her.

"Let's go home," Anna hiccuped through her tears.

—

Huddled in the shadows, a dark figure watched the touching scene between Anna, Xian and Chen. So there wasn't just one obstacle, there were two. The Chinese cunt could have her boy toy; he would dispose of the other, then Anna would be his. Damn that police car for coming when it had; he had been so close to taking her. He would continue biding his time. They would slip up, and when they did, he would be there.

—

Officer Ma was relieved when they found Anna. It would have been a mess if something had happened to her on his watch. He needed to report to Detective Zhào. As they approached Ms. Cassidy, he had seen a man following her but he disappeared suddenly when the lights got brighter. The American author was in danger. They needed to be cautious so there wasn't an international incident now that she had become famous.

章

Chapter 60

Opening the door to the penthouse, the sound of chatting and laughter filled the dining room. On the way up in the elevator, they discussed the explanation they would give their guests. Xian and Chen were embarrassed by their behavior and didn't want Dr. Lin to rake them over the coals for the bonehead move they had made. Anna was all for the plan they'd come up with; she was ashamed of her behavior, running away instead of talking to the guys.

"I hope the food is to your liking," Anna said as she walked into the dining room. Seeing that a sizable dent had been made in the dishes on the table, she guessed they liked it well enough.

"Anna, this food is fabulous!" Wu Feng gushed.

"He liked it so much he is on his third helping of soup and second of the chicken," Huang Hu laughed.

Grinning, Wu Feng lifted his spoon in salute, dipped it into the bowl and shoveled more soup into his mouth.

"Ms. Cassidy, the food is delicious; I would love the recipes for both," said a smiling Mrs. Lin. "The chicken is flavorful. The soup is so comforting. Is it a special recipe?"

"Mrs. Lin, the recipe comes from German-Russian immigrants that went to the States. There are numerous variations; this happens to be my take on it. My daughter and I pride ourselves on the recipe. Chen, Xian, please sit down and eat something. I have more in the kitchen. Please excuse me." Anna turned and headed for the kitchen.

"Let me help you, Anna," spoke the rich tenor voice of Dr. Lin behind her.

"Dr. Lin, you are a guest. You don't need to help me." Anna blushed as she pulled the platter of chicken and vegetables from the warm oven.

The gruff doctor looked closely at Anna, putting a hand on

her arm. "Anna, I said you needed rest with all the emotional roller coasters you've been dealing with. Why are you pushing yourself? And what happened with those idiots? I have an overwhelming suspicion they did something inordinately stupid today."

Anna leaned back against the counter, putting the platter down. "You could say that. It wasn't one of their better days, but to be fair, they did both rescue me from dicey situations earlier. Xian rescued me from a media mob at the market and Chen rescued me from a stalker that followed me from Montana. So, though they left me alone all afternoon and didn't show up until a few minutes before the meal without a hello, I shouldn't be too upset with them." Replaying the day in her head, she was again on the fence if she should let it go or be upset with them.

"The icing on the cake was that they were fawning over the young woman sitting at the table." Tendrils of anger were trying to wrap themselves around Anna again. Why did she care? Neither were dating her; why couldn't they be interested in the beautiful young woman?

Observing Anna, Dr. Lin recognized a green monster lurking behind her eyes. Clearing his throat, he used his hand to cover the smirk he couldn't contain. These three had one heck of a triangle going. Anna cared for Xian and Chen. Her jealousy was refreshing. These men needed someone that cared that much.

"Anna, I don't think you have anything to worry about with the young woman. Those two men only have eyes for you. Why do you think they continually rush to your aid whenever the world goes sideways?" Dr. Lin hoped the three would resolve their issues before everyone was hurt. "Let's get this food out there for the boys to try. Once they find out how amazing a cook you are, good luck trying to get rid of them."

Humbled by the doctor's praise, Anna blushed as she spooned soup into the large tureen. "Thank you for the compliment. I've made these dishes a few times in my life."

"I can tell; you put so much love into the food, you can almost taste it." The doctor put his arm around Anna's shoulders and squeezed gently. "Now let's go feed those two.

The minute they noticed you were missing, it was almost comical. As much as they want to compete with one another, they both want what's best for you. It's difficult to decide which one your heart yearns for more, hmm?"

She looked down at the soup in her hands, watching a carrot float across the surface like a float tube on a breezy summer lake. The fine tremors that wracked her body sent shimmery ripples through the broth. Dr. Lin's evaluation of the situation softened her anger toward the men. They had put their lives on hold, chasing after her, taking her shopping and running errands. Now she was acting like a spoiled brat.

She pasted on a brave smile; Anna's meltdown would come after everyone had left and the guys were in bed. This time it would be because she didn't know what to do. She loved those two outrageous idiots. There was no use denying it anymore.

"I guess we should go and feed them. This was supposed to be a meal to thank everyone and celebrate my great news."

"News? I didn't know about that part of the plans for tonight. I knew you wanted to have this meal as a thank you for everyone's help, but what news?" Dr. Lin's curiosity got the better of him so he asked, "A hint?"

Anna laughed, to see the surly physician so curious was adorable. "I got a new job, that's all I'm saying now. Though I do have a question for you," she said, pulling a straight face from somewhere deep when she wanted to laugh so badly.

Now the older gentleman was more than curious; he was intrigued. "Okay, spill it."

"Would you be my physician while I'm living in Beijing?" Her eyes sparkled with mirth at the expression on his face once the question sunk in.

Staring at her with shock and delight, he asked, "You are moving to Beijing? When?" His excitement was palpable. He wanted to slap his forehead, hadn't Lin Bolin commented on being her assistant when she returned in January?

"Middle of January. Okay, is that enough of a hint? Let's go finish eating so I can serve dessert. It's a special treat I don't make often." Her nerves calmed and her spirit lifted. This doctor didn't just fix the physical, he also had a touch with the emotional part. Anna brushed a quick kiss on his stubbled cheek. "Thank you," she whispered as she shyly blushed and hurried to the dining room with her tureen.

The more time Dr. Lin spent around Anna, the more he could see what Chen and Xian saw in her. Dr. Lin realized she wasn't perfect by any means, but she had a huge heart and compassion that belied her years. If he weren't careful, she would have another conquest and his wife would have his hide. Grabbing the warm platter of chicken and vegetables, he followed the remarkable author.

Anna breezed into the dining room to find her new friends sitting around the table, laughing and talking. Setting the tureen on the turntable in the center, Anna sat in the empty seat across the table from Chen and Xian. She wasn't ready to be close to those two yet. She may have forgiven them in her head, but her heart wasn't entirely on the same page.

Dr. Lin deposited his platter on the turntable and sat beside a sweet-looking woman. Her eyes twinkled when she saw how flustered the doctor was. They had taken longer than expected to just retrieve a few dishes from the kitchen. Mrs. Lin suspected that her husband had worked some of his magic on the young woman. Exact details of what had happened weren't forthcoming, but having been with her husband for thirty-five years, she knew when he had seen a situation and did what he could to fix it.

Anna stood and looked at the men chatting with the young woman seated between them. "Chen, Xian, I'm sorry for delaying your dinner; please help yourself."

Chen and Xian kept speaking with the woman, not paying attention to Anna.

Mrs. Lin was seated next to Chen. Seeing his rude behavior towards Anna, she kicked him under the table. After all the fuss they had made over her leaving earlier and now they ignored her. Chen was lucky she didn't slap him upside the head.

Looking at Mrs. Lin in surprise, Chen was oblivious to what Anna had said. Mrs. Lin's glare showed him that he had done something wrong again. Mrs. Lin scowled at Chen and then looked across the table at Anna, who had sat down and stared at her empty plate. Not only had Mrs. Lin sent him a piercing scowl, but the other table occupants also gave him and Xian the stink eye. Not batting an eye, he went back to his conversation with Xian and their guest.

Embarrassed by his boss and Mr. Xiao's behavior, Wu Feng moved to sit next to Anna. "The dinner is amazing. Will you cook for me when you come back?"

Giving Wu Feng a sad smile, she quietly whispered to him, "I'm not sure I'm going to come back. If I do, I most certainly will cook for you." Reaching over, she patted his hand.

Hearing that Anna wasn't sure she would return, he leveled a menacing glower at his boss and friend. How could he be so dense? After the fuss he had made over Anna, he now ignored her completely.

"Excuse me, Anna, I'll be back in a few moments." He stood up and went to the bathroom, not using it but sending a text message to Huang Hu about what Anna had said. How could their employers both be so dense?

WHAT? Was the reply from Huang Hu.

Knowing he had achieved his goal, he returned to the dining room and gave Anna a side hug before he sat down. Huang Hu got up and sat down on Anna's other side. He placed his hand on hers and patted it. "Whatever you decide, Anna, Feng and I support you completely. If you would prefer, we can help you find another apartment. Don't throw the job with the studio out because we work for exceptionally dense men."

Hearing the support from both of the young men, Anna felt better. Perhaps that would be the best solution. Find an apartment and just step away from Xian and Chen. She had dreamt about writing for a studio; why should she throw away her chance to live in this beautiful city because the men she loved were inconsiderate? "I may take you up on that. Perhaps we can do some looking tomorrow."

Dr. Lin, having overheard most of their conversation, shook his head. When Chen and Xian had rushed from the apartment, the rest laughed and talked about how bad they had it for Anna. Now that she was back, the morons ignored her. This was too much.

"Xian, Chen, may I speak with you in the den for a moment," Dr. Lin spoke quietly. Standing up, he expected them to follow. Noticing they were even oblivious to what he had said, he walked up behind each and swatted the back of their heads. "Den, **NOW!**" Turning, he walked down the hall towards Anna's bedroom and the den she had decided was too masculine and dark for her taste.

Xian and Chen looked at one another, confused. In all the years they had known Dr. Lin, he had never gotten this angry with them. Excusing themselves, they followed Dr. Lin.

He closed the door behind the men after they entered. Dr. Lin gave them both a disgruntled sigh. "So, did you both decide intentionally to drive Anna away? If so, you're doing a bang-up job of it. I believe you're about five minutes from her moving out and never speaking to either of you again."

Xian and Chen stared at one another and back at Dr. Lin. Chen was still rubbing the back of his head, Dr. Lin had thumped him pretty hard. "Why? We went and rescued her, didn't we? Why would she leave?"

Dr. Lin sighed with exasperation, bowing his head and rubbing the bridge of his nose with his thumb and forefinger. "I didn't think you two were that dense. You walked in, sat down and completely ignored Anna, **AGAIN!** Why do you think she left in the first place? She was left alone in the apartment early this afternoon. She cooked a meal, mostly to thank you two ungrateful wretches. You didn't contact her at all this afternoon to see how she was after a media mob threatened her, then she was nearly kidnapped from the place that was supposed to be safe. When you returned to the apartment, you completely ignored her." Stopping, he looked at the bewildered men.

"You need more? How's this? You discover she is missing and dash out of here like the apartment building was on fire, desperate because she disappeared. Now that you've returned her successfully, you completely ignored her again. She brought warm food in for you two from the kitchen and spoke to you. Did you hear her at all? My wife was moments from smacking Chen in the back of the head herself. I'm so disappointed in you two. Is Anna just a new shiny toy for you to play with? Once the novelty wears off, you move on to the next new thing?" Dr. Lin said, intimating that the young woman that came with Xian tonight was the new shiny toy.

Xian sank into one of the chairs in front of the mahogany desk. "Dr. Lin, you're right. We have been absolute dolts. We haven't seen Shuai Ming in years and have been so wrapped up in catching up with her that we have seriously neglected Anna." Xian glanced at Chen to see how his compatriot took the news.

Chen walked to the window and looked out, silent as he ran through the afternoon's events. He had been so wrapped up trying to ensure Anna would be safe from Scott that he had completely neglected her. Xian was right; when he came in and saw Shuai Ming, he was so excited to catch up with their college friend that he had pushed Anna away from his thoughts. His surprise Friday night wasn't going to make up for this one. It might help, but he and Xian had messed up the situation. Could they do anything right when it came to Anna?

"Dr. Lin, have any suggestions on how we fix this? We really made a mess of things today," Xian said as he bent his head forward, resting his forehead on his fists.

"Well, unless you want Anna moving out tomorrow, I suggest you figure it out quickly. Your assistants are close to mutiny as well. Those two young men would throw you both under the bus in a moment if Anna asked. The young man that arrived with us is **HER** new assistant. If looks could kill, you two would already be in the ground rotting. You've even upset my wife and she loves you two." Dr. Lin, having said his piece, turned to leave the room. "Figure this out fast. That woman is one in a million. Unless you would rather have her leave your lives for good; if that's your goal, keep up the good work." He opened the door and closed it softly behind him.

After the doctor left the room, Chen sat in the chair next to Xian. "Wow, we blew this one, didn't we?"

Nodding, Xian replied, "Spectacularly."

Both men sat in silence for a few minutes. Xian looked at Chen for some ideas. "I'd say the flowers you sent her this morning might grant you a modicum of clemency. I'm just screwed," Chen responded to his silent inquiry.

"Ice cream?" Xian tried.

"I don't think there is enough maple nut ice cream in the entire city of Beijing to fix this one," Chen sighed. He knew Anna's favorite ice cream from one of their late-night calls. Her day had been challenging and Chen suggested a bowl of ice cream to improve it. They sat and ate ice cream while Anna poured her heart out. Remembering that night only made Chen feel worse.

"I had thought about taking her car shopping tomorrow; that way, she would have a vehicle when she returned. Maybe that will help?" Xian looked hopeful.

"It's hard to say. Anna isn't a woman driven by money. She is comfortable on her own with what the studio is paying her. Most importantly, we better get out there and try the food she made us if there's any left. If we want to keep our assistants too, we better figure something out soon." Chen clapped Xian on the shoulder as they returned to the dining room.

"Yeah." Xian followed Chen from the room.

Laughter and conversation could be heard down the hallway. Xian and Chen grinned at one another, perhaps the situation had calmed. They heard Anna's distinctive laugh and sighed in relief. Maybe they weren't as bad off as they assumed if she was laughing.

Wu Feng was the first to notice their return; with a glance around the table, he let the rest know that the butt of their laughter had returned. Silence fell over the dining room as Xian and Chen entered.

Looking at their fellow diners' expressions, they were far from being out of the dog house. "Anna, can we talk to you for a few minutes?" Xian asked meekly.

"Sorry, Xian. I don't have time right now." Anna continued as she stood, "I have a special surprise for everyone who has finished eating. If you're finished, please follow Huang Hu." Anna had filled Huang Hu in on her special treat for dessert; they would have it upstairs in the room off the patio. She had spent all afternoon arranging the room in preparation for this evening. Except for Xian and Chen's idiocy, she had enjoyed preparing to entertain guests; it had been some time since she hosted any kind of party.

Bowing slightly, Huang Hu gestured for the guests to proceed with him up the stairs near the dining room. "Oh my, I didn't even notice the stairs." Mrs. Lin giggled.

Heading for the kitchen with Wu Feng in tow, Anna went to

get the dessert she had prepared for the guests. Xian tried to stop her so he could talk with her. She brushed past him, Anna didn't want to deal with either of them at the moment. Dr. Lin, his wife and the other guests had done their best to cheer Anna up. They had almost succeeded until Xian and Chen had returned to the room.

Ducking into the kitchen, Anna grabbed several plastic bags from the refrigerator. "Wu Feng, can you grab the tray from the oven? I have the plates, silverware and serving utensils all set up."

Chen tried this time to get Anna's attention. "Anna, we need to talk to you."

Looking at Chen and Xian resignedly, she said, "Oh, now you want to talk to me? Well, I'm not interested in talking to either of you. You're lucky the rest of the guests talked me out of leaving tonight and spending the rest of my trip at Dr. and Mrs. Lin's home. Clean the table off; that might help. You never even tried the food I made for you." Sniffing, Anna wiped her eye on her sleeve. "Come on, Feng. This dessert is better eaten fresh."

Brushing past the guys, she headed for the second story with Wu Feng following silently behind her.

章

Chapter 61

Dessert was a triumphant success. Anna had spent most of her afternoon making the delicate Pate a Choux pastries. Airy puffs of dough filled with a from-scratch custard or chocolate mousse and topped with fresh berries and whipped cream. Taking special care to make everything by hand, the delicacy was light and airy.

"Anna, oh my word! These are delectable. How did you ever learn to make this?" Mrs. Lin was beyond impressed.

Glowing from the praise, Anna created another chocolate version for Dr. Lin. "I've been making these since I was a kid. My mother taught me when we lived on our farm. We used to cheat back then. I even used a boxed pudding and whipped cream from a packet; funny, since we had a dairy farm."

Everyone laughed while Anna recounted stories of her youth on the dairy farm. They enjoyed the descriptions of the animals and antics she and her siblings had pulled.

Anna looked at the stairs wondering how Chen and Xian were doing with the dishes. Xian probably had no clue how to do dishes; it might have been comical to watch those two trying to deal with the remnants of the meal. Her disappointment with them still clung on. Had they even tasted the food she had made?

At that moment, Xian poked his head over the stairway's railing. "The table has been cleared and dishes are taken care of. Anna, you will need to deal with the food; we aren't sure how you would like it stored. Are we welcome to join now?"

She gave her guests a say in the matter and looked around for their vote. "What do you guys think?" Anna put the query to the group.

While Anna had served the dessert, Shuai Ming had finally introduced herself. Anna had realized some time before that she had seen the woman at the airport talking with Xian when she first arrived. They chatted for a while and got along quite well. If Xian hadn't been such a poor host, he would have introduced them and avoided most of the drama tonight.

They all agreed to allow the two to join the rest; Lin Bolin wasn't thrilled with allowing them to join in again. After his meeting with Mr. Wei earlier in the day, he had been impressed with his concern for Ms. Cassidy. What he saw during the evening made him less impressed. Ms. Cassidy would be his boss. With the fantastic opportunity she had given him, he would be her devoted and faithful assistant.

"Looks like you've been given a dessert reprieve. I have a few cream puffs left." Pulling two plates from the pile on the small table, she set up the desserts. "Chocolate or plain?" she questioned each as they came up the stairs.

"Chocolate for me," Xian answered.

"I'll take a plain," Chen replied, finding an empty spot on the couch.

"You're in for a treat, sir," Wu Feng sighed out. "I could eat ten more of those."

Putting the puffs together quickly, Anna handed the treats to Xian and Chen.

Looking at their plates with the delicate pastry, they both felt worse. All the time Anna had put into the meal and they had all but ruined it for her.

Chen picked it up to eat it with his hands. He wanted to touch, taste, see and smell it to truly appreciate it. Biting into the crisp outer shell, Chen tasted the creamy vanilla custard filling the pastry. Silky whipped cream oozed from where he had taken a bite. With closed eyes, Chen savored the bite as he chewed. Swallowing, he opened his eyes. Chen could taste the love Anna had poured into the delicacy.

Xian watched Chen as he took his bite. He witnessed the exquisite pleasure that Chen felt as he swallowed the sweet. Suppose Chen, who wasn't the biggest sweets fan, had that expression on his face. Then how would he, a consummate patisserie connoisseur, feel about it? Xian cut into the puff; custard, cream and dark silken chocolate oozed from the shell. Scooping a bite into his mouth, the flavor explosion made him realize how much Anna cared for them. Only true feelings could create something so exquisite.

The rest of the guests had finished with their portions. They watched with interest to see how the men reacted to the special treat. Dr. Lin swore he saw a tear roll down Chen's cheek after taking his second bite. Wu Feng and Huang Hu sat back, stuffed with the rich food, smirking at their employers.

Lin Bolin was happily eating his third cream puff. Anna had especially filled it to overflowing. She had felt bad for having Lin Bolin come, and then the whole night went sideways. What must he think of her? Anna planned on talking to him alone before he left for the night. She didn't want to lose this young man as her assistant. He had proved himself while working at the hotel.

Anna sat back and watched Chen and Xian while they dug into her treat. Watching their faces as they finished the dessert gave her more pleasure than she wanted to admit. She was still angry with them, right?

Dr. Lin, feeling the soporific effects of the dessert, tugged his wife's sleeve, motioning that they should take their leave. If he didn't move soon, he would be sleeping on the couch. "Anna, the meal was better than many of the restaurants I've been to. Perhaps we can return the favor when you return?" He poured his hope into that question. Anna needed to return; she was quickly becoming the daughter he never had.

Seeing the high emotions in the kindly physician, Anna rushed to him and hugged him tightly. "*Lin shūshu*, I would be honored if we could continue our friendship when I return," she said, bowing to express her sincere respect.

Trying not to let anyone see, Dr. Lin brushed the tears that had escaped his sharp eyes. They had been through so much that night. Mrs. Lin smiled as she watched her benevolent husband fall apart at the kindness this woman had paid him. Touching Anna's cheek, Mrs. Lin whispered, "You have no idea what you have done for that old man." Winking, she took her husband's hand and led him down the stairs.

Chen and Xian had cleared their plates. Xian went so far as to lick his clean, which caused some raucous laughter from the remaining guests.

Shuai Ming watched the man she had dreamt of for the last

twenty years make a fool of himself for a woman he had only met the week before. Why couldn't he behave that way for her? When they were in college, they had been best friends. Xian would be there for her any time, day or night. The day he met Chandra, things had changed between them. He would still be there, but not anytime like he had before. Events they would typically have attended together, he then went to with Chandra.

Shuai Ming had met Chandra's brother, Chen, soon after. Xian and Chandra had hoped the two of them would hit it off. How perfect would it have been to have best friends marry siblings? It didn't work that way. Chen was still on the heavier side at that point and had little self-esteem. Shuai Ming, a strong independent woman, was turned off by his weak demeanor. He wasn't Xian; robust, confident and handsome. She realized too late that she had loved Xian for some time.

When she heard her father was being transferred to the States, she was ready to go with him. Being around Xian and Chandra was too painful for her. Twenty years later, Chandra was gone, but Xian had found someone else the day she returned to China. How could life be any crueler?

Shuai Ming was surprised when she met Chen again. Gone was the overweight and shy introvert; a handsome, self-assured man was in his place. She had thoroughly enjoyed catching up with Chen. As the evening wound down, she wondered what life might have been like had she stayed with Chen back then. Would she be the wife of an award-winning actor? It wouldn't have been easy; Xian would have been there, just out of her reach.

Wu Feng and Huang Hu hugged Anna, catching her completely off guard. "Are you two drunk?" she inquired while she checked their eyes. "Count backward from ten; walk a straight line."

Laughing, they began picking up dishes and carrying them down to the kitchen. Anna, dazed, watched with odd fascination. Arms reached around her waist from behind, pulling her back into a firm embrace. The soft clean scent of Chen permeated her senses. His chin rested on her shoulder and a knot formed in her stomach. Anna was so torn at that moment; she wanted to hate him so much, but yet, be naked in his arms.

"Anna, can you ever forgive me? I can explain why I didn't call, but it doesn't matter. I could have taken a few moments to check on you. The worst part is that I returned and didn't even acknowledge you. I came in so close to mealtime. You can call me an ass; I certainly was today."

Pulling his arms around her tighter, Anna leaned back against his chest and took a shaky breath. "I will forgive you, but it won't be this moment. I realize I probably hurt you when I claimed you were my fiancé and then took it back. I deserved some of what I got today, but not all of it. Give me some time to let it go." Anna gently pulled from his embrace and walked out onto the patio.

Chen knew he was better off retreating for the night. They had only had two arguments since their friendship had begun; he had been wrong both times but behaved like a pompous ass. Each time Anna had put him in his place and forgave him the next day. They would be fine tomorrow. He would still find a way to make it up to her. Picking up some of the remaining plates, he moped down the stairs. There was much to think about.

Xian watched Anna retreat from Chen and walk out into the chill of the night. Chen seemed resigned to something as he cleaned up some of the plates and retreated downstairs, leaving Xian alone with Anna.

Leaning against the doorjamb, Xian watched Anna as she stood with arms wrapped around herself to fend off the chill. Unbuttoning his jacket, he slid it off as he walked to Anna, then draped the body warmed jacket over her shoulders.

Glad for the warmth and unashamed to accept it, Anna pulled the jacket close around her. Wrapping the warm musky aroma of Xian around her like her favorite Minky blanket back home. "How did you like the dessert?" Anna asked with feigned nonchalance.

"Well, as I saw you laughing along with everyone else while I licked the plate, I think you know how much I liked it."

Quietly giggling to herself, he had looked so cute licking the chocolate from the plate. Having had that stray thought, Anna peered closely at Xian's nose. Sure enough, there was a dot of chocolate on it. Irrepressible giggles erupted from Anna, startling Xian. "Anna? Are you okay? Why does it seem like I'm always asking you that question?"

Gasping, Anna took a moment to try and compose herself. Why that spot of chocolate was so hilarious to her, she had no idea. Unable to help herself, Anna sauntered up to Xian and beckoned him to lean closer. As soon as Xian leaned forward, Anna wrapped her arms around his neck and licked the tip of his nose.

Startled, Xian stumbled backward, pulling Anna with him. Landing against the cement wall, Anna crashed hard into him. Xian wrapped his arms around Anna, holding her tight so she wouldn't fall to the cement. Happy to have her there, Xian pulled her closer and pressed his lips firmly to Anna's. Unable to stop herself, she wrapped her arms around his neck, fingers tangling in his hair as she deepened the kiss.

With a groan of agony, Xian pulled away from Anna. "I can't do this right now. You have been on one mind-blowing, emotional roller coaster today. You're hitting that euphoric peak, and at any time, that downward dip will hit and you may hate me more than you already do. I couldn't handle that. As much as I want you right now, and every moment of the day, we can't do this. Not while you are in this frame of mind. Let's go down and say good night to the rest of the guests." Xian held his hand out to take her hand.

Blinking rapidly, Anna stood there for a few minutes, getting her emotions under check. "I'm sorry, Xian. Excuse me." Stepping past Xian's outstretched hand, she wanted to just retreat to her bedroom. It would be safer there. Trying to brush past Xian so she could rush down to her room, a muscular arm snaked out and grabbed her, stopping her retreat.

"Anna, don't run away from me. I want you to stay, but I don't want you to hate me later because you realize it's not what you wanted."

"You're right; I don't know what I want right now. As angry as I may get at you and Chen, I don't believe I could ever truly hate either of you unless you did something to truly hurt me. What's happened between us can't be normal. How often do people get thrown into the situation we find ourselves in? Part of my problem is that I don't know if you really have feelings for me or just feel protective because I've had so many dangerous situations happen. Chen, I know, likes me for who I am. We don't even know one another that well Xian. You need to give me some time to figure out my heart."

"Just don't run away, okay? If something is bothering you, please talk to me. I'm not sure what we have between us either, but I like what we have. If it becomes more? I would be one of the happiest men in the world. However, if we aren't meant to be, I'll be disappointed but I'll survive. Don't feel pressured on my account." He turned Anna to look at him. "I like you, Anna. I can't change that, but you must have the final say." Brushing his lips on Anna's forehead, he pulled his hands from her shoulders and went down the stairs, leaving Anna alone with her thoughts.

Xian had nailed it on the head, she was coming down from that euphoric high and she would have regretted going further with him. Sleep, that's what she needed; perhaps everything would be less confusing in the morning.

When Anna reached the main level of the penthouse, it was hushed. The table in the dining room had been cleared and was clean. Checking in the kitchen, the food had all been put in containers and placed in the refrigerator. She would need to find out who had taken the effort to put everything away. Xian and Chen had said that the food needed to be put away. Perhaps Huang Hu and Wu Feng had taken matters in their own hands. It looked like no one had been slaving away in that room for the afternoon. Checking the living room, it was empty as well. Did everyone leave?

Checking Xian and Chen's bedroom doors she found both were open, but no one was there. Finding the apartment empty was probably for the best. She was ready for bed.

Entering her room, she saw her phone lying on the bed where she had forgotten it earlier. Several messages were on the screen when she unlocked it.

Xian, We are going to the lounge downstairs for a few drinks. Don't wait up for us.

Chen, Anna, we thought you could use some space and quiet. Going to the lounge downstairs, sleep well.

Huang Hu, Ms. Anna, the meal was amazing; I look forward to trying more Western dishes.

Lin Bolin, Ms. Anna, I hope to see you before you leave. Sorry we didn't get to talk more. Thank you so much for the invitation. The food was fabulous.

Wu Feng, Good Night Ms. Anna. I'll keep an eye on everyone for you. ;)

Anna laughed at Feng's text message. He understood her very well. Good, as long as she knew someone was keeping an eye on them she could relax. Looking in her closet, Anna found a pair of silky pajamas; the shorts and tank top hopefully would be comfortable. She fought the urge to put on the pair of Chen's pajamas. It would have been comforting, but she didn't want to lose his scent on them.

章

Chapter 62

Loud voices and laughter woke Anna. Looking at the time, it was after two in the morning. Wondering what was going on, Anna got up and slipped into her robe —cracking her bedroom door open to see if she could hear anything. Giggles and slurred voices greeted her, then a loud shushing, more laughs and a crash.

Realizing she better go see what was going on before they broke the furniture, Anna followed the noise to the sitting area by the kitchen. Leaning on one another on the couch were Chen and Xian. Both well past the tipsy stage and definitely blatantly drunk.

Wu Feng sat in a chair, running his hand through his hair in aggravation. He had been babysitting those two since they got to the lounge. Wu Feng wasn't sure what set them off, but they were competing with one another again. Drink for drink, they had been doing shots. He was lucky enough that he had at least gotten some water in them between the drinks. After the first five shots, they began extolling Anna's virtues, each trying to find a better trait than the one before. If Wu Feng hadn't known Anna already, he would have thought she was one of the original goddesses with magnificent powers.

Trying to wrangle both of them back up to the apartment was challenging. Xian kept trying to hug him and tell him how much he appreciated what Wu Feng had done for Anna. Chen would then start thanking him as well. They both had it bad for Anna; hopefully, they would make it through the rest of her visit without imploding.

"Wu Feng?" Anna called out softly so she wouldn't startle him.

"Ms. Anna? What are you doing up?" Wu Feng had hoped to get the drunk brothers to bed without disturbing Anna.

"Well, as those two are as quiet as an elephant on roller

skates, you didn't have a snowball's chance to get them to bed without me hearing." Smiling, Anna watched Chen and Xian slumbering on the couch. "It would serve them right to leave them there."

Wu Feng chuckled. "Ms. Anna, that's not nice. I'll get them moved to their rooms. This won't be the first time I've dealt with these two drunks."

"How about this, I'll take one and you take the other. I used to do this with my husband on a rare occasion when he tied a good one on. How hard can these two be to deal with?" Pushing the sleeves of her robe up she said, "Okay, which one should I tackle?"

Not sure if he should allow it or not, he hesitantly replied, "Why don't you handle Mr. Chen? He's closer and a little lighter than Mr. Xian."

Standing in front of the couch, Anna assessed the situation. How would she best move the dead weight of a drunk Chen? She was going to see if he could be woken up enough to get him to his room. "Chen, wake up." Anna shook him gently.

Rubbing his face with an unsteady hand, Chen mumbled something and snorted. Well, that wasn't going to work. Guess she was just going to have to go about this a bit differently. It had been a while since she had done this; the last time was a lightweight boxing champion who had a few too many. She made fifty bucks that night putting him in his car that night. Leaning over, Anna got her shoulder into Chen's stomach and stood up with him over her shoulder. Good thing his room wasn't that far.

Wu Feng watched, gape-mouthed, as Anna carried Chen to his room. He kicked himself for not getting a video of it to send to Huang Hu. Tomorrow he was going to recount the story to his friend. They were going to treat Anna to a special dinner for this, she kept amazing him at every turn. Perhaps he would start an Anna fan club. He could be the president.

A few loud grunts later, Anna sauntered out of Chen's room, brushing her hands together. "Need some help with Xian?" Anna asked with a raised eyebrow.

Wu Feng nodded, he couldn't believe his luck. Now he would get proof. This would be blackmail for those outrageously late nights when Xian was in a mood at the office and wouldn't go home.

Anna repeated the same feat of strength, carrying Xian to his room. Laying him on the bed as carefully as she could, she pulled the covers over him after removing his shoes. Soft snores came from under the blanket.

Smiling, she decided she would be nice and make them some congee for when they woke up. Those two were going to have killer hangovers. Time for her to get back to bed if she was going to get up a little early and cook the porridge. "Wu Feng, I can offer you a couch if you don't want to head home," Anna yawned as she clapped the shoulder of the tired young man.

"That's okay, Ms. Anna. I don't live too far from here. Would you do something for me?"

"What can I do for you, Feng?" Anna asked with curiosity. The unassuming assistant had never requested anything from her.

"Huang Hu and I would like to take you out for a meal tomorrow night. Oh wait, that would be tonight; it's after midnight." Wu Feng looked at Anna with ill-disguised hope.

Appreciating that the poor man had babysat the drunken duo, how could she not agree? "Feng, absolutely. I would love to go to dinner with you two. Do we dare tell our employers? Who knows what those two might do."

"No kidding, but I'd rather tell them than hide it and have them find out. I like my job." Wu Feng wiped a light sheen of sweat from his forehead. Just discussing hiding something from Xian made him anxious.

"I'm just kidding, Wu Feng. I would never ask you to hide something from Xian unless it is a surprise for him." Her appreciation of the young man rose even more.

"When I'm gone, please take care of him. He might seem tough but he's actually a very soft man. I don't want to see him get hurt," Anna said and wrapped an arm around Wu Feng's shoulders. "Good night, Wu Feng. I'll be here all day tomorrow. I have a deadline I need to meet and I didn't get anything written today, so I'll be a boring person tomorrow and work."

"See you tomorrow Ms. Anna." Wu Feng blushed as he

bobbed his head and left the apartment.

Yawning and scratching her hip as she walked to her room, she could have sworn she heard a loud snore from one of her drunken roommates. She couldn't blame them. It had been a rough day for all of them. Crawling under the covers, Anna set her alarm and fell asleep immediately.

Minutes later, her alarm went off. Maybe it hadn't been minutes, but it felt that way. Congee took at least two hours to make; if she wanted to have it ready when the two party animals awoke, she would have to start it early.

Checking on the men, she ensured they were still asleep and closed their doors. She didn't want her work in the kitchen to wake them.

Fifteen minutes later, the pot of ingredients was simmering away. Anna would need to check on it every fifteen minutes, giving it a good stir. The smell of garlic and ginger permeated the apartment and it smelled so good. Anna planned to make a pot of ginger tea when it was closer to breakfast. She missed the spicy beverage. It had been some time since she had it at her friend Ely's restaurant.

Anna dug in and started working on the manuscript that was coming due. It worked well because the breaks when she checked on the meal helped her stretch her legs and mind. With all the drama over the last week, it was easy for Anna to come up with ideas for the final chapters. Before the congee finished, she had completed two chapters with four to go.

Checking her watch, there were about ten minutes left for the porridge to be finished. *Thud!* What in the world? Anna got up, wondering who had fallen off the bed. She knocked on Chen's door first. No answer, so she opened the door a crack to check on him. Chen was sprawled across the bed, snoring lightly. It must have been Xian. Knocking on his door, Anna heard a muffled voice. "Xian, are you all right?" Opening the door, Anna poked her head in and looked for Xian.

"Out damned temptress," came a slurred voice from behind the bed.

"Temptress, am I? Now see here, Sir Xian. You should have your royal arse in that bed," Anna said to play along with Xian's drunken ramblings.

"Milady Anna, I am so sorry. I believed you to be a foul temptress come to relieve me of my soul." The solemn declaration came from a face peeking over the edge of the bed.

Anna managed to hold back a fit of giggles with great difficulty as she watched Xian peer at her. "Sir Xian, may I be of some assistance?"

"How could I ask such a favor of Milady? I am the one that is supposed to ride in on a white charger and save you." Xian raised his arm as though he had a sword and pledged a troth.

Making her way around the bed, Anna offered her hand to the bleary-eyed knight wannabe. "Sir Xian, your hand, please."

Eyeing Anna through cracked eye slits, Xian groused, "I still believe you are an evil temptress; why else would I want to ravish you at this moment?"

It was time to get Xian back in bed and herself out of the room. He wasn't in his right mind at that moment. Grabbing his hand without a by your leave, Anna pulled Xian up and pushed him back onto the bed. Pulling the covers up under his chin, she kissed his forehead and walked out of the room, softly closing the door behind her. Muffled calls of protest came from the room for a few minutes before silence descended over the penthouse once more.

The food was ready thirty minutes later. The spicy and earthy aromas of the garlic and ginger lingered long through the morning. Anna wouldn't have needed to worry about getting up early to make the congee. Noon rolled around before the first of her patients managed to crawl out of their room. Chen shuffled to the breakfast bar and flopped down on one of the stools.

"Morning, Chen," Anna called in a louder than normal voice. Watching Chen cringe, she knew he had one doozy of a hangover. Turning the hot water kettle on, Anna flitted around the kitchen making tea and getting the congee warmed up. Taking pity, she used a softer voice to ask, "Chen, would you prefer coffee or tea this morning?"

"Coffee if we have it, please," Chen groaned as he folded his arms on the counter and laid his head on them.

"That bad?" Anna couldn't help but snicker.

"Yeah, laugh it up. It's not your head that feels like a

cement truck is parked on it. "

"A cement truck, that's oddly specific."

"Well, they are large, loud and that big tub on the back goes round and round." Chen lifted a hand without moving his head and swirled a finger around in circles.

Shaking her head, Anna prepared a cup of coffee for Chen. "Cream or sugar?" she asked quietly as she set the cup down in front of the poor man.

"Black as night." Chen lifted his head just enough to sniff the cup of coffee. "This smells different. It smells better somehow." Lifting the cup to his lips, the sigh of pleasure surprised them both. "It's so good." He pulled the cup into the circle of his arms. It looked to Anna like he was trying to hug the warmth and comfort of the hot brew.

"Coffee! I smell coffee," a hoarse voice croaked from around the corner. Xian ambled into the room and melted onto the chair next to Chen.

"Yes, Sir Xian, you shall have it shortly," Anna said as she winked at the rumpled man.

Both men gave Anna odd looks. What had gotten into her this morning? Seeing the perplexed looks on their faces, Anna couldn't contain her mirth and let out a loud guffaw. Catching Xian's cringe and Chen covering his head with his arms, she apologized, "Sorry, guys. That was a little loud."

Grumbling something about cheerful people in the morning, Xian tried to steal Chen's cup of coffee. Weakly, Chen slapped his hand away and glared at him. "My precious," he said, giving his best Gollum impression. Xian snorted and winced from the pain.

"Don't make me laugh, man," Xian groaned.

"And why not? They say laughter is the best medicine," Anna inquired.

"Just remember how chipper you are when you're hungover and we return your favor," Xian complained until Anna set the cup of coffee in front of him. "Okay, I take it back; you're an angel."

Taking a deep breath of the robust aroma, Chen agreed, "Saint Anna."

Shaking her head again, she finished ladling the porridge

into bowls. Setting a bowl in front of each with a slight drizzle of toasted sesame oil and tamari, she waited for their critique.

Chen lifted his head, sniffing the air. "Is this your congee?"

"Certainly. With how much you two drank last night, I figured this would sit the best on your stomachs. Was I wrong?"

"**NO**," was the emphatic response in unison.

Mixing the liquids into the thick rice porridge, Xian took a spoonful and blew on it before ladling it into his mouth. The warm, soft grain blended well with the garlic, ginger and leeks. "Anna, this is delicious. How did you learn to make such flavorful congee?"

"I've been playing with that recipe for years now. It was one of the only foods I could eat at times when I had digestion problems. It's become comfort food for me now. It was one of the things that started me on my love for Chinese cuisine and culture."

Chen sipped the congee from his spoon. "Mmm, this is so good. What did you add to it? I'm not familiar with having it this way."

"A drizzle of toasted sesame oil and I use low sodium tamari because it can be a bit too salty when I need to cheat and use purchased broth. I've played with other versions over the years, but I tend to come back to my tried and true. If I'm being really adventurous, I'll also add mushrooms or fried onions."

Taking her bowl, she added her flavoring and mixed it well. Taking a sip, she decided it was passable. She wasn't familiar with the broth she'd used, so it was slightly different. The porridge was warm and comforting. It didn't take her long to finish her bowl; she had work to complete.

"I'll leave you two to your meal. Work is beckoning."

"Anna, are we forgiven?" Chen's hangdog look made Anna feel pity for him for a moment.

Looking at the pathetic men, she nodded her head. "Yes. You're both forgiven, especially since we got a video of me putting Xian to bed last night. I did the same for Chen, but we forgot to record it. I suggest you both behave."

"What do you mean by putting me to bed, exactly?"

Wracking his brain, he couldn't remember anything after they went to the lounge.

Anna appraised the situation by standing with her hip cocked and arms folded across her midsection. Should she tell him? Oh yes, she should, she decided. "I picked both of you up and carried you over my shoulder to your rooms, where I deposited you on your beds." Inwardly she had to laugh at the expressions on both men, shock and incredulity. "Don't believe me? Good thing Wu Feng sent me the video." She pulled her phone out and found the video from Wu Feng.

Initially, when she had gotten the video, Anna was annoyed that he had secretly taken a video of her manhandling Xian. Now, she was glad for it. They needed a bit of a reality check that she wasn't as helpless as they tried to believe she was. Holding the phone so they could watch, Chen couldn't help but grin. Xian was dumbfounded; she had indeed carried him to bed.

"I bow to the prowess of Anna," Xian said humbly, bowing to Anna. She was a kick-ass woman; he'd never doubted it. He was even more impressed with her now, having seen the video.

"Well, this strong woman needs to get back to her writing. Deadlines are a drag." Pulling a bottle of water out of the fridge, Anna waved to Xian and Chen on her way out of the kitchen.

Well, they weren't as bad off as she had suspected. The bottles of water with aspirin had hopefully made a difference. She had left them on the nightstands with a note for each. Anna was glad it had helped. Hangovers were the worst; Anna was delighted she had been lucky so far and hadn't suffered when she drank too much at Xian's place.

Sitting at her computer, the words began to pour from her fingers. Her new laptop was great. The monitor, keyboard and trackpad she had picked up made working on the portable computer easier. If the guys let her be, she should make her deadline that afternoon.

章

Chapter 63

Hours later, Anna finally finished the chapters she had worked on so diligently. Earbuds and loud ELO were her writing jam. Once in the groove, the words flowed easily. It was a welcome oasis from the tsunami that had continually threatened to drown her.

Checking her phone, Anna was amazed at how late it was already. Time had gotten away from her while she put her thoughts on the screen. A message from Wu Feng informed her they would be there to pick her up at 6:30 tonight. It was 5 o'clock now, so she had an hour and a half to shower and get ready. Usually, she would be done in thirty minutes, but tonight she felt like making an effort.

After a forty-five minute bath and a quick shower, Anna felt rejuvenated. She didn't look too bad when putting the last-minute touches on her minimal makeup. She was curious about what Wu Feng and Huang Hu had in store. The young men had grown on her. Their help made a massive difference in how this trip could have gone. There was much she owed them.

Anna had chosen a charcoal gray sweater dress and paired it with a pair of knee-high, black suede boots. She looked young and fashionable; her new coat finished off the ensemble. Too bad she didn't have more jewelry with her. Most of hers was taking up space at the police station.

Grabbing her clutch and phone, Anna ventured out of her room to see what the guys were up to. They had been reticent all day. It made her wonder.

Wandering through the apartment towards her office, she heard voices coming from the sitting area by the kitchen.

"What do you mean she's going out without us?" Chen's voice was irritated.

"Wu Feng sent me a message that he and Huang Hu plan to take Anna out for dinner. She agreed, so we have no say about it. I'm not any happier about the situation than you are," came the surly voice of Xian. "We aren't exactly in Anna's good graces at the moment. You will be going out with her tomorrow night and I will escort her on Saturday night. I believe you said you had plans for Sunday evening as well?"

"Yeah, Mama Jing would skin me if I didn't bring Anna in for a meal before she leaves. Mama Jing thinks highly of Anna and keeps pestering me to bring her back." There was an ulterior motive for taking her to Mama Jing's for a meal, but he couldn't let Xian know. He wouldn't be allowed to go alone with her if he had an idea of Chen's plans for that night.

Anna stood out of sight, eavesdropping on their conversation. It wasn't the most adult thing to do, but these two had pissed her off with their high-handedness over the last few days and it was wearing on her. Perhaps this way, she would have a clue what to expect.

"Do you know what time her flight leaves on Monday?" Xian questioned Chen.

"Late, almost 8 P.M. Anna gets in the same day. And before you ask, I ensured her return flight was upgraded to first-class."

"That's good, at least. If I thought Anna would accept it, I'd have my jet fly her back so she wouldn't have to deal with the commercial flights." Anna almost wanted to accept his unofficial offer. A quiet ride on Xian's jet would be a welcome reprieve from the loud chaos of the airport terminal.

Chen's grumpy voice responded, "Let's just wish her a wonderful night and go enjoy the leftovers we missed out on last night. It smelled so good; we were so busy catching up with Shuai Ming that we never really ate any of it. I feel terrible about that, especially after all the work Anna put into it. At least Dr. and Mrs. Lin enjoyed it."

There was a soft murmur of agreement from Xian. "Anna continues to blow me away. Her carrying us and putting us in bed this morning...I'd never have believed it if I hadn't seen video proof. Now I know **NOT** to get on her bad side again."

They laughed and agreed they needed to get back into Anna's good graces. Arms crossed and leaning against the wall around the corner from the sitting area, Anna smiled. It would be interesting to see what they came up with to try and get back on her friendly side. She wasn't that mad at them anymore, but she wouldn't tell them that. Let them sweat it out a bit.

The topic of conversation switched to business. Hearing a notification from her phone, she realized Wu Feng and Huang Hu were more than likely waiting for her. Checking the message, they were indeed in the lobby.

Quietly taking the long way around to the sitting area, Anna then made enough noise that Xian and Chen would hear her coming. Sweeping into the room, Xian and Chen stopped in mid-conversation. She could tell by their faces that they wanted to demand she not go out. It impressed her that they managed to keep the imperious attitudes to themselves.

"Hi, guys," Anna greeted them nonchalantly. "How are you two doing?" They looked significantly better than they had at lunch. Maybe they had taken naps while she was working. Chen was wearing a pair of dark lounge pants with a comic-themed sweatshirt; it was a character Anna wasn't familiar with. Xian had put on a pair of worn jeans and a button-up, long-sleeve pullover; it was the most relaxed she had seen him. It was nice to see them so laid back. "Looking good."

Her perfect night would have been to curl up on the couch between those two and watch a good movie. She had better get going or she wouldn't make it out of the apartment. Wu Feng and Huang Hu were waiting for her.

"Have a good time Anna." Chen smiled, getting up and giving her a hug and a kiss on her cheek.

Xian was right behind him, giving Anna a hug and kiss on her forehead. Raising an eyebrow over Xian's kiss, Chen wondered if they had kissed before. No, he didn't want to know. It would only make things harder to deal with if he thought she had kissed his best friend.

"See you in a while. Don't wait up." Anna winked at them and sashayed to the front door. As the door closed, she could have sworn she heard a groan from one of them.

Reaching the lobby, Anna found her "dates" for the night. Both young men had cleaned up quite well. They weren't wearing their usual business attire. Huang Hu was dapper in his shawl-collared sweater under a suit jacket and a pair of dark jeans. Wu Feng just couldn't get away from the suit. However, he did go for a t-shirt under one of his less formal ones.

"You two are quite handsome. I'm a lucky woman to be in your company tonight," Anna greeted the assistants. Nodding to the receptionist, she sauntered up to the young men. "Are you ready?"

Wu Feng had seen Anna first and his jaw had dropped. Even dressed casually, she was stylish and elegant. He felt seriously outclassed. Elbowing Huang Hu to look up, Wu Feng smiled at the gobsmacked look on his buddy's face. "Wow, Ms. Anna, you look spectacular."

"Okay, you two. Tonight you call me Anna or I go right back upstairs." She wanted to feel a tiny bit of normalcy for a change. Anna turned on her heel to walk back to the elevators to make her point.

"Anna, no, please. We can do that for you tonight. Please forgive us if there is a slip. It's a force of habit." Huang Hu stepped forward, ready to go after her if she went too far.

"As long as we're on the same page. I appreciate that you need to call me that around your bosses, but when it's just us can you please try calling me Anna? It helps give me a slight sense of normalcy."

Wu Feng nodded and grinned. "Then, you can call me Feng when we are alone."

Not to be left out, Huang Hu piped in, "You may call me Hu, Anna."

"Now that's dealt with, let's have a great time. What did you have planned?" She was excited to see what these two had in mind. Anna knew it would be a different experience than when she was with Xian and Chen and was glad.

"Dinner and...karaoke!" he exclaimed with excitement.

Anna couldn't help but chuckle to herself. They had finally figured out a way to get her out to sing karaoke. "Where are we going for dinner?" Anna's stomach punctuated the question with a loud growl, startling Hu and Feng; even the receptionist looked over in curiosity.

Embarrassed, Anna bowed slightly to the receptionist and

asked to be excused for the sound. Smiling broadly, the receptionist waved it off as no big deal. Since the American author had moved in, there had been a bit of excitement.

"I only had a bowl of congee for lunch; my stomach has informed me that it's unhappy with how long it's taking us to find food."

Offering their arms in unison, Anna accepted one on each side and allowed them to escort her to a beautiful gray SUV sitting under the portcullis.

"Would you prefer to sit in the front or back tonight?" Wu Feng asked Anna.

"It doesn't matter. I can sit in the back," she said as she headed for the back door of the vehicle.

"Well, as it's your company car I figured I'd give you the option," Wu Feng said with a slight smirk. This should give Anna a surprise, hopefully one she liked.

She stopped in her tracks and pivoted on her heel to face the young man. "It's what?"

"This is your company car. You know the one that comes with your new job." Wu Feng almost kicked himself for not having a camera ready to catch Anna's expression.

"Is it a good one? I'm not familiar with this make," Anna said as she circled the sleek SUV.

"One of the best. Mr. Wei picked it out personally for you yesterday." He hoped that tidbit would help get his boss out of the doghouse. After his royal screw up yesterday, he needed any help he could get.

"Too bad I can't drive here. Let's take this baby for a spin." Anna got in the front seat; no way she was going to sit in the back for her inaugural ride.

"Your wish is my command." Wu Feng got into the driver's seat and started the engine and the quiet rumble made him smile. He was still shocked that Mr. Wei had told him to take this set of wheels tonight. Seeing Anna's delight was worth it.

Dinner went quickly. Remembering past conversations with Anna, they took that into consideration when they chose their destination. Reflecting on when they discussed what she would like to do if given an opportunity, one of her requests was to eat stall food.

They stopped at some of their favorite shops and gathered several dishes before finding a place to sit down and eat. Relying on the experience of Huang Hu and Wu Feng, Anna let them choose the dishes they would eat. A selection of vegetable dishes with a few seafood options filled the table.

Many dishes and a few bottles of Jiujiang later, the three of them laughed and chatted, discussing her plans for when she returned. It was hard to believe she only had a few more days before returning to her semi-normal life. Everything that had happened in the last week felt like it happened over months, not just seven days.

Finished with their meal, they made their way to the karaoke bar close to where they were eating. Letting the alcohol wear off before they returned Anna to the penthouse would be good. She was slightly tipsy and Huang Hu knew Chen would give him an earful if she were impaired.

Buying an hour's worth of time, the three found their karaoke room. Huang Hu found some water for Anna and sodas for him and Wu Feng, leaving Wu Feng to choose the first song.

Browsing through the catalog, Anna found one piece she kind of knew by a Chinese musician. She was amazed at the number of songs from the States. Picking a few, Anna thought she could do a passable job.

An hour later, Anna, Hu and Feng were breathless with laughter. None of them should quit their day job in hopes of a singing career, but they poured their hearts out. Wu Feng had managed to sneak a few videos of Anna singing for Chen and Xian. He hoped it would get him and Huang Hu out of hot water. Figuring the adorable way Anna belted the songs may soothe their wounded pride.

"So, an odd question, you two. Is there anywhere we can get ice cream at this hour?" Checking her watch, it wasn't late. She hadn't tried Chinese ice cream yet.

"If I remember correctly, there is a shop open later near the apartment complex. I'm not sure there is a huge difference between what you get in the U.S. and what we have here," Feng answered her.

Thinking about it, Anna decided that it was just the comfort of eating ice cream at the moment. "I'm excited to try some of the different flavors you have here. I've done my research." She winked at him.

Smiling, they walked down the street arm in arm. It had been a relaxing evening for a change. Anna hadn't had a mellow day since right after she arrived. It was a welcome change. Having dropped her new wheels off at the apartment, they decided a walk would help any of the residual alcohol burn off completely. The ice cream shop was only a few blocks away.

Stopping and picking up several flavors to take back with them, Anna thought Xian and Chen might want to have a late-night treat with her. Call it an olive branch if you would. Anna would be around both of them most of the weekend, so it would be best if they were back on civil terms. It would be awkward to show up at the wrap party and not talk to one another for the night.

Huang Hu and Wu Feng bent their heads together, whispering so Anna couldn't hear them while they walked. It was the worst thing they could have done. A dark figure broke away from the deeper shadows of the buildings, making a beeline for Anna.

Huang Hu turned just as a dark shape reached out to grab Anna. "Anna! Duck!" he shouted.

Startled, Anna dropped to the ground as a designer shoe sailed over her head. The loud thud of a body hitting the ground overshadowed her gasp of shock. Growling, the body wearing black clothing and a mask stood, making to rush at them again. This time a short boot sailed through the air and caught the man-shaped shadow on the side of the head, flipping the would-be assailant on his back.

Huang Hu was on the phone with the authorities. He had Detective Zhào's number on speed dial. Looking at one another, Wu Feng and Huang Hu mouthed "Scott" to one another. Watching Anna for signs of shock, Wu Feng crouched down and held her so she wouldn't see the groaning body. One night is all they wanted, one quiet night with no drama. It didn't happen, once again.

Moments later, they could hear a siren coming closer.

Perhaps Officer Ma had been on duty at the apartment, so he was much closer than some other officers. Flashing lights soon accompanied the siren approaching quickly. The three of them turned to watch the car arrive. Officer Ma stepped out and saw Anna on the ground.

"Does Ms. Cassidy need an ambulance? Is she okay?" Officer Ma's superiors would have his badge if she was injured while he was supposed to be watching over her.

Doing a cursory inspection, Anna appeared in one piece. "Anna is okay, shaken up but not hurt. The idiot that tried to grab her may need one." He turned to indicate the prone body on the sidewalk, but it was gone.

Pulling Anna's head to his chest and covering her ears, Wu Feng released a string of expletives that would have made Anna proud if she had heard and understood them. Looking around, Huang Hu was explaining what had happened to the officer.

Anna gently pulled Wu Feng's hand from her ear. He had been sweet, trying to keep her from hearing the diatribe he had just spouted. "Feng, I'm fine. Let's talk to Officer Ma. It had to have been Scott again. I feel like he was probably the one who followed me last night too."

Steadying Anna, Wu Feng helped her over to speak with the officer. Once Anna was leaning on the front fender of the officer's car, Wu Feng pulled his phone out and found Xian's number. If he didn't report this immediately, he'd be lucky to ever work in China again. Mr. Wei was that protective of Anna.

"Mr. Wei, good evening," Wu Feng's voice cracked as he spoke. He didn't want to be telling his boss about this. "We had an incident on our way back to the penthouse. Someone tried to grab Anna."

"**WHAT THE HELL!** Wu Feng, you will be fortunate to have a job tomorrow. Explain!" Inwardly groaning, Wu Feng heard Chen's voice asking what had happened in the background.

While Anna spoke to Officer Ma, Wu Feng filled in Xian and Chen. "Get her back here as soon as she's done. Let me know when you're close. I'll run her a hot bath," his boss said.

"We will be on our way shortly. Anna is just finishing up.

Sir, she will get home safely." Wu Feng hoped his words would be prophetic. He needed to get Anna and her ice cream home in one piece.

Later, opening the door to the penthouse, Anna was greeted by two frustrated men.

"How are you doing?" Chen put a hand on each shoulder, looking her over to ensure she was unscathed.

"A bit dazed but otherwise intact. I was closer and more personal with Feng and Hu's shoes. When you told me they knew martial arts, I didn't realize they were **THAT** proficient." Rubbing her shoulder. "Now I'm even happier that I have a spa appointment tomorrow; a massage is just what the doctor ordered."

"Spa?" Xian asked as he walked around the corner.

Anna turned her head and cringed. "Yeah. I have a spa and salon appointment for tomorrow to help get ready for the evening. Xian, should I book a salon appointment for Saturday? I am not equipped to handle getting ready for that alone."

Checking his phone quickly Xian replied, "I have you covered. I have a hair and makeup team coming to the penthouse on Saturday at about 2 P.M. We will need to leave at about 5 o'clock."

Adding an alarm to her phone at least would keep her on track for time on Saturday.

"Chen, do you have what you plan to wear tomorrow night? What time do I need to be ready?" she inquired, checking her appointment times for the next day. Her spa appointment was at 1 P.M. and her salon appointment was at 2:45 P.M. Anna wasn't sure if she could get into her dress alone; she might have to find a female assistant with some hair and makeup experience. "Hmm, I wonder if Liz would move here to do my hair and makeup," she mused to herself.

Chen looked up from reading something on his phone. He had found a seat on the couch in the sitting area while Xian and Anna discussed the gala. Xian taking Anna would be a treat for her, but he still couldn't help but be jealous that it wouldn't be him going with her. There might be a good chance Xian and Anna might run into "them." Xian's parents and his brother usually went to these events. Come to think of it, had Xian even mentioned his family to Anna? If he hadn't, she was in for a shock, to be sure. There may be a few things Xian hadn't told Anna.

"We will need to be at the hotel by 7 o'clock. The studio puts on a pretty serious party. My suggestion is not to drink anything unless I bring it to you. I'm not sure how stiff the security will be at the party. Inevitably, super fans may sneak in and I've already seen some ugly comments on the internet about you and I associating. I don't know, Anna. Perhaps you were right about the dating thing." His agent, Tao Xiuying, had been on the phone that afternoon with him deciding how to spin some of the negative press. Li Ming was doing her best to smear Anna's name altogether.

Anna decided not to ask about the ugly comments or talk about Chen and her potentially dating. Instead, she replied, "Okay, I have it. I'm going to bed, guys. It will be a busy day tomorrow; I feel like something will happen tomorrow for some overwhelming reason. Maybe because I haven't had a day of peace since I arrived? I brought you a treat; I hope you enjoy it." Handing them the ice cream, she kissed both on the cheek on her way to her room. It was time to sleep.

章

Chapter 64

A loud rapping on her bedroom door woke Anna from the first sound night of sleep she had since arriving in Beijing, except for the night she had been drunk. "One minute," she yelled, pulling on a satin dressing gown over her pajama set when the knocking continued. She couldn't wait to get home and back to her usual sleepwear – her birthday suit.

Opening the door, a flustered Huang Hu stood by the door, fidgeting. "Huang Hu? What's going on?" Anna craned her neck to look past the nervous assistant.

"Remember when you asked one of us to accompany you to your appointments today? Think they will have room for two more at the spa? I requested Mr. Xiao stay at the apartment and I'm lucky I still have a head left. Sorry, Anna, Mr. Xiao and Mr. Wei said that if you plan on going back to the Four Seasons, they will accompany you themselves."

"Huang Hu, it's okay. I had a suspicion something like this would happen. I booked two additional spots; it would have been either for you and Feng or Chen and Xian. How did I know I wouldn't get away with a quiet day on my own?" Rolling her eyes, she pulled the tie on her robe tighter and searched for her self-appointed guardians, Huang Hu following behind her with his head bowed.

Watching Anna's slippers slapping angrily on the marble floors made Huang Hu glad he wasn't the one she was annoyed with. He could understand the need for security, but all four of them to guard her? If Mr. Xiao wasn't careful, he would smother the relationship he had built with Anna.

Irritated with the high-handedness of her temporary roommates, the sharp slap of slippers on the marble with each step should have warned anyone she was coming. Inhaling deeply, Anna caught a hint of something that smelled interesting. Her ire was suddenly forgotten as her stomach informed her it was empty and she should be working on filling it.

Poking her head around the wall by the sitting room, Anna was trying to be stealthy as she was on a recon mission. Where were the guys hiding? She didn't believe they had cooked. If they had, someone had gone grocery shopping because she didn't have much here as she didn't want a bunch of unused food left when she was gone.

Noise in the kitchen let her know that one of them was doing something in that room. Which one was it? Chen or Xian? She felt a tap, tap on her shoulder. "Hu, I'm trying to figure out who is in the kitchen." Tap, tap this time on the other shoulder. Waving off the hand tapping her shoulder she ordered, "Hu, be useful and figure out who is in the kitchen for me." Swat! A flat palm hit her left butt cheek. "Hu, you had better run." Anna whirled and ran smack into Xian.

Feeling her face heating up, Anna knew she had to be bright red at that moment. How could she best play this off? "Hi, Xian. I didn't realize you were behind me. You didn't happen to see Huang Hu did you?" She peered around the muscular body blocking her view. If she ran her hands over his chest for a few moments, he wouldn't get mad, right? His warm musky scent tried to overload her thought processes as it surrounded and enveloped her.

Scrambling backward, she came up against a wall, not a solid one but a warm, laughing one. Turning, she was face to face with an amused Chen.

"Do I even want to know what's going on?" Anna asked, raising an eyebrow with a quizzical look. Chen looked around Anna and questioned Xian without words.

Smirking, Xian walked past Anna and Chen and sat at the kitchen counter. "We had a spy among us."

"Spy? What spy? I was just checking what smelled so good." Quickly pulling her innocent face as she stepped around Chen and sat at the counter.

Checking her watch, it was already 10 in the morning. Anna would have time to eat and take a relaxing bath before the spa. Perhaps she might even indulge and read while in the tub. Liz had picked up the latest novel from one of Anna's favorite authors for the trip. She couldn't remember the last time she had picked up someone else's book; writing had consumed most of her time for the previous six months. It would be a pleasure to stretch out and devour some mind candy. Anna's mind candy was supernatural fiction with bawdy humor thrown in.

Knowing the genre's popularity, Anna had tried her hand at writing supernatural romance with poor results. She was much better at sticking with Asian historical fiction and fantasy.

"Hey, space cadet." Xian nudged Anna.

"Huh?" Anna had been wrapped up thinking about a tub of hot water and a good book.

Chen sat a plate in front of her containing bao buns, an egg and scallion crepe and a stuffed sticky rice roll. Looking over the offering, Anna was intrigued by the different dishes, looking to Chen for explanations.

Explaining each of the foods on her plate, Anna tried each and was pleasantly surprised. They were delicious! Now she would need to learn how to make some of it at home. One of the things she would miss the most when back in Montana was the food.

Finished with her meal, still thinking about the book and a soak, Anna cleaned up her plate and wandered back to her room, leaving Chen and Xian to watch her go without saying anything.

"Is she still mad at us?" Chen scratched his head. He was sure Anna had forgiven them, but she seemed so distant today.

Watching her retreat to her room, Xian couldn't say one way or another. Anna had been distracted through most of the meal. He would have given much to be able to see into her mind at that moment. What was she thinking about? Was it the events to come that weekend? Was she still mad at them? He wished she would just talk to them and explain.

Making up his mind, Xian followed Anna to her room. Knocking on the door, there was no answer. "Anna?" Xian called. No answer. He tried sending her a text message to check on her. *Anna, are you all right? You aren't answering your door.* Pacing up and down the hallway, Xian finally decided to find out what was happening. He was worried something had happened to Anna, had she slipped on the floor in the bathroom or shower? No! That couldn't be it.

Trying the bedroom door, it opened to an empty room. "Anna? Are you in the bathroom?" Xian called out again. Still no answer. Checking around the bed to ensure she hadn't fallen, there was only one place left to check. The bathroom door was open, but Xian didn't hear anything. "Anna? I'm coming in."

Rounding the corner into the bathroom, Xian stopped dead in his tracks. A naked Anna was just stepping into the bathtub. Why didn't she answer him? Turning his back to Anna, Xian tried to process what he'd seen. He knew that she had lost quite a bit of weight. He should have known better; hadn't he seen Chen's scars from his weight loss? Did it matter if she had stretch marks and scars? However, it made sense why she was so anxious about wearing certain clothes.

Didn't he see a tattoo on her shoulder blade? He fought the urge to turn and look at it again. Knowing she was okay, Xian left the room as quietly as he could. Should he tell her he had seen her? He would, but not right now. Later.

He needed to go and get ready. He and Chen would go to the spa with Anna; she said she had booked services already in anticipation of someone accompanying her. Xian wondered what services she had booked exactly. A chime broke through his contemplation. Who could be at the door?

Xian opened the door to one of the apartment complex's couriers; a package had been delivered to Anna. Curiosity was eating at Xian, was this her dress for tomorrow? He needed to know to make sure his attire complemented her dress.

Checking to see if anyone was watching, Xian smuggled the large box to his room. Closing the door, he laid the large decorative container on the bed. Untying the bow, he pulled off the lid of the box. Pieces of wine colored chiffon fabric filled it. What must have once been a magical ball gown was now nothing but shreds in the box. Thank goodness he had opened it before Anna got it.

Pulling his phone out, he contacted the boutique the dress came from. "What happened to Ms. Cassidy's gown? I thought you were doing some minor alterations on it." He did his best to keep his tone as neutral as possible; at that moment he wanted to yell at someone, but it wouldn't benefit anyone doing that.

"Mr. Wei, we had the dress sent by courier this morning, and it was in perfect condition," the clerk assured him.

"Give me a number I can send a photo to," Xian demanded. His patience was wearing thin quickly. The clerk promptly gave Xian a number and he sent a photo of the box they had just received.

"Oh my!" a shocked gasp came from the other end of the phone. "One moment Mr. Xian." Soft music came through the phone, indicating he had been put on hold. He would say that they had better have some kind of option. This would devastate Anna to discover that another dress she had been so proud of choosing on her own had been destroyed.

From the fabric's color, Xian was sure he would have loved Anna in this dress. Where in the hell had someone intercepted it? This was going to come to an end.

"Mr. Wei? I'm the owner of the boutique, I was the one that assisted Ms. Cassidy and I'm so disappointed. She looked so beautiful in this dress and she was so excited to surprise you."

"Do you happen to have another gown that could be modified for her?" The chances of that being the case were very slim. Most boutiques didn't carry multiples of the same size for most dresses.

"I already checked; we only have smaller or much larger of that dress. I do have one that would fit Ms. Cassidy's measurements exactly. It just came in, and I had thought to contact Ms. Cassidy about it. I believe it would be even more spectacular for her. The only thing is it's about $10,000 more than she paid for the ruined gown." The poor owner felt so bad for Anna.

"What color is the dress?" Xian wondered if it would compliment Anna's coloring.

"It's an azure blue with gems and stones studding the bodice. I can send a photo if you like."

"Please do." Looking at the photo that came through, the dress was exquisite. Anna would be magnificent in it. "Please send the dress; I will take care of the cost. Do you have a fur-lined cloak in your shop, by any chance? Oh, and out of mild curiosity, what did the wine color dress look like? Could you get one in and make the modifications again?" A minute later, two photos came through to his phone. A white cloak with rabbit fur lining would make the blue gown look magical. The photo of the wine-colored dress bummed him. She would have looked spectacular in that one as well. Still, it wouldn't have been appropriate for the gala. The one he ordered would be more in line with the formal dress of the event.

Xian arranged for Wu Feng to pick up the garments; no outsider would be allowed access to anything of Anna's from this point forward. Chen might not like the idea, but Xian was sending bodyguards tonight.

An hour later, Wu Feng arrived at the apartment with the gown and was accompanied by Liu Chaoxiang. Xian had hired the security officer away from the apartment complex as Anna's personal guard. Liu Chaoxiang was glad to accept the post. He was still annoyed that the horrid man from the other evening had been harassing a guest. From the moment he had met Ms. Cassidy, he had immediately liked her. He was glad it would be his job to protect her.

Xian explained the situation to Liu Chaoxiang; the large man's face grew redder as Xian recounted all of the mishaps and harassment Anna had suffered since arriving. Bowing to Xian, he assured him that Ms. Cassidy would be protected as long as he was on duty. Xian planned to have him move into the apartment with Anna when she returned if there was still trouble. He didn't like the idea of Anna living alone. But it would have to be her decision.

"Mr. Wei, please just call me Liu. Most people have a difficult time with my name. I've been just called Liu for most of my life," Liu explained and then bowed to Xian.

"Liu, glad to have you on board." Xian took the large package from Wu Feng and carried it back to Anna's room.

A knock on her door caught Anna just putting her skirt on. "One moment." Opening the door, Xian stood there with a sizable ribbon-wrapped package. Her dress had arrived! As much as she wanted to surprise Xian, she had better show him so he could coordinate with her. She carefully slid the ribbon off, putting the box on the bed. Holding her breath, she opened it to find an azure blue ball gown with more bling than the Queen Mother's crown.

Stuttering in shock, "Th...This...This isn't my dress. Why? WHY!" Anna screamed.

Three sets of feet came thundering through the apartment. Wu Feng, Liu and Chen all stopped to see a red-faced Anna screaming. She began looking for items to throw across the room. Her anger had been stuffed down for so long that the dam finally broke. Rage overwhelmed her. Wu Feng and Liu looked at one another, turned and fled to the other end of the penthouse.

Chen looked to Xian, trying to understand why Anna had hit Mount Vesuvius level. Xian looked at the box on the bed and down at his phone, sending Chen a photo of Anna's destroyed gown. Seeing what remained of her wine gown, Chen wanted to scream and throw things with Anna. Raising his hands in the universal example of "we come in peace," Chen stepped slowly towards the raging woman.

"Anna, you need to calm down, sweetheart." As soon as he said it, he realized he might have made a mistake.

Turning on Chen, Anna growled and threw a shoe at him. Deciding retreat was the best option at that moment, she needed to cool down some. Chen gave Xian a shrug and escaped as another shoe narrowly missed his head.

"Anna!" Xian's firm tone caught Anna as she looked for something else to throw. Hearing the no-nonsense tone in Xian's voice, Anna calmed down a fraction. The rage turned into sorrow; her screams turned into sobs. Crumpling to the floor, she hugged her knees as she rocked and sobbed. Xian rushed to Anna, crouching down he threw his arms around her, repeating her name softly this time, "Anna, It's going to be okay." He pulled her to his chest, letting the hot tears soak his sweatshirt. "Guess it's good I dressed casually for the spa," he joked, trying to jolly Anna out of her tears.

"Why Xian? What have I done to deserve this?" Hiccuping, Anna leaned her forehead on Xian's shoulder.

Lifting Anna's chin with his fingers, Xian wiped most of the tears from her cheeks. "Anna, the dress you chose was wonderful and it's terrible what happened to it. I don't mean to make it seem trivial, but that dress wouldn't have been good enough for the masquerade gala. The one in the box matches your measurements; perhaps you can try it on so we know if we need to go and find another dress?"

Pulling away from Xian, Anna leaned back against the bed. "Figures, here I was so proud of myself for picking out the gown on my own. I'm just a huge joke." Anna buried her face in her knees and wrapped her arms over her head.

Xian cautiously pried Anna's arms away from her head; taking a hand, he tugged gently, trying to get her on her feet. "Come on, Anna, want me to help you put the dress on?" Waggling his eyebrows at Anna in mock lascivious behavior.

Trying hard not to grin at Xian's antics, Anna snuffled and wiped her eyes with the back of her hand. "Why Xian? One day, why can't I have one day?" Pulling Anna into his arms, he hugged her tightly, wanting to protect her like this forever. Standing there for several minutes, she began to calm down. "Let me try it on. Better find out if this is another fiasco or if it will work." She backed out of his arms and pushed him towards the door. "I'll call if I need help. Out."

Xian let a small smile creep across his lips as he stepped out of the room. Leaning against the wall, he waited patiently for Anna.

Five minutes later, Anna called out to Xian, "Hey, worrywart, come help me with this dress."

Opening the door, Xian froze; his breath had been taken away. Accentuating Anna's curves and coloring, the dress made her look royal. The necklace, earrings and bracelet he gave Anna would perfectly match this dress. Actually, she needed new jewelry. There was one accessory he would need to procure to match the new jewelry. Would his people be able to find one in time?

"Turn around, troublemaker." He wanted her to turn so she couldn't see how flustered he'd become. Zipping the dress the rest of the way, Anna turned, the gems and bangles on her bodice catching the light and sparkling. To him, the dress looked like it fit her perfectly. "How does it fit? Is it comfortable enough?"

"It fits like it was made for me. Xian, I bow to your impeccable taste. I've never seen a gown this spectacular."

"You will be the talk of the gala tomorrow night." Kissing her forehead, he spun her and unzipped the dress. "Get ready; with all this drama, we will be late if we don't get going."

"Careful, Xian. I'll have them wax you within an inch of your life at the spa." Shuddering at the thought, Xian beat a hasty retreat. He needed to get the rest of the kids together so they could leave. Huang Hu was doing errands for Chen, preparing for the evening. He would have Wu Feng and Liu accompany them to the spa.

Walking down the hall to the sitting room, he found Wu Feng explaining to Liu what had been happening in more detail. Shaking his head in disbelief, Liu growled at the worst of the explanations.

"We need to find them and make them pay," Liu's deep voice grumbled.

Wu Feng clapped the mountain of a man on the shoulder. "We are working on it. Mr. Wei has a team looking for them as we speak. After their antics today, he stepped up the search. Ms. Cassidy only has until Monday before she returns to Montana." Looking around to see if his employer was nearby and listening, Wu Feng lowered his voice to say, "I think if Mr. Wei could find a reason to go with her, he would walk away from his company to go."

Liu raised an eyebrow at this news. He was under the impression that Mr. Xiao was Ms. Cassidy's fiancé. Wasn't that what she had told the man in the lobby? Perhaps it was a smoke screen to help her escape the creep. He would observe and see if he was wrong or not. When she stood up for herself, she impressed the war-hardened man. He saw many women harmed during his military service. Many were timid and wouldn't stick up for themselves; sometimes, you needed a more rugged hand.

Xian walked into the sitting room, glad to see Liu getting to know Wu Feng. They would be working closely for a few days when Anna returned. Liu would be Anna's security and Lin Bolin would be her right hand. She would have a staff that

would be able to protect her.
    "Time to go. The spa awaits."

章

Chapter 65

Anna was relaxed and ready for the party when she finished her spa treatment and salon appointment. It was fun to hear the guys grunt, groan and complain about the rough massage. To Anna, it felt amazing. Muscles that had been knotted were now loose and supple.

The ladies at the spa remembered her and giggled when they found out Chen was the one she had made an effort for. They all agreed he was very handsome and they were curious about who the other men were. How do you explain the complex situation that one was a bodyguard and the other was your employer who has romantic feelings for you and is your romantic interest's brother-in-law AND best friend?

After being worked over by the masseuse, Anna went to her salon appointment while Xian and Chen ran some errands. She felt terrible for Liu because he had to sit in a salon with gossipy women.

When Anna discovered that Liu would be assigned to her as a bodyguard, she was first aggravated with Xian for his high-handed decision to appoint someone to her. Though after she thought about it for a while...what she wouldn't have given to have Liu with her when she had been attacked. That thought changed her attitude. Now she was glad for the gruff man's presence.

Watching the mountain of a man sitting in a salon was undoubtedly the topic of gossip. Anna was lucky to get the same stylist she had the first time she came in. She showed the stylist a photo from the studio of Chen and her in their period attire. Gasping, the stylist knew who Chen was and she was a huge fan.

"This is the man you told us about?" Excitement circulated the salon.

Turning pink because of all of the attention, Anna nodded.

"Yes, Chen has been a long-distance friend for over four years. We've spent most of my time here together. I have also become good friends with his brother-in-law, Wei Xian."

A clatter was heard further back in the salon. Someone had dropped a pair of scissors on the floor when they heard Xian's name. Her client had jerked in surprise. Instead of cutting a large chunk of her hair, the stylist had let the sharp implement drop to the floor. The woman craned around, trying to see who had been discussing Wei Xian. Was it the same Wei Xian she knew?

Two hours later, Anna walked out with her hair styled in a braided bun and a silver hairpin matching her dress. She had been lucky the shop had one that would work so well with her cheongsam dress. Turning her head, she could hear the soft jingling of the chain and stones attached to the hairpin.

"Liu, have the guys returned?" Anna questioned.

"I believe they are on their way back. We will wait for them in the lobby and Wu Feng will notify me when they have pulled up to the front." Liu checked his phone for messages; he decided to escort Anna to the lobby, not seeing anything.

Sitting carefully in one of the lobby chairs, Anna pulled her phone out, deciding to do some correspondence catch-up. She had been terrible about keeping up with people.

Checking her messages, Frankie had sent her quite a few, checking to see how her trip was going. Anna sent the photo of Chen and herself dressed in the elaborate hanfu, including a short note that they had much catching up to do when she returned.

Gloria and Dana had also sent notes asking when Anna was returning. With everything that had happened, she just never had a chance to give them a call. Being on opposite sides of the clock made it difficult. Anna had been lucky Liz worked a job that made it easy for her to be up at odd hours. Once she was home, she would have a girl powwow and give them a full blow-by-blow of the trip. For now, they would have to live with a quick message.

The one person Anna needed to speak with was Veronica and they had been playing phone tag for several days now. Having submitted the last chapters for her latest book, she was waiting on the editor for the notes on the rewrite. Veronica had informed Anna that she would have a book tour in the new year, possibly in May. The publish date of the new novel wasn't set in stone yet.

Finally finished with her correspondence, Anna sent Chen and Xian a quick message asking when they would return. While she waited for an answer, she figured it was the perfect time to browse social media. After the awards, Anna hadn't had time to dig into her social media platforms. She checked her accounts and noticed many people had started following her or asked to add her as a friend. It amazed her how much publicity an award in another country could garner.

A message popped up on Anna's phone from Xian. *We're on the way. Be there in five minutes.*

"Liu, they should be here in about five minutes."

"Okay, Ms. Anna." One of the first things Anna did was explain to Liu that if she worked with him, he would need to call her Ms. Anna unless they were in a situation that required him to be more formal. He took orders well. While waiting, she asked Liu some questions to get to know him better. Anna knew that Liu had been in the military in a special force unit until he was injured. The injury didn't keep him from working, but it did keep him from being in the military.

Anna began liking the soft-spoken man as she learned more about him. She started to wonder if he would enjoy a trip to Montana. If they couldn't capture Scott in Beijing, he might return to Montana and Anna would be without security. That would be a discussion she would have before she returned.

Liu was alert, keeping an eye on the guests that came and went while they waited. Once Mr. Wei and Mr. Xiao had given him even more details that Ms. Anna wasn't privy to, he was determined to keep this spunky woman safe. Even more disturbing facts that Wu Feng wasn't privy to.

We're here, Anna received a text from Xian.

"Liu, they're here. Let's get going. I still need to figure out how to get into my dress for tonight." Anna stood and started for the door.

"Ms. Anna, you need to wait for me to go first and make sure the coast is clear." Liu charged ahead of Anna; he took his job very seriously.

Allowing Liu to take the lead, Anna followed close behind. She had been tempted to walk next to her protection, but she realized that would be intrusive if he needed to react quickly.

Arriving at the front door, Anna saw that Wu Feng had the van door open and waiting for her. Liu checked both directions closely before motioning Anna to proceed with him to the vehicle. She quickly entered the van to find that Xian was the only occupant.

"You lost Chen somewhere along the way?"

Xian smiled while typing on his phone. "No, he's picking up a few last minute items. He took his car."

"Was that smart? We're almost certain Li Ming staged that accident. What's to say she won't try again?" Anna wasn't happy with Chen. They were overprotective of her, but Chen could go out and risk himself? The hypocrisy rankled.

"Huang Hu is with him. We are hoping that will be enough of a deterrent. He shouldn't be long; he may get back before us." Xian checked his phone for replies to his text messages.

Wu Feng looked over his shoulder and gave Anna a thumbs up. At least someone appreciated the work done by the salon. Xian hadn't even looked at Anna since she got in the car. Her novelty must be wearing off. Now they were ignoring her after being so attentive. Guess it was a good thing she was returning home soon.

Their drive back to the apartment complex was quiet and quick. As soon as the van arrived, Anna barely waited for it to stop before she bailed. Liu rushed to follow her, not happy with Anna for not waiting on him.

She wasn't going to stay in that van for another moment. Being ignored on the trip back added to her irritation from the last few days. It felt like they only paid attention to her when they felt like playing the hero. Entering the building, she barely acknowledged the woman at the desk as she flew past. Liu had difficulty catching up to her without running.

Finally catching her, Liu grabbed her arm and pulled her to a stop. "Ms. Anna, what is going on? Are you late or something? You shouldn't have bailed and taken off as you did."

"Is there somewhere other than the penthouse where we can talk quietly?" Anna wanted Liu to understand the situation from her end of things.

Pondering the options, Liu came up with a solution. "You have access to the executive lounge. At this time of day, it should be pretty quiet. We can go there to talk with limited interruptions."

"Lead on." Anna gestured for Liu to show her the way. Xian had told her about some of the perks of taking over the penthouse. Anna hadn't had an opportunity to use any of them yet. She would have to explore more when she returned in January. Though, if those two kept pissing her off, she would find an apartment and hire Liu and Lin Bolin on her own.

Entering the lounge, Liu took a right and led Anna down a hall to a semi-private room with tables and chairs. Looking around, Anna liked the spot. Quiet and out of the way, they should be able to have a calm conversation.

"Let me ask you first and foremost, who are you loyal to? Mr. Wei or me?" Anna settled back into her chair, waiting for the bodyguard's answer.

Considering his answer carefully, Liu looked Anna squarely in the eyes and answered, "I am loyal to you first and Mr. Wei second. I realize at the moment that he is paying my wages, but I feel that if push came to shove, you would pay it on your own. I would appreciate any explanation about the situation between you, Mr. Wei and Mr. Xiao. For some reason, it seems rather complicated."

Looking down at the hands folded in her lap, Anna wasn't sure where to begin.

Thirty minutes later and numerous text messages and phone calls from Xian, which were ignored, Anna had explained the whole situation to Liu. He had leaned back in his chair, arms folded and listened intently, interjecting questions for clarification when necessary. Posing the question of possibly traveling with her to Montana, Liu was intrigued. He spoke passable English and had a passport, so there should be no reason he wouldn't be able to accompany her if necessary.

"I suppose we better head up before they send out a posse looking for us." Rising from her chair, Anna held a hand out to

Liu. Smiling, he shook the proffered hand.

"Ms. Anna, I look forward to working with you. For some reason, I don't think it will be boring."

Winking, Anna smiled saying, "Not if I can help it. I've lived scared for most of my life. I plan on changing that."

Arriving at the apartment, Xian expected to find Anna and Liu there. No sign of either had him concerned. Now, where had she gone? At least she hopefully had Liu with her. Wu Feng had told him they went into the building and he had confirmed with the receptionist that they had passed by her and hadn't left. Maybe they stopped at the bar?

He hadn't said much to Anna on the way back to the penthouse. He didn't remember even looking at her after they picked her up. Smacking his forehead with his palm, he had done it again. He should have complimented her, not even seeing how her hair and makeup had turned out.

Hearing the door to the apartment opening, Xian rushed to greet Anna only to find it was Chen carrying a large garment bag.

"Gee, thanks; I missed you too," Chen laughed at Xian's disgruntled expression.

Waving his hand in dismissal, Xian walked back down the hall towards the guest room he had been staying in. Tomorrow he would have to run to his place before getting ready for the gala, he had to pick up parts of his costume.

Xian had been working on another surprise when they had picked Anna up. So wrapped up in what he was doing, he had ignored her.

"Xian, where's Anna?" Looking down the hall towards Anna's room he said, "We need to start getting ready."

"She's not here," Xian growled at Chen.

Chen spun on his heel, giving Xian an undisguised look of anger. "You said you would pick her up from the salon. How did you lose her?"

Running fingers through his hair, Xian wasn't sure how to explain what had happened. He hadn't learned his lesson Wednesday, it seemed. "Well, when we picked her up from the hotel, I was a bit preoccupied with something and didn't take notice of her hair and makeup. I have no idea what she looks like at the moment. As we pulled up to the doors, she barely waited before bailing. Liu took off after that and I would hope he caught her. I'd say I probably am on her shit list again."

Groaning, Chen took his clothes to his room. Returning to the sitting room, Chen pulled out his phone and checked for Anna's location. "She's on her way back up to the penthouse; she's in the elevator."

Xian looked at Chen with surprise. "How do you know that?"

Chen looked smug and pleased with himself, "I enabled a tracking program on her phone. At least if she has her phone on her, we can find her."

Relief that she was safe made Xian almost giddy. What was he going to do after she left? He nearly panicked when she didn't return to the apartment immediately. How would he cope with her being a quarter of the globe away from him? Guess that was a bridge he would cross when it came.

Hearing the door opening, he knew **THIS** time it was Anna.

"Anna, are you all right?" Xian asked as she walked in the door.

Raising an eyebrow at Xian's question, Anna bit her tongue; she wanted to ask why he was concerned now. Instead, she replied, "I'm fine. I'll be in my room getting ready. Is Chen back?"

Nodding, Xian knew she wasn't happy with him. Tomorrow he would make it up to her.

"**CHEN!**" Anna yelled from the foyer.

Liu wiggled his finger in his ear. Wow, did that woman have a set of lungs on her? He was glad she wasn't yelling at him.

Chen poked his head around the wall by the sitting room. "Hey Anna, you're back. It's 4:30 P.M. already. We need to leave in the next forty-five minutes."

"Chen, I'll be ready. I need to put on lacy bits and my new dress. I hope you like it." Anna waved as she turned to walk to her room.

章

Chapter 66

True to her word, Anna was ready to walk out the door forty minutes later. She had to call Chen to help her. The cheongsam was more straightforward than the one she received from the studio; it had a zipper in the back due to all the lace. It wasn't traditional, but it looked amazing on her. Deep blue lace lined with matching blue satin. This dress had a fishtail hem which gave Anna more ease of movement, flaring out versus the typical snug design.

Not sure what to wear for jewelry, Anna decided to get Chen's advice.

Need some assistance, please. Anna texted Chen.

On my way, was the short reply.

Moments later, Chen arrived wearing the men's cheongsam jacket of blue jacquard and black pants. His jacket was nearly the same color as Anna's dress. She realized why women threw themselves at him. *Handsome wasn't quite the right word to describe Chen at the moment. Suave, yeah, that would be more accurate,* she thought to herself.

"We match quite well, Mr. Xiao." Anna would enjoy being with Chen tonight, matching as they did. No one should mistake that they were together; now if only that were the case.

"That was the plan, Ms. Cassidy." Chen winked as he walked behind Anna to finish zipping the back of the dress. "So, was that the only assistance you required?"

"Yes and no. I need some jewelry advice. I'm not sure I have anything that looks good with this style dress."

"I've got you covered," Chen said, reaching into his pocket. He pulled out a blue crushed velvet case and handed it to Anna.

Cautiously flipping the case lid open, Anna squealed like a little girl; catching herself, she sobered quickly. Sapphires and diamonds twinkled back at her. "Chen...they're beautiful. Isn't it a bit much for your wrap party?"

"Not at all. Let me help you with them," Chen said, taking the case from Anna's hand. Draping the necklace around Anna's neck, the large sapphire was surrounded by diamonds just above her dress's collar. Matching earrings added just the right touch to Anna's look. Turning her to face him, Chen was thrilled with how the gems accentuated her beauty.

Excited to see how she looked, Anna dashed to the bathroom. Looking in the mirror, she was awed by the subtle dance of light and color flickering over the perfect stones. Between the necklace Xian had given her and this one, she would need a safe to store them. Where would she ever wear something so extravagant in Montana?

Chen leaned against the doorjamb, watching Anna as she admired the jewels. He would never forget the childlike glee she had shown when she opened the case before her more reserved self took over. If only she would let herself loosen up more often. Perhaps tonight, she would enjoy herself. He was banking on his surprise to make her night.

"You look very elegant tonight, Ms. Cassidy. How did I get so lucky to find a treasure like you?"

"You clean up pretty well yourself." Anna could feel the green-eyed monster trying to rear its ugly head again. Just her luck to find a man who oozed charm and charisma. How would she ever compete with the actresses and other celebrities there tonight? They didn't matter, from what Chen told her, but was that the truth?

Noticing Anna's hesitance, he could tell her self-confidence was wavering. She had gone through so much since she arrived; he wished she could realize her importance to him. Though she couldn't have thought he was doing an excellent job of displaying just how much she mattered to him in the last couple of days; but trying to keep her in the dark about how bad Scott and Li Ming had been was difficult.

Enough, no thinking about those two tonight. Liu would be with them at the party as a backup. Technically, Li Ming was invited to the party as she was the lead actress. Though, with everything she had pulled in the last week, he wasn't sure if she would be allowed to attend.

Wednesday, while he had been investigating Li Ming and her whereabouts, he had spoken to Mr. Shun. When the board met to discuss Anna and her scripts, they had also unanimously decided to buy out Li Ming's contract and block her from further work with their studio. He wasn't sure if they had informed her yet or not. This could put Anna at an even greater risk of harassment because...he knew Li Ming. She would never own up to her faults. She would lay all the blame on Anna.

Wu Feng had informed Chen that he would also attend tonight but would mingle more with the other crew members, watching for any signs of trouble. Liu would keep close to Anna during the evening, especially if Chen wasn't by her side. He wanted her to have a great time but also to be safe. She would return home soon and it wouldn't be good if something happened right before she was supposed to leave.

Taking Anna's hand, Chen placed his other hand on her cheek, turning her to face him so he knew she was hearing him. "Anna, you look remarkable tonight. The actresses and other celebrities will be green with envy because I feel there will be some famous and powerful men falling at your feet tonight. Remember, you are an award-winning writer; you deserve to be there as much as they do."

"Thank you, Chen. How did you guess?" Anna asked, alluding to her sudden bout of nerves.

"Even though we didn't speak face-to-face, I've gotten to know you over the years. You do this when something good comes along. You second guess yourself. That self-destructive streak you have is better than it has been, but still rears its ugly head occasionally."

Sighing, Anna knew he spoke the truth. Perhaps therapy wouldn't be a bad idea. Time would tell if it would be beneficial, but she needed to do something. The panic attack was a rude awakening. It had been quite a long time since she had one that bad. When she was with her ex-husband, that was the last one and it had nearly hospitalized her. Tonight was not the time for reflection on this. She was going to go and have fun.

Anna's whole demeanor changed and Chen could tell. He

watched as her entire body relaxed and she almost started glowing. There was the Anna that had stolen his heart. Her twinkling eyes and mischievous grin let him know they were good now. Now, they could go and take the party by storm.

Taking Anna's hand, Chen led her down the hall to let Liu and Wu Feng know they were ready to head out. Walking into the sitting area where the guys were hanging out waiting, there were whistles of appreciation when they saw Anna. Chen gave them an odd look. This was more casual than he would have expected. Anna's influence on the men around her was beginning to show.

Anna posed for them, turning around to let them see the whole look. "So, what do you think?" She posed the question to Huang Hu, Wu Feng and Liu.

"You are going to blow them away, Ms. Anna," Wu Feng responded first.

In agreement, Huang Hu and Liu nodded. They didn't have to verbalize their appreciation.

"Stunning as always," said an unexpected voice from the hallway. Xian walked into the sitting area and up to Anna, placing a peck on her forehead. "You'll turn heads for sure." Leaning in, he whispered in her ear, "Sorry about earlier. You looked great and I didn't say anything."

"It's okay. I need to have thicker skin. We will have our night tomorrow night." Anna hugged Xian and kissed his cheek. "Are we ready, Chen?"

Checking the silver and blue designer watch on his wrist, he replied, "Yes. We need to get going. Anna, did you have a coat? It's getting cooler at night."

"I do; I picked one up with Wu Feng's assistance. Xian, he's picked up some of your great taste. Give me a moment; I'll go and get it." Grabbing the black cashmere trench coat she had purchased, it was just the right amount of stylish to go with her dress. She had no idea what she would wear tomorrow night as her gown had unusual sleeves.

Coat over her arm, she met Chen in the foyer. "Ready."

"Let's have an amazing night." Chen offered his arm.

章

Chapter 67

Arriving at the party, Anna was astonished at how similar to the awards the party was. Paparazzi and media were camped in front of the hotel. Huang Hu parked the van at the curb and an attendant opened Chen's door. Cameras flashed as soon as they saw who disembarked from the limo van. Holding out his hand, he assisted Anna from the back seat.

If Anna had thought there were flashes when Chen appeared, she was nearly blinded by the cameras' strobe effect when they saw who accompanied him. This was the first chance most media had to get her photo after the award ceremony. Her brush with the media at the market was nothing compared to the number of media present for the party. Holding her hand tightly in his, Chen walked along the open lane to the hotel.

Questions were being shouted from many of the individuals along the path. Chen stopped and signed autographs, shook hands and posed for photos several times. Feeling like she was just along for the ride, Anna quietly stood back and watched as Chen graciously interacted with fans and the media.

"Ms. Cassidy, can we have a photo?" a voice queried from the crowd.

Nodding, Anna smiled and posed. Flashes of light caused her to blink rapidly; tiny orbs danced in front of her eyes. She waved and looked around for Chen. Where had he gone? Anna didn't see him.

A gruff voice came from her left shoulder. Liu was there and casually spoke quietly in her ear, "Mr. Xiao went on ahead. He has been explaining that you were sent together by the studio, not wanting to give the media zoo fodder that you were in a relationship. Once you get inside, he will be by your side the rest of the night."

"Thank you, Liu. I wish he would have told me about that before we arrived." Keeping her composure in these moments had gotten easier. Her previous brushes with the media and paparazzi had given her experience to fall back on now.

Anna entered the hotel, knowing she didn't need to wait on Chen. She had stopped for a few more photos on her way in, not too often as she felt exposed without one of her guys by her side. Having Liu with her helped, but it wasn't quite the same. As she walked, the distance from the curb to the doors felt like a mile; trying not to interrupt other actors as they posed for photos or gave short interviews.

Not having been part of this series, Anna couldn't speak to anything other than what she had gleaned from Chen over the past few months. What she had seen the one day on the set didn't offer much help. Questions about her involvement with the studio bombarded her from both sides. Smiling and waving, Anna could only respond with "No comment" until she had time to meet with the studio and get the official response.

Finally making it into the hotel, Chen talked with a group of people clustered around some chairs in the lobby. Laughter came from the group and Anna smiled. Seeing him in his element made her realize Chen was an actual people person. He put everyone around him at ease.

Anna made her way over to Chen. She recognized the director, Xu Hinge, speaking with him. "Hello, Mr. Xu." She bowed her head in deference.

"Ms. Cassidy, it is a genuine pleasure to meet you again. I hear you will be working with the studio for a while." Xu Hinge smiled as he shook Anna's hand. "I hope I will be working with you in the future."

"Mr. Xu, I would be thrilled to work with you. I had hoped to see you tonight so I could discuss a few things with you. I'll try to keep the work talk to a minimum." She smiled and nodded to the rest of the group.

Chen was impressed. Anna was doing well so far. She made it through the media gauntlet and was already having a conversation. He had been concerned she would try to hide and not talk with anyone. It heartened him to know Anna was resilient and could bounce back from all their drama in the last week.

Xu Hinge grinned and said, "I am looking forward to it. Don't be afraid to discuss work with me tonight. I'm more comfortable talking shop than anything else. May I escort you to the party? We shouldn't just stand out here all night."

"Honestly, I'd be more comfortable staying out here," Anna joked with Xu Hinge. "I'm just a wallflower at heart."

"Trust me, you really want to go to the party; you won't be sorry." He winked at Chen. Had Anna been less distracted, she might have seen the shared look between the two men and wondered what they were up to. Chen had enlisted Xu Hinge to invite a few of the actors who had cameo parts in the series. Getting to know Anna over the years, she had told him about how she had reached out to others besides him but that they had just sent perfunctory responses. Several had appeared in the series with him. Tonight he hoped they could express their true regards towards this exceptional woman.

Chen had opportunities to discuss who Anna was and the current situation with many of them. Most didn't remember getting any correspondence from her. Two of them vaguely remembered possibly having seen her missives. They were two of her other favorites and so she had sent more heartfelt messages to them. Chen had urged them to look into the possibility further; perhaps they were still there even after four years. One had found the messages and wanted to thank Anna in person. He had felt bad that one of his assistants had responded coldly to such a touching, heartfelt email.

Chen wondered if they had arrived yet. He had intentionally dawdled and taken the longest route possible to get to the party, giving his surprises a chance to come before he and Anna showed up. From Xu Hinge's wink, Chen had assumed they were there and in place. He made sure the camera on his phone was ready for the surprise he expected to see on her face once she saw them. He hoped it would make up for some of his enormous mistakes this last week.

Xu Hinge led Anna into a large room with music playing and groups of people talking, drinking and dancing. Looking around the room, Anna recognized a number of the crew members she had met while on the set. Seeing the women from the wardrobe and makeup departments laughing and chatting in a group to the side of the room, she excused herself to go and chat with them.

"Excuse me, may I join you for a little bit?" Anna asked as she joined the women.

"Ms. Anna?" The young woman who had been so inconsolable noticed Anna first. Her face lit up at seeing the sweet American author. "Do you remember me?"

"How could I ever forget you?" Anna smiled. "However, I never got your name while at the studio."

"Sorry, Ms. Anna, I am Wang Chyou. I'm so happy to see you once again. How did your evening go? You looked beautiful when you left."

Shaking her head and laughing ruefully Anna said, "Well, I ended up a bit drunk. Mr. Xiao had to pour me into bed. I'm lucky I didn't end up with a horrible hangover the next morning."

The group laughed at Anna's admission. They weren't used to women admitting they had gotten drunk and were assisted by a man. Ms. Yan came up to Anna and inspected her hairdo. "Ms. Anna, if you have another event to attend and want your hair done in a more traditional style, please don't hesitate to contact me. Whoever did your hair tonight was proficient, but I'm better."

Anna smiled and agreed, adding Ms. Yan's WeChat information so she could contact her. "I will be attending a masquerade gala tomorrow night. Would you be available to do my hair on such short notice? I'm not sure if Xian has someone coming to do it. I'm never sure what he has planned."

Not thinking about mentioning Xian, the women stared at Anna at her casual use of Director Wei's name.

"Ms. Anna, are you referring to Mr. Wei? From the Wei Media Group?" Ms. Yan asked, figuring she would get to the bottom of it for the rest of the curious women.

Anna mentally kicked herself for being so casual with Xian's name. "Yes, Mr. Wei hired me as a liaison between the studio and his company. I will be returning to China in January so we can begin filming one of several scripts they just purchased." Anna could now discuss the movie and series with others, having signed all the paperwork. "I will have creative control of the films, so I must be on set most days."

Claps and cheers from the assembled women made Anna feel accepted and appreciated. She looked forward to seeing these talented women while working with the studio. Knowing that the scripts she sold were historical, Anna hoped Ms. Yan would be working on the production crew. Anna would request that Wang Chyou be on the team too if she had any pull. The young woman had spunk and Anna hoped she could help her get ahead in her career.

The women talked for some time before Chen made his way over to retrieve Anna for her surprise.

"Excuse me, ladies, I must steal Ms. Anna from you. A few people are waiting to meet her." Chen inclined his head in a slight bow. These women were an integral part of the film industry; they were some of the best in hair, makeup and wardrobe. Ms. Yan had won several awards for hair design over the years and Chen enjoyed working with the motherly woman.

"Only if you promise to take better care of our Ms. Anna," Wang Chyou came forward, speaking for the group.

Looking abashed, Chen bowed deeply to the group. "I will do my very best. I haven't been cautious with her. Please accept my apology." He knew these women cared about Anna, but in that moment they looked like they would go to battle for her, showing him how much of a profound impact Anna had made in just one day on the set.

Pulling Chen up from his bow, Anna blushed and assured the group that he had taken excellent care of her. There had just been some misunderstandings. With Anna's assurance, the women wished her the best and told her to return if she could get away later. Promising she would try, Anna allowed Chen to lead her to a large group of people. Murmurs and whispers of excitement greeted them as they made their way through. Coming to the center of the crowd Anna nearly turned and ran the other way.

What were they doing there? Three of Anna's favorite actors were the center of attention. Several studio executives and Mr. Shun talked to the actors and actresses. Chen held on to Anna, sensing her trying to pull away to escape. "Surprise," was all he said as he led her to the group.

"Vengo Gao, Wang Xiao and Dilraba Dilmurat, I would like to introduce Ms. Anna Cassidy, award-winning writer of *The Lost Prince*," Chen introduced and held Anna to keep her from running. These were actors that had been in one of her absolute favorite series. She had also sent them messages when she initially sent Chen's. Theirs had been some of the cookie-cutter responses she had received. Anna couldn't speak. How many times had she dreamt of this moment?

"Ms. Cassidy, it is an absolute pleasure to meet you. I must apologize for my rudeness four years ago. An assistant sent my response to your message. Please forgive me." Wang Xiao was the first to address her. His smile weakened Anna's knees, making her feel wobbly.

Vengo Gao stepped forward and took Anna's hand. "Ms. Cassidy, Chen has told us a lot about you, and we have been sincerely excited to make your acquaintance. We would love to chat with you for a while if that's okay." He smiled down at Anna.

Anna got a grasp of her internal fangirl and did her best to give them a calm response. "I would certainly enjoy having an opportunity to talk with you. Mr. Shun, may I borrow you for a few minutes? I have a couple of quick questions."

Surprised by Anna's request, Mr. Shun nodded his head and broke away from the group to speak privately with her. "What can I do for you, Ms. Cassidy?"

Raising an eyebrow at Mr. Shun's formality, Anna explained that she would like to ask the actors in the circle if they would be interested in her upcoming projects. Perhaps they wouldn't all be a good fit for each script, but Anna had written the one script with Vengo Gao and Wang Xiao in mind. Anna realized there was little chance they would ever have heard about it if it hadn't been for Chen. Mr. Shun, hearing Anna's thoughts, agreed wholeheartedly. These three were a huge draw for their latest projects and if they were excited to be part of Anna's new endeavor, the studio was behind her 100 percent.

"Run it past them; perhaps they would be interested." Mr.

Shun knew better, they had just been discussing the possibility of the three of them being in the sequel to *The Lost Prince*. However, it was good for Anna to assert herself and discuss it with them. She would be working with them for some time once filming began. When Anna had sold the script to the studio, she had informed them of several actors she had hoped would be part of the projects, and here stood three of them.

"Thank you, Mr. Shun. They will be perfect." Her excitement was infectious.

"Is there somewhere quieter we can go and talk? It's difficult to discuss anything with the music and..." looking around at the growing crowd, "...our growing audience."

Mr. Shun laughed to himself. This woman was a sharp one. There were too many eavesdroppers to discuss anything important. "Certainly, Ms. Cassidy, I have a private lounge area for our VIP guests. We can use that for the time being to talk."

"Lead the way, Mr. Shun. With everything happening lately, I'd rather not have extra ears for this discussion." Anna followed Mr. Shun, not realizing that Chen wasn't with the group.

Anna looked around for Chen once they arrived at the VIP lounge as the actors found comfortable seats. Where was he? He was one of the lead actors for these scripts and needed to be involved in the discussion. The actors sitting in the room had her in awe. How would she speak to these stars alone?

"Mr. Shun, we are missing a key individual for this discussion. Where is Chen? He needs to be here." She was becoming nervous about being close to the actors she had idolized for so long.

Mr. Shun looked around the room, not seeing him. "I'll send someone to find him. Curious, as he arranged for our guests to be here tonight." Realizing what he had just said, he wanted to take it back, but he wasn't quick enough.

As though a bloodhound on a scent, Anna turned on Mr. Shun, sniffing out the answer he avoided disclosing to her. "What? Chen arranged all this?" Just when she wondered if there was any chance to salvage their possible romance, he found some way to make her heart melt.

"I wasn't supposed to tell you. Please don't let Chen know I was the one to – how do you Americans put it? 'Spill the beans'."

Touched by what it must have taken to arrange this meeting with the group of actors who'd been another piece of the puzzle that had helped her regain her life, she wasn't going to squander the opportunity. Patting Mr. Shun on the shoulder in reassurance Anna said, "That is how you would phrase the colloquialism. I promise I won't whisper a word of this. I realize he went through a lot to organize this surprise for me."

Smiling, Mr. Shun knew Chen had accomplished his goal. When Chen had started working on this little get-together, he had also enlisted Mr. Shun's help. After explaining everything that had happened in the last week, how could he not help? Looking at the excitement and joy on Anna's face at having the opportunity to visit with these people that had such an impact on her life, it was worth the strings Mr. Shun had pulled to arrange for these actors to be here. There were a few more possible surprises up their sleeves as well. So far, those hadn't panned out either; only time would tell if it happened.

"Go. They are here just for you. If you want to sit in here the whole evening and talk with the actors, as long as they are willing to, enjoy." Mr. Shun winked at Anna and went to find one of his assistants to ensure plenty of refreshments were in the room for their guests.

章

Chapter 68

The evening flew past for Anna. Not wanting to sound too gloomy, Anna had tried to keep her story short. She told the actors about the messages she had sent years ago and how the impact of their acting had helped inspire her not only to write the story for Chen, but to begin screenwriting as well.

Chen did finally make an appearance after a while. Anna could only imagine he had waited to allow her to visit with the three actors. He had added his part of the story to Anna's about how they had become close friends after the letter she had written explaining her situation and what he had done to get her life back to somewhat normal.

Anna was still shocked that these famous individuals had been looking forward to meeting and chatting with her. *The Lost Prince* had impacted quite a few people, it seemed. Curious about what had made them like it so much, she had asked them point-blank. "Thank you so much for being here. I'm still in awe that I'm sitting here and talking to you all. I'm honored and thrilled that you are excited about my upcoming projects. To be quite honest, several of the characters were written with the three of you in mind. But I'm still curious what you all liked about *The Lost Prince* so much?"

"There was an underlying emotion and intensity throughout the movie; even being an actor and performing roles similar to those in your story, it resonated with something deeper inside me. I wanted to be the protagonist in this film, to see the intensity of the love and desire focused on me. Good grief, I have goosebumps just talking about it," Dilraba Dilmurat claimed. "I've played some intense female leads, but yours was something different."

Vengo Gao nodded his agreement. "I've worked with Ms. Dilraba on several projects. Even with the intense relationship between our characters, your movie's main couple had something more tangible and real. It's almost hard to explain."

Anna was satisfied with their explanations and the rest of the evening they laughed and talked about the upcoming scripts. Mr. Shun had returned and had again given Anna permission to discuss her roles in mind for the actors. She would love for Wang Xiao to play a lead role in one of the scripts, while Vengo Gao and Dilraba Dilmurat would be the leads in the other. Anna intended to write parts into *The Lost Prince* sequel for them too, if they were interested.

All three had been excited and requested that Mr. Shun send copies of the scripts to their agents at the earliest convenience so they could read them. They were even more excited to hear that Anna had creative control of the projects and the final say on who would portray the characters. So often in the industry they would get a script they enjoyed and it would end up being changed by the studio, causing the original feel of the project to change. Unfortunately, having signed contracts, they were then stuck, not loving it as much as they had when they initially read it. Anna guaranteed that would not be the case with these projects. Unless there were some exceptional reasons they couldn't film a scene, the scripts would stay as close to the beginning script as possible.

Once the details had been hammered out, and the three had begged her to be a part of the new projects, Anna's inner fangirl emerged and she asked about her favorite historical drama. All three of these actors had critical roles in that series. She had been almost embarrassed to admit she had seen the sequel more than thirty times over the years, and it, to that day, remained one of her absolute favorites.

It didn't take much to get them to regale her with stories about filming the project. Chen had joined in at that point, adding his perspective even though his role wasn't as significant. He knew that Anna hadn't been as drawn to that character. She had been drawn to other parts he had been in.

Laughter rippled through the room as they described pranks and bloopers that the general public wasn't privy to. Anna enjoyed getting to know the actors. She was even more excited about being able to work with these gregarious people. Chen had told her his impression of the actors some time ago; he had enjoyed working with them. Being involved with numerous charities, they offered their time to benefit worthy causes.

A loud commotion from the main room disrupted their fun. Mr. Shun went to the doors to check what might be causing the ruckus.

When Mr. Shun had returned, his face had blanched. He whispered in Chen's ear; Chen looked shocked and took off towards the door. Anna stood, wanting to know what had shaken Mr. Shun and Chen so severely. Thinking she should go and assist Chen with the problem, she headed towards the doors.

"I don't think so, Ms. Cassidy." Liu moved his bulk in front of her, blocking her door access. "Mr. Xiao would skin me if I allowed you to get hurt."

Glaring up at the mountain of a man, Anna stood with fists on her hips, glaring at him. "Move Liu! Who is your employer, Mr. Xiao or me?"

Steeling his resolve, Liu puffed out his chest and straightened to his full height, hoping to intimidate his plucky employer into backing down. He had a bad feeling that wouldn't be an option; from what he had seen of Anna, he would be fighting a losing battle. "You, but I have my orders and at this moment, they supersede yours."

She contemplated kicking the man in the shin. Anna's temper was getting the better of her. Taking a deep breath, Anna closed her eyes, willing her mind to calm before she tried to do bodily harm to her bodyguard. His job was to keep her out of trouble and harm's way. Grumbling under her breath, she stomped back to the sitting area where Gao, Dilmurat and Xiao were chatting.

"Is everything okay, Anna?" Xiao inquired, curious what might be causing her to be so aggravated.

After talking for a while earlier, Anna insisted they use her name instead of Ms. Cassidy. After a week, she still wasn't used to people referring to her that way. She fully understood that respect was what they showed her, but it felt odd when having a casual conversation.

Vengo Gao understood completely and requested that she

use his first name. Wang Xiao smiled and said, "You can just call me by my English name, Lawrence Wang if that is easier." Dilmurat Dilraba wasn't sure what would be the easiest for her, so she left it up to Anna how she wanted to refer to her.

"Xiao, I'm not sure. They aren't letting me go and investigate. I have a bad track record this last week of having odd disasters happen to me. Li Ming has decided she has it in for me and has been causing quite a few issues. That wall is my bodyguard," Anna explained, throwing a half-hearted dirty look toward Liu.

They expressed their dismay as Anna described several situations she had been in. They had even heard about the awards through the celebrity grapevine. When Chen had first approached the actors about attending that evening they had been leery, having listened to many of the rumors Li Ming had started. They weren't sure they wanted to be associated with someone so disreputable. After Chen and Mr. Shun had explained the situation, they were all onboard with making Anna's trip better. The three had agreed they wouldn't work on any project associated with Li Ming.

While Anna explained the situation to the VIPs, Chen dealt with the disaster that blew into the party. Li Ming and Scott had arrived. Li Ming was demanding that she be given VIP status and be allowed in the lounge with her Uncle Shun.

"Li Ming, just what do you think you are doing here?" Why wouldn't this woman leave him alone? "I believe you were asked not to attend the party." Chen stood in front of the doors to the VIP area.

"Out of my way, Chen. I deserve to be here just as much as you do. I was the lead actress for this series; why shouldn't I be allowed?" Li Ming snorted, trying to push past him.

Chen glared at her; how deluded was this woman? She thought she was entitled after all the chaos she had caused? "Well, do you want me to start listing the reasons? I can start rattling them off here in front of everyone. Besides, I believe you are no longer associated with the studio. I was informed they bought out your contract and you won't be working with them any longer. You aren't welcome here."

"Is that cunt in the room?" Li Ming snarled. "Why is she

allowed to be in the VIP area? She had nothing to do with this series and isn't part of the studio, so why the special treatment?"

Chen gritted his teeth, his hands tightening to fists at his sides. It took most of his self-control not to slap the face of the woman who had tormented him since they had been engaged. She had been sweet and kind while they dated; Chen had thought he had finally found that soulmate to spend his life with. She was thoughtful and considerate while working, attentive and adoring in public and private; he had been excited to start his life with her.

After he proposed, she began to change. Chen wasn't supposed to speak to any other woman, so when Li Ming discovered Chen's friendship with Anna, it was almost as though something inside her had snapped. What had been simple irritations with her jealousy became obsessive behavior; she began trying to check his messages and emails, looking for correspondence with Anna. On several occasions, she had even broken into his apartment, stealing items she thought might have been sent from the person she saw as her competition. That had been why Chen had moved from his old apartment to the one he currently lived in.

Finally, Chen had enough and broke off the engagement. Unfortunately, they still had to complete the series they had just finished. Being the lead actors on the project, they couldn't just replace her so far into the series. Sadly, it wasn't just Chen that suffered after their breakup. Li Ming took it out on the whole crew, causing trouble and being rude to everyone. Her behavior was reminiscent of someone with bipolar disorder.

Now, with Anna in China, Li Ming had become entirely unhinged. When she had called Anna a cunt it was all Chen could do not to slap her into next week. Adding insult to injury, she brought Scott with her. Chen was hard-pressed not to resort to violence with the twisted stalker. It was better that they didn't let on that they were aware of his behavior. Earlier in the day, Chen had received a call from Detective Zhao verifying they had seen Scott in the hallway to Anna's hotel room on the security tapes. They needed to get fingerprints from Scott to compare with the ones found in the room.

Watching the psycho looking around the room, Chen could only imagine he was looking for Anna. Chen wouldn't allow that man anywhere near her if he had anything to say about it. The crowd of people who had initially gathered around them began murmuring and whispering, "Is she talking about Ms. Anna?" "Whom is she calling such a horrible name?" "She is such a troublemaker." Chen was getting more and more irritated as the group grew. The last thing Li Ming needed was an audience; she would be insufferable.

Knowing it would get ugly if they didn't move this somewhere more private, Chen grabbed Li Ming's arm and pulled her out into the hallway outside the convention room. "Listen, we are over. There will never be an us. It has nothing to do with Anna, so leave her alone. Get over it and get on with your life; if you keep up this behavior you will never be in another movie or series. Let it go, Li Ming."

"Why should I let it go? That woman ruined my life! She took my man, turned the crew against me and even turned Uncle Shun against me. What do I have to lose? I want her to leave and never return!" Li Ming screeched.

Chen stepped back from Li Ming, disturbed by the craziness he saw in her eyes. This didn't bode well. He needed to talk to Xian and Liu; they would need to step up Anna's security until she returned to the States. He wasn't sure just how far Li Ming would go now. She hadn't been the most stable even when they were together; now, she was almost certifiable. Li Ming was right, though; what did she have to lose at this point? That made her even more dangerous.

"Listen Li Ming, it would be best if you and your guest leave. You aren't going to have access to Anna so it doesn't make sense for you to be here. It can be arranged if you need to hear it from Mr. Shun. Go home!" Chen turned and walked away from her.

Chen entered the main room and heard a piercing scream from the hall. Li Ming wasn't taking the rejection well. Looking around the room he saw Scott lurking near the bar area, his eyes glued to the doors of the VIP room. Scott must have found out that's where Anna was and he was fixated on her. Hearing Li Ming's scream, he set down the beer he had been nursing and went to find his partner in crime. This was Chen's chance to get Scott's prints for the police.

Asking one of the wait staff for a cloth napkin, Chen used the napkin to cautiously empty the bottle and wrap it carefully, preserving the possibility of good prints. He would get this over to Detective Zhào as quickly as possible. If they could find a way to put Scott away for a while, he would be more comfortable. Anna was returning home without them to protect her and that had him worried. She might need to take Liu with her when she goes home. Or perhaps they would need to find a security detail in the U.S.

Knowing Li Ming was on the premises, Chen decided it was time to get Anna home. The rest of the party would be the crew getting drunk and singing karaoke. He had heard from Wu Feng and Huang Hu that Anna had done quite well when they had gone. They had taken a video of Anna and shown it to Chen and Xian. Chen now had the video on his phone; it would be good company when Anna was gone.

While returning to the VIP room, Chen watched closely to ensure he didn't see Li Ming or Scott return to the room. They would need to be cautious about returning to the penthouse. At least Anna had time to visit with people who had also impacted her life. Hopefully, it was enough to get him out of the doghouse.

Anna sat on a couch, talking animatedly with the actors; they looked to be getting along famously. It was good that Anna was meeting and making new friends. She could be close to some of her lead actors working at the studio, making her job much easier. Taking a seat next to Anna, he reached over and took her hand, making a circle on her palm with his fingertip. It was the signal they had planned on the way there to signify something was up and they needed to head home.

Xiao and Gao raised their eyebrows at Chen's familiarity with Anna; giving each other a knowing glance, they smiled and silently wished him luck. They knew he deserved to find happiness. Gao caught Dilmurat's attention and quirked an eyebrow at her, an unspoken signal that they needed to wrap up the conversation. Working with her on such extensive dramas, the signal had come in handy numerous times. Seeing his sign, Dilmurat took Anna's hand between hers.

"Anna, I look forward to working with you in the future. I'm excited to read the scripts you have in mind for us and don't forget to write me a great part in the sequel for *The Lost Prince*." Her smile was genuine and infectious.

"You have no idea how nice it is to make a female friend here. So far, the guys outnumber the girls in my address book," Anna laughingly said and returned her smile.

"Well, I hope you will count Xiao and me as your friends too. Don't hesitate to let us know if there is anything you need. It was an immense pleasure getting to meet you, finally. Chen has gushed on and on about you when we would be on set for our brief appearances." Gao smirked cheekily at Chen, daring him to comment on it.

"Okay, that's enough now that you're making me sound like some lovestruck high school student. Why did I invite you again?" Chen laughed and held his hand out to shake Gao and Xiao's hands; Dimurat gave him a warm hug and he spoke softly in her ear for her alone, "Thank you for what you said to Anna; it means the world to her. I hope you can become good friends."

Dilmurat kissed Chen's cheek and whispered back, "There won't be any problem with that; Anna is fabulous. I'll try to make time when she is back so we can go shopping and have coffee."

Winking at each other, Dilmurat gave Anna a quick hug, telling her to let her know when she was back from the States. Gao and Xiao both gave Anna hugs as well. Anna could almost swear she heard Chen growl under his breath when they had hugged her a little longer than he thought they should.

Gao, Xiao and Dilmurat had exchanged phone numbers with Anna while Chen had been dealing with Li Ming. They had plans to have dinner at Anna's penthouse when she returned. They were happy to make friends with her after realizing what she had gone through.

Mr. Shun arrived in the room just as Chen explained to Anna what had happened and why they should head home. Yawning into the back of her hand, Anna was fine with heading home. She would have an even longer night the following evening, so she wasn't loath to go home and get to bed sooner than later.

Bowing to Mr. Shun, Anna said good night. "Anna, please call me Uncle Shun. If I don't have a chance to see you before you leave, know I look forward to your return. I feel we will work closely together for some time."

Stepping closer to the studio president Anna asked, "If I can call you Uncle Shun, will you allow me to hug you? Uncles are family and I hug family." Not waiting for his answer, she wrapped her arms around him, giving him a slight squeeze before stepping back. "I'll be in touch with the studio about the changes we had discussed at the meeting. Goodbye, Uncle Shun."

Chen bowed to the bemused president and said his goodbyes. Stepping back into the rowdy outer room, Anna looked for her friends from the crew. Seeing them around a table on their way to the door, she stopped and wished them all good night, letting them know she would be looking forward to seeing them when she returned. Since she was making new friends, Anna was torn about returning to the States now, but some arrangements had to be made so she could return to China for an extended period.

The trip back to the apartment was quick; Anna stared at Chen until he finally broke down and explained what had happened with Li Ming. He showed Anna the bottle he had squirreled away with Scott's prints. He would be delivering it to the precinct in the morning.

Anna asked Chen to unzip her dress upon arriving at the penthouse, not caring that Liu was standing there. She had been continually yawning since they left the hotel. She hadn't even noticed the few paparazzi still camped at the hotel's entrance at first; she still waved, smiled and then crawled into the van. Now that she was home, she just wanted to get out of the fancy garb and into her pajamas, perhaps have a small bowl of ice cream and go to sleep.

Scuffing her feet, she shuffled her way to her room to change, leaving a frustrated Chen and an amused Liu behind. "Laugh it up, big man. She will probably ask you to unzip something if you're alone with her; just be forewarned. Anna is not like any woman you're used to."

"I think I can see that already," Liu said and laughed. "If you're in for the night, I'm heading home. I'll check with Mr. Wei in the morning to find out what time we must leave tomorrow evening." Looking at his watch, it was close to one in the morning. "Or rather, later today. Good night, Mr. Xiao." Giving Chen a nod, he excused himself and left the apartment.

"Good God, I wasn't sure you were ever coming back," Xian complained as he came down the hall from his room. "Was it a good evening?"

"We have a lot to discuss. Can you stay up until we are sure Anna's asleep?" The serious look on Chen's face let Xian know something had happened and he wouldn't like it.

"Yeah, I'll stay up as long as we need."

The ice cream didn't happen; Anna didn't make it out of her room. She didn't even bother with pajamas; taking her clothes off, she crawled between the sheets and was asleep in moments.

Xian and Chen, however, were up for a couple of hours discussing their options for when Anna went home. They decided they needed to consult with Liz; perhaps she might have an idea on how they could wrangle Anna while she was in Montana.

章

Chapter 69

Knocking on her door woke Anna up. The room was bright with the sun. One thing she needed to look into was blackout blinds or drapes; she swore being so high up caused the room to get brighter.

"I'm up; come in," she called out, rubbing her eyes to clear the sleep crust.

Chen opened the door and walked in, sitting down on the edge of the bed. "Anna, did you want to get some brunch? Your afternoon is going to be busy with preparations for tonight. We won't go far, just to the restaurant downstairs. I was going to talk to you last night after we got home, but you passed out and I didn't get a chance."

Anna shifted to sit up and stretch her arms; the sheet and duvet slid down to pool in her lap, exposing her upper body. Chen groaned inwardly; oh, how he would love to caress those breasts, teasing each nipple until they...Damn it, if he stayed much longer, they wouldn't make brunch or Chen would need a cold shower.

"Um, Anna, do you feel a draft?" Chen hinted for her to cover up.

"Huh? Oh, sorry, Chen. I was so tired I didn't even think to put pajamas on before crawling into bed." She pulled up the covers, covering the objects of his fascination at that moment. If Chen stayed, they would both be in trouble. He had been so handsome the night before and so sweet to arrange the meeting with her other favorite actors, that it was making it hard for Anna to keep her distance.

"Give me ten, and I'll be ready to go. It's nothing fancy, right? Can I wear a sweater and leggings? I want to be comfortable for as long as I can today before being exposed to the stuffy crowd."

"Stuffy crowd?" Her description of the gala amused Chen.

"Well, having watched a few Chinese and Korean dramas with this kind of event, the crowd is always portrayed as stuffy, hence the 'stuffy crowd'. At least there shouldn't be any chance of Li Ming or Scott showing up, right?"

Chen cringed at the hope in Anna's voice. There was a chance that Li Ming would appear at the gala that night. Celebrities, especially ones in the current news, were invited more often than not. "Let's hope not. Liu and Wu Feng will attend with you, so they can keep her from doing anything physical."

Groaning, Anna didn't want to hear that, but she didn't have much choice. She would have a couple of bodyguards to keep her safe. "You have one of two choices, stay here for the show or get out so I can dress. Three, two, one..." Dropping the sheet and cover, Anna started crawling out of bed.

Torn between the chance to see his love nude and the frustration of seeing her and not being able to touch her, he decided he was better off beating a hasty retreat. "I'll meet you in the kitchen," he said as he closed the door, beads of sweat on his forehead from the exertion of keeping his hands to himself. It took all of his self-control not to walk back into the room, tackle Anna and make love to her for the rest of the day. Slapping himself in the face, he headed for the bathroom by his room; he needed to cool down.

Seeing Chen so flustered had made Anna smile. He was usually more unflappable, but this time he blushed and dashed from the room; though, she had almost wished he would have stayed.

True to her word, ten minutes later Anna was dressed and waiting in the kitchen for Chen. What was taking him so long? He was ready when he came to her room and now he was holed up in his bathroom. She had an inkling of what might have been the problem, but she decided to let it go and just smirked to herself.

Anna had hoped to see Xian around before she went to breakfast, but he wasn't in the apartment. "Hmm, wonder where he went," she mused to herself. Sitting on the stool at the kitchen counter, Anna swung her feet while browsing her social media and waiting for Chen.

"You ready?" The voice brought her back from the world of what her friends were doing. A soft gurgle from her middle verified that she was ready to go and eat. "I swear your stomach talks more than you do some days." Chen laughed at her scowl for that comment.

Sticking her tongue out at him, Anna was almost tempted to go to breakfast on her own if he was just going to tease her.

"Come on, let's go eat." There was a reason Chen was getting Anna out of the apartment. Xian and Chen had conspired to arrange a few surprises for her as it got closer to her departure date. Even though they were rivals for her affection, they both wanted to see her spoiled as much as they could while she was still here. Xian was out picking up what they couldn't have delivered.

Xian was back in the apartment an hour later and several wrapped parcels were laid on Anna's bed. Fresh flower arrangements were scattered throughout the apartment bringing natural perfumes to the sterile rooms. The reservations Xian had made for that evening were confirmed and upon finding out Anna had made arrangements for her hair and makeup, he had canceled the team he'd scheduled.

Mr. Shun had contacted him from the studio asking for the address of the penthouse; the hair and makeup women had found him the night before and asked if they could assist Anna for her big night. More than happy to give Anna a surprise and let the women treat their new friend, he had reached out, so he knew where to send them. The team would arrive in two hours and Anna still needed to bathe.

Laughter and voices alerted Xian to Chen and Anna's return. Xian had suggested that Chen take Anna to the restaurant area in the apartment complex versus taking her out; he wouldn't need to take Liu or Huang Hu with him that way. They had spent a couple of hours the night before trying to find a solution for when Anna returned home. They were able to contact Liz and get her input on the situation.

Her take on it was that she didn't know. It was out of her wheelhouse and she didn't want to risk her mother because of her inexperience. Liz figured Xian might have an idea of a firm to hire in the U.S.; if not, see if her current bodyguard Liu could accompany her. It was hard to determine if Anna would accept that option or not. Knowing that Scott would follow her back, the three agreed they had to figure out something.

Tonight wasn't the time to decide. Tonight was Xian's turn to shine. Chen had tried during the wrap party, but Li Ming had put a wet blanket on his evening. It sounded as though his biggest surprise had gone over quite well. Now, to see how this evening went. The gala was on the far side of town, so Xian had booked a suite at the hotel it was being held at; they wouldn't need to worry about traveling across the city during the night.

While Anna had been out at brunch, he packed an overnight bag for her with her pair of silk pajamas and a silk robe he had purchased to go with it—lighter than the heavy fuzzy robe he had picked up as a comfort option. Looking through the closet, he found an oversized shirt and a pair of leggings; he knew these were Anna's go-to relaxation clothes. They would be the easiest tomorrow for when they returned.

Chen had plans with Anna for the following evening. Mama Jing had been bugging him to bring Anna back for her special supper, so Chen had scheduled it for Sunday night. It was meant as a farewell party for Anna. He was planning on inviting Dr. Lin, his wife and the assistants. He wasn't sure if Chen should ask Shuai Ming; that had been a fiasco when they invited her to dinner at the apartment. Granted, that was on them. It was completely their fault for messing that up. Shuai Ming liked Anna quite well. He wasn't sure how Anna felt about Shuai Ming though.

Chen and Anna walked into the sitting area to discuss something that sounded studio related. Chen had filled Xian in on how well it had gone with his fellow actors. Anna had charmed them as she charmed everyone she met, with the apparent exception of Li Ming.

"How was brunch?" Xian asked, letting them know he was in the room.

Anna grinned widely, looking up from her phone. "It was delightful. It's nice to know that option is easily available when I return. There are days I get so busy I forget to eat; knowing I can call down and have food delivered is a relief."

"That's fantastic. Anna, your hair and makeup team will be here around 2 o'clock; you may want to go and shower or take a bath to be ready for when they arrive. I'd imagine it will take about an hour or two to get dolled up. We have reservations for an early dinner at 5 o'clock. They sometimes have finger foods at the gala, but I'm not guaranteeing anything." Looking at his watch, it was already 12:30 P.M., so she had an hour and a half to bathe.

"Sounds good, Xian. I'll get in the tub now; I could use a long soak. Can you come remind me at 1:30 P.M. so I can jump in the shower quickly? I may just fall asleep in the tub." Smiling, she headed for her room, dancing down the hallway practicing for that evening. Anna hadn't done any fancy steps since she was in high school. That was quite some time ago.

As he watched her antics, he started counting down in his head; five, four, three, two..."**XIAN!**" Bingo, she found the packages. Chen gave Xian an inquiring glance. Smiling, he headed for Anna's room, looking forward to her reaction when she opened the boxes on the bed.

Standing and staring at the bed, Anna wasn't sure what to do.

"You're supposed to open them. Which would you like to start with?" Gesturing to the packages on the bed.

"I'm not sure where to start. Suggestions?"

"Why don't you start with that large one." Xian pulled the long box with a crisp blue ribbon closer to Anna.

Lifting the box's lid, Anna wasn't sure what to think. Fur and fabric filled the large box. Pulling it out, Anna lifted it and found a cloak with fur edging. This was something completely unexpected. She had a cloak back home from when Liz and Sheldon married, they'd had a theme wedding, and the cloak had worked. Anna wore it on occasion when she wore specific dresses. This was so much more elegant than what she was used to.

"This is beautiful, Xian. What's the occasion?"

"It goes with your gown for tonight. I realized that wearing a conventional coat with it might be difficult so I bought the cloak as an option. It will fit very well with your costume. Keep going." He indicated the remaining packages.

Picking the next box, she lifted the cover to find an ornate mask for the masquerade that night. Delicate jewels and feathers adorned the elaborate mask. Letting her ten-year-old self emerge for a few moments, Anna squealed and lifted the mask from the box. "Xian, this is exquisite! Do you have one to match?"

"Yes, I have the dark to your light; I believe we will match quite well. Now for the second to last one." This box Xian picked up and held out for Anna while she lifted the hinged cover. Nestled inside was a crown. It was too large to be considered a tiara, diamonds and blue topaz encrusted the delicate headpiece.

"Xian, how can I wear this? It's too much this time." Growing up, Anna had dreamt of being a princess once or twice. It had never been something she aspired to. This crown would truly make her feel like a princess.

Setting down the case, Xian picked up the final box, a velvet jewelry box. Anna lifted the lid to find a necklace, earrings and bracelet that matched her crown. Blue topaz and diamonds twinkled and shone from the deep blue velvet lining. Looking up at Xian, she had tears threatening to escape her eyes. Liquid pooled in the corners.

Shaking her head, Anna was stunned. Her attire for the night was more than her salary for a year when she worked with her old company building websites. Taking the case from Xian's hands and setting it on the bed, Anna wrapped her arms around the startled man and kissed him on the lips. Coming up for air, she said, "Xian, this is like a dream...I better go shower." Half in a daze, Anna wandered to the bathroom for her soak.

Also dazed, Xian floated down the hallway while setting the alarm for 1:30 P.M. so he could rouse Anna from her bath. Her reaction wasn't entirely what Xian had expected, but it was well-received. He couldn't wait to see her completely decked out in her costume for the night.

The hour flew by faster than Xian expected; before he knew it, his alarm went off. Heading to Anna's room, he called out to Anna from the door, hoping she would be able to hear him from the bathroom. As much as he would like to see more of

Anna, he didn't want a repeat of his earlier error.

After a minute, Anna poked her head out of the bathroom, a towel wrapped around her upper torso. "I'm going to shower; I'll be ready for the ladies by the time they arrive if they aren't early."

"Where would you like them to set up? It might be a bit too crowded in your room."

Thinking a moment, "I believe upstairs would be perfect. Plenty of room and good natural lighting. Are any of the guys around to assist them with whatever they bring?" She was concerned about the women. Hopefully, they didn't need to tote everything up the elevator and upstairs.

"You mean the assistants that you've wrapped around your little finger? I swear those two barely listen to Chen and me anymore. They are both hanging out in the sitting area with Liu waiting on us. Wu Feng and Liu will accompany us this evening; I found them some interesting costumes." He couldn't wait for Anna's reaction when she saw what he had for the men. They were both great sports about it.

"I can't wait. Now get out so I can get showered. Please warn the guys that I'll wander through the apartment in my robe for a bit until I get into my gown." Winking, Anna ducked back into the bathroom and Xian could hear the water in the shower start running.

Tamping down the urge to ask Anna if she needed her back scrubbed, Xian pulled out his phone to ask the receptionist to let him know when the team arrived. He had good timing. The women had just shown up. Sending down Wu Feng and Huang Hu to help them bring whatever they needed to make Anna look like the queen Xian considered her.

Anna stepped out of her room in the satin robe, her damp hair dangling in ringlets around her face. The hair and makeup artists arrived and oohed and awed as they looked around the apartment. Anna was getting excited about personalizing the penthouse to suit her personality. Perhaps she would bring some decor from home when she returned.

Seeing Anna, the ladies requested a quick tour of her place. Anna's room was the last stop so she could show them her gown and the accessories they would need to work with. The laughter tapered off as they became serious and ideas started flying as they tried to decide how to put her hair up to work with the jewels.

Anna reminded the makeup artists that she preferred to look as natural as possible. Wearing minimal makeup had been key to her youthful appearance. Up for the challenge, they went upstairs to where Huang Hu and Wu Feng had set up their cases and tables on the second floor.

An hour and a half later, Anna was ready to step into her gown. Anna started to panic when she realized she couldn't wear her regular lingerie with the dress. Looking through the items Xian had purchased, there wasn't anything that would work.

Racing through the apartment, Anna found Wu Feng dressed in a court jester costume. "Feng, where is Xian? I have an emergency."

"Not sure. Last I saw Mr. Wei, he was helping Liu with his costume. You're going to love it."

"Can you please find him? I can't get dressed until I talk to him." Anna was starting to feel stressed without the proper support.

Wu Feng jumped up from the couch and headed back to Xian's room, looking for his boss. It was just minutes until Xian returned with Wu Feng in tow. Xian was wearing a robe and what looked like tights.

"Anna, what's wrong? Feng said you were having some emergency."

Pulling Xian to the side she whispered to him, "I don't have the right lingerie for this dress Xian. I could go braless if I need to, but I'm a bit more endowed than most and would be uncomfortable to go without."

Giving Anna an appraising look, Xian pulled his phone from his robe pocket. After a quick conversation, he tucked the phone back into his pocket. "The cavalry is on its way. They should be here in fifteen to twenty minutes."

Relief cascaded over Anna with that disaster being averted. *Now, on to the next. Oh, please let there not be another disaster*, Anna thought. "Thanks, Xian. I'm in a holding pattern until I can get my gown on. Let me know when my rescue crew arrives. The guys would probably be more comfortable if I'm not hanging around in just a robe." Inclining her head towards the blushing Wu Feng. Chen and Huang Hu had left shortly after arriving back at the penthouse. Chen said he had some things to deal with.

Twenty minutes later, a harried woman arrived at the apartment with a bag in hand. Xian brought the bag to Anna's room saying, "I believe you'll find what you need here. Think you can be ready in about twenty minutes? If we are much later than that, we will be pressed to make our reservations."

"Shouldn't be a problem. It's mostly just getting into the gown and getting it all adjusted. Why are you still in your robe? Shouldn't you be dressed by now?" A white cravat peaked over the top of Xian's robe and the white tights peaked from below.

Xian gave her a mischievous smile, raised his eyebrow at Anna, and replied, "It's a surprise, dear. I'll go finish getting ready now. You should be ready about the same time I am. Meet you in the dining room in twenty minutes."

Peeking in the bag and seeing a selection of bras, Anna hoped one would be the correct size. "Shouldn't be a problem. They will finish my hair after I get the dress on so it doesn't get disturbed," she said to herself.

Anna dug through the offered bras; several were her size. She found a delicate nude lace bustier that worked with the dress's bodice. Anna was better endowed than most who might wear that dress; it worked well after putting on the ideal foundation garments. Anna had fun with the stockings and garters; the cute ribbons on the garter belt made her giggle.

Finally dressed with the crown situated in her hair and the jewelry added, she slipped into a pair of simple flat jeweled slippers that Xian had found at a costume boutique. Carrying her cloak over her arm, the hair and makeup women trailed her like her court ladies-in-waiting. Walking into the dining room, Anna gasped when she saw Xian, Liu and Wu Feng together.

Xian was dressed in full king's garb of doublet and breeches; Anna was jealous of the knee-high suede boots. The shoulder cloak he wore had silver accents. The colors of his costume matched Anna's well. His crown wasn't as ornate as

Anna's but the stones matched. What was the clincher for Anna was the sword buckled around his waist. He looked royal.

Once she was done drooling over Xian, she checked out Liu and Wu Feng more closely. Wu Feng was the most colorful of the three. His jester's garb was bright blue and silver; he matched his lord and ladies' colors with the mask and hat. Together, you could tell they were from the same party.

Liu was dressed as a knight. Where they were able to find chain mail to fit his bulk...Anna was quite impressed. Oh yeah, Xian was the owner of a vast media firm; he probably had some strings he could pull to find the correct pieces. Liu was handsome and chivalrous looking in his garb. The sword hanging at his side was not as ornate, but still quite lovely.

Curtseying to Xian, Anna blushed when Xian returned a bow to her. Getting into the act, Liu took a knee before Anna and offered her his sword. Recognizing the gesture's significance, Anna took it more seriously than the others around her.

"Are you serious, Liu?" Anna studied the stoic bodyguard.

"Deathly," was Liu's single word reply.

Looking at Xian, Anna couldn't read him. The expression on his face was closed. This was her life and her choice. In Liu's mind, accepting the sword would be him pledging his life to Anna and her safety. "Liu, I accept." Taking his sword, she offered it back hilt first. Curious about what spurred the man to swear to protect her with his life.

Liu accepted the sword and bowed his head. "Ms. Anna, it is an honor."

Anna took Liu's arm and pulled him to stand up. "Does this mean you plan to return to Montana with me? I'll be there for about a month and a half. I don't know anything about your personal life; I understand if it isn't convenient."

Flashing a look in Xian's direction, Liu turned to Anna to answer her question. "I will begin making arrangements to accompany you back to Montana; if it won't be too inconvenient having a long-staying house guest."

"It won't be. I have a guest cabin on my property, so you can have your own space while we are there. I hope you don't mind the snow." Knowing he had been in the special forces, she didn't think he would mind that much.

"Snow doesn't bother me in the least." Liu smiled to reassure her. When Mr. Wei and Mr. Xiao approached him about their idea, he hadn't needed long to think about it. Getting to know Anna, Liu had no problem staying by her side to guard her. His experience with the United States had been limited. He had never been to the mountains there; it would be an exciting experience.

Xian watched as this all played out in front of him. He had arranged it, but it didn't mean he was pleased. Having another man tied to Anna felt like he was just asking for more competition, but her safety meant more to him. They had called Liz that morning and she confirmed the security system was installed in Anna's home so that at least reassured him. Now, they had a way to keep her safe while she traveled and wasn't at home. If only she would just stay in Beijing, he would feel so much better.

"Okay, we will be late if we don't leave now. I booked a private room at the restaurant; I figured the four of us might be a distraction if we were in the main room." Taking Anna's cloak from Wang Chyou, the young wardrobe girl who had liked Anna, he arranged it over her shoulders and tied it loosely at her throat.

"My queen, shall we depart?" Holding out his hand for Anna to take.

The group stood in the foyer, the elevator chiming its arrival. Doors opened to reveal Chen and Huang Hu deep in conversation, barely noticing the group dressed in medieval garb. Xian cleared his throat, catching their attention.

"Oh Xian, glad we caught you before you left. Tomorrow night...." Chen stopped in mid-sentence seeing Anna. "Anna, you look...regal." He stepped forward, took her hand and kissed it, wanting to say so much more but tonight wasn't his night. She would be the center of attention if he knew his Anna.

"Thank you, Chen. What was that you were going to say about tomorrow night?" Curiosity tickled Anna's mind.

"It can wait. You must be getting close to running late."

"We are actually. Huang Hu, can you help the ladies with their cases? They wanted to see Anna off." Inclining his head towards the apartment before walking into the elevator.

"Certainly, Mr. Wei. I'll be glad to." Huang Hu hurried into the apartment.

"See you later, Chen." Anna smiled as the doors of the elevator closed.

章

Chapter 70

Dinner ended up being uneventful. Arriving at the restaurant, they had garnered some attention due to their costumes, but it didn't last. Eating quickly, the group discussed contingency plans if anything happened. Liu and Wu Feng were there to protect Anna so they would be her royal court for the evening.

Xian had whispered an amount in her ear that she had available for bidding. When Anna heard the extravagant sum she stared at him. "Are you sure?"

Xian smirked saying, "That's only a quarter of what I usually spend. I didn't want to shock you too badly. You can spend as much as you'd like tonight, especially if there is something you truly want."

"Wow, Xian. I had planned on spending some of my own money as well." Anna had always given generously to charities at home.

"There's no need. I certainly won't stop you if you truly want to spend some of your own funds. I just wanted you to know what I have set aside to be spent. Please use it." His insistence made her feel less uncomfortable about spending so much.

"If you insist, I'll be glad to help you spend money," she said as she laughed.

After finishing the meal Xian explained to her how things would go at the gala. When they arrived they should have about an hour to view the items offered for auction. Once the auction was completed the dance would start, lasting well into the night.

Pulling up to the venue for the gala, the media and paparazzi were there in force. This time, Anna had some anonymity due to her mask. True to Xian's word, his mask was the dark to Anna's light. Contrasting blue fabric with gems and feathers made both extremely elaborate compared to some of the other masks she had seen.

As the group crawled out of the van, they caused quite a stir. Many of the other guests weren't dressed as elaborately. Many guests had only worn evening wear with a simple mask. But there were still plenty wearing elaborate costumes; someone in a gorilla costume made Anna giggle. She also saw a few people wearing traditional Chinese historical costumes, though nothing as beautiful and ornamental as what she had worn with Chen at the studio.

Making it through the media gauntlet with minimal fuss, they entered the building. Xian showed his invitation and security waved them through with exaggerated deference. Anna raised an eyebrow at the ease they had entering the event. Walking into the reception area they located the tables allotted for registering for their bidding numbers to be used for the auction. They both received their numbers and the catalog with some items that wouldn't be displayed before the auction.

Having looked through the proffered auction items, Anna decided there were several to bid on. Her main objective was to get some gifts to take home and it would be nice to get a present for both Xian and Chen. Anna felt she needed to return the kindness they had shown her. The gifts they had given her were extravagant; how could she ever repay them?

Anna and Xian looked around the room, chatting quietly. The nice thing about the masks was that they weren't pestered by people looking to get attention from Xian. It had happened on occasion when she had been out shopping with him. People recognized him and would try to curry favors—one of the drawbacks of being in charge of such a large company.

As the auction time got closer, more people filled the room. Xian remarked that he recognized a number of them. Turning a corner, Anna couldn't believe her luck when she saw Mr. Shun with a stately woman. They were wearing simple evening wear with elaborate masks and Anna still recognized him right away.

"Uncle Shun?" Anna walked up to the studio president.

Startled for a moment, Mr. Shun looked closely at the bedecked woman standing before him. After a moment, his expression changed, realizing who it was. "Anna?"

Laughing softly, Anna gave him a deep curtsey.

"Ms. Cassidy, what a pleasure to see you. I didn't realize you had planned to attend the gala tonight."

"Mr. Shun, I am a guest of a slightly important man." Anna giggled and winked. Xian spoke to an acquaintance he hadn't seen in some time across the room. He had put Liu in charge of Anna while he had stepped away. Anna was thrilled to know another person in the crowd of 'stuffy people', as she called them.

Mr. Shun smiled, she was there with Mr. Wei and he now recognized Anna's bodyguard Liu. Looking around the room, he spotted a man dressed as a monarch, he figured that had to be Xian. "Ms. Cassidy, this is my wife, Wu Ai. This is Ms. Cassidy; she has just sold the studio some amazing scripts and will be on staff for the next two years, hopefully longer. She was the author that wrote *The Lost Prince*."

"Ms. Cassidy, I have heard quite a bit about you recently. Isn't she a friend of Xiao Chen?" His wife was delicate and dressed in an exquisite cheongsam.

"Yes, that, Anna." Mr. Shun smiled. Chen had gone on at length on more than one occasion about the author he had befriended. Having been around her during the week, he understood why. His crew members were already starting to fight to be involved in her first picture. How different it was from the last project with Li Ming; on that series he had to bribe several key crew members to stay on.

Looking around the room for Xian, she found him having a heated discussion with an older man and woman and a younger lady. Frustration was written all over his face, so much so that she could see it across the room. Curiosity pulled at Anna. Should she try to step in and see what is going on?

"Please take your places; the auction is about to begin," an announcement spoke over the chamber music that was playing.

"Well, I guess it's time to find a seat. I wish you good bidding, sir." Anna made a small curtsey to the couple and took Liu's arm as he escorted her to a set of chairs that Wu Feng guarded. Anna looked around and didn't see Xian; he had been there just a few moments ago. She was tempted to send

Liu to find him, wondering where he might have gone.

Motioning to Wu Feng, she beckoned him to come closer. "Wu Feng, where is Xian?"

"Ms. Cassidy, I'm not sure. I lost sight of him about fifteen minutes ago. Right after you began speaking to Mr. Shun. Would you like me to locate him?" At that moment, the severe expression on his face conflicted with his jester costume.

Craning her neck, she tried to look over the bidders finding their seats in preparation for the auction. Not seeing her escort, she nodded to Wu Feng. "Please. I'm nervous that I don't see him anywhere. He was having a rather heated discussion with a group of people earlier. I'm not sure who they were."

Bowing, Wu Feng shimmied his way through the crowd.

Anna half paid attention as the bidding began on the first items. She had seen a pair of jeweled cuff links that would fit Xian's style. For Chen, there was a tea set from a pottery master that he liked. Anna rechecked the catalog listings; there were several jewelry pieces she hoped to get for the girls back home. One item that stuck out to her was an autographed group of items from a Chinese punk band. Her son-in-law may not know the group, but she figured he would get a real kick out of it.

The cufflinks were up for bid, she waited until it went to the lowest price before she began. Anna was an old hat at this. A few others bid her up, but she won the auction with little effort. The cuff links and tea set Anna would purchase with her own money as they would be gifts for her guys. As for the gifts to take home, she would allow Xian to buy those for her.

Excited to have won the first auction she looked to share it with Xian, but he was still nowhere to be seen.

The auction progressed at a quick pace. Vacation packages, cars, bottles of wine and liquor, jewelry and other exclusive items passed over the auction block. Anna had broken down and bid on two of the vacation packages. She would take Chen on one and Xian on the other, jealousy be damned.

With good luck and a large bankroll, Anna won all the auction items she bid on. Still no sign of Xian though; she hadn't heard anything from Wu Feng either. Glancing at Liu standing off to the side, observing the room with his hand resting on the pommel of his sword, she wondered if he had heard from either.

Anna pulled her phone from her reticule and checked for any messages as the auction finished. Nothing! Where in the hell were those two?

Guests were asked to step into the reception area while the staff rearranged the room for dancing. Anna made her way to Liu, concern bordering on anger hidden by her mask. "Liu, have you seen Mr. Wei? I sent Wu Feng to find him as the auction began over an hour ago. I've had no word from either."

Liu growled at that. When they'd arrived he had gotten a bad feeling. It had been years since his sixth sense had reared its head. They needed to locate Mr. Wei and Wu Feng. "I haven't seen either, Ms. Cassidy. Stay by my side no matter what happens. I like this job and plan on keeping it."

Striding off in the direction of the reception desk, Anna could see that Liu was born in the wrong century. He would have made an incredible warrior in some far-off century. His bearing and stature fit well with the feel of that era. She had to stretch her legs a bit to keep up with the longer legs of her guard.

"Excuse me. We are looking for Mr. Wei. Has he left any messages?" Liu inquired of the women working at the desk.

The assistants looked around the desk and conferred; none had received any message.

Tugging on Liu's chainmail sleeve Anna said, "I'm getting scared, Liu. What could have happened to him?"

Keeping his face expressionless, he couldn't let Anna know he was just as worried, if not more. Being employed by Mr. Wei, he had worked out with both Xian and Feng the past couple days. They were both quite capable martial artists, but that didn't stop a bullet. *Damn it, Liu, no negative thoughts. It's still too early to go there,* he thought to himself.

"Ms. Cassidy, we'll find him. Mr. Wei and Wu Feng are quite capable martial artists. Perhaps he had some kind of work issue come up." He could only hope.

Distraction and fear consumed Anna's mind. "I have an idea." She headed for the venue's front doors and wondered if paparazzi were still lurking.

This time Liu had to stretch his legs to keep up with the freight train that was his employer and principal. He realized she was becoming a friend as well. She wasn't going to get hurt again on his watch.

Anna spoke with the security at the door; none had remembered seeing a man dressed as a king or jester leaving the venue. Strike one.

Anna found several paparazzi hanging around the edges of the building, waiting for notables to exit and hoping to catch something scandalous. "Hey, $1,000 for anyone with proof showing me a man in a king costume leaving the venue," she called out to the group.

Clamoring for attention, all the photographers flipped through their cameras' images. "I have one!" a scruffy-looking man in the back crowed.

Coming forward, he showed a photo of Xian following a man with salt and pepper hair. Wu Feng was close on his heels in one of the following photos. "**FUCK!**" The exclamation startled and shocked several of the photographers.

Liu was there in a moment. He had stood back, trying not to intimidate the people with possible leads. "Ma'am?" He was cautious not to use Anna's name. They didn't recognize her or the men in the photos. He hoped to keep it that way, pulling the photographer aside to speak with him in confidence.

"When were these taken?" Anna asked, trying not to sound desperate. "I believe something must have come up with my date and I haven't been able to reach him."

"It was about forty-five minutes ago. They got into a dark blue sedan. You said something about $1,000?"

Looking to Liu, Anna asked, "Can you arrange his payment?"

Nodding, Mr. Wei had given him several thousand in cash at the beginning of the evening. He had told Liu to spread the bills around to the staff throughout the evening, it never hurt to be a generous tipper. Liu didn't believe he would mind that some of the funds would be used to get information on his whereabouts. Turning his back, he pulled out the stack of bills, thumbed out ten one hundred dollar bills and handed them to the skittish man. Something was still feeling off. It was almost too easy. Why weren't any of the other photographers taking photos of Mr. Wei? Wouldn't he have been a target for pictures with his costume?

"Ma'am, may I speak with you?" Liu motioned for Anna to follow him some distance from the group. "Something feels off. Why didn't any of the other photographers have photos of Mr. Wei? He sticks out like a sore thumb with the elaborate costume he was wearing."

Cursing a blue streak under her breath, Anna pulled her phone out. Trying Xian's number it went immediately to voicemail. Fear gripped Anna; she had recognized the man in the photo that Xian had followed. How had Scott lured Xian and Wu Feng away? She tried Wu Feng's phone next, but there was no luck there either.

Cocking her arm back in preparation to throw her phone in a fit of rage, a firm hand caught her wrist. A soft voice caught her attention, "Anna." Turning, Liu stood there, his mask held in his hand. His eyes were filled with worry for the woman in front of him. "That isn't going to help the situation."

Looking over Liu's shoulder, Anna saw the photographers were watching them closely. "We need to find a more private location to discuss this. I need to locate Mr. Shun." Pulling up her skirt, she dashed back into the venue with Liu hot on her heels. Searching through the milling guests, Anna watched for the one ally she could reach the quickest.

—

Watching Anna lose her composure when the asshole that brought her disappeared made Scott realize his plan just might work, especially if the jerk didn't return. He would bide his time and watch her as she hunted frantically for the man.

He watched as she drank glass after glass of alcohol. Having watched her in Fortine, he knew she didn't drink often, this could get interesting. Now to just bide his time. When the dancing began would be his best chance.

—

Spotting the studio president chatting with a group of men and women, Anna casually made her way to the group. Politely breaking into the conversation and speaking low she said,

"Excuse me, Mr. Shun, if possible there is something pressing I need to discuss with you."

"Certainly, Ms. Cassidy." He turned to the group saying, "Please excuse me; I have something I need to discuss with this young woman." Following Anna to a reasonably unoccupied corner of the room he questioned, "Anna, you're trembling. What's wrong?"

"Xian is missing." Anna managed to get out. She was trembling so badly that she had to clench her teeth to keep them from chattering. Pulling Liu forward, Anna implored him with her eyes to explain. She was having trouble just keeping her composure at that moment.

"**WHAT**?" Mr. Shun's voice carried, causing several guests to look towards the group. Lowering his voice he asked, "What happened?" He looked to Liu for the explanation; he could tell Anna was in no condition to fill him in.

In short order, Liu had explained to Mr. Shun what had happened.

Mr. Shun shook his head saying, "Well, that explains a lot. Normally Xian spends exorbitant amounts of money at this event and he didn't place a single bid tonight. I had chalked it up to him allowing you to do the main bidding for him."

Shaking her head, Anna was finally calm enough that she could add her information to the discussion. "He gave me a sizable allowance for bidding, but he told me it was a fraction of what he planned to spend tonight. What concerns me the most is that Mr. Randall was with him and that means Li Ming is involved."

Anna was impressed with the string of Chinese expletives from Mr. Shun. "If we find any proof she is involved, we will be taking it to the authorities this time. Enough is enough."

Cringing, she had one more alternative, but she knew she would catch an earful. Pulling her phone out again, she tried Xian and Wu Feng one last time before calling Chen and Huang Hu. She had hoped to keep them out of this, but it wasn't possible right now.

Anna waited for the phone to connect. Chen's concerned voice answered the phone, "What's up, Anna?"

"Xian and Wu Feng are missing. There were photos of him

leaving with Scott," Anna said simply.

It was good that Anna pulled the phone away and handed it to Liu at that moment. She could hear the yelling clearly with the phone several feet from her ear. Taking the phone, Liu gave Chen the exact rundown he had given Mr. Shun moments earlier.

"Huang Hu, you need to call Detective Zhao," Chen ordered and stayed on the phone with Liu.

While discussing what to do, Anna saw a server with glasses of champagne walking close by. Grabbing two glasses she quickly downed one, setting that glass back on the tray and keeping the other to drink more slowly, carbonation be damned. Tipping it back and drinking it quicker than expected, Anna looked for the bar. She needed something much stiffer.

Coming back with a double scotch neat, she sipped the drink while watching Liu and Mr. Shun talking with Chen. Where had Xian gone? She couldn't lose him. Her breathing was becoming more rapid. Scott couldn't hurt him; Xian was too strong for him to get hurt. She took another long pull from the glass then a warm hand took the glass from her.

Blearily Anna looked up to find Xian holding the glass, taking a long drink from it. "**XIAN!**" Anna jumped up, throwing her arms around his neck.

Hearing the name, Liu and Mr. Shun turned to find Anna trying to smother Xian.

"**WHERE THE BLOODY HELL HAVE YOU BEEN?**" Anna's loud voice caught the attention of guests nearby.

"Shhh! Anna, I'm sorry. Something came up that I needed to attend to. I should have told you I would be gone for a bit." Xian silently kicked himself; he had almost ruined his own plan. He figured he would have been back long before the end of the auction. Never did he expect Anna to get so emotional about his absence.

Liu strode over and placed Anna's phone in Xian's hand. "Someone would like to speak to you."

Cringing, he had an idea who it was. "Hi, Chen. It's all a misunderstanding. I had something come up and I didn't let Anna or Liu know I would be gone for a little while." Anna could almost hear Chen's angry words on the other end of the phone.

Another waiter with champagne glasses on a tray walked close by so Anna grabbed two more glasses, polishing off one in two gulps and placing the glass back on the tray. Giving her a disparaging glance, he moved off to find other guests. She found a chair nearby and shakily sat down. She had panicked as much about Xian being missing as she had about Chen when he'd been in the accident.

Xian finally cleared up the situation with Chen, Mr. Shun and Liu, then he came to kneel in front of Anna. "I'm so sorry, Anna. Can you forgive me?" Reaching into his doublet, he pulled out a red rosebud.

The small red bud was almost perfect. Anna took the delicate flower in her hands; it was one of the most romantic gestures she had ever experienced. To her, it wasn't the grand gestures that impressed her the most; it was the personal sweet moments like this that melted her heart.

Having had a copious amount of alcohol in a short time, Anna was feeling it. She felt hot, her skin flush with the reaction to the beverages. "Xian, I was so worried about you. When that photographer showed me a photo that looked like you were following Scott, it scared me."

Shaking his head, he would find that photographer. Somehow Scott must have been nearby when he had gone out with Wu Feng to pick up a few items he had needed for later that night. Anna didn't realize they would spend the night at the hotel. He had enlisted Wu Feng to help him stage the room for later. Flowers and candles were ready for when they arrived. Seeing how distraught Anna was, it was probably better that she was getting tipsy.

Leaving Anna with her glass for a few minutes, Xian apologized profusely to the studio president. "I'm so sorry, Mr. Shun, for pulling you into our little drama."

"If you three keep this up, I will option the story and make it into a drama. I'll be rich," said Mr. Shun, laughing silently to himself. This kept getting more and more enjoyable. He couldn't wait to see who made the next move. "If you have everything under control now, I will find my wife."

"Certainly, sir." Xian bowed to the older man.

Liu said, "Mr. Wei, you're lucky you're my employer or I'd punch you right now."

Resting a hand on the bodyguard's shoulder he said, "I wouldn't expect less of you. Now I know you are the right man to keep Anna safe, even if it's from Chen or myself."

His estimation of his employer ratcheted up a few notches, giving him the green light to even protect her from the men who clearly loved her took some serious balls. This was going to be a fascinating job.

"Liu, I booked a suite for Anna and myself and there is a room for Wu Feng and yourself. Things didn't go quite as I had planned. Hopefully, Anna won't stay drunk the whole evening. Let's keep her from drinking for a while. Hopefully, it will help sober her up a bit. Could you find a couple of bottles of water for her? We need to get some liquid into her other than alcohol. I'm starting to kick myself that I haven't gotten a female bodyguard for her."

The reasoning for that became apparent shortly. "I need to pee," the now drunk Anna announced loudly.

Groaning, Xian wondered how they were going to manage this. He helped Anna to her feet as she wasn't very steady. How much had she drunk in such a short time? He had only been thirty minutes late after the auction. "Liu, how much did she drink? I wasn't gone that long."

Snorting, Liu gave Xian a contemptuous glare. "With everything that's happened to her this week, do you think she wouldn't be freaking out if you were gone for even a few minutes, let alone thirty? And you were gone through the whole auction which **SHE DID NOTICE!**" Whew, he nearly lost his composure.

"Okay, I'm an ass. Now we just need to figure out how to get Anna to a restroom."

Had they been in a more private setting, Liu would have just carried the nearly drunk woman to the closest restroom. The biggest problem was getting someone to assist with her costume.

Looking around, Liu located a young female working in the reception area. "Excuse me a moment, miss." Liu struck up a conversation with the giggly young woman once he walked over to the table. Making arrangements with her, he gave her two hundred dollars to help Anna with her costume in the restroom.

"Mr. Wei, arrangements have been made."

They helped Anna make it to the restroom and the young woman helped her wrestle with all of the fabric.

Assisting Anna from the restroom, she handed her back to Liu and Xian. Giving Anna a bottle of water, the men got her to drink it and several more. Instead of being nearly drunk, she started sobering to the point that she was just slightly tipsy.

"I'm so sorry, Xian. I went a tad overboard when you disappeared." Anna's embarrassment at her behavior reminded her why she didn't drink often. From then on, it would certainly not be in public anymore.

"So, do you think you're up for a few dances before we call it a night? It'd be a shame to waste your practice," he teased, winking at Anna. He'd seen her practicing around the apartment when she thought he wasn't looking. She had even enlisted Wu Feng and Huang Hu to help her.

"I believe I can make it through a few dances." Her head had cleared considerably.

"Shall we?" Xian offered his hand.

Taking his hand, he steadied her as they walked to the dance floor, waiting for the current dance to finish. Moments later, the song ended and a waltz started. Nervous, Anna wasn't sure how well she would do. Closing her eyes, she just let herself go and followed Xian's lead. Gliding around the dance floor, they made quite the striking couple. The king and his queen waltzed their way around the room, their eyes only on one another.

When the song finished the crowd around the floor clapped enthusiastically. Xian and Anna had made quite the impression on the other guests. Their chemistry and movements had caused the other dancers to step to the side so they could watch them.

Smiling, Xian bowed and Anna curtsied to the crowd to further applause. Offering his elbow, he escorted Anna from the dance floor. Passing through the crowd on the way to the table they had claimed, they heard whispers of, "Why can't you dance with me like that?", "Oh, my word, who are they?", and "What a picturesque couple. Those two are almost perfect for one another."

Blushing from the compliments, Anna asked for a glass of champagne.

Scowling at Anna, Liu folded his arms over his chest. "You just sobered up; we don't need a repeat of your earlier performance."

"It was the scotch that did me in. I should be okay with just champagne. I need something to help loosen the nerves. They're strung tighter than a hunting bow right now."

Shaking his head, Liu went in search of a waiter.

"Are you sure you'll be okay, Anna?" Xian asked, concerned.

"I'll be fine. I'm having a good time. I won the auctions I bid on, you're in one piece for the moment..." She gave him a threatening look. "And Liu has gone to get me a glass of champagne. I've never felt so sophisticated and elegant. I believe I'm good for at least one more dance." Anna stood; seeing Liu returning she motioned him just to set the glass on the table.

Taking Xian's hand, she pulled him towards the dance floor for one last dance. Taking their places as the music for a Samba began. "Do you know the Samba?" Anna asked.

"Certainly, I enjoyed dancing it with Chandra. It has been a while."

Moving with the rhythm of the music, Xian and Anna found their groove quickly. Looking a little odd dancing the Latin dance wearing medieval garb, they just went with it, enjoying one another. As the music finished a voice came from over Anna's shoulder.

"May I have the next dance?" a deep velvety voice belonging to a man in a magician's costume inquired.

She looked to Xian for guidance; Anna knew declining would be rude but she was nervous about dancing with anyone else. He inclined his head in agreement. There hadn't been any sign of Li Ming or Scott inside the gala. If Anna was okay with it, he didn't see the harm. There were quite a few people around. Would they be so stupid to attempt something with all the witnesses?

"I believe I can spare one," Anna replied.

As a waltz began, the man held out his hand for her to take.

Stepping gracefully around the floor, Anna kept having a niggling feeling that she knew this man. "Do we know one another?"

"How could you not know your soulmate?" came the honey-smooth voice in reply.

Fear gripped Anna. How could she not know it was Scott? Trying to pull away, he grabbed her hand and waist tightly. "Don't think you will get away from me that easily."

Twirling Anna around the floor, he looked for a portion of the dance floor that didn't have eyes watching them. Dancing her to a far corner, he pulled her off the floor towards a door.

Struggling, Anna screamed, "**XIAN!**"

Grabbing the struggling woman, Scott covered her mouth with his hand to keep her from yelling again.

"**MOVE!**" came a bellow from the floor.

Scott looked over his shoulder and trembled as a large man in a knight costume charged toward them. Noticing his distraction, Anna hooked her ankle around Scott's leg, throwing him off balance and toppling them both to the floor.

"**ANNA!**" another shout came over the cacophony of voices.

Scott had landed squarely on top of her, knocking her breath out. She was trying to catch it again when suddenly the heavy body disappeared from atop her. Finally, she could take a deep breath. Gentle hands were helping her from the floor.

"Anna, are you okay?" Xian's worried voice penetrated the haze.

"I believe so. Did Liu get him?" Looking around, Anna found her mountain of a bodyguard holding Scott.

"Yes, Wu Feng is calling Detective Zhao now," there was relief in his voice as he answered her.

"Xian, I need a drink. A real stiff one." Anna sighed.

"I have just the bottle. Are you ready to head to our suite?" Xian asked.

"Suite?" This news caught Anna off guard.

"Sorry, I forgot to mention I got a hotel suite for us; it has two bedrooms. But I figured it was a good idea because of how late these events can go and how drunk I've gotten before." He figured the half-truth would keep some of his plans a surprise.

"Well, as long as a bottle of strong spirits is available, let's go."

Wu Feng charged up, panting out, "Detective Zhao is on his way. He believes that with this kidnapping attempt, they should be able to hold him for a while. They matched fingerprints from the bottle Mr. Xiao dropped off this morning to some in the hotel room. That proves he broke into Ms. Cassidy's room. If we could only prove that Li Ming was involved, it would wrap this problem up quite neatly."

"We could only hope." Xian sighed as he helped Anna through the crowd. Curious onlookers were trying to figure out who the people were.

As they reached the doors, an out of breath Mr. Shun caught them. "Great time for me to need the bathroom. Is Anna okay?"

"She's fine. I'm taking her to our suite for the night. I'll be in touch Monday. We need to try and connect Mr. Randall and Li Ming. I know she's the mastermind behind this; he wouldn't have the necessary resources to pull this off on his own," Xian answered.

"Let me know if there is anything I can do to help." Mr. Shun pulled Anna into a hug. "Take care, Anna. You must return and help me make your stories come to life."

Tears that had been threatening to spill on and off that night managed to escape. "I will, Uncle Shun," she promised, hugging the gruff studio president tightly. "We need to make beautiful stories together."

"Take care of her, Mr. Wei. She isn't just a writer; she's family," he expressed emphatically.

Xian chuckled ruefully. Anna had made another conquest. She was growing a family here in Beijing. "I'll take good care of her, Uncle." Winking at the older man, Xian escorted Anna to the hotel's interior to find the closest elevator to reach their room.

章

Chapter 71

Walking into the hotel suite, Anna was impressed with Xian and Wu Feng's efforts in the room. She could tell that Chen and Xian were close since they had made similar efforts to impress her in hotel rooms. Flowers and candles throughout the room filled it with a strong fragrance.

"So, just casually spending the night at a hotel?" Anna was amused with Xian's sheepish expression.

"You caught me; it wasn't so casual," he answered.

Smiling, Anna looked around the room. "Separate beds?"

"I tried to get a two-room suite; this was what they had available. Don't worry; I'll take the couch." He hoped the couch wouldn't be the only option by the night's end. "So, brandy or scotch? Pick your poison."

Anna mulled it over for a few minutes. "Brandy. It feels like a brandy type of night." She explored the room while Xian found glasses and opened the bottle he had brought.

"I don't suppose you brought swimsuits with you, did you?" She mused as she found the private lagoon pool in the room. Not far from it was a large Jacuzzi hot tub. Oh, she could seriously use a soak in that hot tub. Swim first, soak later.

"Do you need a suit? I'm sure we could find something," Xian replied as he handed her a snifter with amber liquor.

"Not really. I prefer swimming with nothing on if I can get away with it. It's been a bit since I've had an opportunity and this looks refreshing. Possibly a soak in the Jacuzzi after? What a great ending to the night," she said as she sipped the liquor. Warmth slid through her whole body as the potent liquid found her now primarily empty stomach. "If I have anything to do with the water, it better be before I drink much more. I don't do booze and water."

Thinking that sounded like a good idea, Xian sat his glass down and began removing parts of his costume. He had brought the cases for the jewelry with him. They would go into the hotel safe once they were done changing.

"Need some help?" Xian watched as Anna tried to remove her earrings and undo her necklace.

"Please?" Anna replied, tired of struggling with her accessories.

Taking Anna's hand, Xian led her to a chair and had her sit so he could remove her crown and the army of hairpins keeping her hair in the elaborate design. Cautiously he lifted the gem-encrusted crown, setting it gently on a side table. Next, he began pulling pin after pin from her hair, working his fingers through it so he didn't miss any. After removing them all he walked into the master bath and returned with Anna's brush.

Anna raised an eyebrow at the brush and Xian chuckled. "I came prepared. You have an overnight bag with clothes for tomorrow and some essentials."

Thrilling tingles coursed through Anna's body. How considerate, Xian had thought of everything. He began brushing out Anna's hair, long gentle strokes with the brush worked through small tangles formed from the excessive pinning. With the feel of Xian's deft fingers running through her hair as he brushed, Anna felt almost like purring the way her fuzzy roommate would when he was happy.

"That feels amazing, Xian. I'll give you a year to stop." Her eyes closed in pleasure.

Grinning, now he knew one of Anna's weaknesses; she liked having her hair played with. He knew she had a thing for hair; Chen had let that slip while they were talking. He had said that having Anna run her fingers through his hair while she massaged his scalp was nearly orgasmic.

During her last six months, Xian had done Chandra's hair; brushing and braiding it to keep it easily manageable until it fell out from the chemo treatments. He had missed brushing her long hair and taking care of it for her. Perhaps Anna would allow him to braid her hair in the morning before they left. He was glad he had filled Chen in on his plans to get rooms; Xian hadn't told him there was just one room for them to share, however.

After Xian finished brushing out Anna's hair she would need to remove her makeup and then she could get into the pool.

"Well, Milady, you are ready to get wet if you desire. I'll go to the lounge for a while and let you enjoy."

Anna had looked in the overnight bag Xian had packed for her and noticed a pair of biker shorts and a sports bra. Not sure why he had packed them, but it would work for a makeshift swimsuit. "Xian, if you have something you can wear for trunks then you won't need to leave. A couple of the items you packed will work for me to wear in the water."

Xian had a pair of trunks with him. He had remembered at the last moment about the pool in the room and had come prepared; he kicked himself that he hadn't thought of that for Anna. He was glad she had found something in her bag that would work.

"Hey, can you unzip me so I can get out of this gown? I don't think I want to try swimming in all these jewels and translucent material. I'd probably do more sinking than floating."

Anna turned so Xian could access the zipper easily. She suddenly felt timid. It was just the two of them. Fighting her attraction to Xian had become exhausting. Feeling his hands on her back as he slid the zipper down sent wild daydreams of his hands on her naked skin parading through her mind.

Xian wasn't having an easy time of it either. Seeing the glimpse of her bare back sent him into flashbacks of her getting in the tub. He knew her body wasn't perfect; he was more attracted to her personality and how she treated others. Her kindness and care for her friends were what he found beautiful about her.

He couldn't lie to himself; he did find her quite attractive. But Chen loved her. He had sacrificed much for Xian and Chandra. Their families hadn't approved of the marriage and Chen had stood up for them, causing a rift in his family.

Thinking a cold shower might be in order, Xian finished unzipping the dress and turned away. "If you want company, I can go put some trunks on."

"I would love company. The pool is plenty large enough for the two of us."

"Meet you back here shortly," Xian said and fled to the guest bathroom to change.

Ten minutes later, Anna stood next to the pool in biker shorts and a sports bra; it wasn't much different than what she wore swimming in the lakes back home. Xian showed up moments later in a pair of biker-style trunks. Sucking in her breath sharply, she couldn't help but admire the muscular body of her friend and employer.

Xian was equally thrilled seeing Anna; she self-consciously covered her midriff, concerned over the scars and stretch marks her profound weight loss and resulting surgeries had caused.

"Anna, I don't care about your scars or stretch marks. They are part of who you are and you're beautiful. Don't ever feel you need to cover or hide from me."

Feeling the heat rise in her face Anna hurried down the steps and slid into the pool, hoping the water would help cool her heated skin. Ducking below the water, she stayed there until she could no longer hold her breath. Bobbing to the surface, she cleared the water from her eyes to find Xian crouched beside the pool watching her.

"Just making sure you don't drown on my watch. Chen would never forgive me. Come to think of it, seven other men would be just as pissed at me if anything happened to you."

Mentally Anna tried to run through the list in her mind. Chen, of course, Wu Feng, Huang Hu, Lin Bolin and Liu, but who else? "I count five total. Which other two are you referring to?"

"You counted our assistants and your bodyguard?" Anna nodded affirmatively. "Did you also count Uncle Shun and Dr. Lin? They both consider you family. You've been cutting a wide swath through our group. Wrapping us men around your little finger." Once the words left his mouth, he regretted them. Anna hadn't done anything nefarious to garner the love and affection of these men. It was just her innate charm. Hurt was written all over her face. "Anna, I didn't mean it like that."

"I need that drink now." She scrambled out of the pool, grabbing the towel she had hung over the railing.

Smacking his forehead with his palm, *What an idiot!* His words unintentionally hurt Anna. This wasn't how he had envisioned this night. Now all there was to do was get drunk.

Glasses clinking let him know Anna had found the brandy and was helping herself. When he finally dared to face her, she had put a dent in the bottle. Anna, shrouded in the hotel robe, was curled up on the couch staring into the half-full brandy snifter.

"Anna?" Xian called to her tentatively.

"Mmm?" Blearily she looked up at Xian.

"I'm so sorry, dear. It wasn't how I meant it. Can you forgive me?" Kneeling in front of Anna, Xian took the snifter from her hands. The silent tears streaming down her cheeks tore at his heart.

He moved to sit on the couch next to Anna, pulling her into his arms he tried to erase the pain he had caused. Holding her this way made him realize he did truly love this woman. How had he fallen so quickly? Having known this woman for just over a week, Xian knew he couldn't be without her in his life. But what capacity would that be? Friend, lover or just an employee?

A soft snort made him chuckle. Anna had gotten drunk and passed out. Smoothing her damp hair from her face, he kissed her forehead. He sat there for quite a long time thinking about how he would feel about her being gone for almost two months. Time couldn't move fast enough for her to return.

After some time, Xian realized they couldn't stay like this all night. He wouldn't mind, but it would be uncomfortable for Anna. Picking her up, he gently carried her to the bedroom and carefully laid her on the bed. As he started straightening, Anna groaned and threw her arms around his neck, not letting him move.

The position was awkward for Xian, he couldn't stand up but he couldn't exactly lie down either. "Anna, what do I do with you?" Carefully he backed out of her arms. As soon as she lost touch with Xian, Anna began pouting and snuffling as though she was crying in her sleep. What to do?

Running to the bathroom, Xian changed into the pajama bottoms he typically slept in. Throwing the robe on, he stopped by the mini-fridge and grabbed some water. On his way back to the bed, he noticed the over half-full brandy snifter. Picking up the glass, he downed it in a few swallows, the liquor spreading its warmth through his body. His resolve bolstered, Xian returned to the bed to find Anna still asleep with tears leaking from her eyes.

How bad had he been that she was crying in her sleep? Stupid, stupid man, he thought. His careless words must have struck a raw nerve for her. Someday, perhaps she would explain it to him. For now, all he could do was hold her while she slept.

Pulling the covers down, Xian situated Anna in the bed. Her clothes were still damp, so he left her in the robe. Once she was settled, he climbed in and cuddled close to her. After tonight he was going to need a cold shower in the morning.

章

Chapter 72

Anna awoke to find a warm body curled around hers. Why did she keep waking up to strange bodies in her bed on this trip? Though this time something smelled different; it was the warm musky scent Anna equated with Xian. Was she in bed with Xian? Anna squinted her eyes, trying to work the sleep out of them; the room was unfamiliar.

Wracking her brain, Anna tried to remember what had happened the night before. How did she end up in bed with Xian? Wait! Had they...? Oh great, just what she needed to complicate her life more. Lifting the covers, she noticed she wore her sports bra and shorts. *What happened last night?*

"Morning. How are you feeling?" the sleep-roughened voice asked. She could wake up to that warm, velvety voice every morning.

"Well...it would be better if I could remember why I shouldn't feel okay." Her admission cost her. How embarrassing if they had made love and she didn't remember. She was tapping her forehead with her flattened fingers, trying to jog her memory.

A hand slid between her hand and forehead, stopping her attempt to whack some sense into herself. "Please don't do that, Anna. I'll tell you everything once we're up. Can we stay this way a little longer?" The body pressing against her back shifted closer and an arm snaked over her waist and pulled her in tighter. Xian's chin rested on Anna's shoulder as his cheek rested against her ear and hair. The heavenly musky scent of Xian caused things deep in her depths to tighten in anticipation. A cold shower, that's what she needed.

"I don't think we should stay this way too much longer. What will Wu Feng and Liu think? How about Chen? Didn't he say we had plans for this evening?" Panicking, Anna was so close to possibly making another mistake, or had she already made one? Was it a mistake in the first place? She loved Xian, didn't she? But was it the same kind of love she felt for Chen? Anna would need the time back in Montana to help her sort out some of her feelings.

As much as she wanted to go home for a while, she dreaded leaving her new friends. Why couldn't they continue as they had been, Chen and Xian living with her at the penthouse? But that wouldn't be fair to them either. They both had their own lives to live. Anna felt she had been an inconvenience to them since she arrived. Had it only been a week and a half? Somehow it felt like she had been there most of her life.

Shifting so she could turn and face Xian, she looked into the eyes of the handsome man. "Xian, what happened last night? I remember getting in the pool and not much after that. Why was I crying?" She knew she had cried for a while the night before from how her sinuses felt. What had happened now?

Xian sat up, the blanket and sheet sliding down, exposing his well-defined chest and six-pack. Damn, the man worked out. Anna bit her bottom lip; the urge to caress his chest was nearly overwhelming. Being around the guys had kicked her libido into overdrive. Mentally she pictured herself stuffing her desire in a can and jumping up and down on it to tamp the frustration.

"I stuck my foot in my mouth up to my knee," Xian said as he rubbed the back of his neck and avoided Anna's gaze. "I hurt your feelings and you jumped into the bottle of brandy. You passed out on the couch while crying on my shoulder... after finishing over a quarter of the bottle on your own."

Anna sat up to look at Xian. "What exactly did you say?"

"Does it pay for you to know if it hurts you again? I misspoke and it hurt you. You didn't give me much chance to discuss it with you when it happened. I'm not sure what caused the pain I saw in your eyes after I said it."

"Xian, I believe I need to know. It was something that affected me profoundly. However, I know last night the emotions were running high after I was nearly kidnapped for the third time. Please tell me; I believe it's something I need to work through," Anna said and pleaded with her eyes.

Groaning, Xian couldn't help himself. He couldn't refuse

Anna anything; she had some magical pull over him. "I said you cut a deep swath through the men you knew, wrapping them around your finger." Once the words were out of his mouth again, he wondered if there would be continued fallout.

Pulling her knees to her chest, she wrapped her arms around them and rested her chin there. "Now I remember; it's kind of silly, though it does explain things a bit. Sorry Xian, you happened to scrape open an ancient scar. There aren't many that haven't healed; you found one that still has a bit of scab." Sighing, she stared into the distance while memories flooded in.

"When I finished high school and enlisted in the military, I went from men avoiding me to them clamoring for my attention. Unfortunately, they didn't want a relationship; they were after a more fleeting experience. Until I married my ex-husband, that was my experience. Men were more than happy to be my friend or be 'friends with benefits,' but few had an interest in anything beyond that. I don't even know if my ex loved me or just the idea of getting married. I can't explain how toxic that ended up being. Kyle was the first man I felt was truly in love with me for me, not just my looks or for sex. I'm not sure why your comment ripped that particular wound open."

Hearing Anna's story, Xian now understood more about her. Anna wasn't actively trying to seduce any of them; it was just her innate inner beauty that attracted them. His careless comment the night before would have made her even more insecure than she had been. With Chen and himself vying for her attention, she might think it was only because of her looks or for a short-term fling.

"Anna, I am so sorry I said that. It was careless and inconsiderate of me. I don't know about any other guys, but I started falling in love with you at the airport and fell even further when you came to my apartment with Chen. The feelings have only grown stronger since. When I took you shopping—your unrestrained joy when you found clothes that made you feel beautiful. Though you don't need fancy clothes to make you beautiful, it shines through no matter what you wear. It's your inner beauty that draws me. I had hoped to make the gala a special night for you and I failed miserably."

Seeing Xian doubt himself troubled Anna. He had been so self-confident and assertive. How could this pillar of strength look so lost?

"It's okay, Xian. How could we know Scott would find a way into the gala? I'm guessing that was Li Ming's doing once again. They did get him, though, right?"

"Last I heard Liu was waiting on the authorities when we left. I should check in with them and find out what happened. I swear that the excitement of spending a night alone with you shut my brain off," he said as he found his phone on the nightstand. He checked for new messages from either Wu Feng or Liu.

Mr. Wei, the kidnapper, has been detained by the authorities. Wu Feng and I have checked into our room and will be ready whenever you are.

Liu's message was from the early hours of the morning. Showing Anna the message, there was a sigh of relief from her. A lot depended on how long they would be able to detain him. It was hard to say since he was a foreigner.

"So it's over?" Anna said, her voice expressing her fervent hopes that she could relax a little.

"On the Scott front, it seems so, but Li Ming is still plotting who knows what." They were disgusted that they couldn't make anything stick to punish her.

"I'm not so worried about Li Ming. Scott's the one I was worried the most about. When we started dancing, his touch had such evil vibes." She shuddered at the thought of Scott's hands on her shoulders and waist. "I need to go shower. My skin is crawling at the memory of his hands touching me."

"Good idea. I'll use the other bathroom and shower as well. We should get back to the penthouse. You were right. Chen has gone through a lot to arrange the evening. We better try and get something right." Smiling ruefully, he crawled out of bed. At least now he didn't need a cold shower; their conversation had the effect of being doused with water from a mountain stream.

An hour later, showered and dressed in a sweater and jeans, Xian casually lounged on the couch looking through the email he had received from the auction. Per his instructions, they had packaged and would be sending all of Anna's purchases to the apartment. Xian was amused by some of her chosen items, especially the signed punk rock memorabilia. He didn't peg Anna as a punk rock fan.

Emerging from the master bathroom, dressed in an oversized boyfriend shirt under a sweater and a pair of black leggings, Anna looked comfortable and cute. He had chosen well. Xian and Anna had carefully placed their attire from the night before in garment bags. Hopefully, Anna would have another chance to wear the beautiful dress.

"You look quite adorable." Xian sat forward, resting his elbows casually on his knees.

"You have great taste. However, you did overlook a piece of clothing. I had to use one of my garments from last night."

"What? I was sure I had a complete outfit for you," Xian said in a bemused tone, confusion written on his face.

"It's nothing. I just had to use the bra I wore with the gown." Anna giggled as Xian colored slightly. "Why you had the sports bra and shorts was somewhat confusing."

"I had hoped to work out with you before we returned. It might have helped relieve some of your stress."

"Thanks for trying. Though I don't typically work out in a gym, I've missed getting exercise. I have several trails I hike. Hopefully, the snow holds off for a bit after I get home."

"That sounds like it would be quite a bit of fun. Perhaps sometime I can visit your home. From the photos Chen has shown me, it's beautiful," Xian replied wistfully.

"You're welcome to visit anytime. You're family now. No matter what happens." Anna sat down next to Xian. Looking at her watch, it was nearly noon. "We better get back. Let's have one plan go off without a hitch."

"That would be great. Chen is having a rough time because things keep going sideways for him. I don't want to admit it, but he cares for you as much, if not more, than I do."

"Well, let's do our best then." Anna leaned against Xian's shoulder and closed her eyes for a few minutes. "Let's go."

章

Chapter 73

It had taken longer than expected to get back to the apartment. On the way, Detective Zhao had called Xian asking them to stop by the station to file a statement about what had transpired the night before.

Anna gladly wrote an account of how she had been physically grabbed and forcibly dragged across the dance floor. When Detective Zhao read her version of the recent harassment and the numerous attempts to abduct her, he hoped they could detain him. Even though Scott was an American, so it could be complicated. With the severity of the charges, he wondered if he would get the whole possible sentence of life imprisonment or death.

They had verified that his prints were in Anna's hotel room, though there were two other sets they couldn't identify on her laptop.

Hearing that, Anna offered to let them take her prints so they could authenticate whether they were hers or someone else's. One set should be hers, but who else had handled her laptop? Liz never touched it, that she knew of, so it couldn't be her. Had Li Ming been with him when he had broken into her room?

Having given what information they could, Xian, Liu and Anna returned to the van where Wu Feng waited.

"Everything go all right?" Wu Feng asked.

"As well as can be expected. We will have to see what happens. It may cause some complications with Anna's return to the States. It depends if she will have to testify," Xian said, clearly unhappy with the situation. "With the kidnapping charge, he faces a life sentence or possibly death."

After all she had been through, Anna couldn't dredge up any sympathy for the man. She would have to check in with them before leaving the next day. Her possessions wouldn't be available for a while, possibly until after she returned in January. Anna made arrangements so Xian or Chen would be allowed to pick up her belongings when they were released.

"Let's get back to the apartment, it's almost 3 o'clock already and Chen said we had plans at 6 P.M. I want to shower again and get ready," Anna commented from the back seat of the van.

"Okay, Ms. Anna." Wu Feng pulled out into traffic.

Twenty minutes later, they pulled up to the apartment building to find Huang Hu waiting.

"Where have you been? Mr. Xiao is beside himself. He was concerned you wouldn't make it back in time for what he has planned."

"Sorry Hu, I should have called or texted. We had to make a detour to the police department because of what happened last night," Anna responded without thinking.

"What happened last night? Oh, you mean Mr. Wei disappearing?" Huang Hu picked up that comment quickly.

Cringing, Anna sighed and admitted, "No, there's more. Let's wait until we get upstairs so I don't have to repeat myself."

Huang Hu looked at the other men as they climbed out of the van, hoping for some clue. Wu Feng shook his head at him and Liu flat out ignored him and followed Anna and Xian through the front doors leaving Wu Feng to bring the bags.

Arriving at the apartment, Anna barely reached the door before Chen pounced on her. "Where have you been? I expected you hours ago."

"You need to wait until Wu Feng and Huang Hu get here, then I'll explain," Anna said as she headed for her bedroom.

"But Anna..." Chen called after her.

"Just wait a few minutes Chen," Anna snapped at him.

Xian put his hand on Chen's arm to stop him from following Anna. He knew she needed a few minutes to gather herself. "Give her a few minutes, Chen; our evening didn't go much better than your night out."

Chen gave Xian a questioning look.

"She told you she would explain once the guys get back here. Last night was rough for her," Liu said as he positioned himself in the hallway to Anna's room to keep Chen from following her. He knew she needed a few moments.

Chen and Xian looked at one another and back at Liu. "Are you keeping us from Anna?" Xian asked Liu.

"Yes!" was Liu's emphatic answer.

Wu Feng and Huang Hu picked that moment to arrive back at the apartment, coming through the door with the garment bags and cases.

"Good, now perhaps we can get to the bottom of all this?" Chen said impatiently, trying to get around Liu, but the man didn't budge.

"Liu, can you get Anna? Let her know Wu Feng and Huang Hu are back," Xian said quietly to the bodyguard as he pulled Chen into the living room.

Nodding, Liu walked down the hall to knock on Anna's door. "Anna, the others have returned. Chen is very anxious. Can we tell him now?"

Anna opened the door, looked up at Liu and said, "Have them go to the living room. The sitting area is a bit too small for this meeting."

Grunting his reply, Liu turned to gather the other penthouse occupants in the living room.

Anna had taken a few moments to compose herself. She washed her face and thought about how much she should tell Chen. As far as she knew, she hadn't done anything with Xian, but that didn't mean that there might not be some hard feelings. "Deep breath, girl, you have this," Anna said in the mirror.

In the living room, the men were assembled. Xian lounged on the far end of the couch, his arm slung over the back casually. Chen sat on the sofa across from him, his elbows on his knees, fingers steepled in deep thought. Wu Feng and Huang Hu took up positions on the opposite ends of the couches from their employers, both on their phones checking for news from the weekend. Liu had taken up a place behind the wing chair positioned at the head of the couches. The chair was reserved for Anna.

Walking around the couches, she made her way to the chair in front of Liu. Anna gave him a small smile, Liu was taking his oath seriously. He was even protecting her from Xian and Chen. She had heard the interaction in the hallway and was stunned that he would go that far. Would he genuinely return to Montana with her?

When Anna returned from Montana, she would talk to Xian about changing some of the furniture here; the chairs weren't the most comfortable.

"Sorry Chen, I believe you'll understand after I explain what happened last night. During the dance portion of the evening, I was asked for a dance. Everyone was in costumes and masks, so Xian agreed I could accept the dance. It wasn't far into the song when he revealed himself; it was Scott." Anna paused here to gather herself. This attempt had been the closest he had come to succeeding.

"What? How did he get in?" Chen nearly shot off the couch.

Gesturing to Chen to stay put and calm down, Anna continued her explanation. "We aren't sure, but suspect Li Ming helped him. As the song finished, he tried to drag me out of the ballroom. It might not have gone so well if it hadn't been for Liu's quick reaction. Scott was taken to the police department and that's why we are late; we had to stop and make statements this morning. I got rather drunk last night and Xian took care of me." She was embarrassed to admit the getting drunk part.

"Are you okay? Did you get hurt at all?" Chen reached out to take Anna's hand.

"I'm fine. I just had my breath knocked out. It could have been worse, but at least Scott has been detained. It's too bad Li Ming is still at large, however. She is as much trouble as Scott."

Xian and Chen looked at one another. "We will continue to be cautious. I don't believe we've seen the last of her either," Xian commented.

A pained expression crossed Chen's face before he said, "Should we just cancel the plans for tonight?"

Anna could tell it had hurt him to ask that question. She wasn't going to destroy something he had been looking forward to and had planned. So many of their other plans had gone awry; why not have a good night tonight? "Don't cancel the plans. I'm sure everything will be fine." She was so good at uttering famous last words.

章

Chapter 74

Anna dressed in the best casual dress she had found while shopping with Xian. It was a designer dress by Brunello Cucinelli; the color was called Crystal Blue though Anna thought the color was more like Steel Blue. It was a simple design, sleeveless with a belt and pockets. Over the top, she pulled on a black cashmere cardigan she had found. A pair of black, strapped, low heels rounded out the look. She had even taken a few moments to put on a little makeup.

While she had been getting ready for the gala, the ladies had taught Anna how to apply her makeup. It was one of the reasons she rarely wore it; she never had someone to take the time to teach her how to use it for her skin tone. Now, she knew how but she still wasn't a fan of wearing a lot of it or often.

Leaving the peace of her room, Anna ventured out into the apartment. Wu Feng and Huang Hu were waiting in the sitting area, both dressed in suits and ties. Anna began wondering if she hadn't dressed formally enough.

Turning to return to her room and change into something more formal, she heard whistling coming down the hall from Xian's room. Xian arrived dressed in black jeans, a white dress shirt with a simple black tie and a dark gray vest with a gray cashmere coat. He was so debonair in that outfit. It was pretty casual for Xian, so Anna wasn't so concerned about changing now. She wondered why Wu Feng and Huang Hu were dressed so formally.

Anna walked up to Xian and straightened his tie. "You look very dapper tonight. Almost as handsome as last night."

"You look beautiful as always." Xian brushed a strand of hair back from Anna's face.

"Ahem, I hope I look good too," Chen said as he opened his bedroom door. He stepped out of his room dressed in a dark pair of distressed jeans, a dress shirt, a blue tie that almost perfectly matched Anna's dress and a vest with a tweed suit jacket over the top. Could you call a man gorgeous?

Walking up to Chen, she adjusted his tie too, tucking an errant curl from his unruly hair behind his ear. Quietly, so only he could hear she told him, "I'm almost at a loss for words over how good you look. Would you be offended if I said you were gorgeous?"

Looking Anna in the eyes, Chen could see her sincerity. "Thank you. You can call me gorgeous if you like," he whispered to her.

Laughing softly, Anna blushed slightly before stepping back. Clearing her throat, she looked around realizing someone was missing. "Where is Liu?"

"Right here," his deep voice answered from behind her. Anna turned and gasped; Liu wore a black dress shirt and suit with a steel blue colored tie. He looked like he had stepped off the cover of GQ. She was amazed, the tie was nearly the same color as her dress.

"You look very nice tonight," Anna managed to say, not trusting herself to speak more. She looked at the hunky bodyguard in a different light; why hadn't she noticed how good-looking he was? Shaking her head she swore at herself internally, *Anna you slut stop it. You are already in over your head with Chen and Xian.*

Xian and Chen gave one another worried glances. Had Anna found another man that sparked her interest? Had they picked a competitor for her affections when selecting her bodyguard? Who knew the rugged, ex-military man could clean up so well?

"Are we finally ready?" Chen said as he headed for the door. "The evening awaits."

Xian had commandeered one of the larger limo vans from the company so they could all ride together. Huang Hu drove tonight as he knew their destination and the others didn't quite yet. Anna had an inkling they might be headed to Mama Jing's, unless the plans had changed from earlier in the week, so she wasn't saying anything.

Soon Anna started to recognize some of the buildings on the

way to a fantastic restaurant. They were indeed heading to Mama Jing's place.

Parking in the same lot as when Chen had taken her to dinner, the group got out and prepared for the short walk. It felt like more than a month ago when Anna and Chen had taken the same walk. She remembered some of the bright buildings along the route. It looked odd for one woman to walk down the sidewalk with five men, all dressed impeccably. Anna was a fortunate woman at that moment.

It felt great to walk along the sidewalk, laughing and chatting with the men. Liu was leading the way; they had worked out their assigned positions before they left. Chen and Xian flanked Anna and Wu Feng and Huang Hu brought up the rear. She almost felt like royalty being guarded by five handsome bodyguards.

When they arrived, Mama Jing's restaurant seemed quiet compared to her previous visit. Anna hoped nothing was wrong. She was looking forward to the special dinner Mama Jing had promised her. It was thoughtful of Chen to remember and make an event of it. Liu opened the door and held it for the group to enter.

It was so quiet, there seemed to be no one there. "Chen, are you sure she's open? It looks pretty dead." Anna looked around.

"**SURPRISE!**" people yelled from different directions.

"HUH?" Anna's knees buckled. Xian and Chen were quick on their feet; each caught an arm before Anna could hit the floor.

"Sorry. Was it too much?" Chen asked, abashed.

Tears rolled down Anna's cheeks; she was truly touched. She looked around the room and there were her new friends. Dr. and Mrs. Lin, Xu Hinge, Mr. Shun and his wife, Lin Bolin and Wang Xiao. Ms. Yan and Wang Chyou, and a few other ladies from the makeup department were also there. Her new family, the people she had met and grown close to on this trip, except for Wang Xiao. That was probably the biggest surprise, to have the actor be there after having just met him.

Mama Jing bustled out of the back room. "Anna!" She threw her arms around Anna and hugged her tightly. "This is a special going away party; we wanted to let you know how much we will miss you while you're back in the States and we can't wait for your return."

Once Mama Jing released Anna she marshaled her staff, getting them bustling to get the food set out. Anna turned and gave Chen a hug that made breathing a little challenging. She kissed his cheek and whispered, "Thank you so much."

"You deserve this. See how many people you've touched in the short time you've been here? We are all going to miss you terribly while you're gone. Just come back as quickly as possible." Chen's voice cracked with emotion as he spoke fervently.

"Hey, my turn for a hug." Xian tapped Chen's shoulder.

"Certainly, brother," Chen said as he turned and hugged Xian. The group laughed at Xian's expression of disgust.

"As much as I love you, bro, you are **NOT** whom I was asking to hug." Xian laughed and grabbed Anna, whirling her around. "Princess, it will be way too long until you return. How will I live with that insufferable romantic while you're gone? He's going to mope and whine the whole time."

Anna forgot her tears as she giggled and slapped Xian's shoulder. "Okay, put me down." Feet firmly planted on the floor, she hugged Xian and kissed his cheek. "I'm going to miss you too."

Huang Hu and Wu Feng were next to grab Anna, hugging her and wishing her well. They knew they would see her tomorrow, but now it was a joyful moment. It would be more emotional when they saw her off at the airport.

Lin Bolin was nearly in tears. "Ms. Anna, are you sure you will be gone until mid-January? I will be ready when you return and be the best assistant possible. Huang Hu and Wu Feng are taking me under their wings and showing me the ropes."

"Lin Bollin, don't worry, time will go quickly and I'll be back before you know it. I will have high expectations for you," Anna responded and hugged the young man.

The guests gave Anna their good wishes and handed her gifts to remind her why she needed to return soon.

Dr. Lin waited until everyone else had said their piece before pulling Anna to the side. "How are you doing, young lady?"

His voice betrayed the concern he felt for his new friend.

"I'm probably going to sleep for a week when I get home. I think I've packed a couple of years' worth of excitement in a week and a half—nothing like nearly being kidnapped several times to get your adrenaline pumping. I'll check in with my physician, Dr. Diana, when I return. She's been my doctor for years. I'm sure she will read me the riot act over some of my antics."

Chuckling, Dr. Lin hugged Anna. "I think of you as a daughter, just as I think of Xian and Chen as my sons. I expect you to keep in touch once you are home and keep yourself well until you return to my care."

"Yes, Uncle Lin," Anna said, touched when she saw a few rogue tears escape the doctor's eyes.

Finally finished with all of the good wishes and hugs from everyone other than Liu, Anna searched for the surly bodyguard. She found him positioned so he could watch the room and the door. "Liu, come join the party."

"Ms. Anna, we leave tomorrow and I don't want any surprises tonight. I'll relax once we are on the plane taking you home."

"Are you sure you're okay coming back with me? I'm taking you away from your home and family for almost two months."

Liu looked at his charge; how could he be unhappy spending two months alone with this amazing woman? It would be a joy getting to know her without the constant threat of danger. He would be happy to have a relaxing assignment. "Ms. Anna, I'll follow you anywhere. The vow I took last night wasn't a joke."

Anna's heart skipped a few beats. His intense gaze made her flush. "Are you packed and ready to go?"

"I'll be finishing the last bit tonight and tomorrow morning. A friend will take care of my place while we're gone." *Damn*, he thought. The "we're" was a slip up and he hoped Anna didn't notice.

"Sounds good. I need to do some last minute souvenir shopping in the morning and will finish packing in the afternoon. I know the guys want to take me to dinner one last time tomorrow, but I'm not sure if that will be a good idea. It's going to be hard enough to say goodbye as it is. Try and enjoy at least a little tonight, okay? Mama Jing is an amazing cook."

Nodding, Liu returned to being wary and watched for any sign of trouble.

Food had been pouring out of the kitchen; dish after dish, all of it looked and smelled divine. There were several that intrigued Anna, but she couldn't place what they might be. Soon the food was all in place and Mama Jing gave everyone the order to eat.

Anna sat at a place of honor, Xian and Chen on either side serving her choice tidbits of the different dishes. So many delicious foods were available and the guys were terrific at getting her a few bites of each to try them but not get overloaded.

Laughter and loud boisterous voices filled the place. Looking around the room at these special people warmed Anna's heart. When she returned, they would have a party at the penthouse; and this time, Xian and Chen wouldn't ruin it. She wouldn't invite them.

When the dishes emptied on the table and everyone seemed satiated, Mama Jing went to get one more surprise. Bringing out a cake with luscious strawberries and other berries on the top, she set it down in front of Anna. "Anna, my dear, you have made my adopted grandson so happy; please enjoy this special treat." She cut a slice and placed it on Anna's plate. Everyone watched as Anna took a bite.

It was a cake unlike any she had tasted. Unique flavors were melding with the fruit, and the frosting was not sweet, letting the cake and fruit provide the sweetness. "Mama Jing, this is so delicious. I would love the recipe."

"I'm sure I can make that happen." The bubbly woman clapped and several more cakes appeared for the guests.

Anna cut into her slice again but her fork found something hard. She carefully picked through the soft crumbs, licking them from her fingers as she went. Finally, she found the metallic item, which was not what she expected. Checking to ensure everyone was distracted by the dessert, Anna picked up the silver circle and quickly tucked it into a napkin.

Was it a mistake? Did someone's ring fall off when baking the cake? She would check with Mama Jing once she finished. Carefully, she completed her piece of the cake.

She hadn't noticed, but Chen saw her slipping the ring off her plate. Good, he knew he could go through with the rest of his plan. "Anna, can you come with me for a moment?" Chen offered her a hand up.

Glancing at Xian and around the table, Anna stood up and bowed slightly. "I'll be back in a few moments," she said as she followed Chen to a small private dining room. Anna and Chen entered the room to soft music playing. Bouquets and candlelight were placed around the room.

"This is where I would have liked to have dinner with you, just the two of us, but I couldn't deny the others their chance to celebrate with you and wish you well until you can return. So my other option was to sneak you away for a few moments. Did you by any chance find something in your piece of cake?" He gave her a shy look from under his bangs.

"I did. How did you know?" Anna said as she held out the ring.

Taking the silver circle, he cautiously dipped it into a glass of water on the table and rubbed it clean with a napkin. Holding it up in the candlelight, it was stunning, a large diamond in a simple setting. Going down on one knee, he looked up at Anna, his emotions no longer hidden.

"Anna, you have changed my life for the better. You were there for me when I was experiencing some of my darkest moments. I've been there for some of yours. I want us to be there for each other for the rest of our lives. Will you marry me?" Chen held out the ring to her. The love he felt for her was unmistakable in his eyes.

"Oh, my." Anna staggered; this wasn't what she had expected. They weren't even dating. How could he propose to her? "Chen...I care for you so much it hurts sometimes, but I'm not ready to get married again. Whomever I do marry, I want to get to know them for a while before we make that lifelong commitment. We could finally begin dating after my return to Beijing, but I can't commit to marrying you. I'm so sorry, Chen. I just can't say yes yet."

"But you're not saying no, right?" Hope sparked a light in his dark expression. When she didn't say yes right away, his face had fallen. When she said the word "yet", he brightened. "You'll give me a chance?"

Anna reached down and pulled Chen to his feet, wrapping her arms around him. "I'm not saying no; I'm saying not right now. There has been too much happening in the last week and a half. Why don't we try dating when I get back?"

Chen gave her a mischievous wink saying, "I had hoped you'd say yes so I could give you a proper send-off tonight." Leave it to him to defuse the tense situation with humor.

"Mmm, as tempting as that is, it would torture me. The taste I got last weekend was fabulous. I look forward to more possibilities of getting to explore one another further. But that also needs to wait." She kissed his forehead and each cheek. Whispering so softly, she wasn't sure if he would hear her, "I love you."

Chen returned her hug, but before he released her he didn't just kiss her cheek or forehead. His lips found hers. With the heat and intensity he put into that kiss, she would have been on the floor if he hadn't held her so tightly. **WOW**, *talk about toe-curling*, was Anna's only thought.

He took her hand and led her back to the table, letting her go and trying to keep a cheerful facade. She had rejected him once again. He spared a glare at Xian; it had to be because of his best friend. Why else wouldn't she give him a definitive answer? He knew they had gotten close this past week, but didn't realize it had been **THAT** close. Had something happened between them at the hotel? He clenched his fists under the table at the possibility.

The rest of the evening was filled with laughter. Anna listened to the guests' stories and impressions of her, recounting the anecdotes about what she had gone through since arriving. Her guys were good about not revealing some of the most harrowing parts of her trip. She didn't want to remember some of them, but it was fun finding out just how much she had made an impact.

As the night wore on, guests began excusing themselves; they had work the next day. Anna made sure to hug each one as they said their goodbyes, especially Uncle Lin and Uncle Shun. She understood that the honorific "uncle" was mainly used for older acquaintances, but she felt they were indeed uncles to her. They were family.

Before she realized it, everyone had gone home. Anna had been left with her male entourage.

"Mama Jing, you have made my last night in Beijing memorable. I will be back once I return from Montana. I have a feeling you will be seeing more of me. I need to learn some of your recipes." Anna hugged the grandmotherly figure.

"Anna, come with me." She pulled Anna to the room where Chen had proposed. "From the look on Chen's face, you didn't say yes," she remarked.

Feeling like she had let her grandmother down, Anna answered as though she was her grandmother. "I told him I couldn't say yes right now. It wasn't an absolute no, but even though we have chatted and been close over the phone for over four years, we don't know one another well enough to make this commitment. I know here in China that once you are engaged, it's more like you're already married. I'm not ready for that yet. When I return, we will try dating first."

"Good, I was worried when I saw his expression after you came here. I'll keep an eye on him for you. He might mope for a while." She clucked. Chen was going to be a handful for some time. "You know that man truly loves you. He won't admit it to you, but he would give his life for you if you asked." Mama Jing wanted to give Chen as much help as she could. She had seen how happy Chen had been their first night at the restaurant.

"I care for Chen much more than I care to admit. I just need some time. My heart has some decisions it needs to make, and right now, it isn't easy." Anna pulled Mama Jing into a tight hug. "Please take care of him for me. I love him, but don't you dare tell him that yet." She wagged a finger at the matron.

Rolling her eyes, she grumped as she agreed to Anna's terms. "I won't unless I have no choice."

Narrowing her eyes to slits, Anna gave the woman a calculated look. "Pinky promise?"

Laughing, Mama Jing put up her pinky for Anna to hook

with hers and they pressed their thumbs together.

She hugged Anna one more time. "Be safe, young one. Return healthy and unscathed." Mama Jing dabbed at her eyes.

"Please don't cry, Mama Jing."

"I can if I want. My age allows me that luxury." She snorted and led Anna back to the others.

Numerous take-out containers sat on the table, the guys discussing who got what.

"You can't help but take care of these boys?" Anna smiled.

"They get too skinny if I don't. I would have sent even more if you had been here longer." She grinned and hugged all of the men, even the standoffish Liu.

"Now get going. It's getting late and you have a long couple of days coming." She handed bags to Huang Hu and Wu Feng. "Good night."

The group walked back to the van more slowly, full of delicious food.

Liu was again out in front, eyes watching for any sign of trouble. He wasn't wrong to watch out, a car pulled up and a gun pointed out of the dark window. Seeing the barrel, Liu turned and grabbed Anna, taking her down to the ground with him as projectiles flew over them. Xian grunted as something hit him in the shoulder. Chen, Wu Feng and Huang Hu grabbed him and pulled him out of the line of fire.

Seeing that they missed the target, the car sped off. They had prepared for this; there was no plate and nothing to distinguish what car it was.

"Anna?" Liu was frantic; she wasn't answering him. "Chen? How is Xian?" Liu asked.

Wu Feng had his phone out with the light turned on. Xian had been hit by one of the bullets. They tried looking for any blood in the limited light. "I'm confused. He's been hit in the shoulder, but there's no blood," Huang Hu responded.

"I don't believe they were real bullets; they were nonlethal rounds. It doesn't mean he won't have one hell of a bruise for a while. Wu Feng, do you have Detective Zhao's number? Oh, and you better call Dr. Lin and have him meet us at the apartment, Anna's unconscious." Liu was looking for any sign of damage to her.

"Anna?" Xian and Chen both called out in fear.

After a quick conversation with Detective Zhao, Wu Feng said he would stay until Officer Ma could come and investigate. They would also check the CCTV cameras in the area. They should take Anna and Xian back to the apartment and Detective Zhao would find them there to get their statements.

Relieved they didn't have to stay on the street, Liu instructed Huang Hu to run and get the van. He didn't mind carrying Anna that far, but it put them at risk. He also didn't want Xian to walk any further than needed until they were sure how badly he was injured. *Damn it. One night, she deserved one night.*

—

The dark sedan raced off into the night. There was another stop to make. A case full of unmarked currency was in the back seat. There would be another passenger soon.

章

Chapter 75

Liu carried Anna into the apartment and straight to her room, gently laying her on the bed. Chen and Xian were close behind, they had tried to look her over in the van but they didn't find anything. He had loathed putting Anna down once they were in the van. He would have held her the whole way back had he been allowed.

The doorbell chimed right before the door burst open minutes after they'd arrived. "Where's Anna?" Dr. Lin called out.

"Master bedroom," Chen shouted back.

Xian was sitting on the couch at the foot of Anna's bed, Chen leaned against the doorjamb and Liu was pacing through Anna's closet.

Finding the unresponsive woman on the bed, Dr. Liu rushed to her side, checking her pulse and pupils.

"Explain what happened," he demanded as he looked at the men.

"We were walking back to the van when a dark sedan pulled up and a gun was pointed at Anna. I grabbed her and we dropped to the sidewalk; the first projectile whizzed over our heads and the second hit Mr. Wei in the shoulder. I'm not 100 percent sure if more shots were fired," Liu answered, falling back on his military training to report to the doctor.

After Dr. Lin ensured Anna wasn't in immediate danger, he turned around. "And why isn't that shirt off already, Xian?" he barked.

Chastised, Xian pulled off his coat and tie. Unbuttoning his shirt was more of a chore; the shoulder was starting to hurt now.

Seeing Xian's difficulty, Chen went over and helped unbutton the dress shirt and remove it, sucking in a sharp breath when he saw the damage to Xian's shoulder. A deep, purple-black bruise had begun forming on his upper arm and chest.

Liu glanced over and saw the extensive bruising. He knew what had caused this. It was a high-caliber rubber bullet. In most instances it wasn't lethal, but it could do severe damage; and if someone was hit in the right spot, it could indeed be fatal. Xian was going to have a rough go of it for a while.

Dr. Lin tsked as he looked over Xian's shoulder. "This was premeditated. That was a high-caliber rubber bullet. It's typically used in riot situations and is not lethal. Xian, you will hurt for a while and I recommend not using that arm for a day or two. Then, I will give you exercises to help it from locking up. Chen, is there an ice pack in this place?" The doctor spoke the words Liu had been thinking.

"I'll go find something, Dr. Lin," Chen said as he rushed from the room.

"And here I thought we were finally going to have a quiet night," Dr. Lin sighed out. "I'm not sure what is happening with Anna. I believe she was just stunned. Liu, did her head hit the pavement?"

Thinking for a few minutes, Liu shook his head. "No, I've been trained to protect the head when hitting the ground with a body. I may have knocked the breath out of her, however. We did go down rather hard and fast."

"We will watch her and if she hasn't regained consciousness within the hour, we will transport her to the hospital as quietly as possible. If we need to go, I'll make special arrangements."

Chen returned with a bag filled with ice cubes. He stopped in Anna's bathroom and grabbed a hand towel to wrap around the ice. "Here, put this on it." He handed it to Xian.

Xian groaned as the ice pressed on the bruise. Damn, that hurt, but Anna was the one he was concerned about. His shoulder would be fine.

Forty minutes later, a soft groan came from Anna and her eyes fluttered.

"Dr. Lin!" Liu called down the hallway. They had gone to Xian's room and applied some salve the doctor carried with him. It worked well for this kind of situation.

The doctor came at a slow jog, his bag in hand. Sitting

down next to the pale woman, he checked her pulse again. "Liu, get a bottle of water for Anna; she can't drink the tap water," he barked the instruction.

"Shh, not so loud," Anna groaned. Her hand reached up to the back of her head. "Ow."

"Sorry Anna, how are you feeling other than an obvious headache?" Dr. Lin asked solicitously.

"Sore, I feel like a bag of cement fell on me. What in the world happened?" Anna asked.

"I believe Liu can explain that better than I can. You might have a very slight concussion. You'll need to be cautious with your flight tomorrow."

Liu came back to the room with the bottle of water in hand. "Ms. Anna, I'm sorry. You were shot at with rubber bullets; I was a little aggressive when I protected you." He bowed low.

Struggling to sit up, Anna reached her hand out to Liu. "Why should you be sorry when you risked your life for mine? Thank you."

"Anna, don't push yourself to get up tonight. Rest and you should be fine by tomorrow," Dr. Lin said as he checked her over one last time.

"I will, Uncle Lin. I'll let you know when I make it home. Thank you for taking such good care of me," Anna said as she sat up. She was reaching her arms out for a hug from her extended family. "Hopefully when I return you will be able to visit me more for social reasons than medical."

Hugging her, he kissed her forehead and said, "I would enjoy that." Turning he took his leave. He stopped at Xian's room to check his shoulder. "Anna's awake, now don't you two put too much strain on her before she leaves. She will be back soon enough," he said as he patted Xian's good shoulder.

"Thank you, Dr. Lin. We'll take good care of her until she leaves. Thank you for caring for my shoulder as well."

"You're fine, Xian; take care."

Xian crawled out of bed; stopping by Chen's room, he knocked on the door. Hearing a mumble, he cracked the door open. "Anna's up. Want to come with me to check on her?"

"Yeah, give me a moment," Chen said as he crawled out of bed and threw on a robe. He had been sitting in bed reading through the first script they would be filming when Anna returned. Anything to try and distract himself from what had happened. From what he had read so far, it was as good as *The Lost Prince*. He was surprised because he hadn't read this script yet. Usually, Anna let him read everything she wrote.

Chen and Xian softly walked down the hall to Anna's room, trying to be quiet. "Anna?" Chen called softly.

"Come in, guys." Anna realized that Xian was most likely with him if Chen was there.

Xian and Chen came inside. "How are you feeling?" Chen asked as he sat down on the edge of the bed. Xian sat on the couch, gingerly leaning back. His shoulder was aching right then but he didn't want to let Anna know he was injured; she would only worry.

"I have a slight headache and I'm a bit sore. Liu weighs more than he looks, it seems." She tried not to laugh loudly; it hurt too much. "Liu explained what happened. Xian, are you okay?"

Damn it, Liu had tipped her off. He would at least play it down, he didn't want her worrying about him when she would be leaving. "I'm fine, like you a bit sore. Don't worry about me."

After chatting a little while, Anna decided it was better to try and get some sleep. She was going home tomorrow. How much had Anna's life been turned upside down over the last week? "It's my last night; I'm going to miss you two."

"The next couple of months won't go fast enough. Can they be over already? Or perhaps you could just stay and not leave at all?" Chen laughed.

"I wish. Unfortunately, I have so much to arrange if I'm going to be here for a couple of years. Sorry Chen, we will have ample time once I'm back. Besides, we will have video chats." She smiled. "Okay, guys. I am kicking you out. Tomorrow is going to come early enough. Do you have to go to work, Xian? Chen, what is your schedule? I need to do some shopping in the morning; I haven't had a chance to pick up gifts. I'll be in trouble if I forget."

"I have to go to work for a meeting in the morning. I'm all yours in the afternoon until your flight leaves," Xian said once he stood up.

"I don't have any plans for tomorrow. On Tuesday I'll be moving back into my place. It's going to feel odd, it feels like we've been living like this for months, not just one week," Chen mused as he headed for the door.

"I know. I feel the same. Hard to believe I've only been here for a week and a half, it feels like a month or longer. Ok guys, good night. See you in the morning," Anna said as she turned off the lights. How she wished they could have crawled into bed with her. She could have really used the comfort right now.

章

Chapter 76

Morning came and the clouds hung dark and heavy, matching Anna's mood. She was homesick, but she also didn't want to leave. Chen, Xian, Wu Feng, Huang Hu and now Liu had become a huge part of her life. How would she live without them? At least, Liu would be flying back with her, she wasn't sure that she could go back to living alone after everything that happened.

Snorting, as a funny thought popped into her head. Liu was returning to Fortine with her; a tall, buff Asian man in small-town Montana. Hmm, she wondered how that was going to go over. For one thing, she knew Liz would get a royal kick out of it at the very least. Perhaps it would be a good idea if the two of them kept mostly to themselves while they were there.

Anna hadn't told Liz that Liu would be coming back with her. She would need to give her a heads up so she could get the guest cabin cleaned and put fresh bedding on the bed. Hopefully, Liu would be comfortable having his own space.

Picking up her phone from the nightstand she texted Liz. *See you soon. Can you please prepare the guest cabin for some company?* Anna stretched, her head no longer hurt and she didn't feel so sore. If it hadn't been for Liu, she would probably have a severe bruise from the rubber bullet.

She wasn't going to need to pack much clothing-wise to return home. Only a few outfits she bought would take the trip with her. With her returning so soon, it was senseless to take all the new stuff with her when she had plenty at home. Not returning with a large amount of clothing allowed her to pack the large number of gifts she would be taking back with her. The jewelry Anna had been gifted would stay safely stowed in the apartment's safe until her return.

Checking the time, she wondered if Xian had left for the office already. She wanted to spend every possible moment with Xian and Chen before she left. Throwing on her robe, she thought she better find out if there were any plans. Stepping out of her room, Anna was greeted by a delightful smell. Mmm, there was food. Did someone cook? Voices and noise were coming from the direction of the kitchen.

Anna walked down the hall but the doors between the foyer and kitchen area were closed and locked. Well, this was new. She hadn't even realized a door was there. Backtracking, she went through the dining room area, and that door was closed as well though when she tried it, that one opened. What in the world? Opening the door the rest of the way, she understood why they had closed it. The noise from the men trying to work in the kitchen would have woken the dead.

"So, who is trying to burn down the apartment? You realize I'm trained for logistics in the fire department; I don't actually put out the fires, right?" Anna laughed as four men turned, startled to see her.

Huang Hu sitting at the counter got up, grabbed Anna, turned her around and pushed her back through the door.

"What the hell, Hu?" her indignant grumble turned his ears pink.

"Sorry Ms. Anna, you need to wait a bit longer. Why don't you go and work on packing? When it's ready, I'll come and get you." He smiled as he pushed her towards her room.

Looking over her shoulder at the young man, Anna couldn't believe she was being pushed around in her own apartment. Well, not hers quite yet. She would officially take over when she returned, but still. Huffing, she stomped back to her room. Unbeknownst to her, Chen, Xian, and Wu Feng had observed Anna and they were getting a good chuckle over her huff.

Going through her closet, Anna chose the outfit she would wear on the plane. The gray sweater dress she had purchased and her long black coat would suffice. Her outfit differed significantly from what she had worn when she arrived, another reminder of how much had happened since she arrived. Anna chose a few pieces to pack that would work with some of her clothes at home.

Xian had thoroughly spoiled her; she would never be able to shop at a big box store for clothing again. There was certainly a significant difference between off-the-rack and designer. Was she going to need to purchase a whole new wardrobe? Would she ever be able to go back to flannel pajama bottoms and sweatshirts while writing?

Anna dug through the drawers; where was the set of pajamas she had taken from Chen's apartment? She wasn't finding them anywhere. Frantic, Anna looked through each drawer and the hamper with her dirty items. Wu Feng had already told Anna he would be taking care of the dress from Saturday night; once it returned from the dry cleaners, he would put it in her closet for when she returned.

For the short time she would be back in the States, she didn't believe she would need any formal wear. The sweater dress and perhaps the blue dress from the night before would work. They would fit about any situation she might run into in Montana. Unfortunately, the dress the previous evening needed cleaning, especially after being tackled to the sidewalk.

Come to think of it, she hadn't seen Liu before being ejected from the other end of the penthouse. Was he finalizing his arrangements? Maybe he was getting cold feet about the trip? Xian had arranged for a ticket in first-class with Anna on the return flight.

A knock on her door pulled Anna from her distracted thoughts. "Come in."

The bedroom door cracked open and a hand poked through, waving a white napkin. "I come in peace." Huang Hu stuck his head in next. "Is it safe to come in?"

Anna snickered at his apparent attempt at making peace. "You're safe. Come in, Hu."

"Mr. Wei and Mr. Xiao formally request your presence in the sitting area. May I escort you?" He offered his arm.

Surprised at Huang Hu's proper behavior, Anna accepted his arm. "Any hints before I get there? I'm not sure I'm up for any more surprises."

Fighting to keep a straight face, Huang Hu gave her a deadpan answer, "Sorry ma'am, no hints." He whispered to her, "I'd like to keep my job. If I screw this up, Mr. Xiao will have my head; sorry, Ms. Anna."

What did those two have up their sleeve? She didn't have

long to find out. Anna and Huang Hu entered the sitting area; the coffee table had been set with plates and utensils. In the breakfast bar area there were quite a few covered dishes.

Xian and Chen were both wearing aprons, which was so adorable. They weren't making this any easier. "So, which of you two gets packed in my luggage and smuggled home to cook for me?" Anna asked, joking with the two of them.

Looking at one another, it seemed there was some understanding between them.

"Ma'am, if you sit on the couch your meal will be brought to you." Chen bowed slightly.

Raising an eyebrow at the curious antics, Anna complied and sat on the couch. Xian took Anna's plate from before her, placed select bits from each dish and returned to place it in front of her. Looking over the plate, it was a sampling of all of her favorite dishes so far. Curious about why these particular dishes, Anna looked from Xian to Chen. "I appreciate the effort, but I wouldn't normally take some of these as breakfast dishes."

"Let's just say it's a selection of the foods you love, an incentive to remind you what you'll be missing while you're gone," Xian replied.

"Come here, you two. Park it." Anna gestured to the chairs across from the couch.

Taking the aprons off and laying them across the back of the stool at the counter, they each took one of the chairs.

"Thank you two so much for this wonderful gesture. Please don't worry. I'm coming back. I don't think I could stay away now if I wanted to. There are some special people I would miss too much if I did. Beijing is my second home now, not just because I need to return to work. Plus, I never had a chance to explore, I had hoped to at least visit one of the temples before I left, but that will have to wait. If only all four of you could return with me...I realize that is a selfish wish. I'll be back before you know it." She had to fight the tears that threatened her. They had grown so close over the short time she had been there.

"We just didn't want you to forget us," Chen mumbled.

"There will never be a chance of that," Anna assured them.

"You will be part of my life as long as you'll have me. You two are so silly." She got up and walked around the table. Pulling each to their feet she hugged them. If only she could stay like this forever. She was wrapped in the arms of these incredible men.

"Now, I'm going to eat; I have some last-minute things I need to do." Kissing first Chen on the cheek, then Xian. "Can we plan a late lunch before I have to head to the airport?"

Both nodded. Xian headed down the hall to his room, returning with his briefcase. "I need to head to the office for a while. I've been putting this meeting off for over a week. I'll be back as soon as possible." Anna could tell he didn't want to leave.

"Get. The sooner you go, the sooner you can return. It isn't like I'll leave before you come back," Anna said as she sat down to enjoy the spread before her. "Please tell me someone is going to eat with me. I don't want to eat this all alone."

Chen and Huang Hu joined Anna for breakfast. They discussed Anna's ideas for the gifts she wanted to pick up to take back with her. The group formulated a plan and determined it wouldn't take them long.

Liu contacted Anna letting her know he would be there that afternoon; he was taking care of a few last minute arrangements before they flew out. She assured him that was fine, she had some souvenir shopping to finish.

Shopping took only slightly longer than she had estimated. Chen's recommendations had worked well, only requiring two stops to accomplish her goal. She found something special for everyone on her list, even Si Ming.

Returning to the penthouse, Anna was greeted by Liu. "Anna, quite a few packages were delivered while you were gone. I placed them in your room."

Excited, the items from the auction must have arrived. Chen was curious and tried to snoop while Anna checked through the packages. She finally got annoyed and shooed him out. Luckily, she had found his gift and hid it before he could open it.

She called Huang Hu to her room and asked if he could get some gift bags for her. Five would do the trick.

One of the perks of the apartment complex was a nicely stocked market. Huang Hu was able to find what she needed without much effort.

Finishing her packing didn't take long. Most of the items from her shopping spree were packed in the larger of the two suitcases, along with the special gifts she had won at the auction. In the smaller of the two, she packed the clothes she had chosen to take back. When she was done, five gift bags sat on her bed and her suitcases were ready by the door.

She only had her office items to pack when Xian returned from the office. Looking at the time, they had an hour before they would need to leave. They had plans to stop and eat on the way to the airport, at least being in first-class, the food would be decent. Suddenly it was so real. Anna remembered how nervous she had been when she came to Beijing; now she was sad to leave.

After Anna finished packing the laptop and small office items she would need, she left her messenger bag in the foyer with her suitcases. Making one last check through her room and office to ensure she didn't forget something, she picked up the gift bags off the bed and took them to the guys assembled in the sitting area.

Huang Hu and Wu Feng were sitting on the couch; she could tell they were on their phones as a distraction versus doing anything constructive. Xian and Chen sat in the chairs, looking sullen and staring into space. Liu had taken one of the stools next to the counter.

"Hey, you're not going to my funeral." Anna attempted to jolly them out of their funk. "I'm not going to be gone that long."

The answering grumbles and mumbles touched her. They were all beside themselves. Hopefully, her gifts would cheer them up. She passed the bags out to each of the men.

Each was shocked when handed a bag. Xian pouted that Chen's bag was larger than his, which made Anna smile. They were just big kids at heart sometimes. "Stop moping and open your gifts."

The expressions varied from shock to tears when they took out the items she had chosen carefully for each. Liu's was a shocked expression. He wasn't often given a gift, especially one as thoughtful as what he received from Anna. The watch she had gifted him was GPS enabled and could be tracked from any smartphone. It showed dual time zones and a star chart on the back. He had seen a watch like this before and the price tag on them was pretty impressive.

Huang Hu opened his gift to find a signed model of his favorite manga character. He was floored that Anna had remembered their conversations and had found it for him. He was on the verge of tears.

Wu Feng was in tears after seeing his gift. Inside was an open ticket to his hometown. He hadn't been back in some time and had mentioned how his mother's health wasn't the best. Anna had discussed it with Xian and they agreed he should take a week and visit her.

Xian opened the box with his cufflinks and his eyes widened. They were limited edition. Only five sets of the cufflinks had been made. He had been looking for a pair of these for a while now. "Anna, how did you know?"

Winking, Anna replied, "It's because I'm good."

The last to open his was Chen. His was the largest and heaviest of the bags. Inside was an elaborately ornamented case. Just the case alone was a work of art; Chen opened the box, and his jaw dropped. "**ANNA!**" He jumped up and threw his arms around her. In the box was a tea set from his favorite pottery master. The set was the only one the artist had created for the year. Anna had gotten lucky that he had donated it for the auction.

She was thrilled to see the joy each of the men had received from her gifts. Now she knew they would never forget her either.

"Okay, we better get going. Food, then the airport." Anna went to her room and grabbed her coat and purse from the bed. She looked around soaking it all in one last time until she returned.

章

Chapter 77

On the way to the airport, they found a small shop that served authentic dishes. Anna wanted to try a few more foods before she left. The conversation was strained at best. Xian and Chen were both introspective, whispering with one another, ignoring Anna completely. Wu Feng had spent most of the meal texting with his family. Huang Hu kept looking at his figurine; Anna was close to accusing him of playing with dolls, he was so wrapped up in it. Liu was figuring out his new watch, tweaking a dial then reading the instructions, only to tweak another setting.

After finishing their meal, Xian and Chen requested Wu Feng take a slight detour. Checking the time on her phone, they were running ahead of schedule, so she didn't mind. She figured they just needed to pick something up in this part of town since they were there, at least that's what she would have done.

When they stopped, Xian and Chen told Huang Hu and Liu to keep Anna in the van. Under no circumstance was she to put so much as a toe out. Nothing like waving a red flag in front of a bull. Anna tried to open the van door only to have her hand slapped by Huang Hu. "You heard them. No leaving the van."

By the time they returned, Anna was in a full sulk. "Find what you were after?" Anna grumped.

"Why yes, we did," Xian said, a twinkle in his eye. It was a welcomed change from the moping she had experienced most of the morning from him.

"It was even better than we could have imagined," Chen added, a mischievous grin on his face.

Now Anna was curious. What had they stopped to get? It was going to be nice not having mysterious men making her crazy.

"Head for the airport, Wu Feng," Xian directed his assistant.

Arriving at the airport, the group piled out. Huang Hu and Liu unloaded the luggage. Stepping inside the terminal, they waited for Wu Feng to park before they ventured further.

People bustled through the airport; loud conversations and announcements over the intercoms were almost overwhelming for Anna. Glad for the guys, she wrapped her arms around herself. It would be a comfort having Liu with her on the return trip. With all that had happened, Anna wondered if there might not be some PTSD she might need to address. If she didn't know better, she would have expected to see Scott come out of the crowd and try to grab her.

Xian and Chen had finally explained to Anna what they had installed at her house in Montana. At first, she was livid; though, after thinking about it, it was probably the best present they could have given her. They were thoughtful, even if they were a bit overbearing at times. Anna knew they were doing it for her benefit, it would be nice if they consulted her once in a while though. What had shocked her was to find Liz had been their willing accomplice. It explained a few things.

Wu Feng found them and they all went to check Anna and Liu in, checking their luggage and verifying their tickets. Their flight left in an hour and they would arrive back in Montana late Monday night. Thinking about it hurt Anna's brain. They were leaving Beijing at 8:20 P.M. Monday and would arrive in Kalispell at 11:10 P.M. the same day.

All checked in, they headed for the first-class lounge to wait until they were notified they would be boarding. Wu Feng and Huang Hu sat at a table with Liu, asking him to send tons of photos when they arrived. The bodyguard laughed at the younger men. He could tell they were jealous that he was going and they weren't.

Anna sat sipping on a screwdriver, figuring she hadn't gotten drunk on vodka while in China so it wouldn't evoke any memories she didn't want to dredge up at the moment.

Noticing the boys exchanging suspicious looks, Anna finally nailed Xian and Chen down. "What is up with you two? You've been acting odd ever since we ate. Spill it," she demanded.

Realizing their time was rapidly running out, Xian reached

into his pocket and pulled out a velvet box. He handed it to Anna. After Chen's proposal, she was nervous to see what might be in a box that was obviously for jewelry. Looking at both of them before she opened it for some clue, they kept deadpan expressions.

Snorting, she plucked up the courage and opened it. Inside were three identical rings in different sizes. These were decorative bands, not wedding or engagement rings. Confused, she looked back at them for an explanation.

"Anna, you've become part of our family, no matter what happens. If by chance you end up being with one of us, or..." Xian trailed off, and Anna could tell it was difficult for him to say the next part of his statement, "...if you happen to find someone other than us to be with, we purchased these rings to express the bond between us." He took out the middle ring, took Anna's right hand, and placed the band on her right ring finger.

He then took out the largest of the three and handed it to Anna, offering his finger. Anna struggled as she put the band on his finger; her emotions at that moment threatening to overwhelm her. Anna took the last ring and held her hand out for Chen's right hand, placing it on his finger. She kept his hand in hers, looking into his eyes to see how he felt about this. It wasn't the ring he had wanted on her finger. The warm smile he returned showed he was good with it. Xian placed his hand over theirs, sealing the bond between them.

An announcement came that the flight would be boarding in ten minutes. "I wish you would have allowed me to send you on my private jet," Xian commented as he stood.

"Xian, that would be abusing our friendship. I'm good on the commercial flight. Besides, you've spoiled me enough with the few flights I took on your jet."

"Oh, you haven't been on the jet I use for international flights." He gave her a big grin.

"**NOW** you tell me." Anna laughed.

"Well, I'm coming to get you when you move back, especially if you plan to bring Si Ming back. I'm working on the logistics of getting him over here." Xian threw his arms around Anna, hugging her tightly. Before letting her go, he captured her lips with his, kissing her nearly senseless.

Whew, Anna thought to herself. I'm lucky he didn't level that kiss on me at the hotel. We would have been in big trouble.

Chen glared at Xian, mad that he had beat him to the punch. He grabbed Anna's arm, pulling her into a crushing embrace, not to be outdone. Anna knew the kind of kiss Chen was capable of and braced herself. What happened shook her more than if he had tried to clean her tonsils with his tongue. The kiss was tender, sweet and gentle. They were polar opposites.

Breathless, Anna picked up her purse from the table. Looking for Liu as he shook hands with Wu Feng and Huang Hu. Smiling, they clapped him on the back and wished him well, reminding him to take exceptionally good care of Anna, or he would have to answer to them. The threat elicited a laugh from the stern bodyguard.

Anna grabbed each of them, giving them quick hugs, admonishing each to take care of their bosses and let her know if they were moping too much or if anything odd happened. Securing their agreement, she turned one last time to wave. Anna managed to keep her tears in check. They could wait until she was on the plane and the men couldn't see them.

Boarded and sitting in her seat next to Liu, she settled in. Reaching in her purse to grab her book, she could use a bit of light reading to distract her. Inside she found a small wrapped box. Unwrapping the elegant box, inside was a necklace with a jeweled giraffe. "Keep me with you always." Was the note included in...Xian's handwriting?

"Liu, can you help me with this?" Anna handed the chain to her companion.

With the necklace around her neck, it looked beautiful. She wouldn't take it off. Grabbing her phone, she took a quick selfie and sent it to Xian. *I'll wear it always.* Anna sent the message with the photo.

"Please turn off all cellular devices." The notice came over the intercom.

Just as she was going to turn the phone off for the flight, a message popped on her screen from Chen. *Scott escaped. Li*

Ming is nowhere to be found. What the hell?

—

Sitting in cramped seats on a flight that was questionable if it would make it out of the country, let alone across an ocean, Li Ming sat wearing sunglasses and a hat, doing her best to stay inconspicuous. Beside her was a clean shaven caucasian man with freshly colored brunette hair who thumbed through a wrinkled and soiled magazine provided on the flight.

"Are you sure you want to do this?" Scott asked her quietly.

"Do I have much of a choice?" she snapped back. She had dug this hole, time to bury a specific author in it.